and, in 2005, the Prix Femina for *The Falls*. She has written some of the most enduring fiction of our time, including *We Were the Mulvaneys*, which was an Oprah Book Club Choice, and *Blonde*, which was nominated for the National Book Award. She is the Roger S. Berlind Distinguished Professor of Humanities at Princeton University.

From the reviews of *We Were the Mulvaneys*:

'Oates's finest . . . a major achievement'   *Chicago Tribune*

'*We Were the Mulvaneys* works not simply because of its meticulous details and gestures . . . What keeps us coming back to Oates Country is something stronger and spookier: her uncanny gift of making the page a window, with something on the other side that we'd swear was life itself'

DAVID GATES, *New York Times*

'This is a book that will break your heart, heal it, then break it again every time you think about it'   *Los Angeles Times*

'Novelists such as Updike, Roth, Wolfe and Mailer slug it out for the title of the Great American Novelist. But maybe they're wrong. Maybe, just maybe, the Great American Novelist is a woman'   *Herald*

'A brilliantly detailed ... succession of dramat... recognise, and she ma...

By the same author

JOYCE CAROL OATES

We Were the Mulvaneys

A NOVEL

HARPER PERENNIAL
London, New York, Toronto and Sydney

for my "Mulvaneys" . . .

This edition produced for The Book People Ltd,
Hall Wood Avenue, Haydock, St Helens, WA11 9UL

Harper Perennial
An imprint of HarperCollins*Publishers*
77–85 Fulham Palace Road, Hammersmith, London W6 8JB

www.harperperennial.co.uk
Visit our authors' blog at www.fifthestate.co.uk

This edition published by Harper Perennial 2008
1

First published in Great Britain by Fourth Estate in 2001

Copyright © The Ontario Review, Inc. 1996

The quoted passage on page 177 is taken from Ludwig von Bertalanffy,
Problems of Life: An Evaluation of Modern Biological and Scientific Thought
(Pitman Publishing, Ltd, London, 1952), page 103

PS Section copyright © Sarah O'Reilly 2008, except 'What is a Family except
Memories?' by Joyce Carol Oates © The Ontario Review, Inc. 2008

PS™ is a trademark of HarperCollins*Publishers* Ltd

Joyce Carol Oates asserts the moral right to be identified as the author of this work

A catalogue record for this book is available from the British Library

ISBN 978-0-00-781542-5

Printed and bound in Great Britain by Clays Ltd, St Ives plc

This novel is entirely a work of fiction. The names, characters and incidents
portrayed in it are the work of the author's imagination. Any resemblance to
actual persons, living or dead, events or localities is entirely coincidental.

CONTENTS

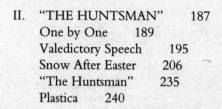

I bequeath myself to the dirt to grow from the grass I love,
If you want me again look for me under your boot-soles.

You will hardly know who I am or what I mean,
But I shall be good health to you nevertheless,
And filter and fibre your blood.

Failing to fetch me at first keep encouraged.
Missing me one place search another,
I stop some where waiting for you.

from Walt Whitman, *Song of Myself*

I
FAMILY PICTURES

STORYBOOK HOUSE

We were the Mulvaneys, remember us?

You may have thought our family was larger, often I'd meet people who believed we Mulvaneys were a virtual clan, but in fact there were only six of us: my dad who was Michael John Mulvaney, Sr., my mom Corinne, my brothers Mike Jr. and Patrick and my sister Marianne, and me—Judd.

From summer 1955 to spring 1980 when my dad and mom were forced to sell the property there were Mulvaneys at High Point Farm, on the High Point Road seven miles north and east of the small city of Mt. Ephraim in upstate New York, in the Chautauqua Valley approximately seventy miles south of Lake Ontario.

High Point Farm was a well-known property in the Valley, in time to be designated a historical landmark, and "Mulvaney" was a well-known name.

For a long time you envied us, then you pitied us.

For a long time you admired us, then you thought *Good!—that's what they deserve.*

"Too direct, Judd!"—my mother would say, wringing her hands in discomfort. But I believe in uttering the truth, even if it hurts. Particularly if it hurts.

For all of my childhood as a Mulvaney I was the baby of the family. To be the baby of such a family is to know you're the last little caboose of a long roaring train. They loved me so, when they paid any attention to me at all, I was like a creature dazed and blinded by intense, searing light that might suddenly switch off and leave me in darkness. I couldn't seem to figure out who I was, if I had an actual name or many names, all of them affectionate and many of them teasing, like "Dimple," "Pretty Boy" or, alternately, "Sourpuss," or "Ranger"—my favorite. I was "Baby" or "Baby-face" much of the time while growing up. "Judd" was a name associated with a certain measure of sternness, sobriety, though in fact we Mulvaney children were rarely scolded and even more rarely punished; "Judson Andrew" which is my baptismal name was a name of such dignity and aspiration I never came to feel it could be mine, only something borrowed like a Hallowe'en mask.

You'd get the impression, at least I did, that "Judd" who was "Baby" almost didn't make it. Getting born, I mean. The train had pulled out, the caboose was being rushed to the track. Not that Corinne Mulvaney was so very old when I was born—she was only thirty-three. Which certainly isn't "old" by today's standards. I was born in 1963, that year Dad used to say, with a grim shake of his head, a sick-at-heart look in his eyes, "tore history in two" for Americans. What worried me was I'd come along so belatedly, everyone else was here except me! *A complete Mulvaney family without Judd.*

Always it seemed, hard as I tried I could never hope to catch up with all their good times, secrets, jokes—their memories. What is a family, after all, except memories?—haphazard and precious as the contents of a catchall drawer in the kitchen (called the "junk drawer" in our household, for good reason). My handicap, I gradually realized, was that by the time I got around to being born, my brother Mike was already ten years old and for children that's equivalent to another generation. *Where's Baby?—who's got Baby?* the cry would commence, and whoever was nearest would scoop me up and off we'd go. A scramble of dogs barking, their eagerness to be taken along to wherever a mimicry of my own, exaggerated as animals are often exaggerations of human beings, emotions so rawly exposed. *Who's got Baby? Don't forget Baby!*

The dogs, cats, horses, even the cars and pickups Dad and Mom drove before I was born, those big flashy-sexy Fifties models—all these I would pore over in Mom's overstuffed snapshot albums, determined to attach myself to their memories. *Sure, I remember! Sure, I was there!* Mike's first pony Crackerjack who was a sorrel with sand-colored markings. Our setter Foxy as a puppy. The time Dad ran the tractor into a ditch. The time Mom threw corncobs to scare away strange dogs she believed were threatening the chickens and the dogs turned out to be a black bear and two cubs. The time Dad invited 150 people to Mulvaney's Fourth of July cookout assuming that only about half would show up, and everyone showed up—and a few more. The time a somewhat disreputable friend of Dad's flew over to High Point Farm from an airport in Marsena in a canary-yellow Piper Cub and landed—"Crash-landed, almost," Mom would say dryly—in one of the pastures, and though the baby in the snapshots commemorating this occasion would have to have been my sister Marianne, in July 1960, I was able to convince myself *Yes I was there, I remember. I do!*

And when in subsequent years they would speak of the incident, recalling the way the wind buffeted the little plane when Wally Parks, my Dad's friend, took Dad up for a brief flight, I was positive I'd been there, I could recall how excited I was, how excited we all were, Mike, Patrick, Marianne and me, and of course Mom, watching as the Piper Cub rose higher and higher shuddering in the wind, grew smaller and smaller with distance until it was no larger than a sparrow hawk, high above the Valley, looking as if a single strong gust of wind could bring it down. And Mom prayed aloud, "God, bring those lunatics back alive and I'll never complain about anything again, I promise! Amen."

I'd swear even now, *I'd been there*.

For the Mulvaneys were a family in which everything that happened to them was precious and everything that was precious was stored in memory and everyone had a history.

Which is why many of you envied us, I think. Before the events of 1976 when everything came apart for us and was never again put together in quite the same way.

We Mulvaneys would have died for one another, but we had secrets from one another just the same. We still do.

I'm an adult telling you these things: Judd Mulvaney, thirty years old. Editor in chief of the *Chautauqua Falls Journal*, a twice-weekly publication, circulation 25,600. I've been a newspaperman or in any case working for newspapers since the age of sixteen and though I love my work and am, I suppose, fairly obsessed by it, I'm not ambitious in any worldly sense. I've been entrusted by the elderly gentleman publisher of the *Journal*, who happens to be a friend of mine, to put out a "good, decent, truth-telling paper" and that's what I've been doing and will continue to do. Moving out and up to better-paying jobs in larger cities evokes only the mildest glimmer of interest in me. I'm not a newspaperman who strives for sensation, controversy. I'd rather be truth-telling and I hope always to be without hypocrisy.

I've constructed a personality that is even and temperate and on the whole wonderfully civilized. People murmur to Corinne Mulvaney, after they've met me, "What a nice young man!" and, if they're women like her, women of her age with grown and far-flung children, "Aren't you lucky, to have such a son!" In fact I suppose Mom is lucky, not just because she "has" me but because she "has" my brothers and sister too, and we love her as much or nearly as much as she loves us.

Mom doesn't know and I hope never will know that two of her sons were involved in a criminal action of extreme seriousness. I'll be direct with you: I've been an accomplice to two Class-A felonies punishable by lengthy prison terms in New York State and I came close to being an accessory both before and after the fact in an actual case of murder and very possibly I would not be repentant if this murder had been committed. Certainly my brother Patrick, who came close to committing the murder, would not have been repentant. Asked by the judge to speak on his own behalf, at the time of sentencing, Patrick would have looked the man in the eye and said, "Your Honor, I did what I did and I don't regret it."

Many times in my imagination I've heard Patrick say these words. So many times, I almost think, in that twilight state of consciousness between sleep and wakefulness, which involves a subtle, shifting, mysterious personality few of us have explored, that in fact Patrick was arrested, tried, and convicted for murder, kidnapping, auto theft—whatever the numerous charges would have been—and had stood before a judge and spoke in just this way. Then I force myself awake, and relief floods through me like sunshine! *It didn't happen, not in that way.*

But this document isn't a confession. Not at all. I've come to think of it as a family album. The kind my mom never kept, absolute truth-telling. The kind no one's mom keeps. But if you've been a child in any family you've been keeping such an album in memory and conjecture and yearning, and it's a life's work, it may be the great and only work of your life.

★ ★ ★

I've said there were six in our family but that's misleading. *Six* is such a small number! In fact High Point Farm was busy and complicated and to a child confusing as a stage play in which familiar and unfamiliar faces are ceaselessly coming and going. Friends, relatives, houseguests, Dad's business contacts, hired help—every day and frequently every hour you could count on it that *something was happening*. Both my parents were sociable, popular people who had little patience with quiet, let alone solitude. And we lived on a *farm*. We owned horses, dairy cows, goats, a few sheep, chickens and guinea fowl and geese and semi-tame mallard ducks. What a barnyard squawking in the early morning, when the roosters crowed! I grew up with such sounds, and the cries of wild birds (mainly jays who nested close about the house in our giant oaks), I came to believe they were part of the very fabric of morning itself. The very fabric of my soul.

Unlike neighboring farms in the Valley, High Point Farm wasn't any longer a "real" farm. Dad's income came from Mulvaney Roofing, in Mt. Ephraim. Originally, the farm property had included three hundred acres of good, fertile if hilly soil, but by the time Dad and Mom bought it, only twenty-three acres remained; and of these, Dad leased fifteen to neighboring farmers to grow timothy, wheat, soybeans, alfalfa, corn. But we had farm animals we loved, and of course we had dogs, rarely less than four, and cats—cats!—always a select number of cats allowed inside the house and an ever-shifting number of barn cats. My earliest memories were of animals with personalities stronger than my own. A horse has a very defined yet often unpredictable personality unlike, for instance, a dog; a cat can be virtually anything. Dad used to complain jokingly that the boss of the household was a certain temperamental, supremely self-absorbed and very beautiful Persian cat named Snowball and the second-in-command was Mom, of course, and after that he didn't care to speculate, it was too humbling.

"Oh, yes! We all feel sorry for poor Curly, don't we?"—Mom teased affectionately, as Dad made a brooding face. "So neglected in his own home!"

Say I counted the animals and fowl of High Point Farm with personalities defined enough to have been named—how many might there have been? Twenty? Twenty-five? Thirty? More? And of course they were always shifting, changing. A new litter of puppies, a new litter of kittens. Spring lambs, goats. It was rare that a foal was born but when a foal was born, after many days and nights of worry (mainly on Mom's part, she'd sometimes sleep in the stable with the pregnant mare) it was quite an occasion. Several families of canaries had come and gone before I was born and it was a fond household tale of the time Mom had tried to breed canaries right there in the kitchen, the problem being she'd succeeded only too well, and at the height of the "canary epidemic" as Dad called it there were three large cages containing a total of fifteen canaries, trilling, warbling, chirping, scolding, sometimes screeching—"And ceaselessly defecating," as Dad said dryly. I remember once when I was very small, Dad brought home a spindly-legged little gray goat because its owner, a neighboring farmer, had been going to shoot it—"Come meet Billy-boy!" Dad announced. Another time, Mom and Mike returned from a trip to the feed store in Eagleton Corners with a large flamey-feathered golden-eyed strutting bantam cock—"Everybody come meet Cap'n Marvel!" Mom announced. My first puppy was a bulldog named Little Boots with whom I would grow up like a brother.

When I think of us then, when we were the Mulvaneys of High Point Farm, I think of the sprawling, overgrown and somewhat jungly farm itself, blurred at the edges as in a dream where our ever-collapsing barbed wire fences trailed off into scrubby, hilly, uncultivated land. (On a farm, you have to repair fences continually, or should.) Getting us into focus requires effort, like getting a dream into focus and keeping it there.

One of those haunting tantalizing dreams that seem so vivid, so real, until you look closely, try to *see*—and they begin to fade, like smoke.

Let's drive out to High Point Farm!

Come with me, I'll take you there. From Route 58, the Yewville Pike, a good two- and three-lane country highway linking Rochester, Yewville and Mt. Ephraim on a straight north-south axis, you pass through the crossroads town of Lebanon, continue for eight miles following the Yewville River and crossing the erector-set new bridge at Mt. Ephraim. (Population 19,500 in 1976.) Continue along what turns into Meridian Street, passing the aged redbrick mill factories on the river (manufacturers of ladies' handbags, sweaters, footwear) that have the melancholy look of shut-down businesses but are in fact operating, to a degree. Take a right onto Seneca Street past the stately-ugly old Greek Revival building that is the Mt. Ephraim Public Library with the wrought-iron fence in front. Past the Mt. Ephraim Police Headquarters. The Veterans of Foreign Wars. The Odd Fellows. Bear right at the square, where most of the tall old elms have been removed, and continue on to Fifth Street, where you take a right at Trinity Episcopal Church.

No—wait. This route is a shortcut to avoid Mt. Ephraim's "downtown" (hardly more than three blocks but the old, narrow streets can get congested). Let's circle around to the far end of South Main Street, another right, and a left, now we're in an area of small businesses and warehouses. There's Mulvaney Roofing—a smallish single-storey stucco building, recently painted an attractive dark green with white trim. On the roof are state-of-the-art asphalt-and-polyester shingles in a slightly darker shade of green.

How proud Dad was of Mulvaney Roofing. How hard he'd worked for it, and to build up his reputation as a man you not only wanted to do business with because his product was so fine but because you liked and respected him as a damned nice guy.

Now back onto Fifth, and continue for three blocks. Passing on the left Mt. Ephraim High where we Mulvaney children all went to school, in turn (factory-style design, flat leaky roof and cheap bargain bricks built in the mid-Sixties and already showing signs of wear) and the school playing fields and at the corner a town ballpark, nothing spectacular, a few bleachers and a weedy infield and litter drifting in the wind like tumbleweed. There's Rose & Chubby's Diner, there's the Four Corners Tavern with the cinder parking lot. Past Depot Street. Past Railroad. Down the long hill past Drummond's Gloves, Inc.—still operating in 1976, skidding just ahead of bankruptcy. (Mr. Drummond was an acquaintance of my dad's, we'd hear of the poor man's problems at mealtimes.) Bear right at the fork in the road past Apostles of Christ Tabernacle, one of Mom's first churches in the area but back before Judd was born, a sad cinder-block building with a movie house marquee and bright pink letters REJOICE ALL, CHRIST IS RISEN! Continue across the train tracks and past the Chautauqua & Buffalo freight yards. You'll see the water tower fifty feet above the ground on what I'd always think were "spider legs": MT. EPHRAIM in rainwashed white letters. (Probably there are Day-Glo scrawls, initials and graffiti on the water tower, too. Probably CLASS OF '76 MT.E.H.S. There's an ongoing struggle between local officials who want the tower clear of graffiti and local high school kids determined to mark it as their own.)

Turn now onto Route 119, the Haggartsville Road, a fast-moving state highway. Gulf station on the left, Eastgate Shopping Center on the right, the usual fast-food drive-through restaurants like Wendy's, McDonald's, Kentucky Fried Chicken all recently built along this strip in the early 1970's. Spohr's Lumber, Hendrick Motors, Inc. Familiar names because the owners were friends of my dad's, fellow members of the Mt. Ephraim Chamber of Commerce, the Odd Fellows, the Mt. Ephraim Country Club. The traffic light ahead marks the town limits. Beyond, on the left, is Country Club Lane that leads back from the busy highway for miles in an upscale "exclusive" residential neighborhood; the Mt. Ephraim Country Club itself isn't visible from the highway but you can see the rolling green golf course, a finger of artificial lake glittering like broken glass. On the right is a similiar prestige housing development, Hillside Estates. Now you're out of town and the speed limit is fifty-five miles an hour but everyone is going faster. Heavy trucks, semis. Local pickups. You're passing small farms, open fields as the highway gradually ascends. Railroad tracks run close beside the road for several miles then veer off through a tunnel that looks as if it's been drilled through solid rock. Beyond a scattering of shantylike houses and a sad-looking trailer village there's a narrow blacktop road forking off to the right: High Point Road.

Now you're in the foothills of the Chautauqua Mountains and those are the mountains in the distance ahead: wooded slopes that look carved, floating. Mt. Cataract is the highest at 2,300 feet above sea level, chalky at its peak, visible on clear days though it's thirty miles away. *It looks like a hand doesn't it?* Marianne used to say *like someone waving to us*. In winter this is a region of snow vast and deep and drifting as the tundra. In my mind's eye I not only see but cringe at the blinding dazzling white hills stretching for miles, tufted and puckered with broken cornstalks. Sparrow hawks circling overhead in lazy-looking spirals, wide-winged hawks so sharp of eye they can spot tiny rodents scurrying from one cornstalk to another and drop in a sudden swooping descent like a rocket to seize their prey in their talons and rise with it again. In warm weather most of the fields are tilled, planted. Hilly pastureland broken by brooks and narrow meandering creeks. Herds of Holsteins grazing; sometimes horses, sheep. You're in the deep country now, and still ascending. Past the crossroads town of Eagleton Corners—post office and gen-

eral store in the same squat little building, farm supply store, gas station, white clapboard Methodist church. Now the character of High
Point Road changes: the blacktop becomes gravel and dirt, hardly
more than a single lane, virtually no shoulders and a deep ditch on
the right. The road rides the edge of an ancient glacier ridge, one of
a number of bizarre raised striations in the earth in this part of New
York State, like giant claws many miles long. And now there's a
creek rushing beside the road, Alder Creek that's deep, fast-moving,
treacherous as a river. Still you're ascending, there's a steep hill as
the road curves, it's a good idea to shift into second gear. When the
road levels, you pass the Pfenning farm on the right, which borders
the Mulvaney property—at last! The Pfennings' house is a typical
farmhouse of the region, economical asphalt siding, a shingled roof
exuding slow rot. The barn is in better repair, which is typical too.
Lloyd Pfenning is Dad's major renter, leasing twelve acres from him
most years to plant in oats and corn. A half mile farther and you pass
the run-down, converted schoolhouse, Chautauqua County District
#9, where a succession of families have lived; in this year 1976, the
family is called Zimmerman.

Another half mile and you see, on the left, a large handsome
black mailbox with the silver figure of a rearing horse on its side and
the name M U L V A N E Y in lipstick-red reflector letters.
Across from the mailbox there's a driveway nearly obscured from
view by trees and shrubs, and the sign Mom painted herself, so
proudly—

> HIGH POINT FARM
> 1849

The gravel drive is lined with tall aging spruces. Around the house
are five enormous oaks and I mean enormous—the tallest is easily
three times the height of the house and the house is three storeys. In
summer everything is overgrown, you have to stare up the drive to
see the house—what a house! In winter, the lavender house seems
to float in midair, buoyant and magical as a house in a child's storybook. And that antique sleigh in the front yard, looking as if the
horse had just trotted away to leave the lone passenger behind—a
human figure, a tenderly comical scarecrow wearing old clothes of
Dad's.

A storybook house, you're thinking, yes? Must be, storybook people live there.

High Point Farm had been a local landmark long before my parents bought and partly restored it, of course. Most recently it had been the secluded homestead of an eccentric German-born gentleman farmer who'd died in 1951 and left it to young, distant relatives living in cities far away with little interest in the property except as an occasional summer place or weekend hunting retreat. By 1976, when I was thirteen, High Point Farm was looking almost prosperous and it wasn't unusual for photographers from as far away as Rochester and Buffalo to come out to photograph it, "historic" house and outbuildings, horses grazing in pastures, antique sleigh and "quaint" little brook winding through the front yard. Each year, High Point Farm was featured on calendars printed by local merchants, the *Mt. Ephraim Patriot-Ledger*, the Western New York Historical Society.

On the wall of my office at the newspaper there's a Historical Society calendar for 1975, opened permanently to October— "Pumpkin Time at High Point Farm!" A glossy picture of the scarecrow figure in the sleigh in Dad's old red-plaid jacket, earflap cap, bunchy khaki trousers, surrounded by Day-Glo orange pumpkins of varying sizes including, on the ground, an enormous misshapen pumpkin that must have weighed more than one hundred pounds. Beyond the figure in the sleigh is the lavender-and-fieldstone farmhouse with its numerous windows and steep-pitched roofs.

I've had the page laminated, otherwise it would long be faded and tattered.

Our house was a rambling old farmhouse of seven bedrooms, verandas and porches and odd little turrets and towers and three tall fieldstone chimneys. Dad said of the house that it had no *style*, it was *styles*, a quick history of American architecture. Evidence showed that as many as six builders had worked on it, renovating, expanding, removing, just since 1930. Dad kept the exterior in A1 condition, of course—especially the roofs that were covered in prime-quality slate of a beautiful plum hue, and drained with seamless aluminum gutters and downspouts. The old, central part of the house was fieldstone and stucco; later sections were made of wood. When I was very little, in the mid-Sixties it must have been, Dad and two of his Mulvaney Roofing men and Mike Jr. and Patrick repainted the wood sections, transforming them from gunmetal gray to lavender with shutters the rich dark purple of fresh eggplant. The big front door was painted cream. (Eighteen gallons of oil-base paint for old, dry wood had been required, and weeks of work. What a team effort! I'd wished I was big enough to use a brush, to climb up onto the scaffolding and help. And maybe in my imagination I've come to believe I had been part of the team.)

Part of the house's historic interest lay in the fact that it had been a "safe house" in the Underground Railroad, which came into operation after the passage in 1850 of the Fugitive Slave Act, one of the most shameful legislative measures in American history. My mother was thrilled to discover documents in the Chautauqua County Historical Society archive pertaining to these activities, and wrote a series of pieces for the *Mt. Ephraim Patriot-Ledger* on the subject. How innocently vain she was! How captivated, as she said, by "living in a place of history"! She'd been born on a small farm about fifteen miles to the south where farm life was work, work, work and the seasons simply repeated themselves forever, never adding up to what you'd call "history."

It was after I started school that Mom became seriously interested in antiques. She'd furnished much of the house with authentic period items, those she could afford, and it became her notion to buy and sell. She acquired some merchandise, set up shop in a small converted barn just behind the house, advertised in one or another local antique publications and painted a sign to prop up beside the scarecrow in the sleigh—

HIGH POINT ANTIQUES
BARGAINS & BEAUTY!

Not that many customers ever came. High Point Farm was too far from town, too difficult to locate. Sunday drivers might drop by, enthralled by the sight of the lavender-and-stone house atop the hill, but most of Mom's visitors were fellow dealers like herself. If in fact someone wanted to buy an item of which she'd grown especially fond, Mom would seem to panic, and murmur some feeble apology—"Oh, I'm so sorry! I forgot—that item has been requisitioned by a previous customer." Blushing and wringing her hands in the very gesture of guilt.

Dad observed, "Your mother's weakness as a businesswoman is pretty simple: she's a hopeless amateur."

Scouring auctions, flea markets, garage and rummage sales in the Chautauqua Valley, not above browsing through landfill dumps and outright trash, about which Dad teased her mercilessly, Mom only brought home things she fell in love with; and, naturally, things she'd fallen in love with she couldn't bear to sell to strangers.

What is truth?—Pontius Pilate's question.

And how mysteriously Jesus answered him—*Every one that is of the truth heareth my voice.*

Once I thought I understood this exchange but no longer.

In setting forth this story of the Mulvaneys, of whom I happen to be the youngest son, yet, I hope, a neutral observer, at least one whose emotions have been scoured and exorcised with time, I want to set down *what is truth.* Everything recorded here happened and it's my task to suggest how, and why; why what might seem to be implausible or inexplicable at a distance—a beloved child's banishment by a loving father, like something in a Grimm fairy tale—isn't implausible or inexplicable from within. I will include as many "facts" as I can assemble, and the rest is conjecture, imagined but not invented. Much is based upon memory and conversations with family members about things I had not experienced firsthand nor could possibly know except in the way of the heart.

As Dad used to say, in that way of his that embarrassed us, it was so direct, you had to respond immediately and dared not even glance away—"We Mulvaneys are joined at the heart."

THE DOE

Like whispering the furtive rustle. *Judd. Judd. Judd.*

I must have been eleven years old, that night I was wakened by the deer, and followed them back to the pasture pond. Wakened not by hooves outside my window (I had no idea the sound was hooves) but by a rustling in the tall dry grasses. *Judd. Oh Judd!*

Judd sleeps so hard, Mom used to tease, *when he was a baby his dad and I would lean over the crib every few minutes, to check if he was breathing!*

It was so: up to the age of about thirteen, I'd sleep so hard, I mean—*hard.* Sunk to the bottom of a deep, deep well.

Wonder why? Weekdays at High Point Farm never began later than 6 A.M. when Mom hollered up the stairs, "WAKE UP! RISE 'N' SHINE, KIDDOS!" And maybe whistled, or banged a pot. Barn chores before breakfast (my God it could take as long as an hour to wash the cows' filth-encrusted milk-swollen udders, hook up the milking machine to each cow, drain their heavy milk bags dry, empty the milkers into pails) and barn chores after school (horses, mainly—as much work, but at least I loved our horses), approximately 4:30 P.M. to 6 P.M. And then supper—in our family, *intense.* Just to hold my own around our table, for a kid like me, the youngest of the Mulvaneys, used up energy, and staying power, like keeping on your toes through twelve rounds of a featherweight boxing match—it might look almost easy to outsiders but it isn't easy, for sure. And after supper an hour or so of homework, also intense (Mom insisted that Patrick or Marianne oversee my efforts: worrying I wasn't the high-nineties student it was her conviction I should be) and more excitement among the family, watching TV for a while if something "worthwhile, educational" was on: history, science and biography documentaries on public television were favored by our parents. And we'd discuss them during, and afterward—we Mulvaneys were a family who *talked*. So when around 10 P.M. I staggered upstairs to bed it was with the gravity of a stone sinking slowly through deep, dark water. Sometimes I fell asleep half in my pajamas, lying sideways on my bed, and Little Boots curled up happily beside me. Sometimes I fell asleep in the bathroom, sitting on the toilet. "Oh, Judd! Goodness! Wake *up*, honey!" Mom might cry, having pushed open the door I'd neglected to lock.

No privacy at High Point Farm.

What with the six of us, and the dogs and cats and frequent visitors and overnight guests (my parents were what's called *hospitable*, and Marianne was always inviting girlfriends to stay the night—"The more, the merrier!" Mom believed)—privacy just wasn't an option.

Patrick was the self-declared loner of the family. He'd read Henry David Thoreau's *Walden* at the age of twelve and often camped out overnight on Alder Creek, in the woods—even so, he'd have one of the dogs with him, or more than one. In his room, there was always a dog or a cat and I'd peek in on him sometimes (the kind of dumb-admiring thing a kid brother does) to see him asleep twisted in his bedclothes with a heavy furry shape slung across his chest, both of them snoring softly.

God, did I sleep hard as a kid! Everything in those days was stark and intense and almost hurtful—I mean, it had the power to make me so *happy*, so *excited*. I'd fall into bed and a switch in my brain turned off and I was gone, out. And if anything suddenly woke me in the night (you'd be surprised, it was never the wind: High Point Farm was buffeted constantly by wind that made the oak limbs creak, rattled windowpanes and whined under the eaves and down the chimneys, but we never heard it, only if the wind died down we'd get a little anxious) it was like someone shone a flashlight into my face. My eyes would fly open and I'd lie in bed with my heart pounding, covered in sweat. The time of quick terror when *you don't know who you are, or where*.

Then I would recall my name, my true name: *Judson Andrew Mulvaney*. Dad liked to hint I'd been named after a "rich, eccentric" relative of his, an "Irish landowner of County Kildare" but I guess that was some kind of joke, Dad hadn't any relatives at all in Ireland that he knew, nor any relatives in this country he'd acknowledge. But what a name for a little boy! What promise of dignity, worth! Just the sound of it, shaping the words aloud—it was like Dad's new overcoat, camel's hair, Mom's Christmas present for him she'd bought on sale the previous March in Yewville's best department store, that coat so many sizes larger than anything scrawny Ranger might wear yet a coat I might grow into one day. Like Dad's classy riding boots, another bargain-sale item, and Dad's fur-lined leather gloves. His Ford pickup, and Mom's Buick station wagon, and Mike's lipstick-red Olds Cutlass and the Jeep Wrangler and the John Deere tractor and other farm machinery and vehicles I might one day be capable of driving. All these, *Judson Andrew Mulvaney* summoned to mind.

Shivering with excitement I stood at my window staring down at the deer. Counting six, seven—eight?—cautiously making their way single file through our yard. They were white-tailed deer probably headed for our pasture pond where it extended twenty feet or so beyond the fence. Where by day our small herd of Holsteins drank, grazed, drowsed on their stolid feet slowly filling their enormous milk-bags, near-motionless as black-and-white papier-mâché beasts, only the twitching of their tails, warding off flies, to give you the idea they're alive.

It was 3:25 A.M. A strange thrill, to think I was the only Mulvaney awake in the house.

There were many deer on our property, in the remoter wooded areas, but it was rare for any to pass so close to our house, because of the dogs. (Though our dogs never ran loose at night, like the dogs of certain of our neighbors and a small pack of semi-wild dogs that plagued the area. Mom was furious at the way people abandoned their pets in the country—"As if animals aren't human, too." And there were miserly farmers who didn't believe in feeding their dogs so the dogs had to forage the countryside.) Mulvaney dogs were well fed and thoroughly domesticated and not trained to be hunters though they were supposed to be watchdogs "guarding" the property.

I wanted to follow the deer! Made my way barefoot out of my room and to the stairs thinking *None of them knows where I am, Ranger is invisible*. Little Boots slept so hard on my bed, he hadn't even known I was gone.

Troy, sleeping somewhere downstairs, didn't seem to hear me, either.

You could do an inventory of the Mulvaney staircase and have a good idea what the family was like. Staircases in old farmhouses like ours were oddly steep, almost vertical, and narrow. Our lower stairs, though, were always cluttered at their edges, for here, as everywhere in the house, all sorts of things accumulated, set down "temporarily" and not picked up again, nor even noticed, for weeks. Unopened mail for Dad and Mom, including, sometimes, bills. L.L. Bean catalogues, Burpee's seed catalogues, Farm & Home Supplies circulars. Back issues of *Farm Life*, *Time*, *Newsweek*, *Consumer Reports*, *The Evangelist: A Christian Family Weekly*. Old textbooks. Single gloves, a single boot. Stiffened curry combs and brushes, thumbtacks, screws, stray buttons. Certain steps had been unofficially designated as lost-and-found steps so if you found a button, say, on the living room floor, you'd naturally place it on one of these steps and forget about it. And there it would stay for weeks, months. For a while there were two blue ribbons from the New York State Fair on the stairs, won by Patrick for his 4-H projects. There was a necktie of Mike's stained with spaghetti sauce and wadded up, he'd tossed down and forgotten. Every few weeks when the staircase got so congested there was only a narrow passageway at the bottom, Mom would declare a moratorium and organize whoever was around to clear it; yet within days, or hours, the drift would begin again, things accumulating where they didn't belong. Dad called this the fourth law of thermodynamics—"The propensity of objects at High Point Farm to resist any order imposed upon them."

At the bottom of the stairs I paused to get my bearings. Except for the rattling and creaking of the wind which I didn't hear, the house was silent.

I tiptoed through the dining room, pushed the swinging door open cautiously (it creaked!) and tiptoed through the kitchen hoping the canary wouldn't wake up and make a noise. Off the back hall was a small bathroom, and across from it Mike's room, his door closed of course. (Mike, the oldest child, was special, and had had special privileges for years. He didn't sleep upstairs with the rest of us but had his own large room downstairs, near the bac[k] had virtually his own entrance, his privacy. Now he years old, working for Dad at Mulvaney Roofing, he w any longer but wanted to be considered an adult. Often ᵁᵉ was out late at night, even on weekdays. I didn't know if he was home even now, at this hour.) The back door of the house wasn't locked, I smiled turning the knob it was so easy!—slipping from the house, and no one knew.

Ranger's the baby of the family but he's got some surprises for us. Wait and see.

How bright, glaring-bright, the moon. I hadn't expected that. Shreds of cloud blowing across it like living things. Almost, the light hurt my eyes.

All those stars winking and pulsing. That look of being alive, too. So many! It made me dizzy, confused. Of the constellations Patrick had been trying to teach me, looking through his telescope he'd assembled from a kit, I could identify only the Big Dipper, the Little Dipper, Orion?—but where was Andromeda? The sky seemed to shift and swim the harder I stared. The wind seemed to make the stars vibrate.

The hard-packed dirt of the driveway was wonderfully cool and solid beneath my feet. My bare feet still toughened from summer when I ran around barefoot as much as I could. Up in my room it hadn't seemed cold but now the wind fluttered my pajama legs and lifted my hair from my forehead, I was shivering. And the moon so bright it hurt my eyes.

There was the rooster weathervane on the peak of the hay barn. Creaking in the wind: looked like north-northeast. It was October already. A smell of deep cold, snow to come.

In the barn one of the horses whinnied. Another horse answered. Those quizzical, liquid sounds. A third horse! What were they doing awake at this hour? It wasn't possible they heard me, or smelled me. Clover, my horse, always knew me by some mysterious means (my way of walking, my smell?) when I approached his stall, before I actually came into his sight.

Something streaked past me and disappeared into the grass—one of the barn cats? Or a raccoon? My heart thumped in immediate reaction, though I wasn't scared. *The night was so alive.*

I was a little worried my parents might notice me out here. The floodlights might come on, illuminating the upper drive. Dad's voice yelling, "Who's out there?" And the dogs barking.

But no. I waited, and nothing happened.

It's like I *was* invisible.

The house looked larger now in night than it did in day. A solid looming mass confused with the big oaks around it, immense as a mountain. The barns too were dark, heavy, hulking except where moonlight rippled over their tin roofs with a look like water because of the cloud shreds blowing through the sky. No horizon, solid dark dense-wooded ridges like the rim of a deep bowl, and me in the center of the bowl. The mountains were only visible by day. The tree lines. By night our white-painted fences gleamed faintly like something seen underwater but the unpainted fences and the barbed wire fences were invisible. In the barnyard, the humped haystack, the manure pile, I wouldn't have been able to identify if I didn't know what they were. Glazed-brick silo shining with moonlight. Barns, chicken coop, the sheds for the storage of machinery, much of it old, broken-down and rusted machinery, the garage, carports— silent and mysterious in the night. On the far side of the driveway the orchard, mostly Winesap apples, massed in the dark and the leaves quavering with wind and it came to me *maybe I'm dead? a ghost? maybe I'm not here, at all?*

But I didn't turn back, kept on, following the deer, now passing the strawberry patch (my sister Marianne had taken over, since I'd done only a mediocre job fertilizing, weeding the summer before) and there was Mom's garden we all helped her with, anyway Patrick, Marianne and me, sweet corn, butternut squash, a half dozen pumpkins still remaining, and marigolds beginning to fade, for we'd had a frost or two already. That look as Mom characterized it of an autumn garden—"So melancholy, you want to cry." Along the fence, the sunflowers crowding one another, most of them beginning to droop, going ragged, heads bowed, swaying in the wind like drunken figures. Birds had pecked out most of the seeds and the flowers were left torn and blind-looking yet still it was strange to me to pass by them—sunflowers seem like people!

I was following the deer though I couldn't see them. The earth was puddled and the puddles glittered like mirrors. Smells are sharper by night—I smelled a rich mud-smell, wet-rotted leaves and manure. I wasn't much aware of my feet, cold now, and going numb, so if they were being scratched, cut by stones or spiky thorns, I didn't know. I was scared, but happy! *Not-Judd, now. Not-known.*

I crept up to the pond, which was only about three feet deep at this end. Draining out of the meandering brook that connected with Alder Creek. Every few years the pond choked up with sediment, tree debris and animal droppings, and Dad had to dredge it out with a borrowed bulldozer.

A single doe was drinking at the pond! I crouched in the grasses, watching from about fifteen feet away. I could see her long slender neck outstretched. Her muzzle, lowered to the water. By moonlight the doe was drained of color and on the pond's surface light moved in agitated ripples from where she drank. Where were the other deer? It was unusual to see only one. They must have continued on, into the woods. The doe lingered, lifting her head alert and poised for flight. Her ears twitched—did she hear me? Maybe she could smell me. Her eyes were like a horse's eyes, protuberant and shiny, black. Tension quivered in her slender legs.

I loved the wild creatures. I could never hunt them. They had no names the way the animals of High Point Farm had names. You could not call them, nor identify them. As soon as you sighted them, by day, they would vanish. As if to refute the very authority of your eyes. Theirs was the power to appear and to disappear. It was meant to be so: not as in Genesis, where Adam names the creatures of the earth, sea, and is granted dominion over them by God. Not like that.

Next month was deer-hunting season in the Chautauqua Valley and from dawn to dusk we'd hear the damned hunters' guns going off in the woods and open fields, see their pickups parked by the side of the road and often on our own property. Every year (this was county law, favoring "hunters' rights") Dad had to post new bright orange NO HUNTING NO FISHING signs on our property if we wanted to keep hunters off, but the signs, every fifty yards, made little difference—hunters did what they wanted to, what they could get away with. Through the winter we'd see almost no deer near the house, and rarely bucks. Bucks were killed for their "points" and their handsome antlered heads stuffed as trophies. Ugly glass eyes in the sockets where living eyes had been. Mom wept angrily seeing killed deer slung as dead meat across the fenders of hunters' vehicles and sometimes she spoke to the hunters, bravely, you might say recklessly. To kill for sport Mom said was unconscionable. She was of a farm family where all men and boys hunted, out in Ransomville, and she could not abide it—none of the women could, she said. Once, long ago, Dad himself had hunted—but no longer. There were bad memories (though I did not know what these were) having to do with Dad's hunting and the men he went hunting with, in the area of Wolf's Head Lake. Now, Dad belonged to the Chautauqua Sportsmen's Club—for "business" reasons—but he didn't hunt or fish. It was Dad's position he called "neutral" that since human beings had driven away the wolves and coyotes that were natural predators of deer in this part of the state there was an imbalance of nature and the deer population had swollen so that they were malnourished, always on the verge of starvation, not to mention what predators they'd become, themselves—what damage they caused to crops. (Including ours.) Yet, Dad did not believe in hunting—animals hunted animals, Dad said, but mankind is superior to Nature. Mankind is made in the image of God, not Nature. Yet he didn't seriously object when Mike wanted to buy a .22-caliber rifle at the age of fifteen, for "target practice," and he still had his old guns, untouched now for years.

The doe was staring toward me across the pond. Forelegs bent, head lowered.

Then I heard what she must have been hearing—something trotting, trampling through the meadow. I heard the dogs' panting before I saw them. A pack of dogs! In an instant the doe turned, leapt, and was running, her tail, white beneath, lifted like a flag of distress. Why do deer lift their tails, running for their lives? A signal to predators, glimmering white in the dark? The dogs rushed into the pond, splashing through it, growling deep inside their throats, not yet barking. If they were aware of me they gave no sign, they had no interest in me but only in the doe, five or six of them, ferocious in the chase, ears laid back and hackles raised. I thought I recognized one or two of our neighbor's dogs. I shouted after them, sick with horror, but they were already gone. There was the sound of panicked flight and pursuit, growing fainter with distance. I'd stumbled into the pond and something stabbed into my foot. I was panting, half sobbing. I could not believe what had happened—it had happened so quickly.

If only I'd had a gun.

The does, fawns, their carcasses we found sometimes in the woods, in our cornfields and sometimes as close as the orchard.

Once, a part-devoured doe, near Mom's antique sleigh. Throats and bellies ripped out where they'd fallen. Usually they were only partly devoured.

If only I had a gun. One of Dad's guns, locked in a closet, or a cabinet, in a back room somewhere. The Browning shotgun, the two rifles. There was Mike's rifle, too. Mike had lost interest in target shooting pretty quickly and Patrick hated guns and Dad hadn't taught me to use either the shotgun or the rifles, hadn't allowed me even to touch them. (Though I'm not sure, maybe I never asked.) Still, I believed I would know how to use the guns.

How to aim, pull the trigger, and kill.

Instead, I ran back to the house crying.

Helpless little kid! eleven years old! Babyface, Dimple!

Ranger, roaming the night. Wiping tears, snot from his face.

In the downstairs bathroom, trembling, I ran hot water in the sink. I was trying not to think what had happened to the doe—what the dogs might be doing to her—what I couldn't see happening, and couldn't hear. Back in the woods it would be happening if she had not escaped (but I did not think she had escaped) but maybe I would never know. *Don't think about it* Mom would say. Sometimes even with a smile, a caress. *Don't think about it, Mom will take care of it. And if Mom can't, Dad will. Promise!*

I was terrified the hot-water pipe would make its high-shrieking noise and wake my parents. *What the hell are you doing downstairs, Judd?*—I could hear Dad's voice, not angry so much as baffled. *Going on four in the morning?*

My damned foot, my right foot, was bleeding from a short, deep gash. Both my feet were covered in scratches. *For Christ's sake, why didn't you put on shoes?* I had no answer, there was no answer. I sat on the lowered toilet seat staring at the underside of my feet, the smeary blood, the dirt. I lathered soap in my hands and tried to wash my feet and there was this *uh-uh-uh* sound in my throat like choking. It came over me, I'd trailed blood into the house! For sure. Into the back hall. Oh God I'd have to clean it up before somebody saw.

Before Mom saw, coming downstairs at 6 A.M. Whistling, singing to herself.

There were some Band-Aids in the medicine cabinet, I tried to put on my feet. Tetanus! What if I got tetanus? Mom was always warning us not to go barefoot. It would serve me right, I thought. If my last tetanus shot was worn out, if I died a slow terrible death by blood poisoning.

Don't think about it: back in the woods, what's happening. Or not happening. Or has happened already. Or a thousand thousand times before even you were born, to know of it.

Outside, Mike pulled up, parked. Quiet as he could manage. He'd driven up our driveway with only his parking lights on, slowly. Getting out of his car, he hadn't slammed the door shut.

I couldn't get away in time, there was my older brother in the doorway, blinking at me. Face flushed and eyes mildly bloodshot and I smelled beer on his breath. Blackberry-color smeared around his mouth, down onto his neck—a girl's lipstick. And a sweet smell of sweat, and perfume. Good-looking guy girls stared after in the street, Mule Mulvaney himself, the one of us who most resembled our father, and with Dad's grin, slightly lopsided, teasing-reproachful-affectionate. Mike hadn't shaved since morning so his beard was pushing out, his jaws shadowy. His new suede jacket was open and his velvety-velour gold shirt was partly unbuttoned, showing matted-frizzed red-brown hair at the V. A zipper glinted coppery in the crotch of my brother's snug-fitting jeans and my eye dropped there, I couldn't help it.

Mike said quizzically, "Hey kid what the hell: what's going on? You *cut* yourself?" There were splotches of blood on the floor, blood-soaked wadded tissues, I couldn't hide.

I had to tell Mike I'd been outside, just looking around—"For the hell of it."

Mike shook his head, disapproving. "You've been outside, this time of night? Cutting up your feet? Are you crazy?"

My big brother, who loved me. Mikey-Junior who was the oldest of the Mulvaney kids, Ranger who was the youngest. Always there'd been a kind of alliance between us—hadn't there?

Mike, who was slightly drunk, like Dad good-natured, funny and warm when he'd been drinking in an essentially good mood, and nobody was crossing him, and he was in a position to be generous, crouched down and examined my feet. "If they know you're running around outside, barefoot, like some kind of weird, asshole Indian, there'll be hell to pay. You know how Mom worries about damn ol' *tetanus*." He gave the word "tetanus" a female trill, so already he was treating this as some kind of joke. Weird, but some kind of joke. Nothing for him to get involved in, anyway.

Of course, Mike wouldn't tell on me, that went without saying. Any more than I was likely to tell on him, mentioning to Mom what time he'd come home tonight.

Lifting me beneath the arms like a bundle of laundry, Mike removed me from the toilet seat, suppressing a belch. Lifted the seat, unzipped and urinated into the bowl with no more self-consciousness than one of our Holsteins pissing into the very pond out of which she and the other cows are drinking. Mike laughed, "Christ am I wasted," blowing out his cheeks, rolling his eyes, "—gotta go *crash*."

Too sleepy to wash his hands, his fly unzipped and penis dangling he stumbled across the hall to his room. The little bathroom, closet-sized, was rank with the hot fizzing smell of my brother's urine and quickly I flushed the toilet, wincing at the noise of the plumbing, the shuddering of pipes through the sleeping house.

I was shaky, felt sick to my stomach. *Don't think! Don't.* I wetted some paper towels and tried to clean the hall, blood-smears on the linoleum which wasn't too clean, stained with years of dirt, as for the braided rug—it was so dirty, maybe nobody would notice. I heard a quizzical mewing sound and it was Snowball pushing against my leg, curious about what I was doing, wanting to be fed, but I only petted her and sent her away and limped back upstairs myself and to my room where the door was half-open!—and in my room where the dark was familiar, the smells familiar, I crawled back into bed beside E.T. who made a sleepy gurgling cat-noise in his throat and Little Boots who didn't stir at all, wheezing contentedly in his sleep. So much for the vigilance of animals. *Nobody knew I'd been gone except my brother who not only would not tell but would probably not remember.*

The wind had picked up. Leaves were being blown against my window. It was 4:05 A.M. The moon had shifted in the sky, glaring through a clotted mass of clouds like a candled egg.

ST. VALENTINE'S 1976

No one would be able to name what had happened, not even Marianne Mulvaney to whom it had happened.

Corinne Mulvaney, the mother, should have detected. Or suspected. She who boasted she was capable of reading her husband's and children's faces with the patience, shrewdness and devotion of a Sanskrit scholar pondering ancient texts.

Yet, somehow, she had not. Not initially. She'd been confused (never would she believe: deceived) by her daughter's behavior. Marianne's sweetness, innocence. Sincerity.

The call came unexpectedly Sunday midafternoon. Fortunately Corinne was home to answer, in the antique barn, trying to restore to some semblance of its original sporty glamor a hickory armchair of "natural" tree limbs (Delaware Valley, ca. 1890–1900) she'd bought for thirty-five dollars at an estate auction—the chair was so battered, she could have cried. *How people misuse beautiful things!* was Corinne's frequent lament. The antique barn was crowded with such things, most of them awaiting restoration, or some measure of simple attention. Corinne felt she'd rescued them but hadn't a clear sense of what to do with them—it seemed wrong, just to put a price tag on them and sell them again. But she wasn't a practical businesswoman, she hadn't any method (so Michael Sr. chided her, relentlessly) and it was easy to let things slide. In the winter months, the barn was terribly cold: she couldn't expect customers, when she could barely work out here, herself. Her breath steamed thinly from her nostrils, like slow-expelled thoughts. Her fingers stiffened and grew clumsy. The three space heaters Michael had installed for her quivered and hummed with effort, brightly red-coiled, determined to warm space that could not, perhaps, be warmed. On a bright winter day, cold sun glaring through the cobwebbed, uninsulated windows, the interior of the antique barn was like the vast universe stretching on, on and on where you didn't want to follow, nor even think of; except God was at the center, somehow, a great undying sun—wasn't He?

These were Corinne's *alone-thoughts*. Thoughts she was only susceptible to when alone.

So the phone rang, and there was Marianne at the other end, sounding perfectly—normal. How many years, how many errands run for children, how many trips to town, to school or their friends' houses, wherever, when you had four children, when you lived seven miles out in the country. Marianne was saying, "Mom? I'm sorry, but could someone come pick me up?" and Corinne, awkwardly cradling the receiver between chin and shoulder, interrupted in the midst of trying to glue a strip of decayed bark to a leg of the chair, failed to hear anything in the child's voice that might have indicated distress, or worry. Or controlled hysteria.

It's true: Corinne had more or less forgotten that Marianne's date for last night's prom (you would not want to call Austin Weidman Marianne Mulvaney's "boyfriend") had been supposed to drive her back home, after a visit at Trisha LaPorte's—or was it perhaps the boy's father, Dr. Weidman the dentist?—no, Corinne had forgotten, even whether Austin had his own car. (He did not.) Corinne prided herself on never having been a mother who fussed over her children; it wasn't just that the Mulvaney children were so famously self-reliant and capable of caring for themselves (Corinne's women friends who were mothers themselves envied her), Corinne had a hard time fussing over herself. She'd been brought up to consider herself last, and that seemed about right to her. She didn't so much rush about as fly about, always breathless, not what you'd call perfectly groomed. Her women friends liked her, even loved her—but shook their heads over her. Corinne Mulvaney was an attractive woman, almost pretty—if you troubled to look closely. If you weren't put off by first impressions. (Those who were invariably asked, with almost an air of hurt, how handsome Michael Mulvaney Sr. could have married *that woman*?) Corinne was tall, lanky, loose-jointed and freckled, somewhere beyond forty, yet noisily girlish, with a lean horsey face often flushed, carrot-colored hair so frizzed, she laughingly complained, she could hardly draw a curry comb through it. On errands in town she wore her at-home clothes—overalls, rubberized L.L. Bean boots, an oversized parka (her husband's? one of her sons'?). She was a nervous cheerful woman whose neighing laugh, in the A & P or in the bank, turned people's heads. Her eerily bright-blue lashless eyes with their tendency to open too wide, to *stare*, were her most distinguishing feature, an embarrassment to her children. Her fluttery talk in public, her whistling. Her occasional, always so-embarrassing talk of God. ("God-gush," Patrick called it. But Corinne protested isn't God all around us, isn't God *in* us? Didn't Jesus Christ come to earth to be our Savior? Plain as the noses on our faces.)

At least, Corinne didn't embarrass her daughter Marianne. Sweet good-natured Marianne who was Button, who was Chickadee, who was—everybody's darling. Never judged her mother, or anyone, with that harsh adolescent scorn that so wounds the parents who adore them.

Marianne's voice was low, liquidy-sweet and apologetic. She was calling from Trisha LaPorte's house, where she'd spent the night. The St. Valentine's prom at Mt. Ephraim High had been the previous night, and Marianne Mulvaney had been the only junior elected to the King and Queen's "court"; it was an honor, but Marianne had taken it in stride. She'd stayed over in town as she usually did for such occasions—dances, parties, football or basketball games; she had numerous girlfriends, and was welcome anywhere. Less frequently, Marianne's friends came out to High Point Farm to spend a night or a weekend. Corinne basked in her daughter's popularity as in the warmth of sunshine reflected in a mirror. *She'd* been a gawky farm-girl lucky to have one or two friends in high school, self-conscious and homely; it was a continual amazement to her, her daughter had turned out as she had.

Michael Sr. objected: you were damned good-looking, and you know it. And you got better-looking as you got older. How'd I fall in love with you, for God's sake?

Well, that was a wonder. That was a puzzle Corinne never quite solved. Thought of it every day for the past twenty-three years.

Marianne was apologizing—*that* was a habit Corinne should try to break in her: apologizing more than was necessary—for being a nuisance. "Trisha's father says he'll be happy to drive me home, but you know how icy the roads are, and it's so far—I really don't want to trouble him." Corinne said, "Button, honey, I'll send one of your brothers." "Is it O.K.? I mean—" "No problem," Corinne said, in a country drawl, "—*no* problem." (This phrase had become part of Mulvaney family code, picked up from some TV program by one of the boys and now everyone said it.) Corinne asked Marianne to say hello and give her warm regards to Lillian LaPorte, Trisha's mother: a friendly acquaintance of Corinne's from years ago, both women longtime P.T.A. members, active in the League of Women Voters, the Mt. Ephraim General Hospital Women's Auxiliary. She was about to hang up when it occurred to her to ask, belatedly, "Oh, how was the prom, sweetie? Did you have a good time with— what's-his-name? And how was the dress—honey?"

Marianne had already hung up.

∞

Later, Corinne would recall in bewilderment this conversation, so matter-of-fact and—well, familiar. So *normal*.

Of course, Marianne had not lied. Concealing a truth, however ugly a truth, is not the same as lying. Marianne was incapable of deliberate deception. If now and then there'd been the slightest trace of what you might call subterfuge in her it was a sign she was protecting someone: usually, of course, as they were all growing up, her older brothers. Mikey-Junior who'd been quite a handful in his teens ("First 'Mule' was our bundle of joy," Corinne used to joke, sighing, "now he's our boy-oh-*boy*!"), Patrick, poor sweet-shy short-tempered Pinch, who'd had a tendency since kindergarten to blurt out things he didn't mean, truly didn't mean, not just to his family, which was bad enough, but to his classmates—even to his teachers! Even, one memorably embarrassing time, when he'd been no more than ten, a cutting, shrewd remark ("How do *you* know, did God *tell you*?") put to a Sunday school teacher at the Kilburn Evangelical Church. (Corinne was a passionate "nondenominational Protestant" as she called herself, with a weakness for remote country churches; she dragged the children in her wake, and they seemed happy enough. Michael Sr. was never involved in these infatuations, of course: he described himself as a "permanently lapsed Catholic," which was religion enough to suit him.)

Of the children, Marianne had always been the most natural Christian. In her flamboyant way that embarrassed her children, Corinne was fond of saying, "Jesus Christ came to dwell in my heart when I was a young girl, but He's been dwelling in Button's heart, I swear, since birth."

At this, Marianne would blush and flutter her fingers in an unconscious imitation of her mother. She sighed, "Oh, Mom! The things you say."

Corinne drew herself up to her full height. Mother of the household, keeper of High Point Farm. "Yes! The things I say are *truth*."

Corinne Mulvaney's terrible vanity: her pride in such *truth*.

She marveled at it: how even as a child of two or three, Marianne simply *could not lie*. It distinguished her from her brothers—oh, yes! But from other children, too, who, telling fibs, instinctively imitate their elders, feigning "innocence," "ignorance." But never Marianne.

And she was so pretty! So radiant. No other word: *radiant*. The kitchen bulletin board, Corinne's province, was festooned with snapshots of Marianne: receiving a red ribbon for her juicy plum-sized strawberries a few years ago at the state fair in Albany, and, last year, two blue ribbons—again for strawberries, and for a sewing project; being inducted as an officer in the Chautauqua Christian Youth Conference; at the National 4-H Conference in Chicago where she'd won an award, in 1972. Most of the snapshots of Marianne were of her cheerleading, in her Mt. Ephraim cheerleader's jumper, maroon wool with a white cotton long-sleeved blouse. The previous night Michael had taken a half dozen Polaroids of Marianne in her new dress, which she'd sewed herself from a Butterick pattern—satin and chiffon, strawberries-and-cream, with a pleated bodice and a scalloped hem that fell to her slender ankles. But these lay on a windowsill, not yet selected and tacked up on the bulletin board.

She, Corinne, had never learned to sew. Not really. Her mother had been impatient trying to teach her—she'd mistaken Corinne's eagerness for carelessness. Or was eagerness a kind of carelessness? All Corinne was good for with a needle was mending, which she quite enjoyed. You weren't expected to be perfect mending torn jeans or socks worn thin at the heel.

How beautiful Marianne was! Alone with no one to observe, Corinne could stare and stare at these pictures of her daughter. At seventeen Marianne was still very young, and young-looking; with a fair, easily marred skin, no freckles like her mom; deep-set and intelligent pebbly-blue eyes; dark curly hair that snapped and shone when briskly brushed—which Corinne was still allowed to do, now and then. It was Corinne's secret belief that her daughter was a far finer person than she was herself, a riddle put to her by God. *I must become the mother deserving of such a daughter—is that it?*

Of course, Corinne loved her sons, too. As much—well, almost as much as she loved Marianne. Loving boys was just more of a challenge, somehow. Like keeping an even course in a canoe on a wild rushing river. Boys didn't let you rest!

A long time ago when they were young married lovers with only the one baby, Mikey-Junior they'd adored, Corinne and Michael made a pact. If they had more babies—which they dearly wanted—they must vow never to favor one over the others; never to love one of their children the most, or another the least. Michael said, reasonably, "We've got more than enough love for all of them, whoever they are. Right?"

Corinne hugged and kissed him in silence, of course he was right.

What a feverish, devoted, you might say obsessed young mother she'd been! Her blue eyes shone like neon. Her heart beat steady and determined. She knew she could love inexhaustibly because she was herself nourished by God's inexhaustible love.

But Michael had more to say. In fact, Michael was argumentative, impassioned as Corinne rarely saw him. He'd come from a large Irish Catholic family of six boys and three girls in Pittsburgh; his father, a steelworker and a heavy drinker, had bullied his mother into submission young and slyly cultivated a game of pitting Michael and his brothers against one another. All the while Michael was growing up he'd had to compete with his brothers for their father's approval—his "love." At the age of eighteen he'd had enough. He quarreled with the old man, told him off, left home. So his father retaliated by cutting Michael out of his life permanently: he never spoke to him again, not even on the phone; nor did he allow anyone else in the family to see Michael, speak with him, answer any of his letters.

"Of all of them, only two of my brothers kept in contact with me," Michael said bitterly. "My mother, my sisters—even my sister Marian I was always so close with—acted as if I'd died."

"Oh, Michael." He shrugged, screwed up his face in an expression of brave boyish indifference, but Corinne saw the deep indelible hurt. "You must miss them . . ." Her voice trailing off weakly, for it was so weak a remark.

Of course she'd understood that relations were cool between Michael and his family—not one Mulvaney had come to their wedding! But she'd never heard the full story. She'd never heard so sad a story.

Michael said quietly, "No more, and no less, than the old bastard misses *me*."

RINGING THE
COWBELL

There was Patrick, shrewd-suspicious Pinch, falling for one of Mom's tricks!

Ringing the cowbell on the back veranda, the gourd-shaped coppery "antique"—as Mom called it—to summon him back to the house and inveigle him into volunteering—"volunteering"—to drive into town to fetch Marianne home.

Like a fool, Patrick had come running. The sound of the cowbell at High Point Farm was understood to be code for *Who's in the mood for an outing? a nice surprise?* Years ago when the family had been younger, Dad or Mom frequently rang the cowbell on summer evenings to announce an impromptu trip for all within earshot—to the Dairy Queen on Route 119, to Wolf's Head Lake for a swim and picnic supper. When the drive-in on Route 119 had still been operating, the clanging cowbell might even mean a movie—a double feature. In any case, it was supposed to signal *an outing! a nice surprise!* Not an errand.

Patrick should have known better. Eighteen years old, no longer a kid dependent upon his parents' whims and moods, he, not one of his parents, was likely to be the one driving somewhere on a Sunday afternoon. In mid-February, it wouldn't be to any Dairy Queen or to Wolf's Head Lake. But the sound of the cowbell in the distance, as he was walking along the frozen creek, one of the dogs, Silky, trotting and sniffing at his side, had quickened his pulse with the promise of childhood adventure.

Of the family, Patrick was the one to wander off by himself. He was content to be alone. At least, with only an animal companion or two. He'd done his barn chores for the day, cleaning out the horses' stalls, grooming, feeding, watering—seven pails of water a day per horse, minimum! Then he'd gone hiking along Alder Creek for miles up into the hills above High Point Farm. He might have been entranced by the snow-swept windswept distances but in fact his mind was tormented with ideas. Ideas buzzing and blazing like miniature comets. In one of his science magazines he'd read an essay, "Why Are the Laws of Nature Mathematical?" that had upset him. How could the laws of nature be mathematical?—only mathematical? He'd read, too, about certain recent evolutionary discoveries and new theories of the origin of Homo sapiens in northern Africa—what had these to do with mathematics? He said aloud, aggrieved, "I don't get it."

Innocently vain at eighteen, Patrick Mulvaney thought of himself as an experimental scientist, a biologist. He'd been awarded quite a prestigious scholarship from Cornell University to study "life sciences" there. His dad, who hadn't gone to college, boasted that Cornell was "one of the great American universities"—embarrassing to Patrick, though surely true. Patrick intended to push on for a Ph.D. and devote himself to original research in molecular biology. His grades in science at the high school were always high A's; his grades in solid geometry and calculus were high A's too, but Patrick sensed his limits, knew he hadn't natural aptitude for higher math. It filled him with dismay and panic to think that the laws of nature might be mathematical in essence and not a matter of indefatigable observation, data, experimentation. It was unfair! Unjust! Yet—was it correct? *Science is a continuous text ceaselessly being written, revised, redacted, expanded and edited, while mathematics is pure and ahistorical. Much of today's science will be refuted, but not mathematics.* Was this so? How could it be so? What could mathematics say of life? the simplest unicellular life? What could mathematics say of the mysterious evolutionary branchings of life through the millions of years of earth's existence? Patrick murmured aloud, "They don't know everything."

A fine powdery snow was blown against his face, from the ground. Above, the sky was clear—a hard wintry blue like ceramic.

Patrick hiked on, and began to smile. Recalling the "exquisitely beautiful watercolors"—Mom's words—he'd slyly tacked up on the kitchen bulletin board, aged fourteen. Mysterious prints of what appeared to be brilliantly adorned suns, moons, comets—whatever? After keeping the family guessing for a few days Patrick revealed what the prints were: magnified slides of the dogs' saliva.

The looks on their faces.

How Patrick had laughed, laughed. All of them, even Mike, staring at him in disbelief and revulsion. As if he'd betrayed them, or some sacred trust. *As if he'd betrayed the dogs!* Patrick demanded to know why the dogs' saliva, teeming with microbes (not so very different from their own) had seemed "exquisitely beautiful" to them one day, but not the next. Never mind, Patrick, Mom had said huffily, just take those things down at once, please.

Now Patrick laughed aloud, remembering. The memory had quite vanquished his anxiety of a few minutes before. "They don't know anything!"—he heard his bemused voice, aloud.

He meant not just the Mulvaneys, but most of mankind.

Hearing the cowbell, a summons from his mom, Patrick cut his hike short and trotted the mile or so back to the house, Silky panting excitedly beside him, but the trick was on him this time—"I'm sorry to bother you, P.J., but Button needs a ride home from the LaPortes. Can you drive in?" Mom was apologetic, smiling, in that shamelessly exploitive way of hers none of her children could resist, Corinne Mulvaney playing at and perhaps even imagining herself as flustered, helpless—so contrary to her true nature, which was all efficiency. She was in the midst of refinishing a piece of furniture and couldn't stop, she hoped he'd understand, she *was* sorry to be intruding on his time to himself after he'd done his chores and did them so well and—anyway—it was a favor for Button, wasn't it? "Take the Buick, hon. Dad's out with the pickup. Here, catch—" fishing the keys to the station wagon out of a deep pocket of her stained coveralls and tossing them with inappropriate gaiety to Patrick, who glared at her with all that he could muster of adolescent irony. "Gee thanks, Mom," he said, shoving his glasses against the bridge of his nose, "—a Sunday drive to Mt. Ephraim and back. Just what I need."

Fourteen miles, round-trip. No, closer to fifteen since the LaPortes lived on the far side of town. It was a trip he took five days a week, back and forth, usually on the school bus.

So he'd driven into Mt. Ephraim, and picked up his sister, and yes he'd possibly noticed that something was wrong, Marianne's smile less convincing than usual, an evasiveness in her eyes, and certainly she wasn't her usual chattery-brimming self, a purely and profoundly and to Patrick's superior mind often exasperatingly girl-self; but frankly he'd been relieved not to hear about the prom and the party and her "date" and her familiar litany of girlfriends Trisha, Suzi, Bonnie, Merissa—how "fantastic" the decorations in the gym, how "terrific" the local band, what a "wonderful, unforgettable" time everyone had had. And how "honored" she'd been, in the Valentine Queen's court. Patrick, a senior, hadn't the slightest interest, not even an anthropological interest, in the frantic febrile continually shifting social lives of any of his classmates. Corinne was disappointed in him perhaps, he'd scarcely known the Valentine's Day prom was the previous night until the commotion and fuss over Marianne and her new dress, Dad taking Polaroids as usual, and the "date" showing up—Austin Weidman in a dark suit that made him look like a funeral director, poor adenoidal Austin who was in fact a fellow senior, a shy frowning nervous-handed boy intelligent enough to have been a friend of Patrick Mulvaney's through the years but was not. Patrick simply wasn't impressed with Austin and smiled coolly at him, looked through him. Why? *Just Patrick's way.*

Marianne had once complained to Mom, why was Patrick so *unfriendly?* so *rude?* to her friends? to her friends who admired him in fact? and Corinne had said soothingly, in Patrick's earshot, *Oh, that's just Patrick's way.* Which had quite boosted his ego.

So he hadn't paid much attention to his kid sister as he considered her, a year younger, a year behind him in school but light-years distant from him, he was sure, in matters of significance. He may have asked her how the dance—"or whatever it was"—had been and Marianne might have replied murmuring something vague but in no way alarming; adding, with an apologetic little laugh, touching her forehead in a gesture very like Corinne's, "—I guess I'm *tired.*"

Patrick laughed, one of those coded mirthless brotherly laughs signaling *So?* He'd tossed Marianne's garment bag into the back of the Buick where it upended, and slid down, and oddly Marianne hadn't noticed, or in any case hadn't reached around to adjust it. In that bag were Marianne's new prom dress, her prom shoes, toiletries. Patrick didn't give it a thought.

Why didn't you tell me? Why, as soon as you got into the car? As soon as we were alone together?

Afterward he would think these things but not at the time. Nor did he think much of the fact (he, who so prided himself in his powers of observation) that when he'd turned into the LaPortes' driveway *there was his sister already outside waiting for him*. Waiting out in the cold. Garment bag, purse at her feet. Marianne in her good blue wool coat. Just waiting.

In truth Patrick might have felt relief. That Marianne's best friend Trisha wasn't with her, that he didn't have to exchange greetings with Trisha.

He'd backed out of the LaPortes' driveway without a second glance, wouldn't have noticed if anyone had been watching from one of the windows, behind the part-drawn blinds. Marianne was fussing with the seat belt, at the same time petting Silky's persistent head as he poked against her from his awkward position in the backseat, forbidden to climb into the front as he dearly wanted, but she hadn't let him lick her face—"No, Silky! Sit." Silky was Mike's dog he was always neglecting now.

Afterward Mom would say, *I thought you and Marianne were so close. Thought you shared things you wouldn't share with Dad or me.*

Patrick hadn't even thought to inquire why Marianne needed a ride home, in fact. Why Austin Weidman—her "date"—hadn't picked her up, driven her. Wasn't that a "date's" responsibility? Marianne often stayed overnight in town with one or another girlfriend and nearly always she was driven home, if not by a "date" then by someone else. Marianne Mulvaney was so well liked, so *popular*, she rarely lacked for people eager to do her favors.

Nor did Patrick inquire after Austin Weidman. It was absurd, that Marianne had gone to the prom with Austin. A dentist's son, fairly well-to-do family, very Christian, bookish. Marianne had agreed to go with him only after consulting her conscience, and no doubt asking Jesus' advice, for though she didn't "like" Austin in the way of a seventeen-year-old girl's "liking" a boy, she did "respect" him; and he'd asked her weeks ago, or months—the poor jerk had actually written her a letter! (Which she'd showed only to Corinne, not to the derisive male Mulvaneys.) Crafty-desperate Austin had dared put in his bid to Marianne Mulvaney, a junior, and hardly a girl who'd encouraged him, well in advance of other more likely "dates." Marianne was so tenderhearted, so fearful of hurting anyone's feelings, of course she'd said yes.

Last year she'd done the same thing, almost. Jimmie Holleran in his wheelchair. Jimminy-the-Cricket Holleran the kids cruelly called him behind his back, a boy in Marianne's class long stricken with cystic fibrosis, in fact vice-president of the class. He and Marianne were friends from Christian Youth and he, too, had asked her to a dance months before. Though even Mom had wondered about that—"Oh, Button, won't it seem like, well—charity?" Marianne had said, hurt, "I *like* Jimmie. I *want* to go to the dance with him."

Impossible to argue with such goodness.

"Button" Mulvaney was so sweet, so sincere, so pretty, so—what, exactly?—glimmering-luminous—as if her soul shone radiant in her face—you could smile at her, even laugh at her, but you couldn't not love her.

As a brother, that is.

Patrick disdained high school sports, most clubs and activities and competitions of popularity in whatever guise, but he could hardly ignore the presence of "Button" Mulvaney at Mt. Ephraim High. (Even as, grinding his teeth, he could hardly ignore the fallout of his similarly popular older brother Mike—"Mule"—"Number Four"—who'd graduated in 1972.)

Not that he was jealous. Not Pinch.

In fact his sister's popularity this past year at Mt. Ephraim High was an embarrassment to him. He squirmed having to watch her with the other varsity cheerleaders at assemblies before games—the eight girls in their maroon wool jumpers that fitted their slender bodies snugly, their small perfectly shaped breasts, flat bellies, hips and thighs and remarkable flashing legs. They were agile as dancers, double-jointed as gymnasts. They were all very, very good-looking. They wore dazzling-white cotton blouses and dazzling-white wool socks and their smiles were identically dazzling-white—such joyous smiles! And all in the service of the school football team, basketball team, swim team. Boys. Boys whom Patrick privately scorned. Grimly Patrick stared into a corner of the auditorium as into a recess of his own labyrinthine mind, as about him hundreds of idiots yelled, clapped, whistled, stamped their feet like a single great beast.

TWO!   FOUR!   SIX!   EIGHT!
WHO DO WE AP - PRE - CI - ATE?
MT.   EPHRAIM   RAMS!!!

Too silly, too contemptible for words.

But try explaining that to Michael Sr. and Corinne, the proud parents of "Button" Mulvaney. As they'd been for four glorious years the proud parents of "Mule" Mulvaney.

Patrick had never told his parents how he dreaded one day discovering Marianne's name in a school lavatory. Whenever he saw obscene or suggestive words, nasty drawings, above all the names or initials of girls he believed he knew, Patrick rubbed them off in disgust if no one was around, sometimes inked them over with a felt-tip pen. How he despised his male classmates' filthy minds! their juvenile humor! Even the nice guys, the halfway intelligent guys could be astonishingly crude in exclusively male company. Why, Patrick didn't know. Every other word "shit"—"fuck"—"bugger"—"asshole"—"cocksucker." Patrick himself was too pure to tolerate the breaking of taboos not wholly intellectual.

Another thing Patrick had never told his parents: how Marianne, for all her popularity, was considered one of the "good, Christian" girls. Virgins of course. But virgins in their heads, too. There was something mildly comical about them—their very piety, decency. A tale was told of how Marianne had asked one of the science teachers why God had made parasites. In the cafeteria, amid the bustle of laughter, raised voices, high-decibel jocularity, Marianne was one of those Christians who bowed their heads before picking up their forks, murmuring prayers of gratitude. Most of these conspicuous believers were girls, a few were boys. Jimminy-the-Cricket Holleran was one. All were unperturbed by others' bemused glances. Or wholly unaware of them.

In conversation, exactly like her mother, Marianne might speak so familiarly of Jesus you'd swear He was in the next room.

The previous fall, one of the popular football players was injured at a game, hospitalized with a concussion, and Marianne Mulvaney had been one of the leaders of a fervent all-night prayer vigil on the field. The injured boy had been admitted to intensive care at Mt. Ephraim General but by the time the prayer vigil ended next morning at 8 A.M., doctors declared him "out of immediate danger."

So you could smile at Marianne Mulvaney and the "good, Christian" girls of Mt. Ephraim. You could even laugh at them. But they never seemed to notice; or, if they did, to take offense.

Why didn't you tell me? Anything.

How could you let me drive you home that day, not knowing what you were feeling. What you were enduring.

* * *

By 5 P.M. the sky was streaked in dusk. Plum-colored crevices in patches of cloud. Blowing, flying high overhead. Patrick tried not to be spooked by the sight of snow-covered vehicles on the roadside, abandoned days before during a blizzard. The Haggartsville Road was fair driving but High Point was basically a single crudely plowed lane. He'd gotten out, so he supposed he could get back. And school again in the morning. That damned school bus he was bored by the sight of.

Saying something of this to Marianne, who was clutching her pink-angora hands on her lap and didn't seem to hear or in any case didn't reply. The stiffness, the tension in her. Was she frightened of her brother's driving? The heavy car skidding? Beneath loose powdery snow the hard-packed snow of High Point was smooth as satin. Treacherous.

That satin dress: cream-colored, with strawberry chiffon trim: St. Valentine's. Mrs. Glover the senior English teacher speaking coyly of Cupid, "romantic love," Eros. Does anyone know what "Eros" means?

At the curve in the road just beyond the Pfenning farm the station wagon's rear tires did spin for several sickening seconds. Patrick quickly shifted gears, pumped the brakes. He knew not to turn the steering wheel in the direction instinct suggests but in the opposite direction, moving with the skid. And in a moment the vehicle was back in control. He'd reached out to shield Marianne from the dashboard but there hadn't been that much momentum and her seat belt held her in place. He saw, though, how stiffly she held herself, oddly hunched and her mittened hands gripped together tight against her knees. Her pale lips were moving silently—was she praying? Patrick had broken into a quick nervous sweat inside his sheepskin jacket.

"Marianne? You all right?"

"Oh, yes."

"Sorry if I shook you up."

Why didn't you tell me about it then? Why, not even a word?

Was it that you didn't want me to become contaminated, too?

Frankly, by this time, miles of driving, Patrick was becoming annoyed, hurt by his sister's silence. And now this silent-prayer crap! An insult.

High Point Road, haphazardly plowed, wound along the ridge of the ancient glacial striation. Out of the northeast, from the vast snowy tundra of northern Ontario, came that persistent wind. Rocking the station wagon as it frequently rocked the school bus. Like ridicule, Patrick thought. Like jeering. Invisible air-currents plucking at your life.

He remembered, in ninth grade. In the boys' locker room. Boys talking of their own sisters. Maybe it was one boy, and the others avidly listening. Patrick had not been among them, rarely was Patrick among these boys but at a little distance from them, swiftly and self-consciously changing his clothes. In that phase of his early adolescence in which the merest whisper of a forbidden word, a caress of feathers, a sudden sweet-perfumy scent, the sound of fabric against fabric, silky, suggestive—the mere thought of a girl's armpit! nostril! the moist red cut between the legs!—would arouse Patrick sexually, to the point of pain. He'd hidden away in disgust, in shame. Hadn't yet cultivated the haughty Pinch-style, staring his inferiors down.

Patrick Mulvaney a genius? Come on! His I.Q. was only 151. In tenth grade he'd taken a battery of tests, with a half dozen other selected students. You weren't supposed to know the results but somehow Patrick did. Possibly his mom had told him, absurdly proud.

Not a genius but still rumors spread. Like the rumor that he was blind in one eye. Did Patrick care, Patrick did not care. Telling himself he'd rather be respected and feared at Mt. Ephraim High School than liked. Popular!

His heroes were Galileo, Newton, Charles Darwin. The Curies, Albert Einstein. The scientists of whom he read voraciously in the pages of *Scientific American*, to which he subscribed. You couldn't imagine any of these people caring in the least about *popularity*.

It did upset him, though, that everyone seemed to know his secret: he was in fact blind in one eye. Almost.

Mom had surely confided in his gym teacher, when he'd started high school. She'd promised she would not but probably yes it had been Mom, meaning well. Not wanting his other eye to be injured—that would have been her logic, Patrick could hear her pleading, could see her wringing her hands. Patrick had had an accident grooming one of the horses, in fact his own horse Prince he'd loved, young high-strung Prince who was both docile and edgy and somehow it happened that the two-year-old gelding was spooked in his stall by something fleeting and inconsequential as a bird's whirring wings and shadow across a sunlit bale of hay and suddenly to his terror Patrick, at that time twelve years old, weighing not much more than one hundred pounds, was thrown against a wall, found himself down beneath the horse's terrible malletlike hooves screaming for help. His left arm had been broken and his left eye swollen shut, the retina detached and requiring emergency surgery in Rochester. Of the experience Patrick recalled little, out of disgust and disbelief. It had long wounded his pride that of the Mulvaneys he was the only one obliged to wear glasses.

Driving, Patrick shut his left eye, looked with his right eye at the snowy road ahead, the waning glare of the snow, the rocky slope down into the Valley. This should have been a familiar landscape but was in fact always startling in its newness, its combination of threat and promise. He was never able to explain to anyone not even to Marianne how fascinating it was, that the world was *there*; and he, possessed of the miracle of sight, *here*. He would no more take the world *there* for granted than he would take being *here* for granted. And vision in his right eye at least. For the eye was an instrument of observation, knowledge. Which was why he loved his microscope. His homemade telescope. Books, magazines. His own lab notebooks, careful drawings and block-print letters in colored inks. The chunky black altimeter/barometer/"illuminator" sports watch he wore day, night, awake, asleep, removing only when he showered though in fact the watch (a birthday gift from the family, chosen by Marianne out of the L.L. Bean catalogue) was guaranteed waterproof—of course. And he loved his shortwave radio he'd assembled from a kit. Plying him on insomniac nights with weather reports in the Adirondacks, Nova Scotia. As far away as the Canadian Rockies.

You could trust such instruments and such knowledge as you could not trust human beings. That was not a secret, merely a fact.

Patrick was driving his mom's Buick station wagon carefully along this final stretch of High Point Road. He was thinking that the horizon he'd grown up seeing without knowing what he saw here in the Chautauqua Valley, 360 degrees of it, was a hinge joining two spaces: the one finite, a substance inadequately called "land" that dropped to the Yewville River, invisible from this distance, and the other infinite, a substance inadequately called "sky" overhead. Each was an unknown. Though Patrick tried to imagine the glacier fields of millions of years ago, an epoch to which had been given the mysterious name *Pleistocene* which was one of Patrick's words reverently spoken aloud when he was alone.

Pleistocene. Mile-high mountains of ice grinding down everything in their paths.

You could see Patrick was hurt, obviously it showed in his face. If Marianne had noticed.

Gunning the motor as he turned up the rutty-snowy drive, racing the station wagon in the home stretch to announce *Here we are!* And parking noisily in front of the antique barn inside which Corinne was working. Marianne might have begun to say, "Thank you, Patrick—" but she spoke too softly, already he was out of the vehicle, in one of his quick-incandescent and wordless furies, and there came Silky exploding comically out of the rear of the vehicle too, to dash about in the snow, urinating in dribbles, shaking his ears as if he'd been confined for days. Marianne was carrying her garment bag in the direction of the back door and somehow the plastic handle slipped from her fingers and Patrick hesitated before helping her to retrieve it and Marianne said quickly, her voice quavering, fear in her eyes that were a damp blurred blue Patrick would afterward recall, "No!—it's fine, I have it." Marianne smiled at him, unconvincingly. Her tall impatient brother loose-limbed and nerved-up as one of the young horses. "Suit yourself," Patrick said. He shrugged as if, another time, he'd been subtly but unmistakably rebuffed, turned to slam into the house, upstairs to his room, his books.

It's fine, I have it. It's fine.

FAMILY CODE

Many things were coded at High Point Farm. Like our names which could be confusing for they depended upon mood, circumstance, subtext.

For instance, Michael Sr. was usually Dad but sometimes Curly and sometimes Captain. He could be Grouchy (of the Seven Dwarves), or Groucho (of Groucho Marx fame), he could be Big Bear, Chickie, Sugarcake—these names used exclusively by Mom. My oldest brother was usually just Mike but sometimes Mike Jr. or Mikey-Junior; sometimes Big Guy, Mule, Number Four (his football jersey number for the three years he excelled as a fullback at Mt. Ephraim High). Patrick was frequently P.J. (for Patrick Joseph) or Pinch. Marianne was frequently Button or Chickadee. My names, as I've said, were many, though predominantly Baby, Dimple, Ranger.

Mom was Mom except for special names which only Dad could call her (Darling, Honeylove, Sweetheart, Sugarcake). Occasionally Mom could be called Whistle—but only within the family, never in the presence of outsiders.

It was a matter of exquisite calibration, tact. Which code name at which time. Especially in Mom's case, for there were times when being called Whistle seemed to vex her and other times when it was exactly what she wanted to hear—she would laugh, and blush, and roll her eyes as if her innermost soul had been exposed.

Why Whistle? Because Mom had a habit of whistling when she believed herself alone, and to those of us who overheard, her whistling was a happy contagious sound. In the kitchen, in the antique barn; tending the animals; in her garden through the long summer and into the fall. Mom's whistling was loud and assured as any man's but with a shift of mood it could turn liquid and lovely as a flute. You'd listen, fascinated. You'd think Mom was speaking to you, without exactly knowing it, herself. Locking stanchions around the thick neck of a cow, scrubbing a horse's mud- and manure-splattered coat, fending off enraged fowl who'd hoped to hide their eggs in the hay barn, especially in the early morning when she and our canary Feathers were the only ones up—there was Mom, whistling. "Faith of Our Fathers"—"The Battle Hymn of the Republic"—"Tell Me Why the Stars Do Shine"—but also "I'm Dreaming of a White Christmas" (a year-round favorite, to Dad's exasperation)—"I'm Forever Blowing Bubbles"—"I'll Be Seeing You"—"Heartbreak Hotel"—"Hound Dog"—"Blue Suede Shoes" (though Mom claimed to disapprove of Elvis as a poor moral example for the young). When she was in the house, Mom was likely to be whistling with Feathers, who, like most male canaries, responded excitedly when he heard whistling in or near his territory. Whistling was a quick expedient way of communicating with the livestock, of course: the horses whinnied alertly in reply, pricking their ears and flicking their tails as if to say *Yes? Time to eat?* Cows, goats, even sheep blinked to attention. Two deft fingers to her mouth, a shrill penetrating whistle, and Mom could bring dogs, cats, barnyard fowl and whatever else was in the vicinity to converge upon her where she stood, usually beneath one of the carports in an area designated for outdoor feeding, laughing and bountiful as the Goose Lady in our well-worn old copy of Grimm's Fairy Tales.

Dad whistled, too. Hummed happily under his breath. But none of his names alluded to his musical ability or lack of ability.

Coded too were the ways in which we sometimes spoke to each other through animals. This was a means of communication that predated my birth, of course. I remember as a very young child crawling energetically on a carpet, and Dad and Mom praising me to one of the dogs—"Foxy, look! Baby is as fast as *you*."

Such a way of addressing one another was a witty, playful means of making simple requests: "Silky, will you trot over and ask Curly when he wants supper, early or late; and when he plans on husking the sweet corn, in any case." Or, in a raised voice, "Snowball, will you please ask Judd to come out here and give me a hand?" It was a favored means for mild scolding: "Muffin, please ask a certain some-body"—this might be Mike, Patrick, Judd, or even Dad—"how long he plans on lounging there with the refrigerator door wide open?" Mostly such remarks were from Mom or Dad. When we kids imitated them, the code seemed somehow not to work, quite. I remember Mike furious at Patrick for some reason, the two of them riding their horses in the front drive, Patrick stiff and upright in the lead, his horse's tail flicking, and Mike calling after, "Hey, Prince: tell your rider he's a horse's ass, thanks!" But both Prince and his rider ignored the taunt, breaking into a canter to escape.

Most of these exchanges, in fact, were inside our house. Now that I think of it, most were in the kitchen. For the kitchen was the heart of our household; where we naturally gravitated to seek one another out. The radio was always on, turned to Mom's favorite Yewville station; there were always dogs and cats underfoot, looking to be petted or fed; of course, Feathers was a permanent resident in his handsome brass cage near the window. Of all the Mulvaney pets, it was Muffin the cat who was the favored medium for such ex-changes; Muffin who was sweetly docile and patient and so unfail-ingly attentive when we human beings spoke, you'd swear he understood our words. With comical intensity Muffin would look from one speaker to the other, and back, and again, like a spectator at a tennis match. His tawny cat-eyes flashed sympathy, concern. It was almost possible to think, as Dad insisted, that Muffin wasn't a cat but a human being in disguise; yet, being an animal, he was ever so much nicer than any human being. "Muffin, you and I under-stand each other, don't we?" Dad would say, stooping to pet the cat, shaking dry food out of a box into a dish for a between-meals snack that was in fact against Mom's household diet rules just as Dad's own forays into the refrigerator between meals were against the rules, "—both of us endomorphs, eh?" Dad was growing ever more husky with the years, his muscular torso thickening, his belly push-ing out over his belt; he would never be a fat man, nor even plump, for there was no softness to him, only a kind of defiant sinewy flesh. Muffin had begun his Mulvaney life as an abandoned kitten, rescued with his brother Big Tom from imminent death by starvation in a landfill off High Point Road, so tiny he could fit into the palm of the youngest Mulvaney's hand; with alarming swiftness he'd grown into a soft heavy adult male, neutered, weighing somewhere beyond twenty pounds. He was by no means a beautiful animal though his coat was silky-white, always impeccably clean, with lopsided mark-ings like a child's drawing in orange, black, gray, brown. His head was round as a cabbage. His tail was ringed as a raccoon's. He'd been Marianne's kitten from the start, but we all loved him. Dad was a little rough showing his affection, hauling the big cat up onto his lap as he sat at the kitchen table sipping coffee and making tele-phone calls. It was Dad's habit to speak craftily through Muffin to certain of his sons—"Muffin, one thing puzzles me and maybe you can clear it up? Why, after I made a simple request five days ago is the tire on the goddamned John Deere *still flat*?" The object of such remarks was usually Mike, who tended to slight his farm chores. So Mike would say to Muffin, with a smile, "Muffin, explain to Dad I'm just a little behind, I'm still mucking out those goddamned stalls. Tell him I'm sorry, *sir*!"

There was a protocol to such exchanges, a logic to the most cir-cumlocutory of maneuvers. When the code was broken the effect was like a slap in the face. That time Marianne entered the kitchen so quietly I didn't know she was there at first, this would have been early evening of the day following Valentine's Day, early evening of the Sunday she'd been at the LaPortes'. Less than twenty-four hours after *it* had happened to her and in that limbo of time when none of us had any idea, any suspicion. I was hurriedly finishing one of my household chores, cleaning out some of the accumulated magazines, newspapers, mail-order catalogues from the kitchen alcove, and Mom was trimming a half dozen plants she'd brought to set on the table, whistling under her breath, and I heard her say in her bright-flirty voice, "Feathers!—what's this I've heard about a certain some-one not getting to church this morning?" There was a moment's startled silence, I turned to see that Marianne had come in. Her back was to me. She wore jeans, a sweatshirt. Her hair was pulled roughly back in a ponytail. She said, so softly I almost couldn't hear, "I—I think it's cruel for that poor bird to be caged his entire life so that selfish human beings like us can be entertained by him. I think it's a *sin*."

Mom was so surprised, the shears slipped from her fingers and clattered to the floor.

Not just that Marianne of all her children had spoken these harsh words but that Marianne had broken the code. When Mom or Dad addressed you by way of an animal, you always replied the same way. Yet, suddenly, Marianne had not.

Mom said, defensively, drawing herself up to her full height as if her very integrity had been challenged, "Why, Button! What do you mean? Feathers is a canary bred for the cage, and so were his parents and their parents going back for generations! Feathers wouldn't have any life if he hadn't been bred for the cage. He was born in that cage, in fact. You could say that the cage is Feathers' life. And it's a lovely nineteenth-century brass cage, an *antique*." Mom's voice was tremulous with hurt and indignation, as when she argued politics with Dad, rising on the reverential word *antique*.

Marianne said, almost inaudibly, "Mom. It's still a *cage*."

Turning then, with a sigh of exasperation, or a muffled sob, taking no heed of me but hurrying out of the kitchen before Mom could protest any further. Mom and I stared after my sister in mutual astonishment as she pushed blindly through the swinging door into the dining room, and was gone.

Did you know, Marianne: how by breaking the code that day, you broke it forever? For us all?

DIRTY GIRL

Mike Mulvaney Jr. was a senior at Mt. Ephraim and he was on the football team and some of his buddies were involved with the girl but he had not been involved. "Mule" heard all about it, for sure. But he had not been involved.

What can you expect of a girl like that. That kind of girl. Her mother, her sisters. County welfare. Runs in the family.

What the Mt. Ephraim guys did after the last game of the season. Three or four guys on the team and some older guys who'd graduated the year before. Sure, they were all friends of Mike Mulvaney's but Mike Mulvaney had not been one of them, that night.

Getting a retarded girl drunk. Doing—you know, things—to her.

Hey: she isn't retarded. Who says that?

The whole family, the Duncans—the mother's an alcoholic, she's got Indian blood. Comes from the Seneca reservation.

That's not what I heard: I heard they're—you know, Negro.

Well it's all the same. That kind of people. At that—what d'you call it—trailer court—

Trailer village. On the Haggartsville Road.

Mule knew all about it, or maybe just a little about it. Guys exaggerate. They were all drunk. In the Mt. Ephraim Cemetery—wild! You can't believe everything you hear. Della Rae Duncan went out with all kinds of guys including guys in their twenties, and older. Or it was her sister, or one of her sisters—the one with the baby. *Baby pitch-black as tar. No, that's the one that died. Wasn't it a hole in the heart?*

On Monday morning we began to hear of it. First on the school bus, then at school. Nobody knew exactly. None of the younger kids knew. Their older brothers wouldn't tell and it wasn't clear if their older sisters knew: they'd frown, look away. There was the exciting promise *something had happened* which was a still more exciting promise *somebody's going to get into trouble.* Either Della Rae Duncan had had something happen to her or she was going to get into trouble or both.

Della Rae was one of the big girls on the bus. Fifteen years old and still in ninth grade. She wasn't in special ed like a cousin of hers, a tall hulking boy with a harelip. Some of us believed she'd started off in special ed, in seventh grade possibly, but she was in regular ninth-grade classes now.

Della Rae was a *dirty girl* we'd hear. It was just something you knew. There were certain *dirty girls* and Della Rae Duncan was one of them. Some of us thought that Della Rae was a *dirty girl* because her skin was dirty, and her clothes. Her skin looked stained, like wood. She was a short heavyset girl with sizable breasts. A bulldog face. Large thick-lidded eyes and a snaky scar on her swollen upper lip. She was almost nice-looking except she was ugly. She was shy except for her quick temper. She wore boys' jeans and a khaki jacket every day through the winter and she smelled of woodsmoke and underarms. She smelled of the inside of a trailer that doesn't get aired. Her hair was stiff with grease and fitted like a cap over her head, not like normal hair we thought. You could see it was black hair yet it didn't look black exactly, more like it was coated with a thin film of dust.

Della Rae wasn't waiting for the school bus with the other kids at the trailer village, Monday morning. Nor Tuesday. Nor Wednesday. Thursday she was back again, same bulldog face. Dark-stained skin. Puffy-lidded eyes. That pea-colored jacket with a drawstring hood that looked like it'd been used to wipe hands on. Della Rae stared through us making her way to the back of the bus where she sat with another girl they said was part Indian or possibly part Negro. Or both.

At the senior high there was talk, but only in secret. Whispering, sniggering. Guys told one another in the lavatories or at their lockers, heads bent, faces creasing in amazement, lewd grins. There was much laughter. There were expressions of incredulity. *How many? How long? When?* The girls, of course, knew nothing about it. Especially the nice girls knew nothing about it. They did not want to know for just to know of *certain things* was to be sullied by the knowledge. It was possible to pray sincerely and passionately for an afflicted person (like Della Rae Duncan) to be aided by Jesus Christ without knowing exactly why.

Maybe, in fact, it was better not to know why? You could feel sorry for that person, and generous. You didn't shrink away in disgust.

A year or so before, an older brother of Della Rae Duncan's was reported killed in Vietnam. His name would eventually be engraved, with other "casualties" from Mt. Ephraim, on a granite marker in front of the post office.

His name was Dwight David Duncan and he was a private first class in the United States Army, twenty years old at the time of his death. Since dropping out of high school he'd worked for Mulvaney Roofing. When his picture appeared on the front page of the *Mt. Ephraim Patriot-Ledger*, Dad exclaimed, "Son of a bitch! Dwight Duncan! Poor kid."

We gathered around to stare at the picture and read the columns of print. Dwight David Duncan was no one we knew, but the fact that Dad knew him, and was so upset, seemed to bring him into the house with us; into the kitchen, where even the dogs moved about uncertainly, worriedly. Private First Class Duncan was a burly, swarthy-skinned boy with heavy-lidded eyes like Della Rae's and lank, straight, Indian-seeming hair. He'd been photographed in his dress uniform, his cap tilted back rakishly on his head; a cigarette slanted from his mouth. Dad was saying what a good, hardworking kid, very quiet, not too bright maybe but able to follow orders with no questions asked, and no complaints. "God spare us, Mikey-Junior never gets called," Dad said, sighing. There was a pause, and he added, as always when he was on this subject, "Still, the war needs to be fought."

This was like tossing a lighted match into a can of gasoline.

Mom said, "*Why* does it need to be fought?"

Dad said, "Darling, we've been through this already."

Mom said, "Yes, but you never change your mind!"

Dad said, calmly, with a wink at us kids, "Well, *you* never change your mind."

By this time Mom would be pacing about, arms flailing, eyes hot with anguish. If there were cats in the kitchen they'd rush out, ears laid back. If Little Boots was present, the most anxious of the dogs, he'd dance about clicking his toenails on the linoleum floor and whimpering up into his mistress's and master's faces, vivid to him as balloon faces. Mom who'd given impromptu, stammering speeches on the subject to relatives, at prayer meetings, at the P.T.A. and in the A & P, would choke back sobs of frustration, saying that the war in Vietnam had to stop, the killing had to stop on both sides, what a terrible thing, what a tragedy. Tearing the country apart! Turning fathers against sons! It was like the 1850s when the Fugitive Slave Act tore the country apart and led to the Civil War and almost four hundred thousand deaths, such a cruel, inhuman, ignorant piece of legislation, and now in enlightened times wouldn't you think our leaders would have learned from the past? "First Kennedy, then Johnson, and now Nixon!" Mom cried. "What we need to save us is a true Christian leader, before it's too late."

"Yes," said Dad, "—but the fact remains, the war needs to be fought."

"No, no it doesn't! You're wrong!"

"Because the Communists have to be stopped, pure and simple," Dad said. He spoke quietly, stubbornly. His broad handsome face glistened, his curly hair caught the overhead light with a glisten too of oil, the color of wood shavings. He was not a tall man but he was a solid, foursquare man, a man of presence, gravity. You knew that, if you pushed hard against his chest, he would stand firm, unyielding. "—Just like the Nazis, maybe worse. Twenty million men, women and children killed by Stalin and his henchmen! Even more millions killed by 'Chairman Mao' and his henchmen! No, darling, the war can't stop until we push the bastards back, and even if a son of mine has to put on a uniform and fight—"

"What! What are you saying?—"

"—or, God forbid, two sons—"

"Two sons! Michael Mulvaney, are you crazy!"

"—it has to be fought. Pure and simple."

Sometimes Mom would stalk out of the house, and go into a barn for the solace, as she put it, of dumb animals; sometimes Dad would stalk out, to smoke a cigarette in the open air; or Little Boots would get so excited he'd have to be placated by both Mom and Dad; or, suddenly, Feathers would begin to shriek, and everyone would turn to his cage in astonishment that so tiny a creature, smaller than the smallest of our hands, could cause such a ruckus.

Of the Mulvaney boys, Mike Jr. was the patriot (though he confessed he "sure as hell" hoped he wasn't drafted into the army, come graduation) and Patrick was the dissident—of course. Though only fourteen at this time, a weedy-lanky boy with a cracking voice, Patrick was an admirer of the war-protesting Berrigan priest-brothers and warned he'd run away to Canada as a conscientious objector if necessary. Dad said ominously we'd see about that if the time ever came, God forbid! Mom wrung her hands saying you see, you see!—the war is tearing American families apart! Patrick, incensed, had a habit of pushing his glasses against the bridge of his nose as if he hoped they'd break, declaring he was a pacifist, he'd been reading Thoreau's "Civil Disobedience," he could not shed blood, not even animal blood let alone human blood, and no mere earthly political power could change *that*.

It was strange, though: Mike and Patrick never quarreled with each other on this issue. Patrick shrank from confronting his big brother (in fact, bigger than Patrick by about twenty-five pounds) and Mike seemed mainly amused by Patrick, regardless of what impassioned words issued from his mouth. Mike just wasn't one for debating abstract issues. ("BS-ing" he called it.) Just laughed and shrugged his muscular shoulders, a mannerism of Dad's that meant *Hell, live and let live.* In this case, *Fight and let fight.* His philosophy was the trustworthy team player's: you do what your buddies are doing, and you don't let them down.

Marianne, flush-faced like Mom, but by instinct the peacemaker in the family, said she hated war, any war, and prayed the Vietnam War would end soon, and all wars would end, forever. And then no one would be mad at anyone else, ever again.

Judd who was eight years old kept his thoughts to himself. He hoped to join the Air Force as soon as he was old enough, and be a bomber pilot.

Private First Class Dwight David Duncan's picture from the *Mt. Ephraim Patriot-Ledger* was carefully clipped out and tacked to the kitchen bulletin board, where it prevailed for months, a smiling and not accusing presence, until, eventually, it was covered over by newer clippings, Polaroid snapshots, Mom's FAMILY CALENDAR, pages of brilliant color from Burpee's seed catalogue.

★ ★ ★

Mike "Mule" Mulvaney, a fullback on the championship Mt. Ephraim football team for the '71–'72 season, had been with some of his teammates that night, but not the guys who did it.

Whatever it was, exactly, they did. With Della Rae Duncan. Or to her.

If you could believe half the wild tales making the rounds! You know how guys exaggerate.

Guys who weren't even there, for Christ's sake.

That night following the game, and the big celebration party, Mike didn't have a car. He was with his buddies Frankie Kreigner, Brock Johnson, some others. Jammed into Frankie's dad's Cadillac and it was true some of the guys were drinking, passing cans of beer to one another, and also a flask of vodka, and somebody's dad's Wild Turkey. So maybe the boys were violating the law, drinking in a moving motor vehicle, but only technically. Nobody was actually drunk, anyway not Mule Mulvaney, not much. Nor Frankie, who was driving.

Mule could be a rough guy sometimes, a tough customer on the football field (you don't get baptized "Mule" by coach, for nothing) but his rep was that of a helluva nice guy. Not mean. Sure he'd hit you square in the solar plexus with his shoulder and lift you off your feet like a cartoon character too astonished to register surprise before you landed, hard, on your ass, but it wasn't to *hurt*, like some guys, it was more to—well, *impress*. So you'd know that he meant business. So you'd respect him. And stay out of his way next time, if you could.

And he was the kind to help you up off the ground afterward, clamp a hand on your shoulder saying *Good play! nice try!*

The most popular guy on the team, practically. One of the best-looking.

A decent guy, and even, if you knew him better, a Christian—sort of. His mother Corinne Mulvaney was a devout churchgoer, at this time a member of the South Lebanon United Methodist congregation. Mule went less and less frequently with her and the others to church services now he was older, but still it rubs off on you. You have to know deep in your heart *Do unto others as you would they would do unto you* is just plain common sense. So he was beginning to get a little scared. Not seriously scared, but a little. Mixing warm Molson with vodka and whiskey didn't help. After the big party at the MacIntyres' (this really cool ranch-style house on the golf course) they'd piled into cars and driven six miles out to the funky County Line Tavern, where there was the possibility, unwarranted as it turned out, of some after-hours drinking, and some "girls." Then word got out that T-T MacIntyre had picked up Della Rae Duncan, the poor bitch was dumb enough and drunk enough to imagine he "liked" her and wanted to be her "steady." They were in Jamie Klinger's van, this gang of guys. Cruising Route 119 as far south as the river, then turning back to Mt. Ephraim. Cruising Main Street, where (it's after 2 A.M.) everything is dead—the Majestic, the Checkerboard Diner. Then into the cemetery off Iroquois. Which was where Frankie Kreigner trailed them. Though not turning into the cemetery but circling the block. Mule Mulvaney was saying, "Maybe we should check them out?—they might be hurting her, or something." Another time he said, like pleading, "Shit, Della Rae, that poor mutt, that's like shooting fish in a barrel." The other guys were divided. Maybe yes, maybe no. There was something exciting about this. Knowing Della Rae was putting out for their buddies, or anyway guessing so. Though they didn't want to investigate, exactly. Della Rae was a pig and she was smashed out of her skull and you didn't want to think about it, Mule felt blood rush into his cock like a faucet turned on: hot.

So what they did was, actually they did nothing.

That's for the cemetery!—the guys would snigger behind their hands.

Hoo! One for the cem-e-tery!—the girls would overhear, perplexed and vaguely embarrassed.

Keep it for the cemetery! Right on!—giving one another the peacenik sign, laughing like hell. Sometimes under their teachers' very noses and if it was a woman teacher, all the more hilarious.

Girls knew nothing about it. At any rate not the good girls. So if one could be enticed into saying, " 'Cemetery'?—why?" this was quite a coup.

In the junior high, where Della Rae Duncan was a student, the girls knew even less. The smartest girls, the leaders, the most popular girls—Marianne Mulvaney, Suzi Quigley, Trisha LaPorte, Bonnie Sherman and their clique. These were cheerleaders, class officers (Marianne Mulvaney was secretary), members of the Drama Club, the French Club, the Quill and Scroll Literary Society, the school chorus. They were Honors Students. They were active in the Christian Youth Conference. Because they were good-girl girls they believed they were not snobbish and they competed with one another in being *friendly*, being *nice*, to the most obscure students; the most pathetic losers; like Della Rae Duncan, and other "trailer-village" kids. Their smiles were golden coins scattered carelessly in the school corridors, their *Hi's!* and *H'lo's!* and *How are you's!* were melodic as the cries of spring birds.

It wasn't until after the Christmas holiday, when school resumed again in January, that Marianne Mulvaney turned a corner in the girls' locker room and saw, to her discomfort—Della Rae Duncan. Just sitting there, slump-shouldered, on a bench in front of her opened locker. Staring at the floor. Della Rae's face was puffy and embittered like a grown woman's. Her lips appeared to be moving. Her oily hair lifted from her head in stiff coils. Gym class had begun ten minutes before, and at roll call Della Rae had been marked absent, but she was in no hurry now, just slouched there in a kind of torpor. Marianne, so fastidious in her personal grooming, saw in dismay that Della Rae was partly undressed, in baggy gym shorts that ballooned about her hips and a frayed, grimy-gray bra (what heavy breasts!) held together by safety pins. Her flesh that looked stained, with its oily glisten, and a smell of talcumy sweat, seemed on the verge of spilling from her clothes.

For all her social poise at the age of fourteen, Marianne was a shy girl; physically shy; never comfortable in the locker room undressing with the other girls, still less in the communal showers. At church, Reverend Appleby spoke in his flushed, impassioned, somewhat tongue-tied way of *sins of the flesh* as *temptations to us all* but Marianne could see little temptation. At home, she would have been mortified with embarrassment had even her mother glimpsed her in just underwear.

Too late to retreat, Della Rae had seen her. Marianne's pretty face lit up in its customary dazzling smile. "Hi, Della Rae!"—the very voice, a lilting soprano, of Caucasian privilege. The girls' eyes locked. Sharp as a blade was Della Rae's black stare: Marianne felt her face burn at once, and her heart kicked as if she'd been shot, like a bird in flight, yet like a wounded bird carried forward by sheer momentum, scarcely faltering in her stride. Marianne had returned to the locker room to get a packet of Kleenex from her locker but she couldn't remain in the other girl's presence, not a moment longer! She retreated, still smiling, her face aching with the effort, as Della Rae Duncan stared at her with undisguised hatred.

But why me? What have I ever done to you? Whatever has been done to you—how is it my fault?

In a daze, as if she'd been slapped—she, Marianne Mulvaney!—Marianne returned to gym class, where a volleyball game was just beginning. Miss Deltz, the gym instructor, asked Marianne if she'd seen Della Rae Duncan, and Marianne nodded yes. Miss Deltz, a short, wiry, white-blond woman of about thirty, regarded Marianne, one of her favorites, with a look of cautious confidentiality. "Those people, they cause more trouble . . . That kind of a girl. Sad!" It was a murmur, more like thinking out loud than actual speech. Marianne stared at her gym shoes, cleanly white, with white laces perfectly tied, white-ribbed woollen socks. She could not think of a word to say.

Della Rae never did show up for gym that day and if any of the girls missed her, not a word was said.

PROVIDENCE

Well then! Don't believe if you choose not to. I know what happened and I know what truth is and God's purpose is not altered whether such as you believe, or not.
And we'd laugh, protesting. Oh Mom.

It was December 1938, between Christmas and New Year's. Corinne was seven years old. Ida Hausmann, her mother, was driving the family car with just Corinne as a passenger, that car that was a battered old 1931 Dodge like a sunk submarine gray and speckled with rust like pimples. They were at about the midpoint returning home from the village of Ransomville, about four miles yet to go, and a storm was blowing up, rain and sleet and then sleet and snow, the sky above the mountain-rim of the Valley a frightening bluish black roiling with clouds like those fleeting distorted faces you see as you're beginning to fall asleep, and the sun a smoldering red eye at the horizon like the last coal in the smithy engorged with flame by the blacksmith's bellows. (Corinne's grandfather Hausmann was a blacksmith, as well as a farmer.) And you could hear a strange sound like the hoarse-breathing *suck! suck! suck!* of the bellows that was the wind sucking at the struggling car wanting to pluck it from the road.

Against her husband's wishes (Mr. Hausmann was parsimonious regarding gasoline and the general upkeep of the family car and did not approve of "jaunts" to town except for practical purposes like shopping) Mrs. Hausmann had driven backcountry crudely plowed roads to visit a sickly older sister who lived in Ransomville; now on the return trip she was beginning to panic, the way the snow was coming down, an unexpected blizzard. Corinne's mother was one of those women susceptible to "nerves"—"agitations"—of unknown origin, and in emergency situations she either took control completely, as when Corinne's twelve-year-old brother lost several fingers in a threshing accident, or broke down completely, talking and moaning to herself, praying aloud, shaking her head as she was now, oh! they'd never make it home, if they were stuck in snow she'd never be able to shovel out (there was a snow shovel kept in the car trunk for such purposes), why had she gone to visit her sister oh why, why! Her eyes began to glisten, she was blinking rapidly. It was Corinne's task to keep the inside of the driver's windshield clean where it steamed up, swiping at it with mittened hands, but the steam kept coming back, and snow and ice particles were sticking to the outside, and Mrs. Hausmann wept and scolded as if it were Corinne's fault.

Corinne was a big girl in her own eyes, not a scaredy-baby, and she didn't cry easily, but the way the wind rocked the car! and sucked at it! and snow was swirling and rushing toward them like a tunnel they had no choice but to drive into, for there was no turning back. And the windshield wipers were going slower and slower, encrusted with ice. And Mrs. Hausmann cried *I can't see, Corinne keep the window clear I told you!* And Corinne wiped frantically at the glass, leaning across the steering wheel, but what could she do?—the ice was on the outside. And Mrs. Hausmann could drive only ten miles an hour, or less. And at a plank bridge over a creek invisible in a haze of seething white there was a ramp so icy-steep the Dodge's tires even with their chains began to spin, and slip, and the Dodge began to slide backward and Mrs. Hausmann gunned the motor and still the car was sliding, then the motor sputtered and died, Mrs. Hausmann screamed as the car tilted off the ramp entirely, the most sickening sensation Corinne would remember all her life as they fell, overturning into a twelve-foot culvert beside the road. *God help us!* Mrs. Hausmann screamed. *God help my baby and me, don't let us die!*

It might have been that God heard, and took mercy: lucky for mother and daughter, the culvert was solid ice at its base, not water. The car upended and came slowly to rest and there was silence save for the wind and the sifting-hissing sound of the snow that was like something alive, and malevolent. Corinne saw that her mother's mouth was bleeding, and her black wool cloche hat, her only good

hat, was crooked over one eye, its sprig of shiny red holly berries
askew. Later, Mrs. Hausmann would discover that two of her front
teeth had loosened, where she'd been thrown against the steering
wheel, but she didn't notice now, she had no time. She panted,
grunted like a man forcing the driver's door open, and outward,
then crawling out, with much difficulty into the freezing snow, her
heavy skirt hiking up revealing lardy-pale thighs and thick-mesh
beige stockings in such a way Corinne had never seen before.
Corinne! Take my hand! Hurry! she cried. Corinne grabbed her
mother's gloved hand and climbed, for all the terror of the situation,
monkey-nimble out of the car into a roaring of snowflakes so fierce
she could barely see her mother only a few inches away.

Then on their hands and knees they crawled back up the incline
to the road now so drifted in snow it was hardly recognizable as a
road. Ice-rivulets began to form on their faces; snowflakes caught in
their eyelashes like living, lashing cobwebs. It was a cold beyond
cold, you couldn't register it, fingers and toes going numb, faces
chill and brittle as ceramic. Mrs. Hausmann shouted to Corinne that
they'd go to the Gorner farm close by—wasn't it close by?—though
she seemed confused about which direction it was. She set out one
way, crossing the bridge, then suddenly halted and reversed, gripping Corinne's hand. She removed her woolen scarf from around
her neck to wrap it around Corinne's head, to protect Corinne from
frostbite. *Don't be afraid! Don't be afraid! Momma will take care of you.*

It would seem afterward that they walked, trudged, for many
miles, heads bent against the wind. Yet they could not have gone very
far at all. Were they walking in circles? It wasn't clear which side of
the creek they were on, Mrs. Hausmann couldn't remember. It was
not even clear where the road was, exactly. There was a high ringing
sound in the air, above the tolling of the wind. Like a voice, the
words so drawn out you couldn't hear them. Like high-tension wires,
except of course there were none along the Ransomville Road, electricity had not yet come to this remote part of the Chautauqua Valley.
Corinne, don't give in! Stay with Momma! Mrs. Hausmann pleaded. She
had never been a demonstrative mother, still less a warm mother,
she'd had four or five babies before Corinne, of whom only two had
lived, and who knew how many miscarriages, "accidents" as they
were elliptically called, never clearly distinguished from other species
of "female troubles," yet now, in the blizzard, she seemed to Corinne
so loving! so loving! hugging Corinne tight, scolding and pleading,

blowing her warm desperate breath into Corinne's face. Corinne was so sleepy, her eyelids wanted to shut. Her knees inside her thick wool leggings were like water—boneless. She wasn't afraid now and wasn't even cold, wanting only to lie down in the shelter of a snowdrift and cradle her heavy head in her arms and sleep, sleep. But her mother kept shaking her, slapping at her cheeks. Her mother's swollen mouth glistened where blood had coagulated into ice. *God help us!* Mrs. Hausmann prayed. *God help us! I'll never drive that car again, nor any car I swear to you God.*

There came then an eerie smoldering-red glow as if the dying sun had slipped its moorings and sunk to earth, buffeted by the terrible wind. It splintered into a myriad of fragments, glowing-red sparks, tiny as fireflies. And in fact—they were fireflies! Mrs. Hausmann saw with dazed eyes what could not be, but was. *Corinne, look! A sign from God!* Mother and daughter stumbled in the direction of the fireflies which led them not as they would have gone (so Mrs. Hausmann swore afterward) but in another direction entirely, and so saved their lives. For within five minutes something dark hulked above them in the blizzard: the schoolhouse! The single-room schoolhouse that was in fact Corinne's own school, closed for Christmas recess. Mrs. Hausmann had no time to wonder how they had found their way to the school, for hadn't she been headed in the opposite direction?—but the fireflies led them on, winking, almost invisible, dancing several yards before them, emitting too (for so it seemed) that strange melodic high-pitched sound that must have been a voice of God, too pure for human ears. At the school, Mrs. Hausmann lifted a rock, and threw it clumsily into a window, so the glass shattered; and she and Corinne crawled through the window, in their numbed, distracted states tearing their clothes on the jagged glass in the frame, but at last they were inside, in a sheltered place, panting and sobbing with relief. Inside it was freezing cold, and dark as the interior of a cave, but Mrs. Hausmann located the wood-burning stove, and Corinne found the tin box containing her teacher's kitchen matches, and Mrs. Hausmann was able with her stiffened, shaking fingers to start a fire, and so—*they were saved.*

They would not be rescued for nearly twenty-four hours, by a sheriff's rescue team accompanying a snowplow along the Ransomville Road, but from that point onward as Mrs. Hausmann would say they were *in the bosom of the Lord.*

Another, less fortunate traveler on the road that day, a neighbor of the Hausmanns, froze to death when his pickup stalled and he tried to walk to shelter. On a county highway, a young couple abandoned their car to the storm and set out bravely on foot, lost their way and crawled into an irrigation ditch to escape the wind, the man lying on top of the woman and so saving her from freezing; he survived, too, but only barely, both legs having to be amputated at the knees. And many head of cattle died in the Valley, trapped outside when the storm swept upon them. Canada geese were said to have dropped like shot out of the air, transformed to ice. Even in the towns of Ransomville, Milford, Chautauqua Falls, and Mt. Ephraim there were deaths and near-deaths. The Yewville River froze so solidly it didn't thaw until late April. Snow endured for months, well into spring, hard-crusted unnatural snow it seemed, acrid and bitter on the tongue, hiding the bodies of numberless wild creatures, revealed only in the thaw. But Mrs. Hausmann and Corinne were spared, the spirit of God dwelling forever afterward in their hearts.

That's why I love fireflies so, Corinne would say, her eyes shining like a seven-year-old's, *they saved Momma's life and mine.*

❧

And some of us would be laughing. Oh Mom!

And Mom would flare up, quick as a cat might turn on you and hiss, her fur stroked the wrong way, "Don't you 'Oh Mom' me! I remember that day as clearly as if it was last week, not thirty-eight years ago. Yes, and I can see those fireflies as clearly as I see *you.*"

Dad, Mikey-Junior and Patrick would try to keep straight faces. The story of Grandma Hausmann and Mom as a little girl of seven, lost in a blizzard on the Ransomville Road, was one of the oldest Mulvaney family stories, and a favorite, but as we got older one by one (except Marianne, of course: she always defended Mom) we came to wonder how accurate it was.

Most embarrassing was when Mom told the story to people she hardly knew like my eighth-grade math teacher Mr. Cole, or some lady she'd run into at the A & P, or friends of ours spending the night at the farm—how God watches over us all, how Mom's life was changed forever by an act of "providence."

Just the way Mom uttered that word: *providence.* You saw a tall black marble column with a cross at its summit. You saw a blue sky so vast and deep you could fall into it forever.

So Dad couldn't help commenting behind his hand, with that

wink that squinched up half his face, it was surely an act of providence that his mother-in-law Ida Hausmann never drove any vehicle ever again—"*That* was a blessing of God's, yessir!"

To us kids, who'd known her only as a nervous-skinny, querulous, gray old woman with thick eyeglasses, the thought of Grandma Hausmann driving any vehicle on the road was hilarious.

But Mom held her ground. Mom was stubborn, and eloquent. She said, in a hurt, dignified tone, that her mother was a country woman of the old days, German-born and brought to America at the age of less than a year; she'd always been a commonsense Lutheran, not given to flights of religious fancy; when such people are confronted by a truth *they know to be true* they never change their minds, ever. Mom said you have to experience certain things to know certain things. Like an explorer to Antarctica, or to the moon—once you stepped foot in such a place, you'd never doubt it existed. Like giving birth—*that*, just once, you'd never doubt. "If you've done it, you know; if not, you don't." Mom would smile beatifically, and fix her glowing blue gaze on us one by one until we'd begin to squirm. Even Dad.

For that was Mom's trump card: she was the mother, and so possessed a mysterious and unquestioned authority. Dad was the boss, but Mom was the power. Mom in her manure-stained bib overalls, or, in warm weather, her MT. EPHRAIM HIGH T-shirt and khaki shorts, an old hand-knit sweater of Dad's pushed up past her elbows, her boots she called combat boots, or hippie-style leather sandals worn with cotton socks. Mom with her frizzed hair that shone a luminous carroty color in the sun. Mom's smile that could turn sweet and teasing, or pucker into her "vinegar" look; her loud neighing laugh that made people want to join in, just hearing it. *Here I am, a funny-silly woman, an ordinary woman, a TV mom, but God has touched my life nonetheless.*

Mike Jr. (who was the most like Dad) might tease, daringly, "Hey Mom: what about Doughnut?"—one of the barn cats—"she's had thirty kittens, what kind of authority does that make *her*?"

And Mom would retort, quick as, at Ping-Pong, she was capable of returning a killer serve, "It makes her an authority on *kittens*."

And we'd all laugh, including Mom. Yet the fact she was our mother remained.

Of us kids it was always Patrick who was most skeptical about the blizzard-fireflies story. (Maybe because Patrick, the smartest of us, wanted so badly to believe?) There was a way he had of leaning his elbows on the table (the kitchen table: where we'd likely be) and shoving out his lower lip, his warrior-stance in Debate Club at school, and saying, "Oh, Mom! Come *on*! Let's examine this rationally. It could not have been 'fireflies' in a blizzard in December. Ple-*ease*."

And Mom would retort, her cheeks reddening, "What were they, then, Mr. Socrates? I was there, and I saw. I know a firefly when I see one."

"How would I know what they were?" Patrick protested. "It might've been a hallucination."

"Two of us? Momma and me? An identical 'hallucination' at the identical moment?"—Mom was incensed, leaning across the table toward Patrick.

"There's such a phenomenon as mass hysteria," Patrick said importantly. "The power of suggestion and wishful thinking. The human mind is—well, real weird."

"Speak for your own 'human mind'! Mine happens to be normal."

Mom was laughing, but you could see by the glisten in her eyes she was getting miffed.

Yet Patrick persisted. Mike might kick his ankle under the table, Marianne might poke him in the ribs and tease "Pinch!", but Patrick couldn't stop. There was something wonderful in the hot harried look in his eyes, especially the bad one. "O.K., Mom, but consider: why would God send a blizzard to almost kill you and Grandma, then rescue you by sending 'fireflies'? Does that make sense?" Patrick's glasses winked with adolescent urgency. His voice cracked like a radio beset by static. Here was an American teenager who *just wanted things to make sense*. "And what about the other people who died that day, in the blizzard? Why did God favor you and Grandma over them? What was so special about you?"

That was Patrick's trump card, he'd toss down onto the table in gloating triumph.

By this time Mom had gone dangerously red in the face, that mottled look you sometimes get without being aware of it, working in the barns on a stifling hot day, even if you've avoided the sun. Her hands fluttered like hurt birds, her words came stammering. All of us, even Dad, watched closely, wondering how Mom would answer these challenging words of Patrick's, to silence his doubts, and ours, forever. Damn old Pinch!—I wanted to punch his smug mouth, making us all anxious, after Sunday supper (Sunday nights were always "super-casserole" occasions, meaning Mom and Marianne would concoct delicious refrigerator-leftovers unique and not-repeatable), and the dogs and cats gobbling away at plate scrapings, in their separate corners, anxious too, with that twitchy animal anxiety that shows as rapacious appetite, muzzles lowered to the bowl. And by this time Feathers would have woken from his early-evening drowse to scold, chatter, chirp in sounds sharp as the twining of a fork on a glass. Patrick took no notice of such upset as he'd himself caused but leaned farther forward, his bony vertebrae showing through his shirt, and he'd shove his prissy John Lennon glasses against the bridge of his nose, and beetle his brow so he'd be staring at Mom like she was some kind of specimen, one of those poor sad dead "nocturnal" moths pinned to a Styrofoam board in his room.

Corinne drew her shoulders up, and threw back her head. However she was dressed, however flyaway her hair, she spoke calmly, with dignity. *Always, you maintain your dignity:* that was Captain Mulvaney's charge to his troops. "I believe what God requires me to believe, Patrick. I would not ask of Him that He explain His motives any more than I would wish that any of you might ask of me why I love you." Mom paused, wiping at her eyes. Our hearts beat like metronomes. "It *was* providence, and it *is*, that I was spared from death in 1938 so that—" and here Mom paused again, drawing in her breath sharply, her eyes suffused with a special lustre, gazing upon her family one by one, with what crazy unbounded love she gazed upon us, and at such a moment my heart would contract as if this woman who was my mother had slipped her fingers inside my rib cage to contain it, as you might hold a wild, thrashing bird to comfort it, "—so that you children—Mikey, Patrick, Marianne, and Judd—could be born."

And we sighed, and we basked in that knowledge. Even Pinch, who bit his lip and frowned more deeply. Yes it made sense, yes it was our truth, Dad grinned and nodded to signal his agreement.

Hell, yes: *providence*.

STRAWBERRIES &
CREAM

That Sunday afternoon, upstairs in her bedroom, Marianne methodically emptied her garment bag of everything except the satin prom dress, her fingers moving numbly and blindly, yet efficiently. She then zipped the bag shut again and hung it in the farthest corner of her closet beneath the sharp-slanting eaves.

Always, you maintain your dignity.

At High Point Farm in the big old house she'd lived in all her life. What began to beat against her nerves was the familiar sound of clocks ticking.

Clocks measuring Time, was what you'd think. That there was a single Time and these clocks (and the watches the Mulvaneys wore on their wrists) were busily *tick-tick-ticking* it. So that in any room you needed only to glance at a wall, or a mantel, or a table, and trust that the time you'd see measured there was accurate.

Except of course that wasn't how it was. Not at High Point Farm where Corinne Mulvaney collected "antique" American clocks.

Not even that she collected them—"More like the damn things accumulate," Michael Mulvaney Sr. complained.

So it was not Time at High Point Farm but *times*. As many *times* as there were clocks, distinct and confusing and combative. When the hand-painted 1850s "banjo" clock in the front hall was musically striking the hour of six, the 1889 "Reformed Gothic" grandfather clock on the first-floor landing of the stairs was clearing its throat preparing to strike the quarter hour after one. On the parlor mantel were a Chautauqua Valley "steeple" pendulum clock of the 1890s and a Dutch-style painted walnut pendulum clock of the 1850s, one about to strike the hour of nine and the other importantly chiming the hour of eleven-thirty. In the family room was a crudely fashioned 1850s eight-day clock with a tarnished brass eagle at its top, that clanged the hour, half hour, and quarter hour with a jazzy beat; in the dining room, a mantel clock of golden pine with a river scene hand-painted (and now badly faded) on its glass case, of the 1870s, and a delicately carved mahogany Chautauqua Valley grandmother clock of the turn of the century, with ethereal chimes. Scattered through the house were numerous other antique clocks of Corinne's, each a treasure, a bargain, a particular triumph. If there wasn't an excess of competing noise from radio, TV, tapes, records, raised voices or barking dogs you could move through the house in a trance of *tick-tick-ticking*.

Of course there were a number of clocks, including the most beautiful, that had long ago ceased ticking completely. Their pendulums had not moved for years; their slender black hands, pointing at black numerals, were forever arrested at mysterious fatal moments.

You would think that Time "stands still." But you'd be wrong.

Always, Marianne had loved the clocks at High Point Farm. She'd thought that all households were like theirs. So many clocks ticking their separate times. Striking the hour, the half hour, the quarter hour whenever they wished. Friends who came to visit asked, "How do you know what the real time is?" and Marianne said, laughing, "Oh, the real time is in the kitchen: Dad's electric clock." She would lead her friends into the big country kitchen where, above the fireplace, was a moonfaced General Electric clock in the design of a sunburst, with fat black hands and bulgy black numerals and a maddening little hum like something grinding its teeth. The clock had been a gift to Dad on the occasion of his forty-fifth birthday from his poker-playing circle. The men of the circle were local businessmen and merchants and their dominant attitude toward one another was one of good-natured bantering. Since Michael Mulvaney Sr. was notorious for being late for many occasions, including even his poker nights which meant so much to him, there was significance in the gift clock.

In any case, here was High Point Farm's "real" time.

Except, of course, as Mom liked to point out, when the electricity went out.

Up in Marianne's room were several more of Mom's clocks, of

which only one "kept time" and that fitfully: a small cream-colored ceramic mantel clock with garlands of tiny painted rosebuds, golden pendulum and delicate hands, a chime like the sweetest of birdcalls. It was turn-of-the-century and a genuine antique, Mom insisted. But its time couldn't be trusted, of course. So Marianne kept a windup alarm clock with a plastic face, luminous green hands and numerals that glowed in the dark. Five nights a week Marianne set the alarm for 6 A.M. though it had been years since she'd needed an alarm to actually wake her. Even in the pitch-dark of winter.

She took up the clock suddenly, wanting to bury it under her pillow to smother its snug *tick-tick-ticking*. But of course she didn't. For what would that solve?

And there was her watch, her beautiful watch, a white-gold battery-run Seiko with tiny blue numerals; a gift from Mom and Dad for Marianne's sixteenth birthday. She'd taken it off immediately when she'd come home. She hadn't examined it too closely, knowing, or guessing, that the crystal was cracked.

How many times compulsively she'd run her thumb over the crystal feeling the hairline crack. But she hadn't actually examined it. And if the minute ticking had ceased, she didn't want to know.

She was not a girl accustomed to thinking, calculating, *plotting*. The concept of *plotting* an action that might be broken down into discrete, cautious steps, which Patrick would have found challenging, was confusing to Marianne. A kind of static intervened. But this was so: Mt. Ephraim was such a small town, if she took the watch to Birchett's Jewelers where it had been purchased, Mr. Birchett might mention the fact to her mother or father if he happened to run into them. He would mention it casually, conversationally. And if she ceased wearing it, Dad who was sharp-eyed would notice. There were other watch repairmen in the area, at the Eastgate for instance, but how would she get there? Marianne felt fatigued, thinking of the problem. Maybe it was wisest to continue wearing the watch as if nothing were wrong, for unless she examined it closely nothing *was* wrong.

Patrick would guess, unless Patrick had already guessed. He frightened her with his talent for seeing what wasn't there to be seen. His mind worked like a calculator: a quicksilver adding of digits, an immediate answer. He had not asked her much about the previous night because he knew. In disgust of her he held himself stiff against the knowledge. Not a word about Austin Weidman. *Why isn't your "date" driving you home?* Under normal circumstances her brother would have teased her but these were not normal circumstances.

Cutting his eyes at her, outside when she'd dropped the garment bag in the snow. And she'd murmured quickly, shamefully, it's fine, I have it, it's fine. And he'd walked away, not another word.

You know you want to, Marianne—why'd you come with me if you don't?
I'm not gonna hurt you for Christ's sake. Come on!
Nobody plays games with me.

And this was a strangeness she'd recall: how when she entered her room which was exactly as she'd left it the day before, yet irrevocably changed, she'd known what a long time she'd been away, and such a distance. As if she'd left, and could not now return. Even as, numbly, she stepped inside, shut the door.

"Muffin! Hello."

Her favorite cat of all, Muffin, fattish, very white with variegated spots, lay dozing in a hollow of a pillow on her bed, stirring now to blink at her, and stare.

Away so long, and such a distance.

She unzipped the garment bag and removed her toiletry kit, her badly stained satiny cream-colored pumps, wadded articles of underwear and the ripped pale-beige stockings, placed everything except the toiletry kit in the bottom of her wastebasket without examining. (The wastebasket was made of white-painted wicker, lined with a plastic bag for easy disposal; Marianne would be emptying it into the trash can herself in a few days, as usual. No one in the family would have occasion to see what she was throwing out, still less wonder why.)

She didn't remove the crumpled satin-and-chiffon dress from the garment bag. Didn't glance at it, or touch it. Quickly zipped the bag up again and hung it in the farthest corner of her closet, beneath the sharp-tilting eaves. Then rearranged her clothes on hangers, not to hide the garment bag exactly but simply so that it wouldn't be seen, first thing she opened the closet door.

Out of sight, out of mind!—one of Corinne's cheerful sayings. Not a syllable of irony in it, for irony was not Corinne's nature.

In the closet, three white cotton cheerleader's blouses on wire hangers. Long full sleeves, double-button cuffs. If you were a cheerleader at Mt. Ephraim High, generally acknowledged the most coveted of all honors available to girls, you were required to buy your own blouses and maroon wool jumper and to maintain these articles of clothing in spotless condition. The jumper was dry-cleaned of course but Marianne hand-laundered the blouses herself, starched and ironed them lovingly. Inhaling the good, familiar, comforting smell of *white*.

Which she stooped now to inhale, closing her eyes.

Love you in that cheerleader's costume. Last Friday. You didn't see me I guess. But I was there.

Corinne was so amusing! Like a mom on TV. She'd tell stories on herself, to the family, or relatives, or friends, or people she hardly knew but had just met, how she'd have loved to be a housewife, a normal American housewife, crazy about her kids, in her heart she loved housewifely chores like ironing, "calming and steadying on the nerves—isn't it?" yet in the midst of ironing she'd get distracted by a telephone call, or a dog or cat wanting attention, or one of the kids, or something going on outside, she'd drift off from the ironing board only to be rudely recalled by the terrible smell of *scorch*. "It's my daughter who's the real homemaker: Button loves to iron."

That wasn't exactly true, though almost. She'd taken pride as a young girl of ten or eleven, ironing Dad's handkerchiefs at first, and then his sports shirts, which didn't require too much skill, and finally his white cotton shirts, which did. And her own white cotton blouses of course. Like sewing, ironing can be a meditation: a time of inwardness, thoughtfulness, prayer.

Not that she'd tell her girlfriends this, they'd laugh at her. Tenderly, affectionately—*Oh, Button!* Even Trisha, who was such a good girl herself.

He'd said there was no one in Mt. Ephraim to talk with, about serious things. Except her.

Whether God exists? Whether God gives a damn about us, if we live or die?

She couldn't remember when he'd said this, asked this. If it was before leaving the party at the Krausses', or after, at the Paxtons'. Before or after the "orange-juice" cocktails. The tart stinging delicious taste coating the inside of her mouth.

Sometimes I wake up in the middle of the night, y'know?—and I'm so scared, almost I want to yell something weird, crazy—Why'd you screw me up so, God? What's the point?

His earnest moist heavy-lidded eyes. Some girls thought them beautiful eyes but Marianne shied from looking at them, into them, too obviously. There was his quickened breath, the sweet-liquor smell. The heat of his skin that was rather pallid, sallow. A shrill girl-ish giggle escaped her, didn't sound like her but like an anonymous faceless girl somewhere in the night, between houses, in a boy's car or staggering drunkenly between cars in high-heeled pumps and un-buttoned coat in blurred swaying rays of headlights.

Oh Zachary what a way to speak to God!
She shut the closet door, hard.

The cat was pushing himself against her ankles in an ecstasy of yearning. He seemed to sense, or even to know. How long she'd been away, and how far. How hazardous, her return. Temporary.

She knelt, hugging him. Such a big, husky cat! A sibling of Big Tom, yet heavier, softer. Head round as a cabbage. Long white whiskers radiated outward from his muzzle stiff as the bristles of a brush, and quivering. His purr was guttural, crackling like static elec-tricity. As a kitten he'd slept on Marianne's lap while she did her homework at her desk, or lay across her bed talking on the phone, or read, or, downstairs, watched TV. He'd followed her everywhere, call-ing her with his faint, anxious *mew?*—trotting behind her like a puppy.

Marianne petted him, and scratched his ears, and stared into his eyes. Loving unjudging eyes they were. Unknowing. Those curious almost eerie black slats of pupil.

"Muffin, I'm fine! Go back to sleep."

She went to use the bathroom, she'd been using the bathroom every half hour or so, her bladder pinching and burning. Yet there was the numbness like a cloud. She locked the door, used the toilet, the old stained bowl, aged ceramic-white, the plumbing at High Point Farm needed "remodernization" as Corinne called it, the bath-rooms especially. But Dad had laid down some handsome vinyl tile of the simulated texture of brick, a rich red-brown, and the sink cabi-net was reasonably new, muted yellow with "brass" from Sears. And on the walls, as in most of the rooms at High Point Farm, framed photos of family—on horseback, on bicycles, with dogs, cats, friends and relatives, husky Mikey-Junior clowning for the camera in his high school graduation gown twirling his cap on a forefinger, skinny Patrick, a ninth grader at the time, diving from the high board at Wolf's Head Lake, arrested at the apogee of what looked to have been a backward somersault, maybe a double somersault. Button was there, Button smiling for the camera that loved her, how many times Button smiled for the camera that loved her, but Marianne, wincing as she drew down her jeans, her panties, and lowered her numbed body to the toilet seat, did not search her out.

"Oh!—oh."

As sometimes, not frequently but sometimes, she'd whimper aloud with the strain of a painful bowel movement, a sudden flash of sensation almost too raw to be borne, now the sound forced itself from her, through her clenched teeth—"Oh God! Oh Jesus!" She seemed fearful of releasing her weight entirely; her legs quivered. The pain was sharp and swift as the blade of an upright knife thrust into her.

You're not hurt, you wanted it. Stop crying.

Don't play games with me, O.K.?

I'm not the kind of guy you're gonna play games with.

At first when she tried to urinate, she couldn't. She tried again, and finally a trickle was released, thin but scalding, smarting between her legs. She dared not glance down at herself out of fear of seeing something she would not wish to see. Already seen, in vague blurred glimpses, at the LaPortes', in the hot rushing water of a tub.

The pain was subsiding, numbness returning like a cloud.

Flushing the toilet, she saw thin wormlike trails of blood.

That was all it was, then!—her *period*.

Of course, her *period*.

That was how Mom first spoke of it, warm and maternal and determined not to be embarrassed: *your period*.

It was all routine, and she was one who responded well to routine. Like most of the Mulvaneys, and the dogs, cats, horses, livestock. What you've done once you can do again, more than once for sure you can do again, again. No need to think about it, much.

Still, Marianne's hands shook, at the first sighting of menstrual blood she'd feel faint, mildly panicked, recalling her first period, the summer of her thirteenth birthday, how frightened she'd been despite Corinne's kindness, solicitude.

I'm fine. I'll take care of myself. In her bureau drawer a supply of "thin maxi-absorbent sanitary pads" and snug-fitting nylon panties with elastic bands. She realized she'd been feeling cramps for hours. That tight clotted sensation in the pit of the belly she'd try to ignore until she couldn't any longer. And a headache coming on—ringing clanging pain as if pincers were squeezing her temples.

It was all routine. You can deal with routine. Ask to be excused from active gym class tomorrow, which was a swim class, fifth hour. After school she'd attend cheerleading drill but might not participate, depending upon the cramps, headache. Always in gym class or at cheerleading drill there was someone, sometimes there were several girls, who were excused for the session, explaining with an embarrassed shrug they were having their periods.

Some of the girls with steady boyfriends even hinted at, or informed their boyfriends, they were *having their periods*—Marianne couldn't imagine such openness, such intimacy. She'd never been that close to any boy, had had countless friends who were boys yet few *boyfriends*, with all that implied of specialness, possessiveness. Sharing secrets. No, not even her brothers, not even Patrick she adored.

Her cheeks burned at the mere thought. Her body was her own, her private self. Only Corinne might be informed certain things but not even Corinne, not even Mom, not always.

She shook out another two aspirin tablets onto her sweaty palm, and washed them down with water from the bathroom faucet. In the medicine cabinet were many old prescription containers, some of them years old, Corinne's, Michael Sr.'s, there was one containing codeine pills Dad had started to take after his root canal work of a few months ago then swore off, in disgust—"Nothing worse than being fuzzy-headed."

Well, no. Marianne thought there could be lots worse.

Still, she took only the aspirin. Her problem was only routine and she would cope with it with routine measures.

Marking the date, February 15, on her *Purrfect Kittens* calendar.

She'd been a tomboy, the one they called *Cute-as-a-Button*. Climbing out an upstairs window to run on tiptoe across the sloping asphalt roof of the rear porch, waving mischievously at Mule and P.J. below. Her brothers were tanned, bare-chested, Mule on the noisy Toro lawn mower and P.J. raking up debris. *Look who's up on the roof! Hey get down, Marianne! Be careful!* The looks on their faces!

Roof-climbing was strictly forbidden at the Mulvaneys', for roofs were serious, potentially dangerous places. Dad's life *was* roofs, as he said. But there was ten-year-old Button in T-shirt and shorts, showing off like her older brothers she adored.

It was a good memory. It came out of nowhere, a child climbing through a window, trembling with excitement and suspense, and it ended in a blaze of summer sunshine. She'd ignored the boys calling to her and stood shading her eyes like an Indian scout, seeing the mountains in the northeast, the wooded hills where strips of sunshine and shadow so rapidly alternated you would think the mountains were something living and restless.

And Mt. Cataract like a beckoning hand, for just Button to see. *Here. Look here. Raise your eyes, look here.*

In the warmly lit kitchen rich with the smell of baking bread there stood Corinne leaning against a counter, chatting with a woman friend on the phone. Her blue eyes lifting to Marianne's face, her quick smile. The radio was playing a mournful country-rock song and Feathers, incensed as by a rival male canary, was singing loudly in rebuttal, but Corinne didn't seem to mind the racket. Seeing Marianne grab her parka from a peg in the hall she cupped her hand over the receiver and asked, surprised, "Sweetie? Where are you going?"

"Out to see Molly-O."

"Molly-O? *Now?*"

That startled plea in Corinne's voice: Don't we prepare Sunday supper together, super-casserole? Isn't this one of the things Button and her Mom *do*?

Outside it was very cold. Twenty degrees colder than that afternoon. And the wind, bringing moisture to her eyes. It was that slate-colored hour neither daylight nor dark. The sky resembled shattered oyster shells ribboned with flame in the west, but at ground level you could almost see (sometimes Marianne had stared out the window of her bedroom, observing) how shadows lifted from the snowy contours of the land, like living things. Exactly the bluish-purple color of the beautiful slate roof Michael Sr. had installed on the house.

In the long run, Dad said, you get exactly what you pay for.

Quality *costs.*

Marianne's heart was pumping after her close escape, in the kitchen. There would be no avoiding Mom when they prepared supper. No avoiding any of them, at the table.

Yet how lucky she was, to have a mother like Corinne. All the girls marveled at Mrs. Mulvaney, and at Mr. Mulvaney who was so much fun. Your parents are actually kind of your friends, aren't they? Amazing. Trisha's mother would have poked her way into Marianne's room by now asking how was the dance? how was your date? how was the party? or was it more than one party? did you get much sleep last night?—you look like you didn't. Another mother would perhaps have wanted to see Marianne's dress again. That so-special dress. Even the satiny pumps. Just to see, to reminisce. To examine.

One of the rangy barn cats, an orange tiger with a stumpy tail, leapt out of a woodpile to trot beside Marianne as she crossed the snow-swept yard to the horse barn. He made a hopeful mewing sound, pushing against her legs. "Hi there, Freckles!" Marianne said. She stooped to pet the cat's bony head but for some reason, even as he clearly wanted to be petted, he shrank from her, his tail rapidly switching. He'd come close to clawing or biting her. "All right then, go away," Marianne said.

How good, how clear the cold air. Pure, and scentless. In midwinter, in such cold, the fecund smells of High Point Farm were extinguished.

No games. No games with me.

Just remember!

At the LaPortes' she'd bathed twice. The first time at about 4:30 A.M. which she couldn't remember very clearly and the second time at 9:30 A.M. and Trisha had still been asleep in her bed, or pretending to be asleep. The gentle *tick-ticking* of a bedside clock. Hours of that clock, hours unmoving beneath the covers of a bed not her own, in a house not her own. Toward dawn, a sound of plumbing somewhere in the house, then again silence, and after a long time the first church bells ringing, hollow-sounding chimes Marianne guessed came from St. Ann's the Roman Catholic church on Mercer Avenue. Then Mrs. LaPorte knocking softly at Trisha's bedroom door at about 9 A.M. asking, in a lowered voice, "Girls? Anyone interested in going to church with me?" Trisha groaned without stirring from her bed and Marianne lay very still, still as death, and made no reply at all.

Later, Trisha asked Marianne what had happened after the party at the Paxtons', where had Marianne gone, and who'd brought her back, and Marianne saw the worry, the dread in her friend's eyes *Don't tell me! Please, no!* so she smiled her brightest Button-smile and shook her head as if it was all too complicated, too confused to remember.

And so it was, in fact: Marianne did not remember.

Unless a giddy blur, a girl not herself and not anyone she knew. Coughing and choking dribbling vomit hot as acid across her chin, in a torn dress of

cream-colored satin and strawberry-colored chiffon, legs running! running!
clumsy as snipping shears plied by a child.

❧

Out in Molly-O's stall, at this hour? But why?

This safe, known place. The silence and stillness of the barn, except for the horses' quizzical snuffling, whinnying.

Marianne wondered if, back in the house, Corinne was consulting with Patrick. *Is something wrong with—?*

Judd, too, had looked at her—strangely.

He was only thirteen, but—strangely.

Marianne took up a brush and swiftly, rhythmically stroked Molly-O's sides, her coarse crackling mane. Then lifted grain and molasses to the wet, eager mouth. She clucked and crooned to Molly-O who had roused herself from a doze to quiver with pleasure, snort and stamp and twitch her tail, snuffling greedily as she ate from Marianne's hand. That shivery, exquisite sensation, feeding a horse from your hand! As a small child Marianne had screamed with delight at the feel of a horse's tongue. She loved the humid snuffling breath, the powerful, unimaginable life coursing through the immense body. A horse is *so big,* a horse is so *solid.* Always, you respect your horse for her *size.*

She loved the rich horsey smell that was a smell of earliest childhood when visits to the horse barn were overseen scrupulously by adults and it was forbidden to wander in here alone—oh, forbidden! Brought in here for the first time in Dad's arms, then set down cautiously on the ground strewn with straw and walking, or trying to— the almost unbearable excitement of seeing the horses in their stalls, poking their strangely long heads out, blinking their enormous bulging eyes to look at *her.* Always she'd loved the sweetish-rancid smell of straw, manure, animal feed and animal heat. That look of recognition in a horse's eyes: *I know you, I love you. Feed me!*

So easy to make an animal happy. So easy to do the right thing by an animal.

Molly-O was nine years old, and no longer young. She'd had respiratory infections, knee trouble. Like every horse the Mulvaneys ever owned. ("A horse is the most delicate animal known to man," Dad said, "—but they don't tell you till it's too late and he's yours.") She wasn't a beautiful horse even by Chautauqua Valley standards but she was sweet-tempered and docile; with a narrow chest, legs that appeared foreshortened, knobby knees. Her coat was a rich burnished-red with a flaglike patch of white on her nose and four irregular white socks—Button's horse, her twelfth birthday present. There is no love like the love you have for your first horse but that love is so easy to forget, or misplace—it's like love for yourself, the self you outgrow.

Marianne hid her face in Molly-O's mane whispering how sorry she was, oh how sorry!—since school had started she'd been neglecting Molly-O, and hadn't ridden her more than a dozen times last summer. Her horse-mania of several years ago had long since subsided.

It had been a mild horse-mania, compared to that of other girls of Marianne's acquaintance who took equestrian classes and boarded their expensive Thoroughbreds at a riding academy near Yewville. Flaring up most passionately when she'd been between the ages of thirteen and fifteen, then subsiding as other interests competed for her attention; as Marianne Mulvaney's "popularity"—the complex, mesmerizing life of outwardness—became a defining factor of her life. Competing in horse shows wasn't for her, nor for any of the Mulvaneys. (At the height of his interest, at fifteen, Patrick had been a deft, promising rider.) Dad said that the "great happiness" in horses, as in all of High Point Farm, was in keeping it all amateur—"And I mean *real* amateur."

It was more than enough, Dad said, for a man to be competing in business with other men. Maybe an occasional golf game, squash, tennis, poker—but not seriously, only for friendship's sake, and sport. A man's heart is lacerated enough, being just an ordinary American businessman.

Of course, Dad admired certain friends of his, business associates and fellow members of the Mt. Ephraim Country Club who were "horsey" people (the Boswells, the Mercers, the Spohrs), but the thought of his daughter taking equestrian lessons, competing in those ludicrously formal horse shows, was distasteful to him. It was rank exhibitionism; it led to fanaticism, obsession. You don't want animals you love to perform any more than you want people you love to perform. Also, it was too damned expensive.

The Mulvaneys were in fact "well-to-do." At least, that was their local reputation. (Despite the way Corinne dressed, and her custom of shopping at discount stores.) High Point Farm was spoken of in admiring terms, and Michael Mulvaney Sr. cut a certain swath in the county, drove new cars and dressed in stylish sporty clothes (no discount stores for him); he was generous with charitable donations, and each July Fourth he opened his front pasture to the Chautauqua

County Volunteer Firemen's annual picnic. But in private he fretted over money, the expense of keeping up a farm like High Point, leasing as much land as he could, supporting a family as "spendthrift" as theirs. (Though Michael Sr. was the most spendthrift of all.) From time to time he threatened to sell off a horse or two—or three—now the older children's interest in riding had declined, but of course everyone protested, even Mike Jr., who rarely poked his head into the horse barn any longer. And Mom became practically hysterical. *That would be like an execution! That would be like selling one of us!*

Well, yes.

In the next stall Patrick's gelding Prince was knocking about, whinnying and snorting for Marianne's attention. And so Clover and Red were stirred to demonstrate, as well. *Here we are, too! Hungry!* And a gang of six barn cats was gathering around Marianne, mewing and suggestively kneading the ground. *Love us! Feed us!* All these creatures had been fed twice that day, by Patrick and Judd, but Marianne's appearance threw their routine off kilter, or so they wished it to seem; and Marianne was far too softhearted to disappoint. As a little girl she'd made rules for herself: if she petted or fed one animal in the presence of others, she must pet and feed them all. It was what Jesus would have done had He lived intimately with animals.

What would Jesus do?—that's what I ask myself. I try, and I try, but my good intentions break down when I'm with other people. Like with the guys, you know?—it's like there's the real me, that being with somebody like you brings out, Marianne, and there's the other me that—well, that's an asshole, a real jerk. That makes me ashamed.

His eyes lifted shyly to hers. The heavy lids, the narrow bridge of the nose, the lank hair fallen onto his forehead. His skin looked grainy, as in an old photograph. He was stretched on the step below her, his shoulders rounded, so she'd wanted to poke at him as she might have poked at Patrick to urge him to straighten his backbone, lift his shoulders. Music pounded and pulsed through the walls. It was loud enough to influence the beat of your heart, to make you sweat. He'd been drinking but wasn't drunk—was he?—and seemed instead to be speaking frankly, sincerely, as she'd never heard him speak before. Oh hadn't he meant it, any of it? Had it solely been to deceive, to manipulate?

She could not believe that, could she?

Not Marianne Mulvaney in whose heart Jesus Christ had dwelled for the past seventeen years, or more.

As she left the barn, the thought touched her light and fleeting as a snowflake. *Am I saying good-bye?*

Now the sky was cracked and cobbled and glowed in the west with a mysterious bruised flame on the very brink of extinction. In the front windows of the antique barn lights winked, and Marianne thought for an uneasy moment that Corinne was inside; but it was only reflected light.

Marianne unlatched the door of the antique barn with cold-stiffened fingers and let herself inside. Switched on the overhead light, hoping no one in the house would notice. Hoping Corinne wouldn't grab a jacket and run out to join her.

She'd had a thought of—what was it?—not a dream exactly but a vivid memory of a framed reproduction, a wall hanging?—one of Corinne's "bargain treasures." Suddenly it seemed urgent to find it.

But where, amid this clutter?

Marianne hadn't been in her mother's shop for a while. There must have been new acquisitions, it looked as if Corinne was stripping down and refinishing a weird armchair of twisted, gnarled tree limbs, like a torture machine, and there was a Shaker-style rocking chair positioned on a worktable, but Marianne couldn't be sure.

A smell of paint solvent, varnish, furniture polish, oil-based paint (Corinne had been painting the interior of the barn a bright robin's-egg blue but hadn't quite finished the task), mouse droppings, dust. That comforting smell of old things, of the past. *So happy here, things are so calm and sane here* Corinne would exclaim, brushing away cobwebs, dodging a drip from the ceiling, gamely clearing space for visitors to walk through the clutter, her eyes glistening like a child's. All the Mulvaney children were involved in Corinne's obsession from time to time, particularly Marianne, eager to be Mom's helper, though lacking her mother's unquestioning passion for old things, the mere look and feel and smell and heft of them; the fact, to Corinne endlessly fascinating, they were *old*. And *abandoned* by their former owners.

Michael Sr. took a characteristic humorous view of High Point Antiques: to him, Corinne's stock was basically junk. Some of it "O.K. junk" and some of it "not-bad junk" but most of it "just plain junk" of the kind you can find in anybody's attic or cellar if not the town dump. The mystique of *old* and *abandoned* was lost on him. "In my business," he said, "you provide the customer with state-of-the-art goods and labor or you're out on your ass."

Marianne guessed that the antique barn was Corinne's haven from the continuous intensity, the carnival atmosphere, of family life. Especially when Marianne and her brothers had been small children. There was cram and clutter and a look of a tornado having blown through in both the house and in the antique barn but in the antique barn it was quiet, at least.

Heavy rusted wrought-iron garden furniture, a "gothic revival" settee, a "rococo revival" chair of exquisite cast-iron filigree, willow ware settees and headboards, that twisty furniture made of gnarled tree limbs with bark still intact—"naturalistic style," of the turn of the century; native willow and imported rattan and much-varnished aged wood that looked as if it would disintegrate into its molecules if anyone's weight was lowered upon it. There were dining-room sets, battered drop-leaf maplewood tables and matching chairs with split rush seats; there were stacks of dust-limp lampshades, lamps of yellowed carved ivory, free-standing gilt-stenciled "Doric columns," even a broken-stringed harpsichord with keys the color of English breakfast tea. There were lacquered surfaces, grimy-fabric surfaces, splotched-mirror surfaces, porcelain and marble and stone and concrete (urns, dogs, horses, a ghastly white-painted "darky" holding out a fingerless hand for an invisible horse's rein). There was a counter of shoe boxes stuffed with aged postcards dated 1905, 1911, 1923, handwritten, in the scrawled and faded and frequently indecipherable hands of strangers; penny postcards bearing vista-views of the Chautauqua Valley, photographs painted over to resemble watercolors in romantic pastel hues, selling for as little as one dollar a dozen. (If Corinne could sell them at all.) Marianne couldn't resist, pulled out a card at random, a sunset scene of canal barge, yoked mules and mule driver titled *Erie Barge Canal at Yewville, N.Y., 1915*. On the reverse was a message in near-invisible blue ink, in a woman's flowery hand: *Hello Rose! Suppose you think I am dead. But I am not, very much alive instead. How are you all? & are you still in the same house? Let me hear from you. All O.K. here except for Ross & grandma, no change. Love to all & the baby too. Yr. sis. Edna.* It was dated Fri. P.M., July 16. Hastily Marianne put the card back in the shoe box and moved on. If she began reading through these old cards she'd lose herself for an hour.

Some of them she'd stolen away to keep in her room. They sold so cheaply, it seemed a shame. Such tragically real and unique and irreplaceable documents. Corinne agreed they were precious but then everything in her antique barn was precious wasn't it?—that was the point of antiques wasn't it?

Behind stacks of water-stained and -warped old books—James Fenimore Cooper's *The Pathfinder*, Winston Churchill's *A Modern Chronicle*, Hamlin Garland's *A Son of the Middle Border*, *A Children's Garden of Poesy* and several volumes of *Reader's Digest Books, Information Please Almanac 1949*—partly covered by a kerosene-smelling ratty old quilt, Marianne found what she was searching for. A framed reproduction of an antiquated painting by an unknown artist, titled *The Pilgrim*: a romantically twilit vista of mountains, a woodland lake, light radiating from a likeness of Jesus' face in the sky falling upon a robed figure kneeling in a meadow of grazing sheep and lambs beside the glistening water. The figure was barefoot and seemed to have made her way across a rocky terrain; her profile was partly obscured by a plait of faded gold hair and a shawl modestly covering her head. Beneath the title was the caption, which Marianne found thrilling: *He that loseth his life for my sake shall find it.*

Corinne had brought *The Pilgrim* home years ago from a flea market and hadn't sold it though the price had been lowered several times, rather conspicuously—$25, $19.98, now $12.50. (How did Corinne determine these prices, anyhow? She seemed to have, as Michael Sr. observed, an unfailing instinct for keeping them just high enough to discourage potential buyers.) Marianne recalled Patrick saying of the reproduction, *What cornball stuff, Mom!* and she supposed she had to agree, yes it was sentimental and silly, bad as the worst of Sunday school Bible cards, Jesus floating in the sky like a balloon, the lambs gathered around the pilgrim like wooden toys with disconcertingly humanoid faces. Still, Marianne found the image fascinating, like a riddle to be decoded. Many times she'd asked Corinne who was the pilgrim, and where had she come from? She was alone—why? She seemed quite young, only a girl. Was she about to die, and that was why Jesus smiled down upon her from the clouds? Yet she did not appear injured or exhausted; in her very posture of humility, head bowed, hands clasped and uplifted in prayer, there was a suggestion of pride. Clearly the pilgrim was praying to Jesus, unaware of Him though His rays of light illuminated her out of the shadow.

Corinne found *The Pilgrim* fascinating, too. She had the idea it was based on some German folktale, she didn't know why. And the caption wasn't accurate, exactly: it should have been *She that loseth her life for my sake shall find it.*

Marianne drew her fingers across the glass, trailing dust. She squatted beside the painting, staring avidly at it, her eyes misting over in tears. She felt a surge of happiness sharp as pain in her heart.

She hadn't actually seen *The Pilgrim* in a long time and had more or less forgotten it. Yet, evidently, she'd been thinking of it the previous night, soaking in Trisha LaPorte's bathtub. Numbed, dazed. Her thoughts flying rapidly and fluidly and without weight or seeming significance. *Jesus help me. Jesus help me.* Like scenes glimpsed from the window of a speeding vehicle, lacking depth and color. Like those strange fleeting faces, strangers' faces, some of them distorted and grotesque, we see as we sink exhausted into sleep. So, amid the steaming water, above a limp-floating naked girl's body, a body at which Marianne did not look, *The Pilgrim* rose, took shape. It hovered suspended until finally it faded into numbness and oblivion, a gouged-out hole in the very space of consciousness.

So much to talk about! So many interruptions! Laughter, and Judd scolded by Dad for passing sausage-bits to Little Boots beneath the table, and Mom scolded by Dad *Honeylove will you for God's sake stop jumping up every five minutes?*—and the discovery, midmeal, that the oven was still set at four hundred degrees and the Mexican chicken-shrimp-sausage casserole was beginning to burn. Marianne had helped Mom prepare supper as usual as if nothing were wrong, so perhaps nothing was wrong. In addition to the super-casserole there was grilled Parmesan-dill bread, baked butternut squash sprinkled with brown sugar, a giant tossed salad with Mom's special oil-and-vinegar dressing, homemade apple-cinnamon cobbler with vanilla ice cream. How many suppers, how many meals, here in the big cozy country kitchen at High Point Farm: you might bear the memory into eternity, yet each occasion was unique, mysterious.

In a haze of smiling, nodding, chewing, swallowing Marianne navigated the hour-long meal. Not quite so talkative, smiling, happy as usual but maybe no one noticed? (Except Mom?) Mikey-Junior was away with his girl Trudi Hendrick (*Are* those two getting serious?

Mom's worried, wondering) but all the other Mulvaneys were in their usual seats. And all hungry.

You know you want to, why'd you come with me if you don't?

Nobody's gonna hurt you for Christ's sake get cool.

Talk swirled around Marianne's head like confetti. She was listening, yet seemed not to hear. Did they glance at her oddly?—or not notice a thing? There was a buzzing in her ears remote as wasps, in summer, under the eaves. That ache like weeping in her loins. (Don't think: *va-gin-a*. Ugly words like *ut-er-us, clit-or-is*.) Marianne leapt up to save Mom a trip, carrying the heated casserole back to the table; passed the newly replenished bread basket back to Dad, the salt-free margarine, the hefty gleaming "Swedish" salad bowl. Mom was telling them excitedly of the candidate she and church friends intended to campaign for, in the upcoming Presidential election, Jimmy Carter—"A true Christian, and an intelligent, forceful man." Dad murmured in an undertone, with a wink for the kids, "Rare combo, eh?" but Mom chose to ignore the remark; tried never to argue at mealtimes, on principle. Next was talk of the icy roads, Monday morning's predicted weather (snow flurries, windchill temperatures as low as minus twenty). Talk of upcoming dental appointments (Patrick, Judd—both groaned), a vet appointment (for poor Silky, whose teeth were getting bad). Dad brought up the subject of the bid Mulvaney Roofing had made last Monday to the contractor for the St. Matthew's Hospital addition, one of seven bids from local roofers, so far as he knew; a decision was due soon, maybe this week. With a shrug of his burly shoulder meant to disguise the hope and anxiety he felt, Dad said, grinning, "Well, as the fella says, 'No news is good news.' Right?" Mom interjected in her way of thrusting her head forward, gawky-girl style, with her neighing laugh, " 'No noose is good noose'—as the condemned man said on the scaffold."

"Oh, Mom!" everyone brayed.

Except Marianne, who smiled vaguely. Knowing she'd hurt her mother's feelings earlier, that exchange about Feathers. Though she couldn't remember any longer what either of them had said.

Patrick tried to initiate a discussion of time travel but Dad laughed scornfully, pointing out it was bad enough we have so many useless overpriced places to travel to now, let alone going *back* and *forward* in time. Mom remarked it would make her so nervous, plunging into the unknown—"The 'known' is about all I can handle." Patrick sulked they never took anything seriously and Dad said in fact they took everything seriously except not at mealtimes. Going on then to tell a new joke ("There's these identical-looking skunks, one's a Republican and the other's a Democrat, meet in a bar") he'd heard in the club locker room that afternoon and everyone laughed, or made laughing-groaning sounds, and Marianne too smiled though preoccupied with passing the salad bowl. And replenishing the bread basket lined with bright pumpkin-decorated paper napkins from Hallowe'en. Patrick observed dryly, "Is Homo sapiens the only species that laughs? What's the evolutionary advantage in *laughing*, does anyone know?"

Mom said thoughtfully, "Laughing is a way of getting out of yourself, laughing at yourself—mankind's foibles, pretensions." Dad said, "Hell, it's a way of letting off steam. Nervous tension." Judd said, "It's just something that *happens*, you can't force it." Patrick said, "But why? Why does it *happen*? What's the point?" Mom said, sighing, laying a hand on Patrick's arm, "Oh, well, Pinch—if you have to ask, you'll never know." And everyone laughed at Patrick who was blushing, embarrassed.

Everyone except Marianne who was at the counter cutting more slices of bread. She smiled, and returned to her seat. What had they been talking about?

It's as if I am already gone. Just my body in its place.

She'd seen Patrick glancing at her, sidelong. Not a word from him.

There was the Mulvaney cork bulletin board on the wall. Festooned with color snapshots, clippings, blue and red ribbons, Dad's Chamber of Commerce "medal," dried wildflowers, gorgeous seed-catalogue pictures of tomatoes, snapdragons, columbine. Beneath what was visible were more items and beneath those probably more. Like archeological strata. A recent history of the Mulvaneys. The bulletin board had been there forever, Mom's contribution to the household. At its center was a large calendar with the handprinted ★ ★ ★ WORK SCHEDULE ★ ★ ★ above. High Point Farm had to be run like a boot camp, the elder Mulvaneys believed, or chaos would sweep in and bear them all away like a flood. So painstakingly, with the judiciousness of Solomon, Corinne drew up each month a schedule of chores—house chores, mealtime chores, trash-related chores, all variety of outdoor/seasonal chores, horse chores, cow chores, barn chores, pet chores, and what was unclassifiable—"misc." chores. (These, the Mulvaney children agreed, could be the most treacherous. Helping Mom clean out the cellar, for instance. Helping Mom sand, scrape, caulk, paint in the antique barn. Helping Mom put flea collars on all the dogs and cats in a single afternoon.) Like any month, February 1976 presented itself to the neutral eye as a phenomenon of white squares arranged symmetrically along proportionate grids as if time were a matter of division, finite and exacting; each square mastered by Corinne Mulvaney's meticulous hand-printing. Corinne was famous for her terrible fair-mindedness, as Dad said she spared no one the worst, not even herself and him.

True, the Mulvaneys sometimes made deals with one another, switched chores without Mom's approval. So long as the chores got done there was no problem but when the ★ ★ ★ WORK SCHEDULE ★ ★ ★ failed in any particular, as Dad said there was hell to pay.

Still it was nice wasn't it, comforting. Knowing that at any time you could check the bulletin board, see exactly what was expected of you not only that day but through the end of the month.

Most prominent on the bulletin board as always were the newer Polaroids. Button in her pretty prom dress. Before the luckless Austin Weidman the "date" arrived in his dad's car to take her away. *Strawberries 'n' cream!* Dad teased, snapping the shots. But of course he was proud, how could he not be proud. And Mom was proud. Pride goeth before a fall Mom would murmur biting her lower lip but, oh!—it was hard to resist. Marianne had sewed such a lovely dress for her 4-H project, not due until June for the county fair competition. And Marianne was so lovely of course. Slender, high-breasted, with those shining eyes, gleaming dark-brown hair of the hue of the finest richest mahogany. In one of the shots Marianne and Corinne were smiling at Dad the photographer, arms around each other's waist, and Corinne in her baggy SAVE THE WHALES sweatshirt and jeans looked wonderfully youthful, mischievous. The white light of the flash illuminated every freckle on her face and caused her eyes to flare up neon-blue. She'd been photographed in the midst of laughing but there was no mistaking those eyes, that pride. *This is my gift to the world, my beautiful daughter thank you God.*

The meal was ending, they were eating dessert. Talk had looped back to Dad and his triumphant or almost-triumphant squash games that afternoon. Marianne listened and laughed with the others. Though her mind was drifting away and had to be restrained like a flighty unwieldy kite in a fierce wind. *No telephone calls for Button that day. Not one.* Corinne would surely have noticed.

Dad was being good, amazingly good for Dad—eating a small

portion of cherry cobbler and stoically refusing another helping. He complimented Mom and Marianne on the terrific supper and went on to speak of his friend Ben Breuer whose name was frequently mentioned at mealtimes at High Point Farm. Mr. Breuer was a local attorney, a business associate and close friend of the Democratic state senator from the Chautauqua district, Harold Stoud, whom Michael Mulvaney Sr. much admired and to whose campaigns he'd contributed. "Ben and I are evenly matched as twins, almost," Dad was saying, smiling, "—but I can beat Ben if I push hard. Winning is primarily an act of *will*. I mean when you're so evenly matched. But I don't always push it, you know?—so Ben thinks, if he happens to win a game or two, he's won on his own. Keeping a good equilibrium is more important."

Patrick pushed his wire-rim schoolboy glasses against the bridge of his nose and peered at Dad inquisitively. "More important than what, Dad?" he asked.

"More important than winning."

" 'A good equilibrium'—in what sense?"

"In the sense of friendship. Pure and simple."

"I don't understand." Patrick's mild provoking manner, his level gaze, indicated otherwise. A tawny look had come up in his eyes.

Dad said, pleasantly, "Friendship with a person of Ben Breuer's quality means a hell of a lot more to me than winning a *game*."

"Isn't that hypocritical, Dad?"

A look of hurt flickered across Dad's face. He'd been spooning cherry cobbler out of Mom's bowl which she'd pushed in his direction, seeing how he'd been casting yearning glances at it, and now he said, fixing Patrick with a fatherly patient smile, "It's sound business sense, son. That's what it is."

After supper there was the danger of Corinne knocking at her door. Of course the door could not be locked, impossible to lock any door at High Point Farm and violate family code.

In fact there were no locks on the children's bedroom doors. For what purpose, a lock?

God help me. Jesus have pity on me.

During the meal Marianne had had a mild surge of nausea but no one had noticed. She'd conquered it, sitting very calmly and waiting for it to subside. As Dad said, *An act of will.*

But it was there, still. The nausea that had spread through her body like that species of thick clotted green scum that, if unchecked, spread through the animals' drinking pond and despoiled it each summer. Microorganisms replicating by an action of sunshine, Patrick explained. Only drastic measures could curtail them.

But the nausea remained, and a taste of hot yellow bile at the back of her mouth. Like acid. Horrible. It was the vodka backing up, vodka and orange juice. She hadn't known what it was, exactly. Zachary prepared the drink for her saying it was mild, she wouldn't notice it at all. How happy she was, how elated! How easily she'd laughed! *You're so beautiful Marianne* he'd said staring at her and she'd known it was true.

Jesus have pity on me, forgive me. Let me be all right.

As soon as she'd come home that afternoon she took two aspirin tablets. To get her through the ordeal of supper, two more. It seemed to her that the pain in her lower belly, the hot sullen seepage of blood in her loins had lessened. Her skin was hot, her forehead burning. If Mom had noticed she would have said in her usual murmurous embarrassed way, dropping her eyes, that it was just her period. A few days early this month.

How to examine her dress without touching it or smelling it.

The left strap was torn from the pleated bodice but did not appear to be otherwise damaged, it should be easy to mend. More difficult would be the long jagged tear in the skirt, upward from the hem on a bias. She could hear still the shriek of the delicate fabric as if her very nerves had been ripped out of her flesh. *Nobody's gonna hurt you for Christ's sake get cool.* Where she'd gently hand-washed the dress with Pond's complexion soap in lukewarm water in Trisha's bathroom sink the stains were still visible, blood- and vomit-stains. The satin was still damp. When it dried, it would wrinkle badly. But she would try again of course. She would not be discouraged.

Picking up the dress between her thumb and forefinger as if she feared its touch might be virulent, she turned it over on the bed.

Oh. Oh God.

The scattered bloodstains across the front of the dress were light as freckles but the darker stains on the back, a half dozen stains as long as six or seven inches, had turned a sour yellowish shade, unmistakable. Like the stained crotches of certain of her panties which Marianne scrubbed, scrubbed by hand to rid them of traces of menstrual blood before drying them in her closet and dropping them into the laundry chute. Ashamed that Corinne, who did the laundry, might see. Oh, ashamed! Though Corinne would never say a word, of course—Corinne who was so kind, so gentle. There's nothing to be embarrassed about, Button, really, Mom insisted, perplexed at her daughter's sensitivity. But Marianne could not help it. These panties weren't disreputable enough to be discarded yet were not fit to wear; especially on gym days at school. One by one they'd collected at the back of Marianne's underwear drawer in her bureau, to be worn, if at all, only in emergency situations.

Look, you know you want to. Why'd you come with me if you don't? Nobody's gonna hurt you for Christ's sake get cool!

At the prom she'd been photographed with the Valentine King and Queen and the Queen's "maids-in-waiting" of whom Marianne Mulvaney was the only girl not a member of the senior class. Up on the bandstand. Smiling and giddy. The band was so loud! Sly-sliding trombone, deafening cymbals and drums. The Valentine King who was a tall blond flush-faced boy, a basketball star, kissed Marianne—full on the mouth. There was a smell of whiskey, beer, though drinking on school property was forbidden. Confetti caught in her hair. The band was playing "Light My Fire." She was dancing with a senior named Zachary Lundt and then another senior named Matt Breuer who was the son of Dad's close friend Mr. Breuer. In the excitement she could not recall with whom she'd come, which "date." Then she caught sight of Austin Weidman's long-jawed glum face and waved happily.

Her friends had come out to High Point Farm to see her dress and to stay for supper. Mom loved Marianne's girlfriends—how lucky Marianne was, Mom said, to have such good friends! Such sweet girls! Her own girlhood had been lonely, she'd been a farmer's daughter of the kind who had to work, work, work. That way of life was past now, like kerosene lamps, outdoor privies, snow chains on tires.

In her room, Marianne modeled the dress for Trisha, Suzi, Merissa, Bonnie. They were themselves very pretty girls, from well-to-do families in Mt. Ephraim, they were "good, Christian" girls—generally. Suzi and Merissa were cheerleaders like Marianne. Bonnie was class secretary. Trisha would be editor, the following year, of the school newspaper. They all had "dates" for the prom of course but their "dates" were with boys they'd gone out with in the past, boys of a certain quality. They teased Marianne about Austin Weidman whose name they pronounced in four flat-stressed syllables—

"Aus-tin Weid-man"—as if it were the funniest imaginable name. Suzi who was the boldest of them said slyly, What a shame, Button wasting that dress on Aus-tin Weid-man. All the girls laughed, including Marianne who blushed fiercely. She'd been prancing about her room in the shimmering satin dress with the strawberry-pink chiffon netting at the waist and hips, the finely stitched pleated bodice, elegantly thin straps. (Yes, she would have to wear a strapless bra beneath! Imagine.) She'd parodied the sexy arrogant pelvis-thrust stance of a fashion model, lifting her arms above her head, but now froze in that position, confused.

Nobody's gonna hurt you, Marianne.

"*Marianne Mulvaney*"—*hot shit.*

You're pissing me off, you know it?

Everyone in the school had voted for the Valentine King and Queen and the names of the eight finalists were announced on Friday morning over the intercom in each homeroom and Marianne Mulvaney was the only junior in the list and her friends had shrieked with excitement and hugged, kissed her. Marianne had been dazed, disoriented, a little frightened. Who had voted for her? Why would anyone vote for *her*? This was not like being elected to the cheerleading squad for which she'd practiced tirelessly for weeks, nor was it like being elected secretary of her class which might have been perceived as an honor few others would have coveted. This was grace falling from above, unexpected. This was high school celebrity.

Was it a sin, such happiness? Such vanity?

Later, she would try washing the dress again in the bathroom sink. She would have to wait until everyone had gone to bed. And then she would have to be very quiet, stealthy. If Mom heard. If Mom knocked on the door. If Mom whispered, *Button*—?

Quickly Marianne folded the dress back up, to the size of a T-shirt. A spool of thread among her sewing things she'd spread on top of her bed went rolling, and Muffin leapt to pursue it. He'd been watching her from across the room. The dress was still damp, but Marianne placed it on a high shelf in her closet beneath some summer clothes. Zipped up the garment bag and hung it in a corner of her closet. Out of sight.

Fortunately Marianne hadn't a mother like Trisha's. Poking about in her room. That look in Mrs. LaPorte's eyes, that nervous edge to the voice.

I'm fine, thank you. Really!
A little tired I guess. A headache.

That look passing between Trisha and Mrs. LaPorte. They'd been talking of Marianne of course. Last night, those long hours she'd been out. Hadn't returned with Trisha and the others. Went where?

O Jesus truly I do not remember. I have sinned but I do not remember.

Between her legs she was bleeding into a sanitary napkin. Her lower abdomen ached. There was comfort in this ache which meant cramps: something routine. A few days earlier this month but nothing to be alarmed about, was it. Take two more aspirin before bed. Put your mind on other things.

It was too early for bed. The telephone had not once rung for her, all that Sunday.

She sat at her desk. Opened her geometry book. The printed words, the figures began to swim. She read, reread the problem and even as she read she was forgetting. The cat batted the spool of cream-colored thread about on the carpet until Marianne could not bear it any longer and scolded, "Muffin! Stop."

Cruel and unfair, certain of the rumors at Mt. Ephraim High. That the "good, Christian" girls—the "popular" girls—the "nice" girls—if they were pretty girls, in any case—were subtly upgraded by their teachers. Marianne was sure this was not true—was it? She worked hard, she was diligent, conscientious. True, her friends were happy to help her with problems of math, science that gave her trouble. Boys in her class, senior boys. Not often Patrick, though: Patrick disapproved.

At the thought of Patrick, Marianne began to tremble. She was convinced that he knew. In the station wagon, driving home—the way he'd glanced at her, frowning. Certainly he would know by the end of homeroom period tomorrow morning. Or would no one dare tell him? There would be, in any case, murmured jokes, innuendos for him to overhear. *Mulvaneys! Think you're so good don't you!*

At Trisha's she'd bathed twice and a third time since returning home that afternoon and now at 10 P.M. yet a fourth time cautiously lowering herself, her clumsy numb body, into water so hot it made her whimper aloud. The bathroom was filled with steam so she could barely see. The tub was an enormous old-fashioned claw-footed vessel of heavy chipped white porcelain. As a child, Marianne had been lost in it, giggling just slightly frightened as the buoyancy of the water lifted her feet and legs, tilting her backward. Mom had bathed her in this tub, careful not to run too much water into it, and to keep the water from getting too hot. Scalding water issued from the right-hand faucet, cold water from the left. You would not want to lift your foot experimentally to that right-hand faucet.

Nothing happened you didn't want and ask for.

So shut up about it. Understand?

He'd shaken her, hard. To stop her crying, sobbing. Choking-vomiting. The stink in his car that made him furious.

In the tub the currents of scalding water twined and twisted with the currents of cold water. A noisy gushing that muffled any other sound. Her heart was beating strangely as it had beat the other morning when she'd heard her name—*her* name!—over the loud-speaker. She shut her eyes not wishing to see her naked arms and legs, milky-pale, floating like a dead girl's. Her pale bruised breasts, floating. The ugly plum-colored bruises on the insides of her thighs. Especially she did not wish to see any thin tendrils of blood.

O Jesus have pity, Jesus let me be all right.

Always, you maintain your dignity. You're a Mulvaney, you will be judged by different standards.

It came to Marianne then, late in the evening of that windy-frigid Sunday in February, that you could make of your pain an offering. You could make of your humiliation a gift. She understood that Jesus Christ sends us nothing that is not endurable for even His suffering on the cross was endurable, He did not die.

Dissolving then like a TV screen switched to an empty channel so there opened before her again that perfect void.

SECRETS

In a family, what isn't spoken is what you listen for. But the noise of a family is to drown it out.

Because Judson Andrew Mulvaney was the last-born of the Mulvaney children, because I was Babyface, Dimple, Ranger, I was the last to know everything—good news, or bad. And probably there were lots of things I never knew at all.

This was long before the trouble with Marianne, I mean. When I was a little cowlicky-haired kid all eyes and ears like, if you'd imagine me as a cartoon figure I'd be a fly with big bulging eyes and waving antennae. For years I was undersized for my age, and a quiet boy, so to compensate sometimes I'd chatter loudly and importantly at school and, if it was just Mom and me, or Mom, Marianne and me, at home. I'm embarrassed to remember, now. And maybe I still behave that way, unconsciously, now. In imitation of Mikey-Junior who was my hero until I was in high school.

Secrets excited me, secret talk! What I'd understand was *not for Ranger's ears.*

How many times I'd overhear Dad and Mom talking just out of earshot—their lowered, conspiratorial voices, mostly Dad's—and Mom murmuring what sounded like *Oh! oh yes!* and occasionally *Oh no!*—and my heart would contract like a fist—what was wrong?—no joking?—no outbursts of laughter?—*Dad and Mom not laughing?* The memory of it makes me uneasy even now.

Say Dad and Mom were upstairs in their bedroom with possibly the door ajar, but I'd be scared to eavesdrop, scared of being discovered. Or they'd be in the kitchen with the stove fan roaring and rattling to drown out their conversation. (At least I'd think that was its purpose.) Or they'd meet up (accident? not likely) in one of the barns, or out in the driveway, strategically far enough from the house or any outbuilding, and they'd talk, talk. Sometimes for as long as an hour. *Serious adult talk.* Once I was crouched peering over the railing of the screened-in back porch and Patrick crept up behind me and we observed Dad and Mom talking together, out of earshot, for a long time. They were standing in the driveway by Dad's Ford pickup, one hot-gusty summer afternoon: Mom in manure-stained jeans and dirty T-shirt and a bra strap showing, raggedy straw hat, dabs of white Noxzema on her sunburned face, and Dad in his summer town clothes, short-sleeved sports shirt, loosened necktie, neat khaki trousers with a braided belt fitting him snug around the waist. Dad was rattling his ignition keys in that way of his (had he just returned home from Mt. Ephraim? or was about to drive out again?) and talking rapid-fire, and nodding, not smiling though not exactly grim either, like a stranger to Patrick and me, one of those adult men you'd see in town or on TV speaking with another adult man or woman not as he'd speak to a child or a young person but in that special way like it was a different language, almost. Dad was a good-looking man in those days built like a steer (we kidded him) with a thick neck, solid torso, somewhat short legs in proportion to his body; he always took up more space than anyone else; his speech and gestures, even when he was confused, had an air of authority. A man you would not want to cross. A man you would want to please. Probably he was discussing money with Mom—*money-problems* were a major category of such private conversations, or, what was about the same thing, some vehicle or machine or household appliance in need of repair or replacement ("Everything's collapsing on this goddamned farm!" Dad would groan, and Mom would reply, "Not *everything*, Mr. Mulvaney!—speak for yourself"—a line that doesn't sound so funny in retrospect but was guaranteed to crack up anybody who happened to overhear); or, maybe, what was most unnerving, one of us. That day I asked P.J. in an undertone what did he think Dad and Mom were talking about like that?—and P.J. said with a shrug, "Sex."

I was nine years old. Too young to know what "sex" was or

even what a kid of fourteen, P.J.'s age, might imagine it was. I looked at my brother amazed. "Huh?"

"Don't you know, Babyface, everything is about sex? It's the primary law of nature of living things—what keeps us *going*."

P.J. was the reader of the family, hidden away much of the time with science books and magazines and his "projects"; he'd discovered biology in eighth grade, and believed that a man named Charles Darwin who'd lived in the nineteenth century had had "the answer." Half the things he said were purposefully inscrutable: you never knew if he was serious, or just being, as we'd say, *Pinch*.

I asked, "Keeps who going? How?"

"I don't know *how*," P.J. said loftily, looking over my head, "—I just know it's *sex*. Like if a man and a woman are arguing, or whatever, it isn't about money or needing to get things done or—whatever: it's about *sex*."

Which impressed me, but also scared me.

Because as I've said, you never could trust Pinch to say what was serious, or even what was true.

But there was the time years before, when I was really small, maybe three years old, wakened at night by a bad dream or by the wind banging something against the house, I ran next door into Dad's and Mom's bedroom uninvited and unexpected and their bedside light was on and I climbed right in bed with them, burrowed against them, so focussed on my own childish fear I hadn't the slightest awareness of surprising them, annoying or embarrassing them, in the midst of what I could not have named, at the time, robust *lovemaking*. I can remember only the confusion, the creaking of bedsprings and Dad's exclamation (I think it was "What the hell—!") and Mom quickly pushing Dad from her, his bare sweaty shoulders and back, covered in frizzy hair, his bare buttocks, and hairy muscular legs, both my parents breathing hard as if they'd been running. Mom gasped, "Oh Judd!—Judd, honey—is s-something wr-wrong?" trying to catch her breath, shielding herself, her naked breasts, with the sheet, even as I continued to burrow blind and whimpering against her, and Dad flopped onto his back beside us with a forearm across his eyes, softly cursing. I said I was afraid, I didn't want to be alone, I kicked and wriggled and of course Mom comforted me, possibly scolding me a little but her naked arms were warm and her body gave off a wonderful yeasty odor. Above my head Mom whispered to Dad, "I thought you said you locked the door," and Dad said, "*You* locked it, you said," and Mom said, "Judd's had a scare, Michael—he's just a baby," and Dad said, "Fine! Good night! *I'm* going to sleep." And Mom whispered to me, and got me to stop crying, and we giggled together, and Mom switched off the light, and soon we all fell asleep together, a warm sweaty tangle. And it wasn't until years later I realized how I'd intruded upon my parents in their secret lives, and it was too late to be embarrassed.

And if I force myself to think of it, maybe I'd have to admit that I'd done this more than once, as a small child. And each time Dad and Mom relented, and took me in. *He's just a baby.*

(Corinne and Michael Mulvaney were so romantic! All the while we kids were growing up, until this time I'm telling of when things changed. Mike thought they were embarrassing but sort of funny, you had to laugh, smooching like kids like they were just married or something; P.J. was plain embarrassed, and sulky, turning on his heel to walk out of, for instance, the kitchen, if he'd walked in upon Dad and Mom kissing, or, as they sometimes did, breaking into impromptu dance steps to radio music appropriate or not—a dreamy-dithering fox-trot, or a faster, less coordinated step, what they called "jitterbugging," poor Feathers in his cage trilling wildly. When Dad and Mom met in public, even if they'd been apart only a few hours, and where they were was a Friday night football game at the school, a hundred people milling around, Dad would greet Mom with a big grin and "Hello, darling!" and he'd lift her hand to his lips to kiss it tenderly—even Marianne cringed at the sight, it was too, too embarrassing. Once, one of Mom's women friends asked what was the secret of her and her husband, and Mom replied, in a lowered voice, "Oh, that man isn't my husband. We're just trying things out.")

Secrets! As a child you come to see the world's crisscrossed with them like electromagnetic waves, maybe even held together by them. But you can't *know.* Not, as kids say, *for sure.* And if you blunder by accident into a secret it's like you've pushed open a door where you thought was just a wall. You can look through, if you're brave or reckless enough you can even step inside—taking a chance what you'll learn is worth what it costs.

This other time I'm thinking of, when Mike Jr. was a senior in high school, and a star player on the football team, his picture in the local papers often and the name "Mule" Mulvaney famous in the county—I did barge in on a secret, sort of. Dad was talking to Mike and P.J. in the family room, the door shut against intrusion (you'd have to know that our family room door was *never* shut, I'd have thought there wasn't even a door to the room), and I came downstairs and overheard just enough to arouse my curiosity, something in Dad's usually congenial jokey voice that was low and earnest and quivering with emotion and exciting because I understood this was *not for Ranger's ears.* I went to crouch by the door and pressed my ear against it. Dad was saying, "—I don't care who the girl *is.* What her reputation is, or people say it is. Or she herself thinks it is. No sons of mine are going to be involved in behavior like that. If anybody's treating a girl or a woman rudely in your presence—*you* protect her. If it means going against your friends, the hell with your 'friends'—got it?" Dad's voice was rising. I could picture his creased forehead, the set of his jaws, his eyes that seemed, at such times, to snap. Just—*snap!* You'd feel the sting of his glance like a BB pellet in the face.

Now I know it must have been Della Rae Duncan Dad was speaking of, in such outrage. Word was spreading through town, half the Mt. Ephraim football team had "had relations" with the drunken girl, after the Rams had won the Chautauqua County high school championship.

Finally Mike was allowed to speak, pleading, "But I wasn't with those guys, Dad! I d-didn't know anything about it until afterward." Dad asked skeptically, "Oh yes? How long afterward?" and Mike said, "I—don't know, exactly." "An hour? Five minutes?" "Gosh no, Dad—the next day, I guess." Mike's voice was weak and scared and I'd guess he might be lying. Or maybe Dad just scared him so, he was breaking down. It was fascinating to me to hear my big brother Mule speaking to our father like a small child—like me, aged ten. The thought came to me *Don't we ever grow up?* For some weird reason this was consoling.

They talked a while longer, Dad and Mike, and finally Dad relented, saying, "All right, Mikey. But if I ever learn you were involved, even just that you *knew,* at the time, I'll break your ass. Got it?" Mike murmured, "Yes sir," like he was grateful! All the while P.J. must have been sitting there, stricken with alarm and embarrassment, only fifteen at the time and not what you'd call "socially mature" for his age—Dad must have figured he was old enough to learn certain facts of life, even if they didn't immediately apply to him.

Dad said, winding things up, "O.K., guys! Enough for one day.

Any questions?" Mike and P.J. murmured *no*. "Just so you know your old man loves you, eh? Just so you know."

I hurried out of Dad's way, hiding around a corner, and after he'd left I tiptoed back to the doorway, and there were my brothers standing with a shared look as of witnesses to an accident. They didn't see me but I didn't hide from them, exactly. Mike was wiping at his eyes, kind of solemn but excited, shaking his head, "—You can't lie to Dad, it's the weirdest thing. I mean, you can try, but it doesn't work. It's like he *knows*. It's like he can hear what you're thinking. He always understands more than I tell him, and more than I know."

P.J. had removed his glasses and was polishing the lens on a shirttail. He said petulantly, "*I* don't know anything about it! Why am *I* being blamed?"

Mike said, "You're *not* being blamed. Blamed for what? *I'm* not being blamed, am I?—not that I deserve to be, I don't."

P.J. said, "Those guys are your friends, not mine. I don't even know what they did."

"Well—I don't, either."

"Yeah, I bet."

"I *don't*." Mike was pacing around, running both hands through his hair. He looked a little like Dad, from the back. He said in a rueful voice, "It's a funny thing, how you always know more than you say. I mean—a person does. What you say is always less than you know."

"What's that supposed to mean?"

"Just what I said! Like if I say, 'I went out with the guys, we went from point X to point Y, from point Y to point Z'—well, I'm telling the truth, but I'm saying less than I know."

P.J. looked confused. As if Mike was saying things of the sort P.J. was known for, and P.J., thrown in the position of listener, was at a disadvantage. "But—why?"

Mike said excitedly, "Because to say a thing is just to state a fact. If I say, 'My name is Mike Mulvaney' I'm saying a whole lot less than I know about myself, right? It's impossible to say who I *am*, where'd I begin?—and where'd I *end*? So I wind up saying my name."

P.J. said, "That's true about any statement we make, isn't it? We never tell as much as we know."

"Right! So we're lying. So almost every statement is a lie, we can't help it."

"Yeah. But some statements are more lies than others."

This, Mike didn't seem to hear. He'd stopped his pacing and was looking toward the doorway, not seeing me; his face glistened with sweat but he smiled suddenly, as if something had just become clear. "It's weird, man—it's like a discovery to me. It means I'm not going to be telling much of the truth through my life, or even know what the truth *is*. And, for sure, I'm not going to be able to tell Dad anything he doesn't already know."

P.J. snorted with laughter.

Later I found Mom out in the antique barn and asked her what was going on, what had Dad been talking about with my brothers, and Mom said she had no idea, none at all—"Why don't you ask Dad, Ranger?"

I asked Marianne instead. *She* didn't know, she told me quickly. Not a thing.

THE REVELATION

"Cor-rinne! *Hello.*"

Wednesday morning, a harried errand-morning, and there was Mrs. Bethune the doctor's wife approaching Corinne, with a smile and a wave of greeting, in the Mt. Ephraim Post Office. *Not* one of Corinne's women friends.

Keep in motion, don't slacken and you'll escape Corinne instructed herself, smiling vaguely at Mrs. Bethune even as she lifted a hand in an ambiguous gesture—hello, or hasty good-bye?

Lydia Bethune was one of the inner circle of the Mt. Ephraim Country Club, to which the Mulvaneys had belonged for the past three years; always perfectly dressed and groomed, one of that species of attractive, capable women whose very being seemed a reproach to Corinne. For an ordinary weekday morning in Mt. Ephraim, Lydia was wearing, not wool slacks and a soiled parka, like Corinne, but a lovely soft russet-dyed rabbit-fur jacket, one of those unspeakable "fun" furs, and expensive-looking leather boots that shone as if they'd been polished only minutes before. Her hair was beauty-salon frosted-blond, cut stylishly short; her makeup was impeccable; thin smile-lines radiated outward from her pink-lipsticked mouth like Muffin's whiskers, that seemed to quiver with emotion when he looked up at you. Lydia was a familiar Mt. Ephraim presence, active in charities including of course the hospital women's auxiliary of which Corinne was a member; her daughter Priscilla was in Patrick's class at the high school, a flashy girl with a sullen smile—pretty enough, Corinne granted, but thank God not *hers*.

The inward-swinging door of the post office kept opening, customers kept coming in, Corinne's escape was blocked. No choice but to stand and chat with Lydia Bethune who was a nice woman, a well-intentioned woman, but who carried with her an aura of perfumed complacency that set Corinne's teeth on edge.

"Corinne, how *are* you?"

"Oh, well—you know, busy."

"Bart says he sees Michael at the club often, on the squash court especially, and I have lunch there sometimes, about once a week. But we never see *you* there."

Corinne murmured a vague apology. True, she rarely went to the Mt. Ephraim Country Club, despite the ridiculous six-hundred-dollar yearly dues Michael paid. She wasn't a woman who golfed, in warmer weather; she had no use for the tennis courts, or the indoor or outdoor pools; if she wanted exercise, she had plenty of house- and farmwork to do. Above all, she wasn't a woman who "lunched"; the thought made her smile. Dressing up to have expensive lunches, with drinks, with women like Lydia Bethune and her friends!—not quite Corinne Mulvaney's style. Every few weeks, Michael insisted that they have dinner on a Saturday evening with one or two other couples, or maybe Sunday brunch, with the children, but that was about the extent of Corinne's involvement. And even then she went reluctantly, like one of her own adolescent children dragooned into something against his will, complaining that she hadn't the right clothes to wear, or her hair wasn't right, or she had nothing to say to *those people*.

Don't be ridiculous, Michael chided, we're *those people* ourselves.

Lydia Bethune was chattering, smiling—a smile that made Corinne uneasy, it looked so forced. "Priscilla says Marianne was *so* pretty at the prom. I saw the pictures in the paper—"

"Oh, yes." Corinne's cheeks burned. Her daughter was so much Corinne herself, how could she accept such a compliment?

"I hope you took photographs?"

"Well—yes."

"And—" Lydia was a bit rattled, breathless, "—how is your family?"

"My family?" Corinne drew a blank. "Why, the last I knew, they were *fine*."

What an awkward encounter. Corinne stood miserably balancing a heavy grocery bag in the crook of one arm and her catchall tote bag crammed with library books in the other. Her parka hood had slipped so she had to tilt her head at an angle to look at Lydia Bethune; if they were to continue their conversation, she really should lower the hood, out of courtesy. Oh but she yearned to escape! Lydia had dredged up another subject, a mutual woman acquaintance who'd just had a cyst removed from a breast, and Corinne murmured yes Florence *was* lucky it had been benign, trying to back off, edging toward the door. She glanced at her watch and gave a little cry of alarm—"Oh, my God! The parking meter!"

So Corinne made her escape, probably rather rudely. She heard Lydia Bethune call "Good-bye" after her but she did no more than waggle a hand, not glancing back.

Now what had that been all about? She discovered she'd been perspiring inside the nylon parka. Damp circles the size of silver dollars had formed on the palms of her hands.

Not those kind of people. We're not!
Everyone and everything associated with the Mt. Ephraim Country Club made Corinne uneasy. And when she was uneasy she was resentful, even angry.

She hadn't wanted to join, of course. It had all been Michael Sr.'s idea.

Already Michael belonged to the Mt. Ephraim Chamber of Commerce, where for years he was one of the younger, more vigorous and more active members, and he belonged to the philantrophic-minded if not very effectual Mt. Ephraim Odd Fellows Association, and he belonged to the Chautauqua Sportsmen's Club for "social and business" reasons, but for more years than he would have wished to acknowledge (at least fifteen) he'd wanted very badly to be invited to join the Mt. Ephraim Country Club which was the most "selective"—the most "prestigious"—certainly the most expensive—of all; where the richer, more prominent and influential of local citizens belonged, some of whom Michael Mulvaney did in fact count as friends, or anyway friendly acquaintances—the Boswells, the Mercers, the MacIntyres, the Spohrs, the Lundts, the Pringles, the Breuers, the Bethunes. There were not many prominent families in Chautauqua County, still fewer in Mt. Ephraim, but Michael Mulvaney knew them, knew the men; they knew him, and liked him; it wasn't really an exaggeration to claim they were all *equals*. This, Michael felt strongly in his heart. He deserved to be a member of the Mt. Ephraim Country Club. He deserved the privilege of playing golf there if he wished, of bringing his family to the Sunday brunch buffet, of having dinner in the elegant atrium dining room overlooking the golf course, of playing poker with like-minded friends, of watching his children play tennis on the courts, of dropping by after business hours for drinks, a cigar, in the Club's Yankee Doodle Tap Room. *Strictly for business* Michael insisted, but Corinne understood this was only part of her husband's motivation, and surely not the largest part.

Oh, she should have been more sympathetic!—Michael Mulvaney, a disowned son of a Catholic working-class family in Pittsburgh, had reimagined himself as a small-town American businessman who owned property, had money and influence, was "known" and "liked" and "respected" in his community. He'd been a loner in his late adolescence, and was now a "family man." If he'd never be one of the wealthier citizens of Mt. Ephraim and vicinity he had a chance of becoming one of the "well-to-do"—"something of a country squire." Or, if not quite even that, at least a friend, a friendly acquaintance, a *social equal* of such. At first Corinne in her awkward way tried to tease him—"Darling, aren't *we* enough for you? Your family, your animals? High Point Farm and its debts?" But Michael had only grimaced, hadn't laughed. Nor was he in a mood to be consoled when, year following year, into the 1970s, on or about March 12, the membership committee of the Club proposed its candidates for balloting, and Michael Mulvaney was overlooked.

Secretly relieved, Corinne would say, incensed, "Those snobs! Self-important, selfish snobs! What do you care? *We* love you."

Michael would only shrug irritably, and turn away. No kisses from Whistle right now, no hugs and jokes. No thanks.

Corinne would glimpse her husband outside, in his work clothes, lugging bales of hay, buckets of water into the horse barn. Exercising the horses in the back pasture, with the boys. He'd rise early to clean out the horses' stalls, feed and bathe and groom the horses—these arduous, least-favorite chores the responsibility, of course, of his children. But there Michael was, working off nervous energy in the barn. *He's that hurt, that furious* Corinne thought, shocked. It struck her to the heart, left her weak, disoriented, that, to Michael Mulvaney, after all, his family wasn't quite enough.

Then, March 1973, a call came, from the Club, followed by an absurdly self-important registered letter, and Michael Mulvaney was *in*.

(No secret that Michael's sponsor was his old friend and business associate, a fellow officer in the Odd Fellows, Morton Pringle. Mort who was chief counsel for the First Bank of Chautauqua and who'd hired Mulvaney Roofing for work he'd admired, and recommended to his well-to-do friends. One day, Michael would inadvertently learn that his candidacy at the Mt. Ephraim Country Club had not been unanimously supported. Out of deference to Mort Pringle, and because Michael was, in fact, a well-liked person in Mt. Ephraim, no one had actually blackballed him; but several members hadn't voted. They'd gone onto the record as *abstains*.)

Corinne wasn't happy about the invitation, still less about her husband's excitement at receiving it, at last. Where was his pride? Where was his *character*? How could he want to waste his hard-earned money (twenty-five hundred dollars for "induction fees," six hundred dollars annual dues!) when High Point Farm's expenditures were relentless, not to mention the children, a family of four healthy active children *costs*. "We've gotten along for almost twenty years without belonging to the Mt. Ephraim Country Club—why join now? *Who cares?*" Corinne demanded.

Clearly, Michael Mulvaney cared.

Corinne, a Democrat and a liberal, the sort of Protestant who allowed no one to stand between her and God, argued, furthermore, that the Club was un-American, unchristian, immoral—"For whites only! And all male! Women can belong only as adjuncts to their spouses or male relatives!"

"So what?" Michael said.

"So *what*? Don't you understand?"

"Corinne, it's a private club. It's friends who've gotten together, who want a clubhouse, essentially. When the Club was founded, in 1925, there were only twelve men—they were *friends*. And, eventually—"

"Stop! I can't believe what I'm hearing! You, Michael Mulvaney—a bigot. A sexist. A *snob*."

"What the hell, Corinne?—*I* can't join the Women's Garden Club, or the Women's League of Voters—"

"League of Women Voters—"

"I can't join a Negro fraternity, or the Knights of Columbus.

There are exclusively Jewish country clubs, there are Italian-American clubs, what's the problem?"

"It's un-American, that's the problem!"

"It's *American*, in fact: all kinds of organizations, private clubs, even secret clubs. It's people making their own decisions about who they want as friends."

" 'Friends'?—it's as much about keeping people out. It's cruel, it's discriminatory. Look how they kept you waiting for years—how hurt you were. How you tried, you campaigned—"

Heatedly Michael said, "Never mind about me! We're talking principles here. First principles. The right of a group of people to—"

"To exclude others, for their own self-promotion. For 'business' purposes. And to *drink*. I've heard tales about those country club bashes—"

"Corinne, everybody drinks. Anybody who wants to, drinks. Our friends drink."

"*Your* friends drink—"

"They're your friends, too! Drinking is hardly a monopoly of the country club set."

"Michael, this ridiculous club discriminates against two members of your own family! Marianne and I, being 'female,' can't even enter by the front door! We have to enter by a side door, through the 'family entrance.' Were you aware of that?"

So they argued. For days, for a week. The quarrel would flame up, then subside; like a treacherous marshland fire it would seem to have been extinguished, when it had merely gone underground. Corinne sulked, and Corinne was sarcastic, and Corinne was morally, spiritually dismayed. She knew, she knew *she* was right! But the children weren't eager to come to her defense. And there was Marianne's question, put to Corinne one day with dazzling simplicity: "Mom, don't you want Dad to be happy? *We* do."

For even Marianne wanted to belong to the Mt. Ephraim Country Club. Especially Marianne—so many of her friends' families belonged.

So Corinne, who was a good sport after all, bought a CONGRATU-LATIONS! card for Michael, got the kids to sign it, and added smudged paw prints with dogs' and cats' names attached; added a warning, in parenthesis, *A woman convinced against her will is of the same opinion still.* She signed the card LOVE ALWAYS YOUR 'WHISTLE ' and dropped it off with a bottle of champagne at Mulvaney Roofing.

So Michael Mulvaney was inducted into the Mt. Ephraim

Country Club one evening in May 1973. And quickly became an involved, active member, generous with his time, eager to serve on committees, offer his practical advice on such matters as building maintenance, plumbing, public relations. You would think your father is running for political office, Corinne observed dryly to the children, he's become such a *handshaker*. Watching affable Michael Mulvaney, smiling, gregarious, in his navy blue blazer with brass nautical buttons and his bright plaid necktie, moving about in the atrium dining room at Sunday brunch, greeting friends, being introduced to potential friends, shaking hands, laughing, flirting with women who clearly adored him—all very innocently of course (of course!)—Corinne had to acknowledge with a sigh that the Mt. Ephraim Country Club made her husband glow with pleasure in a way that High Point Farm, for all its beauty, no longer could.

Am I disappointed with him?—oh just a little.

Corinne did admire the Club, from a distance: the colonial-style building of fieldstone and spotless white clapboard, overlooking the golf course of gently rolling, sculpted-looking hills; the fir-lined gravel driveway with the ominous sign at the entrance: MT. EPHRAIM COUNTRY CLUB   PRIVATE   MEMBERS AND GUESTS ONLY Of course, there were numerous decent people who belonged, people she knew well, and liked very much, as they liked her, quite apart from the Club. It was just that she couldn't overcome her prejudice against it. People whom she could respect outside the Club she did not, somehow could not, respect there. How would Jesus Christ fit in, in such a milieu? Would *He* have been blackballed for membership, year after year? Over time, Corinne visited the Club less and less frequently, and then only when Michael insisted. "Oh Mom, you're not *trying*," her shrewd children objected. But why should she *try*? Whom was Corinne Mulvaney hoping to impress, or deceive? True, women like Lydia Bethune were friendly enough to her, but probably (almost certainly) out of pity; she felt their eyes crawling over her, assessing. Who was Corinne Mulvaney but a gawky farm wife trying to pass herself off as someone she wasn't; someone who belonged in overalls, jeans, polyester slacks or shorts, not cotton pastels, linen skirts, "chic" black, shoes with ridiculous heels and fussy little straps. She was miserable at the Mt. Ephraim Country Club, couldn't her family see? Michael compounded her misery by insisting she was a "damned attractive woman" except why didn't she have her hair cut and styled? wear a little makeup, at least lipstick? smile more? buy some new clothes? Marianne said, "Mom, you're just as nice-looking, *nicer*-looking, than any of the women your age at the Club." When the other Mulvaneys laughed at this innocent slight, Corinne the loudest, Marianne quickly said, blushing, "I mean, Mom, you look just as nice as *anybody*. You *do*."

The Mulvaneys, a family who loved to laugh, hooted with laughter at such a notion.

Thinking of such things, smiling and grimacing to herself, Corinne wasn't prepared for—yet again!—Lydia Bethune appearing suddenly before her. Corinne came to a dead stop on the sidewalk, staring at the woman. What *was* this? What on earth did Mrs. Bethune the doctor's wife want with her? So commanding a presence in her russet rabbit-fur, her sleek frosted-blond hair, glowing makeup. She was smiling uneasily at Corinne, knowing how close Corinne was to bolting past her. "Corinne, please?—let me *tell you*—about your daughter?"

Corinne stared at Lydia Bethune, blinking. Her luminous blue eyes had gone hard and blank and opaque and she was gripping her packages and tote bag as if fearing the other woman might snatch them from her. "What—what about Marianne?"

Lydia Bethune swallowed. "Well, I don't know, exactly," she said apologetically. "It's just something Priscilla mentioned and I—I've been seeing her, by accident, not in school. I mean, during school hours. I'm wondering—is anything wrong?"

Corinne asked evenly, "Where have you been seeing Marianne?"

"In St. Ann's Church. You know—on Bayberry. Yesterday afternoon, when I dropped by. And I think today—I mean, I happened to see her go in, this morning around eleven." Lydia tried to smile at Corinne, one mother of an adolescent girl to another, but the pink-glossy smile disintegrated like wet tissue. The women regarded each other with raw, perplexed eyes.

Corinne bit her lip, and said, trying to keep her voice from shaking, "Well. Thanks, Lydia. I do appreciate it."

Driving to St. Anne's Corinne thought, calmly *So this is how it will be revealed to me: by a stranger.*

BABIES

Memory blurs, that's the point. If memory didn't blur you wouldn't have the fool's courage to do things again, again, again that tear you apart.

Labor was the right word for it. You surely do *labor*. Like pushing a wagon loaded with cement blocks uphill, three wheels stuck. Grunting, sweating, straining like a sow to *give birth* as it's called. There came a high-pitched roaring, and a muscular contortion not to be believed *like pulling yourself inside out, like you're a glove*. And then suddenly, after how many hours it would always seem suddenly, a rushing out of the tunnel into blazing, blinding light.

Here I come, here I come, oh! here! I! COME!

Michael Mulvaney her husband grinning and gritting his big teeth, droplets of sweat gleaming on his face like shiny transparent beetles. Oh his bloodshot eyes! No sleep for eighteen hours! *Push! push! push! uuuuhhh!* he and the nurse were urging like demented cheerleaders. Veins stood out on the young husband's forehead, close to bursting. *Corinne I love you, love love love you, that's my girl thatagirl! that-a-girl! PUSH!*

Then suddenly it was out of her, and in others' rubber-gloved hands. The baby!—she'd almost forgotten, that was the point of this ordeal wasn't it, so much fuss—the baby, squirming and red-slippery as a sea creature, incongruously lifted into raw air. Where did so much lung power, so much volume, come from? What if the baby had begun to wail like that, that loud, inside the womb? Corinne laughed at the thought, drunk and dazed. Jammed her scraped knuckles against her teeth and laughed, wept behind her hand. *Oh God, am I worthy? Are You sure You didn't make a mistake?*

Four times Corinne would *give birth*. And never grow wiser. In fact each time it would seem more preposterous—she'd done so little, and reaped so much. Were she and Michael Mulvaney really good enough, strong enough, smart enough, *deep enough* to be entrusted with babies?

That first time, in the Rochester hospital, March 1954, euphoria swept over her like a drug. Red-slippery baby in her arms: a boy. A boy! Michael Jr.! (In fact, was Corinne drugged? What was it— Demerol? She'd been brave and brash asking the doctor please not to sedate her, please no thanks but maybe with her anxious husband's complicity he'd dosed her anyway on the sly? guessing it would be a protracted labor he'd hoped to maintain her screams at a respectable decibel level, was that it?) And there was her husband, her Michael Mulvaney she'd married after only a few months of knowing him, loving him more than her life, her life she'd have tossed into the air confident he'd catch it, yes and she'd *given birth* to this astonishing kicking-crying boy-baby for his sake.

Joking amid the sticky bedclothes, lifting the tiny baby in her arms, for always they were great kidders, a comic duo to crack up the nurses—"See what you made me do, Michael Mulvaney!"

They were married, it was quite legal. But Corinne had removed her plain, worn-gold, pawnshop-purchased wedding band months before, worried she'd never get it off her swelling fingers. The only mother in the maternity ward with no ring, just—fingers. So Michael couldn't resist quipping, loud enough to be heard through the room, "Well. Guess I'll have to marry you now, kid, eh?"

The looks on those strangers' faces.

So Corinne was a new mother: slightly touched by new-mother craziness. She hoped to dignify herself by commenting sagely to the doctor (always, you want to impress them: men of authority) about "the sucking reflex"—"the bonding instinct"—and similar clinical-anthropological phenomena. She wanted to impress this man she hardly knew, she'd been a college student after all, even if it was only at Fredonia State, and she'd dropped out between her junior and senior years to get married. She wasn't some immature girl like others in the maternity ward with her—seventeen, eighteen years old, just *kids*. She, Corinne Mulvaney, was a mature young wife of almost twenty-three.

Plucking at the doctor's sleeve as he was about to move on, "Oh! doctor, wait!—one thing!" and he'd smiled at her breathlessness, "Yes, Corinne?" and she'd said in a rush, stammering, "Y–You don't think God made a mistake, do you? That He might change His mind, and take our baby back?"

Marianne, the third-born, the sole daughter, was to be the *miracle baby*.

You only get one of them, once. If you're lucky. But most people aren't lucky. (So you mustn't gloat, of course.) Corinne and Michael Mulvaney seemed to understand, though they were still young parents when their daughter was born, in their twenties. This was in June 1959.

Already, they had two boys. Two boys! But where Michael Jr. and Patrick Joseph had been screamers and thrashers virtually from birth, strong-willed, stubborn, crying through the night in a contest of wills ("Pick me up! Nurse me! I know you're there!"), their intransigent male selves assertive as their tiny, floppy penises, Marianne was sweet and amiable, an angel-baby, a *friendly baby*. A baby, as Michael Sr. observed, who actually seemed to be *on our side*. Within two weeks of coming to live with them at High Point Farm, this baby slept seven hours through a night, allowing her exhausted mother and father to sleep seven hours, too. Corinne and Michael grinned at each other. "Why didn't we try one of these, right away?"

Not that they weren't crazy about their sons, too. They were, but in a different way.

Boy-babies: unpredictable surges of animal-energy, even in the crib. Mauling and bruising Corinne's milk-heavy breasts. With sly goo-goo eyes *Love me all the same!* When they slept, they did sleep hard. Especially Patrick, in his first six months. But more often there were thumps, crashes, the sound of breaking glass. Earsplitting heartrending baby-shrieks. Kicking and splashing bathwater, refusing food, refusing to be diapered, flush-faced, flailing like beached little sharks.

Mikey-Junior, the firstborn, the biggest baby (nine pounds, two ounces) would come to seem in time the most distant: he'd been born, not in Mt. Ephraim, but in Rochester; in a "big-city" hospital; brought back to a rented duplex in an almost-slummy neighborhood near downtown, not to High Point Farm like the other babies. This seemed to cast him, in retrospect, in a kind of gritty urban light; amid traffic noises, frequent sirens, the isolated and mysterious shouts of unknown men in the middle of the night. Sometimes it almost seemed that Mikey had been born to strangers—young, clumsy, frightened parents who hadn't yet decided exactly whether they wanted to have children; whether all this they'd set into motion by their passion for each other was *serious*.

Michael Jr., Mikey-Junior, Big Guy, one day to be called "Mule" and "Number Four": *all boy* as a certain kind of sausage might be said to be *all sausage*. Uncanny how he'd resembled his young (twenty-six, and scared) father, already in the delivery room: the puggish nose, the squarish jaw, the close-set warm-chocolatey-brown eyes, the dark-red curls like wood shavings. The belligerent mouth that turned, when kissed, to sugar. Within his first year alone Mikey got his head so stuck between stair railings (in the rented duplex) his terrified father had had to remove one, to free him. He'd snatched at and trapped in his hand a bumblebee (yes, he was stung); tackled a young cat and was scratched above his right eye; hung on his mother so much she'd begun to be lopsided, with a chronic aching neck. His first words, in comical imitation of his parents' admonitions, were *Mikey! Baby!* and *Noooo!* As soon as he grew teeth he used them: gnawing at newspapers like a hungry rodent, gnawing at his crib railings, biting through a toaster cord—fortunately, the toaster hadn't been plugged in at the time. Very quickly, being mechanically-minded like his father, he learned to switch on the radio, the TV, the washing machine; to unplug the refrigerator and start it defrosting; to pick his father's jacket pockets for loose change, which with gleeful squeals he'd toss rolling and bouncing across the floor. More dangerously, he learned to turn on stove burners and the oven, to strike matches into flame. He was comically aggressive in "protecting" his Mommy when visitors dropped by. Once the Mulvaneys moved to the country (what a wonderland for an active child, the many rooms in the old house, the outbuildings, fields and woods) he cultivated a habit of escaping parental vigilance, climbing out of his playpen and wandering off, sniffing like a dog, inexhaustibly curious. Always, Corinne was calling, "Mikey! Mikey where are you!" and trotting after him. Once, aged two, he drifted out of her sight when she was working in the garden and disappeared for ninety minutes—only to be discovered peacefully asleep in a dark, stiflingly hot corner of the hay barn by his distraught parents. Mikey-Junior was as finicky an eater (Corinne joked) as Porky Pig. Indeed, he had a cast-iron stomach: if he didn't vomit immediately after gobbling down some problematic food (for instance, rancid dog food) he digested it with no evident side effects. He weathered falls, cuts, bruises, insect bites, poison ivy and poison oak. Bouts of furious weeping passed swiftly as storm clouds scudding overhead, no sooner gone than forgotten. Like an amphibious creature, he seemed already to know how to swim before, at the age of three, he was led gently out into shallow water at Wolf's Head Lake, hand in hand with his Dad. By the age of five, he was diving unassisted into the lake, nimble and monkeylike in imitation of Michael Sr. (at that time almost-slim, boyish, with powerful shoulders, arms and strongly muscled legs that propelled him through water hell-bent as a torpedo). A sunny, uncomplaining, good-natured child—"but, wow!" as Corinne so frequently sighed, "—two handfuls."

By contrast, Patrick, born when Mikey-Junior was four, was a fretful, nervous baby. The kind that flails and kicks as a mode of expression. They'd laughed at him, in delight—his oddly long, narrow little feet like flippers. His pale blue bug-eyes, earnest like Corinne's. Fair brown hair growing in peculiar little tufts on his eggshell head, like inspired thoughts imperfectly formed. A baby with high standards, the Mulvaneys boasted. A baby to keep you on your toes. *Think-think-thinking* like a clock ticking in your hands. Yet capable of heartrending sweetness—that was Patrick, little "Pinch." By eleven months teetering on his feet and chattering high-decibel nonsense with the aplomb of a baby Mozart, to the astonishment of his parents. Corinne was enchanted, mystified. Her infant son was as opinionated and as assertive in expression as his father, and as strong-willed. He wanted his "own" way yet, a moment later, dissolved in tenderness, he wanted only to be hugged, comforted. He might have been overwhelmed by his older brother Mikey except he was in awe of Mikey—so much more physical and forcible than Patrick. No doubt he couldn't distinguish, for some time, among "Mommy," "Daddy," and "Mikey" as figures of household authority. Even as a baby Patrick had an instinctive sense of *right* and *not-right*, and frequently embarrassed his parents by screwing up his earnest little face at people he didn't like, as if in the presence of a bad odor. Patrick would rear back, thrust out his lower lip, point and jabber disapprovingly. "No like, no like" he seemed to be declaring. Overly made up or perfumed women disturbed him, Reverend Earkin (of the First Baptist Church of Eagleton Corners) who spoke in a high-pitched, nasal voice, people who spoke too emphatically, or laughed too loudly, or condescended to him, or overstayed their visits at High Point Farm. In those years before he'd settled into knowing who Michael Mulvaney was, in Mt. Ephraim terms, Michael Sr. was friendly with a number of local men—Wally Parks, for instance, who operated a small airport in Marsena, "Haw" Hawley who owned a tavern at Wolf's Head Lake and was stocky and black-bearded and smoked a bitter-smelling ropy cigar. These men Patrick particularly disliked, and let his feelings be known. "Lucky the kid approves of *me*," his father said dryly.

Then came, unexpected, Corinne's third pregnancy. Her third!—so soon after Patrick's birth. Breathless, a bit dazed, Corinne told her little boys that God was sending them a surprise because they'd been such special babies, He wanted to make more of them to send to High Point Farm. Mikey was thrilled, but Patrick was too young to comprehend. When, one day, the tiny girl-baby was brought home, and presented as "your baby sister Marianne," he'd stared at the infant, thrust out his lower lip, and, wide-eyed, began to jabber excitedly.

Years later Patrick would insist he remembered that day. He'd thought his baby sister was a baby pig.

So came the *miracle baby* to High Point Farm, the Mulvaneys' little girl.

Corinne joked that God had sent Marianne a little quicker than they'd anticipated (yes, they were practicing birth control—sort of) to prove that a baby could be, well—an experience just a little different from the usual.

It was no exaggeration: Marianne was a beautiful sweet-natured baby with gray-blue eyes, dark curly hair, features exquisite as a ceramic doll's. So lovely, Corinne hung over her crib just to stare and stare and stare. A baby who slept, and woke, with a smile. Who nursed at the breast, and allowed herself to be bathed, her wriggly little body dried and powdered and diapered and dressed, with a wet cooing-clucking sound as of perpetual surprise and delight. *Why, life is fun! I love you!* Her crying spells were infrequent, her tantrums rare and brief. (Unlike Patrick, who'd raised the art of tantrum-throwing to new heights.) As soon as anyone, dogs and cats included, entered her field of vision, Marianne raised her little arms eagerly to be hugged or lifted. There were older women, mothers with grown children, who, to Corinne's embarrassment, burst into tears at the mere sight of her, as of memories too precious to be borne.

Those years. They'd still been young, and they'd certainly seemed to themselves blundering, humble, groping, inexperienced; inventing their lives as they went. *You Mulvaneys! how lucky are you!* the refrain went. (For Michael was proving himself as a Mt. Ephraim merchant, too, at this time—a dynamo of energy guiding Mulvaney Roofing.) Such pronouncements left them, Corinne in particular, uneasy, apologetic, vaguely guilty. *Yes but we don't deserve. Do we?* Their beautiful Baby Marianne, their precious Patrick and Mikey—already, as in a dream, they'd harvested of their love *a family*.

Lying beside her husband in bed, at night, as his breathing slowed and thickened, Corinne tried to sleep, for she was always exhausted, yet she couldn't prevent her mind from racing—flying—sorting through the memories of the day as one might rummage through a drawer in search of some utterly commonplace household object; as if searching for a clue; and suddenly, awake after all, Michael would murmur, "Of all of them"—requiring no preamble, no explanation, as if simply voicing Corinne's worries, a continuous stream of thought flowing through both mother and father, parents, "—it's her I wonder about." *Her: our baby girl Marianne.* (Asleep in her crib a few feet away.) And Corinne would say quickly, "Wonder what?" The more uneasy Corinne was, the lighter, more jovial-joshing her middle-of-the-night tone. Michael would say, shrugging in the dark, "Oh hell, it's hard to explain, it's a little crazy I guess—like God is trusting us with something we're possibly not good enough, not strong enough, to deserve." And Corinne would laugh, sliding an arm across her husband's burly, warm chest, feeling the prickly-wiry hairs through the thin cotton of his T-shirt and nuzzling against him. "Michael Mulvaney, what a thing to say! As if God doesn't know what He's doing. That's about the silliest thing I've heard from you, yet." Her eyes starkly open in the dark, her lips drawn back from her teeth.

And what, in this recitation of Mulvaney babies, of "Judson Andrew"? I'd almost forgotten to speak of myself. It's easy for me to forget myself! I'm told I was a "perfectly adorable" baby, by which I think is meant a "perfectly ordinary" baby—no distinguishing features, no memorable acts. A predilection for wakefulness, a puppy-like devotion to my older brothers and sister. There are snapshots of the three of us—I mean, the four of us—in which Mikey-Junior, a husky curly-haired little boy, cuddles me, a small infant, in his arms, with a dazzling grin at the camera; there are snapshots of the four of us posed with family pets, or perched atop porch railings, or ponies—Dad or Mom steadying the smallest of us from behind, crouched out of sight. One of my favorite snapshots, which I'd stolen away with me when I left High Point Farm, is pencilled on the back in Mom's handwriting, *Chickadee & Baby Judd, Xmas 1964;* it shows my beautiful five-year-old sister, all smiles and bouncy curls, posed with me, a rather odd-looking, astonished-appearing toddler in a green playsuit, posed amid a glittering mound of Christmas presents.

Marianne was "Little Mother"—helped take care of me, feed, bathe, clothe me. Mom boasted that "Little Mother" was as capable as "Big Mother" in many ways. Changing diapers, helping with toilet training. On the potty, Baby Judd had been "eager to please" and what that meant exactly, I didn't want to know. Naturally there are fewer snapshots of me than of the other babies in the overflowing family album, which I didn't interpret as a lack of interest in me personally (I know Mom loved me, a lot) but a diminution of *baby* as a subject. After all, who could blame my parents? To announce my birth, Mom sent out several dozen brightly inked cards she'd made herself, depicting a cartoon caboose at the end of a long, winding freight train:

JUDSON ANDREW MULVANEY
July 11, 1963
7 lbs., 4 oz.
brown hair, brown eyes, pug nose
PRAISE GOD THE MULVANEY CABOOSE HAS ARRIVED!

DAMAGED GIRL

I hadn't known, God help me I hadn't guessed. Yet I think it must have been partly my fault. I'm her mother, it must have been partly my fault. I'm waiting, O God I'm hoping to understand.

St. Ann's Roman Catholic Church, at the hilly crest of Mercer Avenue, a snowy-glaring cemetery behind it, was one of the few Mt. Ephraim churches Corinne had never once stepped inside. Not just that St. Ann's was a Catholic church (and Corinne, Protestant to her fingertips, had a nervous apprehension of the Holy Roman Faith) but, somehow, she and Michael Sr. didn't seem to have any close friends in the parish who might have invited them to weddings, baptisms, funerals.

Corinne wondered: Did Marianne have a special friend in St. Ann's?—was that the connection?

She parked the station wagon hurriedly in front of the church, one wheel up on the curb and she hadn't even noticed. Thank God, her husband wasn't a witness. Thank God, the church parking lot was almost empty, no mass at this hour of midafternoon, no one around. Corinne hoped. She brightened at the thought that the heavy wooden doors were probably bolted shut from the inside.

St. Ann's Church was large by Mt. Ephraim standards. Dark red brick, weatherworn; aged, but dignified; bell tower overhead. Mourning doves fluttered about its eaves and their droppings were like ossified tears, streaking downward. The church was in an affluent residential neighborhood in north Mt. Ephraim, attractive tree-lined streets of single-family dwellings in acre-sized lots. A neighborhood in which many members of the Mt. Ephraim Country Club lived. Corinne felt a tinge of old, automatic dismay and had to check herself. There came Michael Sr.'s laughing-chiding voice in her head: *Look, kid, you're one of those people yourself.*

It occurred to Corinne, a bit desperately, that the LaPortes lived only a block or so away. Trisha was Marianne's closest friend. Might that be the connection?

A stained-glass rose window overlooked the sidewalk. Corinne had a love of stained glass, especially old pieces. So beautiful, if skillfully executed, especially seen from inside a building, sunshine behind it. Maybe that was what attracted Marianne to a Catholic church?—things to *see*? Stained glass, statues. Altars decked with gold leaf. The somber little wood-frame country churches to which Corinne took her children (the First Church of Christ of South Lebanon was their current place of worship) were all so plain and spartan and scrubbed-looking. Not much for an adolescent imagination to seize upon. But wasn't that the point, after all?

Jesus is a spirit in us. Not an object to behold.

Corinne tried one of the heavy doors, cautiously—it opened. Her heart was beating painfully. She stepped inside the dim-lit vestibule and a sweet-rancid odor made her nostrils pinch. Incense. An undercurrent of mildew. That unmistakable smell of so-aged-it-can't-really-be-cleaned-any-longer linoleum tile. As if rehearsing a way in which to speak of this adventure, a way of most artfully recounting it to make her listeners laugh, Corinne thought *Why, you know right away it isn't one of our churches, it's one of theirs!*

In a flash it came to her: of course she'd known something had been wrong with her daughter, these past few days. Something not-right. Since Sunday. Since the telephone call. A mother always knows, can't not know. But Corinne had been so busy, hadn't gotten around to investigating. And hadn't she always been proud she wasn't the kind of mother to "investigate"—on principle. *I want my children to trust me. To think of me as an equal.*

A cruel counterthought mocked *No, you're just afraid of what you might discover.*

A new church is always forbidding and St. Ann's with its high ceiling and ornamental interior seemed to Corinne not-welcoming. There were statues positioned along the walls, statues meant to represent Jesus, His mother Mary, and other saints—richly robed, life-sized, Caucasian. To be worshipped as pagans might worship: the eye fastened to an object, confused about what an object *is*. And the spirit indwelling. Near the back of the church was a miniature side altar before which votive candles had been lit, their flames flickering. An elderly woman knelt before this altar, head bowed, whispering prayers with a rosary clutched in her fingers. Up the wide aisle, at the front, was the main altar, prominent as a stage, glittering with gold or gilt; draped in satiny white, with much ornamentation, and vases of flowers beginning to wilt. Overhead was a large cross upon which was impaled Jesus Christ, crowned with thorns, dabbed with blood, a dark-haired dark-bearded tender-eyed Savior, contorted in an ecstasy of suffering. Corinne stared. The wonder and horror of the crucifixion swept over her anew.

Jesus forgive us, we know not what we do.

In fact, St. Ann's was not deserted. There were several persons scattered amid the wooden pews. At the far right, in a slanted net of pale amber light from a stained-glass window, sat Marianne. She was wearing her sky blue parka, the hood lowered; her hair was unkempt and her head sharply bowed, a hand lifted to her eyes. It looked as if her lips were moving silently. Corinne tiptoed to her and leaned over. "Marianne?" she whispered, straining her mouth in a smile. "Honey—?"

It was as if she'd shouted into the girl's ear. Marianne started, drawing back. Her eyes were puffy-lidded and glassy and she seemed scarcely to show, in that first instant, any sign of recognition.

"Honey? It's just—me."

Marianne stood, and a book fell from her lap, noisily to the floor—Marianne's own Bible, a long-ago Christmas present to her from Corinne.

Instinctively, Corinne reached out to touch her daughter. She drew a shaky hand across Marianne's matted hair, smoothed it from her forehead. Corinne's heart was beating terribly hard now. She knew, she knew—but what did she know? Wanting to close her arms tight around her daughter, poor child, poor unhappy child, but she didn't dare. Others were watching. And Marianne, with a teenager's finesse, eluded her, groping to pick up the Bible and to gather gloves, bookbag, purse beside her on the seat. You might almost have thought, observing, that Marianne had been waiting for her mother to come by, pick her up and drive her home as she so frequently did.

"Well. Maybe we should—go?" Corinne whispered. She was smiling so hard her face seemed to her, from inside, one of those ridiculous happy faces.

Never beg any child of yours, Corinne's mother had warned her, long ago. *Of all things, never that.*

What a strange, unexpected remark for Ida Hausmann to have said, impulsively, to her own daughter.

As if she, Ida Hausmann, had ever begged any of her children—for anything.

Yet here Corinne was, confused, hopeful, pleading with her daughter whose vague eyes, grainy skin, windblown hair frightened her—"We'll just go home, honey? Yes?"

Going home, to High Point Farm: Corinne's remedy for any sorrow.

She was driving the Buick station wagon along streets she barely saw. Keeping up bright, nervous chatter. And the radio was on, to her favorite station—WYEW-FM out of Yewville. No point in upsetting Marianne, or herself, so she spoke gently, repeating her simple questions: What was it? Had something happened? Why wasn't Marianne in school? What was *wrong*?

Stiff beside her in the passenger's seat, like a stranger in dread of being touched, Marianne seemed scarcely to hear. Her lips were dry and chapped; her skin that was always so smooth and fresh looked shadowed, a sad-tinctured skin. Puffy eyes—she'd been crying. Of course, crying. And her hair, the child's lovely wavy hair, matted, tangled, needing to be washed—how had she ever left the house that morning, without Corinne noticing? Was Corinne *blind*?

To her questions, Marianne murmured, near-inaudibly, what sounded like *I don't know, Mom.*

Corinne asked, more daringly, "Is it about last weekend?—the prom? Did something happen at the prom—or after?"

Marianne shook her head, not emphatically but as one might shake one's head to clear it. She was hunched in the seat, her sky blue parka zipped to her chin. A wintry light, qualified by the splotched windshield, so badly in need of cleaning, made her appear diminished, child-sized. On her lap, clutched in both hands, was her plain black simulated-leather Bible, Chickadee's Bible crammed with brightly colored Sunday school cards and bookmarks.

"Did you have a—quarrel? Disagreement? With one of your friends?"—Corinne persisted. "Honey, you can tell *me*."

Recalling with a sensation of dismay how, the previous evening, instead of sitting down at dinner with her family, Marianne had stammered some excuse, a headache, cramps, she'd taken a bowl of cottage cheese with mashed banana up to her room, but how could Corinne know she'd actually eaten it? And that morning, rushing at the last minute, a hurried breakfast or perhaps none at all, in the commotion of the morning kitchen, who could tell? And what about the previous morning?

Was Corinne *blind*?

"Does Patrick know? I mean—that you've been missing school, and—whatever it is, that's wrong?" Corinne spoke confusedly, suddenly furious at her son. Patrick who rode the school bus into Mt. Ephraim five mornings a week with his sister, Patrick who might have noticed she wasn't attending classes. Even granted they were in different classes, he should have known. Damn that Pinch, so wrapped up in himself!

If Marianne replied, Corinne hadn't heard. She was approaching a railroad crossing, braked to avoid colliding with another vehicle— winced, and waved, with a contrite smile, as someone, a man (anyone she knew?—the pickup truck looked familiar) sounded his horn at her irritably. "Oh! Sorry, honey." She looked anxiously at Marianne who was turned from her, gazing sightlessly out the side window. A hurt girl, a damaged girl. A girl Corinne didn't know.

If only she'd turn to Corinne, give the slightest sign, Corinne would have seized her in her arms and held her tight.

Instead, Corinne continued driving, bumping across the Chautauqua & Buffalo track, approaching the shabby edge of downtown Mt. Ephraim without exactly knowing where she was, now saying, in her anecdotal manner, "—Lydia Bethune—you know *her*!—happened to mention to me—we'd run into each other in the post office—she'd seen you in the church?—where apparently *she* goes?—not in school—and I said, 'There must be some mistake. I'm sure Marianne is at school. She never misses a day of school.' And *she* said—'Well, I thought you'd want to know, Corinne. I would want to know if it was my daughter.' So I said—" Corinne's voice rushed, plummeted. As if she could not stop the flow of words, as if Marianne's silence were a space that had to be filled; the interior of the station wagon (so cluttered in the rear with family debris, it was shameful) had to be filled. She heard herself say, in a wounded tone, as one might speak to a very young child, "Now what a surprise that was, Marianne: to learn about something so private—I mean, it should be private, kept within the family, shouldn't it?—from a total stranger. Oh not that Lydia Bethune is a *total* stranger, but—"

And on and on, breathless. Trembling, her tongue absurdly numb, cold. Though the heater was on full blast, in her face. And she was fumbling with the radio dial: the announcer's overloud phony-excited voice reading an ad (and the announcer was Ted Wintergreen she'd known back in high school: in those days a timid sallow-skinned farm boy) was distracting. Beneath the grungy overpass and up the steep potholed hill past the Blue Moon Café where, years ago, when he'd just started the business, Michael used sometimes to have lunch—the Blue Moon Special, he'd joke about, kidding Corinne she should make it at home, greasy-salty hash with ketchup, a big plate of it, absolutely delicious. There was the dilapidated rear of the old Civic Center, a brownstone slated for razing, rebuilding with county funds. (The builder was a friend and associate of Michael Mulvaney's and the understanding was, Mulvaney Roofing would get the contract.) FOR SALE/LEASE signs like sprouting weeds. So many aging buildings. Even the Odd Fellows Lodge, a "historic" local mansion donated for tax purposes—shabby amid heaps of tattered snow.

Corinne turned up a backstreet, parallel with South Main. Passing from the rear (it looked as if a delivery was being made, from a big tin-colored truck) Mulvaney Roofing. Only later would Corinne realize she'd never so much as considered saying to Marianne, *Shall we go see Dad?*

Now on Fifth, passing the YM-YWCA with its new, spiffy façade fronting an old stone building of the 1940s. Corinne recalled how, a lifetime ago, when she'd been a young teenager, she'd used sometimes to swim in the dank chlorine-smelling bluish water of the Ransomville YM-YWCA pool on one of her infrequent outings in town. If you were a country girl, a farmer's daughter, you valued such outings in ways no Ransomville children did. What thrilled you—a gift from providence!—was just routine to them, taken for granted. Boring, even. Like graduating from high school (Corinne Hausmann was the first in her family), like insisting upon going to college at Fredonia (what an audacious step that had been). With a pang of sentimental, embarrassed affection Corinne saw herself hurrying along the street, a tall lanky rawboned girl with cheeks that looked perpetually windburned, bright eyes, heart brimming with excitement for—oh, everything! For life. For love. Falling in love. Marrying, and having babies.

All that, in her shyness, so doubtful of herself, Corinne Hausmann had known could never happen to *her*.

Marianne had taken a much-wadded tissue out of her purse and was wiping her nose with it surreptitiously. Corinne restrained herself from saying, in her practiced-mom's way, take a fresh Kleenex out of my purse, please. Instead she looked at Marianne with a smiling frown, not wanting to appear anxious. All this while she'd been chattering, had Marianne even listened?

"Honey? Please? Look at me—what *is* it? Are you sick? Is it the—flu?" She paused, hopeful. How her mind was set to run, run with this new, plausible notion. "Some new strain of flu has been going around town, I guess. Plus strep throat. Strep throat is dangerous. Shall we take you to see Dr. Oakley?"

Dr. Oakley was the Mulvaneys' family doctor, a gentlemanly old G.P. they'd been seeing forever. Just the thought of Dr. Oakley was a solace—wasn't it?

Marianne murmured quickly, "Mom, no."

"But if you're not feeling well, honey? You certainly don't look well. I mean—you don't look like yourself."

"I don't want to see Dr. Oakley."

"But—" Corinne felt as if she were sinking, drowning, "—*what's wrong?*"

Marianne shook her head with surprising stubbornness, swiping at her nose with the wadded tissue. "I—I just don't feel like being in school right now."

But that isn't like you. I know my Marianne and that isn't like her. Instead Corinne said, "But to behave so secretively, hiding away in a Catholic church of all places!" The attempt at a joke fell dismally flat. "Well. I think we're going to see Dr. Oakley before we go home. I think that's best."

"Mom, *no*. Please." A look of panic registered in Marianne's sallow face. "I just—I just want to go home, Mom. I'll be all right if—I can just go home."

"You're sure?" Corinne said doubtfully.

"Yes, Mom. Oh yes."

Corinne's mind ran with this new thought: bringing her daughter home to make her well again. Was it that simple?

She drove, nervously humming to herself. Possibly she wasn't aware of humming to herself. Or of repeatedly touching her chin, her nose. Her nose itched! The sky overhead was a harsh deep blue tracked with filmy clouds like cobwebs: reminded her of a certain corner of the antique barn, back behind stacks of furniture she hadn't been able to reach, to clear of cobwebs, in a long time. The sun was bright but seemed to give no warmth. Over the radio came one of those earnest-sadistic announcements of "bitter cold" impending— wind from the northeast out of Canada, expected low minus twelve degrees Fahrenheit and a wind-chill factor of minus twenty-five. But how cozy the Mulvaneys would be, at High Point Farm. Dad could make a fire in the big fieldstone fireplace in the living room, Marianne could curl up on the sofa with a book, Muffin in her lap, Troy stretched on the floor in front of the sofa. But no: if Marianne really had flu, she had better stay upstairs in her room. Warm as toast in her flannel nightgown in her pretty white-rattan bed beneath the hand-knit quilt Corinne had found in a Chautauqua Falls second-hand shop. Such beautiful, fine work! A rag-quilt of dozens of squares, rectangles and oblongs, a rainbow of colors. Just because it badly needed dry cleaning, no one had cared to buy it, probably hadn't even examined it carefully until sharp-eyed Corinne Mulvaney came along. She would always recall Marianne's surprise and pleasure opening the present, for her thirteenth birthday: Oh Mom! It's so beautiful! Oh thanks! And a hug and a kiss for Mom, and a sly-teasing query, Did you sew it yourself, Mom?—so all the family laughed, including Mom.

That was a lovely memory. A memory to be treasured.

Yes, Marianne would doze up in her room, and Muffin beside her. Corinne would bring her hot soup (chicken-corn chowder?— so rich, so delicious) and buttery baked rolls and a tall glass of milk. Marianne no longer drank milk, no longer ingested enough calcium, Corinne was sure. That might be part of the problem. Vitamin deficiency. Obviously the girl had allowed herself to become exhausted, pushed herself too hard. Those school activities! The cheerleading alone was terribly time-consuming. (Corinne's mind was working rapidly now, constructing a narrative, an anecdote. She'd be on the phone telling her women friends for days.) Oh and you know what teenaged girls are like—dieting continuously. So self-conscious, such emphasis upon being thin. Marianne had never been thin as a young girl, but entirely normal according to the weight charts. So she'd allowed herself to become run-down, her resistance weakened. So she'd caught this flu that's making the rounds. And the excitement over being elected to the Valentine's Day prom court—the only nonsenior to be elected. You know what high school celebrity can be—exhausting!

Why hadn't I seen the signs, have I been blind?

Am I blind?

And this Weidman boy, what was his first name, an awkward, well-intentioned and stiffly courteous boy, who'd written that pathetic but somehow pushy, aggressive letter to Marianne—was he possibly in love with her? Exerting pressure on her emotionally? Marianne was not the type to speak of such things, she'd worry she was betraying the boy's confidence. But if the boy was pursuing her, so much more doggedly than other boys had pursued her, Marianne would be terribly distressed. Nothing worried her more than the possibility she'd hurt someone's feelings. *But why didn't Patrick seem to know about any of these things?*

Corinne depended upon her second-oldest child to inform her of "situations." He'd long been her ally, in his prickly way. A kind of miniature adult as he'd grown up, surrounded by children and childish behavior. (Yes, Dad and Mom frequently behaved childishly. That was a fact.) Corinne wondered if in all families of a certain size and heft there are those who, regardless of age, *know*; and those who carry on obliviously, happily, because they *don't know.* The blissful well-being of the latter depends upon the complicity of the former—but what if the complicity breaks down?

Corinne was leaving Mt. Ephraim, picking up speed. This familiar reassuring route. Like a horse knowing its way home. Past the Eastgate Shopping Center (where Corinne had intended to shop, at Kmart and T-J's, no time for that now) and the fast-food restaurants, gas stations, car wash. (Oh, she'd promised the family she would have the Buick washed, hadn't she. Well—another time.) There was Spohr's, Hendrick Motors, Harvey's Fence City. Country Club Lane and Hillside Estates—expensive houses looking like cardboard in their snowy nearly treeless lots. In the front yard of a rundown old Victorian farmhouse once owned by friends of the Mulvaneys, now rented by strangers, was a red Olds Cutlass sedan FOR SALE!

BARGAIN! resembling an older beat-up model of the very car Mike Jr. had bought, and was making exorbitant payments on each month, to his dad's disgust. Thank God Route 119 was reasonably dry and clear, they'd be home soon. Out here, you could breathe! Snowy fields stretching away for miles like the tundra, stubbled with broken cornstalks. You never outgrow the landscape of your childhood, Corinne supposed. What's oldest in your memory you love best, cherish. She hoped she and Michael had provided their children with a landscape that would accompany them all their lives. A solace, a comfort.

If in fact they actually left the Chautauqua Valley. But why? Why would they ever leave?

Corinne was about to ask Marianne what sort of soup she'd like when they got home, there was chicken-corn chowder left over in the refrigerator, always more delicious the second time, how's about that?—turning to Marianne with a smile, but seeing the girl's face registering horror. What? What was wrong? Corinne was confusedly aware of something dashing in front of the station wagon at the crest of a hill—a gray-furry shape blurred with speed—and before Corinne could think to brake the vehicle's front wheels ran over it with a thud—and beside her Marianne began to scream, and scream.

THE LOVERS

They'd met in the summer of 1952, at Schroon Lake in the Adirondacks. Corinne was waitressing at a resort hotel, Michael had summer employment with a local construction crew. It had not been love at first sight except as each would insist afterward. Perhaps Corinne was telling the truth—she'd flushed and stammered in Michael Mulvaney's presence when they were first introduced. *My God, of course I knew! How could I not know!* Michael would recall and retell with zest, how many times, how he'd first laid eyes on his wife-to-be in a loose, giggly group of girls, summer employees at Schroon Lake including the girl with whom he'd been "involved" at the time. (Michael Mulvaney's second "involvement" of the summer, in fact—and the season had scarcely begun by July 1.) *Hey sure I knew! One look, even with that hair of hers, I knew.*

Though had he noticed her at all, really? A shy, awkward girl who wore her carroty-fair frizzy hair in tight, tidy braids wound around her head like a maiden in a Grimm fairy tale. Too tall for his taste—nearly his own height, five feet nine. (Short men go for short women, no mystery why.) Corinne Hausmann was twenty years old, a college girl at Fredonia State with a 3.7 (out of 4) average, yet she might have passed for fifteen. Not a very experienced or self-confident fifteen. Rangy and rawboned and disappointingly small-breasted, freckled as if someone had playfully splattered paint drops across her, face and forearms especially. No need to ask if she was a farm girl! Her smile was slow and shy as if there were something shameful about her teeth (only a slight gap between the two front teeth) and her fingers and eyelids were fluttery, her laughter breathless. Clear wide luminous-blue eyes given to shifting evasively when anyone, a young man for instance, a good-looking darkly tanned sexually aggressive young man for instance like Michael Mulvaney, stood too close, or spoke too pointedly.

Well, I was afraid of you! I couldn't help it.

Hey, I was afraid of you—the virgin milkmaid!

And Michael would laugh, laugh. Happy-hyena laugh, you had to love him. Poor Corinne blushing to the roots of her carroty hair.

The truth was that Michael Mulvaney, when he'd first met his wife-to-be, was crazy about a girl named Donna whose last name he'd quickly forget but not his wild adventures with her, making love where and whenever they could, often in risky places like the backseat of a stranger's fancy car, in a just-vacated room at the hotel, on an isolated stretch of beach. This was not an era in which good girls or even not-so-good girls succumbed to sexual pressure from men but Donna (from Glens Falls: "speedcar capital of New York State") was a notable exception. She too was a college girl, a third-year nursing student at Cornell. Liked to drink and got high— "high" not "drunk" which didn't sound so good—and meltingly amorous. How could Michael Mulvaney keep sweetly shy Corinne Hausmann in mind, or even, to be frank, remember her name, overwhelmed as he was by Donna? Her supple hips and pelvis, her bold exploring hands, her astonishing mouth that was so ardent, beyond even his lurid ex-Catholic-boy fantasies—Michael was prone to fall into an open-eyed stupor in the midst of work (roofs his specialty, from the start: being short-legged, compact, deft and muscular, with a strong tolerance for working in the sun, had its distinct advantages) contemplating Donna, the night-before and the night-to-come. He was just twenty-three years old and had been living on his own, parentless, family-less, for the past five years. His "real" life. He was a fast, reliable worker but clearly too smart to remain only a worker, you'd naturally give Michael Mulvaney more responsibility than you'd give the rest of the crew who were older, dumber. It helped that he was in peak physical condition (he swam, he dived, loved to show off at the lake) so he could subsist on four or three, occasionally two, one or even no hours of sleep, after a night of drinking and lovemaking with Donna before showering and hurriedly shaving and dressing and beginning the next long, so very long (you had to be at the work site by 7:30 A.M.) workday.

He'd have to admit: his attitude toward females, especially college females, was predatory. It wasn't just the Fifties, it was Michael Mulvaney. He bore a grudge against his several sisters for reasons we won't go into, still more against his mother about whom he'd never speak, so don't ask. But college girls! He resented them almost as much, and as unfairly, as he resented college boys, contemptible in his mind as mere *boys* while he, on his own for years, was a *man*.

Also he was determined he'd make his way with no need for a college degree or any of *that*.

So, in July 1952, when Michael Mulvaney first met Corinne Hausmann, he wasn't in love with Donna what's-her-name, or any of them. He was hot-blooded, tireless, even after a day of hammering and tarring roofs in the Adirondack sun (so crystal-clear it seemed to be filtered through a pane of magnifying glass), a pumphandle of a kind wild to spurt seed, liquid seed, enough to populate a small city. Oh yes! Summers in the Adirondacks, everything is *temporary*—what happiness in *temporary*! It suited him just fine. All he had to be cautious of was knocking up a girl, otherwise just take and enjoy, take what you can while you can, no regrets and don't look back and after Labor Day he'd be hundreds of miles away. Hadn't his own asshole old man kicked him out, shut the door after him?—and his mother and sisters he'd thought had loved him, his sister Marian three years younger especially, and all but two brothers ceased to know him?—just wiped him out of existence, at the old man's bidding? *Can't trust them, can't trust women* he blamed them, the women, the most.

Jesus! his veins beat with rage just to think of it! so he rarely thought of it, at least while sober. And when not sober Michael Mulvaney was in the presence of amorous females ninety-nine percent of the time so he rarely thought of it then, either.

Now somehow it happened, never did figure out the connection, Michael's girl Donna was a friend of a friend of Corinne's; or, if not a friend, a friendly acquaintance. (It puzzled Michael, maybe it puzzles most men? how girls and women can befriend each other so quickly? intimately?) So after he'd broken up with Donna who'd been putting the screws on him and she'd gotten what you had to call *upset, distraught*, one early evening there came the tall carroty-haired girl from the hotel (Carol? Cora? Corinne?) to the boarding-house where Michael was staying, and she bore him a message from all the girls, she said, except Donna, who didn't know anything about it. "She's so hurt! She loves you."

Michael was so surprised, he had to take a step back.

Stammering, "N–No, she does *not*."

"Of course she does! You should hear her talk about you."

"I don't want to hear her talk about me—I've heard it."

"We're afraid she might hurt herself, somehow. She's a nurse, she knows too much!"

Michael broke into a sweat, imagining Donna dead: the girls at the hotel accusing him, the police arresting him, his picture in the papers.

He said, gaining a little more control, "She's exaggerating, and you're exaggerating. Donna might imagine she loves me but she *does not love me*—she's too shallow for love."

"Too shallow for love! Listen to him—what an authority!"

Corinne was literally breathless, her cheeks flushed as if she'd rubbed spots of rouge on them quickly and carelessly. She trembled with indignation, fingers and eyelids fluttering. The ridiculous braided hair weighed upon her head and slender neck like a crown of a kind a demented child might fashion and in her off-hours sum-mer clothes—dime store sleeveless T-shirt, blue cotton "pedal push-ers" and straw made-in-Japan sandals—Corinne did resemble an overgrown child, excited and audacious and—well, dangerous. *No telling what this babe might say!*

Michael took her arm, her firm upper arm in his firm fingers, led her panting and protesting out of the boardinghouse, walked with her—who knows where: he'd have liked to steer them to one of the lakeside places where they could get beers, sit down and discuss this like rational human beings—in a park, around a kind of lagoon, where families were picnicking, barbecuing, the kids running around, people tossing bread pellets and other treats to a noisy flock of ducks, Canada geese, resident swans with their brood; *life as usual* in the background which is usually the case when your own life is being decided without your knowing it; walked, and grew earnest in conversation, for Michael Mulvaney at twenty-three was in his deepest most secret heart a serious and not-predatory young man, perhaps not even a young man as he appeared but already beyond youth, impatient for the next phase of his life to begin. On their third or fourth time around the lagoon their attention was drawn to a tremendous squawking and wing-flapping in the water, a big white goose had gotten snarled in some nylon fishing line, his legs, webbed feet, and even his bill entangled, and Corinne cried, "Oh, look! That poor goose! We'll have to help it!"—with no hesitation, as if she'd been primed for just such an emergency, wading out into the brackish thigh-high littered water, taking it for granted that Michael, whom she hardly knew, would follow. Which, what the hell, he did. Dozens of geese and even killer swans honking, hissing, flapping their wings as these importunate strangers invaded their territory. But there was no choice, was there? Michael cursed, stumbling in Corinne's wake, and grabbed the afflicted bird, its eyes glaring in panic, wings flapping like a deranged windmill until Michael managed to pinion them against its sides, and deft-fingered Corinne, quicker and stronger than any girl Michael had known, managed to untangle the nylon line, maybe six feet of it, not an easy task in these circumstances, as, attracted by the commotion, a small appreciative crowd gathered on the bank of the lagoon to shout encouragement and break into cheers and applause when at last the goose was freed, and half swam half flew amphibian-airplane style to join the other indignant, honking and wing-thrashing birds at the far end of the lagoon.

Michael muttered, "Bastard didn't even thank us!"

Corinne said, "*I'll* thank you, Michael Mulvaney!"

Not a kiss, as he'd hoped, but a handshake. A good strong man-to-man handshake.

So it began: what he wouldn't have wished to call *love* exactly—at least not so soon. He cringed at the thought of seeming, or actually being, weak and sentimental. *How'd we meet?—over a goose, for Christ's sake! In the middle of a goose-pond! No, I'm not kidding.* He had to admit that this odd pushy prim (and virginal) farm girl possessed an abundance of what you'd call *character* of a kind he hadn't previously encountered in any female of his acquaintance; certainly not in such easy-lay girls as Donna the nursing student, nor in his own pious-Catholic sisters. And *character* could be sexy in its own way—oh, boy!—you'd arouse opposition, resistance, for sure—nothing *easy* about Corinne the freckled farm girl from Ransomville, New York.

How many times, how many years Michael Mulvaney would joke and tease about the goddamned goose, the kind of guy who doesn't let things go, but the fact was he'd been impressed by the way Corinne went for that goose to save it—hadn't been capable, you could figure, of looking the other way, passing it by like most people would. She'd recognized the situation as calling for immediate moral involvement. He, Michael Mulvaney, showered for the second time that day and dressed in clean pressed chinos and a sports shirt and new crepe-soled canvas shoes, might easily have passed by the goose—well, not easily, maybe guiltily, but, well—he could have. Probably would have. (He'd have gone to look for a park cop—maybe.) By way of this train of thought he concluded that Corinne Hausmann was morally superior to him, as a woman should be morally superior to any man; and that this fact would be of benefit to him one day, as you might assume that the friendship of rich people might be beneficial, who knows exactly how.

So, aged twenty-three, working at Schroon Lake for good summer wages, not a thought in the world for any immediate future that included a woman, let alone marriage, Michael Mulvaney fell in love. *Hell, I was relieved it was so easy, after all. Didn't hurt a bit.* There was the added enticement that Corinne confessed she'd been about to become engaged, to a fellow student at Fredonia State. Immediately Michael flared up, "Don't tell me anything about him, Corinne! Not even his name." Corinne said, astonished, "But, Michael, there isn't much to tell. Jerry is a sweet, quiet, serious boy—he's majoring in music education, plays the—" Michael interrupted, in anguish, "Corinne, *no*. As long as you didn't—well, sleep with the guy—that's all I want to know." Corinne said, hurt, "But you had girlfriends, Michael. *I* don't expect you not to have had girlfriends!" By this time Michael was on his feet, pacing about, grabbing at his hair. He said, "Honey, what a guy does, what men do—it isn't anything like what a girl like *you*—your quality—does, or even wants to know about. Believe me!"—adding, excitedly, as it flew into his head, " 'Judge not, that ye be not judged.' " When Michael quoted the words of Jesus Christ to her, Corinne grew grave, glowing, transfixed. (Was he conning her?—she seemed never to catch on, if that was so.) She said, taking his hand, "Anyway, I didn't love Jerry, I see that now. Oh, let me say it! What I felt for him wasn't one ounce of what I feel for you, Michael Mulvaney!" Michael's heart swelled. He said, joyously, "One *iota*, honey. You mean one *iota*. That's a helluva lot less than one *ounce*."

Still, Michael was unforgiving. Stubborn as a balking goat. When, after they'd become engaged, Corinne had wanted to see her friend one final time to explain what had happened, Michael was obdurate in opposition: *no*. Hadn't Corinne written to the guy, hadn't she spoken with him on the phone? She wouldn't be returning to Fredonia in the fall, what difference did it make? He'd broken off completely with his ex-girlfriends, hadn't the slightest interest in seeing any of them ever, ever again.

So when Corinne hesitantly suggested inviting Jerry to their wedding, as a gesture of goodwill and friendship (it was to be a small church wedding at the Ransomville Lutheran Church, all but a few of the guests Corinne's), Michael vetoed it at once. Grabbed her in a bear hug so tight it squeezed the breath out of her, kissed her and said, "Darling, you love *me*, Michael Mulvaney. I'll show you I'm more than enough for you."

Is nothing lost? Corinne wondered. Twenty-four years later, thinking these things, in a consulting room in Dr. Oakley's office, she heard again her young lover's ardent voice ringing in her ears and saw again the distinct webbing of shadow and light on the wall of the room (Michael's room at the boardinghouse), the outline of a lilac tree outside the window that fixed these words permanently in her memory.

Love me! I'm more than enough.

IMMINENT MORTALITY

S he would have wished him not to know. Never to know. For once he knew, once they shared the bitter knowledge, never again would he be able to look at her in the old way. The old loving kidding-around *How'd all this happen?* way. (Meaning High Point Farm. The kids. The animals. The whole *shebang* as Michael Sr. called it. Plus the mortgage.) Never without each of them thinking *Our daughter! our baby girl!*—eyes snatching at each other's, helpless, in fury and unspeakable hurt.

She waited for him not in the house in the warm-lit kitchen where Patrick, Judd, the animals would be crowding her, but in the converted barn. HIGH POINT ANTIQUES. Space heaters thrummed heroically but emitted little palpable heat beyond a few feet, their red-heated coils like X rays of raw nerves. The stark overhead light caused ugly shadows to veer upward from the floorboards. Her cold-stiffened fingers moved fumblingly, varnishing the hickory armchair. Varnish fumes so sharp her cheeks were streaked with tears.

Keep busy! Just keep busy. Wisdom of the Hausmanns who'd been farm people for centuries.

Marianne was upstairs in her room, sedated, calm and possibly sleeping. She was all right, she'd be all right. HEAD HEART HANDS HEALTH the watchword of the American 4-H movement HEAD HEART HANDS HEALTH and Marianne Mulvaney would be all right.

Corinne hadn't been able to pray, not exactly. As if, if she did, she might reproach God? blame Jesus? for what had happened to her daughter? For what had been allowed to happen to her daughter? Instead the words repeated HEAD HEART HANDS HEALTH like a flashing neon sign she couldn't turn off.

Michael was late coming home. It was dark as midnight by 7:20 when at last his headlights ascended the bumpy drive. Corinne had called him at work from Dr. Oakley's office but he'd been out, his secretary said, on a work site miles away, a Valu-Right Drugs in a new shopping center on Route 119 where a five-man crew was putting in a hot asphalt roof. That was at 4:30. Again she'd called him from home but he was still out. He'd told her that morning he'd be late for supper, he was meeting some men friends at the Club, the taproom. Business he'd said. But he'd be home by seven at the latest.

She hadn't wanted to call him at the Mt. Ephraim Country Club. Hadn't wanted to risk upsetting him in front of his friends. And the situation was under control now wasn't it. Marianne safely home, upstairs in her room. Sweet throaty-purring Muffin snuggling beside her on top of the quilt.

The wind was out of the northeast, gaining strength. A powdery glisten to the windowpanes, fine gritty sandlike snow blown against the glass. And there stood Michael in the doorway, in his good camel's-hair coat and the jaunty fedora with the tiny pheasant feather in the rim, looking puzzled, concerned. "Hon, what the hell are you doing out here? Something wrong?"

Michael's cheeks were ruddy, healthily flushed from the cold and the two or three drinks he'd had, his eyes quick, staring. Those eyes, Corinne used to say with a shivery laugh, like X-ray eyes seeing what you'd never expect them to see.

The varnish brush had slipped from Corinne's fingers unnoticed. She'd been squatting by the armchair on its messy outspread newspapers and now stood, trying to smile but in fact she'd begun to cry. Exactly what she'd vowed she would not do.

"Jesus, Corinne—what is it?"

He came to her, she fumbled to take his hand. Michael's hand she'd long ago teased was the size of a bear's paw. It came to her then—when there was disturbing family news (Patrick's terrible accident with his horse had been the worst, but there'd been others—oh, others!) it fell to Corinne the mother to inform Michael the father. How Corinne came by such knowledge, such cruel expertise, was a mystery. Softly she said, "It's Marianne, darling. Something has happened to her."

"Marianne? What? Where is she?"

She gripped Michael's hand tighter, to steady him. There was no way to say this, yet she would find a way.

"She's all right now—she's upstairs in her room. I mean, she isn't in danger, and she isn't ill. But something has happened to her."

That sick, sinking look in Michael Mulvaney's face. He was a man, he knew.

The father of a seventeen-year-old daughter. He knew.

After the front wheels of Corinne's station wagon ran over the creature, there was nothing for her to do except make an emergency U-turn on the highway and speed back into Mt. Ephraim, to get medical help for Marianne who was sobbing convulsively—choking, breathless, hysterical. Hyperventilating! Corinne was in such a distraught state she hadn't seen what she'd hit—thank God she hadn't had an accident, swerving and weaving on the highway as she tried to comfort, with one groping hand, the weeping, thrashing girl in the seat beside her. Like a woman in a dream she sped back into Mt. Ephraim tapping her horn to clear a way for herself when necessary. In the exigency of her need, her need to get help for her daughter, she might have struck other vehicles, pedestrians—might have killed Marianne and herself both. *God help us, God take care of us. God we are in Your mercy.*

What had she struck back there on the hill, a dog?—but the creature had seemed too small for a dog, and wrongly shaped. A cat? It hadn't a cat's shape, either—more like a raccoon, bulky and waddling side to side in that way of raccoons—but you rarely saw a raccoon in winter, still less in bright daylight.

On hilly Cassadaga Street just inside the town limits there was Dr. Oakley's old gray-shingled house. Corinne parked, and half walked half carried sobbing Marianne inside and explained to the astonished nurse-receptionist that her daughter needed immediate medical attention. And of course Dr. Oakley the Mulvaneys' old friend took Marianne into the back at once, before the half dozen other patients seated hushed and staring in the waiting room. (Corinne, accompanying Marianne into the rear, had no time to take notice of these staring witnesses except one or two were familiar faces, from P.T.A. perhaps, acquainted with the Mulvaneys, surely. And so this episode, Corinne Mulvaney bursting into Dr. Oakley's office with her hysterically weeping young daughter, would be murmured of, spoken of, relayed by telephone and in person like an electronic news bulletin flung in myriad directions simultaneously through Mt. Ephraim before Michael Mulvaney would have heard of it himself.)

In Dr. Oakley's consulting room, as Corinne would tell Michael that evening, Marianne grew calmer. It was a familiar place, and Dr. Oakley urged her to sit, offered her a tissue, spoke comfortingly to her. Corinne pulled up a chair close beside Marianne's and held her hand as she spoke. Marianne's face was streaked with tears that glistened like acid and her skin was drained of color and she could not bring herself to look at Dr. Oakley behind his desk, nor at Corinne. She said in a small almost inaudible voice that she'd been "hurt."

"Hurt, Marianne?" Dr. Oakley asked. "How?"

The other night, after the prom. Very late after the prom. It might have been three o'clock in the morning.

"And where did this happen, Marianne?"

In a boy's car. In a—she couldn't recall exactly—parking lot somewhere. Behind some buildings. By a row of Dumpsters. She'd been drinking, and she'd been sick. Her memory was confused and she would not wish to speak in error.

"Who was the boy, Marianne?" Dr. Oakley asked quietly. "What did he do to you?"

Marianne didn't reply at first, then said, in the same near-inaudible voice, that she did not wish to say the boy's name. She did not believe that what had happened had been his fault to any degree more than it had been her fault. She'd been drinking at the party, and she had never been so sick in her life. She had made a mistake to drink and believed that friends had warned her but she could not remember clearly. She could not remember much of what had happened and even the memory of the prom itself had become blurred like a dream you know you've had yet can't recall. It was there, it was real, yet she had no access to it. And she did not wish to speak in error.

Dr. Oakley said, frowning, "But something was done to you, Marianne? You've been—'hurt'?"

There was the evidence she'd discovered, Marianne said slowly, of certain injuries. On her body. She had struggled with him, the boy whose name she did not wish to say, but he'd ripped her dress, and might have struck her—unless she'd fallen, slipped and fell in her high heels, on icy pavement. Trying to run from his car. It had been very cold and windy and she didn't know where her coat was and she'd been sick. She had never been drunk before but believed that that was what had happened to her—she'd been drinking some- thing made of orange juice and she'd been warned but had not lis- tened, or could not remember having listened, and could not remember who'd warned her. She did not wish to name any names and to involve her friends or anyone for no one was to blame except possibly herself. She might have been running and stumbling from the boy's car because she was going to be sick. Ashamed to be sick, vomiting in his car. She'd believed they were parked in the La- Portes' driveway because the boy had said he would drive her there but apparently they were somewhere else and she could not say where. Afterward, he had driven her to the LaPortes'. Yet she could not speak in absolute certainty about any of this: whether in fact the boy had said he would drive her to Trisha's house or whether she had misunderstood. For the past few days she had been praying and meditating upon what to do, and she had decided she must do noth- ing, for it was she who had made the mistake and not the boy and she must not bear witness against him. And Marianne began to cry again, helplessly. And Corinne hugged her, herself in tears, as Dr. Oakley looked on, and Corinne wept, wept as if her heart had bro- ken. And Marianne sat stiff yet unresisting, allowing her mother to embrace her but not returning the embrace until, after a short while, Marianne said calmly, looking now at Dr. Oakley, "I'm ready to be examined now, Dr. Oakley, I guess."

Dr. Oakley's nurse escorted Marianne into an examining room and Corinne would have accompanied them but Dr. Oakley sug- gested it might be better if she waited here. And Corinne waited, and after what seemed like a very long time Dr. Oakley reappeared, and his expression was grim, sympathetic—"It appears that your daughter has been sexually abused."

Corinne was on her feet, anguished. "Oh God. Oh Jesus. She's been—raped?"

Dr. Oakley paused. Licked his lips. His thick bifocals, which left such deep indentations on the bridge of his nose, reflected an opaque light. He held a sheet of paper in his tremulous hands and frowned at it, as if his own handwriting perplexed him. "There is evidence of 'forcible penile penetration,' yes. The hymen has been ruptured and there are bruises and lacerations in the vaginal and pelvic area and bruises elsewhere—thighs, abdomen, breasts. It's been several days since the assault and so there wouldn't be—I'm sure—" and here Dr. Oakley, the most gentlemanly of elder men, faltered, "—any traces of semen remaining. But I've taken a smear, and we'll see."

"Raped? Marianne?"

"Corinne, she doesn't say—that. She hasn't said that, dear, you see."

"But of course that's what it is, Dr. Oakley! *Rape*."

Dr. Oakley was shaking his head, visibly nervous, frowning at the report in his fingers. He was a man whose courtly, warmly gracious manner could sometimes shade into awkwardness—he was an old-style general practitioner, of an era that preceded what he perceived as trendy psychologies, "therapies." He said, carefully, "I've prescribed painkillers for your daughter, and something to help her sleep. She's a brave young woman, and it may be that you and—and Michael—need to listen to her, and not—" again he paused, with a fastidious licking of his lips, "—do anything rash."

These things Corinne reported to Michael in as calm and measured a voice as she could manage. She dreaded his rage, his terrible temper that erupted rarely, yet with alarming force. *The bastard! I'll kill the bastard!* she'd anticipated his words for hours. *Tell me who it is, I'll kill him!*

Yet, initially, what frightened Corinne more, Michael took the news as one might take news of one's imminent mortality. He did not interrupt, he did not speak at all. He was having difficulty breathing and grasped at both her hands, his face suddenly ashen, eyes an old man's eyes, watery and incredulous. He seemed to have lost his balance—stooped, and swayed—sat heavily on an upended wooden box. One of his gloves had fallen from his overcoat pocket and his jaunty fox-colored fedora lay on the floorboards at his feet. Quickly, pleading, thinking he might be having a heart attack or a stroke (his blood pressure was high—oh why hadn't she remembered!), Corinne said, "Michael, darling, it's all right—*she's* all right. Marianne's very brave, and Dr. Oakley says she needs to rest—she wasn't hurt badly, really!—I mean—" Crouched in Michael's arms, the clumsy embrace of his arms in the sleeves of the camel's-hair coat, pressing her anguished face against his.

They looked up, to see Patrick bareheaded and shivering in the doorway, staring at them. His voice quivered with boyish reproach and alarm. "Dad? Mom? What's wrong? Why're you two out *here*?"

EVERY HEARTBEAT!

That time in our lower driveway, by the brook. I was straddling my bike staring down into the water. Fast-flowing clear water, shallow, shale beneath, and lots of leaves. Sky the color of lead and the light mostly drained so I couldn't see my face only the dark shape of a head that could be anybody's head. Hypnotizing myself the way kids do. Lonely kids, or kids not realizing they're lonely. The brook was flowing below left to right (east to west, though at a slant) and I stood immobile leaning on the railing (pretty damn rotted: I'd tell Dad it needed to be replaced with new planks, we could do it together) until it began to happen as it always does the water gets slower and slower and you're the one who begins to move—oh boy! we-ird! scary and ticklish in the groin and I leaned farther and farther over the rail staring into the water and I was moving, moving helplessly forward, it seemed I was moving some-how upward, rising into the air, helpless, in that instant aware of my heart beating *ONEtwothree ONEtwothree!* thinking *Every heartbeat is past and gone! Every heartbeat is past and gone!* A chill came over me, I began to shiver. It wasn't warm weather now but might have been late as November, most of the leaves blown from the trees. Only the evergreens and some of the black birches remaining but it's a fact when dry yellow leaves (like on the birches) don't fall from a tree the tree is partly dead. A light gritty film of snow on the ground, darkest in the crevices where you'd expect shadow so it was like a film negative. *Every heartbeat is past and gone! Every heartbeat is past and gone!* in a trance that was like a trance of fury, raging hurt *Am I going to die?* because I did not believe that Judd Mulvaney could die. (Though on a farm living things are dying, dying, dying all the time, and many have been named, and others are born taking their places not even knowing that they are taking the places of those who have died.) So I knew, I wasn't a dope, but I didn't know—not really. Aged eleven, or maybe twelve. Leaning over the rotted rail gaping at the water hypnotized and scared and suddenly there came Dad and Mike in the mud-colored Ford pickup (Might as well buy our vehicles mud-colored to begin with, saves time, was Dad's logic) barreling up the drive, bouncing and rattling. On the truck's doors were neat curving white letters sweet to see MULVANEY ROOFING (716) 689–8329. They'd be passing so close my bike might snag in a fender so I grabbed it and hauled it to the side. Mike had rolled down his window to lean out and pretend to cuff at my head— "Hey Ranger-kid: what's up?" Dad at the wheel grinned and laughed and next second they were past, the pickup in full throttle ascending the drive. And I looked after them, these two people so remarkable to me, my dad who was like nobody else's dad and my big brother who was—well, Mike Mulvaney: "Mule" Mulvaney— and the most terrible thought came to me.

Them, too. All of them. Every heartbeat past and gone.

It stayed with me for a long time, maybe forever. Not just that I would lose the people I loved, but they would lose me—*Judson Andrew Mulvaney*. And they knew nothing of it. (Did they?) And I, just a skinny kid, the runt of the litter at High Point Farm, would have to pretend not to know what I knew.

THE ASSAULT

*B*ut Mort Lundt is a friend of mine.

Amid a rush of emotion almost too powerful to be borne, that was the first thought that came to Michael Mulvaney Sr.

Reckless and desperate he drove, that night, giving no warning to the Lundts, into Mt. Ephraim, at high speeds along the icy roads, to the Lundt home (whose fieldstone ranch house, on Elmwood Lane near the Country Club, he'd visited as a guest once or twice)—arrived at about nine-thirty, in a light snowfall, to find a Chautauqua County sheriff's vehicle parked in the driveway. And there was Eddy Harris, one of the deputies, an old friend of Michael's, waiting for him.

Michael bounded out of the Ford pickup without shutting the door behind him, coatless, bareheaded, and Eddy Harris quickly climbed out of the cruiser to meet him. Eddy was embarrassed, hesitant. "Michael, hey—how's it going?"

"What the hell are you doing here?"

"Corinne called me, she told me you might be headed here. You got a problem, eh?"

Michael saw someone at the Lundts' front door, a tall figure—Mort Lundt. He said, excited, "Not me, it's those bastards in there who've got a problem," pushing past Eddy who tried to block his path, "—I'm going to have a little talk with them."

Eddy said, taking hold of Michael's arm, "Just a minute, Michael—" and Michael shrugged him off, furious. "Who the hell's side are you on?"

The door opened, and Mort Lundt called out shakily, "I'm not afraid to speak with him, Officer. We can clear this up right now."

Michael Mulvaney Sr. bounded up the steps, ignored Mort Lundt's extended hand. How strange for the two men, accustomed to handshakes, warm and even effusive greetings, encountering each other in such very different circumstances, to be sizing each other up now! Michael Mulvaney was an inch or so shorter than Mort Lundt but some thirty pounds heavier and in every way more physical, more intense; adrenaline, thrumming through his veins, gave him a heated energy, a clammy-white radiance to his face. The men were approximately the same age, approaching fifty, but Mort Lundt with his thinning filmy-gray hair and bifocal glasses appeared older, more tentative. He shrank back from Michael as if he feared a blow to the face. Michael cried, "Right! Right now! And where's your son? *He's* the one I've come to see."

Mort Lundt said, stammering, "Zachary is—isn't here right now."

"The hell he isn't! We'll see about that."

For some five or ten minutes the men stood talking disjointedly together, in the Lundts' foyer. The sheriff's deputy remained close by, not involved in the conversation but listening. Mort Lundt, by training an investment banker, by temperament a man given to excessive courtesy, tried to speak rationally, calmly, though his voice cracked; Michael spoke loudly and not always coherently, as if, as it would be said of him afterward, he'd been drinking. Mort acknowledged that yes, he'd heard some disagreeable things about a party after the prom the previous weekend, he'd heard there'd been "underage drinking" and some "pretty wild behavior" and he'd questioned his son, and disciplined him: Zach was grounded for six weeks, denied the use of his car, an 8 P.M. curfew. Michael interrupted, "Your goddamned son, he hurt my daughter, my little girl, last Saturday night. *Hurt* her!—*abused* her! Do you know about it, Mort? Did the little bastard tell you *that*?"

Mort protested, "Please d–don't call my son such—"

Michael cupped his hands to his mouth and shouted into the interior of the house, "Are you listening, you little bastard? Fucker! Get your ass down here or I'll come get it!"

"Just a minute, Michael—"

"Michael, wait—"

Both Mort and Eddy tried to restrain Michael, and he threw

them off, staggering, furious. He said to his friend Eddy, "You! Call yourself a man of the law! You should be arresting this kid for *abuse—assault*."

Shortly after this exchange, Zachary Lundt appeared on the stairs. He wore bleached jeans, a Grateful Dead sweatshirt. His long, lank hair fell forward into his eyes. If he'd meant to confront Michael Mulvaney defiantly, or even bravely, resolutely, all strength drained from him as Michael bounded to the stairs, grabbed him by the arm and began to shake him. "Bastard! Punk! What did you do to my daughter! I'll kill you—"

Mort Lundt and Eddy Harris intervened. Michael shoved at both men, striking Mort on the side of the face and sending his glasses flying; in the struggle, Zachary Lundt slipped, fell, would have fallen onto Michael except Michael seized him in a bear hug, cracking several ribs, and flung him against a wall where his nose was broken, bloodied.

It had all happened so swiftly! In another part of the house, Mrs. Lundt was frantically dialing the Mt. Ephraim police.

THE PENITENT

They said, *Tell us*.
　　She said, *Only what I know*.
　　They said, *Tell us!—so that justice can be executed*.
　　She said, *I was drinking. I was to blame. I don't remember. How can I give testimony against him!*

How many times Marianne Mulvaney was to repeat these words. To her parents, to anyone who questioned her. Including two Mt. Ephraim police officers when, the morning following Michael Mulvaney's "disruptive and disorderly behavior" at the Lundts' house, they came to High Point Farm to question her in her parents' presence.

I was drinking. It's so hard to remember. I can't swear. I can't be certain. I can't bear false witness.

Her many hours in solitude, in St. Ann's Church, had given her a strange stubborn placidity new to Marianne Mulvaney. She'd been reading the Gospels, she'd been praying. Opening her heart to Jesus as she'd never done before—oh, never! He had instructed her in the way of contemplation; of resisting the impulse to rage, to accuse. And, in truth, drunk as she'd been, sick, staggering, confused and frightened as she'd been, she could not clearly remember what had happened between her and Zachary Lundt.

So Marianne told the Mt. Ephraim police officers, her parents looking on, subdued, silent.

(Michael Mulvaney had been arrested, the previous night. Charges of assault were "pending.")

Yet: what could be proven against Zachary Lundt, with no witness except Marianne?—her words against his? Zachary's friends would rally around him—she knew. She was not bitter but she knew. It was clear to her, logical as a chess game in which you see your opponent's devastating moves to come but are helpless to prevent them. (Patrick had once tried to teach Marianne to play chess, but soon gave up on her—she was too nice, too unaggressive, no competition for wily Pinch.) Quietly, calmly repeating *I was drinking—there's so much I can't account for, can't remember. How can I bring criminal charges against him. I am as much to blame as. Can't bear false witness.*

As if this litany were the most basic, the most irreducible of knowable facts. As if it were all that might be granted her by way of understanding. As if, wakened from a cruel enchantment, she'd discovered in her hands a wide, ragged, rotted net, a net with enormous tears and holes, yet her sole solace, her sole hope, was to cast this rotted net out again, again, again and draw it in breathless and trembling to discover what truths it might contain. But they were always the same truths. *I was drinking. I was to blame. I don't remember. How can I give testimony against him!*

Given to understand, too, that if she declined to bring charges of sexual assault against Zachary Lundt, Zachary Lundt and his father Morton would not bring charges of assault against her father.

So it was, and had to be. She'd peered deeply into her soul.

Her soul she'd never truly examined until now. Her soul she'd scrubbed, scrubbed, scrubbed as, in the hot, hurting water at the La-Portes', she'd scrubbed her offended flesh. And if there was pain in such abrasion, there was satisfaction, too. Even a muted joy. *Resist not evil: but whosoever shall smite thee on thy right cheek, turn to him the other also.* Jesus' voice had never been so vivid to her, so specially directed to *her. Observe all things whatsoever I have commanded thee; and lo, I am with thee always, even unto the end of the world.*

She didn't return to school until the first Monday in March. By that time she'd thought, thought long and hard, much of the time in solitude in her room, and healed herself. Of course, she kept up with her school assignments—she was diligent, even obsessive about that. (It was Corinne who called Marianne's teachers, virtually every day.) She did most of her household chores, eager to follow Mom's

★ ★ ★ WORK SCHEDULE ★ ★ ★ which was the very essence of family life at High Point Farm. Schoolwork, chores—as if nothing was wrong. For, after all, now she was recovered, even the nastiest of the bruises fading, nothing *was* wrong.

Bless them that curse you. Pray for them that despitefully use you.

The Lundts did not file charges against Michael Mulvaney Sr. Marianne Mulvaney did not file charges against Zachary Lundt. These facts were distant, impersonal as radio voices fading in and out of coherence. *The Kingdom of God is within.* Her bare knees on the floorboards of her room, her hands grasped tight, tight together and her eyes shut streaking tears. *Jesus! Jesus! Jesus!*

It was a secret thing from the first. After what he'd done to her, inside her, deep and up inside her, using his fingers snatching, digging, clawing *You bitch! cunt! don't tell me you don't want it, cunt!* pushing her down onto the backseat of the Corvette, the new-smelling leather upholstery, the cold fabric, and his furious pale face leaning close, shoving her legs apart, her thighs, the dress ripping, and she too weak too terrified to resist, even to utter *No!*—and after, brought to the LaPortes', slipping in quietly in stealth and shame and guilt and in the sparkling-hot water scrubbing herself sobbing and murmuring to herself and even laughing, giggling—biting her lip to keep from making too much noise, waking Trisha and her parents. A secret, and a revelation.

Blessed be they that mourn: for they shall be comforted.

She could not speak of the joy that arose from such hurt, stirring her to excited wakefulness in the night, so she climbed from bed, knelt on the bare, hard floorboards, flung herself against the edge of the bed and prayed, prayed. A cold-glaring full moon suspended in the sky like the unblinking eye of God. And the wind, the wind that never ceased at High Point Farm, above the Valley!—twining into the very ventricles of her heart.

Jesus! I thank You, I am alive. I thank You for this life, this breath.

For Zachary might have strangled her, after all. He might have dragged her limp body out of the car, pounded her head against the icy pavement, hadn't that been a possibility? an unspoken (unless it was a spoken) threat?

She harbored such secrets, such revelations. Dared not speak of them to her father (so upset, distraught, he was making himself sick) but spoke elliptically of them to her mother (who hurried to Marianne as if summoned, so powerful was the connection between them, and the two knelt and prayed together, weeping, sometimes laughing, clutching hands like young sisters, the simplest of prayers *Our Father Who art in Heaven hallowed be Thy name* until their cheeks were streaked with tears, the color returned to their faces). For there was comfort to be taken in such hurt—Jesus knew, on the cross. Public shame and humiliation. Knowing of course how everyone must be speaking of her, pitying her—at the high school, and in town. Through the Chautauqua Valley. Zachary Lundt would have told his buddies, of course, would have boasted—yet even if he had not, news of it, of Marianne Mulvaney and her father's intervention, the arrest, the police, would have spread, irrevocable.

You Mulvaneys. Think you're hot shit don't you.

Few of Marianne's friends had called to ask after her. Though she'd been absent from school for days. No boy had called. Trisha who was her closest friend, since fifth grade, hadn't called. Well, yes—Trisha had called, on Tuesday of the second week Marianne had stayed out of school, and Corinne had answered the phone, but when Marianne called back, hours later, Trisha wasn't in. And Mrs. LaPorte spoke so stiffly to her, so—oddly. As if she scarcely knew who Marianne was. Marianne said quietly, "Please tell Trisha I'm sorry she's involved in any way, in this." After a startled pause Mrs. LaPorte said, "Involved? My daughter? My daughter isn't involved in anything. I haven't the slightest idea what you're talking about."

So she prayed, and by degrees healed herself. The bruises and abrasions were gone, or almost gone. A second visit to Dr. Oakley and there remained only coin-sized discolorations on the insides of her thighs. Where Zachary had torn at her with his furious fingers, where he'd poked, pushed his blood-engorged penis—again, again, again, again—was healed. At any rate, the bleeding had stopped. She would not know for another several weeks if her regular menstrual pattern would resume but she wasn't thinking of that now.

I was drinking, I was to blame. If I could relive that night but I can't. How can I bear false witness against him?

One day Mom removed the soiled, torn prom dress from the back of Marianne's closet where it was hidden. She hadn't needed to ask Marianne where the dress was. Found it, unerring, without wishing to examine it; wadded it into a ball and stuffed it in a paper bag with other household trash. Mom's eyes gleaming with tears but she wasn't crying nor was Marianne. Not a word uttered.

Bright-glaring snowdrifted winter mornings at High Point Farm! It would be Marianne's last winter here, she seemed to know. Two mornings in succession, the last week of February, the school bus couldn't get through, so Patrick and Judd stayed home. That air of excited childish expectation, listening to WYEW-FM radio as they'd done for years, years, years on blizzard mornings, waiting to hear of county school cancellations. Though Marianne was upstairs when the Mt. Ephraim district was announced and P.J. and Ranger cheered in unison.

Not that P.J. much liked to stay home—"quarantined" as he called it—amid so much snow, silence.

Winter silence. His eyes avoiding hers, young face ravaged in shock, pity, distaste.

(How much did Patrick and Judd know? Presumably, their parents had told them something. And Mike, an adult, knew. He'd known from the first, the evening of the day Corinne had taken Marianne to Dr. Oakley.)

Marianne had agreed to see Dr. Oakley another time, at Mom's urging. On the examination table steeled herself against pain shutting her eyes *Jesus! Jesus! Jesus!* as beads of sweat formed at her hairline but there was no pain. Jesus had helped her banish pain. Afterward dressing herself, articles of clothing slipping from her fingers numbed and without sensation like strangers' fingers weirdly annexed to her hands. She'd overheard a man's voice in the room next door. "—made the right decision, under the circumstances. An ugly, messy prospect—" but she'd stopped listening.

There was Michael Mulvaney Sr.: Dad. Tried not to think about Dad.

After that first night when he'd gripped her hand, so hard. And cried. The shock of seeing Dad cry! She was terrified, her heart was breaking. So she vowed not to think of it afterward, with Jesus' help. For there was nothing to be done. She could not testify against Zachary Lundt for she could not recall, with any degree of accuracy, the sequence of events of the early hours of Sunday February 14 nor even herself during that time. It was like a movie where something has gone wrong with the film, images continue to flutter past, but dim, confused, out of focus. Nor could she accompany her father as he wished (where? to the Chautauqua County district attorney's office, in Chautauqua Falls?)—simply, she refused.

Could not, could not. God forgive her, she could not.

And so it became a household of silence. As if in the aftermath of a violent detonation. No wonder Mom played the radio so loudly in the kitchen, her brothers turned the TV up, even the dogs barked at the slightest provocation—a flock of noisy crows in the pear orchard, a helicopter with propellors *chop! chop! chopping!* the air on a mysterious early-evening flight through the Valley.

There was the discovery she'd never actually *looked at*, never *seen*, Michael John Mulvaney, Sr., until this time. For always he'd been Dad. Or Captain, or Curly. (Though not "Curly" for years— one of the names he'd outgrown.) Seeing him now, *Dad*, yet *Michael John Mulvaney, Sr.*, when she could not look at him directly, at all. For his eyes shifted uneasily in his sockets when she appeared. If she entered a room in which he stood or sat, he would shortly leave. Forehead creased, eyes shifting so he need not see her.

He'd aged a decade in ten days. Heavy-footed on the stairs, turn a corner and there he was—*who?* A bearish man, shoulders slumped, rubbing a fist into an eye and panting like a winded horse trying to catch its breath. His face like uncooked, flaccid dough.

Daddy I'm so sorry.

Daddy what can I say.

Can't remember, can't testify. Daddy I'm so ashamed.

She did not wish to hear but sometimes (by chance, in the bathroom adjacent to their bedroom) she heard. And there was Dad's voice lifting in anger, incredulity and Mom's voice quieter, pleading. The quarrel subsided, you would think it had been extinguished, but like a smouldering swamp fire it had simply gone underground and would soon erupt again, another night. The quarrel was as much a matter of silence, withheld speech, as it was speech itself. And suddenly Michael Sr. who was Dad, her Dad, stalked from the room not giving a damn who heard, Marianne, Patrick, or Judd, down the shuddering stairs and out the back door, a dog or two scrambling across the kitchen floor in his furious wake, toenails clicking on the linoleum. A few seconds later came the sound of the Ford pickup revving into life, the battery turning over, catching, tires spinning in the packed snow, catching too, and Dad would be halfway down the drive before switching on the headlights.

Those red taillights: Marianne would watch from her bedroom window. If she'd risen from bed, to stand and see. Smaller and smaller the lights like rapidly receding red suns (dwarf stars, Patrick called them) in her vision blurred with moisture until they disappeared.

Strange: how when a light is extinguished, it's immediately as if it has never been. Darkness fills in again, complete.

Those days when the phone rang a number of times in succession (for Dad—he took the calls in his study, door shut) and other, more frequent days when Dad was in town and the telephone never rang. Or if it did Mom might call out, in her cheery general-bulletin yodel, for anyone to hear who was interested: "Wrong-num-ber!"

There were few calls, these days, for Corinne Mulvaney, as for her daughter. What had happened, so swiftly, to their popularity? She could count her friends on the thumbs of both hands, Mom joked.

Though Mom didn't joke much, these days.

Rarely whistled, even to call the household brood to be fed.

Sometimes in an open-eyed frowning trance she'd pass by Foxy, or Little Boots, or Troy, or tremulous Silky gazing up at her with widened hopeful doggy eyes and tails beginning to thump in happy anticipation, sometimes she'd collide with one of the cats, in particular Big Tom whose aggressive habit it was to block her way in the kitchen in order to shunt her in the direction of the bowls in the cats' corner. Just didn't seem to see these creatures, *not at eye level*. "Oh, you! Hungry so soon? Didn't I just feed you?" Automatically pouring dry kibble into a bowl taking no heed of the cat or dog staring up at her in mute animal perplexity.

Yes and Feathers might burst explosively into song, aroused by the whistling teakettle, or wild birds tittering at the feeder outside the window, but he'd sing alone. His marvelous trilling rising-and-falling soprano, but he'd sing alone.

Some mornings, you'd hardly guess Corinne Mulvaney was in the house.

They'd asked her about Austin Weidman, how many times. And how ashamed she was, about Austin!

And about Zachary Lundt.

Can't bear false witness. Because I can't remember. If I could relive but I can't.

Playing upon her vanity. Her pride. So shrewdly. That she alone,

Marianne Mulvaney, younger than he, in all ways less experienced than he, had had the power nonetheless to bring him, a sinner, Zachary Lundt, Zachary of the lank dark hair and dreamy heavy-lidded eyes, to Jesus Christ, their Savior. *Like there's the real me, Marianne, being with you brings out. Not the mean dumb asshole I usually am.*

Hunched like a broken-backed snake on a step beneath her, at Bobbi Krauss's party. His thin handsome face, sallow skin and intense eyes. Unnerving to see boys in tuxes like adult men, and Zachary Lundt most of all—but then, he was two years older than Marianne. His bow tie removed and stuffed carelessly in a pocket, stiff white collar unbuttoned. Drinking beer, straight vodka, Zachary Lundt even the senior girls watched sidelong but were wary of, his reputation, tales you'd hear of Zach and his buddies, a wild circle, well-to-do kids and most going on to college though their grades were low-average and their school activities virtually nil. That gang of five or six guys hadn't exactly been invited to Bobbi Krauss's after the prom but sure Bobbi was flattered, sort of, when they showed up—Zach in his new-model Corvette (but lacking his prom date, poor Cynthia Slosson—he'd taken her home early?) and Ike Rodman in his dad's Caddy with some of the guys. They'd been drinking already, and ready to party. And right away Zach moved onto Marianne Mulvaney, staring at her, in that way she'd noticed him (impossible not to notice *him*) staring at her, unsmiling, at basketball games and pep rallies where "Button" Mulvaney and her sister cheerleaders performed. And shortly afterward they were observed in earnest conversation in the Krausses' rear hall, then seated on the stairs that led to the second floor, Marianne in her beautiful creamy satin dress with the strawberry-colored netting seated on the third step, Zach on the second, leaning on his elbow peering up at her. As if seeing in her (her heated face that felt swollen? her small so-distinct breasts in the pleated bodice he'd accidentally brushed with his wrist, handing her a drink?) a way of salvation. Salvation!

Oh how could she confess to her mother, to any of them: such shame.

Yet she'd believed him sincere. How, otherwise?—*Sometimes I wake up in the middle of the night scared as hell, Marianne why are we here on earth if we're just gonna die?*

Urging her to drink the "orange juice cocktail" he'd made for her so delicious "screwdriver" somebody called it she'd never tasted anything quite like it, better than champagne, sweeter than champagne she'd had several times, far sweeter than any of Dad's and Mom's beers she'd sipped out of curiosity, and her throat was parched from the hours of dancing, she was so dizzy so happy! (But wait: was this at Bobbi Krauss's or was it possibly at Glen Paxton's—had they gotten to Glen Paxton's, at all? She would not recall afterward.) Austin Weidman was whining he had to leave by 12:30 A.M. to take Marianne to the LaPortes' so that he could get home by 1 A.M. which was his curfew (they laughed, laughed at him—a 1 A.M. curfew, for a senior boy) and kept hovering in the rec room doorway his bow tie crooked, his dirt-colored hair stringy where it had been fine and feathery at the outset of the long evening and his eyes behind thumb-smudged lenses aggrieved. Zachary said politely he'd drive Marianne to the LaPortes' where she was spending the night with Trisha (who'd already left the party) and Marianne stammered blushing not knowing what to say and there was the sick look in Austin Weidman's face as if he'd been kicked in the belly as it began to sink in at last how he wasn't wanted. Chewed-looking lips, black plastic glasses like his father's. If you looked at him head-on you saw he was a nice-looking boy but who wished to look at Austin Weidman head-on? He had dabbed a sort of flesh-colored ointment over a pimple on his chin, and sweating had made it run. His breath too had a medicinal odor, like tooth fillings. He believed himself in love with Marianne Mulvaney, though he hadn't dared tell her, or anyone. Hoping instead to impress her, bragging, as an adult man might brag, about "future plans": he intended to be a dentist like his father, here in Mt. Ephraim; their sign would say T. WEIDMAN, D.D.S. & A. WEIDMAN, D.D.S., FAMILY DENTISTRY. At the prom Austin had danced awkwardly with Marianne, perspiring, staring at her in wonderment and holding her loosely, as if he feared stepping on her delicate size-six satin pumps with his size-twelve black leather dress Florsheims—but he'd stepped on them anyway. Marianne had spent much of the time talking and laughing with her own circle of friends, as Austin looked on smiling, like an elder brother. And of course she'd danced with other boys all evening. Lots of other boys.

Marianne! I need your help, you're the only person who can help me.

Touching her knee, his warm fingers on the smooth satin skirt, lightly, as if merely in emphasis as he spoke, spoke with such urgency, and a sudden sensation swelled like a balloon between her legs. *Will he kiss me? Is that what will happen next?* But he did not kiss her. Perhaps seeing something in her face, her startled eyes, that dis-

suaded him. He leaned close to her, his elbow now on the step beside her, looking up at her speaking quietly, earnestly and she'd sat
transfixed staring at him not daring to speak nor even to breathe.

The only person, the only person who can help me.

Immediately afterward, or was it much later?—Marianne was
laughing so hard, tears leaked unbecomingly from her eyes. Rock
music—Mick Jagger's brawling voice—was deafening, so loud you
couldn't hear it. *Beat beat beat* burrowing into the heart like heart-
worm. They were in the Krausses' rec room where in summer glass
doors slid open onto a flagstone terrace and a pool overlooking the
Country Club golf course—Marianne had come swimming here a
few times, though she wasn't a close friend of Bobbi Krauss, one of
the glamorous senior cheerleaders. It was time to leave, time for the
next party—where? Zach's friends who were all seniors Marianne
didn't know were laughing saying piss-pot Weidman had gone home
in his old man's piss-pot Dodge which was a car that for some reason
elicited derision. Marianne's friends were gone. Zach was red-faced
losing his poise muttering in an undertone *Fuck off, assholes!* when his
drunken buddies tried to detain him and Marianne at the door, tugging at Marianne's arm, even her hair, and at Zach who shoved them
away laughing and angry. *Hey can we come along? Hey Zach: ain't gonna
forget your buddies are you?*—bawling like hyenas.

The first stab of nausea hit her, *Oh! oh God!* as Zach, cursing under
his breath, carried Marianne's coat, helped her walk to his car, her
knees weakened suddenly so he had practically to support her. Helped
her climb into the freezing car not seeing or not caring how her skirt
was caught in the door when he slammed it shut. Marianne swallowed
down bile, gagged, choked. Where was her little beaded purse, with
tissue in it? Something hot and stinging spilled from the corner of her
mouth as Zach gunned the Corvette motor, jerked away sliding from
the curb. Marianne's head rolled on her shoulders like crockery.

After that, Marianne didn't remember.

You Mulvaneys think you're hot shit don't you.
No. She didn't remember.

Always, you maintain your dignity.
Monday she'd be returning to school, she was determined.

It was still February, that morning, barefoot, in her flannel nightgown, Marianne descended the stairs quietly, making her way through the slumbering house drawn by the bitter cold, thin whistling wind. All night dreams had cascaded at her like snow avalanches in the mountains. She wasn't taking the chunky beige pills Dr. Oakley had prescribed to *aid sleep* nor was she taking the sleek green-and-black capsules Dr. Oakley had prescribed to *help restore appetite* (like Mom "restoring" one of her "antiques"?) but that was Marianne's secret, one of her secrets.

At the rear of the house, she looked out to see—yes, the space where Dad's pickup was usually parked, in front of the garage, was empty. A light burned there, Mom had left on all night. He hadn't come home.

(Of course, there were reasons why Michael Mulvaney Sr. sometimes stayed overnight in Mt. Ephraim, usually at the Odd Fellows Lodge where there were two or three rooms available for members. Treacherous driving conditions—hadn't it been snowing hard the night before?—it was snowing now, in snaky coils and tatters blown against the windows, drifting up against the back porch where, only yesterday, Patrick and Judd had shoveled.)

"Dad, I'm sorry"—her lips moved, she wasn't sure if she'd spoken aloud.

She had opened her heart to Jesus, and He had consoled her. Yes it was Marianne Mulvaney's fault that *it had happened*. But it was not her fault that she could not *give testimony, bear witness* against the boy who was her assailant.

Strange to be awake at this hour, and downstairs, alone. The big old farmhouse creaking in the wind. How many people had lived here, died here. Since 1849. You thought such thoughts in solitude, before dawn. Before the life of the household began. Now there was only the wind, and the *tick-tick-ticking* of a dozen clocks to indicate that Time is a joke, doesn't exist. Yet you need to believe.

The first time Trisha came to stay overnight at High Point Farm, when they were in fifth grade, she'd said, shivering wide-eyed *Oh! is it like this all the time, doesn't it scare you, Marianne?* as if the wind in the chimney were a ghost, hoo-hoo-hooing through the night. Marianne had laughed, feeling flattered, superior. Everything at High Point Farm was special, even a ten-year-old knew that.

It was true she'd be returning to school. Next week. That was arranged. First, she would have to meet with Mr. Hendrie the principal of Mt. Ephraim High and Mrs. Langley the guidance counsellor. Marianne and her parents, that is. At least Mom, if Dad refused to come. There were so many rumors circulating, Mr. Hendrie had told Mom, so many unverified, disturbing things being said. About Marianne, and Zachary Lundt. And a group of seniors involved in drinking, late-night partying . . . sexual misconduct. Mr. Hendrie and Mrs. Langley hoped to discuss these matters before Marianne resumed classes and Mom would be involved, of course. Marianne had the idea that her mother had already spoken with Mr. Hendrie and Mrs. Langley on the phone at length, possibly she'd even gone to see them. Marianne didn't ask, and didn't know.

There was also the therapist "Jill James" recommended by the minister of the little country church in South Lebanon. "Jill James"—she insisted you call her that, no formalities—was a Christian therapist, a rarity in our secular times, with a master's degree in adolescent and family counselling from the State University at Port Oriskany. She was Mom's age, maybe older, stout and big-boned with a broad, shiny face colored like Crayola and a handshake brisk and hearty as Dad's. Her office at the Eastgate Shopping Center was bright cheery colors, too, hanging ferns and macramé on the walls and piped-in soothing music. Marianne had seen "Jill James" just once, and was scheduled to see her again, this very day. She'd prepared certain words she must say, repeat, offered like small semiprecious gems, all she had to offer. *I don't remember. I'm as much to blame as. I was drinking, I'm so ashamed. My pride and vanity. Can't bear false witness.* "Jill James" had her own words to offer, of course. For that was what they did, adults: uttered their words prepared beforehand, as you uttered yours.

If she walked barefoot in the snow, it might be a test. In her numbed, exalted state she'd become invulnerable!

She was standing at the window, looking out. It was still snowing, but more thinly. The wind had lessened. Beyond the barns, the eastern sky was lightening in that cracked, cobwebby way of winter mornings. A dull sun barely penetrating cloud. Marianne could not see Mt. Cataract from here, but she knew its location, its promise. *A hand! A hand raised in greeting!* If she set out for Mt. Cataract, thirty miles away, how far would she get?

You Mulvaneys. Hot shit. The bunch of you.

She would have to move swiftly, before Mom woke. Before

Patrick, Judd, Mike woke. Before the day began, the clamor and commotion of early morning at High Point Farm.

There was Troy, the border collie, handsome dog, stretched out asleep on the dog-haired carpet along the interior wall, near the heating duct, of the living room; wheezing faintly, utterly content. He hadn't noticed Marianne at all: what a watchdog. And in a sag-bottomed easy chair, gazing at Marianne with unperturbed slate-blue eyes, was beautiful Snowball, purely white, with her Persian-pug nose and thick, fur-tufted paws. Snowball had been watching Marianne all along as if it weren't out of the ordinary, Marianne in her nightgown, barefoot, prowling the shadowy house.

Can't. Can't bear false witness. Don't you understand!

She would have said, yes of course she'd be returning to school on Monday, even as she made her way through the dining room, through the kitchen (there was Feathers on his perch, puffed out to a filmy yellow ball twice his size, tiny head tucked beneath tiny wing), into the back hall strewn with boots, curry combs, stacks of newspapers, items in transition from useful to trash, to the back door. She would open it quietly, she would step outside. *Jesus! Jesus!* He was beckoning to her, He would guide her. He had been guiding her all along.

But: she'd stepped on something, something grisly, a small rubbery thing, about the size of a grape. Stepped on it with her bare right foot and recoiled, in disgust.

She knew what it was, before switching on the light. Ugh! Un-unmistakably, a rodent's heart.

One of the cats had left it there on the carpet. He, or she, had caught and devoured a mouse, all but the inner organs, left scattered about the house like morbidly prankish offerings. Marianne felt a stab of nausea even as she thought calmly *It's what cats do: their nature*.

Hadn't Mom explained to Marianne when she'd been a little, little girl. Cats aren't cruel deliberately, they're carnivores, hunters, it's their nature to catch mice, rats, even rabbits (especially, at High Point Farm, baby rabbits), and birds. If you loved a cat you would have to look the other way, accept his nature and forgive him. Like the dogs, capable of such cruelty sometimes. Even Troy, even Silky. Hunting winter-weakened deer in the woods, circling a stricken pregnant doe tearing at her belly with their teeth to bring her down. Yelping, yipping. A frenzy of bloodlust in the snow. Muzzles wet with blood. Marianne had never witnessed such a horror, but she'd seen part-devoured deer carcasses, she knew. Dogs you love, who love you, with their savage need nonetheless to dig at, gnaw at, even roll luxuriantly in the carcasses of once-living things.

Why? Marianne had asked.

Because, Mom had said.

Yes but why? Marianne asked.

Because it's nature, honey, Mom said. *And nature isn't evil.*

Snowball, fluffy-white, elegant, with her disdainful pug face and fastidious ways, had followed after Marianne and was twining herself around Marianne's leg, hoping to be petted. Marianne whispered, "Snowball, did you do this? Aren't you ashamed!" The white cat sniffed at the rubbery-red thing on the carpet with a show of slightly repelled innocence.

Another of the cats, lean rangy bony-headed E.T., leapt from his perch on top of the refrigerator, to hurry and join them. E.T. was a neutered tom with a crackling, inquisitive purr. "E.T., did *you* do this?" E.T. too sniffed at the rodent remains as if he'd never seen anything quite like it before, but was not actively interested. As Corinne, the mother of the household, the keeper of the family, would have sighed in these circumstances, Marianne sighed. There was relief in her annoyance, as if she'd awakened from a disagreeable trance. She had a chore to be done, however distasteful. All thought of leaving the warm house, drifting off in subzero winds into the woods beyond the back pasture, had vanished.

With some tissue, she lifted the tiny heart from the stained carpet, and located other part-devoured innards amid the clutter in the hall, part of a sinewy little tail, and carried them at arm's length into the bathroom. Did not look at what she held but dropped it into the toilet, and flushed. A stab of nausea returned, like a fist rising from her bowels, and she saw again the shadowy backseat of the Corvette, a boy's thin-cheeked, contorted face and angry eyes. But she did not weaken. She did not gag, begin to vomit. She was all right.

Not all the rodent remains had been flushed away so she tried again, wincing at the noisy plumbing, the groaning pipes so like merriment, derision. This time, thank God, everything disappeared forever in a splashing swirl of bluish-tinged water.

Blessed be they that mourn: for they shall be comforted.

ASK DAD

No one would be able to name what had happened, or would wish to name it: *rape* was a word that came not to be spoken at High Point Farm.

What were the words that were spoken? I remember *abuse—assault—taking advantage of—hurt.* Those were words I heard, or overheard, though these too were not uttered openly (that is, in the presence of Patrick or me) as one might not speak openly of cancer, of death.

The perpetrator, who was Zachary Lundt the son of Morton and Cynthia Lundt, was always referred to as *he, him.* Unless Dad was speaking, raging. *The bastard. The son of a bitch. The fucker.* (When Dad had been drinking, I mean. Other times, he wouldn't be talking much at all.)

Eventually, of course, I would come to know what had happened to Marianne, or at least a certain sequence of "facts." At the time, however, as the last-born of the Mulvaney children, I was the last to know anything. And even then, such was our family speech code, I didn't exactly *know.* One morning, in the stable, I asked Patrick what was going on and Patrick squinted at me through his round wire-rimmed glasses, not missing a beat as he combed Prince, and murmured, "Who wants to know?" (This was a Mulvaney euphemism for "Mind your own business.") I said, "*I* want to know, for God's sake: what's going on, why's everybody tiptoeing around, what's wrong with Marianne?" Patrick moved to Prince's other side as the deep-chested mahogany-brown gelding shook his mane, shook and lifted his tail and released a torrent of steaming-hot piss. "I'm one of you," I said, hurt, "—why can't I *know*?"

Patrick peered at me over Prince's sleek ripply back. He was wearing a green wool cap yanked down over his ears that gave him a squeezed furious look and his cheeks were flushed with cold. He mumbled sullenly, "Marianne's had some trouble I guess but she's O.K. now."

"Some trouble? *Marianne?*"

This was just so surprising to me, I didn't know how to react.

Patrick shrugged. His face closed like a fist, that was the most I'd get from *him*.

I knew: Marianne hadn't gone to school lately and, at least when I was home, she seemed to be hidden away in her room, with the door closed. I thought she must be sick, but Mom assured me, with a bright quick smile, "Oh, no! Button's had flu but she's just about recovered. You know this family—" Mom's fingers were fluttering the air like deranged butterflies, "—we get sick fast, and we get well fast. She'll be returning to school—oh, tomorrow. Or the day after."

Mom was backing away, I tried to detain her. "Mom? How come Dad's acting so strange, too?"

But Mom was in motion. I'd caught up with her in the back hall as she was zipping up her parka, stamping her feet into whichever pair of boots happened to be handy. Grabbed her car keys, she was late for—whatever. Called over her shoulder at me, with a worried smile, "Dad's had the flu, too. 'Cap'n Mulvaney'—he'll be himself again *soon*!"

Finally I cornered Mike. After supper one night when it was just Mom, Mike, P.J. and me at the table. Marianne upstairs and Dad away "on business" as Mom explained vaguely. We'd had a strained meal, poor Mom jumping up to answer the phone twice—three times—but it was never the call she expected, if in fact she expected any call. P.J. was brooding over something, staring into his plate as if into one of his fancy concepts—"infinity." Mike shoveled in his food with an angry appetite it seemed. He had a date that night with one of his girlfriends and near the end of the meal he was moving his shoulders twitchy and impatient as if he'd been sitting on the bench waiting to be called into the game and the waiting had gone on too long. As soon as he finished eating he was on his feet mumbling

"Excuse me, Mom! Thanks!"—and Mom looked after him hurt, like she was always looking hurt these days. Mike shaved for the second time that day; then in his room he was banging around looking for something, yanked off one shirt and put on another, combed his oiled hair compulsively staring at himself in his bureau mirror and liking what he saw, but just barely. Silky nudged against Mike's legs gazing up at him with lovelorn doggy-brown eyes, but he ignored him; I wandered into Mike's room uninvited, lounged on the bed and petted Silky, a kid brother hanging out in his big brother's room. I was too shy to ask any question of Mike that might violate the code. For instance, the kid brother is risking something just initiating a conversation with a big brother who clearly has other more significant things on his mind.

"Shit." Mike spoke softly, but angrily. Yanking off the shirt he'd just put on, pawing through his closet for something else. He'd shaved so roughly there were pinpricks of blood on his jaws. His eyes had a yellowish cast. How long he'd ignore me, I had to wonder. It was almost fascinating, like one of P.J.'s weird experiments with pond algae.

On the walls of Mike's room and on his bureau and windowsills were photographs, clippings, plaques, all sorts of memorabilia of his four years as a star high school athlete. (The big brassy shiny trophies were out in the living room, of course. On permanent display. "MULE" MULVANEY MOST IMPROVED ATHLETE 1971, MT. EPHRAIM CHAMBER OF COMMERCE SPORTS NIGHT. MULE MULVANEY OUTSTANDING SENIOR ATHLETE MT. EPHRAIM HIGH 1972. And more.) As a small kid I'd been in awe of my big brother Mule in his football gear, snug-fitting pants, maroon number four jersey bulked up with padded shoulders. That shiny helmet that makes players look like astronauts. We younger kids knew the players didn't have those bodies really, so padded-up, yet we reacted as if they did—so strong-looking, so *confident*. That was why seeing one of the players suddenly fallen and writhing with pain on the football field, like the time Mike was struck down with a broken ankle, was such a sobering sight, a terrifying sight I'd remember vividly all my life. There were cries, screams. The referee's frantic whistle. Dad already pushing his way through the crowd, descending the bleachers, and Mom on her feet crying, "Oh Mikey! Oh no!"

Mike Mulvaney was ranked one of the two or three best football players who'd ever graduated from Mt. Ephraim High, but it was generally acknowledged that his playing was erratic, reckless. He'd suddenly lose control and judgment and that's when he would get hurt. Luckily his injuries were mostly minor. What was said about him, in print and word-of-mouth, was what a "great sport" he was. Never played dirty like some of the others, never complained bitterly after a losing game. In interviews, Mike graciously attributed his sportsmanship to "ideals fostered by my dad and mom." He gave credit to Coach Hansen. He gave credit to his teachers, his minister. You'd have thought he was one of the "good, Christian" boys but the real Mike was rowdy and irreverent. When the Mt. Ephraim Rams lost a game, which was rare, it was Mike who cheered the other guys up, and Mike who dared tease Coach himself, a bull-like local character with a notable tendency to turn sullen and morose if things didn't go quite as he wished. "Hey, Coach: lighten it!" Mike once yelled, in my hearing, "—here today gone tomorrow, what the hell?" As if this were a happy insight. And Coach and others standing around looked at Mike and laughed.

His senior year of high school Mike had offers of football scholarships from Michigan, Minnesota, Notre Dame, Colgate as well as each of the New York State universities, couldn't make up his mind for weeks then settled on SUNY Buffalo but didn't return after the first semester claiming college wasn't for him, and that included college football. Maybe the coach there didn't appreciate him? Maybe the university was too large? Maybe his grades, in business administration, weren't good? Whatever, Mike returned home and started work immediately at Mulvaney Roofing with Dad. Dad had wanted Mike to get a college degree but, frankly, he admitted he couldn't see how a diploma would make the slightest difference if you knew what you were doing in your trade and if you did it better than anyone else.

That was his formula for success. The formula that had worked for Michael Mulvaney Sr.

Finally Mike glanced at me, not glowering exactly but not smiling either. I took this as an invitation to speak. I said, "Is something going on with Marianne?" Mike was roughly zipping up a blue velour sweater, a gift from his girlfriend Trudi, and said, hotly, "Yes, something's wrong. Something's pretty fucking goddamned wrong." He turned back to his mirror, peering critically at himself. "Some son of a bitch hurt her, some guy at the school." This was such a surprise to me, so astonishing, I stammered, "Huh? *Who?*"

and Mike said bitterly, "Some guy. In P.J.'s class. Some cocksucker's gonna pay for it." "But—what did he do?" I asked. Mike was running his comb another time through his curly-kinky russet-brown hair; then he slipped the comb into his back jeans pocket, like a secret weapon. He said dismissively, "Ask them. They don't want *me* to talk about it. To anyone." "But who was it, Mike? What happened?"—I was excited, scared. I was old enough to know of certain ways in which a girl could be *hurt* by a guy (I knew what *rape* was, more or less) but it was difficult for me to comprehend that my sister Marianne, my sister everyone liked so much, especially guys at the high school, could have been *hurt* in such a way.

Mike left his room, went to grab a parka from a bed in the back hall. "Mike, hey—why won't anyone talk about it? Why's it such a secret?" I asked. Mike stomped his feet into leather boots, taking his car keys out of his pocket and impatient to be gone. At the door he paused, looked at me, considered how to reply, his eyes narrowed and damp like Mom's as if he, not Marianne, had been the one to be *hurt*. Whatever this obscure and mysterious *hurt* was.

He said, "Ask Dad."

BOYS WILL BE BOYS!

A morning in March, room 209 of Mt. Ephraim High: Madame Lederer's classroom. On Marianne Mulvaney's desk seat in first-year French there was drawn, in red Magic Marker, a curious tubular thing about five inches long labeled LE COCK. One tip of the thing was swollen like a balloon and annotated, in smaller letters, THIS SIDE UP.

No one knew who'd drawn LE COCK. (Of course, someone knew.) The girls were embarrassed, unsmiling; would not look toward the offensive desk, nor at certain of the boys who were exchanging glances with one another, grinning, wriggling their shoulders, embarrassed, too, but more than that, excited. *What a cruel thing to do, for God's sake. That isn't funny, you guys.* But who could erase the drawing, at such short notice? And with Madame Lederer already in the room, writing the next day's assignment on the blackboard? And who wanted to get involved, anyway? *That's disgusting. What an asshole.* But maybe she wouldn't notice. Maybe Madame Lederer wouldn't notice.

Boys will be boys!

A second after the bell, when nearly everyone was in the classroom, settling into their seats, Marianne Mulvaney entered, in the new, measured way of hers; not, as in the past, gliding into the room with friends, smiling and calling out hello, but alone, and shyly; uncertainly, like a convalescent on her feet just a little too soon, disoriented in the world of the healthy and trying not to show it.

The girl was Marianne Mulvaney of course, and yet—*was* she?

Except for Madame Lederer at the blackboard, back turned to the classroom, everyone was watching covertly, avidly. *Poor Marianne! So sad. How can you guys be so nasty.* It was noted that Marianne's face was oddly triangular, sallow-skinned and witchy; her downcast eyes were overlarge in their sockets; her directionless smile was strained, lips pulled tight across her teeth. *Look: she asked for it. Come on!* Making her way to her desk in the third row, almost dead center of the room, Marianne stumbled over Ike Rodman's size-thirteen sneakered feet in the aisle, murmured what sounded like "Excuse me," and Ike said quickly, his face reddening, "Yeah, sure." Everyone watched as Marianne approached her desk, and lowered her bookbag to the top; slipped into the seat without seeing LE COCK, in that way of hers she'd had since returning to school a few days before, vague-eyed, almost in slow motion, but always with that smile *that pathetic smile!* like a permanent grimace.

Sighs of general relief, a few scattered titters. Madame Lederer, a chesty, overdressed woman in her late thirties who imagined herself chic, turned to welcome her first-year class with her customary grandiloquent gestures and sweetly-glamorous big smile. *"Bonjour, mademoiselles et monsieurs!"*

Almost too loudly, with mock eagerness, came the response: *"Bon-jour, Madame Lederer!"*

At her desk in the third row, center of the room, Marianne Mulvaney fumbled to open her French text, opened a spiral notebook, took out her pen and squinted at the smiling, gesticulating woman at the front of the room. There was nothing more to look at, no more interest in Marianne, the morning's meager drama had fizzled out.

PHASE

How apprehensive she'd grown of the telephone ringing. Especially at night if Michael Sr. wasn't home.

As so often, since February, unaccountably he was *not* home.

So often, these weeks. As winter yielded by slow, resistant degrees to spring. The harsh windy snow-pelleted spring of upstate New York, daffodils' bright-yellow shocked faces coated in ice, their stems broken, fallen. So Corinne thought: Nothing progresses in a straight line, it's more—well, *imbricated*. The way a roofer lays tiles, shingles, overlapping one another, for strength.

Where did he go, under the spell of his obsession?—Corinne could ask, of course, and he'd answer. Always, there was a ready answer. *Dropping by some old friends. Just driving around, clearing my head.* With a hint of his old bad-boy jocularity, *Hey, who wants to know?* Or, winking, *Come with me, sweetheart, and you wouldn't have to ask.* (As if he'd want her with him! As if Corinne his wife, his children and High Point Farm, weren't part of what he needed to escape *from*.) But the ready answers were never the right answer, where their eyes might lock, Corinne's and Michael's, and she'd know he was speaking the truth.

Welcoming her into his heart.

Even the pain, the hurt, the rage of his heart—why couldn't he let her in any longer?

She wanted to cry to him: *I'm her mother! I've been violated, too.*

★ ★ ★

He was letting Mulvaney Roofing slide, that much Corinne knew.

What Michael Mulvaney had so tirelessly, so single-mindedly and with such hope built up for the past twenty years, what, apart from his family, he'd lived for ("To be respected as the best god-damned roofer in the Chautauqua Valley") he was letting slip like sand between his fingers.

Worried calls from his foreman Alex Flood—8 A.M. and a crew was at the work site and where was Mr. Mulvaney; worried calls from his secretary Leah, midmorning and supplies were being deliv-ered, important calls coming in—where was Mr. Mulvaney?

Bright as a blue jay Corinne heard herself quip (even as her fists were clenched so tightly, her nails dug deep into her palms), "Why ask *me*?—I've only known the guy twenty-three years."

Laughing her breathless neighing laugh, in the face of startled silence.

During one of these unsettling calls (in fact, at 4:40 P.M. and the call was from a customer with a complaint), Patrick entered the kitchen, and overheard Corinne on the phone. When she hung up, he touched her arm gently. "Hey, Mom. Hey."

Was she crying? She hadn't even noticed!

No embarrassment so keen, so cringing-painful, as that endured by an adolescent in the presence of his parents. Especially a nerved-up self-conscious high-I.Q. eighteen-year-old boy in the presence of his thoroughly rattled forty-five-year-old mom.

Patrick was saying in a bright buoyant strained way that re-minded Corinne of herself, "He'll be O.K. You know Dad."

"Oh, that's right. I know that," Corinne said quickly.

"He's just going through a—" Patrick grinned, shoving his glasses against the bridge of his nose, "—a phase."

They laughed together. Just a little too loudly. The joke being that the Mulvaney parents were forever saying of the Mulvaney children that one or another, or all of them collectively, were *going through a phase*.

"Well. That's right," Corinne said, wiping at her overheated face, "—that's true for all of us! Amen."

With the yearning eye of, almost, a bereft lover, Corinne gazed af-ter her tall fair son, her mysterious second-born. In his soiled sheepskin jacket, headed quickly outside to his barn chores. *Wants to get away from me: can't blame him*. Patrick was dutiful about his chores, uncomplain-ing as Marianne; far more reliable and efficient than Mikey-Junior had been at that age. Corinne's heart swelled with love of Patrick—love, and a sense of loss so poignant it left her weak. Was it sinful, God, to feel such emotion for your own child? Seeing how tall and lanky Patrick had grown, inches taller than she, taller even than his father. Patrick was a beautiful boy, no matter that chronically crinkled brow, that habit of squinting, staring, pursing and sucking his lips. But she dared not touch him, of course. It was one of the astonishing discoveries of Corinne's middle years as a mother to learn that, inside her own family, she could pine for the attention of a boy who was her own son!

Almost the way, as a lonely, homely-gawky high school girl, a farmer's daughter, she'd pined for the attention of just such boys— tall, fair, aloofly handsome. Their eyes boring through her with no recognition.

As for Mikey-Junior, her firstborn—she'd had to give him up, in the emotional, intimate sense, years ago. He even winced now if she called him "Mikey-Junior" and not "Mike." Not just that he'd begun to shrug away embarrassed at his mother's touch but—clearly— he'd begun what Corinne understood was a secret sexual life, a sexually intense life, with how many girls Corinne would have grown sick and silly by this time trying to count.

Not that Corinne was a jealous mother. Not in *that way*. Like certain of her women friends, confessing how obsessed they were with their son's probable secret lives.

Patrick, though. Patrick hadn't discovered sex, yet. Corinne wondered if he was attracted to girls, dreamt of girls, at all. Thank God she could trust *him*.

But: she'd have liked a little more courage! To sit down with Patrick, just the two of them. And speak, for once, frankly. *How are you taking this terrible episode in our life? Has your sister confided in you? What do you know, from other sources, of what happened? What are people saying of us?* (But did she really want to know? Her heart beat rapidly at the thought, as if she were in the presence of danger.) Yet she knew it wasn't possible. No longer. Patrick was eighteen, and soon to leave home. She saw sometimes in the very lenses of his glasses distant landscapes. Rarely now did he, or the others, linger downstairs in the kitchen with Mom as they used to. That was all gone, suddenly.

It *was* all gone, wasn't it? Corinne hadn't quite realized. The boisterous half hour or so when all the children, home from school, crowded into the kitchen breathless and excited exchanging the day's news, teasing, joking, laughing, headed for the refrigerator—the dogs barking ecstatically, for it was the high point of their day, too. (Habit-ually, the dogs waited for the school buses at the foot of the drive. On afternoons when Mikey-Junior had team practice, poor Silky would continue his vigil, alone, as the other dogs trotted with the children up to the house.) Those wonderful years when Mikey was still in high school, and Judd still in elementary school. Mikey-Junior, P.J., But-ton, Ranger. And good old Mom glowing with pleasure even as, mom-style, she scolded: "Hey! You scavengers! Don't you dare ruin your appetites for supper!" As if growing boys could ruin their ap-petites. These boys ravenous with hunger, devouring peanut butter sandwiches, chocolate chip cookies, slices of American cheese, stale buttermilk biscuits smeared with jam. Mikey who was "Mule" and "Number Four" had the appetite of a young steer, swallowing down a full quart of milk in a half dozen gulps. Marianne who was forever "watching her weight" joined them drinking diet soda, nibbling dain-tily at carrot sticks, celery. All of them flirting with Mom. Vying for Mom's attention, bragging to Mom. Like the dogs eagerly wagging their tails, like the cats hoisting their tails erect kitten-style. *Hey Mom look at me! at me, at me!*

Now, all was changed. Irrevocably?

Of course, Corinne acknowledged that the older boys had long ago begun to resist her hugs, kisses, crooning baby talk. Brushing hair out of their eyes, dabbing spots of dirt from their faces. A boy's resistance to his mom seemed to start at about the age of five—so young! By nine, by eleven, you had to be careful, really careful how you approached him. (The shrewd thing was to wait for a boy to come to you, which, when circumstances were just right, he would. Grounded by a football injury, right ankle in a cast for weeks, aged sixteen, Mikey had reverted almost to babyhood, at such times when only his Mom was around to tend to him. She'd loved every moment!) By thirteen and beyond, though, they weren't children any longer. Nor even boys, exactly—their voices changing, tiny prickles of beard beginning to push through. Michael Sr. joked he could smell Michael Jr.'s hormones all over the house, mixed with the rich, ripe smell of sweat socks and sneakers.

Going through a phase.

Aren't we all? Amen!

Corinne thought, inspired: Maybe that was it? They *were* all go-ing through a phase, the entire Mulvaney family, and they'd come out of it, soon? *Just a phase*—the very words made everything suddenly hopeful again.

Not long ago Michael Sr. had been capable of sleeping through gale-force winds; now he slept fitfully, only a few hours at a time. He'd become so addicted to his damned cigarettes, he'd wake every three or four hours to go downstairs to smoke. (Pretending he was only going to use the bathroom. As if Corinne, sharing the same bed with the man, didn't know.) Sometimes, at dawn, Corinne would seek Michael out downstairs, wanting to locate him before the children woke. His snoring—raspy, wet, arrhythmic—would lead her to him, in the family room, or the kitchen, or the minimally furnished, badly cluttered room that was his at-home office. There, Michael Mulvaney Sr. slumped on a sofa or in a chair, occasionally even on the floor, head fallen so sharply to one side it looked as if his neck might be broken. A sag-eyed ashen-faced man sprouting gunmetal-gray whiskers, his muscular shoulders, arms, midriff going to fat. There would be a scattering of beer bottles at his feet, possibly a depleted bottle of whiskey—Early Times, his favorite. An ashtray heaped with ashes and butts. What a smell! Corinne would stomp to a window to shove it open, the colder the air, the better. How hurt she felt, and how vindictive!

One of the dogs, usually Troy, who slept in this part of the house, would be close by, having stationed himself near his master through the night. Angular collie-face, moist eyes you wanted to believe intelligent, consoling. *Don't worry, it's only a phase!*

∽

This, Corinne knew: one of the places Michael was slipping off to in secret (yes, she'd discovered a matchbook in his pants pocket—she'd gotten that desperate) was the Wolf's Head Inn at Wolf's Head Lake twelve miles away.

Dear God, no. Not again.

Michael's old friend "Haw" Hawley owned the place, or owned a mortgage on it. The Wolf's Head crowd, Michael's oldest friends in the Chautauqua Valley, predating by years his Mt. Ephraim connections. Some of the men also belonged to the Chautauqua Sportsmen's Club—Wally Parks, Rick Shires, Cobb Connor. Getting Michael Mulvaney to go on their notorious hunting weekends with them, deer-hunting season in November–December. Not just the shotguns terrified Corinne who hated hunting in any case, but the long nights of drinking, poker-playing, carousing. When Michael returned from one of these expeditions to the foothills beyond Wolf's Head Lake he'd be hungover, a guilty glaze to his eyes. Corinne doubted he'd ever shot any deer, but the men concocted tales to protect and enhance one another in the eyes of the women back home. (In Michael's office at Mulvaney Roofing, there were photographs of Michael and his hunting buddies standing before the strung-up carcasses of deer, shotguns proudly erect. Corinne wouldn't allow any of these in the house though she did, being practical-minded, agree to prepare venison steaks and stews.)

Eventually, after a few years, Michael had sickened of the hunting expeditions. He'd never come out and admitted to Corinne that she was right, morally or otherwise, but Corinne guessed he'd become revulsed by the idiotic bloodshed and his friends' behavior.

"Haw" Hawley! Corinne's feelings about him, and his wife Leonie, were complicated. She granted they were *fun*—rowdy, vulgar, slapdash, lively. Never a dull moment at the Wolf's Head Inn, those long summer twilights and nights. Corinne knew how Michael enjoyed that hard-drinking crowd, but she hadn't been able to like them, much. Hadn't ever felt comfortable. Though, as a young wife eager to please her husband, she'd surely tried. Both Haw and Wally Parks had flirted with Corinne when Michael wasn't present, and she'd never known if they were serious or just kidding around. (Or both.) Corinne had chosen to interpret the flirting as *kidding around*, though she'd never told Michael about it.

Haw was a big-bellied wild-bearded alcoholic who drank along with his customers, Wally was a rail-thin blond-Presley type who managed the Marsena Airport and had cooked up for himself a local reputation for having been a World War II bomber pilot in Japan, an alcoholic, too—oh, why mince words, *they were all alcoholics* and Michael Mulvaney had been well on his way to alcoholism, the years he'd seen that gang regularly. As a young wife, with young children, Corinne had a recurring nightmare vision of the husband she adored, the father of her children, sunk to his armpits in the black sludgy-muck of Wolf's Head Lake's northern shore, slowly sinking from view.

Dear God, please no.
I'm not young enough, or strong enough, this time.

It was Corinne's belief, never shared with anyone, that she'd had to struggle for her husband's very soul, those years. A shudder ran through her—how close she'd come to losing Michael to that filthy black muck.

Yet, she had to admit, there'd been a certain shabby glamor about Wolf's Head Lake, and the Inn, in the days they'd all been young, and good-looking. An erotic undercurrent to virtually every exchange between a man and a woman not married to each other. The sexy *beat! beat! beat!* of the jukebox in the barroom. The Wolf's Head Inn was a country tavern built on a promontory above the lake, a boat-rental concession operating out of its ground floor. (How the Mulvaney children loved those leaky, cumbersome rowboats, clamoring to be taken out Sunday after Sunday! The memory made the corners of Corinne's eyes crinkle—that blinding glare on the lake at sunset. A ghost-pain darted between her shoulder blades. Until Mikey-Junior was old enough to be trusted with a rowboat and the younger children, it fell to Mom to take the crew out, while Dad drank beer and played cards with his friends on the Inn veranda. You could hear them laughing and hooting like hyenas a hundred yards out on the lake.)

Inside, the Inn was dim-lit on even the sunniest days. There was a long battered bar that put Corinne in mind, fancifully, of a locomotive. There were flyspecked screened windows overlooking the lake, there were unfinished floorboards littered with cigarette butts and package wrappers by the end of the night. And the smell!—her nostrils pinched at the memory. Sharp, distinctive, unmistakable: beer, tobacco smoke, disinfectant-and-stale-urine at the rear, where His and Hers rest rooms opened off a dank alcove. Yet the Inn had a seedy glamor, your heart quickened when you stepped inside. There was a small dance floor, there was an ever-glowing jukebox. How many nickels Corinne had dropped into it, herself! Every other song you heard was Elvis Presley. Playful-rowdy Elvis ("Hound Dog"), dreamy-maudlin Elvis ("Heartbreak Hotel"), sexy-seductive Elvis ("Love Me Tender"). Corinne had been a dreamy young wife in her twenties, she'd drunk beer, too, till her head swirled and she laughed at the slightest provocation. A quick squeeze of Michael's fingers on her wrist could send a tinge like electricity to her groin—oh, yes!

Wolf's Head Inn, Wolf's Head Lake, NY—discovering the matchbook in Michael's trouser pocket, the crude logo of a wolf's head in silhouette, brought this back to Corinne, with a shiver.

Of course, the lake *was* beautiful. All of the rural Chautauqua Valley was beautiful. Back in the Fifties there had been relatively few cabins, cottages, cheap motels at the lake (development was to come, with a vengeance, in the Seventies) and you could walk without distraction along the shore, through the pine woods, gazing across the placid surface of the lake to the dense woodland on the opposite shore a mile away, lifting into the fir-covered Chautauqua foothills and the slate-blue hazy mountains beyond. Of course, the children loved it. Of course, it was their favorite, favorite place. And Michael's.

Yet Wolf's Head Lake had seemed to Corinne a place of surprises and danger. She was a young mother, she exaggerated—maybe. Much of its shore was rocky and unsuited for swimming; even at the periphery of the main beach, where a lifeguard was on duty, you sometimes stepped into repulsive soft muck like quicksand. A quick storm could blow up, turning the water into harsh choppy waves; if you were in a rowboat halfway across the lake, and if the wind was coming at you, the return could be desperate, and exhausting. Or, on hot, muggy days, the lake glittered sickly-slick, like molten plastic. There were ugly stinging flies, clouds of droning gnats and mosquitoes. Even (thank God, Corinne had never actually seen one!—she'd never have stepped into the lake again) water snakes, in the wilder inlets. And wasn't the sunshine harsher at Wolf's Head Lake than at home? All the Mulvaneys had suffered sunburn at one time or another, even Michael Sr. who tanned darkly. Once, Button was five or six, playing on the beach and wading in shallow water one afternoon for hours, and the sky had been pebbled with cloud and yet, by the end of the day, she was whimpering in pain—her slender shoulders and back flaring lobster-pink, burning to the touch. And there were so many loud, rough, combative children at the beach, running and splashing in the water, tossing sand, mouthy boys whose every third word was a profanity. And the girls!—young teenagers in flimsy bathing suits flaunting their remarkable little bodies, plastic sunglasses and bright makeup worn even in the water, precocious hussies eyeing Corinne's own Mikey-Junior when he'd been no more than twelve! Just as their mothers and older sisters frankly eyed Michael Sr. who was so good-looking.

That way, infuriating to Corinne, signaling *Hey: look at me, here I am!*

At Wolf's Head Lake, Corinne had been made to realize a truth that seemed to have eluded her until then—it's one thing to marry a man, and another thing to keep him.

That time, late one Sunday evening, the children ready to go home for hours, even Mikey-Junior drowsy, falling asleep in the back of the station wagon, and Corinne, exasperated, went back into the Inn another time to get Michael, only to discover him with scrawny platinum-bleached-blond Leonie Hawley giggling like idiots on the dance floor, all but necking!—as Corinne would accuse Michael afterward. Michael and Leonie pretended absolute innocence, of course. But Corinne knew, *of course she knew*. Her husband and that flirty brazen woman, an obvious attraction between them, everyone else knew including Haw Hawley, how shameful! There was Leonie with her wide-innocent eyes, there was Michael guilty-defiant, his face darkening with blood. Driving back to High Point Farm the elder Mulvaneys had quarreled while the children slept, or pretended to sleep, in the back of the station wagon. Michael, his voice slurred with drink, became increasingly defensive, angry— "Your imagination is working overtime, sweetheart! And I don't like to be spied on." Corinne said, "Damn you, Michael Mulvaney, do you think I'm a complete fool?"—pausing to draw breath, not knowing if she was about to burst into tears, or laughter, "Or an incomplete fool?" Harsh horsey-sounding laughter erupted from her throat, but Michael, grim behind the wheel, didn't join in.

Following that, Corinne rarely went back to Wolf's Head Lake with the children. Or, if she did, it was just for the day—swimming, boating. For a while Michael went on his own, hanging out at the Inn, then gradually he stopped going, too.

These were the early years of Mulvaney Roofing's prosperity. The Mulvaneys made new friends in Mt. Ephraim, a new class of friends. Everyone liked Michael Sr., and most people came to like Corinne, once they adjusted to her quirky mannerisms, her odd admixture of shyness and brashness. Michael was one of those persons who, entering a gathering, make people smile in anticipation—like switching on a light, Corinne observed, in a dim-lit room. Men gravitated to him to pump his hand, women's fingers fluttered to their hair and their mouths shaped quick smiles. An up-and-coming Mt. Ephraim businessman who worked, sometimes, a twelve-hour day, rushed home to rapidly shower, shave, get dressed in suit, white shirt and tie, and rush out again to attend a meeting of the Mt. Ephraim Chamber of Commerce, the Mt. Ephraim United Way, or, with Corinne, the P.T.A.

A new adventure, and the Mulvaneys thrived.

So it happened, Michael saw his Wolf's Head Lake friends less and less frequently. He'd already given up hunting, though he kept his guns and his membership in the Sportsmen's Club. Where once he'd seen Haw, Wally, Rick, Cobb and the rest every week or so, now he

saw them every six weeks, every three months, every six months—
there just wasn't time. If the Mulvaneys gave a big party, their July
cookout for instance, Michael would invite the Wolf's Head Lake
crowd—maybe. (Corinne wisely didn't say a word. Her strategy was
to let Michael see how his old friends simply didn't fit in with the
new.) Once, Michael told Corinne how he'd run into Rick Shires at a
farm supply store and Rick had seemed almost shy of saying hello to
him, as if he'd feared Michael might snub him—"I felt so damned
guilty, should've suggested we go somewhere for a drink, but—"
Corinne said consolingly, "Rick must know you're busy, honey. I'm
sure he understood." Another time, only a few years ago, Corinne
hadn't relayed to Michael how she'd run into Haw at the Kmart on
Route 119, shocked to see how ravaged and gray-balding he'd become, wearing bifocals, his drinker's face a cobwebby map of broken
capillaries, yet pushy with Corinne, on the edge of nasty. Corinne
asked how was Leonie? and Haw said sarcastically why ask *him*, they'd
been divorced for five years and never saw each other. (Maybe
Corinne had heard this, she couldn't recall! So embarrassing.) After a
few awkward minutes Corinne backed off, with the vague murmur
that she'd tell Michael they met, maybe they could get together sometime that summer, and Haw virtually snorted in derision, made a gesture with his arm that was meant to indicate Mt. Ephraim and said,
"*That's* where the money comes from, eh?" Winking, and smirking,
as, wounded as if Haw had spat in her face, Corinne limped away.

Thinking in triumph, *At least I have saved him from you. From
turning into you.*

Or had she only postponed Wolf's Head Lake in their lives?—
that nightmare vision of Michael Mulvaney sinking to his armpits,
to his chin, sinking helplessly in that soft filthy black muck.

❧

How obsessed poor Michael had become, with *it*.

In the winter and spring of 1976, how heavily *it* weighed upon
all their lives.

Though with the therapist Jill James, and, to a lesser degree,
with her minister and his wife, and one or two women friends (yes,
they'd begun to drift back—hesitantly), Corinne could discuss what
had happened to Marianne, or what had probably happened, she
could not, would not, utter the word *rape*; would have denied ever

uttering it in Dr. Oakley's office. What had happened to their daughter was *assault, molestation,* occasionally *sexual assault.* To Michael, who had a difficult time speaking of the incident at all, and whose resistance to speaking of it seemed to be increasing with the passage of time, it could only be referred to as *it.*

The way, Corinne understood, you don't speak of *death* to grieving people. If you wanted to speak to them at all, you had to discover other words.

What frightened Corinne was the change in Michael. Where once he'd been completely reliable, now he was unreliable. Oh, he might be telling the truth about where he'd been, working late—then again, he might not. (It was turning Corinne into the kind of wife who checks on her husband continuously—discreet telephone calls to his office, questions innocently posed, pockets searched. How could this be happening to high-minded Corinne Mulvaney!) Michael's moody silences, his nocturnal prowling, drinking, compulsive smoking. His mysterious telephone calls. His short temper with his sons. (Never Marianne. He was stiffly smiling, cordial and distant with her.) And his new habit of secrecy, that alarmed her the most.

What was he planning?

After that terrifying night he'd rushed to the Lundts' house and was arrested, might have been charged with assault, fined or sent to prison—that episode so like a nightmare Corinne could barely force herself to recall it—she hadn't been able to shake off the conviction that something worse was to happen. She tried not to let her imagination run wild, didn't want to make herself ill with worry. (Of course, there were days when Corinne *was* ill with worry. But she meant to keep going just the same.) Yet it was impossible, in weak moments, not to envision an alternate scenario: if Eddy Harris hadn't been at the Lundts' to stop Michael in his rampage, he might have done more than only crack Zachary Lundt's ribs and bloody his face against a wall. He might have done as much to Mort Lundt, too.

My husband is not a violent man, he is not a murderer.

Dear God, You know his heart. Help us!

She'd called Eddy Harris, out of desperation that night. She lived in dread she'd have to call him, or other police officers, sometime again.

Neither in reproach nor in gratitude had Michael ever mentioned to her the fact she'd called Eddy Harris to head him off. It was as if he'd forgotten.

Had she betrayed him, in his eyes?

I only did it because I love you, she prepared to tell him. *Because we aren't that kind of people.*

Imagining his reply, *Aren't we? Who says?*

Especially disturbing, yes and infuriating, was Corinne's discovery that Michael was making secret decisions that involved them all. Decisions involving money—God knows how much! Without giving so much as a hint of his intentions, Michael met several times with a Yewville attorney named Costello, of whom Corinne had never heard. She learned of this simply by chance, overhearing a telephone conversation. When she confronted him, Michael said evasively, "Hell, Corinne, a man can always use a lawyer. These are litigious times in the U.S. of A."

Corinne said anxiously, "Michael, what are you planning? Not some sort of civil lawsuit? It would destroy Marianne—it would destroy us all—if this becomes any more public than it already is! Imagine Marianne testifying in court, having to say such awful things, then being cross-examined by some merciless, vicious lawyer! Oh, Michael, promise me, please, *no.*"

Michael shook his head vehemently, backing off from her, bent on escape. He had work to do, calls to make. He was a damned busy man. Not looking back at his distraught wife wringing her hands like any distraught wife on TV, tears streaking her face.

"Trust me!" he called back. Jamming the fedora with the jaunty little feather onto his head, rushing out. A cold April rain was being blown slantwise against the house. Michael's khaki raincoat was rumpled behind as if he'd been sleeping in it.

Then, a week or so later, Corinne learned, again by chance, that Mr. Costello, whoever he was, hadn't "worked out"—he'd been "terminated." But instead of feeling gratitude, immense relief, Corinne steeled herself to wonder, *Is he hiring another? What are his plans?*

Corinne knew: Michael was sick not just with *it,* with what had happened to Marianne, but with what he felt to be the betrayal of their Mt. Ephraim friends. He told her bitterly, one night as they lay in bed, in the dark, unable to sleep, "Between Mort Lundt and me, naturally they're choosing Lundt. Siding with him. Because the bastard's got money and connections, he's one of *them.*"

"Don't think of it that way, darling," Corinne said fumblingly,

"—think of it that, well—they just don't want to get involved. You know how people are."

"I guess I didn't, actually," Michael said. "But I'm getting to know how our friends are. Our 'friends.' " Corinne could imagine his mouth twisting in the dark. "Fucking 'friends.' "

She cringed as if he'd struck her. It was so unlike Michael Mulvaney to utter any obscenity in a woman's presence.

Michael claimed that people avoided him downtown. At the Odd Fellows', at the Sportsmen's Club, most of all at the Country Club. (Oh, but why go *there*? Corinne wanted to protest.) "Am I a leper? Am I the Walking Dead?" Michael laughed. They saw him, he said, and quickly looked away. Shaking his hand was a chore, he could see it in their eyes. He could feel it in their grip. Why, that hypocritical old fraud Ben Thorsen, who'd bellyached to Michael he couldn't pay straight-out for the roofing repairs he'd had done on his house, so Michael had agreed to monthly payments, at *no interest*—he was one of the worst. "But you never did like Ben Thorsen," Corinne objected, as if that were the point.

Mulvaney Roofing hadn't gotten the contract for the Civic Center renovations. Nor for the St. Matthew's Hospital project. Maybe he'd demand an investigation—why a certain rival roofer's bid was accepted and his rejected. Just maybe!

Suddenly, too, Ben Breuer never had time for squash with him, or a quick drink. Nor Charley MacIntyre, Jake Spohr. If he dropped in somewhere for lunch, one of the clubs, or the Blue Moon Café where everyone knew him, he'd be made to feel how unwanted, how unwelcome he was. Oh of course he'd be invited to sit down at a table—if there was room—but it was obvious that Michael Mulvaney's presence dampened the mood. Laughs subsided, there was nothing to talk about except weather, politics, sports.

What were they talking about before he'd joined them?

What did they talk about when he excused himself to use the men's room?

"People have their own lives," Corinne said gently, caressing her husband's shoulder. "They don't always—think of how others are perceiving them. You don't want to exaggerate this, Michael. You know you have a tendency to—"

Michael continued, contemptuously, as if he hadn't heard. Telling of how, that day, for the hell of it, he drove out to Spohr's Lumber to have a few words with Jake. If anybody knew about the Civic Center and St. Matthew's deals it would be Jake. Hadn't he, Michael

Mulvaney, always gotten along fine with Jake Spohr?—the two weren't close friends by a long shot, but they respected each other, had what you'd call a reciprocal relationship, throwing business each other's way, and Jake came from a background like Michael's—he'd moved to Mt. Ephraim from Buffalo, no roots in the Valley and no fancy education, just a reputation for doing good work. So Michael asked Jake point-blank what was going on behind his back?—was he being squeezed out, or what? And Jake shook his head like this was a question he couldn't comprehend, much less answer. Jake acknowledged there was probably "personal politics" behind the contracts but wasn't there always? (Spohr's Lumber had the contract for the hospital wing, but not for the Civic Center.) Michael then asked what was being said about him and his family?—*what was being said about his daughter Marianne?* "And Jake looked me straight in the eye, Corinne, and said, 'Not a thing.' And I was sweating like a winded horse, scared as hell but I had to push it asking was he sure? and there was a beat, and I could see Jake swallow, but he said, still looking me in the eye like we were brothers or something, going way, way back so for sure I could trust him, 'Sure I'm sure, Michael. I'd tell you if I knew anything.' "

Beside her in the dark Michael began suddenly to laugh—hoarse, wheezing laughter so the old wickerware bed creaked as if laughing, too. Corinne lay stricken in dismay amid such merry laughter she could not join.

Sometime after midnight, then, groggily aware of Michael easing from bed. She sighed, turned, shut her eyes tight, pretending to be asleep, yes she *was* asleep, burrowed in sleep as in salvation.

She would find him in the family room. Or the kitchen. Or his office. If she looked. She'd discover an empty Early Times bottle in the trash, beer conspicuously missing from the refrigerator. If she looked. Probably there'd be an empty glass somewhere on the floor, tipped on its side: Michael wasn't troubling to hide his tracks, much, any longer. Too angry, and since anger wears you out, too exhausted.

Her worst fear: the telephone ringing.

At 12:50 A.M., and Michael not home.

It was late April, after Easter. Corinne was in bed upstairs, propped up with pillows, too anxious to sleep; reading, or trying to read, one of

Patrick's science magazines. Though every cell and nerve ending in her brain quivered with wakefulness, she could not concentrate on a passage she'd read, reread how many times. . . . *No evidence either in the living world of today or of past geological epochs for a continuous transition of species . . . what we actually find are separate and well-distinguished species . . . intermediate stages from one species to another which should be found . . . are not met with. The worlds of organisms, living and extinct, do not represent a continuum but a discontinuum. . . . Certain conditions of stability exist not only for the individual genes but also for genomes. . . . A "species" represents a state in which a harmoniously stabilized "genetic balance" has been established, that is* . . . Thinking of Marianne who was so deeply unhappy at school. Yet never spoke of it. Poor Marianne with so few friends now, few telephone calls, and all that visiting the girls had done back and forth at one another's houses—suddenly, for Marianne, all that had ceased as if it had never been. She'd quit the cheerleading squad, rarely attended club meetings or her Christian Youth meetings. Her grades had dropped to C's but seemed to have levelled off. She was happiest at church, so far as Corinne could judge. Singing hymns in her thin, sweet soprano voice—"Rock of Ages," Corinne's favorite hymn of all time, was Marianne's, too. It was the only public place she felt comfortable: the First Church of Christ of South Lebanon was a one-room foursquare white-shingled church miles from Mt. Ephraim; the congregation was mostly country people; no one knew the Mulvaneys except as relatively new churchgoers, Corinne Mulvaney and her three children. Corinne drove to church in the mud-splattered rust-speckled Buick station wagon with the bumper sticker 4-H: HEAD HEART HANDS HEALTH and, on a rear window, a frayed decal FUTURE FARMERS OF AMERICA 1974. No one would have judged her the wife of a prosperous businessman, or, maybe, anyone's wife at all. If there was a Mr. Mulvaney, no one had ever sighted him in South Lebanon, nor would.

It was a tenet of the First Church of Christ not to judge one's brothers and sisters in Christ. *Let him that is without sin first cast a stone. John 8.*

Corinne knew she was neglecting her sons. The youngest especially—poor Judd! Babyface, Dimple—Ranger. She loved the boy but hardly dared hug him, now he was thirteen. A quiet, good-natured child, all but lost in the ferocity of Mulvaney family life; he'd stopped asking about Marianne, stopped asking about his father. *Only a phase* Corinne would tell him. *God sends us sorrow sometimes to strengthen us.*

Do I believe that? Corinne wondered.

Of course, I believe. I must.

Then there was Patrick. Haughty P.J.! The child least like either of his parents. It was a mystery to Corinne how Patrick continued to accompany her to church services at the little South Lebanon church, now he was eighteen years old, a tall, restless, skeptical-minded young man. "Monosyllables of wisdom" Patrick cruelly and wittily described their minister's sweetly simple sermons. The congregation he called "the flock"—if you know animals, you know there's nothing dumber, less attractive, than an adult sheep. As a boy he'd tried to take part in hymn singing but now he seemed merely to be mouthing the words, his mind elsewhere. He was visibly embarrassed when "witnesses for Christ" came forward; he shuffled to the communion rail with an expressionless face, like a stoical child taking his medicine. His participation in "clasping of hands in Christ" was distinctly less than enthusiastic. Yet, he continued to accompany his mother, sister and younger brother to church; it was their custom for Patrick to drive the station wagon home, so that Corinne could sit quietly beside him, fingers to her eyes, adrift, her soul almost palpably buoyed by the love of Jesus Christ she'd taken into her heart anew. Patrick was being, Corinne guessed, *a good son*. *Mom's good son*. Acquitting himself dutifully and with a measure of good humor, just possibly counting the days until he left High Point Farm for college and could leave his Christian faith behind. It worried Corinne terribly, but—well, she just knew!

What her sensitive, easily offended son was thinking about *it*, what experiences he was having at the high school in the wake of *it*, Corinne shrank from imagining. She knew what adolescent boys could be like—what cruelty, dirty-mindedness, mockery of those perceived as weaker, or as outsiders. Yes, and girls, too! The cruelty of the barnyard: how chickens peck fiercely, relentlessly at an afflicted chicken in their midst, pecking to the raw flesh, seeking blood. She supposed Patrick must suffer as Michael Sr. suffered. She supposed he couldn't help but overhear remarks about his sister and Zachary Lundt; he'd have to see the Lundt boy every day, Mt. Ephraim High was so small, only a few hundred students. Yet he was managing, he was quiet but resolute. If he shared his innermost thoughts with anyone, it was no longer Mom.

As for Mike—eldest son, firstborn baby, so *grown*. Mikey-Junior who'd turned twenty-one—no: twenty-*two*—last month. Corinne had been stunned by Mike's abrupt decision to leave home and live in Mt. Ephraim, just at the time of his birthday. But why? Corinne had asked, for to her High Point Farm was paradise, and why would one leave paradise willingly? Mike said, Well, it's time. Corinne asked again, But why? and Mike said, shifting his shoulders restively, clenching and unclenching his fists, It makes sense to live where you work, right? and Corinne said, Yes but you could ride in with Dad instead of driving in yourself, the way you used to—how can that be a reason? and Mike laughed and said, Mom, you just don't get it, and Corinne said, hurt, I guess I don't. Michael Sr. didn't approve of the sudden decision, either. Why the hell did Mike want to move to town, to an apartment! *A mere apartment.* And in a cheaply flashy stucco building in the new Riverdale section of Mt. Ephraim where the Mulvaneys knew no one. Corinne tried for a lighter tone, teasing Mike about how he'd prepare his own meals?—for Mike was the biggest eater of the Mulvaneys, always hungry. Mike said with a shrug he'd eat in restaurants mostly, and Corinne said, chiding, Restaurant meals!—they aren't very nourishing, and they're expensive. And Mike said, in that winking way he had with his mom, as if there were a subtext to their conversation she hadn't been getting, Hey Mom: it all depends upon the restaurant.

All depends upon the restaurant.

It was then, waking Corinne from sleep, the telephone rang close beside the bed.

But she hadn't been asleep—had she?

Fumbling to lift the receiver, the palm of her hand already damp with panicky sweat, she knew, just knew it must be bad news.

"Corinne? Hey sorry—did I wake you? It's—"

The voice was familiar, gratingly—Corinne recognized it even as she struggled to comprehend what she was being told.

Haw Hawley. At Wolf's Head Lake. Calling to say that Michael had had an "accident"—"Nothing too serious, but he shouldn't be driving tonight. We thought we'd better let you know, so you wouldn't worry."

Corinne was already out of bed. "Is he hurt?"

"Hurt?"—as if the idea hadn't occurred to Haw. "Well—not really. I mean, he's mainly sleeping. We put him in one of the rooms, in bed."

"I'll come get him," Corinne said.

"Now? So late?"

"I said, Haw, I'll come get him."

* * *

So Corinne drove to Wolf's Head Lake, arrived at 1:25 A.M. in hastily thrown-on jeans, sweatshirt, sneakers without socks. She had not so much as glanced at herself in a mirror, hadn't had time to splash water onto her face or drag a comb through her hair, rushing off, calling to the children (of course, they'd been awakened—or had they been asleep, at all, waiting too for the telephone to ring?) that things were all right, their dad was all right, at Wolf's Head Lake and she was going to get him.

How strange to be driving alone at night, arriving alone at the darkened lakeside. Buildings made unfamiliar by night, their lights extinguished. The faded red neon WOLF'S HEAD INN extinguished. There were only two vehicles in the tavern parking lot, one of them Michael's pickup. Haw was waiting for Corinne on the Inn veranda, beneath a bug-swirling light, a tall, burly, apologetic man who made no effort to shake Corinne's hand, or touch her to comfort her—that wasn't his way. "Michael got in a, kind of a disagreement with a local guy," Haw said, "—they'd both been drinking and they shoved each other around. But nothing serious." Corinne entered the near-darkened tavern, diminished and melancholy it seemed without patrons, even the jukebox turned off, but, oh!—that smell. She would know it anywhere. "How badly drunk is he?" Corinne asked. "Sick-drunk? Passed-out drunk?" She was trying to be matter-of-fact. She was trying not to sound furious and reproachful, a raging wife. Wasn't she a farm woman, after all—she'd had plenty of experience with emergencies. Telling herself, *As long as he's alive. He's alive.*

A light was burning at the rear of the tavern, beyond the bar and the shabby old-fashioned kitchen, beyond the stinking alcove, and Corinne hurried in that direction, not waiting for Haw, who was short of breath, to lead her. He lumbered close behind her, squinting at her through smudged glasses, smelling of beer himself, male-sweat and beer. Saying, "Michael looks worse than he is. Don't be upset." But when Corinne saw her husband sprawled atop a bed, his face swollen, his upper lip swollen and bloody, shirt stained and eyes shut, snoring, she began to cry. It took some time to wake him and when she finally did, crouched beside the bed in a posture of abnegation and appeal, stroking his heated face, she had a sense of going in and out of focus in his eyes, a hapless female figure in a cartoon.

The room was minimally, shabbily furnished and smelled of insecticide and stale tobacco smoke. It had an adjoining cubbyhole of a bathroom, however, and Haw was kind enough to provide a rudimentary first-aid kit, so Corinne could tend to Michael—washing his face, putting iodine and Band-Aids on his cuts. He groaned, cursed, thrashed about; he was deeply ashamed, disgusted with himself. Saying, "I don't know what the hell happened, honey. One minute I was O.K. and the next—" His arm lifted, only to fall back limp onto the bed.

Haw said, "You're both welcome to stay the night—of course. Drive back home tomorrow. That way, you won't have to both come again, to get Michael's pickup." He was hanging about in the hallway, awkward, apologetic, yet trying for an amiable tone. *Old-friends-who've-been-through-worse-than-this-together* tone. Corinne remembered their encounter in the Kmart and felt a physical, visceral dislike of the man.

Stiffly she said, "Thank you, but I want to take Michael home tonight."

"But—"

"No! Tonight."

She was close to clamping her hands over her ears, like one of her children.

"Corinne, come on," Haw said, scratching at his beard, "—d'you hate it here that much? Hate *me*?"

Corinne stared at Haw, wiping her eyes. A wave of shame came over her: how could she, Corinne Mulvaney, whose sense of herself as one privileged by God had defined her entire adulthood, acknowledge hating any living person, let alone this sad, hopeful, raddle-faced and lonely old friend? One of the few men of Corinne's life who had desired her, as a woman? "Well, all right," she said, relenting. "You're right, I suppose. But we'll pay you for the room."

"Corinne, what the hell—"

"I said *we'll pay you*."

Surprising, how tough she could be, even in her nerved-up exhausted state. She'd almost forgotten how good it felt.

Brisk, capable, fueled with purpose as a mom should be, Corinne telephoned home to assure the children that everything was under control. Patrick answered the phone on the first ring. He asked how was Dad and Corinne said Dad was fine and Patrick persisted, what had happened?—and Corinne said that nothing had *happened*. "It's just Dad isn't up to driving right now. But he'll be fine by morning. We'll both be home by midmorning." Still Patrick asked, reproachfully,

"What's *wrong* with Dad? I've got a right to know." Corinne said sharply, "We'll talk about it tomorrow, Patrick. Good night!"

As long as he's alive. Alive.
I give us both over to You, God. Protect us!

They lay together exhausted. Only partly undressed, their shoes off. Not in, but on top of, the dank-smelling bed that was hardly more than a cot, pushed into the corner of the cramped little room. Michael's left eye had swollen almost shut and promised to be luridly blackened. There were cuts in his eyebrows, his upper lip was swollen, the color of an overripe plum. His knuckles, too, were skinned and swollen. A jittery sobriety had overtaken him by 3 A.M. just as Corinne sank toward sleep. "Jesus, honey, I'm sorry!" Michael murmured. Corinne murmured, "Well." She was holding him in a way she'd held him frequently, after lovemaking, in the early years of their marriage: her arm slipped beneath his heavy shoulders, his head on her shoulder, his arm slung across her. Seen from above, they would appear to be huddling together like dazed and desperate children. With an air of dogged incredulity that seemed genuine Michael was saying, "—just don't know what happened." Corinne said, taking the tone she'd taken with Patrick, "It isn't what *happened*, Michael, it's what you've *done*." The schoolmarmish edge was a way of keeping herself from more tears, or worse than tears. Adrenaline had pumped through her veins for a long time and was beginning now to wane and Corinne knew that, when it did, if she wasn't safely unconscious, she would be washed out, despairing.

God protect us!—we're your children, too.

She wished Michael, willed him, to sleep. To relinquish shame. The tattered remnant of his pride. A man's pride, carried like a burden on his back. But vaguely, wonderingly he continued to speak. Corinne had not inquired what the quarrel with the stranger had been. Haw claimed not to know and Corinne did not think it had had anything to do with *it*—Wolf's Head Lake was a considerable distance from Mt. Ephraim. But she preferred not to know, would never ask. There was the relief of her husband's *living self*. When the telephone had rung waking her from her stuporous sleep she had had the instantaneous terrified conviction that Michael had been killed, or had killed; that he had transgressed beyond his capacity to return. But that was not so. With God's love, it would not be so. She could save him, would save if only God showed the way.

Now, the comfort of his warm, perspiring body heavy against hers. Her arm growing numb from his weight. His damp hair, the hard intransigent bone of his skull. A smell of his body and breath— beer, whiskey, sweat. It was a smell she savored as, a farmer's daughter, she'd learned to savor, young, the smells of the barnyard, the smells that meant home. Well, yes—they were *stinks*, sometimes. Exacerbated by rain and humidity. Yet, still, they were familiar, they meant home. They meant *what is known*. *What is given to us, to know*.

The light in the room was extinguished. There was a window beside the bed, no blind to draw so Corinne was aware of the starlit sky above Wolf's Head Lake; a faint-luminous pearly moon that seemed to be pulsing. Unless it was an artery in her brain that was pulsing. Confused, she mistook it for—what? A streetlamp. Somehow, that was logical. There were lights on poles in Haw Hawley's parking lot turned off for the night and somehow this was one of them except floating. And there was a streetlamp in a famous painting of a jungle, a dream-jungle, a French painting of the previous century Corinne had seen years ago but could not now identify, yet recalling the jungle flat as wallpaper and clearly a dream and the artist had inserted a streetlamp in it because *that is the nature of dreams*.

She'd believed that this heavy perspiring man huddled against her was asleep but suddenly he began to speak. A low, aggrieved, jarring voice she could not escape. "—This thing that I did I didn't tell you, nor the lawyer either, fuck him, fuck them all, think I don't know how they talk about me behind my back? take my money and ridicule me?—so I acted on my own, yesterday morning I went to the Chautauqua County district attorney and demanded the S.O.B. talk to me in person, Birch himself, big-deal Democrat, *I* voted for him for Christ's sake, so I demanded he bring criminal charges against the kid who'd assaulted my daughter, she could not testify herself so we would have to bring charges on the strength of her doctor's records, Dr. Oakley's records could be subpoenaed and he could be made to testify—couldn't he? Isn't that the law? Where a felony has been committed against a minor? A medical man, a man who knows exactly what happened to my daughter! He could be made to testify, he would have to tell the truth. And Birch listens, or pretends to listen. Saying then it did not seem to him a 'winnable' case. Just to take it to a grand jury—not a 'winnable' case. If the victim refuses to testify. And I say but what if the victim had been *killed*? You would charge the murderer wouldn't you? What kind of criminal justice system is this for Christ's sake? And Birch asks why won't my daughter testify, has she made a statement to the police?—and so on. Questions like that. Fucking lawyer questions! Pretending he's sympathetic. Saying, 'In such cases the defense will argue "mutual consent." All but impossible to convince a jury where it's a female's word against a male because the jury must deliberate evidence and can convict only beyond a reasonable doubt. Unless the young woman has been seriously injured and can't testify, and her injuries documented, and maybe a semen swab matched with the young man. It would be a rare case, possibly if the victim was retarded, where she refused to testify or was ruled incapable, and a grand jury would indict. Not "winnable," Mr. Mulvaney. You'd only be opening your daughter and your family to public humiliation. If the defendant didn't cave in and there's no reason he would in such circumstances, in fact his lawyer would move to dismiss and a judge would probably concur. This is Chautauqua County,' Birch says, 'we had a hell of a time getting an indictment against a man in Milford—you read about it, maybe— who beat and kicked his pregnant wife a while back—juries don't like to "interfere" in domestic cases. In male-female cases. If sex is involved, especially. Remember that trucker who shot his wife and her boyfriend with a shotgun?—the grand jury did indict, but on second-degree manslaughter—the jury acquitted him—"not guilty by reason of temporary insanity." Probably you wouldn't know, Mr. Mulvaney, "sexual misdemeanor" and assault and rape cases are reported all the time, including pretty brutal rapes, but these cases rarely get to trial. Even if a grand jury indicted which I don't believe they would it would be impossible to conduct a trial without your daughter and if she did testify it would destroy her'—and I'm listening to this bullshit and can't hold back any longer saying 'I want the fucker punished! I want justice! I see this kid around town, my daughter has to see him in school, and my son—*he's getting away with it, with the hurt he inflicted on us.*' I was getting excited, I guess. I was yelling at Birch saying 'We deserve better in this town, my family and me!' And these deputies came in, guards—"

Corinne was holding Michael feeling his heart beating through his body. Madness! He was mad. Yet she held him, the corners of her eyes leaked tears stinging as acid. "Oh Michael, oh my darling, oh no oh no," she whispered, though he didn't hear, wasn't listening, locked in his grief, a fanatic grief, yet childlike too, saying, "God help me, I don't know what else to do. If I can't protect my own daughter. My own children. My family. If I wasn't a coward I would exact my own justice. I can't live with it. We'll have to sell the farm and move away. We're like lepers. We—" Corinne shut her eyes tight: she saw High Point Farm on the very edge of High Point Road, the steep drop along its most dangerous stretches, thinking *Why we will fall over, fall to the bottom and be lost*. Michael was saying, pushing from her arms now, sitting up, rubbing his face, his swollen eyes, half sobbing, incredulous, "It isn't just my daughter it's all of us. She can't be blamed but it's all of us. I vowed I would love them all equally—I did. I tried. When they were babies, I tried. But the girl—she ran away with my heart. She can't be blamed, but that was how it was. Always I'd be thinking *I would kill for her, my baby girl*. But—"

Corinne said, sitting up beside him, "Michael, no! Don't say such things. It's a sin to say such things."

"—I'm not strong enough, I'm a coward. How can I live knowing that! God help me, Corinne, I can't bear the sight of the girl any longer." Michael began to sob helplessly, despairingly, in Corinne's arms. It seemed to her she could not hold him tight enough, enclosed enough; she would have wished to envelop him with her body, as one might a small child, an infant, drawing him somehow inside her, stilling the terrible agitation of his thoughts. Oh, if she could swallow him up! Save him! "I wish to God I never had to lay eyes on her again," Michael whispered, in horror of what he was saying. "God forgive me! It's so."

Corinne heard herself whisper in reply, hesitating only a fraction of a second, "I know, darling. I know." She began to croon, rocking him. His hot heavy pulsing body. His maleness, his very bulk. That weight turned to despair, so heavy. How had she been blind for so long, these weeks?—how had she missed understanding?—here was her first love, her firstborn. The others, the children born of her body, even Marianne, were hardly more than dreams, ripples on the surface of a dark impenetrable water. From this man, from his body, their bodies had sprung. He was her first love. "Darling, I know," Corinne crooned softly, as if it were a lullaby. Seeing the goose comically entangled in nylon fishing line thrashing its wings, struggling in desperation. *But I will save you: with God's help*.

So Corinne and Michael Mulvaney clutched at each other desperately in a room at the rear of the shabby Wolf's Head Inn at Wolf's Head Lake, in the early hours of a day in April 1976, until at last, mutually exhausted, they lay back down together in the narrow dank-smelling bed and slept, slept.

GONE

What a morning it must have been of swift, inspired arrangements! What bargaining, bartering, pleading and coercing by telephone!

For when Patrick and I returned home from school the following afternoon, we discovered that our sister Marianne was gone.

Just—*gone*.

Mom had driven her, the Buick station wagon packed with as many of her things as it could hold, to Salamanca, New York, a hundred miles south and west of High Point Farm, where she was to live from now on with a Hausmann relative, a cousin of Mom's who, we were assured, was a very very nice, very good-hearted Christian woman who'd never had children of her own.

We must have stood there gaping for Mom added quickly, as if this were a crucial point, that of course Muffin had gone with Marianne—"On her lap all the way, purring." Fixing us with a beaming neon smile.

II
"THE HUNTSMAN"

ONE BY ONE

One by one, we went away.

It's the story of American farms and small towns in the latter half of the twentieth century: we went away.

First of the Mulvaney children, even before Marianne went to live with a cousin of Mom's in Salamanca, was my older brother Mike: to live in Mt. Ephraim initially, and continue to work at Mulvaney Roofing, until the business encountered "fiscal setbacks" (Dad's term) and relations between father and son became strained, and more than strained, and Mike quit and joined the Marines.

That would be in November 1977. Approximately a year and a half after the events I've recorded. After *it*.

By the time Mike had his final nasty quarrel with Dad and slammed out of Mulvaney Roofing forever, his life had become what you'd call complicated. He wasn't a reliable worker for Dad, sometimes arriving at the work site late, or failing to show up at all. He didn't get along with certain of his co-workers, nor with Alex Flood who was Dad's right-hand man. Nights, he ran with a wild, hard-drinking crowd, some of them guys he'd known in high school who like him hadn't gone to college, or in any case hadn't graduated. There were rumors that some of these guys dealt in drugs, or associated with dealers who operated out of Port Oriskany, Rochester, Buffalo. Half-drunk, late at night, Mike was several times stopped in his Olds Cutlass by Mt. Ephraim police or sheriff's men, and let off with a warning; the cops knew "Mule" Mulvaney who'd been a star of the Mt. Ephraim Rams and they knew Michael Mulvaney Sr. and liked him or anyway felt sorry for him, damned sorry for what had happened to his daughter. To Mike they said, "You don't want to get into any more trouble, son," and Mike said, wiping his face, in the way he'd had of speaking to his high school coach, "Officer, I sure don't! Thanks for telling me that." Still, he had two D.W.I. citations by the time he totalled the Olds Cutlass one rainy autumn night out on Route 119, escaping with minor bumps and lacerations himself but causing the girl who was with him serious injuries, a broken collarbone and ribs, a shattered kneecap, facial lacerations so disfiguring she would have to undergo a series of cosmetic operations.

Twelve days after the accident, Mike made the break with Dad, left Mt. Ephraim, signed up at Marine recruiting headquarters in Yewville without telling anyone beforehand. We were all amazed—you'd have thought Mike might have hinted to Patrick what was coming, but he hadn't. Mom was heartbroken, deeply hurt. She hadn't understood how estranged Mike and Dad had become, though it had distressed her how infrequently Mike came to the farm to visit, even for his favorite meals. Unless they weren't "favorite meals" any longer and Mom hadn't been informed.

Most of this, I didn't know at the time. I understood that things weren't good between Mike and my parents and I understood that Mike was making a break with his family which included his brothers, too. I believed that Mike had been shamed by what had happened to Marianne because it meant that "Mule Mulvaney" no longer counted for much in certain quarters of Mt. Ephraim. Zachary Lundt and his pals Rodman, Breuer, Glover. Phil Spohr too ran with that crowd. By treating Marianne as they had they were showing their contempt for her big brother, too. Weren't they?

Some cocksucker's gonna pay for it Mike had promised. But a long time had passed and no one had paid.

There were weeks when I didn't see my older brother except to catch glimpses of him in town, usually in his car—he'd honk, and wave, grinning out at me yelling "Hey there Ranger!" but not slowing down as he passed by. I'd look after him, waving, my smile fading on my face like some pathetic cartoon character fading right out of the frame. One October afternoon leaving school I ran into him on Meridian Street, saw this tall good-looking reddish-haired guy emerging from a 7-Eleven in black T-shirt and chinos and work boots, two Molson six-packs in hand and a cigarette drooping from his mouth and one of his adoring girls waiting in the idling lipstick-red Cutlass coupe that had to be the sweetest, coolest car anybody could want to drive, ever. "Ranger!—how's it going?" Mike called out. He introduced me to the girl as his kid brother and she smiled at me out the car window, a pretty thin-faced blond with frizzy hair and lips made up to look like luscious raspberries. "Is 'Ranger' your real name?" she asked, and Mike said, "Hell, no: his real name is 'Dimple.' Smile for us, kid, and show why." My face burned. I didn't know if I loved it or hated it when Mike teased me in that way of his that was rough, pushy, almost-mean, like Dad. In fact, if you didn't look to see it was Mike at such times, his voice so resembled Dad's, and his manner, you'd swear this *was* Dad.

The girl's name was Marissa King. She was nineteen years old, the daughter of a customer of Mulvaney Roofing, a farmer who owned hundreds of acres in southern Chautauqua County. Mike had met her while working for her father, repairing barn roofs for several weeks that summer; there had been talk, though none of us Mulvaneys knew it, of the two of them getting engaged. But Marissa was the girl in the Olds Cutlass with my brother, the night it was totalled on Route 119.

And Marianne of course was gone.

Living a hundred miles away, on the other side of the mountains, with a cousin of Mom's none of us knew; in the town of Salamanca none of us, except Mom, had ever seen. Weeks passed, and months, and though Mom had promised Patrick and me we'd drive down to visit Marianne soon, somehow we never got there. And Dad never spoke of going, in fact he never spoke of Marianne in my hearing, at all.

This cousin of Mom's was named Ethel Hausmann and she was unmarried, a longtime receptionist and bookkeeper for a Salamanca podiatrist. Mom was vague about the woman, apologetic and enthusiastic at once—"Ethel isn't easy to know but she's a deep spiritual good woman I would trust with my life. I *would*." Since Marianne's *vanishing* Mom had become yet more nervously extravagant in her speech, eyelids and fingers fluttering.

Each Sunday at 8 P.M. Mom would telephone Ethel Hausmann and speak with her for several minutes, and then with Marianne, in private; after fifteen or twenty minutes she would call Patrick, and then me, to speak with our sister. "Keep the conversation short, please," Mom would whisper. "This isn't a local call."

So strange—talking with Marianne on the phone. I could almost believe it was one of our old games. The "telephone game" when I was very small, three or four years old, and Marianne and I would pick up phone receivers and talk and giggle on different floors of the house, playing at being adults. A game we could only play when Dad and Mom weren't around. How distant Marianne sounded now, her voice thin and flattened. *Because the mountains are in the way* I thought. Possibly Marianne had been crying while on the phone with Mom—Mom would resolutely *not* have been crying: eyes bright, perfectly clear and dry—but she'd make an effort to be cheerful while speaking with me. I was reminded of certain of our hymns we'd sing like marching songs chanted through clenched teeth. "Judd! How are you?" Marianne would ask eagerly, and the question confused me: it isn't one sisters and brothers ever ask of each other as kids. It's an adult question, one of the phony ones. Except I guess Marianne meant it. I'd mumble, embarrassed, "I'm O.K., I guess," shrugging as if she could see me, and Marianne would cry, "Oh, Judd! Gosh I miss you! I can't wait to see you. Mom says—" I wouldn't know how to reply, just stood there gripping the receiver in misery, because Mom had warned Patrick and me not to discuss future plans with Marianne; never to speak of *the future*—"It will just get her hopes up, and that would be cruel."

Marianne would inquire after the animals one by one, always beginning with Molly-O. Oh, she missed Molly-O! She dreamt she was riding Molly-O all the time. She dreamt Molly-O was just a filly, a baby, just brought to High Point Farm. And how was Prince?—how was Clover?—how was Red? And how were the dogs—Foxy, Little Boots, Troy, Silky? And the cats—Big Tom, E.T., Snowball, Marmalade? And Feathers? She was always imagining she heard Feathers in the early morning, when she was just waking up. And how were the goats Blackie and Mamie? And the barn cats? And Cap'n Marvel and all that crew? And the cows, and the sheep? Marianne always reported that she and Muffin were fine but missing the family, it was so quiet and somehow so *small* there. We always assured Marianne that everyone was fine at High Point Farm, too. (In fact, Silky had died of a cancerous tumor in his stomach, but none of us wanted to tell Marianne. Mike had left Silky behind when he'd moved to town, said his apartment building didn't allow pets, and poor Silky pined away at the end of the driveway for weeks waiting for Mike to return then abruptly sickened and died and Mom, P.J. and I had a little ceremony burying him in the front yard, not far from the brook, where, as Mom said tearfully, he could wait for Mike forever.)

Last of all, Marianne would draw a deep breath and ask after Dad, as if she hadn't already asked Mom and Patrick, and I'd stand sweating and the words I wanted to shout jammed in my throat and Marianne's voice became plaintive, pleading, "Judd? There isn't anything wrong with Daddy, is there? He never seems to be home when Mom calls." I stammered I didn't know, I didn't think so, Dad was working hard these days. Marianne would begin to sound desperate, asking, "Does he ever say anything about me, Judd? Does he ever—say my name?" and I would mumble yes sure I guessed so, and she would ask, suddenly pleading, "When can I come home, Judd? Do you know?"—but by this time Mom who'd been hovering close by, nervous as a cat, would take the receiver gently from me and say into the mouthpiece in a playful-Mom voice, "Sor-ry! This is your long-distance operator and *your time has run out.*"

Patrick left to enroll at Cornell in early September 1976 and would never live at High Point Farm again except for brief periods. That first Thanksgiving when we were all looking forward to seeing him he shocked us by not coming home—"Too much work," he explained tersely. Lab courses in biology, organic chemistry, physics. And at Christmas, he was home for only a few days of the long recess—not only did he have too much work to do, he'd been hired as a biology lab assistant. The following summer, he was home only two weeks, returning to Ithaca to work in the lab. (This, Dad didn't like at all. He'd been counting on Patrick to "do his share" on the farm. Already, Dad had had to hire part-time help, and these were not very reliable farmworkers, like the Zimmermans, father and son, who lived down the road in the old renovated schoolhouse.) But Patrick had his own life now, and he certainly had his plans. His talk was all of "amino acids"—"genetics"—"cellular biology." He had little to say about Cornell University itself, meeting new people, making friends—his manner was stiff, polite, distracted. He endured Mom's effusive talk and as much as he could of her affection; his smile was the old Pinch-smile, a corner of his mouth tucked down, in a look of virtual pain—but it seemed unconscious, it meant nothing.

He hadn't any interest in hearing news of his fellow graduates of the Class of '76 nor had he much interest in his own photograph in the *Mt. Ephraim Patriot-Ledger* above his name and the caption, "Area Youth Achieves Dean's List, Cornell." Mom, of course, had provided the newspaper with the information.

Unlike Marianne, Patrick rarely inquired after the animals. He never seemed to have time to visit with Prince, still less to ride. When Mom muttered glumly about Dad wanting to sell Prince, Red, Molly-O, Patrick frowned but did not protest.

Damn you, don't you care? Why don't you care? I wanted to shout.

Always I'd be waiting for Patrick to spend some time with me, just me alone. His kid brother who missed him so. His kid brother at High Point Farm pining away like poor Silky, left-behind and lonely. Once I came into his room where he was (damn him: he hadn't been home three hours) studying a chart with the heading "Mendelian Inheritance in Man" and I asked him if he'd spoken with Marianne, or seen her? and he sort of shrugged and looked embarrassed. (Meaning yes, he had?—or no, he hadn't?) "Why does Dad hate Marianne so? Why doesn't he want to see her, or even talk to her?" I asked, and Patrick said, frowning, "Dad doesn't hate *her*. It's just she reminds him of—you know." Lifting his arm in a way of Dad's that signaled *What the hell? what can you do?*—spreading the fingers, letting the arm fall limp.

I said, "But that isn't Marianne's fault!"

Thinking I could hate Dad, if Patrick gave me a sign.

But Patrick said, soberly, looking at me for the first time since he'd come home, "It isn't Dad's fault, either."

VALEDICTORY SPEECH

Before Patrick Mulvaney left Mt. Ephraim, he gave us all something to remember.

At first he'd debated not showing up for his high school commencement in June, though he was valedictorian of his graduating class, and the "honor" fell to him (as he was told repeatedly by Mr. Hendrie the school principal, and by his teachers) to deliver the valedictory speech. His grades through high school had been in the high nineties; he'd several times had perfect scores in math, chemistry, biology, his favorite subjects. His S.A.T. score was in the highest percentile and he'd been offered scholarships to a number of excellent universities. Since *it,* however, he'd been more withdrawn than previously, preferring to spend time alone, at home, in a makeshift laboratory he'd set up in one of the old barns. (The lab was out-of-bounds to Patrick's kid brother Judd, which didn't mean I'd never poked my nose into it, at times when Patrick wasn't around. Examining beakers containing strange soapy liquids, lemony-acid-smelling chemicals, corked bottles, vials, and jars. Prominent on the workbench was Patrick's mail-order microscope he'd laboriously assembled from a kit. On a wall was a poster of the "periodic calendar" of chemicals—to me, an eighth grader, exotic as a foreign language. I was in dread of high school science, where I'd be expected to learn such things, but, worse yet, I'd be measured against my brilliant older brother.) Patrick never missed a day of school, sitting quietly in his classes, frowning at his teachers who admired rather than liked him, a thin-limbed, lanky boy with a penetrating steely-blue stare. Because his left eye was so weak, he sometimes narrowed it almost to a slit. *Pinch's laser-ray.*

Of the eighty-nine students of Mt. Ephraim High's 1976 graduating class, all but a handful had always been wary of Patrick Mulvaney; uncomfortable around him as of an adult in disguise in their midst. They admired him, and feared him, and did not much like him; he responded by looking through them, when he could not avoid looking at them. This included even the three or four who'd once counted themselves his friends.

Whatever Patrick's classmates were thinking of Marianne, now mysteriously departed from Mt. Ephraim, and of Patrick who was her brother, *Patrick did not know and did not wish to know.* Of course, Zachary Lundt was a classmate of Patrick's, who would be graduating with him on June 19, ranked sixty-five in his class. And there were Zachary's buddies, his circle. Patrick seemed not aware of them at all. Even entering the cafeteria, or the boys' locker room, or descending a flight of stairs to overhear—what? Murmured remarks, crude jokes. Muffled laughter. Words intended for Patrick Mulvaney to hear which in fact he might have heard yet somehow did not, was spared, as if the very airborne syllables might be repelled by an act of his superior will.

When, at a May assembly, Mr. Hendrie made the proud announcement that one of their seniors was among the first-prize winners of the annual New York State High School Science Fair, and that senior was Patrick Mulvaney, there was a distinct pause, a collective intake of breath, before the clapping began. Patrick, forced to rise in his seat, flushed deeply in embarrassment, or chagrin. He would be one of those who aggressively seek honors, yet shrink from their public acknowledgment.

And now: the valedictory speech.

Should he, or shouldn't he? Conform, or—?

Give them something to remember—maybe?

Patrick, in true Pinch-style, brooded over it for weeks. What *honor* was there, for God's sake, in being merely the best of the Mt. Ephraim High class of 1976? Just possibly, as soon as he took the podium and began to speak, certain of his rowdier classmates would immediately register boredom and contempt—did he dare to give them the opportunity to mock him?

Maybe, Patrick fretted, he should refuse to deliver a speech at all. There was no precedent at the high school for such rebellion but—how could he be punished, at this date? What could Hendrie and the others do, since commencement was only a ritual, and actual graduation a matter of state records, diplomas issued from Albany and sent through the mail? And what an absurd ritual it was, adolescents in caps and gowns! "It's a cartoon situation, essentially," Patrick said. "I can only be degraded by participating."

With Pinch, you never knew how serious he was. After all these years, Mom still couldn't gauge. She said, protesting, " 'Degraded'! Oh, Patrick, how can you say such a thing? We're all so proud of you—it will break my heart if you stay away from your own graduation."

Patrick winked at me. "I could call in sick that morning, Mom, and tell Hendrie I've got rabies."

"Patrick, that isn't funny," Mom said, almost pleading. The way she stared at my brother sometimes, now that Mike and Marianne were gone, the way her eyes sort of clung to him, dragged at him—it was weird to see, and made me uncomfortable.

Patrick said, "I'll say I have rabies but I want to come to graduation anyway and give my speech, on the way to the hospital. See what old Hendrie says then." In fact there had been several recent cases of rabies in the Valley, spread to human beings by infected raccoons and house pets. But Patrick's joking meant he was probably going to relent. Mom laughed, and chided him for his "morbid Pinch-humor," leaning over to brush a strand of limp sand-colored hair from his forehead.

She said, "Patrick, you know all of Mt. Ephraim will be eager to hear your valedictory speech."

As late as the night before graduation, Patrick was still brooding over the speech. I asked him how it was coming along and he glared at me and said, "Who wants to know? *You?*"

Graduation day was a Monday, a warm windy splotched-sunny day. The ceremony was set to begin promptly at 11 A.M. at the school and, to our relief, Patrick did appear downstairs in his cap and gown, and he'd apparently prepared a speech, on a long sheet of yellow scrap paper carelessly folded and stuffed into his trouser pocket. Mom asked what the title was and Patrick just shrugged. He might have been embarrassed, or nervous; the skin beneath his eyes had a sallow, shadowy cast, as if he'd been awake much of the night. He gave off a sourish-acrid odor as if his sweat had a chemical component, reacting against the fine-knit dark wool of the absurd ankle-length gown that fitted his lanky frame loose as a tent. Patrick insisted upon driving to the school an hour before the rest of us, saying he had last-minute work to do on his speech. "But why can't we ride *together*? Aren't we a *family*?" Mom shouted after him, perplexed and annoyed.

Patrick drove off in the Jeep Wrangler and an hour later the rest of the family followed, in Mom's station wagon. We were down to the three Mulvaneys for Patrick's graduation: Mom, Dad, and me.

Mike was with a roofing crew on a work site out the Haggartsville Road. (Mom had asked Dad if Mike could be excused for the day, to come to his brother's graduation—but nobody felt very strongly about him coming, including Mike himself. And Patrick.) No mention was made of Marianne. I'd asked Mom a few days before if she'd been invited and Mom said, "Why of course, Marianne has been invited to her own brother's graduation!" adding vaguely, "—but my cousin Ethel is counting on her to help out around the house and not be gadding all about the countryside, so—probably— we shouldn't expect her."

Are we lepers? We, Mulvaneys?—lepers?

Climbing the front steps of Mt. Ephraim High School, entering the foyer, passing by the glass trophy case where "Mule" Mulvaney's photo was still proudly displayed, I saw how eyes shifted upon my parents and shifted away, so fluidly you'd think it was the same motion. As Mom gaily chattered, waved, called out, "Hello! Hel-*lo*!"

The crowd seemed to part for us. Fascinating: how people who'd known Corinne and Michael Mulvaney for twenty years seemed now not to see them, or, unable to reasonably not see them, smiled vaguely, with a pretense of enthusiasm, then turned away to greet others, shaking hands and embracing others. Most instructive for a thirteen-year-old who'd be a journalist one day, to observe.

Yes we feel sorry for you Mulvaneys but no, no!—don't come talk to us, don't spoil this happy occasion for us, please.

It was a high school graduation like any other, I guess, in the beginning. Except for how we Mulvaneys were being ignored, and maybe I'm actually exaggerating that, since one or two of Patrick's

teachers said hello on their way into the auditorium, and may even
have exchanged more words than that with Mom while Dad stared
on stonily, as if unhearing. There was much milling about in the
foyer as, in the auditorium, to hurry us on our way, the Mt.
Ephraim Marching Band played jubilantly—was it the school anthem, or the national anthem, or a John Philip Sousa march in quick
time? Though there was to be a reception after graduation, seniors
in caps and gowns were being photographed now, with one another, with members of their families, with obliging teachers and
Mr. Hendrie. Here and there I saw to my chagrin classmates of mine
from junior high with their families—we shrank from recognizing
one another, here. What a din! It was like a pep rally in the gym,
voices and laughter reverberating from floor, ceiling, walls, and the
music blaring.

And where was Patrick Mulvaney?—his mother rushed about
searching for him, asking whomever she encountered, whether she
knew them or not, had they seen her son?—ushers, teachers, fellow
parents, Mr. Hendrie himself. "Patrick is valedictorian, you know—
he's been working on his speech for days—he's such a perfectionist!" Mom managed to lament and marvel simultaneously. Her eyes
shone a radiant, unnerving blue and her skin looked as if she'd been
overexposed to sun. She would have been an attractive woman except for something too eager, too hungry and almost haggard in her
face, and her lunging, oddly cranelike posture that made others draw
back. Mom was never comfortable in high heels, yet at such a time
she felt duty-bound to wear them: old-fashioned round-toed glar-
ing-white pumps that looked whitewashed, with a two-inch heel.
Her hair had been so vigorously shampooed that morning it lifted
from her head in an astonished frizz, carroty-red mixed with gray
like the underside of those layered, dense clouds called cumulonim-
bus. Her outfit, selected that morning after much anxious deliberation, was a silk polka-dot dress that fitted her loosely, marble-sized
red dots on a white background; the bodice was a mass of buttons,
the skirt long, swishy. This was a rare "feminine" costume of
Corinne Mulvaney's, no doubt purchased at the Second Chance
Shop sponsored by the Mt. Ephraim General Hospital Women's
Auxiliary. (It was one of Mom's recurring nightmares that the original owner of one of her extravagant secondhand outfits would recognize it on her; yet this possibility, real enough in a community the
size of Mt. Ephraim, seemed never to discourage her from wearing

these outfits in town.) Her very audacity quickened her sense of play, her reckless vitality.

By contrast, my father was somber, unsmiling amid the congratulatory crowd; his head slightly lowered, eyes hooded and his shoulders rounded, as if he hoped, through a fury of compression, to draw his very skeleton inward, and make himself smaller. He must have shaved quickly, or carelessly that morning—a still-moist red-beaded scratch of about two inches glinted beneath his jaw. He was wearing a dark blue serge business suit that, too, fitted him loosely, as if its original owner had been a larger man. His shoes were brown leather, not recently shined. His necktie had a bronze sheen. Awkwardly, he and I stood together just inside the front door, ignored by everyone, yet stubborn and immobile as rocks in a stream of sociability that broke and flowed about us. It was strange to me, that my father Michael Mulvaney Sr. who had always been the center of others' attention was now an invisible man. Yet there was a bitter comfort in it! *Lepers! lepers! we Mulvaneys—lepers!* Dad's mouth was shut tight as if soldered yet I could hear those words, and I heard them in his gravelly baritone. While Mom, under the pretext of searching for Patrick, went boldly up to people with hand extended, neon-happy smile—"Why, Lydia! Hello!" I heard her call out to Mrs. Bethune, who blinked at her startled, "—have *you* seen my son Patrick?—the valedictorian?"

The Lundts were at the far side of the foyer, entering the auditorium talking and laughing with friends. Mort Lundt, his wife Cynthia, an elder couple who must have been grandparents. If Michael Mulvaney saw, he gave no sign nor did he budge from his position near a glass trophy case.

Seniors were lining up for the procession in a corridor to the right. A *Patriot-Ledger* photographer was taking flash shots. Congressman Harold Stoud appeared amid happy cries and exclamations. Directions were being given over loudspeakers. Most of the crowd had filed into the auditorium. Rows of seats were rapidly filling. If we didn't hurry, we'd be late! Mom had given up on Patrick when at last she sighted him, already in line, partway down the corridor; she waved to him, blew a kiss, mouthed a message Patrick icily ignored. "Let's go! Oh, why are you two just *standing there*!" Mom sighed, pulling at Dad and me who were balky as goats. With no shift of rhythm or tone, the band was playing "Pomp and Circumstance." Ushers held out programs, urging us and other late arrivals to hurry inside. The forty-eight-year-old man who was Michael Mulvaney Sr. stared and blinked about himself like a man in a dream. It's possible he did not know precisely where he was, or why; or, knowing, had retreated from full consciousness, even as Mom, breathless and excited, linked an arm through his, and an arm through mine, leading us into the auditorium. We sat in the fourth row from the back. A blinding mist seemed to surround us, protect us. If any of the Lundts were close by, or the parents and relatives of Zachary Lundt's friends who had taken his side, and said such things of Marianne Mulvaney, or any of those friends of friends whose names, faces, histories Michael Mulvaney had memorized, *his enemies! his enemies!*—we would be spared seeing. Already the capped and gowned seniors were marching by us down the aisles to the front reserved rows. More flashbulbs popped. Small children pointed at their older brothers and sisters. "There's Patrick!" Mom whispered. She nudged me, as if I were a small child, needful of being reminded of my connection to my brother. Dad was sitting tense, downlooking, the stiff-paper program rolled into a cylinder in his hands.

This commencement, Patrick's graduation, would pass like a blur before my eyes, for I seemed to know beforehand that something would happen and could wait only for it to happen, and all that preceded was confusion. There were delays at the start—Mr. Hendrie appeared, in his academic regalia, parting the heavy maroon velvet curtains, and mock frenzied cheers erupted. It was 11:10 A.M., and it was 11:20 A.M. Again Mr. Hendrie appeared, greeting the packed assemblage ebulliently, and the band shifted to the national anthem and we rose to our feet and sang, some of us, loudly and happily, though others stood silent, for there are always those others in our noisy happy midst, waiting for whatever it is, to end. Next, a "moment of silence" presided over by a local Unitarian minister. Then the Mt. Ephraim High anthem, words spliced to the vigorous "John Brown's Body," led by the school's choir director. Again, we were all enjoined to sing. Mr. Hendrie returned to the podium and introduced Coach Hansen, a popular Mt. Ephraim presence, who began, amid applause, laughter, and whistles, to read off the names of prizewinners of the senior class in various categories—numerous prizewinners, in numerous categories. The auditorium had grown warm, people were fanning themselves with their programs. Ventilators were turned up, rattling and vibrating. I saw that Dad's putty-colored face was slick with sweat. The program had slipped from his fingers to the floor. He was sitting on the aisle, Mom between us, Mom straight and alert staring at the stage, a fixed smile on her face. *Can't we be proud? Don't we deserve this, this day of pride? He's our son!—our son!* I seem to have heard these words through one of the vents of our house earlier that morning. Mom's hushed, sibilant voice, and no voice responding. Dad must have murmured something, some words, in Mom's ear, before rising shakily to his feet and turning to slip away—suddenly he was gone, up the aisle and through a rear door and gone, his seat empty. (Gone where? To the men's room, and he'd be right back? Outside on the front steps, for a quick cigarette? Out to the car in the parking lot, where just maybe he had a bottle hidden in the trunk?) Mom continued to sit very straight, head uplifted, proud profile, white pearl button earrings, polka-dot silk dress, shining eyes fixed upon the stage in defiance of Mr. Mulvaney's abrupt departure. *She* was the mother of the valedictorian of the Class of 1976, and nothing could change that fact.

The president of the senior class spoke. A popular teacher of drama spoke. More awards were announced: outstanding citizenry, outstanding musical ability, outstanding scholastics, outstanding scientific work. Patrick Mulvaney was called to the stage to receive gilt-embossed certificates not once but twice, in immediate succession—much applause ensued, as if the boy had played some sort of trick upon the announcer, pretending to be twins, or, just maybe, twins pretending to be one boy. Mom was clapping frantically, whistling. Yet Dad's seat remained empty. Congressman Harold Stoud appeared and again there was much applause. Mt. Ephraim's most notable public servant, the "voice of common sense in Albany." Here was the commencement speaker—"Facing the Future as Young Americans"—reading from a prepared speech and delivered in a florid voice and time stretched and pleated and began to slowly turn upon itself like the Möbius strip Patrick had made of silver-striped wrapping paper, to hang from the ceiling of his room. *See, Ranger? Infinity, in my hand.* Still Michael Mulvaney Sr. who was Dad did not return to his seat. Congressman Stoud's words grew heavy and gritty and there came to be a thickness to the air in the auditorium, a strange choking dirt-tinctured air issuing from the vents even as the audience applauded the speaker, cheered, whistled, stamped their feet to hurry the garrulous old fart from the podium. And the tall fair-skinned senior boy who was valedictorian ascended rapidly to the stage and crossed to the podium in his cap and gown, his posture, manner, stride suggesting an upright and very mobile pair of scissors. And still Dad's seat remained empty.

But—what was wrong?—panicky sensations ran like ripples through the audience—the air! the air! poison! poison gas! a terrible sludgy stink like rotten eggs!

There was a moment's collective disbelief, incredulity, as of a single great breath withheld—then eruptions of coughing, choking, outcries of astonishment and terror. Beside me Mom was gagging—tears streamed from her eyes—yet she had the presence of mind to grab me, pull me from my seat, and within seconds we were stumbling up the aisle, rushing from the auditorium gasping, choking—ahead of the crowd—bursting out into the fresh clear June air. Oh, what had happened? What terrible sabotage had been done to disrupt Mt. Ephraim High's 1976 commencement?

Within minutes the verdict was: *a stink bomb.*

Prankish seniors must have set off *a stink bomb,* to rout their own commencement. Was such a thing possible?

Close by, only a few blocks away, the siren at the Mt. Ephraim Firehouse began to wail, as the first fire truck careened out of the garage to speed westward along Fifth Street.

Luckily, no one of the more than five hundred persons in the auditorium, which included very young children and numerous senior citizens, was injured in the stampede to escape. Exit doors were quickly flung open, rows of coughing, choking people filed out onto pavement or grass to recover within minutes. The most extreme symptoms were vomiting and hysteria. Most victims were merely nauseated, not incapable of breathing but revulsed by the foul air they had no choice but to breathe. The greatest concentration of the chemical bomb (hydrogen sulfide: ingeniously implanted in the building's basement ventilating system) was at the front of the auditorium where the eighty-nine graduating seniors, their teachers and school district administrators were seated. By the time the *Patriot-Ledger* printed its front-page article on the mysterious event, two days later, declaring in broad headlines STINK BOMB DISRUPTS MT. EPHRAIM H.S. COMMENCEMENT, the prevailing theory was that the prank had not been committed by Mt. Ephraim seniors, not even the rowdy, sometimes malicious boys who might have wished to pull off such a brilliant stunt (their teachers swore they simply weren't capable of concocting such a chemical bomb, let alone shrewdly timing it to detonate well into the ceremony and not at once) but by senior boys from one or another of their sports rivals in the valley—Yewville High, for instance.

There'd been bad blood between Mt. Ephraim and Yewville since the smaller school, Mt. Ephraim, had won the Valley basketball championship that spring; obscene graffiti had been scrawled on both school buildings, and there had been several fights, and numerous threats— the more Mt. Ephraim considered it, the more it seemed obvious the stink bomb had to have been set off by Yewville, for—who else?

Though no one had seen strangers lurking about the high school before the ceremony. And no mocking acknowledgment of the prank had come from any Yewville source.

There were other, less convincing theories, all of them investigated by Mt. Ephraim police and school administrators. An individual malcontent, for instance? A senior embittered by low exam grades, a romantic disappointment, failure to get admitted to the right college? Dislike of his teachers, his classmates? Over the weeks, months, even years, numerous theories, speculations would be discussed, for the stink bomb of June 19, 1976, at the Mt. Ephraim High commencement, was one of the most famous events of local history. But nothing was ever proven. There was no incriminating evidence, there were no informers. No one ever stepped forward to take credit.

"Oh my goodness, Judd!—are you all right? Oh where is Patrick?"

Mom was blinking dazed in sunshine, groping for my hand. I told her sure, I was O.K., I'd recovered almost immediately, whatever the gas in the auditorium was hadn't been any poison just a terrible stink. And funny—wasn't it? A joke! People were streaming out onto the grass beside us, coughing, choking, some of them trying not to vomit, wiping their faces on their sleeves; a few were cursing; some of the seniors were laughing, recognizing it as a prank—"Wow! Wild! Far out!" Ike Rodman marveled. Along the periphery of the gathering crowd came my brother Patrick loping like a track runner, though unhurried, in starched white shirt and chinos, and bareheaded—already he'd derobed, leaving his cap and gown on a sidewalk near a rear entrance of the school. He sighted us, Mom and me, ignored all others, frowning as if perturbed. His Pinch-frown, more a meditative glower than strong emotion. Or was he frowning in order not to smile? I stared at him in awe but he refused to meet my gaze. Mom rushed to embrace him and he let her hug him, stiff and embarrassed, looking over her shoulder; his left eye squinted nearly shut. Clever Patrick Mulvaney! He must have escaped from the stage as soon as the virulent odor began to waft from the vents, he'd even happened to have a handkerchief to press over his mouth and nose, a wetted handkerchief in fact, and he'd run immediately backstage, through a fire exit and outside, just possibly the first person to escape.

Mom exclaimed, "Oh, Patrick! Thank goodness, you're safe." She laughed breathlessly, twining her arms around him as if, in fact, he might have been in danger. "What a catastrophe! You never got to give your speech. Oh but it *is* funny, isn't it? Who would ever think of such a trick!"

Patrick said indifferently, "Some moronic classmates of mine, obviously."

On our way to the parking lot to meet up with Dad, I sidled close to Patrick to nudge him surreptitiously. My eyelids were puffy and my lips swollen and bruised as if I'd been pummelled. Coils of nausea stirred in my guts. Yet it was unqualified admiration, it was awe I felt for him. I whispered, "Jesus, P.J., did you—? Was it—you?" but Patrick merely glanced at me coolly. "Who wants to know? *You?*"

As if the idea amused him, merely.

It would be the most P.J. ever confided in me of the stink bomb episode.

There, in the station wagon, was our father waiting for us, or in any case waiting, sitting, behind the driver's wheel but facing outward, the door open. Legs crossed, his left calf showing a raw hairy dead-white stretch of flesh between sock and pants-leg. The glary bronze necktie was unloosened and his blue serge coat was unbuttoned. Dad was smoking, brooding; tallying up figures on a pocket calculator and jotting them down on a notepad. More than Mom's hair, his was threaded with gray like mica. It did not appear that he had been drinking—at least, no bottle was in sight—but much of the strain was gone from his face and his cheeks were splotched, jowly. When he saw us, the remains of his family, Mom trotting in the lead in high-heeled white pumps, bursting with news, and Patrick in casual clothes again, and me, skinny Ranger, tagging behind, Dad blinked several times like a man who has misplaced his glasses.

"Back so soon?"

SNOW AFTER EASTER

G od damn!—despite his best intentions, he was late.
He'd explained politely to Dr. Herring's assistant that he
would have to leave the lab promptly at 5 P.M., which
was the time at which, under the terms of his employment, he should
have left in any case, but the young professor, new from Harvard, kept
finding more and more work for him to do; always there was more
work for Patrick Mulvaney to do, sterilizing lab equipment, carefully
incubating cultures, wiping up spillage and even (this afternoon!)
sponge-mopping a section of the floor. And helping to record data of
such exacting minuteness, Patrick felt, as he often felt in the midst of
such experiments, which were essentially the counting of microbe cells
with a high-tech hemocytometer, as if he were an intruder in a world
that, if he descended into it for a split second, would devour him rapa-
ciously, reducing him to mere chemicals and a throbbing current called
"life." Gazing through the powerful microscope he had to look up frequently, to break the spell; to escape a vertiginous sensation that was
part dread, and part longing.

There, the *not-human*.

Marianne's bus was due at 5:05 P.M., in downtown Ithaca. Patrick
had told her he'd be a few minutes late, unavoidably. But now he was
very late, unable to get away from the university building until after
5:30 P.M., and it was another eight minutes running to the lot where
his Jeep was parked, and another fifteen minutes getting downtown,
on traffic-clogged one-way streets. He could have wept, he was so

angry! Angry at himself, mainly, for not being more assertive with Herring's assistant, who, he guessed, disliked him anyway, as a twenty-year-old undergraduate he couldn't quite intimidate.

Don't make enemies! Patrick counseled himself uneasily. *You will need all the help you can get.*

Since high school biology, Patrick's sophomore year, he'd known what he wanted to be: a research biologist. Not a teacher—he couldn't see himself in such a role, he hadn't the patience, or the sympathy and identification with others, younger versions of himself. God, no!—the vision filled him with dread. (If he didn't get a Ph.D., if he had to fall back upon, for instance, high school teaching.) Pursuing truth of an unemotional, essentially unhuman nature, in the silence and isolation of the laboratory, suited him; or would suit him once he was independent enough to oversee his own ambitious experiments. *He* would not be inconsiderate of his young assistants, especially hapless undergraduates, though he would not get to know them personally. He would evoke no emotion in them at all.

What plans Patrick had! Sometimes he could not sleep, for speculating. He wanted to study the evolutionary history of a single species in its natural habitat, over a period of millennia—the development of a simple animal. Or, he wanted to study the relations between selected species and their ecology, the process of Darwinian evolution. (As the son of a devout Christian, he was fascinated by the theory of "natural selection" in which all serious scientists seemed to believe, with a very nearly religious conviction. A mindless, purposeless, mechanical process, devoid of meaning, theological or otherwise!) Or, he wanted to study cellular life, the relations between types of microbes. (Dr. Herring's work, funded by the federal government and the National Science Foundation, was a massive project in the development of new antibiotics.) Or, he wanted to study a single body organ, for instance the eye, the remarkable design of the eye, in diverse species.

Well, more than Patrick Mulvaney could name, he wanted!

Sometimes he realized he was arguing with Corinne, and with Marianne, not consciously, not coherently, but with much emotion. Like a young, aggrieved boy, furious at such ignorance. *Don't you see how ridiculous it is to believe "man is made in the image of God"?* he wanted to shout into their startled faces. *How ridiculous people like you are, to believe?*

Corinne had been right: as soon as Patrick left home, aged eighteen, he ceased attending church, church of any denomination. He ceased being a Christian, nor did he so much as think in wonder or defiance or satisfaction *I have ceased being a Christian*. It simply fell from him, like a heavy overcoat he'd shrugged off, no longer needing its warmth or bulk to protect him.

In late April 1978, Patrick was completing his second year of college at Cornell and his grade-point average was just .06 shy of perfect. He was proud of being alone in Ithaca, in an off-campus rooming house in the heterogeneous neighborhood known as Collegetown, yet never, or almost never, lonely; proud of keeping the Mulvaneys at a distance—the obsessive thought of *family*. He loved them all yet had no wish to see them frequently nor even to speak with them often. (Corinne wanted him to call weekly, Patrick compromised by calling every two or three weeks, never at the same time; he dreaded falling into a pattern that would soon become an obligation, a duty, a ritual. Since he didn't have a phone in the two-room apartment he rented, and claimed not to have access to any phone, no one could call him.) He hadn't seen Marianne since the previous June when he'd gone (the only Mulvaney!) to her graduation at Salamanca High. He hadn't seen his parents and brother Judd for almost eight months: when he'd discovered, to his disgust, that, another time, Marianne hadn't been invited home for Christmas, he'd decided not to go home himself, calling home to deliver a chilly little message saying he had too much lab work to do. Corinne said, on the verge of tears, "Oh, Patrick—how can you?" and Patrick said stiffly, "Well, Mom—how can *you*?" And Corinne said, weakly, "If you mean about your sister it's just that your dad isn't ready to see her yet, I'm doing a lot of concentrated praying about it, Patrick, I want you to know, and Marianne does know, and I told her I'm sure your dad will be ready, he'll be strong enough, in a little while—maybe Easter. Patrick?" Patrick said curtly, "Good-bye, Mom. And Merry Christmas."

Hanging up quickly before Corinne could say a word more.

On the phone with Marianne for over an intense hour, Christmas Eve, Patrick meant to console her for the inexplicable cruelty with which their parents were treating her, but as usual with Marianne she'd ended up consoling him. "Patrick, don't worry about me, please! I'm happy. Of course I'm waiting for them to call me back but I'm not, you know, only just that—waiting. I have plenty to do. I'm living my life, and I'm happy."

Patrick ended up believing her. At least, while they were on the phone together.

Weird: meeting Ethel Hausmann, Corinne's cousin, with whom Marianne was living in Salamanca. "Aunt Ethel"—as she'd asked them, with a forced smile, to call her—was like a second, not-very-convincing mother in an amateur play whipped together by Corinne herself. As if she'd grabbed hold of clumsy Ethel Hausmann—*Now Ethel, you play me. Of course you can do it! Don't be bashful, for heaven's sake just try.* Aunt Ethel turned out to be a big-boned, stoic, kindly woman of about fifty-two with a creased face whose habitual expression was a sad, wan *hope*—a look that carried with it the full won't-be-surprised expectation of disappointment. Aunt Ethel smiled, too, and often, but it was a melancholy smile, such an effort you almost could hear creaking. "Why's she so sad all the time?" Patrick asked, and Marianne put a finger to her lips to shush him, "Oh but she isn't, Patrick, not this weekend."

Aunt Ethel had the Hausmann features Corinne called "lethal"— she was long-jawed, long-nosed and horsey-toothed, with pale blue protuberant eyes. (These eyes were uncannily like Corinne's, except the light had drained from them.) Where, for all her slapdash ways, Corinne was a good-looking woman, Aunt Ethel was frankly homely. She was slope-busted, stout, with a smell as of rusted nails. One of those whom life has passed by as if literally she'd been standing on the weed-edged sidewalk in front of her aluminum-sided "bungalow" in Salamanca and watched helplessly as it passed, a procession of fascinating strangers without the slightest interest in, or awareness of, her.

Not married, no child. Unlike her cousin Corinne, Aunt Ethel wasn't even a faithful churchgoer.

For all of her adult life, three full decades, and more, Aunt Ethel had worked for Dr. Briscoe, a local podiatrist—"He prefers not to be called a *foot* doctor." Just the way Aunt Ethel spoke, defensive yet proud, with a wistful undercurrent of hurt, Patrick understood that the woman was in love with Briscoe, whoever he was.

"You mustn't laugh at Aunt Ethel," Marianne told Patrick when they were alone. "She's a good, generous woman, just like Mom said. She let me keep Muffin!"

"That *is* good of her," Patrick said neutrally.

Near as he could gather from his three days, two nights as a not-very-comfortable houseguest of Aunt Ethel's, all she really provided for Marianne was a dreary little room at the rear of her dreary little house that smelled (oh why did he have this notion?—yet it was un-shakable) of rusted nails. In exchange, Marianne was an uncomplaining, bright and tireless and reliable servant.

Or, maybe, slave?

"Oh Patrick, *no*." Marianne's eyes brimmed with tears when Patrick made this suggestion, Pinch-style, rather mean and sly out of the corner of his mouth.

Ethel Hausmann had spoken vaguely of "hoping to assist" with Marianne's college expenses but in the end, apparently, near as Patrick could gather, nothing came of it. (Nor could the Mulvaneys help, much: by summer 1977, Mulvaney Roofing was in what Corinne nervously called a "temporary slough" and Michael Sr. was hoping to sell five or ten acres of farmland "if he can get a decent price." By fall 1977, Red, Prince, and Molly-O had all been sold.) Now Marianne worked part-time, was a part-time student at Kilburn State College, in a small rural town near the Pennsylvania border, two hundred miles south and west of Ithaca. Patrick had intended to drive down to see her but always he'd been busy, distracted by work of his own. On the phone he chided Marianne, "You deserve better than Kilburn State, for God's sake," as if it were Marianne's fault she'd ended up there and not, for instance, at glamorous Cornell. Marianne insisted she was happy at Kilburn, she'd made friends and liked all her professors and believed they liked her. And please remember that her high school grades hadn't been spectacular. At Kilburn, Marianne was enrolled in a history-education program, and lived in a co-op, miles from campus, to economize on expenses. When they spoke on the phone, Patrick could hear energetic voices in the background, a dog barking, a clatter of kitchen noise, radio music. Often he had to ask Marianne to speak louder, he couldn't hear. "It sounds like a railway station," he complained.

What he meant was it sounded like a big noisy happy family.

By the time Patrick drove to the bus station, parked his Jeep and rushed into the Trailways waiting room it was almost 6 P.M. As in one of his nightmares, he'd arrived so late!—and he'd been thinking uneasily of Marianne all day, in fact for days, since they'd made arrangements the week before. What would she think, that Patrick had forgotten her after all? He'd told her not to take a taxi, not to spend the money, he wanted to pick her up, he'd be there.

Entering the waiting room, Patrick almost collided with passengers on their way out. An announcer's nasal voice intoned *Albany! White Plains! New York City!* Where was Marianne? He didn't see her. A girl turned, pretty, snub-nosed—not his sister. Another girl, a young woman carrying a baby. Their eyes lighted upon him, friendly and curious. But Patrick was too distracted to take much notice. He stood in the center of the crowded waiting room, peering about. He was breathless, excited, irritable; he imagined (but was it only imagination?) his hands, even his hair stank of the lab. (He had a habit of running his fingers swiftly through his hair sometimes as he worked.) His glasses steamed faintly. The peripheral vision in his left eye was weak, and weaker still when he was exhausted or rattled, so he turned unconsciously to his left, turning his entire body, frowning— where was Marianne? Hadn't she come to Ithaca, after all?

The thought that she might not have come, and he'd be alone that evening, filled Patrick with dismay.

Or—something had happened to her? In Kilburn, or on the bus, or here in Ithaca? *He* was the one who'd arrived almost an hour late.

The interior of the Trailways bus depot in downtown Ithaca was a shabby slipping-down sort of place, connected with a diner; there was a prevailing odor of cigarette smoke, griddle-grease, wet wool (it had been a chill, rain-darkened April day, rife with puddles) and inadequately washed human bodies. An odor of the left-behind, the losers of America: everyone who could afford it traveled by air now. Or, poor even as Patrick Mulvaney, drove his own car. Passengers for the now-boarding bus shuffled out of the depot and only a few parties remained. An elderly black man muttering to himself, trying to get a locker open; a very pale teenaged boy, with short, spiky hair and spindly limbs, nodding off against a rear wall; two light-skinned black girls, giggling and whispering together; a middle-aged woman with her heavyset, apparently retarded son, Patrick's age; a sailor, duffel bag on his lap, smoking, and casting furtive glances at the giggling girls—or was it at the sleeping boy beyond, who looked about twelve years old? A disheveled man smelling of burnt orange peels approached Patrick with—what?—a ballpoint pen to sell—but canny Patrick turned away and pushed through the doors to the outside. There were benches here, and a few stragglers sitting on them, but no Marianne.

He realized how much he wanted to see her, now she wasn't in sight.

He realized how much he was depending on this visit of hers, he who had so few friends—well, no friends at all, exactly.

Prowling the bus-boarding area, circling the depot to check all the buses in sight. Thinking just possibly he'd gotten the time wrong and Marianne was only now due, 6 P.M.?—but she wasn't here, wasn't anywhere. He stared grimly as a northbound bus, up from Binghamton en route to Syracuse, discharged passengers. All strangers. The Erie, Pennsylvania bus, with its Kilburn connection, had obviously come and gone an hour ago. Patrick saw an Ithaca patrolman talking with a security guard and approached them to ask if they'd seen Marianne but at the last moment he passed on by, he was too confused. He could not think how to describe his sister! His mind had gone blank and his last clear memory of her was of the radiantly smiling cheerleader in the maroon jumper and long-sleeved perfectly starched white cotton blouse, eyes shining, curly-brown hair bouncing as in an advertisement for American happiness itself. "Button" Mulvaney. Immortalized on Mom's bulletin board.

Except: hadn't those snapshots been discreetly removed, hidden away or even destroyed. Two years ago.

Patrick pushed through the swinging doors into the waiting room another time and to the ticket counter. Asked the severely frowning middle-aged woman behind the counter if she'd happened to see a girl come into the waiting room, after the 5:05 P.M., bus from Erie? A girl about nineteen? The woman said no, not that she recalled, with a shrug of one shoulder to indicate she wasn't trying very hard to recall, Patrick's question was naive. "Well, she'd look younger, I guess," Patrick said, faltering. "My sister. But she doesn't look much like me, she's sort of—" Again his mind went blank. It was like a blackboard carelessly erased, by hand. The ticket-counter woman shook her head, whether meaning "no" or in bemused pity of Patrick who was visibly perspiring, glasses sliding down his nose.

It was 6:07 P.M. And then it was 6:12 P.M. Patrick had Marianne's number to call at the Green Isle Co-op, Kilburn, New York but he dreaded making the call, as always there would be happy frantic mealtime-sounding noises, and whoever would answer, male or female he couldn't always determine, would yell *Mari-anne! Hey Mari-anne! Who's seen Mari-anne! Telephone for Mari-anne!* and he'd shut his eyes tight bitterly resenting this stranger who so familiarly called his sister's name; resisting the impulse to imagine her life there amid young and presumably attractive, idealistic men and women like herself, in the

Co-op's residence which Marianne had described to Patrick as a big old ramshackle inn with several greenhouses, two acres of good rich soil where they grew their own vegetables, communally-owned cars and a pickup truck. The residence, in "condemned condition," had been bought by Kilburn College, then leased to the Co-op for a token payment, one hundred dollars yearly; the Co-op members had repaired it, furnished it, made it "like home." No, Patrick didn't want to call the Green Isle Co-op just now.

It was 6:20 P.M. Patrick circled the waiting room, asked a woman if she'd go into the women's rest room to check if his sister was inside but of course she was not. His lips moved silently. *Marianne. Marianne!* He should have sought out Zachary Lundt, long ago, and killed him. In his fantasy, a smart-boy A-student fantasy, he'd force his sister's rapist to swallow poison—Lysol: flaming agony, mouth, esophagus, stomach, liver. It would look like suicide! And not detectable, as the hydrogen sulfide stink bomb, the proudest project of Patrick Mulvaney's high school career, had not been detected, so far as he knew. (No, Patrick hadn't made any inquiries about who the prankster might be. That was what guilty parties always did: couldn't resist. But Patrick, who was smarter than smart, could resist, for all his life. Just watch!) Weak, breathless, he leaned against the badly scratched wall of lockers, too shaky to continue pacing yet not wanting to sit down amid the shabby, torn plastic seats and relinquish his advantage which was the advantage of height. But his left eye, which always betrayed him, was dimming with fatigue. The day had begun so long ago, in a rainy, snow-gritty twilight before dawn, in dreams in which Marianne and his Biology of Organisms lab were mixed together—he could scarcely remember. Awake before dawn in his third-floor room in the stucco house on Cook Street, waking beneath the eaves of his dormer bedroom, as at High Point Farm, his quick-pulsing nerved-up body waking him in lieu of an alarm. Sometimes in this strange place in Ithaca hundreds of miles from home he heard in his sleep a rooster crowing, and another rooster crowing in reply. Now it was spring, the early-morning cries of red-winged blackbirds, cardinals. And *Wake up kiddos! Wake-up time kiddos!* and Mom's friendly whistle. Smelled frying bacon, for always Mom insisted upon good, solid, hot breakfasts, no going with just cereal dumped in a bowl, breakfast was the most important meal of the day Mom and Dad both insisted. He'd hear the dogs' toenails excitedly clicking on the kitchen floor as quickly he descended the stairs, Mom whistling to Feathers who trilled and warbled in return. And that damned radio station, out of Yewville, the announcer Mom swore by, her favorite. And Marianne would be downstairs already in the kitchen helping Mom get breakfast on the table, the two of them talking and laughing together, almost if he shut his eyes very tight he could see her: his lost sister.

The man in the waiting room Patrick had assumed was a sailor obviously wasn't—he wore a navy-blue nautical-looking jacket, and biker's boots, and his dark hair grew long and greasy onto his neck. He was about thirty, unshaven, with quick-darting eyes and a damp mouth. As Patrick watched, the man rose stealthily, not straightening to his full height, carried the duffel bag with him and went to sit two seats from the oblivious sleeping boy.

But the boy wasn't a boy!—Patrick saw, to his astonishment, that this was Marianne, his sister—her hair cut cruelly short, face waxy-pale and mouth slack, so without expression, in the daze of sleep, he hadn't recognized her. She looked so young, so—childlike. She wore a thin corduroy jacket, unbuttoned, and slacks with a stretch-band waist, and a flimsy white cotton T-shirt stamped in green GREEN ISLE CO-OP; her left breast, the size and apparent hardness of a green pear, was sharply outlined by the ribbed white fabric. On her feet, badly worn sneakers and no socks. On the seat beside her was a grimy canvas bag, also stamped in green GREEN ISLE CO-OP, stuffed with items. Patrick saw to his disgust the man in the nautical jacket staring at his sister and in that instant saw her through the man's hungry eyes—a girl-boy, sexually tantalizing because sexually ambiguous, vulnerable, unprotected, provocative.

"Marianne!"

Marianne's bluish-bruised eyelids flew open, as if she hadn't been fully asleep.

Pinch-style Patrick scolded, "What the hell!—I've been waiting around this dump for you, for an hour! *What are you doing asleep?*"

Cook Street, in heterogeneous Collegetown, near an edge of the gigantic Cornell campus, was one of Ithaca's numerous steep-banked streets: Patrick estimated it at about seventy degrees. His two-room apartment at 114 Cook was at the top of a moldering stucco house long ago partitioned into "apartments" for students, mainly foreign graduate students. Patrick had moved there the previous summer, from an even shabbier place on College Avenue. His fellow tenants were all young men, from India, China, Pakistan, studying science or engineering; they were as fanatic as he about work and quiet, shyly friendly with him but not inquisitive—not very real to Patrick as, he guessed, he wasn't very real to them. Patrick might have lived more conveniently in a residence hall on campus, within closer walking distance of his classes, but he valued privacy, relative isolation. And he couldn't tolerate his fellow undergraduates' juvenile behavior, noise at all hours, binge-drinking, vomiting and brawling, ceaseless rock music.

His problem was, and would always be *I hate my own kind.*

The ugly scrawls in red Magic Marker on the lavatory walls, inside the toilet stalls, at Mt. Ephraim High School. Patrick Mulvaney, trembling with rage and humiliation, had tried to rub them off with his bare hands.

MM: MARYANN MULVANY. MMMMM SUCKS COCK.

At Cornell, no one knew the name MULVANEY. Twenty thousand students. When Patrick had driven through campus, Corinne beside him in the station wagon loaded with his things, he'd been dazed and euphoric contemplating *size, distance, anonymity* while Corinne wrung her hands in her lap fretting like any mom *But you'll be lost here, oh Patrick you'll be lost here, no one will know who you are!*

At the rooming house on Cook Street, Patrick parked his Jeep at the curb. Expertly turned the wheels inward, put on the emergency brake. Marianne who had been exclaiming happily over the Cornell campus (Patrick had driven her through the main campus, along elegant East Avenue and down the long hill to Central Avenue and back then to Collegetown, wanting her to see the enormous sloping hill behind the dignified old buildings, windswept, beautiful even at twilight in drizzle) stared up at the smudged stucco house that was so ugly, so melancholy and *squat*—and seemed to be at a loss for words.

Patrick laughed. "Not quite the 'purple' house, is it?"

Marianne murmured it was certainly a wonderful location, only a few blocks from campus.

Inside, they climbed the stairs to the third floor. Patrick carried Marianne's bulky Green Isle bag over his shoulder. A cloying, oily odor of cooking wafted upward from the kitchen at the downstairs rear. There was a pervasive smell of mildew, mice, drains, Airwick. Patrick hoped that one or another of the other residents might be around so that he could introduce Marianne, but all doors were shut. *My life here. My life now. I'm no Mulvaney, see?—I could be anyone. Citizen of any country.* Since their meeting, and their embrace, in the bus depot, Patrick had been telling Marianne, almost boasting, how much he liked Cornell. His courses, his professors, his work. He'd been singled out for praise frequently enough, the vast impersonality of the campus, which so upset other undergraduates, didn't faze him. In fact, it suited him. After the small-town claustrophobia of Mt. Ephraim—yes, it suited him. Here he worked, worked. He'd become infatuated with his work because it was meaningful, it was important, *real*. A course called Biology of Organisms—so exciting! He'd found a home you could say. A spiritual place. The more he concentrated on his work the more guaranteed his reward. Of course, he didn't work for a "reward"—exactly. But there was, he believed, a direct correlation. As there isn't always, in life. Between what you do and what happens to you. What you deserve and what you get.

Seeing Marianne's quizzical smile, Patrick quickly added that he didn't always work, of course. He had a few friends, he'd gone out with a few girls. No one special, but—he didn't always work. Sometimes when he got restless he went running—across Cascadilla Creek and down Central Avenue below the hill and over to Fall Creek, to the gorge (he would show her the gorge tomorrow: the famous suspension bridge from which suicidal students threw themselves) and across and around Lake Beebe and back to Cook Street—how many miles, he didn't know. He ran in a kind of trance, his mind stilled. In rapid motion, his body seemed to catch up with his metabolism, he felt right. And he didn't mind bad weather—"Reminds me of home." Other nights he'd go downtown, to State Street, where there was a cheap movie house, old and crummy and smelling of rancid popcorn, he'd see whatever was playing, the last show ended after midnight and he'd return home and work for maybe another hour or two—by the time he hiked up from State Street, the movie would have faded from his consciousness. He loved how *unreal* movies were, like certain people.

Marianne looked at him oddly. "People?" They were in Patrick's apartment now, switching on lights. "But, Patrick," Marianne said, "people are *real*."

"That's what I said," Patrick protested, with brotherly impatience, "—movies aren't *real*, the way people are *real*. You know—" setting Marianne's bag on the table, where a vase of fresh-cut flowers had been placed for Marianne's arrival, "—*too real*. Take themselves too seriously."

He spoke with a boyish vehemence Marianne didn't seem to understand. But he was happy, couldn't have been happier. What

vast relief *Marianne was there with him, and safe.* And would be returning to Kilburn the following afternoon.

To prepare for Marianne's visit, Patrick had hauled the residence
vacuum cleaner up two flights of stairs and thoroughly vacuumed
both his rooms. He'd dusted windowsills, lampshades, blinds.
Whistling, he'd mopped the floors. He'd been in a good mood:
mildly apprehensive but not anxious. *Oh Patrick I can't wait, I miss
you so! But are you sure you have time for me?* He'd washed his several
old-fashioned loose-fitting windows not only inside, top to bottom,
but outside, as well as he could manage with Windex and paper
towels, leaning out backward from the sill. (Told himself he was a
roofer's son: accustomed to climbing on roofs, helping out Dad,
he'd grown up unafraid of heights.) He'd scrubbed his miniature
kitchen sink with steel wool and vacuumed, cleaned, scrubbed the
third-floor bathroom Marianne would have to use, which Patrick
shared with two other residents. (In theory, this bathroom was kept
clean by the custodian, who lived on the ground floor; in fact, it was
often dirty, unspeakably dirty, and Patrick didn't intend for his sister
to see it in such a state.) He'd left his windows open a few inches to
air out the rooms. *Are you sure you have time for me Patrick, I know you
work so hard. But I'd love to see you!* He'd repositioned some of the
artworks he'd taped to his walls, and added more: Xerox color re-
productions of stained cell slides, many times magnified, bold primary colors and dreamy melting hallucinatory shapes, as striking, to
Patrick's eye, as anything painted by Cézanne, Matisse, Picasso. Yet
they were only lab slides, of cellular life as common as the grains of
sand of all the oceans of the world.

The first time he'd looked through a microscope, in seventh
grade, he'd been shocked, and perplexed. *So beautiful, it almost hurts.*

Of course, he knew *beauty* doesn't exist. He hadn't known then
but he knew now. *Beauty* is a matter of perspective, subjectivity.
Cultural prejudice. You require a human eye, a human brain, a human vocabulary. In nature, there's nothing.

Still, *beauty* gives comfort. Who knows why?

Maybe Patrick Mulvaney would discover the answer, some day.

He'd removed from his bed the handmade rag quilt, red white
and blue squares elaborately sewn together, of contrasting fabrics
(cotton, denim, velvet, taffeta, corduroy, muslin) Corinne had given
him from home; folded it and hid it away in his closet. Because he

couldn't be sure that their mother had given Marianne anything quite so nice to take with her to Salamanca.

On Dryden Road, at a florist's, he'd bought a dozen fresh-cut flowers. Yellow daffodils he hoped wouldn't remind Marianne too much of High Point Farm where they'd grown in wild profusion, multiplying each spring, bulbs planted by Corinne along the driveway, in the front lawn, out near the road. And hyacinth too Corinne had grown, cutting sprigs to bring into the house, the sweet smell, so sweet. And jonquils with their papery petals. In a glass vase Patrick set these flowers on his single table, to greet Marianne.

So she'd exclaim, as soon as she entered the room, *Oh Patrick how nice*. Wiping lightly at her eyes.

He dreaded her crying. He was not going to cry, himself.

Never cried. Couldn't remember the last time. When Prince had trampled him, practically knocked out his eye? God damn making him a freak for life.

Still, no one's fault. In nature, no one's to blame.

"Snow after Easter—it doesn't seem fair, does it?"

Marianne was stirring a rich dark minestrone soup in a battered pan on Patrick's hot plate, as Patrick set the table for their meal; she peered out the window where, in the streetlight below, damp snowflakes swirled like agitated moths. She hadn't sounded complaining, only wistful. Patrick said, incensed, "I don't much notice weather now. That's one thing I'm freed from, now I'm not a farm kid."

Farm kid just slightly mocking. For of course the Mulvaneys of High Point Farm had never been only just *farmers*.

Marianne said, "I'll never change, I'm sure. Staring up at the sky, trying to figure what's coming."

Patrick was briskly laying out plates on the table, a folding table in the center of the book-cluttered room that was his study: the plates, slightly chipped, were cobalt-blue stoneware of some well-known American stock, pressed upon him by Corinne when he'd moved to Ithaca. *But you have to eat off something, why not something nice?* The thick-plied yellow cloth napkins were from home too, and the stainless steel cutlery with the chunky carved-bone handles. Marianne had noticed, smiled, murmured something Patrick hadn't heard. Patrick was saying, in the high-toned, nasal, insufferable mode of a brother scoring points against a sister who'll always be younger than he, "But why should you *care*? We're free of all that. If there's a drought, or so much rain the seeds rot in the soil. If there's an infestation of tent caterpillars in the orchard, or Japanese beetles. We don't have to be superstitious, like primitive people. God, what a relief, to live in a place like this, where I'm not connected, I'm not responsible, I can walk away without a backward glance. What a relief, not to have to care who you *are*."

Marianne said hesitantly, "But, Patrick, you must care—?"

"What? Why?"

"Who you *are*? You must care."

Patrick said impatiently, "I said *where you are*. It's a relief not to have to care *where you are*. All that pride we had, at home, and anxiety. Keeping up some kind of—I don't know—model family life. Not that we were aware of it, even Dad and Mom. Especially Dad and Mom. As soon as I left I discovered how big the world is, you only have to reposition yourself in it. *Where* is just temporary, you'll be moving on."

Making little speeches, to his perplexed sister. He supposed he was overstating the case for her sake. *Look: you aren't missing much. Do I miss them?*

Supposed that Marianne's presence in these cramped quarters where he was accustomed to being blissfully alone, in truth rarely thinking of *back home*, of *them*, of *it*, was making him say extravagant asinine things he didn't exactly mean.

Marianne, however, took every statement of Patrick's seriously. He remembered that from the past: years, years, years of playing elder smarter more cynical brother to his adoring, unquestioning sister. It was flattering, but occasionally annoying. Provoking anger, you could not predict when, like the hot pounding anger he'd felt in the bus depot, seeing his sister, *his own sister he loved*, through the eyes of a sexual predator. Marianne was saying slowly, "I suppose I'm different. More literal. Every place I *am*, like, now, the Co-op, and Kilburn—I can't think it's temporary. Even if I left, it would still be there. The place, and the people."

Patrick let the subject pass. He had yet to inquire much about the Green Isle Co-op apart from knowing that it provided off-campus room and board for Marianne at Kilburn State and that, by working there, she could defray sixty percent of her college costs. Just possibly he resented his sister's tender tone in speaking of it and of the companions she'd known only the previous September but clearly liked, very much. Brothers and sisters they were to her, apparently. Patrick knew the names, *Abelove, Birk, Felice-Marie, Val, Gilb* or was it *Gelb*. A mixed-breed spaniel named *Teardrop*.

This information seemed to him more than sufficient.

Patrick had wanted to take Marianne out to dinner that evening, to a Chinese restaurant on State Street, but she'd insisted she would make their meals while she was here. She'd seemed so emphatic over the phone, he'd given in—"Though it's a lot of trouble for you, to bring food on the bus. Couldn't we buy it here?"

"Oh Patrick, *no*."

Sounding almost hurt. In just Corinne's tone, if one or another of her children hadn't been hungry for a meal, or hadn't wanted to take time to sit down at the table and eat with the family.

So Marianne had brought with her on the Trailways bus, in the canvas bag, two quarts of a tomato-based soup stock, raw vegetables, and macaroni; two loaves of bread she'd baked herself, zucchini-walnut and nine-grain whole wheat; a jar of Green Isle raspberry jam; even, in a plastic bag, salad greens and vegetables. Preparing the meal in Patrick's alcove kitchen (no stove, but a double-burner hot plate, a squat little Pullman refrigerator on the floor, a small aluminum sink, a single counter and cupboard) she'd chattered to him, glowing with pleasure and purpose. Almost, she was Button Mulvaney. If Patrick didn't stare at her.

In the bus depot, God he'd been shocked! The sight of her going through him like a sharp blade.

Marianne?—was it possible?

In the room here when she'd removed her jacket. He'd swallowed hard, how thin she was. Upper arms no larger than his wrists. Collarbone jutting and breasts tiny as a twelve-year-old's and anyone who would gaze upon such a child with lust was sick, depraved, repellent. The spiky hair, brutally shorn at the back and sides. Faint blue veins at her temples and eyes threaded with red as if she'd gone without sleep recently. Or had been crying.

Equally disturbing, the odd clothes. Discount-store clothes. Like no clothes worn by Cornell students, even those eager to define themselves as "characters," "freaks." The flimsy white cotton T-shirt with the thin, loose straps and, in green stamped letters

GREEN ISLE CO-OP

on the front. Sarcastically Patrick asked, "Are you in disguise, Marianne?—as what?" He'd meant to be funny but Marianne only stared at him, confused. She'd touched her hair nervously as if trying to smooth it down. It occurred to him that she didn't know what she looked like.

Patrick had read about rape victims, he'd done research in his methodical Pinch-style, in the Cornell psych library. *It is common for a rape victim, female or male, to avoid mirrors and direct confrontation with all images of the "self." As if, where there had been a person, there is now no one.*

Patrick offered to help Marianne prepare supper but she said she didn't need help. The minestrone was her own recipe, never the same twice. Patrick murmured he wasn't used to being waited on any longer, it made him uneasy, and something in his voice tipped off Marianne, who laughed, teasing, asking who'd been cooking for him lately? a girl? and Patrick blushed and said no one.

Marianne smiled. "No?"

It was true in a way. No one had cooked for Patrick here, in his own kitchen.

They sat down to eat. Marianne's minestrone was the most delicious soup Patrick had ever tasted: steaming-hot, in stoneware bowls, a thick broth seasoned with fresh basil and oregano, containing chunks of celery, tomato, carrots, red onion, beans, chickpeas and macaroni. The nine-grain whole wheat bread was crumbly, chewy, delicious, too. And a green salad with red leaf lettuce and endive, cucumber, pepper, alfalfa sprouts, a vinegar-and-oil dressing flavored with dill. Patrick was surprised at his appetite, his hunger. Usually he prepared for himself quick meals out of cans, dumped in a pan or stir-fried in a skillet. Sat at his desk and worked as he ate, hardly tasting his food, washing it down with numerous glasses of fruit juice. Lean-limbed, lanky, with a flat stomach, Patrick had always had nearly the appetite of his heftier brother Mike but no one had seemed to notice. He ate, ate, ate and retained only ropey muscle on his bones. Marianne had always been slender, small-boned; she'd eaten sparingly, as she ate now, taking pleasure in Patrick's appetite and his reactions to her meal—"Wow. Terrific. This is really good."

Marianne blushed: like Corinne, she was uneasy receiving praise.

Saying, disparagingly, "—I think I put too much oregano in the soup. If it's overdone—"

"Hell, no," Patrick said severely, "—it's perfect."

Marianne smiled, laughed nervously. In the overhead light her eyes were enormous and the sockets deeply shadowed.

Patrick reiterated how happy he was at Cornell, how rarely he was lonely. Marianne's wistful smile seemed to inquire *But don't you miss me?*—he took no notice. He was feeling rather boastful, a quiet boy running at the mouth, in the way of stiff shy vain young men who imagine themselves brilliant, and are so perceived by others. He spoke warmly if vaguely of his fellow tenants in the house, foreign students so much more serious than most American students. Civilization, for them, was a very different matter than it was for Americans, Patrick believed. We tend to take it for granted, it's just *there*. We tend to think it's *for us*, a gift. But others, from the East especially, seem to know something else. "Almost, when you talk with them," Patrick said earnestly, "you get the impression they're shielding us—I mean, a kid like me. Typical spoiled American kid like me."

"Oh, Patrick," Marianne laughed, with sisterly reproach, "—you're hardly typical."

Patrick said loftily, "I don't want to be. But I see the world through the prism of my culture, not through 'objective' eyes."

"But why would anyone else be more 'objective'? I don't understand."

"Because their civilizations are older, more fatalistic. It's like contingency in evolutionary theory—sheer chance. There seems to be design, in fact it's ingenious design, no mere human brain could have devised it, there seems to be 'intelligence' manifested—but it's the accidental, mechanical accumulation of 'natural selection' over a period of millions of years. No God, only just nature. And accident." Patrick spoke dogmatically, in the tone of Dr. Herring in the lecture hall. Marianne was sitting meekly hunched at the table, bone-sharp elbows on the table, eyes downcast and forehead creased. She'd virtually stopped eating.

Shyly she said, "My friend Abelove—that's his last name, he's called by his last name—he's executive director of the Co-op—he says that evolution and creation can be reconciled. Evolution through nature and creation through—"

"God?—don't be silly," Patrick said, snorting in derision.

"—I'm not sure how to explain it—"

"I'm sure you aren't!"

"It's just that there are different ways of perceiving the same thing," Marianne said uncertainly. "I mean—aren't there?"

"There are scientifically demonstrable ways, and there are superstitious, self-deluding ways," Patrick said curtly. "You can choose one or the other but not both."

Marianne stood from the table, shakily. Patrick thought she was going to walk away but instead she went to slice more bread, he'd eaten all the slices she'd laid out.

When Marianne returned to the table, Patrick made an effort to speak more moderately. Really, he wasn't a bully, so hotheaded!— he'd be ashamed of himself afterward. It was *Pinch-instinct*, screwing up his face like a spoiled brat. There were excellent reasons why people like his sister—and his mother, and her mother—in fact, most of humanity—believed what they believed, in the face of reason itself: they *believed* because, like children, they were terrified of the dark. Mistaking the luminosity of an inhuman and implacable Truth for mere dark.

In high school, Patrick had read Charles Darwin's great works *The Origin of Species, The Voyage of the Beagle.* James Watson's *Double Helix* which his biology teacher had given him, as an acknowledgment of Patrick's special status. Darwin the visionary, Watson and Crick the careerists. Well, science was both, wasn't it?—*he*, Patrick Mulvaney, didn't intend to separate the two.

Marianne was an avid listener as Patrick spoke of his courses, his professors, his work; she didn't inquire into his grades, but Patrick informed her—all A's, through three semesters of five three-credit courses each, except for goddamned organic chemistry where he'd managed only an A-, in a pack of premed majors some of whom were rumored to have cheated on the final—well, not only on the final.

But Patrick, flush-faced, indignant, didn't want to go into *that.*

The cheating, dishonesty, cynicism, beer-drinking drug-taking sexual promiscuity of his undergraduate classmates—not all, but a sizable percentage—no, Patrick didn't want to go into *that.*

Instead he told Marianne of his hopes for a career: after his B.A. he would enter a Ph.D. program, possibly here at Cornell where he could work with Maynard Herring, one of the most distinguished of living microbiologists (who'd already singled out Patrick Mulvaney as bright, promising); he would win a fellowship, or if not a fellowship a teaching assistantship; he would complete his Ph.D. in three years—"If all goes as planned." Earnestly Patrick spoke of certain mysteries of science that intrigued him: why viruses can't replicate themselves, for instance, but have to insert their genetic information into a host and force the host to reproduce the virus; how can so many totally disparate components—microorganisms, chemicals, atoms—constitute an individual human being, with a unified personality? And what is "personality," given such a galaxy of components? Why have so many plant and animal species become extinct?—more than ninety percent of all species that have ever lived. And what does it mean in evolutionary terms that the maternal egg is so much more influential in reproduction than the paternal, thousands of times larger than the paternal, and containing all the cellular mitochondria? And how did such an extraordinary organ as the eye evolve, in so many disparate species of creatures, through millions of years, out of sheer blind undifferentiated matter?

Marianne interrupted to ask, with sisterly solicitude, "Your eye, Patrick—is it all right?"

Patrick stared at her. "My eye? What?"

"Your—you know," she said, faltering. "Your injured eye."

Patrick scowled, shoving his glasses against the bridge of his nose. He was huffy, indignant. "We're not discussing my ridiculous eye," he said, "—we're discussing the phenomenon of *eye*. It's so amazing. How a mechanism so intricate and ingenious evolved out of blind matter. Who could have imagined an *eye*, *eyesight*, in the dark?"

Marianne had risen unobtrusively to clear the table. She shook her head, with a wan smile. "Someone with an ingenious imagination," she said softly.

"Hmmm! Very funny, Marianne."

Vehemently Patrick continued to speak, not knowing what he said or why, at this moment, he was driven to say it; the words long pent-up, the solitude of his life erupting suddenly, in a passion he hadn't known he possessed. Marianne moved quietly and surely clearing the table, rinsing the dishes, all the while listening to Patrick, murmuring words of assent or surprise, occasionally wincing as if his sharp words hurt. Somehow Patrick had swerved from the subject of science's great mysteries to humankind's collective failure. These were thoughts he'd had numerous times, in high school even, but he'd never spoken of them to another person before. "Look, it's so damned depressing! Why after all this time, all that science has discovered, the human race is so *ignorant*. So *superstitious* and *cruel*. Consider: the Nazis murdered sixteen million men, women, and children; Stalin murdered twenty million; even more millions—*more!*—were victims of Chinese Communist 'ideology.' Just in the twentieth century alone. Our civilized century. That's the mystery, not nature—why human beings are so vile."

Marianne had come to stand staring at Patrick, her eyes almost frightened. "Patrick, you sound so angry."

"Shouldn't I be? Why aren't *you*?"

Patrick had risen from the table, trembling. He'd had no idea he was so angry, a pulse beating in his left eye, furiously.

Quickly, without a word, Marianne came to him. Gripped his arms and on her toes leaned against him, pressing her cool, thin cheek against his. Not quite an embrace but it was comforting, consoling.

I love you. We love each other. That's enough.

He wanted to believe her, she insisted she was happy.

She *was* happy, her soul shining in her deep-socketed eyes.

Last time Patrick had spoken with his mother on the phone, mentioning Marianne's upcoming visit to Ithaca, Corinne said evasively, guiltily, *Oh give Marianne our love! She's doing very well at that little college, she'll make a wonderful teacher I'm sure. Judd and I are going to drive down some weekend soon.* A pause and a choked-pleading voice, *Hon, I wouldn't interfere with your sister if I were you* and Patrick said coolly, *Yes, but you aren't me, Mom. And I'm not you.*

What secrets lay between them, Mom and Button?—mother and daughter?

Just possibly, none.

MMMMM SUCKS COCK! That time, at the start of gym class, at the high school, Patrick swung around the row of lockers and saw a friend of his hastily rubbing something off the corrugated front of Patrick's locker with the flat of his hand, a look of distaste on his friend's face and Patrick walked by pretending he'd seen nothing. Afterward unable to face the friend. Could not recall whether, from that day until graduation, he'd ever spoken to him again.

Would he die for Marianne, yes he believed he would.

Yet: had he ever confronted Zachary Lundt, or any of the pack of guys who were Zachary's friends and who, it was rumored, would "stand up for Zach" if the police investigated?—no, he had not.

That wasn't Patrick's way. That wasn't Pinch's way.

Aloof and furious and deeply unspeakably hurt.

Nor had he confronted his father, with whom, since February 1976, he'd scarcely spoken. *You go your way and I go mine.* His father seemed to him mad: it was pointless to talk to him, still less argue. He'd banished Marianne from the household and from his life so that he could banish her from his thoughts. It was simple as that, and Patrick understood. He understood, but couldn't forgive. To Corinne he said *It's cruel, it's ridiculous, I hate him, how can you?* and Corinne said angrily, *You don't hate your father, Patrick!—you know that. As for Mari-anne, she's happy and she's adjusted, her faith sustains her just as it sustains me. Don't interfere!*

But Pinch would interfere, if only at a distance.

He wanted to believe her, she insisted she was happy.

Didn't want to sit staring at her, trying to figure out what was her life now.

Life after high school: cheerleader, prom princess.

He didn't want to interrogate her yet had to ask: how had her first semester at Kilburn gone?—and when, another time, she told him with girlish enthusiasm, plucking at her shorn hair, how happy she was at the college, how much she'd been learning in her classes, especially a course in American history, focussing upon the Aboli-tionist movement, readings in Thoreau, Emerson, Frederick Doug-lass, Patrick interrupted to ask, "But, Marianne, how did you *do*? I mean—your grades?"

Crude blunt Pinch.

Marianne had been smiling and now her smile faltered. Her bruised-looking eyelids began to flutter, so like Corinne's. Is there a gene for such related mannerisms, or are they purely learned, condi-tioned? She said, quietly, so quietly Patrick almost couldn't hear, "I—didn't exactly complete two of the courses. I had to take incompletes."

"Why?"

"Well—" Marianne squirmed, pulling at her spiky hair. "Things sort of came up. Suddenly."

"What kind of things?"

"An emergency at the Co-op, just after Thanksgiving. Aviva who was assistant store manager got sick—"

"*Store?* What store?"

"Oh Patrick, I must have told you—didn't I? In Kilburn, in town, we have a Green Isle outlet. We sell preserves, fresh produce in the summer, baked goods—my zucchini-walnut bread is one of the favorites. I—"

"And you work in this *store*? How many hours a week?"

Marianne dipped her head, avoiding Patrick's interrogative gaze. "We don't think in terms of hours—exactly," she said. She was sitting on Patrick's sofa (not an item from home, part of the dull spare slightly shabby furnishings of the apartment) while Patrick sat facing her, in a rather overbearing position, on his desk chair, his right ankle balanced on his left knee in a posture both relaxed and aggressive.

Thinking Pinch-style *I have a right to ask, who else will ask if I don't?*

"What terms do you think in, then?"

"The Green Isle Co-op isn't a—formally run organization, like a business. It's more like a—well, a family. People helping each other out. 'From each what he or she can give; to each, as he or she requires.' "

"Who said that? P. T. Barnum?"

"Oh Patrick, *no*." Dutifully Marianne laughed at Patrick's adolescent sarcasm, as a sister must. For an instant they were twelve and thirteen years old, and Pinch was being dourly witty at the supper table. "It's the Co-op motto, it's Abelove's, derived from some nineteenth-century philosopher I think."

"Karl Marx."

"Whoever."

Marianne smiled anxiously, forehead creased. Since Patrick had picked her up at the depot she'd been plucking at her hair, half-consciously; stroking the nape of her neck as if it were tender, and ached; groping to make sure the flimsy straps of her T-shirt were in place. You would wonder (Patrick would wonder) why a young woman of nineteen would wear such a shirt, and nothing beneath it; why, when it was only just April in upstate New York, and far from summer. And why the pebble-colored slacks with the elastic waist, in so synthetic a fabric it had no weave at all, smooth as Formica—slacks that might have been bought in a bargain basement children's department. *I am so small and inconsequential, please don't be angry at me.*

But Patrick was angry. Bristling with anger. He said, " 'From each, what he or she can give'—sure. Who's helping *you*?"

"But Patrick—"

"You're clerking in a store? You're baking bread? What else?"

"Patrick, these people are my friends. You'll have to come visit us—maybe the weekend Mom and Judd drive down? Kilburn is a small place, the town and the college, nothing like Cornell. No one is suspicious of anyone else there. No one would ever *cheat*, for instance."

Patrick let this pass. He listened in silence as Marianne spoke of how she'd been approached by some of the Green Isle people on her second day at Kilburn, she'd been wandering in the bookstore sort of lost and confused, to tell the truth she'd been almost crying, the textbooks cost so much, even the used textbooks, and the first thing

Felice-Marie and Birk said was hey don't worry, there's probably some of these books out at the house, we have a library, you can use ours. She spoke of the "wonderful old" house that had once been the Kilburn Inn "going back to stagecoach times." The greenhouses they'd restored to almost perfect condition, the pear orchards, meadows, fertile soil—"Mom would love." She spoke of the Co-op membership, currently twenty-three, of whom eighteen lived in the house. They had a single bank account, they pooled all their finances, if they worked outside the Co-op (as, sometimes, Marianne did, shelving books in the college library) they pooled their earnings. Green Isle was synonymous with "honor system." Green Isle was a "communal oasis in an American capitalist-consumer desert." (These were Abelove's words, reverently quoted.) In just five years since the Green Isle Co-op had been founded by Abelove, it had acquired an excellent local reputation, and many loyal customers at the store. In fact, Kilburn State was itself a customer: Abelove had negotiated a contract with the food services department.

Patrick resisted his Pinch-instinct and asked casually, politely about Abelove. And of course Marianne spoke warmly, at length; describing this "wonderful, dedicated" person with a "wonderful, kindly sense of humor"; a musician (guitar, banjo); an artist (clay sculpting); an organic gardener (no artificial fertilizers or insecticides); but primarily an intellectual, a theorist with advanced degrees in psychology and anthropology. Abelove had been an assistant professor at Kilburn who'd become disillusioned with the "straightjacket conformity" of the academic world; he'd dropped out to found the Green Isle Co-op, a private vision he'd had as an idealistic teenager camping alone on Mount Katahdin which is somewhere in Maine.

Patrick interrupted to ask, "How old is this person?"

"Old? Why, I don't know—in his early thirties maybe."

"I'd guess he just didn't get tenure at Kilburn State. That's why he 'dropped out.' And where are his 'advanced degrees' from, do you know?"

Marianne plucked at her hair, trying to recall. "Somewhere in Boston, I think."

"Harvard?"

The question was very lightly, ironically put. Marianne missed the tone and said, "Yes, I think maybe. One of them, at least. Actually Abelove won't talk about himself. Things are known about him—people talk about him, because they admire him so—but he rarely talks about himself."

Patrick said stiffly, "The Green Isle isn't some sort of ridiculous cult, is it?—and 'Abelove' some sort of megalomanic guru?"

"Oh, Patrick, *no*."

Patrick sucked at his lower lip. Harvard, really! He very much doubted Harvard. He said irritably, "Well, is there a religion involved? Do you all 'worship' together?"

Marianne said, hurt, "You know I have my own religion, Patrick. I've been attending a wonderful little church in Kilburn—actually it's outside of Kilburn a few miles. 'The Church of the Apostles.' It's a farm community congregation—Mom would love Reverend Hooker and his wife who's this 'free spirit' type, sort of like Mom in fact. We—"

Patrick interrupted, "Marianne, what happened to your courses last semester? You're in Kilburn to study and get a degree, aren't you?—not to work for this Co-op as an indentured servant."

"But—I have to help out, if there are emergencies," Marianne said pleadingly. "It happened so unexpectedly! Poor Aviva had some sort of—breakdown. She just disappeared from the house—we didn't know where she'd gone—I mean, at first—I volunteered to take over her duties and of course I had my own—and my classes—and, well—things got complicated." Marianne paused, smiling at Patrick; she was sitting with her legs drawn up beneath her, in what could not have been a very comfortable position. "I only just did what anyone would do, Patrick, in such circumstances."

Patrick let this pass. "Are you making up those courses now? This semester?"

"Well—not exactly."

"What's that mean? No?"

Marianne said softly, "I'm going to enroll in summer school, in about six weeks. The dean of students has been very understanding."

"You mean—you're not taking classes now?"

"Well—no. I just haven't had time, with so much—"

"You've dropped out of school? God, Marianne!"

"I haven't *dropped out*, didn't I just say I'm going to enroll in summer school? Why are you so angry, Patrick? I don't get angry at *you*."

"Wait. Those incompletes are on your transcripts now as *F*'s, aren't they? If you didn't make them up."

Marianne sat wordless, plucking at her hair.

Patrick sighed heavily, removing his glasses. Rubbed his eyes roughly. But what point in anger, really. *Wouldn't interfere with your sister. If I were you.*

Strange, Patrick thought. He, Patrick Mulvaney, was this young woman's brother: they'd been *brother-and-sister* through all of their conscious lives: each was more closely related to the other genetically than either was to either of their parents. Yet he believed he scarcely knew Marianne at all. He loved her, but scarcely knew her. Members of a family who've lived together in the heated intensity of family life scarcely know one another. Life is too head-on, too close-up. That was the paradox. That was the bent, perplexing thing. Exactly the opposite of what you'd expect. For of course you never give such relationships a thought, living them. To give *a thought*—to *take thought*—is a function of dissociation, distance. You can't exercise memory until you've removed yourself from memory's source.

An image of a broken cobweb, glistening-sticky across his knuckles, came to Patrick. As he'd walked through the tall grass behind the horse's barn. Once you see a web in such a way it's too late. It's no longer a web.

It was late, past ten o'clock. Not late by Patrick's usual schedule but it felt late, the visit with Marianne had drained so much energy from both. Yet, unpredictably, Marianne jumped up from the sofa saying she had a surprise for Patrick she'd almost forgotten—in fact, two surprises.

She'd brought dessert, lemon tarts, from Kilburn, another of her specialities. Patrick protested he wasn't hungry but found himself eating three of the tarts. Marianne picked sparingly at hers, eating crumbs and licking her fingers. Her sallow complexion glowed as Patrick complimented her—"You never made anything like this at home, did you? Terrific."

And she had a packet of snapshots of High Point Farm that Judd had taken to send her, at Easter.

Mulvaney family snapshots! At such a time.

Patrick swallowed nervously. He dreaded looking through these with Marianne—but how could he refuse?

Such family snapshots had always fascinated Patrick. The only ones he ever felt comfortable with were those he'd taken himself—there would be a reason, a logic, why he, Patrick, wasn't in a picture. Any snapshot that included him was naturally of intense interest—though usually, being vain, and in his own eyes homely, gawky frowning be-spectacled Pinch, he yearned to tear such snapshots into pieces; yet a snapshot that excluded him aroused even more anxiety. *Where am I? Didn't I get born? Has it all happened without me?* He wondered if there was a region of the human brain, somewhere in the cerebral cortex, specifically in the visual cortex at the back of the brain, that was trig-gered to register metaphysical anxiety over such absences.

How close we've all come, to never having been born. Out of what unfathomable infinity of possibilities, the slender probability of a single egg's fertilization by a single sperm.

It was something Patrick did not want to contemplate.

These two dozen Polaroids, taken by Judd over the past several weeks, excluded both Marianne and Patrick, of course. And Mike, now in the Marines. Patrick's fingers were damp and shaky as he held them, each in turn, and Marianne, who'd surely looked at them a hundred times already, was breathless, wiping at her eyes. Repeat-edly she exclaimed, "Look! Oh, Patrick, look here—" at familiar sights somehow unfamiliar, exotic. There was Troy with his nar-row, intelligent head cocked at an odd angle, doggy-brown eyes shining; there were two drowsy cats luxuriantly lying together on one of Mom's quilts—"I didn't know Snowball and E.T. could get along so well, did you?" Marianne observed, as if this were quite a revelation. There was Mom, irrepressible Mom, clowning on the back porch in a shabby old plaid parka of Mike's, gripping a thick five-foot stalactite icicle descending from the roof, grinning at the camera; overexposed in the sunshine of late winter, harsh lines bracketing her mouth. Another of Mom taken in the kitchen, ap-parently unaware of the camera, poised in chatty conversation with Feathers in his cage, the canary a blur of yellow. And there was Dad glimpsed unaware of the camera too, bareheaded, graying, in his camel's-hair coat, seen through a kitchen window as he was about to climb into the Mulvaneys' new gleaming-silver car. ("New car? I thought Mulvaney Roofing was having financial problems," Patrick protested to Corinne on the phone, when she'd informed him that his father had gotten a great deal on a secondhand 1975 Lincoln Continental, from a car dealer in New Canaan where he'd done some roofing work—"You know your wily old dad, 'Make me an offer I can't refuse.'") There were shots of the dun-colored late-winter landscape taken from Judd's bedroom window, views of the barns, the weathercock, Mt. Cataract in the distance; shots of interiors of High Point Farm, an empty—and oddly long—living room, the cluttered staircase seen from the second floor, Little Boots gazing up expectantly as the camera flashed. And, in his stall, Judd's cockeyed little horse Clover, snapped in midchew, hay burgeoning from his rubbery-damp mouth.

The other horses were gone, only Clover remained. Did Marianne know? Of course, Patrick thought, she must know—Molly-O is gone.

Molly-O, Prince, Red. Our childhood.

Neither spoke of the horses.

One of the snapshots was of Blackie and Mamie the handsome mated goats, in their pen: how quizzical their expressions, as the camera flashed. Another, somewhat blurred, was of several browsing cows by the pasture pond. Another was of Mom glimpsed outside, through a kitchen window, in conversation with—could it be Dad? in khaki-colored jacket?—no, probably a hired man, maybe Zimmerman from down the road.

Patrick sorted through the snapshots with a mounting sense of alarm. His left eye ached. Something, someone was missing.

Marianne said, wiping at her eyes, as if he'd spoken aloud, "I wish Judd had had Mom take a picture of *him*. It just seems so—" she paused, not knowing what she wanted to say, "—strange and sad without him."

Without us, Patrick thought. Any of us.

But he said nothing. His left eye was watering seriously. He was wearing his glasses of course, shoved against the bridge of his tender nose. He saw that Marianne was trembling; pale with strain and exhaustion. Why didn't she put the snapshots away? Why had she brought them at all? Did she imagine that he was as obsessed with the Mulvaneys as she?

Softly Marianne said, "I was disappointed there weren't more of Mom and Dad, too. Judd didn't actually take a real picture of Dad."

Strange on her bloodless lips: *Dad*.

Dad, Dad. Who is *your* Dad?

Is a *father* a dad, always? Is Dad a *father*?

Is Dad a *dad*, or just a *father*?

Patrick said abruptly, "What a ridiculous word—'Dad.' Did you ever hear it, actually?" He laughed, a sound as of dry twigs snapping.

Marianne was replacing the snapshots in the envelope, slowly.

"Patrick, I think Dad will be calling me home sometime soon."

Patrick wasn't sure he'd heard correctly. He didn't ask Marianne to repeat her words.

Marianne began to speak, not quite coherently, of the last time Corinne had called, Easter Sunday it had been, in the evening, she'd called at the Co-op and Marianne picked up the phone herself, what a surprise, what a wonderful surprise, to pick up a ringing phone just knowing *It can't be for me, it would never be for me,* and such knowledge completely matter-of-fact, not at all disturbing—and it was Corinne, it was Mom! With a just-perceptible air of childish pride Marianne said, "We talked for a long time—forty minutes! And before she hung up Mom said, just out of nowhere, 'If Dad was home right now, Marianne, I think maybe he'd like to speak with you.' I didn't know what to say, I was so—scared. Mom said, 'Marianne, are you listening?' and I said yes and she said, 'It might be Easter or it might be just—the time. I shouldn't talk like this maybe, I'm just guessing but it's what I think.' So I asked if I should call them later that night when Dad got home? when should I call? and Mom started crying, I think—I think she was crying—and *I* was crying—" Marianne laughed, shaking her head. Her deep-socketed eyes glistened with tears. "Oh, Patrick, it was so—wonderful. I couldn't sleep all that night."

Patrick thought, Don't say a word.

Patrick stood, almost overturning his chair. Marianne cowered before him, seeing something terrible in his face.

" 'Dad'!—how can you call him 'Dad'! He's a blind, selfish man. He's cruel. He's crazy. The way he's treated you—crazy! Why care about him, or her? Let them go."

Patrick slammed out of the room—into his bedroom, blindly— didn't know what he was doing—couldn't believe his anger. It had erupted so suddenly, out of—where?

Immediately he was ashamed of himself. Why frighten Marianne, his sister? To what purpose, saying such things to her?

She, to whom such a filthy thing had happened.

The terrifying possibility came to Patrick: our lives are not our own but in the possession of others, our parents. Our lives are defined by the whims, caprices, cruelties of others. That genetic web, the ties of blood. It was the oldest curse, older than God. *Am I loved? Am I wanted? Who will want me, if my parents don't?*

"No. Bullshit!"

It was very quiet. Few in the rooming house played music, there were few audible conversations. There was not even the incessant whining of the wind of High Point Farm. Patrick, badly trembling, sat down hard on his bed—flat, lumpy mattress—threw off his glasses and rubbed his eyes. He tried to calm himself. He was not one to give in to emotion. Hadn't a girl called him *icy-cold* not long ago and the very words had thrilled him. *Damn you, Pinch: why interfere? Your sister has Jesus Christ. She doesn't need you.*

How she'd stared at him, when he'd shouted at her. Cowering, shrinking. The packet of snapshots had slipped onto the floor unnoticed by her.

Patrick had intended that Marianne sleep in this room, in his bed; he would sleep on the sofa, uncomfortable as that would be. He'd changed the sheets, plumped up the single pillow which was a goose-feather pillow from home. The room was hardly larger than a closet, space enough for the bed, a bureau of drawers, a wicker stool he'd brought from home, painted robin's-egg blue. It smelled of damp, and of the night—he'd left the window open several inches.

Patrick halfway expected Marianne to knock timidly on his door but there was no knock, no sound at all from the other room. He went out, to discover his sister nodding off on the sofa, limp-limbed, her head drooping and swaying. The skin of her face was waxy-white and looked tight as the skin of a drum. Her mouth was slack, her eyelids fluttering. Of course, poor Marianne was exhausted. She'd travelled hours by bus, she'd had to wait for Patrick in the depot, she'd made supper, she'd cleared and washed the dishes; she'd endured her brother's self-besotted talk all evening. Patrick went to get Corinne's rag quilt after all, from where he'd hidden it. Why not? It was warm, it was beautiful, it even smelled faintly of the dried potpourri Corinne tossed into drawers at home, like a secret blessing. He covered Marianne with the quilt, tucking it in around her shoulders. He switched off the overhead light but stood for a while watching her in the dim light of the other room, as if guarding her. The packet of snapshots lay beside her on the sofa.

How could Patrick put his sister back on the Trailways bus tomorrow afternoon at 5:20 P.M.? How could he surrender her to—whatever was there, in Kilburn, in the Green Isle Co-op? Yet he knew he was going to.

You have no choice Pinch instructed himself. *You have your own life.*

"THE HUNTSMAN"

My brother Patrick first saw the German woodcut "The Huntsman" when he was eleven years old, sorting through a box of things Mom brought home from a farm auction in the Valley. These were the days when we kids would search eagerly through Mom's "treasures" and if we liked anything especially, Mom would promise not to sell it.

Sometimes, Mom took us along with her to flea markets, rummage sales, secondhand shops in the Valley, even to auctions—for years on Saturdays in summer we'd drive out, not Dad and rarely Mike but Mom, Patrick, Marianne and me. There's nothing like an auction for excitement, at least for a young kid, and people like my mom who've been "bitten by the bug." A professional auctioneer striding across a platform, microphone or megaphone in hand, booming voice like an old-style preacher's, capable of rousing your interest in the weirdest items you'd never in a million years give a second glance to except he's singled them out—an old handwringer washing machine, for instance, a tattered-yellowed wedding veil of sixty years ago you'd mistake for a mosquito netting except, in the auctioneer's words, it's *one-hundred-percent-authentic-antique-Americana*. A shrewd auctioneer knows how to draw people into bidding against one another, almost it doesn't matter sometimes what the item is, you're in a bidding war that can escalate like a firestorm *Twenty dollars I've got twenty dollars do I hear twenty-five? do I hear twenty-five?*—peering out into the audience and there's a hand suddenly raised—*Twenty-five! I've got twenty-five do I hear thirty? do I hear thirty? ladies and gentlemen do I hear thirty? Going, going—Ah, thirty! I hear thirty! For this prime piece of antique-Americana I hear thirty! Do I hear thirty-five? Do I hear thirty-five? Ladies and gentlemen, do I hear thirty-five?*

And so on.

The summer I was six years old, Mom took me with her to a farm auction at Milburn, and among the items being sold was a palomino rocking horse, and I asked could I have it, and Mom said we'd see, so when the bidding started Mom raised my hand for me whispering *Go on, Judd! You show 'em, Baby!* and suddenly there I was, bidding in an auction! The auctioneer grinned in our direction, took my bid and continued the bidding, the price jumped from $20 to $35 within seconds, and Mom raised my hand for me another time, and another time the auctioneer took my bid, the rocking horse was going now for $40, there were ten or so people scattered through the crowd bidding on it but as the price climbed, $45, $50, $65, everyone dropped out except a Yewville antique dealer, a woman Mom knew as a friendly rival, and me, six-year-old Judd Mulvaney at his first auction. Every time the auctioneer bawled out *Do I hear—? Do I hear—?* one of us would lift a hand, until at last, quicker than you'd have had time to absorb, the price for the rocking horse was $80—it was my bid—Mom whispered in my ear and I jerked my hand into the air and our "friendly rival" sat mute and unmoving—*I'd won the palomino rocking horse!*

At least, there was the feeling I'd won, a kind of anxious elation. Mom hugged me and smiling people sitting around us shook my hand. *I'd won!*

When we brought the rocking horse home, and Dad inspected it, it didn't seem like such a prize. A lot of the paint was flecked off and the wood was termite-ridden so the first time I tried to rock on it, the left hindquarters fell off. "Eighty dollars for a piece of junk," Dad said, shaking his head mournfully. Mom defended what we'd done saying it was excellent practice for children—"To learn to bargain for what you want in life, and not to be cowed by other people." Dad said, "Sure, if what you think you want is what you really want. Not just termite-ridden merchandise somebody's hoping to unload on a sucker."

Pulling a long face and winking at us kids. *All right! I give in. Your mom's crazy but I love her. I give in.*

All the while I was growing up, High Point Farm was filling with "treasures" Mom had promised never to sell. Or she'd fallen in love with herself and couldn't sell. Mainly clocks—all kinds of clocks—Mom described herself as a "fool about a clock"—but also odd pieces of furniture (Colt Willow Ware, antique-Americana ca. 1880s, was a favorite), watercolor landscapes of the "Chautauqua Scene" of the turn-of-the-century, mismatched Wedgwood china, music boxes that eked out raspy, rusty melodies ("Three Blind Mice" was my favorite), mirrors that yielded of their depths subtle distortions of perspective. And every kind of practical-seeming, moldering book—*Butterfly Lore*, *Living with Horses*, *Restoring Antiques for Fun & Profit*, *Crazy for Cats!*, *Forty Years of Bird-Watching: A Log*, *Organic Farming Made Easy*, *Canine Capers II*, *How to Improve Your Vocabulary 365 Days a Year*, *Home Remedies: Family Health Handbook 1957*. Marianne most loved miniatures—ceramic clocks with delicately painted faces and almost inaudible chimes, porcelain dolls, a Gothic Revival dollhouse, glass paperweights and figurines. Patrick preferred maps, an Atlas world globe (copyright 1938), isolated volumes of *Encyclopaedia Britannica* and *Information Please!*; a carved ivory chess set missing only a few pieces, a magnifying glass, a beautifully carved, now paintless wooden mallard decoy, an intermittently functioning battery-operated radio. In his tower room, over the years, dozens of previous items came and went, for Patrick was both hard to please and fickle, his Pinch-instinct was as much to reject as to accept, and by the time he left for Cornell only a few "treasures" remained—a tall cherrywood chest of drawers, the robin's-egg blue wicker stool (of a set scattered through the house, Mom had painted). For a long time "The Huntsman" hung on Patrick's wall beside his desk and when, his senior year in high school, he removed it, he didn't discard it but put it away in a closet. He'd outgrown it, but wasn't ready to part with it.

"The Huntsman" was a reproduction of a woodcut measuring about twelve inches by fifteen, in a cracked wooden frame, a real bargain as Mom claimed—only $2.99! It was intricately drawn, striking in its details, seeming very *real*. Now, I'd guess that the unknown artist had been influenced by Dürer. There was the same sort of high-voltage intensity, nervous concentration. The huntsman and his prey drew the eye like a narrative about to explode into action, not just a static picture to hang on a wall. Patrick wasn't like Mike, had no interest in owning a gun, but he became fascinated by the youthful figure of the huntsman on a rocky promontory, aiming his rifle at a mountain ram in the near distance, on a facing promontory. The drawing had been executed in the instant before the huntsman pulled the trigger—so it seemed. But was the huntsman really going to shoot? Or, just possibly, was he contemplating the handsome animal, about to change his mind and lower the rifle? *Don't shoot!* you wanted to shout. It was that kind of drawing: the more you studied it, as Patrick did, frowning distracted from his homework, the more like a riddle it became. The young hunter was blond, beardless, hatless, in plain clothing of a bygone era; the mountain ram was a magnificent beast with curly black wool, remarkable curling horns, a high-held head. Both huntsman and ram were similarly depicted—fastidiously drawn, in approximately the same posture. The artist surely intended them to be twins of a kind. Both were heroic figures, very male. *No don't shoot!* you wanted to shout. But the strain was so palpable, almost more than you could bear.

Yet there was more, much more to see in "The Huntsman." The sky was lightly marbled with cloud. Mountain peaks (Alps?) were ringed with shreds of cloud. In the intricately rendered foreground was a woodland scene, a reflecting pool and tall rushes, grasses, ferns. If you looked really closely (as Patrick pointed out to me) you could see, in the left, lower corner, unnoticed by the huntsman, a crouching hare. And this hare too was so meticulously drawn, so *alive*—you'd start to wonder was that the artist's point, somehow, the hidden quivering unguessed-at life, which required patience and shrewdness to observe, wasn't being seen, at all?

As soon as he'd discovered "The Huntsman" amid Mom's things, Patrick knew he had to have it. He asked Mom what it was and Mom said as far as she knew it was German—"All these things seem to be German." She examined the woodcut front and back. Probably just a cheap mass-reproduced item, somewhere between real art and kitsch, but Mom would never denigrate anything she'd brought home. Patrick used his magnifying glass to discover the date 1879, numerals fine as hairs, in the grassy foreground.

To him, "The Huntsman" was real art.

Or, maybe, something more.

It was after Marianne's visit to Ithaca, in April 1978, Patrick began to think of the woodcut. He was sure he hadn't thought of it in a long time.

In that way you recall, suddenly, sharply, in daylight, a trace of a dream of the previous night—but even as you recall it, it begins to fade.

Patrick didn't even know where "The Huntsman" was, he was sure—stored away somewhere at home. In a closet, in the attic. Or had he taken it out to Mom's antique shop, and given it back to her? He didn't think so. But he wasn't sure.

Romantic-corny. Of course it was kitsch. Noble figures silhouetted against the sky. The young German-blond huntsman, the handsome black ram. A young male as hunter, warrior, killer. No wonder the woodcut thrilled, even if you rejected hunting as an atavistic practice, a remnant of primitive behavior, cruel, contemptible, in contemporary terms impractical. Even if you dreaded the trigger being pulled, wanted the ram to wake from his trance and bound suddenly away, to safety.

Patrick sat at his desk and gazed out the window into a space he could not name that filled with a luminous tawny-golden light. On Cook Street were new-budding trees, fragrant and hazy with pollen. He was here, in Ithaca, in his new life; also, so strangely, he was *there*—the place he could not name.

Am I coded, too, to hunt? Kill? Is that my inheritance, male Homo sapiens?

He laughed aloud—"Bullshit." He was twenty years old, not eleven. No longer living at High Point Farm and would never live there again.

PLASTICA

Why?—he'd hoped to be more *normal*.

What passed for *normal* in his generation. In America, in the late 1970s.

It was an experiment, of a kind. An immersion in *normal*.

When Patrick called me to tell me what he was planning, in that way of his you couldn't judge *Is he serious? is he kidding?* at first I couldn't believe it. Wondered if it was some weird Pinch-joke. Not that Pinch bothered to joke with me much anymore, hardly took time to call home at all. Now he was a junior at Cornell and I was a sixteen-year-old high school sophomore in Mt. Ephraim. (This was in October 1978. We—Dad, Mom, and I—had seen almost nothing of Patrick over the summer. We hadn't yet moved from High Point Farm, nor were even planning any such desperate move, that I knew. Sure I was scared, selling the house might come next. All but four acres of the farm had been sold or long-leased and most of the cows sold and only my horse Clover remained of the horses we'd loved and still Mulvaney Roofing's profits were in decline. But what my parents were planning, worriedly in secret, I didn't know.)

So Patrick called to say, "Guess what, Ranger: I'm going to a rock concert next Friday. First time ever." And I laughed, "Come on, P.J.! You're kidding."

"No. I'm dead serious."

Asked if I'd ever heard of a band called "Plastica" and I told him sure everybody's heard of Plastica—"But you aren't going to like the sound." I shook my head imagining my snobbish brother screwing up his face as the Plastica sound washed over him, cringing in his seat until he couldn't stand it any longer and had to escape, hands over his ears. I laughed saying, "Well—good luck." Patrick didn't like me laughing, I guess, he got angry saying, "It's an experiment, I'm serious—the hell with you." And hangs up. Like that!

Now think: *If he hadn't gone to that rock concert, if he hadn't seen who he thought he saw.* All that followed from that night, my brother's desperate criminal behavior, and my complicity, would never have occurred.

I believe this.

But on October 25, 1978, Patrick Mulvaney went to hear the rock group Plastica perform on the Cornell campus, to a clamorous sellout crowd of six thousand. Many of the fans were drunk, or high, or both, and Patrick, too, was mildly drunk, beer-belching and grimly determined *to have a good time*.

For that was, of all things, *normal*: the wish of a young healthy male *to have a good time* amid a seething, writhing, ecstatic hive of specimens like himself.

In the adaptation of species to environment it is *normal* that survives, passes on DNA to the next generation.

Normal thrives. *Normal* enters heaven.

Certain obsessive thoughts and dreams, these past several months were beginning to frighten Patrick, and even distract him from his work. Maybe that was it: needing to be *normal*.

Not just guilt about Marianne. Though he felt guilt, plenty of guilt, about Marianne.

A few weeks ago, a girl Patrick had liked, and admired, had informed him he was "icy-cold." At first he'd been actually flattered. Somewhat hurt but flattered, his maleness flattered. But later, of course when he thought about it, and he thought a good deal about it, not so flattered. *That's just Patrick's way*.

Back home he'd rather enjoyed his reputation: the Mulvaney who wasn't somehow a *Mulvaney*, exactly. But now, he wasn't always so sure.

The young woman's name was Arlette and she was three years older than Patrick, a Ph.D. graduate student in biology whom he respected as much as anyone he knew and surely (he inwardly protested) had not wished to insult. Had not wished to hurt or disappoint. Seeing now to his chagrin, in the biology building, in the library, often on the street, her quickly averted gaze, her stiffened profile. *Don't speak to me. Please don't call out my name.* Had Arlette begun to love him, and he'd misunderstood? Or had he not wanted to understand? Away from her he would begin to feel attracted to her, too—or maybe to the idea of her. No, Patrick believed he wanted *her*. If only there could be ease, laughter between them and not such self-consciousness! Touching her, Patrick was suffused with feelings of tenderness, anxiety—thinking always of Marianne, Marianne's violated injured body. He didn't want to hurt any girl, did he?—never. But how did you touch, how did you make love, without the possibility of—hurt?

Better not to think about it. Concentrate on your work, that's why you're in college after all.

But how could he not think about it?—there was Arlette, even if avoiding him she did *exist.*

Arlette was one of those bright science-minded girls who are both outspoken and shy; rather nervous in company, with a tendency like Patrick to frown more easily than smile. They'd had lengthy exciting conversations together following Dr. Herring's lectures—Arlette had come to Cornell specifically to study with Herring—and they'd gone out together several times and at last they'd touched each other, if awkwardly; they'd even kissed—experimentally, it seemed. Such cool thin tight-pursed lips! Such self-consciousness! Eyes shut tight in a kind of horror! Neither, obviously, was much experienced in such things. High school romances hadn't been their forte. At twenty-three, Arlette might have been a girl in her mid-teens. So it was daring of her to invite Patrick to her apartment on Quarry Street and to prepare a meal for him which he'd eaten hungrily enough, and with gratitude. And afterward when their conversation began to falter—oh, Patrick's face suffused with blood at the memory! How Mike would have laughed at him, too shy to press forward. Too intimidated by the female body.

Like an animal who has wandered out of safe territory without quite realizing it, Patrick panicked, and fled.

"Icy-cold" Arlette had called him afterward.

She was an intellectual young woman, a graduate of Barnard. If she was to take revenge upon him, a young man who'd apparently spurned her, it must be an intellectual sort of revenge. She'd typed out for him a mysterious aphorism, source unnoted, and slipped it into his lab box. *So cold, so icy, that one burns one's fingers on him! Every hand that touches him receives a shock. That is why some think he is burning hot.*

Sure, it was flattering. Making so much of old Pinch who in secret made so little of himself.

And so, hoping to be *normal*. As Mike used to say, and Dad in the old days when he was good-natured, always genial, *Why not? for the hell of it?*

As he'd told Judd (he *was* close to Judd though rarely calling him) it was an experiment. Patrick Mulvaney behaving in a *normal* way and maybe it would take his mind off other things that were beginning to contort his thoughts in the way that a rod lowered into water appears contorted—you know it isn't, but it seems so.

So: the initial *normal* act was standing in line, a surprisingly long line, with other undergraduates, strangers to Patrick, waiting to buy a ticket. Studying the lurid psychedelic posters advertising PLASTICA! that vaguely amused him, revulsed him. Then, handing over twenty dollars for a ticket. To a rock concert! Patrick Mulvaney! Who listened to string quartets, woodwind trios, piano sonatas on the local classical music station, when he listened to music at all. Usually he didn't, it distracted him from his work. His plotting, tireless calculating. *What information am I lacking that I must be in possession of, to live my life as it's meant to be lived?*

It sobered Patrick Mulvaney to consider that all he might be, could possibly be, was already coded in his genes, and had been so since the instant of his conception; a set of hieroglyphics unreadable by him yet in theory readable, as any language, however mysterious, is in theory readable if one has the key.

The cold drizzly night of the Plastica concert, Patrick was stunned at the size of the crowd pushing into the hall. He'd assumed that, having bought a ticket well in advance of the concert, he would be spared further waiting. How like insects!—like a particular species of beetle that mates in great promiscuous swarms!—the rock fans were, all in their twenties or younger, happily jostling together, shuffling into the hall, and into the amphitheater, under the supervision of grim-looking security guards. Patrick's instinct was to turn away in disgust, hand his ticket to a stranger or, better yet, tear it into pieces. *This isn't for me. I hate my kind.* But he'd arranged to come to the concert with a group of others, friendly acquaintances from his science classes, all unattached young men like himself; they'd eaten together in a noisy pizzeria on College Avenue, and had a few beers, *normal* for a Saturday night in a college town. Inside the hall, however, Patrick began to taste panic. Just finding their seats amid so many others, in a rear, far-left row, a very long distance from the stage. Taped rock music blasted out of a speaker close by.

Why am I here, am I this desperate? What am I trying to escape?

By the time the concert began, thirty-five minutes late, the crowd had grown rowdy, noisy, about to veer out of control like sloshing waves. The headache-buzz at the back of Patrick's skull from the several beers he'd drunk had intensified though he felt, oh Christ how sober. Keenly aware of his misery. He'd never had any experience being seasick but he felt seasick now.

The crowd began to clamor: shouting, catcalling, clapping hands and stamping feet in rhythm. Patrick leaned forward in his seat and made a feeble effort to join in. *Normal* to be in such a din in such a place on a Friday night in Ithaca if you're twenty years old, not in his room as usual, squinting over a book, taking notes as if to save his life. *Normal* to cheer with thousands of others as, at last, amid blinding swirling lights and drums shrill as jackhammers, the members of Plastica bounded out on stage. Patrick gritted his teeth staring in amazed disgust at the half dozen scrawny male specimens in ludicrous black-leather costumes, trousers low-slung to show their navels, skintight to show the outline of their testicles. They wore armbands, ear-clamps, nipple-rings. The leader singer Traumeri was alarmingly emaciated, his chest sickly-pale, virtually concave, covered in an oily film. His bony-pouty face was made up pasty-white, his thick lips crimson, druggy-glassy eyes outlined in black mascara; his dyed black hair, braided in long dreadlocks, flew about his head as he threw himself about the stage with the manic abandon of an epileptic in a seizure. Traumeri and others of the group had recently been arrested on drug charges in London, evidently this was part of Plastica's reputation, why such crowds turned out to see them perform. Exhibitionist freaks whom the middle-class frat boys and sorority girls of Cornell would snub if they encountered them in real life.

What noise!—almost, Patrick could not hear. Drums, deafening guitar chords amplified a thousand times, throbbing hammering primitive repeating notes, bawling voices, sheer force-field of energy.

He did not see how he could endure, beyond five minutes.

Patrick glanced nervously seeing on all sides how the audience, most of whom appeared not very different from himself, identifiable to any foreigner as belonging to the same subspecies as he, was wholly entranced by Plastica. Not even the rapt fervent country congregations of the little churches to which Corinne had taken her children had exuded such ecstatic bliss, such unquestioning rapture. *Normal*, was it? And to hold oneself apart, questioning, critical, Pinch-style—*abnormal*?

These thousands of young men and women, Patrick Mulvaney's contemporaries. Like greedy infants at the breast. Patrick wished he might lose himself, if only for a few minutes, in the pandemonium—lose himself in the crowd, the hive. Feel his prickly Pinch-self melt and run like mercury into these other melting selves. And through all pulsed the hammering-throbbing current so like a galvanizing charge animating matter. Patrick tried to listen to the words Traumeri was spitting out amid convulsive bony-pelvic thrusts, as if words might redeem such blasting noise. *Lemme be lemme be lemme be yr sav-yur. Lemme be lemme be lemme be yr Gaw-d. Washed in the blood baby washed in the blood bay-by washed in the blood bay-by of the Lamb.* These words were shrieked yet oddly not exclamatory, as if Traumeri, galvanized by the same electric current that pulsed through the audience, were merely stating a fact.

Patrick couldn't believe he'd heard correctly. A grotesque parody of a Christian hymn? *Lemme be yr sav-yur. Washed in the blood of the Lamb.* Maybe Traumeri's background wasn't so very different from Patrick Mulvaney's. Unless Patrick had heard incorrectly, amid all the noise? Or was it mockery, self-mockery? Or play, as naughty children play? Knowing no one takes them seriously? Patrick had no idea.

He wondered what Marianne would make of such words. His sister who seemed never to judge others, nor even herself. How could you live that way? Was it a form of higher consciousness, in imitation of Jesus Christ, or was it a self-deluding, fatal weakness? *Resist not evil: but whosoever shall smite thee on thy right cheek, turn to him the other also.*

No, Patrick thought. Not me.

Plastica moved on to the next set. An old favorite evidently, judging from the howls and foot-stomping of fans. Patrick gave up trying to decipher words, meaning. It was the throbbing beat that mattered. Pounding in his eyeballs, increasing his heart rate like a viral infection. Those mysterious microorganisms that, lacking the capacity to reproduce on their own, must insinuate themselves into the genes of the host-victim. Who could understand Nature? Covered in rivulets of sweat, shock-haired Traumeri and a fellow guitarist were thrusting their bony pelvises at each other in jackhammer motions that reminded Patrick of nothing so much as the headless body of the male praying mantis copulating the body of the female praying mantis after the female has decapitated the male. He shut his eyes. Saw himself safe in the lab, in his stained smock, bringing his good eye to the microscope, frowning. Yet the frantic Plastica beat had got into his blood. Idiotic *beat! beat! beat!* like a nursery tune thumped on a log. He shut his eyes tighter, and thought of Darwin; of evolutionary theory that was so beautiful in its simplicity, yet so perplexing. *All living things are connected by patterns of descent to all other living things.* But there was a realm of not-being, too. The not-living, never-realized species. Hypothetical creatures that might have evolved, given the odds of probability. Possibility. Horned birds, flying reptiles, feathered Homo sapiens? Homo sapiens with eyes set on either side of the head, so that each eye gives a different image, Homo sapiens with the wonderful "echolocation" powers of bats? Patrick smiled, stubborn Pinch, daring to argue with the young assistant professor from Harvard who was Dr. Herring's protégé: What if? Why not? Isn't there genetic possibility? Maybe it was a character flaw, but he couldn't help his curiosity. Since grade school. Not just curiosity, impetuosity. Arlette and some others in the department admired him. (They said.) Others did not. Couldn't seem to resist questioning his elders, squinting and frowning. Always, Patrick Mulvaney had a further query, a doubt. In high school Mr. Farolino would say smiling, "Yes, Patrick?" even before he'd raised his hand to make a query. But the other morning at the end of Dr. Herring's lecture Patrick had dared to inquire, "Isn't 'existence' a needlessly reductive category, with 'genetic possibility' so vast? Assuming evolution has no end, no limit? No goal?" And the renowned biologist stared at Patrick for several painful seconds, in silence.

Patrick had thought, panicked *For Christ's sake Pinch you've gone too far this time. You'll sabotage your own future.*

Finally, Dr. Herring merely said, with a polite smile, "Your question is purely theoretical, Mr. Mulvaney, I assume."

What was wrong?—Patrick opened his eyes, disoriented. Like waking from a crazed dream—the deafening rock music had ended. Intermission.

He could escape! He'd tried *normal*, and failed miserably.

So Patrick stood, dazed and lurching with others in his row out into the aisle. Many fans had smuggled beer into the hall and were what's called *wasted, zonked-out.* Patrick shouted at his companions, "I'm leaving!—g'night." In the din, it wasn't clear if they heard. He was trying patiently and then not so patiently to clear a path for himself to a side exit when he saw in the crowd ahead a familiar, troubling face in profile—Zachary Lundt!

Was it possible? Here at Cornell? *Zachary Lundt?*

A flame passed over Patrick's brain. The Plastica *beat beat beat* urged him forward. He hadn't seen his sister's rapist since the day of their graduation but he realized he'd been thinking of Zachary Lundt compulsively, even when his mind was rigidly fixed on other things. *Zachary Lundt. The rapist. Never made to pay.* He wondered what frenetic strung-out Traumeri would make of the situation, how would *he* react? Patrick had heard that Zachary had enrolled at the State University at Binghamton despite his mediocre grades and that he'd pledged a fraternity. Of course—just the type. Probably Zachary was visiting fraternity brothers at Cornell. A girlfriend at Cornell. He appeared to be in a noisy group of young people, several clearly drunk. Patrick elbowed his way in Zachary's direction ignoring the curses directed at him. The Plastica beat pulsed murderously in his head. What would he do to Zachary if he caught hold of him? The rapist! The son of a bitch! Hurting Marianne, ruining Marianne's life! Patrick gritted his teeth, must have looked ferocious since people who saw his face made an effort to avoid him. He was imagining his enemy's nose, which his father had allegedly broken, his enemy's eyes which could be pounded with Patrick's fists, blackened, injured. And his mouth, those smiling teeth—Patrick had an ecstatic vision of a jack-o'-lantern spitting blood.

At the exit, Patrick lunged forward shoving others aside to grab Zachary's arm—"Just a minute! Wait!" Then he saw, stunned, that this wasn't Zachary Lundt after all. He muttered, embarrassed, "Oh, sorry. I thought you were—somebody else."

The young man was about Zachary's height, which was Patrick's height, and had Zachary's longish lank dark hair and narrow foxy face, but he was a stranger. He stared at Patrick, clearly frightened. Even at a Plastica concert, where violent throbbing uncensored emotions are celebrated, you aren't prepared to be accosted by a madman.

Patrick escaped. Running then across the darkened campus. His heart was *beat-beat-beating*. Afterward he would wonder why he wasn't ashamed of himself, why not stricken with remorse. But in fact he felt excited. Elated. That scared twenty-year-old hadn't been Zachary Lundt but that didn't mean Zachary Lundt wasn't somewhere else, this very night.

Patrick had come so close to—what, exactly?

DIGNITY

*P*ride goeth before a fall. But it was not a matter of pride.

It was a matter of simple integrity. Dignity. You're a man fifty years old, a father of a daughter and sons, and an American—without dignity, you're nothing. And he'd been led to believe these men were his friends. He'd been led to believe they accepted him, Michael Mulvaney, as one of them. Invited him to be a member of the Mt. Ephraim Country Club. And he'd accepted, one of the happiest days of his life. He'd been inducted into the membership, paid his initiation fee and his dues faithfully, the first of September each year. Michael Mulvaney was one member they could rely upon, and they knew it. And he knew it. And he knew he wasn't mistaken about any of this, wasn't the kind of man to make mistakes in life, building a business out of virtually nothing, without being a shrewd judge of other men's characters. That was a fact.

So one day, one hour, he's had enough. Walking into the bar at the Mt. Ephraim Country Club, shortly after 6 P.M., a Friday. Yankee Doodle Tap Room: men only. Removing his dark glasses to adjust his eyes to the dimness. And glancing around to check out who's here, twelve, fifteen men approximately, at the bar and in the booths, all familiar faces, and there's Ben Breuer in one of the red-leather booths, and Charley MacIntyre, the two exchanging a quick startled glance—a look of *warning*, *caution* passing between them—and there's a third man, his back to Michael, Michael doesn't recognize at first then sees it's Gerry Kirkland, the district court judge.

Kirkland is about sixty, solidly built, with a square-ruddy face creased from a career of hard smiling. His hair, the color of pewter, is thinning patchily at the crown exactly like Michael Mulvaney's. Michael knows Kirkland from the Club mainly, just well enough to shake the man's hand, exchange friendly greetings and inquiries after their respective families. Michael always asks after Jeannette Kirkland and in turn Kirkland asks after—is it Carol? Coralee?—never can quite remember Corinne Mulvaney's name, and why is that? *Fucker*.

That *warning*, *caution* glance swift as a firefly's spark passing between Ben Breuer and Charley MacIntyre. And one of them has murmured to Kirkland, warning him, too. So he doesn't turn to glance over his shoulder, to see who's just come in.

Michael ignores them and goes to the bar, hoists himself up on a stool. Empty stools on either side. Conversations, laughter. Television above the bar. A roaring in Michael's ears but he hasn't had a drink for hours. The bartender is saying, "Hello, Mr. Mulvaney! The usual?" Michael stares at the man, saying, "What do you mean 'usual'? I'll have—" naming a brand of beer he rarely drinks. Embarrassed, the bartender murmurs, "Sorry, Mr. Mulvaney," and ducks away. Michael is sitting alone at the bar squinting up at the television screen without seeming to see it. Tapping his fingers, thick dirt-edged nails on the bar. Edgy, impatient. Feels himself being scrutinized, yet knows if he turns they'll look immediately away. When he'd come in, a few men nodded toward him, smiled vaguely *but not one said hello, not one smiled and called out my name, invited me to sit down*. A glass of foaming beer is brought and Michael lifts it slowly to his mouth. Like a man lost in contemplation of a profound, elusive truth. Not a man whose hand is trembling, who's breaking out in prickly sweat inside his clothes. He turns, can't resist turning. Breuer, MacIntyre, Kirkland. *Think I don't see you? hear you? Fuckers*.

The glass in his hand is drained, empty. Beer so bland he hasn't tasted it at all. But signals to the bartender for another. An anxious heat inside his clothes, flushing up into his face. He hadn't had time to shower that morning, wanting to get out of the house before Corinne came downstairs in search of him. Where he'd spent much of the night, in Mike Jr.'s old room, with Troy. Hair stiff as quills, and he hasn't shaved in two days. Whiskers growing in the color of tin filings, old-man's beard. The second foaming beer is brought to him and he sips at it gratefully then abruptly eases his weight from the stool and approaches the three men in the booth so resolutely *not looking* in Michael Mulvaney's direction. Michael Mulvaney in a rumpled camel's-hair coat, Michael Mulvaney swaying on his feet. Face furious, darkened with blood. Tauntingly he says, "H'lo, Ben—how's it going?" and Ben Breuer glances up guiltily, as if he's just now seen Michael. And Michael says, grinning, "Charley?— great to see *you*." And Charley MacIntyre, startled, smiles weakly at Michael, almost fearfully. "And, Gerry—" Michael lets his hand fall on the judge's right shoulder, a friendly-seeming gesture, but hard, heavy. And Kirkland eases away saying, "Excuse me—!" And Michael stares down at him seeing the undisguised alarm, disapproval, dislike in Kirkland's face, for here's an elder of the Mt. Ephraim Country Club and a prominent citizen of the community in no mood to humor Michael Mulvaney, or any other drunk. And Michael says, "Fucking S.O.B., *you*—!"

And empties his glass of beer in Judge Gerald Kirkland's face.

REVERSE PRAYER

I *need your help, Judd.*
    Or possibly he said *I need help, Judd.*
    The words ran through me like an electric current! No one had ever uttered such words to me in earnest. Until you have heard such uttered to you by someone you love, and are bound to by ties of blood and memory, you can't know how powerful, how thrilling they are.
    Help I need help. Your help, Judd.

Always when Patrick called home it was to tell us, inform us, of nothing. His life in Ithaca was private, and we weren't to inquire. Almost shyly Mom would ask if Patrick might be coming home to visit sometime soon? or when? and Dad had learned to be as polite and impersonal to Patrick as Patrick was to him. If there was something Patrick wanted us to know, he might mention it just before hanging up, as an afterthought: he'd been awarded a summer research grant, he'd made another 4.0 grade average, he was just recovering from an attack of winter flu. If you asked Patrick a direct question, he'd nimbly sidestep; murmur something you couldn't quite hear, maybe yes, maybe no, maybe undecided.
    I'd about reconciled myself: no brothers.
    Where once I'd had two big brothers, now none.
    Thinking *I don't particularly like Pinch, anyway. The hell with Pinch.*
    Where Mom used to proudly tack up newspaper clippings of good-looking "Mule" Mulvaney the star fullback and his Mt. Ephraim

Rams teammates, and, for a while, so long ago it seemed like another lifetime now, where the obituary of Private First Class Dwight David Duncan *killed in action, in the service of his country* had been prominent, on the cork bulletin board in the kitchen, now she tacked up newspaper clippings of Patrick. Mom was a friend of "Tweet" Philco, a Mt. Ephraim woman who composed the regional news section of the *Mt. Ephraim Patriot-Ledger*, the part of the paper given over to items about local engagements and marriages and births and deaths, retirements, anniversary celebrations and reunions, students' activities and honors, athletes' victories, scholarships, prizes, visits abroad—any news however trivial or ephemeral that was suitable for these much-scrutinized pages which, like such pages in all small-town newspapers, constitute a sort of community family album. Naturally, Mom passed on to "Tweet" every particle of good news pertaining to her son Patrick who'd gone to Cornell and was so clearly excelling in his difficult and ambitious field of study. You'd have thought, seeing Mom's bulletin board, that Patrick was her favorite child—maybe her only child. The photo of Patrick that was used repeatedly in the *Patriot-Ledger* was from his high school yearbook, and this—a stiffly posed, faintly smiling Patrick, hair unnaturally combed back from his forehead—glowered over that corner of the bulletin board.

It wasn't often that Patrick spoke with me on the phone but when he did he'd usually talk in a light, bantering, slightly distracted way, calling me Ranger or kid, but as if his mind was on something else. Maybe I'd call him P.J. It wasn't up to me to break through to anything deeper. If I wanted to ask about Marianne, had he spoken with her recently, had he seen her, I'd feel shy about bringing up the subject. I'd have to wait for the right moment and maybe the moment wouldn't come.

This time, though, when Patrick called, and it was late, after 11 P.M. of a weekday, I picked up the phone on the first ring (just happened to be downstairs, in the family room switching through TV channels, volume low so Mom upstairs in bed wouldn't hear) and right away he was serious, none of the Pinch-crap. First thing he asked was, 'D'you think anyone else is on the line?" and I'm surprised as hell, I say, "What? *Who?*"—because it could only be Mom or Dad, as far as Patrick would know. (He couldn't have known that Dad was in Marsena on business, staying the night.) So right away Patrick backs off a little, saying he just wanted to be sure. And there's this beat or two, just silence; I'm holding the receiver to my ear not hearing a thing. I wonder if he's hung up. "Patrick? Is something wrong?"

His voice comes low and mean, like he's angry with me. "There's lots of things wrong."

"You mean—about Dad?"

This is a week after Dad tossed his beer into the judge's face. In front of twelve witnesses in the Yankee Doodle Tap Room of the Mt. Ephraim Country Club. And he'd been arrested, and taken to Mt. Ephraim police headquarters, and booked for assault and disorderly conduct and resisting arrest (there'd been quite a struggle when police officers came to pick him up). And District Judge Gerald Kirkland isn't going to drop the charges because he's angry as hell at my father and we don't know if Dad will be going to jail (he could be put away as long as two years); or if he'll get a suspended sentence and a fine; and if it's a fine, how much. The Monday morning after the arrest there was delivered to Michael Mulvaney Sr. at High Point Farm a certified letter containing a formal notification from the Mt. Ephraim Country Club, signed by each of the Club's twenty trustees, revoking his membership and by extension "all rights and privileges" of said membership as had been enjoyed by the family of Michael Mulvaney Sr.

The expelled member's annual dues of six hundred dollars, paid in full for 1978–79, were returned to him in full, in the same envelope.

As Mom said bitterly, not once but many times *What the hell do we care!*

Now Patrick says these words that shake me up: "I need your help, Judd."

It isn't just the word *help* that's such a surprise, coming from my brother. It's my name *Judd*, my real name and not *Ranger*, or *kid*; as if, serious for once, he's had to break the family code. As if, in this instant, we're equals.

I'm cautious, I wonder if I've heard right. "What kind of help, Patrick?"

He sounds angry, as if I should know. "Executing justice! Taking care of—you know: Lundt. Zachary Lundt. I mean—I'll do it." Patrick speaks carefully but his words seem disconnected, as if he's been drinking. It's the way Dad talks when he's been drinking if he talks to us at all. "I'll be the one. But I need your help. Judd?"

"Y-Yes?"

"Dad's still got his guns?"

"His *guns*?"

"Or Mike? That .22 of Mike's? Locked in the cabinet—you know?"

I'm holding the phone receiver and I'm starting to sweat. Sick with fear and excitement.

Patrick's saying, "The .22? Could you get it?"

"Get it—?"

"For Christ's sake, Judd, you sound like a parrot." Patrick laughs. It's obvious now, and this scares me as much as what he's been saying, that he has been drinking. "Oh, shit. Never mind."

"Patrick, wait—"

"Forget I called! It's the wrong goddamn time. It's—" There's a sound like he's dropped the phone receiver, he's scrambling to pick it up again. "—not the right time, yet. Fuck it."

Next I know he's hung up. And I'm sitting there on the sofa staring at a corner of the ceiling. My brain numb and empty of all thought as if I've been hit over the head with a sledgehammer.

Three days later, Patrick calls again.

Around suppertime, anyway what used to be suppertime at High Point Farm. But now if it's just Mom and me not knowing for sure when Dad might show up we don't exactly sit down at the table as in the old days because Mom says it makes us nervous, as Mom says it's just as easy to eat standing up or somewhere not the kitchen at all. This is about 6:30 P.M. and the phone rings and Mom answers quick and worried as she does when Dad's out but—it's Patrick!—and I hear her talking with him—talking *and laughing*—for ten, fifteen minutes! Trying not to eavesdrop, hanging around the kitchen with the dogs and cats nudging their heads against my legs and it's amazing to me how Mom and Patrick seem to be talking, Mom so relaxed telling Patrick about her latest plans for "expanding" High Point Antiques so that she can bring in serious income, now that Dad is negotiating to sell his property in Mt. Ephraim and "relocate" the business in Marsena and of course they'd be selling the farm—"relocating"—maybe Patrick had heard of the Marsena Antique & Flea Market at the fairgrounds there, every weekend in good weather? one of the oldest and largest markets in the Valley? antique dealers and well-to-do customers come from as far away as Rochester, Port Oriskany, Buffalo? And—

I can't believe I'm hearing Mom utter such words *selling the farm* in a rapid stream of words as if they were of no more significance than the other words and all words sheerly air, gesture. As if *selling the farm* is but the crude expediency for the acquisition of a leased booth at the Marsena Antique & Flea Market. As if *selling the farm* is already past tense, a kind of history not to be questioned.

When Dad was arrested, booked and arraigned, the *Patriot-Ledger* published a picture of him above the headline HIGH POINT FARM RESIDENT ARRESTED FOR " ASSAULT" AT COUNTRY CLUB. The article did not appear in the regional news section of the paper but prominently on the front page. Dad's photo was from the paper's file, I guess, showing him in suit and tie at some awards ceremony, the Chamber of Commerce or the Tuscarora Club, maybe ten years ago. He looked good, he looked handsome and happy though not smiling broadly, the camera's flash caught in his eyes in that weird way like light reflecting in an animal's eyes in the dark. This, Mom didn't clip and tack up on the bulletin board.

I'd sent a copy to Patrick, at Cornell. Figuring he'd like to know.

So there's Mom chattering about her plans. I'd run away to hide in one of the barns except Mom darts after me, grabs my shirt collar like a mom on TV. Her face is flushed, eyes bright as neon. "Oh, Ranger! Say hello to P.J.!"

And Patrick says to me, sort of quick and breezy, "So how's it going, kid?" and I shrug as if he can see me, I'm blinking tears out of my eyes I feel so rotten, "O.K., I guess," and Patrick says, "It's really bad there? like Mom says? they're going to sell the farm? you think so?" and I mumble something maybe yes, maybe no, and Patrick says, "The other night, Judd, what I said—" and there's a pause and I'm waiting for him to say *forget it please, that was crazy talk* but instead I hear him saying, "—I meant it, I'm going to do it, execute justice. I don't know when but—sometime. And I need you, O.K.?" and I'm trying to get my breath, trying to smile, act normal, since Mom's close by at the sink whistling under her breath, "Sure, Patrick. Any time." And Patrick says in his low anxious voice, "Judd, you're the only person I can trust in the world." And I'm saying, stammering, "Well—that's good." And Patrick says, "I just need to get in focus about it. I'm not ready right now. My mind is—not ready, right now." And I say, that sick feeling in my gut, scared but excited, trembling, "O.K., Patrick. I'm your man."

After we hang up Mom says, wiping at her eyes, "Wasn't that nice of your brother to call, Judd! So sweet, and thoughtful. He doesn't know I've been willing him to call all week, in my thoughts—sending him little messages sort of daring him *not* to call. Have you ever tried that, Judd? It's like prayer in reverse. And it works."

THE ACCOMPLICE

In this way I became, at the age of sixteen, a sophomore in high school, an accomplice to my brother Patrick's premeditated crime. I was what you'd call an accessory before the fact and an accessory after the fact. I was what you'd call a co-conspirator. I became an accomplice not at the time of our initial conversation, nor at the time of the second, when Patrick confided in me that I was the only person in the world he could trust!—but in the interim between the conversations. In a trance of several days, day and night. Thinking *Whatever he wants I'll do it. If he wants me to pull the trigger myself I'll do it.*

I believed I'd always known that Zachary Lundt would have to be punished. I'd thought it would happen the way lightning strikes, that someone would do it—my father, or Mike Jr. I hadn't thought that Patrick would do it, or that I would be involved. Me, Judd! But as soon as Patrick confided in me, I understood that Patrick was the only Mulvaney capable of executing justice in the way it required execution. Not as a sudden, impulsive act of violence, like wildfire springing up to consume us all, but as a coolly premeditated act from which the perpetrator would walk away unscathed. For nothing less than *perfect* would satisfy Patrick.

There wasn't an hour in all the hours to come, between my decision in early December 1978 and the "execution" itself in March 1979 that I once thought of not helping Patrick; of backing out, telling him I'd changed my mind, I was scared, or disapproving. I thought *It will be dangerous!* I thought *We could both be hurt!* But I never thought *No I can't do it, I won't.*

My life away from High Point Farm was the dream and my life at High Point Farm and in my thoughts was the real life.

Like, even now, so many years later, I'm at my place of work—in this space that's designated mine—and I'll glance up, I've maybe forgotten the time if I've been working late, past dark—and I think about going home—*home*: to High Point Farm.

At Mt. Ephraim High, Judd Mulvaney was a quiet, skinny kid with a sly sense of humor. Already, as a sophomore, a co-editor of the school newspaper and features editor of the yearbook. Possibly good enough for the junior varsity basketball team but he didn't try out—told the coach he had too many chores to do at home, which was true. His grades were high in some subjects (English, history) and about average in others (math, science). A habit of drifting off at lunchtime, not eating in the cafeteria and maybe not eating at all. A habit of frowning in class, running his fingers over his jaws that were broken out in dull reddened bumps. Brown hair, mud-brown eyes. I guess I wasn't bad-looking for my age but I shrank from being seen. I turned down invitations to parties in town figuring my class-mates, especially the girls, weren't serious—why bother with *me*? At the same time I was goddamned vain, my heart pounded in rage I wasn't more special, as I deserved. *Judson Andrew Mulvaney.*

In the foyer of the high school, in the big glass trophy case that's like a church altar, there was the photograph, still, of "Mule" Mul-vaney and his padded-jersey teammates, Tri-County Football Champions 1972. Every one of my teachers remembered Patrick, for sure, and wore me out asking after him. ("Most brilliant kid I ever taught," Mr. Farolino was forever saying, with a droll shake of his head. "He could be a real pain in the rear, though!")

If my teachers remembered Marianne, they didn't ask after her.

Nor did they ask after Dad and Mom as they'd once done. After Dad's arrest, and the hearing, and the two-year "probation," and a fine of fifteen hundred dollars, and all the stuff in the local papers—not a word. After Mom resigned her P.T.A. office and stopped coming to meetings—not a word.

So I'd want to scream at them. Damn you all! Don't you pity *us*. *We're the Mulvaneys.*

★ ★ ★

It was true, High Point Farm would have to be sold.

Except: at what price? Who would buy? To pay off Dad's debts and keep Mulvaney Roofing afloat, my parents had been selling the property piecemeal, only four acres remained. The house, which Mom spoke of as a "historic monument," and the outbuildings, most of which needed repair.

On a farm, everything needs repair continuously. Buildings, machines, orchards, fences. You can calculate the health of a farm by its fences. When things start to go bad, fences are the first to show it.

The days were long gone, when Mom would organize a "scout team" of us kids, to tramp the fields checking out the fences, repairing what we could. What we couldn't, Dad would repair. And what Dad couldn't, he'd have done by someone who could.

Now, even the front split-rail fence bordering High Point Farm was falling down in sections. It hadn't been white in years. More the color of damp moldering newsprint, overgrown in a tangle of briars and vines.

The house that was so beautiful in our eyes wasn't beautiful really. The shutters had begun to sag, the slate roofs needed repair. The pale lavender color Mom loved so wasn't practical for our climate and faded after two or three years. It must have been at least five years since the house had been painted so Mom fretted: how could we hope to sell the house for a decent price if it looked bad on the outside? On the other hand, why spend money and time repairing a house you won't be living in much longer? Could we really afford fifteen to twenty gallons of expensive oil-base paint, the kind required for old, dry wood? And the labor? (Long gone too were the days when Dad would recruit his crew of Mulvaney housepainters, Mike, Patrick, me, and Dad our foreman, and devote six weeks in the summer to radical home improvement.) The orchards needed pruning, the ponds needed dredging. Every one of the farm machines had something wrong with it. The local men Dad hired to help out were unreliable if not dishonest, pilfering hand tools, buckets of grain and seed, even hens' eggs out of the coop. (Mom swore she'd caught old Zimmerman with broken eggs in his overall pockets, yolks seeping through the denim. Mom said, You can't trust these men, don't leave me alone with these men, they're drinkers, they're wife-beaters, I'm terrified of them. Which wasn't like Corinne Mulvaney who'd never been afraid of anyone in the past, laughed at the notion of locking any door, at any time.

Now she was forever calling, "Judd? Where are you? Is that you? *Judd?*")

I won't go into the health of the livestock. If you know farm animals, you know all about that.

In these desperate months when he was (a fact I wasn't supposed to know) trying to stave off bankruptcy, my father hadn't time for farm chores; or was impatient to a point just short of mania if he had to do them. He was breathless, panting, angry. His disheveled graying hair like steel wool, carelessly shaved jaws, a glisten at the corners of his mouth like spittle. His clothes were the same sportily stylish clothes he'd always worn but they were rumpled, as if he'd crushed them in his fists, and in need of laundering or dry cleaning. His boots were mud-spattered, his shoes in need of shining. The glamorous almost-new Lincoln he drove was mud-spattered too. I'd hear him start the engine, turning the key in the ignition in some weird way that made a squealing sound as of protest, as if he'd forgotten the rudiments of driving, or was distracted by malevolent thoughts. Once he stormed into the house where I was doing something in the kitchen, tossed his car keys onto the table and said, glaring at me, "Take the pile of shit, you're welcome to it." Slammed upstairs and half hour later slammed down again, looking for the keys, of course, and they were exactly where he'd tossed them onto the table, untouched by me.

Where always in the past Dad had been courtly to Mom, to the point of embarrassing us kids, now he was indifferent, or rude; or worse. He didn't like her questioning him and grew into the habit of cutting her off in midsentence—"No!" he'd say, or "Who wants to know?" Once I saw him shove Mom aside when she'd dared to touch him, just her fingers on his arm. Another time I saw him lean close to her, his boiled-looking face brought to within an inch of her face, and he said something to her in a low, contemptuous voice that made her wince as if he'd kicked her in the stomach. (If I asked Mom afterward what had happened, Mom would say, hurt, "Nothing 'happened.' And I'll thank you not to spy on us, young man!")

This I remember vividly: seeing my father pitching manure in the barnyard, in the awkward, uncoordinated way of a man who's never held a pitchfork in his hands before, and suddenly in disgust throwing the pitchfork against the side of the hay barn with such force that for several fantastic seconds the heavy object actually held, quivering, before falling to the ground.

I'd just emerged from the stable. I couldn't help clapping—I guess

I was a smart-ass, unless I just wanted to pretend that such wild, futile behavior on my dad's part was for laughs as in the old days it might possibly have been. *Way to go, Dad! Betcha can't do that again!*

But Dad hadn't heard. Already he'd stalked off, gone to climb into the Lincoln and drive the hell away from High Point Farm and all it had come to mean to him.

I told Mom, "I'm scared of Dad. I wish he'd go away somewhere by himself and *stay*."

Mom said, her eyes welling with tears, "*You! You* go away if you're not happy in this house."

News of such incidents I would relay to Patrick, who'd given me a secret telephone number I could use to call him. (Actually, it was a lab number. Sometimes he was there, and sometimes not, and if not I was to hang up without identifying myself.) "I'm scared of Dad," I said, aggrieved. "I wish he'd go away somewhere by himself and—" Patrick interrupted, in cool Pinch-style, "Look, Judd, our father is just a casualty. He's one of those frogs whose life is sucked out of them without them having a clue what's going on, by a giant water spider."

Michael Mulvaney Sr. escaped going to Red Bank Correctional Facility for Men but he didn't escape what he'd come to call his fate: to be dragged publicly through shit, to *be* shit in others' eyes. It was not his belief and would never be his belief that he'd committed any crime when he'd tossed a few ounces of beer into Judge Kirkland's face, still less that he'd committed any crime when, the previous year, he'd slammed Zachary Lundt against a wall—these were "provoked" acts for which he felt not the slightest repentance. He'd paid a fine of $1,500 but this fine was what he called a "mere fraction" of his punishment. For he'd become involved in the hiring and firing of lawyers like an obsessed man—hiring the "initial error," as he said, and firing its "compounding." Yet he kept hiring lawyers, and each lawyer Dad hired he had to pay, pay, pay. One week he'd be speaking rapturously of someone from Yewville named Costello, the next week someone from Rochester named Elder; the next week, Costello and Elder were out, and Fenwick, "a real shark," was in. Lawyers terrified my mother because she perceived that they thrived on others' misery; she was the daughter of farmers and could not tolerate a profession that "produces nothing, but only takes." She who hadn't wept when three of our horses were taken away to auction (at least, she hadn't wept in front of me) wept when my father boasted of his legal strategies to her. He was going to sue that hypocrite Kirkland! He was going to sue the Mt. Ephraim Country Club! He was going to sue the Mt. Ephraim police—for false arrest! And the *Patriot-Ledger*, for libel! Each lawyer provided my father with hope of redressing his terrible hurt; but it was hope lethal to him as solid food to a man whose stomach has shrunken from starvation. There was even a week or so in January 1979 when Dad was initiating a suit against one of his former lawyers charging "legal malpractice" and during this time my parents quarrelled as I'd never heard them quarrel before in my life. My mother was furious that my father was squandering money on lawyers and my father insisted he could win it all back, and more—didn't he have justice on his side?

At the same time Dad seemed to have no illusions, and no hope. By day, cold sober, he had no hope. He was a man going through the motions of attacking others, a man with no hope. He seemed to have forgotten Marianne entirely, what had been done to her that was the cause of all our trouble, his excited focus was a small circle of men in Mt. Ephraim who'd wronged him, and continued to wrong him. He warned me, "As soon as you're involved with the law, son, they've got you. Like a rat trapped in a corner by dogs. Innocent or guilty, you're going to be punished because you have to hire a lawyer, and as soon as you hire a lawyer you're going to pay, pay, pay. It doesn't matter if you're innocent and you win—you lose. You pay, pay, pay."

In the end, in spring 1979, High Point Farms would be sold thousands of dollar below the realtors' suggested price, to pay my parents' debts, thirty-two thousand dollars of which were legal debts.

❧

After Christmas, Mom and I drove to Kilburn to visit with Marianne. Again, my sister hadn't been invited home for the holidays. I did most of the driving in Mom's Buick station wagon and kept hearing Patrick's voice *Judd you're the only person I can trust in the world Judd you're the only person I can trust in the world* beneath Mom's nervous chatter.

Three hours and forty minutes driving to Kilburn in the extreme southwest corner of New York State, most of the trip along two-lane country highways (sometime stuck behind snowplows moving at twenty miles per hour); almost that long again, driving back home that evening. Mom was anxious about staying overnight in Kilburn—

"At this time of year, you can't tell what the weather might *do*." It was a snowy windswept landscape, the air bright and glittering with cold. No immediate snow was predicted but Mom envisioned the two of us snowbound in Kilburn, trapped until the spring thaw.

I wondered if she'd told Dad where we were going. If he would notice we'd been away. If she and Dad ever discussed Marianne at all.

The former inn, painted mint-green with white trim, that was the Green Isle Co-op hadn't changed much since Mom's and my last visit. There were Christmas decorations in all the windows and, in the front room which was a combination parlor and office, a lop-sided evergreen tree trimmed with handmade paper, tinsel, and cloth ornaments in primary colors. The mood of the Co-op at 11:20 A.M. of a weekday was busy, bustling, even frantic—people rushing about, up and down the stairs, a telephone ringing and a dog barking excitedly. This was an atmosphere hospitable to my mother who wandered inside, smiling and calling, "Marianne? Marianne?" until someone yelled, "Marianne! Visitors!" and Marianne appeared out of the rear of the house where she'd been working in the kitchen, wiping her hands on her apron. She wore baggy khaki pants, a red-plaid flannel shirt with sleeves rolled to the elbows, an oversized stained apron. When Marianne and Mom hugged they began to cry in a soundless way you'd almost mistake for laughter; then Marianne hugged me, her thin, surprisingly strong arms around me as I stood self-conscious, embarrassed—a clumsy kid of sixteen not knowing what to do or say. "My goodness, Judd, you keep growing! You've actually grown *inches*!" Marianne cried breathlessly. Her bones seemed light as a sparrow's and her hair was cut shorter than mine; her skin looked sallow, grainy. But her eyes, glistening with tears, were my sister's beautiful eyes—I almost couldn't bear to look into.

Marianne seized our hands and led us upstairs to her room on the third floor, talking excitedly. Her room was one we'd seen before but now she had a new roommate, a girl named Felice-Marie who smiled but didn't exchange more than a half dozen words before she made her escape. "What a—an attractive girl—" Mom said breathlessly, though Felice-Marie was heavyset, dark-browed, rather sullen. Marianne said, "Oh yes Felice-Marie is a wonderful *person*. She's a speech therapy major, I've learned *so much* from her." It was that radiant high school enthusiasm that ricochets off surfaces, dazzling and feverish and not to be examined closely.

The room Marianne shared with Felice-Marie was smaller than

her room at home, with only a single window; a straw-colored woven rug on the floor, fishnet curtains, a mix of furniture of the kind you see at garage sales, strewn across someone's lawn. There was a yeasty, not-very-fresh smell. Clothes on hangers, crowded on a rod in a corner of the room. Except for a few books here and there, and a spiral notebook on the windowsill, it didn't look much like a room shared by two college students. And there, on Marianne's bed, on her hand-knit quilt, was Muffin blinking up at us, tawny eyes widened and luminous. Marianne cried, "Muffin! Look who's here!" Mom cried, "Muffin! Do you remember us?" Mom embraced the cat, who'd begun to purr deeply. "He hasn't changed at all, Judd, has he?" Mom asked. Her eyes were brimming with tears and her smile was wide, teeth-baring, tense.

In fact, Muffin had lost weight. His fur was sleekly white and colored in patches but the flesh of his belly hung slack and his backbone was prominent.

While Mom and Marianne chattered together I sprawled on Marianne's bed petting Muffin, stroking his belly as he rolled over onto his back. He purred, purred. What solace in animals, I thought. What refuge. Muffin nudged his head against me, tried to burrow beneath my arm. There was something frantic in his affection. I wondered—could he smell his lost brother Big Tom on me, or any of the other cats? Was the entire world of High Point Farm evoked in his cat-brain by my smell, quick and ephemeral as a bubble?

Marianne would not yet know the farm was to be sold. Would she?

I heard her ask shyly about "things at home" and Mom murmured "Oh you know—everything happens at once!" And Marianne asked about Dad and Mom said quickly, "Oh you know Curly!—his left hand doesn't know what his right hand is doing, I swear." She laughed, a sound of fond exasperation.

Curly! No one had called my father that in years.

I knew from Patrick that he'd told Marianne about the terrible things that had been happening: Dad's arrest at the Country Club, the ugly publicity, the lawyers; the two-year suspended sentence and probation and the fifteen-hundred-dollar fine. The Mulvaney family turned inside out for everyone to contemplate.

Marianne smiled weakly, and looked at me, but I was scratching Muffin under the chin, *I* wasn't going to butt in.

Adroitly then Mom changed the subject, asking Marianne about her college courses, and Marianne said vaguely yes she was learning *so much*—but she'd had to drop one of the courses, American history, she hadn't been able to keep up with the work. Next semester, though, she vowed—she wouldn't let herself fall behind, not by a single assignment. "Well, good!" Mom said brightly. "We can't all be like your brother Patrick, a whiz kid who doesn't have to study to get all A's."

Marianne had to hurry downstairs to finish preparing the midday meal, as it was called, where we'd be guests of course, but before she rushed off Mom explained awkwardly that we wouldn't be staying the night in Kilburn and Marianne said, hurt, "Oh, but I thought— you were planning to, this time? There's a choral concert some of us are singing in—at my church—I told the minister my mom and brother were coming, and—" Mom said hurriedly, "Yes, honey, but it's the weather, you know—you just don't know what weather this time of year will *do*. And, well—" her voice faltered, her eyes searched Marianne's face, "—we're expected back home tonight."

Marianne tried to smile, biting her lower lip. "Well. Next time you visit us, then."

"Absolutely!" Mom beamed at us all, Muffin included.

Promptly at noon a gong sounded and Mom and I trooped downstairs and into the dining room for a cheerful, noisy, confused meal at a long table with as many as twenty-five people (their numbers kept shifting as people arrived, departed). Marianne introduced Mom and me and one by one around the table the members of the Co-op gave their names and said "Welcome!" and "Happy holidays!" Even as these smiling strangers, young men and women in their twenties, called out their names, I was forgetting their names, awkwardly self-conscious in their midst. They were so *friendly*. They were so *inquisitive*. Mom was in her element in such boisterous company, jumping up every few minutes to accompany Marianne back into the kitchen, insisting upon helping serve the meal even as others cried, "No, no! Mrs. Mulvaney, you're a *guest*." Mom basked in the attention, loving every moment. It was clear that Marianne was much liked by her friends but she seemed oddly shy; it would have been easy to overlook her. But not Mom, who announced to the table, "When I was a young mother, mealtimes at our house—we have a farm, in Mt. Ephraim—maybe Marianne told you—were *wild*, I mean *wild*. At harvesttime there'd be as many at my table as— right here! We had our own babies of course and visitors would come to the farm with their babies and I remember one Sunday supper we had three high chairs at the table—or was it four, Marianne?" Laughing then, slapping her hand against her forehead like a TV comic, "Oh!—Marianne wouldn't know, *she was one of the babies*."

I was starved and ate everything that was passed to me. Steaming-hot lentil soup with walnuts, fresh-baked buttermilk bread. Some chalky-pale cheese that hadn't much taste, and some runny white yogurt that had even less. There was spinach macaroni, there was a rice-and-vegetable casserole. Mom kept exclaiming how delicious everything was, asking who'd baked the bread (Marianne) and who'd made the lentil soup (a thickset boy named Birk) and was the spinach macaroni made on the premises (it was, by a girl named Edie) and she promised to send the Co-op some raspberry preserves she'd canned, and some Bartlett pears from her orchard. So much did Mom talk, and so exuberantly, she scarcely touched her food, just pushed it around her plate and at a strategic moment switched her plate with mine, which was not only empty but had been wiped clean with chunks of buttermilk bread. (This was something I'd seen Mom do with Dad's plate lots of times. Like at our old July Fourth cookouts, where Dad would clear his plate in five minutes, eating and talking simultaneously, and Mom would unobtrusively switch plates with him and Dad would continue eating and talking, taking no notice he'd been given a new plate, more food.) The more Mom talked, the more Mom performed for the Co-op, the more sullen I became. I was sixteen years old and in some ways mature for my age but in other ways still a young, callow kid. I seemed to be seeing Mom through Patrick's eyes. *She's a casualty, too. She's sad, pathetic. Not to be blamed.* Not that Marianne wasn't overjoyed—she was. It was obvious how she loved us, her mom and kid brother. Not that Marianne's friends didn't like Mom, obviously they did, laughing at her jokes, flattering her with questions about the farm. Almost, I expected Mom to stand up, hands on her hips, and start whistling.

For the visit, Mom was wearing wool slacks and one of her old hand-knit sweaters she'd acquired at a secondhand shop, heavy as a ski sweater, with ribbed shoulders and a starburst design in bright orange and green—it reminded me of Number Four's football jersey. For a festive touch she'd added chunky turquoise earrings and dabbed rouge onto her cheeks. As long as she kept talking, laughing, a girlish glow in her face, she looked young, but when she was quiet, her face in repose was lined. I guess she'd lost weight, too. The heavy sweater disguised her thin arms, flattened chest. Seeing her through strangers' eyes I saw that her hair wasn't what you'd call carroty-colored any longer, but a dull grayish brown. Her eyes were pale blue and startling but had a tendency to shift out of focus as if she was distracted in the midst of talking. There was even a faint purplish bruise on the underside of her jaw and it went through me like a knife blade *Dad did that.*

It wasn't a thought I could hold on to. The table was being cleared for dessert, platters of date-nut brownies (baked by Marianne that morning) were being brought in, pots of herbal tea. And Abelove, the Co-op director, had just hurried in, late for the midday meal, no time for the midday meal, but taking time to shake hands with Marianne's mom and kid brother—"Welcome to Kilburn! Great to see you!" Abelove was like one of our teachers at the high school, a youngish guy exuding "personality." He was in his mid-thirties maybe, stockily built, a round head and thick neck and pale blond hair, goatee and shimmering locks to his shoulders like a blond Jesus Christ. The kind of guy you resent like hell until he singles you out for attention, lets his hand fall on your shoulder (as he did with me calling me "Judd" as if we were old friends, and equals), at which point you melt and go crazy for him. When he praised Marianne for her "tireless spirit of optimism" in the Co-op I saw my sister's eyes film over with tears of gratitude.

How many girls in the Green Isle Co-op were in love with this character, I didn't want to speculate.

Patrick said of Marianne she didn't know, or didn't want to know, when she was being exploited. She didn't know what evil was. She'd cheated herself of knowing because she forgave too soon.

When Patrick uttered the word *evil*, it made me shiver. I never knew exactly what he meant. What is *evil*, after all? I'd asked him if he believed in Satan and he said irritably no he did not, he'd outgrown Satan as he'd outgrown the Christian God. I asked him how can there be evil without Satan? and Patrick laughed saying who did I think invented Satan, if it wasn't human beings?

That day in the Co-op dining room in Kilburn, this Christly Abelove in his green nylon parka, burly chest and beaming smile and blond-glimmering beard, made me think of such things. I'd rather not have thought of them. Like thinking of my father hitting my mother, his fist striking out as if, maybe, in his mind, it was self-defense. Bruising her jaw and she'd be quick to invent some slightly comical explanation *Oh I walked into a door, daydreaming as usual!*

Nor did I want to think of what my brother Patrick might be planning, calculating to do to Zachary Lundt. *Executing justice!*—what a weird, unlikely notion, in the company of so many good-natured smiling Green Isle people, these cheerful strangers my sister now lived among as if she was one of them.

The things we didn't say. We three Mulvaneys.

That strange, dissatisfying visit. Who would have guessed it was the last time Mom and I would visit Marianne in Kilburn?—she was so far from graduating.

I knew from Patrick how he felt about the Green Isle Co-op: he disapproved completely. I should have asked Marianne more about her classes, what she was majoring in, what she planned to do when she graduated. Teach public school? High school, junior high, what? As Patrick had said, she seemed to be spending most of her time working for the Co-op. Mom should have pressed her on these matters too but of course Mom didn't. Through the afternoon Mom talked of far-flung subjects, passionately she defended Jimmy Carter's adversarial position with Congress, declaring to Marianne and me that President Carter was being "stabbed in the back" by his fellow Democrats—the United States government was at the mercy of special-interest groups, lobbies like the National Rifle Association and the American Medical Association, the automobile and oil industries, every kind of defense manufacturer, how could democracy be served? *What is democracy?* Mom demanded to know. *How can the American people be so deceived, by their own elected legislators?* Poor Jimmy Carter, practically the only honest man in Washington!

So Mom talked, talked. Until suddenly it was late afternoon, nearing dusk, almost time for us to leave.

Why, it was almost the New Year 1979!

Marianne, for her part, laughed a lot. Smiled, plucked at her short, scrappy hair. She was careful not to ask awkward questions— about Dad, or the farm. Chose her words guardedly when asking about the animals. Once, when we were alone together for a few minutes, she remarked again how much I'd grown, how "handsome" I was getting, and I rolled my eyes like any kid brother. *This is how you act, with your sister. Isn't it?*

"I guess—I really miss you, Judd," Marianne said softly. There was a look almost of fear in her face. "I wish—"

"Yeah, I know."

"But I'll probably be home this summer, for sure. Mom was saying."

"Great."

"Muffin sleeps curled up here, now." Tenderly Marianne indicated the hollow of her neck and shoulder. "He's lost his extra weight. He's beautiful, don't you think?"

There was Muffin perched on Marianne's desktop, between us, looking urgently from Marianne to me, from me to Marianne. His nose was pale pink, whiskers clean and bristly-white. The tawny eyes with the black-slitted pupils, intelligent-seeming, alert. I thought—He hears things we aren't saying. Marianne petted Muffin, and his purr became a loud crackling rumble like a motor. She said happily, "He hasn't slept against my neck since he was a kitten. So it's good he's lost that extra weight."

"He's looking great."

"He's just the most wonderful *cat*."

"Well," I said, laughing, miserable suddenly and eager to be gone from Kilburn, "—they all are."

Mom wanted to speak with Abelove before we left, downstairs in his office. She wanted to tell him how impressed she was with the Green Isle Co-op—such wonderful, idealistic young people. Above all she insisted that Abelove accept payment for our meal—she pressed bills into his hand with the fluttery-anxious air of a wealthy woman eager to rid herself of loose cash. "*Please* accept this, just a small token!" she begged. As if Abelove had somehow to be placated as well as paid. "You were so generous to include us at your table."

Abelove said, with his big broad smile, "Marianne's family is family of ours. You're always welcome here. But, well—thanks!" He took Mom's money and smoothed the bills out on top of his desk—it looked like about fifty dollars. "Green Isle can use whatever donations any friends can spare. Kilburn State doesn't give the Co-op any financial support apart from leasing the property to us for a hundred dollars a year. Was it run-down, when we moved in!"

Smiling eagerly, Mom said, "Marianne was explaining—'From each, whatever he or she can give; to each—' "

"—'as he or she requires.' "

"Oh but you've all done such a marvelous job here! You live plainly and simply, you eat wholesome food, *no meat*—I wish I could get my husband to give up meat—you're like the early Christians. Before the sects split off, and there was so much rivalry—quarreling. I think, deep in our hearts, we *know*—we don't require theology. There's such happiness in this house, such a sense of—well, family." Mom was worked up, spots of color in her cheeks. It was the way she'd been speaking of President Carter shortly before. "I wish I'd had such a friendly place to live in, instead of just a dorm, at Fredonia State, when I was in college. My daughter is so *lucky.*"

Luckily Marianne didn't hear this. Or Mom didn't notice me slouched and waiting outside Abelove's door. Rolling my eyes. *Geez, Mom.*

It was then that Mom's and Abelove's chummy-chatty exchange took a disastrous turn. How often at this time in all our lives, conversations with Corinne Mulvaney or Michael Mulvaney Sr. took disastrous turns and you'd never be prepared.

Expansive and beaming like a man who's practiced his smile since babyhood, Abelove was seeing Mom to his door. They'd been getting along one hundred percent: Abelove was obviously impressed with Marianne's unexpectedly feisty good-sport mom in slacks, gaudy ski sweater, her hair flyaway yet not unattractive, and Mom was just perceptibly giddy in the younger man's robust masculine presence. Not a sexual energy between them, but almost. Then Abelove made the mistake of saying, "Mrs. Mulvaney, I mean Corinne—you must be very proud of Marianne. She's a special young woman. We call her our *peacemaker.*"

"Do you!" Mom said, her smile going faint. "Well. My daughter has always been a—special person."

"Your daughter possesses a remarkable purity of heart. She has faith in God and in mankind, in equal measure." Abelove's voice dipped warmly, like a preacher's. "She just requires a little more faith in herself."

Marianne was out of earshot, still; down the hall, talking with someone.

Mom said sharply, pressing a hand against her heart, "What? I don't understand." She drew herself up to her full height, stood staring eye to eye with the startled young man. "I'm not in the habit of discussing my daughter with strangers, Mr. Abelove."

Abelove blinked at my mother, surprised. He tried his smile

again, easing it out like something on a leash. "But, Mrs. Mul-vaney—Marianne is not a stranger to any of us."

"*You* are a stranger to me, Mr.—oh, that silly made-up name!" Mom's fingers lifted fluttering to her hair. "Please, this conversation has gone on long enough."

Mom walked quickly away, snatching at my arm in passing. Abelove rolled back onto his heels like a boxer who's taken a hard, unexpected punch to the midriff. He looked at me pleadingly but I just glowered at him, "Good-bye! Thanks for lunch!" and stalked off after my mom.

Coatless in the thin, freezing wind, her eyes shifting, Marianne kissed us good-bye, hugged us and wept and made us promise we'd stay overnight next time we visited Kilburn, by then the weather would have turned warm. I'd slid behind the wheel of Mom's Buick station wagon which was looking kind of grim these days, rust-flecked, low-slung, one of the rear windows mended with masking tape. I was impatient to get out of Kilburn: the sky had darkened in rapid, shifting patches, like a jammed-up ice floe. By the time we reached the foothills of the Chautauquas and twisty-treacherous High Point Road, it would be dark as midnight. Marianne was ask-ing Mom another time to please say hello to Dad, and give him her love, and tell him she was thinking of him all the time; and the same to all the animals! And—did Muffin look all right? or did he look, maybe, a little thin? and Mom said brusquely, "When cats age their kidneys start to fail, you know that. Toxins build up in them and they lose their appetites, even the big, husky eaters, and they lose weight and you'll have to be realistic, Marianne. Muffin isn't a young cat any longer. He must be—how old?"

Taken by surprise, Marianne blinked at Mom. "I—don't know. Six years? Seven—?"

"That cat is eleven if he's a day," Mom said severely. "You'll just have to be realistic, Marianne."

I ducked my head, couldn't look at my sister's face.

Backing the station wagon then out of the deeply rutted drive-way, skidding briefly on an icy patch and then we were on the road aimed for home even as Marianne ran after us in the driveway to stand at the road waving eagerly, braving the wind, a small lone rapidly vanishing figure in the rearview mirror.

BROTHERS

"Mainly what I'll need from you, Judd, is one of the guns. From out of Dad's cabinet."

I murmured *Yes, all right.*

"One of them is Dad's .12-gauge Browning shotgun I've never fired. I held it once in my hands, though. It's heavy—lethal. Double-barreled. It could blow a man's head off at close range. Also there's the .22-caliber Winchester rifle of Mike's—remember? He got me to shoot it a few times. Target practice back of the barns. I remember Mike was surprised, I actually hit the target—beginner's luck, he said."

I didn't remember this. I'd have been too young. My brothers wouldn't have wanted me tagging after them. Or maybe it had never happened? I had the idea, if I telephoned Mike at the Marine base in Florida, he'd laugh and deny it. *What, Pinch? Blind in one eye? He couldn't hit the broad side of a barn.*

Patrick was saying, marveling, "It's strange to be talking like this Judd, isn't it? But it seems right. I've been more at peace since I've started planning what has to be done. Other things, that used to crowd my mind, make me anxious and keep me awake—they've fallen into perspective now, they've lost significance. Is it the same way with you?"

I murmured *I guess so. Right!*

If I spoke so, aloud, it must have been true.

Patrick said, "I couldn't go on with my life. My 'normal' life. Until justice is executed. Until our enemy is punished."

Each time Patrick spoke with me on the phone, through December, January, February, his plan for the *execution of justice* seemed more defined, elaborate. It was as if, away in Ithaca, he was contemplating a map on his wall the details of which he could only hint at, to me. He had scheduled the *execution* for April, at Easter when he assumed Zachary Lundt would be home in Mt. Ephraim. Patrick's plan was to surprise Zachary after dark, take him away at gunpoint, preferably in Zachary's own car. There was a place Patrick would force Zachary to drive (he wasn't sure he wanted me to know where, just yet—didn't want me "incriminated" unnecessarily) where they would be isolated and where whatever was to happen would happen. "I'll demand from him an acknowledgment of guilt. Yes, he raped my sister. Yes, he's a rapist and a liar, he's evil and deserves to be punished. You can believe in evil apart from the devil. There's no Satan but there *is* evil. Evil is genetically programmed into our species, like our rapacity against nature, our greed and superstition and stupidity—I mean, the inclination. We have a choice of activating the evil within, or not. We have free will. *I* have free will, and so does Zachary Lundt. He chose evil, he destroyed my family and he has to be punished." Patrick spoke matter-of-factly. I listened mesmerized by these words which were like no other words ever uttered to me in my life. "I don't mean that I'll use the gun. I might be forced to, if he refuses to come with me. I'm aware of the danger—a bullet or bullets could be traced. So if it's an actual execution, if it comes to that," Patrick spoke quickly but calmly, "—I'll use a knife. Maybe I'll let him live and be disfigured. I might castrate him, like a pig. I'm not sure. I haven't decided. I've chloroformed and dissected plenty of lab specimens. But I'll need a gun, Mike's rifle let's say, so that Mike has a hand in this, too, as I think he'd like, don't you? I need to let Zachary Lundt know I'm serious, in the first few seconds. That's the crucial time, when he could call for help, or try to escape." Patrick paused. The northeast wind sweeping across the Valley that sounded like a waterfall down the roofs and sides of our house seemed to be inside the telephone line, making my brother's voice shimmer and echo. "Judd? You're still there?"

I said *Sure. Sure Patrick!*

Gripping the telephone receiver so tight, my knuckles were waxy-white.

"You'll get Mike's gun for me, won't you? You'll bring it to me? And some ammunition, just in case? Somewhere we won't be seen. *I* can't be seen. Anywhere near Mt. Ephraim, I mean. I'll need to be in two places at once, because I can't be caught and what I'm going to do can't be repeated. It's an experiment that can be performed only once." Patrick spoke in measured, thoughtful sentences. He was both my older brother P.J. whom I adored and feared and someone I didn't know, whose face I could not imagine except for the squinty left eye, the glasses shoved against the bridge of his nose. "You'll have to unlock Dad's cabinet with his key, you can't force it. If you force the lock—well, you can't. We'll find some other means of getting a gun."

I was staring at the shadowy corner of the room where Dad's cabinet was. One of Mom's "antiques" with a glass front, made of a hardwood riddled with knots like eyes.

I told Patrick *yes*.

"So—what's your weather like there?"

Weather? I listened: wind. Possibly snow. It was 3:10 A.M. and I was speaking to Patrick ninety miles away on the phone in the family room, in the dark and with the door shut and Troy sleeping and wheezing contentedly at my feet. Upstairs, Mom was sleeping. She'd taken a long hot bath at eleven and I was pretty sure she was sleeping. I didn't know Dad's exact or even approximate whereabouts but I reasoned that if he drove up the driveway his headlights would precede him and I'd have no trouble escaping back upstairs to my room.

"It's a blizzard here," Patrick said. He sounded pleased.

Patrick reiterated that his plan for Zachary Lundt was just about complete in his mind but he hesitated to inform me of many details because he wanted to spare me involvement more than was necessary. He was certain he would not be caught by police, whether Zachary Lundt lived or died *he* would not be caught, still he was anxious to protect me, his brother. He said, with an air of regret, "No human action can be one-hundred-percent predictable. The future just isn't *there*, to be predicted."

I swallowed hard. Told Patrick I wasn't afraid. I would do whatever he wanted, whenever he wanted.

"It's a matter of simple coordination. You'll meet me at X, and you deliver the gun and ammunition. Mike's .22, my good-luck rifle. The only gun I've ever fired. You return home immediately and you stay home and you're totally uninvolved. Next thing you know you'll be hearing from me, you can pick up the rifle at Y, and return it to the cabinet. It won't be fired, I'm sure. If I realize I have to— well, kill him—hurt him—I'll use a knife. Just an ordinary steak knife. I'll buy one weeks ahead of time at a hardware store here— just a knife. Something that can't be traced. But I might not hurt him actually. Unless it happens. He'll be a coward, he'll beg for his life. He won't put up a fight. I know him. I know all of them— Zachary Lundt and his friends. They were going to lie about Marianne, to protect him. I wish I could punish all of them but I can't. Not just his friends but his father, too. And Dad's friends."

The bitter intonation of *friends*. The way Patrick spoke the word, curled his lip in disgust like Dad.

I whispered agreement. My voice was quavering. I felt a deep shuddering thrill as of someone in love, the first terrible time when you don't know it's love.

I thought, *I have a brother! I am a brother! This is what it is—to be brothers!*

Often when Patrick was about to hang up he would change his mind and leap onto another subject. The way, with a wildfire, a wind-borne spark can leap ten, fifteen feet in an instant, to start a fresh blaze. "Judd? You know how in evolutionary theory intelligence isn't a cause of nature, but only an effect, an accidental effect?—that's a hard concept to believe, I mean really. I've been arguing about it with my professors lately. I mean, I do believe, of course, but—"

I was dazed with exhaustion. Just five minutes of Patrick wore me out. Worse than mucking in the barnyard in ninety-five-degree heat. Worse than any memorization of equations in chemistry, physics. I was ready to burst into laughter. I was ready to ask why you couldn't believe anything you wanted to believe, wasn't it a free country? But I knew this was an ignorant response that would disappoint my brother.

I said *I guess so Patrick*. Said *I don't know*.

There was silence at the other end of the line. Just the wind that had gotten into the telephone somehow. I could imagine my brother's squinty eye, his look of exasperated patience. All Patrick wanted was someone, a brother, worthy of him. I can see that now. I must have disappointed him, for all my good intentions.

CROSSING OVER

You raped my sister he would say.

He would accuse *You raped my sister, you destroyed my family.* At gunpoint holding his cringing, cowering enemy *Did you think you would never be punished?*

That winter, except on the most bitterly cold windswept days, Patrick ran, ran for miles. He was too restless to stay in his room for very long, nor even to work at the lab as he'd once done, lost in concentration, staring down into the magnified, teeming world of microorganisms. He'd grown impatient with that world which had so little to do with his own. That anonymity, so without mind or purpose save its own infinite replication.

His fellow residents at 114 Cook rarely saw him except as he passed them on the stairs, or on the front walk, a tall hooded figure in a sheepskin jacket, wool muffler drawn up to cover the lower half of his face. There were numerous fanatic runners in Ithaca: Patrick Mulvaney would not have considered himself one of them, he believed his bouts of running, sometimes twice daily, were but extensions of consciousness. Where he couldn't any longer think clearly in his cramped little room, nor in the fluorescent-flickering lab whose smells gave him a headache, he could think with enormous clarity in the outdoors, in motion.

What pleasure in his body! his young lean-sinewy body! hard muscles of his calves, thighs! and his upper arms and shoulders, from the metronome-movement of his arms! His route was unvaried so that he didn't have to think about it. So that his mind was freed to think of other things. Up Cook's steep hill to College Avenue and north on College to Central Avenue crossing the Cascadilla Creek, and downhill to West Avenue and to the suspension bridge above Fall Creek, eastward then to frozen Lake Beebe, along the icy-reed-thick shore of Lake Beebe where at dawn juncos and chickadees pierced the air with their sharp, inquisitive cries and he recalled the wild birds at the feeders of High Point Farm, waking to those identical cries, the mysterious speech of birds mixed with his childhood sleep. For miles then along the lake and as far east as the Cornell Plantations, swinging back through the village of Forest Home that reminded him, the close-built wood-frame houses, the narrow streets and sidewalks, of an older area of Mt. Ephraim near the high school where he'd walked, alone, impatient with the din of lunchtime in the cafeteria, long before *it* had happened. Long before *it* had entered their lives. And always, what solace in aloneness! in his body's rhythmic motion! Through Forest Home he followed the southern shore of the lake, curving back to the Cornell campus which he reentered below the Newman Laboratory of Nuclear Studies, ascending then through the campus which was densely built here, his least favorite part of the run, where he might see and be seen by someone he knew, his identity as *Patrick Mulvaney* thrust rudely upon him like something shoved in his face. But his steely gaze, his high-held head and unswerving forward-motion discouraged friendly greetings, if any were imminent. And so back to Cascadilla Creek and down College to Cook. By this time perspiring, exhilarated and exhausted. And filled with hope.

Running revealed to him such truths! *Each moment in time has been one of wonder and dread and not-knowing.*

At the end of March, from a public telephone in Ithaca, Patrick called the Lundts, in Mt. Ephraim. It was five in the afternoon of a weekday. A woman answered on the fourth ring. Patrick introduced himself as a high school friend of Zachary's, naming a name ("Don Maitland") that might sound plausible to Mrs. Lundt, for there was in fact a "Don Maitland" who'd been on the periphery of Zachary's circle, and Patrick guessed the young men wouldn't be in contact, not after several years. Patrick asked for Zachary's address, telephone number, and so forth, and Mrs. Lundt provided the information readily enough, yes he was at SUNY Binghamton, yes studying business administration, no he wouldn't be graduating this year he'd taken a couple of semesters off but he was serious now, working very hard and she and her husband expected Zachary to get his degree possibly as early as next spring. Mrs. Lundt was pleasant-voiced, polite enough to ask "Don Maitland" how he was, what he was doing, and Patrick provided a plausible response, "Don Maitland" too had dropped out of school for a while but was back now, at Oswego Tech, studying electrical engineering. He asked, "Will Zachary be home over spring break? Around Easter?" and Mrs. Lundt said, "Certainly, yes," and Patrick said, "Great! Us guys can all get together, then, like last time," and Mrs. Lundt said, with a mild motherly laugh, "I'm sure you will."

Patrick might then have said good-bye and hung up. But he heard himself ask, with sly naiveté, "How's that girl of Zach's?"

Mrs. Lundt was immediately guarded. "Which girl?"

"I don't remember her name, exactly. A Tri-Delt, I think, at Binghamton. Blond—kind of tall—"

There was a moment's silence. Then Mrs. Lundt said, coolly, "If it's the girl I'm thinking of, I don't know."

Patrick said, with boyish admiration, "Zach's always been lucky with girls. Since junior high. When he wants them, he gets them; when he's done with them, they disappear. Us guys always tease him—what's he got that we don't?"

Mrs. Lundt laughed. Was "Don Maitland" flirting with her? "What do you know, Don, that I don't know about Zachary?"

Patrick said, "Hey, I don't want to be telling tales on Zach. Forget what I just said, Mrs. Lundt."

"*I* don't know what Zachary's private life is. *I'm* only his mother."

"Hey, that's what my mom says. I mean—about me."

Patrick and Mrs. Lundt laughed together. Patrick said, "Well, Mrs. Lundt—thanks! I'll be calling Zach, and I'll sure be looking forward to seeing him in a few weeks."

"—one of them, a girl named 'Joellen'—do you know her, or about her?"

"Who?"

" 'Joellen' something. I don't remember the last name."

"Maybe. From Binghamton? In a sorority?"

"*She* had her nerve. Calling *here*, wanting to speak to *me*."

"Uh-oh," Patrick said sympathetically. "When was this?"

"About six weeks ago. I mean the calls started then. She'd call any time—7 A.M., 10 P.M., once 2 A.M.! Of course we'd just hang up. We were thinking of changing to a private number. But finally I guess she was discouraged, she stopped. 'Joellen'—something. I'm sure she wasn't a college student really."

"Did you talk to her?"

"I most certainly did not! Not after a few seconds, the first time. When I realized who it was and what she wanted."

"What did she want?"

"—to tell lies, slander about my son. To *accuse* him—to his own mother."

"Accuse Zach of what? Geez."

"Oh—who knows? *You* know what girls can be like, a certain type of girl, chasing after boys. You must have the same problem?"

Patrick laughed. "Well, Mrs. Lundt, like I said—I don't have Zach's luck, I'm not what you'd call good-looking like Zach. *He's* got some way about him, just walks into a room . . ." Patrick's voice trailed off in admiration.

Mrs. Lundt said pleasantly, "Well. Zachary takes after his father. When Mort was young, I mean. And had his hair. But Mort, goodness, was never like Zach! He didn't have his poise. But of course things are changed in America now. After the Sixties."

"Yeah. People say."

"As early as eighth grade, girls were chasing Zach. Calling him at home here. Imagine—a girl of thirteen calling a boy at home. When I was in school, we'd have been mortified to do any such thing. We'd have died of shame."

Patrick chuckled sympathetically. "Yeah. My mom. too."

"We got him his own line, finally. Mort said—'Self-defense.' "

"I remember a girl, senior year. She wasn't a girlfriend of Zach's exactly, but—"

"Oh, there were so many. We didn't always approve."

"A cheerleader, I think—"

"Some of them were so brazen, you wouldn't believe it."

"This girl made some crazy accusation about Zach?—after a prom?"

"I don't remember that."

"We were all at a party, at Bobbi Krauss's, she tried to say us guys weren't invited but we *were*. And—whatever happened afterward, after this girl left with Zach, wasn't too clear."

"No. I don't remember."

Mrs. Lundt was speaking quickly, anxiously. About to hang up and Patrick didn't want to arouse her suspicion but he heard himself say, incensed, "This girl's dad, he was a farmer or something?—he came to your house? Zach told us, he was scared as hell. *You* called the police, though, Mrs. Lundt—"

Mrs. Lundt said, in a low rapid voice, "I—don't remember exactly. It was a confused time. The man was drunk and violent and threatened to kill my husband and son—"

Patrick said, "Hey look, us guys were all on Zach's side. For sure. If it'd come to a—you know, trial—we were going to testify for Zach."

"Oh, yes. We so appreciated it, Mort and I. We were so terribly upset. But the girl *was* lying, and exaggerating, and nothing came of it."

Patrick said, incensed, "Zach always knew he could count on his buddies. We didn't need for any lawyer to talk to us, to tell us what to say."

Breathless Mrs. Lundt said, "Oh yes, Mort and I did appreciate it—your loyalty. It was a terrible, terrible time—"

Patrick said, "Hell, Mrs. Lundt, if there's anybody a guy can count on, it's his buddies."

"We were terrified that madman—the father—would come back here, and—do something violent. The police said they couldn't keep him in custody and he wouldn't listen to reason."

"Geez. Whatever happened to him, and the girl?"

"The girl moved away, thank God. Her family sent her away. The man—I'm not sure." Mrs. Lundt was breathing quickly, audibly. She seemed on the verge of bursting into tears. "I think I'm going to have to hang up now."

"Hey, I'm sorry if I upset you, Mrs. Lundt. I didn't—"

"I'm going to hang up now. Good-bye, Dan."

Patrick said, "Thanks for Zach's number, Mrs. Lundt. See you!"

As if he'd been in terror of a bridge. A suspension bridge for instance. Fear of stepping out onto it, a narrow high-swaying bridge like the one across Fall Creek. And to his astonishment he discovered no danger in it—none at all. Crossing the bridge scarcely aware of what he did and he was safe on the farther side.

★ ★ ★

Hard to believe that Patrick Mulvaney was making such mistakes.

Three times, before Thanksgiving, he'd changed his research topic for his senior honors thesis in biology. First he'd been working on a problem of membrane biogenesis, then on a problem of invertebrate genetics, both topics suggested to him by his supervisor Professor Herring. But he couldn't maintain his initial interest. He tried, tried very hard. He understood that a young research biologist must work under the guidance of his elders. You're part of a team, you do what you're told and don't question why. But Patrick became discouraged and impatient, tossed away his data.

His third topic was more theoretical than the first two, and would involve massive amounts of reading in areas new to him, and less lab work. This was an application of mathematical game theory to Darwinian evolutionary theory. Patrick wanted to analyze the concept of the "forced move" in evolutionary design: the biological imperative in which, in order to survive, a species must adapt along a line of X and no other. (Examples were parasites that become exclusively dependent upon a single host-species, the phenomenon of English sparrows dependent upon areas of dense human habitation, short-term gestation in certain species, long-term gestation in others, odd features like eyes on stalks, or recessed eyes, exoskeletons, minute brains.) The "forced move" was a metaphor from chess. You make your move as a species in crisis, brilliant, desperate, lucky or doomed—you have no choice. In retrospect, if you survive, it could be hypothesized from a future vantage point that you'd "adapted" to an altered environment. You'd exercised biological "specialization." The record might seem to show, or one might argue it did show, an unconscious DNA-design. Purpose, intelligence.

Unless the record argued utter randomness, chance. In which case species survival isn't an essence of species but mere accident.

When Patrick spoke of such matters to Professor Herring, in Herring's office in Lydall Hall, the elder man regarded him with bemused eyes. Frequently, he interrupted Patrick to ask him questions which Patrick fumbled to answer—"That's one of the things I want to know." Herring was a vigorous man of middle age, with a reputation in the department for caprice and cruelty, for exploiting disciples who eagerly did scut-work for his protégés among the younger faculty; but he was a brilliant man, generously funded by the National Science Foundation and by the university, known to be remarkably kind to certain of his students, foreign as well as American, but all young men, whom he treated virtually like sons. For three years, Patrick Mulvaney had been a favored undergraduate of his. He'd arranged for Patrick to receive summer research grants, work-study grants, he'd written a surely strong letter of recommendation for Patrick, for graduate school; he'd given hum consistently high grades of course, while singling him out at times for harsh criticism. "You can do better than this, Mr. Mulvaney. *You* can do better," he'd said. And so Patrick did better, without fail. He was grateful to Herring, admired Herring beyond any of his other professors, but he was uneasy in the man's presence. As he was uneasy in the presence of all older strong-willed outspoken and physically robust men who reminded him of his father.

It's basically an uneasy position, to be grateful to an elder. Patrick wasn't sure he liked that position at all.

As Patrick spoke, at what would be their final conference, in January, Herring appeared to be listening with a growing air of discomfort. Patrick had turned up at Herring's office with a sheath of unnumbered sheets of paper covered in close-typed paragraphs and equations, diagrams, and graphs; he was unshaven, eye red-rimmed and gritty from lack of sleep. He'd rushed ahead on a new subtopic before he'd discussed, with Herring, the chapter he'd handed in the previous week. (He could see his earlier work, marked in red, on Herring's desk, waiting to be returned to him. Oh but what did he care about *that*, he'd all but forgotten *that*.) Patrick's reading in mathematical game theory was enormously exciting to him and he was floundering and flailing like a drowning man but—game theory was the key, he was sure! Joining Darwin and John von Neumann and John Maynard Smith—he was sure! Why is it that there exist organisms so similar in design to other organisms they're virtually indistinguishable from them, yet have wholly different DNA? What of the role of mass extinctions in evolution? What is the relation of "natural selection" to "adaptation"? Above all—how could life, which is highly complex biochemical activity, ever have arisen out of nonlife, which is chemical simplicity? *What sense does that make?*

Patrick's voice echoed in the large, high-ceilinged space of Herring's office. The walls of the office were lined with bookshelves and several garishly painted, tusked and black-haired African tribal masks. Eyeless, the masks gazed at Patrick with expressions of mild incredulity. What are you saying! How dare you speak like that! *What sense does it make?* Stricken with embarrassment, Patrick was reminded of the tale that made the rounds at their high school, that Marianne had put up her hand in biology class and asked Mr. Farolino why did God make parasites?

Professor Herring was pushing Patrick's last-week's chapter in his direction across his desk, a signal that the conference was over. The new chapter lay on a corner of the desk, yet untouched. Annoyed yet managing to smile, in an almost kindly voice, as one might speak to a bright, impetuous twelve-year-old, he said, "Why do you assume, Patrick, that there is 'sense' to be 'made' of any of this? Still more, that you're capable of making it?"

Next day, Patrick was notified by a departmental secretary that he'd been assigned a new thesis advisor. A white-haired associate professor whose speciality was philosophy of science, one of the "popular" lecturers whom the serious scientists in the department scorned.

Help me! Help—
One night in early April, fifteen days before he planned to drive to Mt. Ephraim to confront Zachary Lundt, Patrick woke terrified from a nightmare of—what? Quicksand dragging at his legs, seething steaming black muck, getting into his nose, his mouth! Into his eyes! He leapt from bed, stumbled and fell, his heart pounding. He was sobbing like a child. *No, no—help!—what is it!—leave me alone—* He'd confused his damp twisted bedclothes with black muck. Yet it seemed his bed *was* black muck. Liquidy as melted tar, roofing tar, the tar his dad used, yet living, a living organism, seething and sucking at Patrick Mulvaney greedy to pull him down inside it.

He switched on his bedside lamp with shaking fingers. Stared at the alarm clock not registering the time at first—4:35 A.M. And rain. Rain blown against his windows, a chilly draft from the window now that it was April and Patrick had removed the masking tape he'd been using as insulation. Now it was officially nearing spring, the landlord at 114 Cook was more grudging with heat; Patrick's room was as cold as if it were winter. Yet he'd been sweating in his sleep, in such terror of being suffocated. He wiped at his eyes imagining lashes were stuck together with black muck. Christ, how disgusting!

It must be nerves, that was all. Yet Patrick was certain he hadn't any nerves, really. His plan for the *execution of justice* was complete except for a few minor details. Nothing could deter him.

He'd vowed he'd be willing to trade his life, if necessary, in order to *execute justice* against his sister's rapist. Nothing could deter him.

Patrick went out into the bathroom in the hall, used the toilet and splashed handfuls of cold water onto his face. There were his eyes, finely threaded with blood, seemingly enlarged without his glasses, regarding him in the splotched mirror above the sink. Were those the eyes of a twenty-one-year-old capable of murder? Patrick smiled at himself saying, "Yes. Right."

It served him right, he'd had a nightmare. Boasting to Judd earlier that night how well he'd been sleeping lately. How deep and restful his sleep. He wasn't even thinking of his goddamned academic work he'd let slide, classes he'd ceased attending. He'd been provisionally accepted into the Cornell Ph.D. program in biology, depending of course on his final grades; he'd missed the deadlines, or lost the application forms entirely, for admission to the University of Chicago, the University of Michigan, Berkeley and one other where Herring had, last fall, encouraged him to apply. But he didn't lose any sleep over any of this. Nothing could deter him.

Judd had said, maybe not meaning to be insolent but it struck Patrick that way, "Lucky you."

Patrick flared up at once. "Hey kid, if you want to back out of this, go right ahead. I can do it alone."

Quickly Judd said, "No! I'm in it one hundred percent."

"Just let me know, if you're afraid."

"I *am* afraid, sure. But I'm in it one hundred percent."

"If you don't trust I can do this right. If you're having second thoughts."

"Hey P.J., *no*."

"Forget that 'P.J.' crap!" Patrick said. He'd meant to make a joke, a species of joke only another Mulvaney would get, for its daringly mutinous tone, but his voice was quavering. He went on, hurriedly, in the schoolboy-pedant style he'd developed at the Mulvaney kitchen table, impressing his family with his precocious ways, even as he'd made them laugh, "We didn't get legal justice. We couldn't. Dad tried, and failed. Because the legal justice system is just a social institution, and it's inadequate as an expression of morality. The way of 'legal justice' is to apply to a third party elevated above the 'victim' and the 'perpetrator' and their respective families and sanctioned by the people—the State. The State administers justice. But who *is* the State? Just more people. Specimens of Homo sapiens. And why should these specimens be elevated over others? Why should we grant to strangers a moral authority beyond our own? I've given a lot of thought to this, Judd. I'm not acting impulsively. Always at the back of my mind I see Marianne—abused, vilified, exiled *even by her family*. Like we're some primitive tribe, for Christ's sake! Like our sister has become a carrier of taboo! It's ridiculous, it's intolerable—*I won't tolerate it*. I'm not a Christian any longer but by God I'm a Protestant—a rebel. *I'll execute my own justice, because I know what it is.*" Patrick paused, embarrassed at the passion of his speech. Such talk, aimed at his kid brother. "Judd? Hey, sorry—are you still there?"

Judd must have been moved by Patrick's high-flown words. He said, quietly, "I'm always here, Patrick. Count on me."

Back in his apartment Patrick stood for a while at his window, fearful of returning to bed. The sheets would be damp and twisted, smelling of animal panic. That unmistakable sweat-smell. He thought of Judd, a casualty too of Zachary Lundt's rape of Marianne. The poor kid stuck at High Point Farm in its waning, disintegrating days. He and Mike had cleared out, and Marianne was exiled, and Judd, the baby of the family, was left behind. In the past several months, in these nighttime telephone conversations, Patrick had grown closer to Judd than to anyone else in the world—except, maybe, Marianne. (He loved Marianne intensely. But with Marianne you didn't speak directly, couldn't speak the kind of truth a brother could speak to another brother.)

Strange: growing up with Judd, Patrick hadn't taken him seriously. Almost, he'd never looked at him. A kid brother is just someone who's *there*. Difficult to think of a kid brother as an individual with a life, his own secret thoughts, motives. But now, at the age of sixteen, Judd wasn't a child any longer and he'd become Patrick's friend and ally. Patrick liked him—very much. And respected him for his integrity and courage. Respecting a kid brother—what a novelty!

Yet Patrick wondered if, living together at High Point Farm, face-to-face, always, as in any family, competing for the attention of their father and mother, they'd be capable of such frankness and intimacy as the telephone allowed.

Sitting now at his desk, papers shoved aside. Head, which ached dully, in his hands. Jesus, what a close escape. Almost suffocated in that black muck. It had been, possibly, tar—molten tar—the tar he'd worked with, summers, on Dad's roofing crews. (What grueling, demeaning work. Laboring like slaves, for hourly wages, bare-backed on roofs.) But it was also, he seemed to see, a bog—a bog off Route 58, going toward Yewville. That dismal swampy area where a shallow creek emptied into the Yewville River north of Mt. Ephraim. Cattails and jungle vines and those brilliant purple wildflowers—phlox? loosestrife?—grew there in profusion in summer but most of the trees had been dying for years, as the water table rose, bark peeling off their trunks in tatters. At any hour of the day patches of sickly mist hovered over the bog. There was a pervasive odor of rot, of sewage. Just possibly, raw hog sewage seeped into the bog from a large corporate farm a few miles away. As a boy Patrick had never explored the bog, nor had anyone he knew. It was much too far to have bicycled to, from High Point Farm. Even in bright sunshine it retained a look of sinister desolation. In warm weather it was teeming with birds, frogs, water snakes, insects—microorganisms in unfathomable numbers. Now, in April, in the spring thaw, the liquidy black muck would be stirring into life after its long winter hibernation.

"Jesus!"—Patrick shuddered, feeling a pang of nausea. He rubbed, rubbed, rubbed his eyes where something was sticking to his lashes.

THE HANDSHAKE

H *e won't want it, maybe? This is just to test me?*
Noon of April 16, the Saturday before Easter Sunday 1979, the brothers met at the spot Patrick had designated: an unpaved stretch of Stone Creek Road, near a railroad embankment, ten miles east of Eagleton Corners. The area was mainly scrubland, no houses. In deer-hunting season men in fluorescent-orange hunters' dickeys came in carloads to prowl through the woods but it wasn't deer-hunting season now.

When Patrick drove up in his battered, mud-splotched Jeep, there was Judd anxiously waiting in the Ford pickup with the .22-caliber Winchester rifle, wrapped in a strip of canvas, on the passenger's seat beside him. Judd's heart lifted at the sight of his brother whom he hadn't seen for some time. If this was a test of Judd's loyalty and faith in Patrick, he knew he'd done well.

So far as Corinne knew, Judd was on an errand to a farm supply store in Eagleton Corners. Neither Corinne nor Michael Sr. had any idea that Patrick was anywhere near home.

Patrick slowed the Jeep but continued past the turnoff where the pickup was parked. Deftly turned in the road, and drove back to park close by Judd, facing the opposite direction. He swung open his door as Judd opened his but neither brother climbed out of his vehicle. In these quick confused seconds Judd had absorbed the significant fact that both the front and rear license plates of Patrick's Jeep were partly obscured by mud. "How's it going, kid?" Patrick asked. The voice was not Patrick's voice. From their many telephone conversations Judd had come to know Patrick's voice as intimately as his own but this voice, loud, aggressively cheerful, was not that voice. Chill sunshine fell from directly overhead through the Jeep's not-very-clean windshield and onto Patrick's pale, sharp-chiseled face. He looked older, scarcely recognizable. He was wearing wire-rimmed sunglasses so dark as to appear black and his jaws were covered in whiskers of approximately a week's growth. He was wearing an army fatigue jacket and his hair was completely hidden beneath a dark woolen cap pulled down low on his forehead. Judd stared, fascinated. "What's wrong, kid? Don't you know your old brother Pinch?" Patrick seemed pleased.

"You do look sort of different."

"That's my intention."

"Well. I brought the—what you wanted."

"Great! Give it here."

Stone Creek Road was empty of traffic in both directions, so far as Judd could see. He handed Patrick the rifle in its canvas wrapper and Patrick examined it on his lap, behind the steering wheel. He stroked the polished stock and drew his fingers slowly along the long slender barrel. He lifted the rifle to his shoulder, aimed it beyond Judd's head, frowning through the scope. Judd steeled himself preparing for Patrick to pull the trigger. Who knew if Mike's old rifle could even fire, after so many years? Judd hadn't dared to test it, himself. Patrick had said he didn't want the rifle fired, no evidence of recent use, if that could be avoided.

Weird: P.J. with a beard. How Mom would laugh. Though she'd say Patrick was handsome, too. Any new thing the brothers did, like Mike slicking his hair back oiled in high school, or P.J. getting his round wire-rimmed eyeglasses instead of those Mom had selected, she'd make a fuss initially, declaring she'd never get used to it, what an unsettling sight, then come around after a few days to marveling how handsome her sons were, after all. As if she'd made the choice, not them. And maybe she'd remember it, she *had*.

Watching Patrick, Judd began to recognize something. Those bristly brown whiskers. The tight-lipped expression. Patrick reminded him of one of those Hebrew prophets from their Sunday school Bible cards! They'd been given so many of them, as children, at one or another of the churches their mother had taken them to. Judd's favorite when he'd been a little boy was someone named Amos because on his card, in bright primer colors, Amos was tall, manly, sharp-eyed and fanatic in his bushy beard and herdsman's clothes and the caption beneath his picture was *The LORD will roar from Zion. Amos 1:2*.

Judd was saying, "I was worried I wouldn't be able to locate the key to the cabinet but it was in the kitchen drawer, Mom had tagged it. 'Cabinet, family room.' Just like Mom."

Patrick didn't reply. He was examining the rifle like a finicky customer. He'd opened it, peering at the bullets; extracted a bullet to hold it to the light. Judd saw, or believed he saw, that his brother's hands shook slightly. Patrick said, "Did you bring any more bullets?"

Judd had forgotten: a box containing two dozen bullets, never opened, he'd found in one of the cabinet drawers. "Oh, yeah. Here."

"I doubt I'll be using them, but—" Patrick smiled, taking the box from Judd, "—you never know. 'Chance follows design' but not invariably."

" 'Chance follows design'—what's that mean?"

"You make careful plans, and 'chance' seems to favor you. Things go your way that look to a neutral observer like luck. But it's luck you've engineered."

"That sounds good."

"But not *invariably*. Because design can collapse, no matter how carefully it's been planned."

Patrick shut up the rifle, covered it with the canvas and laid it on the seat beside him; put the box of bullets into the Jeep's glove compartment. His movements were brisk, methodical. He was preparing to drive away. They'd been together scarcely five minutes. Judd felt a stab of panic—wasn't there more to be said, explained?

He thought *If it's only a test it can end now.*

Patrick named another out-of-the-way location, about equidistant from Mt. Ephraim and High Point Farm, where Judd could retrieve the rifle the next day. This was the old abandoned cemetery on Sandhill Road, surrounded by a crumbling stone wall where, at the rear, if you approached it from the rear, there was a niche the gun could be shoved into beneath the wall. Patrick said, "You'll be going to church with Mom? You won't be able to get away until later but pick up the gun as soon as you can. If there's any change of plans I'll try to call you. But it should be all over by then."

How lightly *it* sounded on Patrick's tongue. But what did *it* mean, exactly?

Patrick lifted his dark glasses to look at Judd. His eyes were star-tling—not eyes that went with the beard but young eyes, quizzical and alert. "How's the sale of the farm coming along? Any luck?"

Judd shrugged. It was too painful to talk about somehow in the open air. "Mom says we can buy it back sometime. She says that at least once a day."

"But is anyone interested in buying?"

"Sure, people are interested. A doctor and his family drove out from Yewville last week. If we're home, the realtor tries to keep out of our way. Usually we're not home. Mom makes it a point not to be home. So weird to see people you don't know, strangers, being shown . . ." Judd's voice trailed off, *weird* was so juvenile and inade-quate a word to express what could not be expressed but only endured.

"How's Mom taking it?"

"She's all right. She's the one negotiating on the phone, mainly."

"Does Marianne know yet?"

"She must know."

"*I* didn't tell her."

"Well, she must know. Mom's always saying Marianne should be 'realistic.' "

"And Dad, what about Dad? He's 'realistic'?"

"He's negotiating to move the business to Marsena, unless he's negotiating to file for bankruptcy. He isn't home much but when he is he's on the phone with lawyers."

"Is he drinking, much? How's he behaving to Mom?"

Judd thought *What about to me?*—the other day, he'd asked his father please not to shout at his mother and his father had come close to striking him in the face. "Look, Patrick, drop by and see us sometime. It's only ninety miles from Ithaca, it isn't the dark side of the moon."

Patrick looked away. He said, quietly, "Not just yet. Not for a while."

"Yeah. You said."

"I can't forgive them, for Marianne. Him, especially. It's never going to be the same again and Mike feels the same way. I was talk-ing to him a couple of weeks ago—he feels the same way."

"Marianne forgives them. She isn't even thinking of it."

"Of course Marianne is thinking of it! Don't be ridiculous," Patrick said irritably. "Marianne doesn't think of anything else."

Judd said, suddenly angry, "I thought you said Dad and Mom

were 'casualties.' Why blame them for treating Marianne like shit if they're just—what's it?—frogs sucked to death by water spiders."

"For the same reason Dad blames Marianne. You just have a gut feeling, you don't want to see too much of a person."

"What about me? I live there."

"You'll be leaving in a couple of years."

"Going where?"

"To college. Anywhere."

"But it's our *home*. It's where we *live* for Christ's sake."

"Judd, what the hell are we talking about? What's wrong with you?"

Judd wiped at his eyes. He was losing Patrick, he couldn't help what he said. "I don't know what's wrong with me. I just don't want—any of of this. I wish—"

"Sure." Patrick leaned over to touch Judd's arm. The touch was remarkable, as if it had materialized out of the very air. "Where do you and Mom go to church these days?"

"Just this little country church in Milford. Church of Christ Risen. They used to be Methodists but broke away for some reason. They're nice people, good people. Mom mostly sits in the pew at services and prays. She sings the hymns, really loud. Like she's happy, and it matters to show it. Sometimes she cries a little. A hymn like 'Tell Me Why' can set her off. It's like she has a breakdown every Sunday morning, then blows her nose and smiles and we talk awhile to the minister and his wife and some others and I drive us back home and that's Sunday."

"Well. Tomorrow's Easter."

"Sunday of Sundays."

Judd was going to ask Patrick about the knife, had he brought the knife, but he couldn't summon up the words. And at that moment Patrick leaned over to shake Judd's hand. His handshake was strong, frank, unhesitating but his fingers were cold. Judd smiled, taken by surprise. It was the first time either of his brothers had ever shaken hands with him.

They said good-bye. Turned their vehicles around to drive in opposite directions: Judd back to Eagleton Corners, Patrick to the far end of Stone Creek Road. Judd waved out the window at his rapidly departing brother. He wondered what Patrick would do between now and dark; between now and *it*. He told himself *It was a test. It is! And almost over.*

THE BOG

*C*hance *follows design.*

He wanted to believe that. It did seem to be so, after his many weeks of fevered planning.

Sitting now, at eleven that night, moon-bright Saturday eve of Easter Sunday, in his Jeep at the rear of the crowded parking lot of Cobb's Corner Inn where Zachary Lundt and three of his high school buddies had been for the past forty minutes. The Jeep's motor was off, no headlights. Beside Patrick on the passenger's seat, hidden by a strip of canvas should anyone pass close enough to glance inside (but no one did, or would: Patrick had parked just far enough away from other vehicles, partly on the grass) were Mike's .22-caliber Winchester rifle, several yards of rope, a roll of black duct tape, a powerful flashlight and a fishing knife with a double-edged eight-inch blade acquired at a Sears in Whitney Point, New York weeks before. Except for the rifle all were anonymous items, randomly and anonymously purchased.

You would not really use that would you P.J. The knife, or the gun.

You would not be so cruel, or so desperate.

A half dozen times Patrick climbed out of the Jeep to stretch his legs, pace restlessly about in the damp gravel. The parking lot was a busy place: vehicles arriving, departing. No one glanced at him, he might have been anyone. Older than twenty-one, probably in his thirties. The army fatigue jacket added bulk. The bristly beard was not a college student's beard. Patrick was restless but not at all anxious. He might even have whistled to himself, through his teeth, thinly. *Whistle while you work!* It was only practical advice to be cheerful, optimistic. That was Mom's fervent belief and Mom was the daughter of farm people, knew you had to persevere with a smile until you couldn't and then it no longer mattered, you're done. You're gone. But until that moment have faith. Patrick was surprised, he was so calm: his thoughts floated on a placid surface without ripples, no rough current, no urgency. He knew what he would do though he did not yet know when he would do it, what the exact steps would be. *Chance follows design.* A state of pure waiting, suspension—as before an exam for which you've thoroughly prepared and are anticipating now you'll be thoroughly tested, and excel.

It was a clear, startlingly bright night. Smelling of wet grass, gravel. Beery fumes and greasy cooking odors from a vent at the rear of the tavern. Earlier, Patrick had slipped inside Cobb's in the wake of a company of noisy young people, stood unobtrusively by the bar searching for Zachary Lundt. His nostrils pinched at the smells of beer, cigarette smoke, barbecue sauce, pizza. COUNTRY & WESTERN DISCO was advertised but there was no disco tonight, only deafening rock music from the jukebox. Was it Plastica? Patrick wondered, bemused. He wouldn't have known. Hadn't given Plastica a second thought. Rock bands all sounded alike to him, pulsing hammering thrilling noise that worked itself into your heart like a screw.

Patrick knew that Zachary Lundt was at Cobb's. An hour before he'd telephoned the Lundts to learn the whereabouts of his friend Zach, "Don Maitland" just home from Owego, or was it Oswego, eager to join his friends for the evening, and Mrs. Lundt who'd answered the phone in a girlish voice had seemed to remember him, or maybe hadn't, in any case provided the information Patrick needed. Later, maybe the rest of her life she'd regret it but—who could have known, at the time? *We never suspected. How would we have suspected!* Mrs. Lundt had told him Cobb's Corner at ten, asked if he knew where that was, and Patrick said, "Know where Cobb's Corner is? Hell, Mrs. Lundt, everybody knows that."

Patrick stood not quite at the bar, not a customer but just someone who'd strolled in looking for a friend. His wool cap pulled down low on his forehead, wearing now his daytime glasses, and the collar of the army jacket turned sharply up. In the beard that felt like thistles on his face, in his steely-blank expression, he believed himself disguised. In fact, there was no one who looked at him for more than a glancing moment, not even one of the bartenders. There was no one in the tavern, so far as Patrick could determine, whom he knew, except, in a booth against the farther wall, Zachary Lundt and his friends. They were drinking beer, laughing together, smoking.

It was the first time Patrick had seen Zachary Lundt since high school graduation. The day when, unable to avoid passing close by his sister's rapist, he'd fixed his gaze on Zachary's forehead, his face taut and expressionless as now. If the other boy had blushed, or stared defiantly at him in turn, Patrick hadn't noticed. So frequently had Patrick imagined Zachary since October, since his obsession had overcome him, he had to force himself to realize, no, he hadn't seen Zachary, not in person, since June 1976. And Zachary did look slightly altered: hair differently styled, face thicker at the jaws. Still there was the sly foxy narrowness at the eyes. The heavy-lidded eyes. Girls had found him attractive and Patrick supposed he could see why. Except how broken-backed Zachary appeared, leaning his elbows on the sticky tabletop, laughing his hyena-laugh with the others. He was smoking a cigarette, expelling smoke from his grinning mouth. Patrick remembered—hadn't he smashed his fist against those teeth, once? Hadn't he drawn blood? Maybe not. Maybe it hadn't happened yet. He felt a thrill of excitement in the pit of his belly. In his groin. It was a sensation Patrick Mulvaney had never had before. Except possibly in his dreams.

Zachary Lundt. Now a student at SUNY Binghamton, studying business administration. Out drinking with his old high school pals Ike Rodman, Budd Farley, Phil Spohr. Pizza crusts lay scattered on the table before them, beer cans, glasses. Crumpled napkins. They all deserved punishment, not just Zachary. He'd wait for them in his Jeep and when they left Cobb's, one by one he'd pick them off with the rifle. Execution of justice. Calm, methodical. Irrevocable.

Was Patrick Mulvaney capable of such an act? A forced move, one time only. You wouldn't know, would you, until you tried?

Sometime, maybe. And the father, too—Morton Lundt. Even the mother, Mrs. Lundt. They too were involved. They too were guilty. Defending the rapist, slandering the victim. That breathless admission *Mort and I did appreciate it—your loyalty.*

Patrick backed off from the bar, unseen. Left Cobb's, returned to the Jeep, to wait. Thinking how unsuspecting they all were—his enemies. They had no reason to be otherwise. He himself could not have said why now, why such passion on his part now, after such a long time. The Mulvaney men had long shirked their responsibility, that was it, and it was unsaid—Mike Jr. had fled all the way to the Marines where he boasted he was a new man now, soon to be shipped to the Mideast. Michael Sr. had fled—God knows where. But there was Patrick. He was not the Mulvaney man you'd have expected to exact revenge but there was no other, and no choice.

At 12:10 A.M. at last Zachary and his friends appeared, leaving Cobb's by the side door. Beneath the lights of a concrete walkway bordered by crude stucco latticework. The young men stood talking and laughing before going to their cars—Patrick might have picked them off one by one. How unsuspecting they were, unknowing. Oblivious of danger. Patrick thought of the fantastic wingless birds of New Zealand that had intrigued the young Charles Darwin. No mammal predators for millennia—a heaven of birds, of countless species. As if all of creation were exclusively birds, yet birds not birds—unable to fly, helpless against predators when predators arrived. Easy prey.

Zachary crossed the lot to his car, a Corvette. He walked carefully, as if resisting the impulse to sway. He'd been drinking beer for hours, he was drunk. His friends pulled out of the lot while Zachary stood fumbling in his pocket, searching for his keys—no, it was a pair of glasses he took out, and put on, after his friends were gone. So Zachary needed glasses to drive. So his vision wasn't perfect.

Patrick started the Jeep, waited until Zachary's Corvette pulled out of the lot and followed him. A left turn, a quarter mile and a right turn, headed for Zachary's house in north Mt. Ephraim near the Country Club. Zachary drove cautiously, not very steadily, weaving in his lane. He seemed unaware that only his parking lights were on, not his headlights. Patrick waited for the strategic moment—as Zachary turned onto Depot Street, through a darkened stretch of overgrown vacant lots, boarded-up warehouses—before overtaking him, passing him on the left and blocking his way. The Corvette came to an abrupt halt. Patrick leapt from the Jeep, rifle raised to his shoulder and aimed at Zachary's head. "Don't move! Stay where you are."

As if, taken so utterly by surprise, mouth gaping in cartoon astonishment, Zachary Lundt could have behaved otherwise.

Quickly Patrick came around to the passenger's door of the

Corvette and climbed inside, keeping the rifle trained on Zachary Lundt's face. In mere seconds that face had drained of blood. Zachary appeared paralyzed. His staring eyes, the slack of his mouth, his very posture that seemed to have caved in upon itself—he was in a state of panic, totally disoriented. "Don't shoot, please don't shoot," he begged, "—oh please don't shoot me, you can have my w-wallet, my car—anything you want—*please don't shoot*—" His voice cracked, there was no volume to it. He'd begun to tremble convulsively so Patrick felt the tremors of his body as if they were his own.

Is this all there is to him?—the thought pierced Patrick like a knife blade.

After so long, years—this is all?

It was not a thought Patrick could retain. He had his plan, his strategy. He would not be deterred.

Patrick said, "Drive up ahead. See that underpass? On this side of it, turn in, drive the car up that lane, go ahead. Go!"

For a dazed moment Zachary sat unmoving. Patrick was losing his patience. He tried to speak reasonably, "Come on, drive. You won't be hurt if you do as I say." Patrick's voice was deep, guttural, a voice to match the beard, the wool cap, the army jacket. "Come on, for Christ's sake *move*."

Zachary whispered, blinking rapidly, "P-Please don't hurt me— don't shoot me—you can have my m-money—my car—please!—I won't t-tell the police—I won't tell anyone—I p-promise—"

There was a sharp smell of urine. Zachary had soiled himself.

"Drive where I told you!" Patrick said. "Don't be such a coward."

Like a disgusted elder brother, Patrick prodded Zachary with the rifle barrel. In his endlessly rehearsed scenarios of this event he would never have pleaded with his enemy, would never have touched his enemy with the gun; the Zachary Lundt of his imagination, wily and quick as a fox, would have seized the barrel and wrenched the gun out of Patrick's grip and shot him point-blank in the face. But this was a different Zachary Lundt entirely.

He didn't seem to recognize Patrick. His eyes brimmed with tears behind his glasses, he seemed incapable of focussing upon Patrick's face.

"I said—don't be such a coward!"

"Let me go—please! Don't—"

"Drive up to that lane and turn in, now."

Zachary fumbled at the transmission, the steering wheel as if he'd forgotten how to drive. He was sobbing to himself, his breath in shuddering gasps. But he did manage to follow Patrick's orders. He drove the Corvette haltingly forward to a lane that led off Depot Street into a desolate back lot of junked cars and other debris. The moonlight was vivid: the dump looked like an impromptu gathering of fantastical creatures. Hulks of rusted vehicles, part-burned mattresses, gutted sofas and chairs and broken lamps, refrigerators toppled onto their sides with doors gaping open like mouths. Patrick was reminded of Darwin's first glimpse of the Galapagos Islands, the bizarre species and subspecies of animals he saw, a young man just a year older than Patrick. *What does it mean, chance has singled me out for such visions?*

Beyond the dump was a railroad embankment. A quarter mile away, the dimly illuminated water tower, MT. EPHRAIM in ghostly white letters. More vivid were scrawls emblazoned by teenagers, CLASS OF '78 in bold Day-Glo orange. Patrick wondered if anyone from the Class of '76, reckless enough to climb the tower, had left a boastful memento behind. Before tonight he might have credited Zachary Lundt and his friends with such exploits.

Patrick's initial plan for *executing justice* against his enemy was to execute it here. Whatever he'd do to Zachary, he would do here. Later, he'd changed his mind. He had a new idea, incompletely formed. But this spot, hidden from the street, in a sparsely inhabited part of Mt. Ephraim, was ideal for leaving Zachary's car without driving it far. With luck, the Corvette wouldn't be discovered for a day or two. And then only because a search would be out for its owner.

It was as if Patrick had spoken aloud. Zachary pleaded, "Don't hurt me, please?—you can have anything you want, I p-promise I won't tell anyone—"

"Oh for God's sake shut *up*." Patrick was both disgusted and embarrassed.

His nostrils pinching, at the smell of urine. Human piss so much more vile, he'd always thought, than horse piss.

"Turn off the motor," Patrick said. Zachary obeyed, and Patrick took the keys from the ignition and pocketed them. He would toss them away somewhere, later—unless he returned to get Zachary's car and drive it to some desolate spot, maybe into a lake or a river. This was one of his contingency plans. "All right, get out," Patrick said. Keeping Zachary at gunpoint, soldier-like in resolve, he marched him back to the street. In the shadows, in the rutted lane, Zachary kept stumbling, whimpering. He seemed to have shrunken in upon himself, inches shorter than Patrick remembered, shoulders bent and his head at a craven angle. He walked like a man whose legs are about to buckle beneath him. Like an invertebrate prized from its shell, naked, vulnerable, twisting into a coil for protection against the touch of the dissecting knife.

Was it possible, Patrick wondered, he himself would collapse so quickly, so ignominiously, confronted by a stranger with a gun? Is none of us any stronger, despite the heroics of TV, movies? Patrick didn't want to think so. He didn't want to think that his enemy, Zachary Lundt, whom he'd so long despised and in a way feared, was no more than this trembling whimpering boy who'd wet his jeans.

Still Zachary was begging, "Don't hurt me, please"—Patrick shut him up by prodding him between the shoulder blades with the rifle barrel. They were in the street, which was deserted, no light except moonlight and that light interrupted, as filmy clouds were blown across the moon's bright face. At an intersection not far away a lone car stopped for a red light. Patrick half hoped the car would turn this way—quickly he'd discover how he would handle the emergency situation, hiding the rifle by holding it lengthwise against his body, commanding Zachary Lundt to behave as if nothing were wrong. Would Zachary have had the courage to run for help? It might be his only chance to escape. Yet, Patrick guessed, Zachary wouldn't have the courage. Helplessly he'd watch the car pass, meek in the face of another's power over him.

But the car continued through the intersection. The street remained empty.

At the Jeep, Patrick ordered Zachary to get into the driver's seat, he was driving. "Ever handled one of these before?—you'll learn."

Zachary stared at Patrick, cowering. "W-Where are we going? What do you want with me?" His face was oily with sweat and his glasses were crooked on his face. Though he stared at Patrick, it did not seem that he recognized him; terror had blinded him. "Please let me go! Don't hurt me! My parents are waiting at home for me! They'll give you anything you want—they'll pay you anything you want—oh please, sir—*please*—"

Patrick said contemptuously, "I've got other plans for you. Rapist."

How many times, countless times since October he'd heard the voices. His, and his enemy's.

Say it: I'm a rapist.

I'm a—rapist.

Say it: I deserve to be punished.

I—deserve to be punished.

Say it: I deserve death.

And here Zachary Lundt would stare at him speechless. In knowledge of what was to come: his just punishment.

Beyond that, however, the vision was unclear. Patrick wasn't sure where it might lead. *The knife. An eye for an eye, a tooth for a tooth.* But possibly just his fists, he'd never used his fists against any person, a few times in exasperation shoving at his older brother Mike who'd shoved him, much harder, back, but never his fists, not Patrick Mulvaney. Yet he might—he would—how badly he wanted to!—strike his enemy, smash his enemy's mouth. Malicious grinning mouth he'd seen in the corner of his eye, how many times in the corridors of the high school, on the stairs, in the locker room, Zach Lundt and his friends, yes and other guys too, hinting of "Button" daringly in Patrick's presence, punching one another's biceps in glee, bursting into ribald jeering laughter. Almost out of earshot the coarse voices *Look she asked for it, drunk out of her mind and all over Zach begging for it, got what she deserves she was drunk trying now to blame Zach but we were there, we saw* unless Patrick imagined them, in his pride bearing himself tall, impervious to the presence of such others, inferior in every way to a Mulvaney. But he had not imagined the ugly drawings and block letters MM: MARYANN MULVANY. MMMMM SUCKS COCK. He had not imagined these, or his deep abiding shame, valedictorian of the Class of 1976, scholarship to Cornell, state science prize, aren't we hot shit his classmates murmured of him, laughing behind their hands. *Mulvaney, Mulvaney—look, he's a Mulvaney.*

In a rage, in his dream he'd begin to beat Zachary Lundt, as Zachary fell to the floor he'd kick him, kick him with booted feet, heard the crack of bone, the cartilage of the nose, saw the bright blood—but immediately the vision began to fade. As soon as he touched his enemy, the vision began to fade. Like a dream of whatever ferocious intensity, dissipating upon waking, dissolving even as the dreamer tries to retain it, with what yearning, what hunger.

On the way into the country, north on Route 58, and following the Yewville River, as terrified Zachary Lundt drove the Jeep unsteadily, between thirty and thirty-five miles an hour, Patrick thought of such things. *Executing justice. At last. He deserves—all I can give him.* Patrick had to force himself. His rage at Zachary Lundt seemed to have faded. Almost, he felt sorry for Zachary. How beaten, how defeated! Crotch of his jeans dark with piss. The smell of it. His backbone curved, teeth chattering. *He's already been punished, exposed* a voice advised Patrick. But this was not Patrick's plan.

He would not, he vowed *he would not* be deterred from his plan.

His plan how like an artwork he'd created, out of his guts, the anguish of his Mulvaney pride. He, Patrick, fussy P.J., intolerant touch-me-not Pinch his family had loved to tease, gazing in rapt fascination at the German woodcut of the huntsman he'd affixed to the wall of his room. The tall handsome manly blond youth with his rifle lifted to his shoulder, aiming at a magnificent black-curly ram with extraordinary horns. The finely drawn mountains, clouds that seemed somehow alive, quivering grasses, hidden hare in the foreground, all of Nature a setting for that moment when the huntsman pulled the trigger of his rifle—or did not pull it. In adolescent ardor Patrick stared, stared. He had never understood the riddle of the drawing and he had never understood why he seemed to care so much about it.

Signs flashed by in the darkness, illuminated by the Jeep's bright headlights—SLOW CURVE 35 mph—STEEP GRADE TRUCKS USE LOWER GEAR—YEWVILLE 65 mi. They were about ten miles north of Mt. Ephraim. To the right the Yewville River was dark, near-invisible behind dense banks of trees. This was not an area Patrick Mulvaney knew well yet unhesitating he'd instructed Zachary Lundt to drive north on Route 58. *Chance follows design.* Yet how much more readily than Patrick had imagined. Those many weeks of running in Ithaca, in air so cold it pained his lungs, as if preparing himself for an extraordinary test of strength, he'd believed his enemy would be cunning, dangerous, a match for him. He could not have guessed that the abduction would be so easy. Zachary Lundt who'd had such power over him, and over Marianne, ruining the happiness of their lives, so unresisting! It was as if Patrick had strode up to a door and knocked on it, hard, and—the door swung open.

Both the Jeep's front windows were rolled down, chill fresh air rushed in, to dissipate Zachary Lundt's stink. Panic-stink, not just urine but sweat. Oily beads of sweat rolled down his narrow face. Yet Zachary seemed to be trembling less now, he'd entered a secondary state of terror, a suspension of logic. In childlike obedience to his captor he sat gripping the steering wheel tight, his hands near the top of the wheel, leaning far forward and squinting out the windshield in a pose of utter unswerving concentration. Without hesitation he'd followed each of Patrick's commands, driving them out of Mt. Ephraim and into the countryside. Patrick was sitting with his back against the passenger's locked door, the rifle in his lap, aimed at Zachary Lundt's head. The dead-white face, beaky nose, slightly receding chin. *He thinks if he obeys me he won't be hurt* Patrick thought. The thought revolted him as if it were an acknowledgment of his own weakness.

Patrick said, "Up there, that gravel road, see?—turn off."

Zachary did as he was told. Braked the Jeep carefully, slowed *and put on the turn signal* turning off the highway onto a badly puddled gravel road hardly wider than a cow path, leading into the wilderness. Where did he think he was being taken? What could he envision for himself that would not be disastrous, in such desolation, alone with an armed man? Yet he did as Patrick instructed. Murmuring what sounded like *Yes, yes sir.* Like an animal hypnotized by its predator, a rodent about to be swallowed by a boa constrictor, putting up no resistance to its fate. As if the throbbing protoplasmic life of the prey had already been assimilated by the life of the predator, in allegiance with its terrible hunger.

Patrick thought *I won't weaken. I won't be deterred.*

The bog. The dying trees denuded of leaves, peeling bark the color of damp newsprint. Smell of rot, sewage. It was only mid-April and so the teeming thrumming life of the bog had not yet begun yet there was an atmosphere of density, crowdedness; as if invisible, ravenous shapes, all mouth and gullet, hovered near. How quickly a body would decompose here, Patrick thought. It was the first he'd had this thought.

"Do you know where this is?" Patrick asked, almost casually. He didn't want his deep guttural voice to weaken, with excitement. He didn't want to sound like a college kid, a boy Zachary Lundt's age. "Do you know who I am?" But Zachary seemed not to hear. All his concentration went into driving: wincing as the Jeep, even with its shock-absorber tires, lurched and bucked. "I know who you are—Zachary Lundt. That's why you're here."

The Jeep continued, slower and slower, until the gravel road became a spit of muddy land between stretches of bog and Patrick said, poking Zachary's shoulder with the rifle barrel as if to wake him, "Shut off the motor, we're here."

Zachary did so. Patrick pocketed the keys. It was very quiet now that the Jeep's motor was turned off and in that quiet Zachary had begun to cry again, softly.

The Jeep's headlights were still on, illuminating a cattail-choked marsh that stretched into darkness punctuated by slivers of light reflected in water. Patrick climbed out of the Jeep and switched on the flashlight. "Get out. Don't look back, Lundt, just *walk*."

Zachary climbed down uncertainly from the Jeep. He was sobbing, wiping his face on his sleeve. He whispered, "No, please— don't make me—"

"*Walk*. If you can get to the other side, you can live."

Was there another side? The headlights, Patrick's flashlight, the mottled light of the moon seemed to illuminate the same expanse of bog, replicated out of sight.

"W-Why? Why are you doing this to me? I don't know you—"

"You know me, sure you do."

"I—I don't. Please—"

"Rapist. Raped my sister. Now you know."

"Your sister? Who—"

"Now you know!"

"I never—never raped— Who?"

"There've been so many, is that it? So many girls?"

"No—"

Patrick began shouting, "Just *walk*, Lundt. You son of a bitch, you filthy bastard, ruining people's lives, a coward like you, filth like you, you don't deserve to live, you're filth and you belong in filth, *get going I said*." Patrick jabbed Zachary between the shoulder blades with the gun barrel, forcing him forward into the bog where he stumbled, whimpering as if desperate now to escape. Up to his ankles in the soft black muck, then to his knees. It was cold: his breath steamed. Patrick shouted at him, cursed—"You bastard, keep going! Don't look back or I'll blow your head off." He watched as, about fifteen feet out, lunging forward, Zachary fell; trying then like a frenzied animal to crawl forward through thistles, reeds, cattails.

Patrick heard bubbles softly popping, the black muck stirred to life, sucking at Zachary. Was it possible, as in his nightmare? The bog was quicksand? Zachary's terrified voice was barely audible. "Help!—help me—"

Patrick cried, raising the gun, "Help yourself, you son of a bitch! Rapist!"

Elsewhere, the bog was still, silent. A faint wind through the trees, what remained of the trees. Bearing an odor of rot.

Beginning to slant in the sky, the bright moon, mad-glaring moon, past which strips of filmy cloud were blown.

Patrick thought *He knows who I am, sure.*

Patrick thought *I have executed justice.*

Patrick thought *What an awful way to die.*

In that instant changing his mind, as if a key had turned in a lock, abandoning his plan though not immediately understanding that this was so. He'd sunk to his heels, squatting in the muddy soil, aware suddenly of his breath steaming, hands pressed against his ears so he wouldn't have to hear his enemy pleading for his life. *Let him die let him suffocate in filth it's what he deserves: rapist! Murderer!* Shutting his eyes tight, rocking on his heels as if mourning his own impotence, his failure for the object of his hatred wasn't the young man sinking in the bog but the high school boy of years before, smirking, conscienceless, a coward unknown to himself, unexposed and arrogant. And that object, that enemy Patrick could not reach. Rocking in anguish on his heels as once, a child of two or three, he'd seen his own father in what unimaginable extremity of emotion, what unarticulated anguish, having to put down a young filly who'd shattered both forelegs in a freak accident. This memory was so old, retrieved from so great a distance, a fossil record of Patrick's soul, Patrick was astonished—had he forgotten so much, even as he prided himself, above all the Mulvaneys, on his extraordinary powers of mind? He thought *I love my father, how can I hate him?*

It came upon him in a flash: he didn't want anyone to die, not even his enemy.

He pushed through undergrowth, spiky reeds and cattails, approaching the struggling figure from higher ground. How like a giant slug, a mud-creature, feebly flailing, its head and face mired in mud. Patrick snatched up a fallen tree limb about four feet in length and held it out to Zachary—"Hey! Lundt! Take hold! I'll pull you

out." Zachary was so exhausted, or dazed, he didn't respond at
once, until Patrick continued to shout at him; lifting, then, his head
with an effort. His pale face, mottled with mud, seemed on the
verge of dissolution, like tissue in water. His glasses were gone and
his eyes, rapidly blinking, looked both enormous and blind. He
lifted his right arm with great effort, straining to close his fingers
around the tree limb, but he was inches short. Patrick said, disgusted, "Grab hold for Christ's sake! God damn you!" But Zachary
couldn't grab hold, his fingers flailed helplessly, so Patrick had no
choice but to step out into the bog, his feet immediately sinking in
the soft bottom, he was wearing boots but only to his ankles and the
mud came to midcalf, loathsome cold muck seeping into his boots.
He muttered, "God damn you! God damn! Fucker God damn!"
leaning out as far as he dared, knowing the soft shelf of land would
drop away sharply, he held the limb out trembling to Zachary who
again tried to reach it, too weak to lift his arm for more than a few
seconds at a time. Zachary was sobbing, moaning. Patrick inched
farther out. His face was contorted in rage, self-disgust. He could
not believe he was doing this! He, Patrick Mulvaney! Rescuing
Zachary Lundt! After all he'd vowed, his proud plan of *executing
justice.*

It was then that Patrick lost his footing and fell heavily into the
bog, averting his face just in time to avoid a mouthful of mud. Unspeakable hideous filth, black muck. He gagged, he spat. By sheer
strength managing to lift himself, pushing out the limb to Zachary
who at last managed to close his fingers around it, weakly, then with
more strength, the strength of desperation, trying to pull himself to
solid ground. Patrick tugged at the limb, at Zachary, the dead
weight of Zachary, imagining himself sinking too into the bog, as in
his nightmare, as he deserved, betraying his own pledge, Patrick
cursed steadily, words he wouldn't have known he knew, rolling off
his tongue as if he'd been uttering them all his life, until after what
seemed like a very long time but must have been less than ten minutes he was able to haul Zachary close enough to seize his hand, his
arm, his shoulder and help him to firmer ground.

"There! You bastard."

Zachary lay senseless, choking and gagging, bringing up an acid-
smelling liquid from his guts. Patrick crawled from him, got shakily
to his feet. Where were his glasses? He wiped muck from his face,
out of his eyes, eyelashes. He wiped muck from his hands onto grass.

A loathsome smell covered him like a film. He was shivering in the cold, his teeth chattering. Furious as if a malicious trick had been played on him. "Lundt, you fucker! You don't deserve to live but—here you are." Patrick groped about the ground for his glasses, couldn't find them, then found them, thank God they weren't broken, he lifted them quickly to his face and fitted the earpieces in place, pushing the glasses against the bridge of his nose.

Now he could see again. Now he'd be all right.

"I let you live, fucker. I could have let you die and I let you live—remember that."

Zachary lay motionless on the ground, breathing in shuddering gasps. He squinted up at Patrick, with that look of being blind, helpless.

"D-Don't leave me here, please—"

Patrick cursed, and tossed Zachary's car keys at him. He located the rifle where he'd dropped it, and the flashlight, and climbed back into the Jeep, jammed the key in the ignition and started the motor. He was boiling over with fury, stinking of muck, and in no mood to humor Zachary Lundt any longer. Let the rapist find his own way back to Mt. Ephraim—hitch a ride in the morning out on Route 58. Let the rapist invent a story to explain what had happened to him, what had so fantastically happened to him, a college boy who'd met with high school buddies for a few beers at Cobb's Corner and next morning was discovered exhausted and dazed and covered in stinking black muck staggering along Route 58 ten miles from his car left parked in a dump off Depot Street, Mt. Ephraim—or let the rapist tell the truth, if such a coward dared tell the truth.

Quickly before pity weakened him further, Patrick backed the Jeep out of the bog, and escaped. The prospect of actually returning and helping Zachary into the Jeep and bringing him back to Depot Street to his car—no, no! He would not, *would not*. The experiment hadn't gone as he'd planned but it was over, outside him now. He was feeling good suddenly. He was feeling elated! How simple it had been after all, how easy once he'd begun. He'd known what to do and he had done it and it was done now and could not be revoked. *I could have let you die and I let you live.*

He and his enemy Zachary Lundt would remember those words all their lives.

III

"THE PILGRIM"

TEARS

There came Mom's excited voice *Dad is ready to see you now, honey.*

Or, no: Mom would surely say *Honey we're driving down to fetch you, just stay where you are.*

Muffin would trot excitedly into the room, hearing Marianne's happy voice. She'd snatch him up and kiss him on the nose, whiskers and all. And rush in a flurry about the room she shared with Felice-Marie preparing to leave the Green Isle Co-op (though she loved it here, she'd surely miss it—miss her friends terribly) and return to High Point Farm.

Marianne was waiting for that call from Mom. She was waiting, and she wasn't impatient.

It's true she was hurt. In secret. Never admitting to Mom, or certainly to Patrick over the phone. She did cry occasionally, even after so many months (how many? better not to count)—more than was healthy. Crying is nothing but a childish indulgence, crying is mostly self-pity—Marianne knew. Mom was never patient with nuisance crying as she called it. If you have hope, and faith, and enough work to keep you busy, you won't cry. So Marianne hid her tears, and believed that no one at the Co-op knew. Weeping in the kitchen amid so much commotion as she chopped onions, dozens of onions—that was a tactic. Marianne Mulvaney was always volunteering to chop onions! Sometimes too she was observed weeping while preparing bread, kneading the tough dough so energetically it about wore her out, so crying had some logic; and her salty tears fell into the dough, moistening it, and that was said to be why Marianne Mulvaney's breads (her specialties were nine-grain, zucchini, yogurt-and-dill) were everyone's favorites.

Another shrewd tactic for disguising her tears, at least Marianne believed it was a shrewd tactic, was to work out-of-doors as much as possible in cold weather. Preferably when the wind blew! Naturally, her eyes smarted from the cold and tears spilled down her cheeks—couldn't be helped. There she was, observed through a window, furiously raking leaves or spreading mulch in beds, in a chill autumn wind; or, more famously, the sole girl in the Co-op to volunteer for the Snow Removal Brigade, eager and energetic on bright snow-glaring winter mornings shoveling the front walk and the ridiculously long curved drive with a crew of muscle-armed males. Marianne in her blue-tasseled hand-knit cap and matching blue mittens traded jokes with the boys like a sister, wisecracks and friendly insults. Her face glistened with shiny rivulets of tears even as she laughed her dimpled laugh, wiped her cheeks roughly on her mittens. Who among the Snow Removal Brigade was in love with Marianne Mulvaney, the most mysterious, elusive member of the Green Isle Co-op? He, or they, watched her covertly, respectful of her shyness. What a good sport she was, even as she wept; she couldn't keep up with even the slowest of the boys but snow flew unstintingly off her shovel and they all joined to praise her—*For an eighty-nine-pounder, Marianne Mulvaney is tops*. It wasn't so funny, however, one January morning when the thermometer outside the kitchen window hovered at zero degrees, and tear-rivulets froze on Marianne's frosty-pale cheeks, and two of the boys insisted she go inside with them at once to thaw her face before frostbite set in. Marianne said scornfully, "Frostbite? That's never happened before." And, inside the house, "Frostbite? *I* don't feel a thing." But it was so, her tears she'd believed secret had turned to ice for all to see.

She had no choice but to allow her friends Felice-Marie, Amethyst, Val Allan to fuss over her, as Birk and Hewie looked on, administering lukewarm water to her cheeks that were porcelain-white and cold, gently dabbing with soaked cloths, not rubbing (rubbing could lacerate the skin! Hewie warned) but pressing, until after a few minutes blood flowed back throbbing into the capillaries and color returned to her cheeks and Marianne was all right, though wincing with pain. And embarrassment. It made her so angry! She knew she wasn't weak and here they were hovering over her treating her as if she were!

She said, "I'm a farmer's daughter from the Chautauqua Valley and a teeny little snow and cold weather don't scare *me*."

Though afterward, alone, she was transfixed by a sudden terrible fear. It was The Fear. The Fear that overtook her after people, well-intentioned of course, made too much of her. Especially if they worried aloud about her, and touched her. A wise voice warned *If you accept kindness undeserved, even worse will happen to you.*

How much, Marianne wondered, did Abelove know? What exactly had her mother said to him, in his office, shortly before she'd stormed out of the house, a shamefaced Judd in tow? It was believed, not very seriously of course but entertained as a possibility, that Abelove, Founder and Director of the Green Isle Co-op, knew everything there was to know about each of the members. You could only join if Abelove approved you, after an intense private conversation (not an "interview"), and though Abelove had been tactful and gentle and not at all prying with Marianne, she'd had the sense that—oh, it was silly, she didn't truly believe it—his greenish-gray eyes could so penetrate hers, he could read her mind.

Once to Marianne's extreme embarrassment she succumbed to one of her crying episodes working in the greenhouse, seeding flats of lettuce (romaine, red leaf) to be planted in early April, after the thaw. It was work she loved, but some random commingling of smells, fertilizer, crumbly earth, the heat of sunshine magnified by greenhouse glass on a filth-stiffened gardener's glove exactly like Mom's reminded her of High Point Farm, and she hiccuped, and wept, and laughed, and wiped at her eyes protesting she didn't know what on earth was wrong! must be an allergy! but the seizure didn't stop and didn't stop and her face grew smudgy and smeared from dirt where she wiped at it and at last Amethyst who was working with her slipped away to fetch Abelove who was overseeing the dumping of rich black topsoil into a bed and immediately Abelove came rushing into the greenhouse, bristling with authority and rubbing his hands with that air of someone eager to put things right and confident he's the man to do it. Marianne was so ashamed, she cried all the harder. Abelove squatted beside her, teasing, "Uh-oh. Amie was saying, you've gotten the soil all muddy with tears," indicating the soil in the flat which was in fact dotted with moisture. "What's wrong, Marianne?" Abelove always took up more space than his actual physical being required. A few inches away, he'd seem to be touching you. The fine hairs of Marianne's bare arms lifted like filings to a magnet. Abelove irradiated a powerful masculine heat, his somewhat ragged blond goatee and shoulder-length shimmering blond hair giving off light and Marianne was dazed by his nearness, stammering, "Oh, you k-know—just nothing." And Abelove, gazing at her with his greenish-gray teasing eyes, said in his kindest voice, as if speaking to a small child, "Hmmm. If *nothing* can cause such tears, what might *something* someday do?"

Which made Marianne weep all the more.

GREEN ISLE

She was waiting, and she was patient, but she couldn't deny even in her prayers she *was* hurt. It just didn't do any good to think about it. Alone in the room she shared with Felice-Marie, when Felice-Marie was away, hurt prickling her like the start of poison ivy and she'd find herself moving blindly, pacing the narrow floor, not knowing where she was or when it was only knowing the hurt whispering aloud "Don't you love me?—I'd thought you all loved me," working up silly tears, nuisance tears as Mom called them, recalling for the ten-thousandth time the errors she'd made, one-two-three-four-five, after the prom going to that party instead of back to Trisha's house and accepting that drink from Zachary Lundt she hadn't wanted and after that her head swirling and giddy and—next thing she knew she and Muffin were being bundled off in Mom's station wagon and driven hundreds of miles to Aunt Ethel's melancholy little bungalow in Salamanca—"Why can't you forgive me? Why can't I come home?" But the sight of her pouty flushed face in a bureau mirror made her laugh.

She'd hug Muffin who'd been perched atop the bureau all this while, watching her with a look of concern. "Oh, who cares? Right, Muffin? We've got work to do." At least, Marianne did: fifty—or was it sixty—hours a week at the Co-op, in the house or out-of-doors or in the store, which was thriving, in town. And studying and writing papers for her course, the single course she was taking this semester, at the college.

Well, she'd signed up for the course, anyway. "Introduction to English Literature"—required for all teachers' ed. majors. What with one emergency at the Co-op (there was poor hair-straggling-in-her-face Val Allan desperate because she had baking duties all day, dozens of cherry tarts to prepare on order, and an exam at 8 A.M. the next morning, so naturally Marianne volunteered to make the tarts though she herself had a term paper due in forty-eight hours) or another (there was Abelove's perpetually frantic assistant Birk rushing about looking for someone to help him deliver crates of fresh produce to the Pennysaver Food Mart at the Kilburn Shopping Center—something had happened to whoever was scheduled to help him, it was an emergency situation and naturally Marianne volunteered though she'd set aside a precious morning for schoolwork which was weeks behind) it didn't look promising that she'd complete the course, let alone get a decent grade in it. Her professor had called her in for a conference, he'd expressed concern she'd missed so many lectures, warned her she'd have to get a "high, solid A" on the final just to get a C in the course, and Marianne had stared at the floor, shamefaced and tongue-tied. She wanted to say *Oh but this isn't like me really. In high school I never missed any classes. I did all the work and my grades were A's and B's and I was never scolded, never.* Instead she murmured a whispery apology and slunk away in disgrace.

If Patrick knew! Well, Patrick didn't have to know.

Patrick had such high, impossible standards. It just wasn't realistic to expect so much of *her.*

Returning sometimes to the house, to her room, in the afternoon, so tired! her head spinning! especially if it was a day spent clerking in town at the store, where the cash register's *ring-ring-ring-ringing* wore her out, having wakened at 5:30 A.M. and by 5:30 P.M. exhausted, about to fall sleep on her feet, but it was a normal tiredness she supposed, a healthy tiredness, preventing her thoughts from flying off in the wrong direction. Despite the commotion in the house at this hour of day, raised voices, footsteps pounding the stairs, telephone ringing and dog barking, Marianne would gather up Muffin and slip beneath her quilt on her bed, curl up luxuriantly to sleep, twenty minutes was all she required, or only ten. Only five! Cradling the soft-furred lanky cat in her arms and pressing her cheek against his side so that his deep resonant purr entered her being, thrummed along her nerves and quieted them. Within seconds she was deeply and dreamlessly asleep.

Avidly Marianne read Charlotte Brontë. Not just the assigned *Jane Eyre* which she'd already read in high school, which she loved, and which made her cry, but *Villette* as well—what an unexpected heroine, the passionately chaste Lucy Snowe. And a collection of Charlotte Brontë's letters. Out of which she copied,

>   *Out of obscurity I came—to obscurity I can easily return.*

Marianne was so happy at the Green Isle Co-op, where everyone liked and respected her, maybe sometimes took advantage of her trusting nature but nonetheless respected her—sometimes she felt guilty about wanting in secret to go *home*.

Not that she ever uttered the word *home* aloud. She gathered that certain of her friends thought it strange that, virtually alone among them, Marianne was the one who never, at holidays and even in the summer, went *home*. Sometimes only two or three Green Isle members remained in the house during recess, and Marianne was always among them. But they'd learned not to ask. "Oh, Marianne, aren't you going home?"—for Christmas, Easter, whatever. Marianne knew, to her embarrassment, that they talked behind her back; the last time the question was asked, by a girl named Beatie, stuffing clothes into a suitcase at the start of Christmas recess, Beatie clamped her hand over her mouth and stared at Marianne in horror, like a child who has uttered a forbidden word aloud. "Oh, sorry—excuse me, Marianne.'"

Marianne laughed, though a needle was turning in her heart.

"I guess I'm not going home right now, I have so much work to do here."

It was a gracious answer. She hoped Beatie would relay it to any others who were curious about her.

Most of the Co-op members, male and female, from the youngest who was eighteen to the eldest who was in his thirties, complained of *home*. It was fashionable among the Kilburn College students generally, Marianne noted, to complain of *home, family*. Her professors made witty jokes about "domestic American rituals"—Thanksgiving, Christmas gift-giving, family summer vacations—in such knowing ways, everyone in class laughed; or almost everyone. Marianne perceived that to be without a family in America is to be deprived not just of that family but of an entire arsenal of allusive material as cohesive as algae covering a pond.

There was her roommate Felice-Marie, who wore day following day the same shapeless dungarees, Green Isle sweatshirt, and combat boots—the daughter of an Amherst, New York physician, and very well-to-do. Felice-Marie made Marianne swear to secrecy the fact that her mother insisted upon giving her ridiculous Laura Ashley dresses, cashmere sweater sets—"Nobody in the real world wears sweater sets! In 1979!" There was pretty, sarcastic Amethyst who was majoring in women's physical education despite her mother's certainty she'd never find a husband in such a restricted field—"She worries I'll become a *lesbian,* can't bring herself to utter the word but that's what she means, we just quarrel all the time and it wears me out!" There was Val Allan whose parents embarrassed her because they were such old parents, having had her in middle age, and they were forever turning up in Kilburn hoping to take her out to dinner, or to buy a new coat—"It's so pathetic, I could cry, Mother and Daddy can't accept I've sloughed off my bourgeois ways forever, I practically have to scream at them and then they *don't hear!*" There was Birk, the bundle of nerves, funny-frazzled Birk who'd been drifting through Kilburn College for eight or nine years, whose father was a lieutenant colonel in the New York State National Guard and a "neo-Nazi disciplinarian." There was Gelb whose mother was a superintendent of schools in Albany—another "neo-Nazi disciplinarian." Jill, Flann, Dwyer, Smith—all had *homes, families* that provoked curled lips, derisive smirks and eye-rollings, or pitying head-shakes and the murmured sigh, "That generation, they still believe in Vietnam for God's sake it's *hopeless.*"

Abelove, however, never complained of *home, family.* At least not that Marianne knew. Rarely did he speak of personal matters; rarely was he critical of others, let alone scornful. He was capable of losing his temper, boiling over as he called it, impatient with the slowness or incompetence with which his ideas were executed, but he shrank from passing judgment in any categorical way—" 'Let him that is without sin cast the first stone.' "

Uttering these words, thoughtfully, gravely, stroking the wiry-gleaming blond hairs of his beard, Abelove was a thrilling presence. The only person of Marianne's acquaintance who could quote Jesus Christ's words as naturally as if they were his own.

★ ★ ★

Then one day late in the winter of 1979, Abelove's assistant Birk disappeared—"Vanished off the face of Earth," as Abelove said in a dazed, hurt voice. Birk, long entrusted by Abelove with crucial responsibilities, had made the early morning's round of deliveries to area stores, handed out invoices and collected revenue, returned the pickup truck to the Co-op, and vanished. Nothing appeared to be missing from his room which was a clutter of old clothes, textbooks and papers dating back nearly a decade. He seemed to have left no message of farewell. The house was in an uproar as a rumor spread that five hundred dollars was missing from the Co-op's accounts, unless it was fifteen hundred, but Abelove insisted that no money was missing at all. As the agitation peaked, Abelove called an impromptu meeting of the members, stood on the stairs and shouted for them to be quiet—to cease at once spreading such a demoralizing rumor for even if it was true, which it was not, the tacit accusation that their friend and brother Birk was a thief was unfair to Birk since he wasn't present to defend himself.

Abelove was plunged into such low spirits, so distracted for days afterward, Marianne summoned up courage to volunteer for some of Birk's duties. Abelove said, with a faint smile, "*You?* Why, thank you, Marianne, but I doubt you'd be capable."

True, Marianne probably didn't look capable. Not that morning, at least. In her familiar elastic-waist corduroy slacks, a moth-eaten red wool sweater rescued from the communal rag-bin, her size-five canvas sneakers faded to dishwater gray, and a Buffalo Bills cap, also from the rag-bin, covering most of her short-trimmed hair.

Marianne laughed. "Abelove, it isn't fair to judge beforehand!"

The founder and director of the Green Isle Co-op blushed, stroking his beard. If there was one quality Abelove publicly cultivated, it was *fair-mindedness*.

Quickly then Abelove apologized. He assigned Marianne, with an optimistic smile, certain of Birk's duties. For instance, he and Birk each "expedited" deliveries to Kilburn College Food Services and to the half dozen area markets that stocked Green Isle baked goods, prepared foods and fresh produce; Marianne was to take over Birk's half of these duties. Much of "expediting," Marianne discovered, was performed over the telephone, and the telephone was—what?—something magical in her hand, like a wand, or a mask. A cheerleader's bright megaphone that allowed you to speak to complete strangers in a voice not exactly your own—louder, clearer, happier, more assured. Marianne Mulvaney's shyness evaporated as soon as the party at the other end of the line lifted the receiver and said, "Hello?"

Within ten days she astonished Abelove by adding a new store to their list, a farmer's market willing to stock Green Isle baked goods to see if their customers would buy. And Marianne was enthusiastically "expediting" one or two others.

The duty of Birk's which he'd most neglected was keeping the roster of Co-op assignments up-to-date. Each member had his or her special area of responsibility but each had other, rotating duties as well. The "roster" was a large accountant's ledger in which were listed, by hand, names, duties, dates and hours (kitchen/meal-preparation / cleanup / baking / house maintenance / grounds, etc.); members consulted the roster, or were supposed to consult the roster, to see what their duties were. They were supposed to sign in, and sign out, like employees. But Birk had disliked the task, for obviously it caused occasional friction; he'd become increasingly negligent, and many assignments went undone, or half-done; or were done spontaneously, as in a large family in which responsible, capable members step forward while others purposefully hold back. As soon as Marianne took over the roster, she disposed of the old ledger entirely. What a dull, dreary thing! It had made Co-op duties seem like—duties! Within days there was a new roster; on a bulletin board in the kitchen, amid colorful decorative touches, dried wildflowers, snapshots of Co-op activities, sunburst ribbons, were smiling crayon drawings of the members' faces, and beneath the faces were notecards listing their duties, thumbtacked in place. "Oh, Marianne! Did *you* do this?"—how many times the identical remark was uttered, Marianne had to laugh.

Overnight, as everyone marveled, the emphasis had been switched from *duties* to *people*. The roster had been transformed into a work of art—or almost.

And wouldn't they all be eager to perform their duties, seeing the roster was so attractive?—presided over by an arc of smiling faces?

At midday meal of the bulletin board's first day, when Marianne came rushing breathlessly into the dining room, she was greeted with applause from all her friends. And there was Abelove at the head of the table, rising to toast her—with a glass of Green Isle Elderberry Wine (nonalcoholic). "To Mari-anne Mul-van-ey. Expediter par excellence."

Marianne halted just inside the doorway, paralyzed with shyness. Abelove had to come to lead her to the table, to a seat beside his, his big warm hand light on her shoulder as a perching bird.

Abelove, Abelove! That was the man's true name. His first name was something odd and awkward like "Charlesworth"—an old family name, never used by Abelove himself.

Where Abelove's *home* was, his original *home,* no one seemed certain. He never spoke of himself. He was a man of ideas and action and he lived in the present, not the past. One of his favored sayings was, " 'God culminates in the present moment, and will never be more divine' "—was it Henry David Thoreau? It might have been Abelove's very voice. *Past* wasn't urgent, *present* was. *Past* can't be changed, *present* is still in the making.

Still. There were rumors. One Marianne had heard when she'd first moved into the Co-op—that Abelove had been married when he'd come to Kilburn as a faculty member, and that he had children somewhere, was maybe still married though long separated from his wife. A rumor he'd had a love affair with a (married) woman in town. A rumor he'd had a "tragic" love affair with a woman potter, now deceased, who'd lived just across the state line in the rolling Pennsylvania hills. A rumor Abelove was the disinherited son of a wealthy New England businessman. A rumor he'd been a Jesuit seminary student in the Sixties, who'd fallen under the spell of the charismatic activist Berrigan brothers. A rumor he'd been arrested more than once at antiwar rallies and had even spent some time in jail—maybe. A rumor—but Marianne laughed and clamped her hands over her ears. No more!

Once at the dining room table brash gap-toothed Beatie, who'd long had a crush on Abelove, dared to ask him point-blank where his home was, and Abelove said, frowning, " 'Home'? Why, right here. Where else would it be?"

Everyone who'd heard, including Marianne, glowed with happiness at this answer, wanting to applaud.

Keeping the Green Isle Co-op financially afloat in the wake of continual crises (the antique plumbing in what had been an old inn was always breaking down, the mausoleum-like cellar leaked as unpredictably as the roof, the chimneys backed up smoke and the furnace needed replacing and there was an invasion of brisk militant black ants—and more) was a full-time job for the Director. Abelove had had, against the grain of his own temperament, to branch out into what he disdainfully called "venture capitalism"—borrowing money from a local bank at a ridiculously high interest rate, investing in bakers' ovens, a huge kitchen range with twelve electric burners, freezers large enough to accommodate horses. Investing in farming equipment, tons of topsoil, seedlings and plants from area nurseries. Buying a new Ford pickup! And there was insurance!—property, vehicles. And what of medical coverage?—oddly, there were frequently accidents at the Co-op, you wouldn't believe the mishaps.

In 1976, Abelove had had to swallow his pride—"Like swallowing a large apple, whole"—and go out into the community of Kilburn in search of donors—"benefactors"—to help the Green Isle Co-op survive. He'd learned, he said, with a chagrined smile, to present his Mount Katahdin vision as if it were a commodity worthy of being supported by strangers. At least, he'd had some luck—there was indeed a small but distinguished roster of Green Isle Benefactors, most of them well-to-do widows or well-to-do elderly couples. Abelove's handsome face and earnest manner, his shimmering-blond hair and forthright gaze must have dazzled them. " 'From each what he or she can give; to each, as he or she requires' "—weren't these Christ's very words, or almost?

What worried him, Abelove confessed, was that he might start to enjoy seeking wealthy benefactors. For it turned out he had a talent for it—"Where talent takes us can sometimes be dangerous!"

Of his several years as an assistant professor of psychology at Kilburn College, Abelove rarely spoke, and then only with embarrassment. (Birk, who'd been one of his students, had said that Abelove was a wonderful lecturer—"Unforgettable.") He'd had to quit his position of privilege when it became clear to him that the process of evaluating—"grading"—his fellow human beings was inherently cruel, an intellectual extension of the cruelty of Darwin's "natural selection," the survival of the fittest, extinction of the weak. Abelove believed passionately in what he called Anti-Darwinism—"Because we are human beings, and endowed with spirit, in place of mere appetite, we can counteract nature. We can help the weak, and thereby help ourselves. All good rebounds. There is no paradox."

These words rang in Marianne's head, for Abelove spoke them often. *All good rebounds. There is no paradox.* What profound insights! She was sure she understood what Abelove meant, yet when she repeated these statements to Patrick, he'd naturally questioned her immediately—"Just what the hell is that supposed to mean?" Fixing her with his Pinch-squint. And, faltering, fumbling, she hadn't been able to explain. *All good abounds, there is no paradox.*

It *was* true, wasn't it?

And was Marianne in love with Abelove, like so many of the others?

Most of the young women of the Green Isle Co-op, and several of the young men?

Sometimes she thought *yes*, sometimes *no*. It was true her heart fluttered—absurdly, literally!—when he smiled at her, shone his eyes at her, pronounced her name—"Marianne." Sometimes, as if it were a poem he'd just invented, so melodic—"Mari-anne Mul-van-ey." Except he smiled at just about everyone in the same way, when he was in a brimming-happy mood at least, and pronounced their names in that way. He smiled at Teardrop the mixed-breed spaniel who was always wetting, in nervous sparkling flurries, the downstairs carpets—"Teardrop! Uh-oh! Maybe we should change your name to something other than 'Tear'?" He smiled at Muffin who mewed at him across a distance of ten or more feet, tail hoisted upright, ears pricking, eyes tawny-wide and alert. What a kindly sight, Abelove pausing in his rushing-about to hunker down to pet Muffin—"Muf-fin. Muf-fin. Handsome boy!" Of course, Muffin adored Abelove. Flopped down shamelessly at Abelove's feet, rolled over to expose his dazzling-white stomach for tickling. Marianne watched, biting her lower lip. It made her—well, anxious—her nerves tightening—watching the shimmering-blond, husky Abelove tickle Muffin, stroke the cat's uplifted chin with strong, deft fingers. And how Muffin purred! There was something frantic in such happiness.

Marianne watched. She laughed at herself—a schoolgirl crush, and she wasn't a schoolgirl any longer. Marianne Mulvaney was a young woman of twenty. And not so young any longer.

THE PILGRIM

So, of *home*, and of *family*, Marianne Mulvaney never spoke. If her friends in the Green Isle Co-op speculated about her, and whispered of her behind her back, she wouldn't have known, would she?—she couldn't believe anyone would care much, anyway. *Out of obscurity I came. To obscurity I can return.*

Except, this. Late one afternoon in May 1979 as Marianne rushed into the house, returning from a ten-hour stint at the Green Isle outlet in Kilburn (she was "acting manager" there until Abelove could get someone to take over permanently) and frantic to study for her Introduction to English Literature final exam scheduled for the morning after next, a worried-looking Felice-Marie told her that an unknown woman had called and asked for her, not five minutes before. "But she was breathing so strangely, and I guess crying, and sounded angry—I couldn't understand much of what she said."

Marianne halted in her tracks, tasting cold. "A—woman? Crying? Who?"

"Well, I just don't know," Felice-Marie said apologetically, frowning at something she'd written on a scrap of paper. "I don't think it was your mother—I've met her, I wouldn't forget *her*—but it was someone that age, sort of. 'Hahn'—'Hann Eschl'?—she was crying and she sounded almost angry, seemed to think *I* was *you* though I'd explained I wasn't. I'd guess maybe someone in your family has—" Felice-Marie paused, sucking at her lip, not wanting to say *died*.

Marianne said, " 'Aunt Ethel.' That's who it was."

Heart knocking against her ribs like a wide-winged bird desperate to escape confinement, Marianne rushed to the phone in the parlor, and dialed Ethel Hausmann's number, and to her dismay the phone rang, rang. *Oh please answer! Oh don't let it be*— Even in the exigency of such distress Marianne was clear-minded enough to reason that whoever had died, it could not have been Michael Mulvaney Sr.—for Aunt Ethel would not have wept for him. —*Mom. Dear God, don't let it be Mom!* A sickening realization swept over her, how she'd disappointed Corinne: every turn of her life since Valentine's Day of 1976, she'd disappointed her mother, wounded her mother deeply and now—what if it was too late to make amends? She hung up the phone, and with shaking fingers dialed again, this number she'd memorized years ago and would never forget though the several times she'd called Ethel Hausmann since leaving Salamanca, the older woman had been guarded and evasive speaking to her—maybe fearing Marianne was calling to ask for money? (And Marianne couldn't very diplomatically begin a conversation by quickly explaining, "Aunt Ethel, I don't want a thing from you, honestly! I'm just calling to say hello—" as she'd told Patrick who, in any case, hadn't been sympathetic—"Why call that old sourpuss 'aunt,' anyway? What's she to us?" in that sneering Pinch way, as if he was jealous of his sister calling anyone but *him*.) The phone rang—eight, nine times. Then on the tenth ring it was picked up, and there came Ethel Hausmann's breathless, excited voice— "Hello? What? I'm just leaving the house! It's an emergency, who is this?"

"Aunt Ethel? This is—"

"*Who? What?* 'Aunt Ethel'—? I'm nobody's aunt! I'm just leaving the house! I can't talk now!"

"—this is Marianne. Oh, what has happened?"

"Marianne." Ethel Hausmann came to a full stop, panting into the phone receiver. "Oh, yes—I called *you.* I'm just leaving the house, driving—by myself—to Ransomville—but maybe I should wait until tomorrow morning? All the family is there, they need me, but I've never made the trip after dark, only by day—I'm driving alone—what if my car breaks down?—the funeral is day after tomorrow, at eleven—" Ethel Hausmann spoke in the fevered high-pitched voice of a spinster lady to whom nothing has happened in a very long time. Marianne thought, dazed: *Ransomville. Not High*

Point Farm. She felt weak with relief; then guilty, at her relief. She managed to interrupt Ethel Hausmann to ask who had died, and Ethel said, with grim satisfaction, "Your Grandmother Hausmann." Marianne murmured, "Oh!—" her eyes welling with tears, for though she and her grandmother had not been close, Ida Hausmann was Corinne's mother, and Corinne would surely be upset. "Yes, my Aunt Ida is dead," Ethel said. "Seventy-nine years old! A stroke, they said, just this morning! She was chasing some stray cat away with a broom and—gone! Like that! My mother died the same way, so suddenly—I mean, it was slow for a long while—then, at the end, so sudden—twelve years ago next week. Now it's like it's happening again, Marianne, only with her sister. My aunt. And Uncle Will has been dead for *just years.* Your mother was on the phone saying 'That generation is nearly vanished, Ethel—who will take their places?' We're next, I suppose. Oh, it's a terrible, cruel thing—first you're young, and that takes up such a long time you think it's forever, then suddenly you're not young, and you never get used to it—and, oh dear, there's just the one way out."

Marianne listened respectfully as Ethel Hausmann rattled on. She interrupted only with difficulty, to ask about the family, and the funeral. What a shock—Grandmother Hausmann was dead! Marianne would never see her again! Yet she hadn't, in fact, seen her grandmother in years, nor even spoken with her on the phone since leaving High Point Farm. She had the idea (well, Patrick had been blunt about telling her) that the old woman had disapproved of her; of what Marianne had "done" with some high school boy or what "had happened to her"—whatever. Something embarrassing, shameful, to which no name need be given.

Of course, Marianne had sent Christmas and birthday cards to Grandmother Hausmann, year after year. But her grandmother had never replied.

Another person I've disappointed. No wonder Mom is so ashamed of me.

Ida Hausmann, Will's wife. Of the old Ransomville farm. That generation of German immigrants, settlers in the Chautauqua Valley in the 1880s. Rarely had Marianne's grandparents driven to High Point Farm to visit Corinne and her family—"Too far to drive, for a meal," they said. Of course, they wouldn't have considered an overnight visit. They were farm people, after all. You know what disasters can happen on a farm, if you turn your back for five minutes.

So the Mulvaneys had had to drive to Ransomville, for Sunday dinner, once or twice a year. It always seemed more often—"Oh, already?" the children would cry. There was Grandmother Hausmann no one called "Grandma"—Grandmother who was Corinne's mother, but so different from her!—rarely smiled, still more rarely laughed, and then it sounded like thistles being cracked. Her hands smelled like onions and hadn't there been something oniony about her eyes? She complained of arthritis in a reproachful way so you'd know she blamed you for not having arthritis. Silly and sad, Marianne's mother offering up a litany of aches and pains, colds, mishaps to the older woman, to cheer her up. What was Grandmother Hausmann's secret, she seemed so tight and settled inside herself? She, too, believed in Jesus as her savior, but He was an angry Savior, an overseer of Hell.

Driving to Ransomville, approaching the Hausmann farm, Michael Sr. would clown wickedly, wrapping a muffler around his neck—"Brrr! I'll sure be needing this!" Corinne would slap at him, hurt, or pretending to be hurt, as the children dissolved into giggles—Marianne, Mikey-Junior and P.J. in the back of the car, Judd squeezed up front between Dad and Mom. Mom would cry, "Michael Mulvaney, that isn't the least bit funny!" and Dad would wink into the rearview mirror at his adoring audience in the backseat, "It sure isn't, honeybunch. Brrr!"

Once, Dad had actually worn a muffler during the visit, claiming, convincingly, that he had strep throat.

Oh and what a stiff, solemn, smile-and-get-through-it Sunday meal. Going to church services at the Lutheran church a few miles away never seemed to lighten the day for the elder Hausmanns. Marianne recalled grimly chewing gristly pork roast laced with fat, trying to moisten lumpy mashed potatoes with a thick, porous gravy. String beans, boiled to a mush. Winter squash. Of all the delicious pies you could bake, Grandmother Hausmann favored rhubarb.

But afterward, on the long, two-hour drive home, how good to be just themselves again, the Mulvaneys! Giddy with relief and happiness in a vehicle driven by Dad! Dad would lead them singing "Take Me Out to the Ball Game" with a much-repeated refrain—

Buy me some pea-nuts and CRAC-KER JACK!
I don't care if I NEV-ER COME BACK!

Excepting Mom, who frequently had a headache, everyone shrieked with laughter; even Marianne who knew it wasn't very nice to make fun of her grandparents. Dad was merciless, now he was free to work off steam, "Some households you have to leave to appreciate, eh?" and, "The taste of *begrudged food* is unmistakable, isn't it, kids?" Mom slapped at Dad across Judd until finally she too broke down in giggles. "Oh, well," she said, sighing. "It's just an older generation's way, I think. Not the Mulvaney way, thank God."

"Amen to that," Dad said loudly.

As a reward for all they'd endured, Dad would swing over to Mt. Ephraim instead of coming directly home. To the Tastee-Freez, or the Royal Ice Cream Parlor next to the movie theater. A cheer would go up from the back seat. "Yayyyy Dad-dyyyy!"

A nasal voice inquired suspiciously, "Marianne? Are you *there*?"

"Y-Yes, Aunt Ethel." Marianne was crying in that breathless hiccuppy way she hated.

"The funeral is Thursday at eleven, as I've said. At their church." A pause. An intake of breath. "But your mother doesn't want you to attend, I'm afraid."

"Excuse me? What?"

Primly Ethel Hausmann said, like one obliged against her wishes to deliver the worst news, "Corinne does not want you to come to her mother's funeral, please don't ask me why. She doesn't know I'm calling you, even. But I thought I should. I do feel some moral obligation. After all, Ida Hausmann was your grandmother." There came a sound of a nose being blown, a moist peevish sound.

Marianne was stunned. She couldn't think of a single thing to say except a faint, "Oh."

"Yes, I thought you would want to know. Your Grandmother Hausmann is *dead*." There came another weighty pause, an intake of breath. Then, more curiously, "Do you even have another grandmother, Marianne? A Mulvaney grandmother?"

The words *Mulvaney grandmother* had a strange, surreal sound in Aunt Ethel's mouth. Like the improbable name of one of Patrick's microorganisms.

Marianne stammered, confused, "I—don't know."

"Don't know if you have a grandmother! Your father's own mother! Really, Marianne. There's a sorry tale there, I don't doubt." Ethel Hausmann spoke both reproachfully and with satisfaction. "I have to hang up now, Marianne. Don't tell your mother I called? She might object to me interfering in her precious family."

"Y-Yes?"

"Well, I'm not! I just think it's a decent Christian thing to do."

"Thank you, Aunt Ethel, I—"

"I'm not really your 'aunt,' you know, Marianne. To be technical, we're just cousins twice removed."

Ethel Hausmann hung up. Marianne stifled a sob that turned into laughter sudden and lunatic as a sneeze.

She would go to the funeral! She would be welcome!

Marianne hurried from the parlor, tears dimming her eyes, not quite seeing where she was headed so that she nearly collided with a young man squatting just outside the door. It was Hewie, one of the Co-op members, repairing a collapsed step with hammer and nails. Had he been eavesdropping on Marianne's conversations? He squinted up at her as she was about to fly past, remarking, "Marianne—if you need a ride anywhere, like to a funeral or anything, I can drive you. I've got a car."

Marianne's face stung with tears. She hadn't time to consider Hewie's offer. Or the way he looked at her. She laughed and said, halfway up the stairs, "Oh, yes—thanks!"

❦

So it happened that Marianne slipped away, at 6:00 A.M. of an overcast May morning, to be driven to Ransomville, to Ida Hausmann's funeral to which she was not invited, riding with Hewie the Co-op carpenter in his big old battered-plum boat of a 1969 Dodge. Did she imagine it?—a vague impression of someone peering at them out of a downstairs window of the house.

Yes of course Marianne was going to miss her final exam, Marianne was going to fail the course, she hadn't given the exam a second thought. Farewell to Introduction to English Literature! She thought, *Out of obscurity I came.* Wasn't that solace enough? It was!

So by 11 A.M., at about the midpoint of what would have been the exam, she found herself three hundred miles away in rural Ransomville, west of Mt. Ephraim in the Chautauqua Valley. Thank God, Hewie wasn't a talker! Nor a questioner! He was a taciturn young man with brooding dark eyes and a chronic downturned mouth, usually unshaven, like the elusive Birk a Green Isle member who'd been taking courses at Kilburn State for years, nowhere near graduating. There were things whispered of Hewie that Marianne hadn't heard, nor cared to hear. She didn't believe in gossip. She'd warned Hewie at the start of their trip, "I might be—oh, I don't know—behaving kind of—strangely. It's my grandmother dying and this funeral and—you know. I hope—you won't judge me harshly?" Hewie stared at Marianne as if he hadn't heard correctly. He muttered, almost inaudibly, with a scowl, "Hell, I wouldn't judge you at all, Marianne." He seemed annoyed at the suggestion.

By 11 A.M. the wind had been blowing boiled-looking clouds across the sky in a vivid procession and it had turned into a mild, fragrant, dazed sort of spring day. At least Marianne felt dazed. Staring avidly at everything she saw, rubbing her eyes to see if her vision was real. Why, she hadn't been in Ransomville for—four years? Yet the little crossroads town seemed unchanged, same two-pump gas station, convenience store and tackle shop combined, a teenager's long-faded sign NIGHT CRAWLLERS BARGINS! The same post office—volunteer firemen's building, the same elevated railroad tracks, several wood-frame churches, surrounding farmland. The two-lane blacktop highway leading out into the country, to the remote Hausmann farm, was more cracked and potholed than Marianne recalled. And where was the Lutheran church, hadn't it been at a fork in the road? How many miles from town?

Marianne was beginning to tremble, felt the need in her fingers to dart about, plucking at her hair or, like Mom's, fluttering. She clasped them, icy-cold, together in her lap.

She would be welcome at her own grandmother's funeral, with the other Mulvaneys—wouldn't she?

Mom would give a little cry and run to hug her, squeeze the breath out of her—wouldn't she?

Ransomville was in a remote corner of the Chautauqua Valley, far from the more populous Mt. Ephraim and the far more affluent, expanding area of Yewville and Route 58. Until the mid-Fifties, many farms didn't have electricity, let alone indoor plumbing. *A place time has forgotten* Corinne used to say, and Michael Sr. was quick to quip, *Right! and we know why.* In fact, the landscape was beautiful and possibly intimidating to a self-styled city boy. The rolling hills and abrupt glacier-ravines, the fast-running pebbled creeks, the sudden sweeping views, vast skies susceptible to change within minutes from overcast to clear, from clear to stormy, were very like the rockier, wilder stretch of High Point Road beyond the Mulvaney property where the asphalt became gravel. *Human beings always think* Patrick once said *how, on the other side of their property line, civilization ends.* Marianne couldn't have explained what Patrick meant by that but she guessed he might be right.

So strange, and distressing—about Patrick. He'd telephoned her just after Easter, the previous month, a midnight call when Marianne was groggy with exhaustion, wakened by Felice-Marie for this "emergency" call from her brother, and she'd been scarcely able to comprehend Patrick's excited rushed words, let alone what they meant. He wanted her to know, he said, that *justice had been executed*; and that he was dropping out of Cornell before graduating, he'd decided not to go to graduate school just yet but to forestall making any decisions about the future. He was going to travel, he said— maybe the Southwest, the Rocky Mountains. Marianne listened in horror. She'd stammered *Yes but Patrick aren't I coming to your graduation? Aren't all the Mulvaneys coming to your graduation? I've got May 30 marked on my calendar, oh Patrick wait—*

Afterward, the call had seemed like some bizarre dream. Marianne was increasingly susceptible to bizarre dreams now that she'd taken on so many of Birk's duties in the Co-op and fell into bed exhausted every night. But the most bizarre thing about Patrick's call was that he'd sounded so happy, so relieved, so—un-Pinch-like. Yet he'd been delivering catastrophic news, hadn't he?

Now that Hewie had actually turned onto Marianne's grandparents' road, now that they were actually approaching the Lutheran church at the crossroads—there, suddenly, it was: dull gray stone, gaunt and so much smaller than Marianne remembered—Marianne began to feel panic. It was that fear, her special fear. A cold sweat beaded on her forehead and in her armpits. She heard herself plead in a whisper, "Hewie, I guess I—can't." The young man, driving the rattly Dodge in his careful, steadfast way, leaned an ear toward her. "—I guess I'm not ready." What a shock to see amid a dozen or so vehicles parked at the church Corinne's old Buick station wagon— 4-H sticker on a rear window, faded ELECT CARTER-MONDALE '76!!! on the rear bumper. Several people, black-garbed, stood in the church doorway—*Is one of them Mom? Is one of them Dad?* Ludicrous among farmers' modest cars and pickups was a long black hearse out of place as a giant fancy polished boot from a fashionable store window.

Grim-faced oniony-smelling Ida Hausmann, with her disdain for what she called showy earthly vanities, squired about the Ransomville countryside one final time, in *that*!

Marianne pleaded, hiding her face so she couldn't be seen by anyone at the church, "Oh, just drive by, Hewie! Please! I—can't."

Waiting for Hewie to reason with her, for hadn't they come a long distance only to rush on by like fugitives, wasn't the older, male presence always one to reason with her—but Hewie didn't utter a word. He was like that at the Co-op, too—broody eyes and mouth so you'd imagine he was thinking deep thoughts, contrary thoughts, even mutinous thoughts (Abelove often cast uneasy glances at Hewie, while presiding over meetings), but Hewie never made trouble, rarely spoke at all. He scowled, that was about it. Yet you couldn't judge whether Hewie's scowls were meant to be smiles, or not meant to signal anything at all, just nervous tics. He was good-looking in a carved-walnut way, his dark hair grown shaggy past his ears. A man like that is so *frustrating*! Amethyst complained, sighing. Marianne was genuinely baffled. Frustrating? Why?

Atop the hill beyond the Lutheran church there was a rutted cow lane, Marianne asked Hewie quick to turn off, he maneuvered the Dodge in and parked behind a screen of straggly trees. In such a confused state she halfway forgot anyone was with her, and might be wondering at her sanity, Marianne hurried out of the car, stumbled into a field, thistles and briars tugging at her clothes. Stealthily she made her way downhill behind the church to the edge of the cemetery; crouched there to wait for her grandmother's funeral to proceed to the grave site—you could tell poor Ida Hausmann's destination, a gouged-out angry-seeming red-dirt rectangle in the moist earth. Oh, what a heartbreaking sight! *If it wasn't for Jesus Christ, and His Love, and His promise of Heaven and life-everlasting—it couldn't be looked upon at all.*

Was she hidden well enough?—behind a partly collapsed wall of rocks dragged from the fields and cemented together decades ago, and one of the largest tombstones in the cemetery, a granite pedestal and a human-sized stone angel with weatherworn but soaring wings. All about Marianne mayflies and gnats and what looked like junior honeybees droned and buzzed. Hewie descended the hill behind her, near-silent in his soiled running shoes as a deer. Marianne was aware of him yet not aware of him, at the same time—she'd shut her eyes tight, clasped her hands together, bowed her head in prayer. Inside the stone church, a minister was intoning words of scripture over Grandmother Hausmann's casket. Whatever exactly the Lutheran service was, it would be prayer, humble submission to God's will and Jesus' love. *Lo, I am with you always, even unto the end of the world.*

Marianne told herself: if Corinne knew she was crouching out here hiding behind the cemetery, she couldn't truly be angry, or even embarrassed, so long as none of the others knew. That was always the case with Mom—it was Marianne who'd fussed, fussed, fussed over her 4-H projects, hand-stitching her hems perfectly or tugging out the thread and beginning again, preparing her baked goods from scratch and never, never using a mix, while Mom took the position, which she claimed was the American-pragmatist position, that if things work just fine who's to know exactly how they're working, and what business is it of other people's, anyway? They all loved Mom's slapdash cooking that was delicious, you didn't need to know that she'd rushed into the kitchen just in time to wrest chicken pieces from a cat's mouth, or hastily scraped up from the floor, where it had fallen in an appalling heap that might nonetheless be reshaped by hand, some pie, pudding, casserole or quiche. The last time Marianne had spoken with her mother, the evening of Easter Sunday, Corinne had evaded Marianne's shy questions about the farm (was it truly for sale? were they really thinking of moving across the Valley, to Marsena?—but they didn't know anyone in Marsena, did they?) and made some cheery glimmering remark about Marianne's *rag-quilt life* at the Green Isle Co-op, she'd sounded halfway envious, *You young people! practically in a hippie commune and having the time of your life, not like my generation, I was training to be a public school teacher and your father had been on his own, working, self-supporting since the age of eighteen.* Marianne had smarted at the allegation, somehow the term *hippie* didn't strike the ear right, or justly, for Marianne like most of the other Co-op members worked very hard even if, academically, she hadn't all that much to show for it after five or six semesters. But of course she hadn't objected, just laughed uneasily as Corinne chattered on. *Rag-quilt life:* was that how her life was adding up to, in the judgment of her mother? *Rag-quilt life:* well, maybe that was apt.

But Marianne had made an effort to improve her usual appearance for the occasion of Grandmother Hausmann's funeral—surely Corinne would note, and appreciate, that? She'd shampooed her hair until it shone, scrubbed her hands and dug dirt out from beneath her broken-off nails, soaked in the big claw-footed tub on the top floor of the Co-op (not much used, you had to scour the tub with steel wool afterward to remove the stains, no one had time for anything much except showers) until she was *clean, clean, clean.* For the first time in a long time. (Except now, nervous as a cat, sweating—what a sight she probably looked!) On her head, not exactly straight, was a wide-brimmed black straw hat with a crinkly black straw band from the Second-Time-'Round Shop in Kilburn, and from the same shop an ankle-length long-sleeved waistless dress of a similar soft-crinkly fabric, midnight blue that could pass for the black of mourning. Unfortunately the dress was too large for her and had a dipping boat-neck that showed her sharp collarbone so, inspired, in haste, she'd wrapped a strip of black velvet around her throat with a tiny glass ruby pasted on it—a "touch," Amethyst insisted, the dress badly needed. On her feet were a pair of black "ballerina flats" and she wore gauzy black-mesh knee-length stockings. Seeing Marianne rush downstairs that morning, where he was already waiting, Hewie glanced up at her startled, his downturned mouth actually dropping, as if he'd never set eyes on such a person before.

Apologetically Marianne murmured, "I guess—I'm in mourning, Hewie. I hope that's all right?"

At this, too, Hewie glared at her, his mouth working, but in silence. As if her question had annoyed, even offended him. He'd stalked out to his car and started the motor.

After about forty minutes, the funeral party left the church and proceeded into the cemetery. Marianne spied on them shamelessly, biting at her thumbnail, peering out from behind the soaring stone angel. Now and then a gust of wind threatened to knock her hat askew so she had to clamp it down on her head, mashing the crown. Hewie must have been crouching somewhere behind her, peering into the cemetery, too, but Marianne had forgotten him. There was the minister who didn't look quite like Reverend Schreiber who'd been pastor of the Ransomville Lutheran Church for decades, and there were the pallbearers, four men, must be Hausmann relatives but Marianne could recognize only the youngest, a cousin of her mother's now bald and stoop-shouldered. The coffin was a shock— maybe coffins are always shocks, to the unexpecting eye?—such a shiny-glary black, like the hearse. Such ostentation and fuss weren't

Grandmother Hausmann's *style*. And there were several elderly female relatives Marianne recognized, unsteady on their feet in the spongy soil, and darting among them a tall lean elbowy woman who managed to assist all three simultaneously, a woman in what appeared to be a shiny black vinyl raincoat and a wide-brimmed black hat (straw?) tied tight beneath her chin with a black ribbon. Marianne stared—it was Corinne! It was Corinne of course, and behind her was a skinny boy in a dark blue suit, uncomfortable-looking, fawn-colored hair stirring in the wind—Judd. Marianne jammed her knuckles against her mouth, emitted a small unconscious cry like a kitten's mew. *Mom! Mommy!*

But where was Dad, wasn't Dad there, Michael Sr. not at his own mother-in-law's funeral, oh, what did that mean?

Yet it was logical her father wasn't there, for Marianne had so deduced from seeing her mother's station wagon parked in front of the church; if Dad had driven, he'd surely have taken his own car, not Mom's. It was a newly purchased car Patrick had described at length over the phone: one of those overpriced ostentatious American gas-guzzlers, a Lincoln Continental of all things, wouldn't you think a man on the verge of bankruptcy and in this era of gas shortages would have more sense than to buy such a relic?—Patrick had gone on and on as if he'd not only seen the infamous car, but ridden in it, but Marianne gathered he had not. Anyway—that car, and not Mom's battered old Buick, would have been out front if Michael Sr. had been present.

Marianne didn't care to consider why her father wasn't at the funeral. A gust of wind blew at her hat, she clamped it down fiercely, and blotted out any further thought on the subject.

Staring at Corinne, now at the grave site, head bowed as the minister continued with more prayers, and at Judd, her heart suffused with love for them. Her mother, and her brother. *Run to them! Run, now! Before it's too late!* Oh where was Dad, where were Mike and Patrick? What heartbreak for Corinne, what an embarrassment, no one but her youngest son there beside her at her own mother's funeral; and in the watchful presence of the Ransomville Hausmanns, among them grim-bulldog-cousin Ethel. *Go, run! Mom will hug you, Mommy you know she really loves you, there's a love that never wears out. You know that—don't you, Button?*

But Marianne had more sense. Resisted temptation, squatting on her heels down behind the crumbling rock wall, not watching the grave site but jamming her knuckles against her mouth, crying now openly. Squinched all together like a deformed pretzel, her hat tumbling off and would have blown away except Hewie grabbed it, spinning like a wheel through the tall grass. Hewie must have squatted on his heels a few yards away, and just waited. Offering no predictable words of comfort, solace, commiseration, just let Marianne weep her heart out hunched in pain, long as required.

When finally Marianne dared peek up again over the wall, she saw that the cemetery was deserted—even Corinne who'd probably lingered at the grave, shedding bitter tears, was gone.

Somewhere out of sight a wood thrush sang, four throaty, liquid notes.

Resisting temptation. Marianne hadn't known she was strong enough but yes, she was.

And again, that afternoon in Mt. Ephraim where she'd asked Hewie please to drive slowly along South Main Street. Too upset to explain what on earth she'd been doing, crouching and cringing and hiding and skulking like a fugitive, at that country church and now in town. Her voice was hoarse and cracked from crying, her eyes were swollen, she wouldn't have dared glance at herself in any reflecting surface. Where once (as a cheerleader, as "Button" Mulvaney) she'd been the silliest vainest shallow person, now she could barely force herself to contemplate her reflection, not just in a mirror but in her mind's pitiless eye.

Part of downtown was a pedestrian mall—what a good idea! Marianne caught a glimpse of the old Woolworth's which looked unchanged, Rexall Drugs at the corner, across on Fifth Street the movie house showing *The Deer Hunter*—not a new film. She had a vague sense of things not quite the same, a one-way street where there'd never been one before, then suddenly, abruptly there was Mulvaney Roofing!—the squat building familiar as if she'd last seen it the previous week, not four years ago. The green stucco building with white trim, needing a new coat of paint, oh but what was wrong?—an ugly yellow-and-black sign FOR SALE OR LEASE—Marianne wasn't prepared for the sight though hadn't Patrick warned her? Or Judd.

Having seen the sign MULVANEY ROOFING, Hewie braked to a slow crawl, five miles an hour. Unperturbed when other drivers honked impatiently at him, cast derisive glances at his big old boat of a Dodge. Marianne had crouched down in the passenger's seat, straw hat jammed down on her head so that the brim hid most of her face; she peered fearfully up over the rim of the car door, a single eye exposed. Heart pounding like crazy. Beads of sticky sweat on her face. *What if—? What if—? Dad steps outside, and sees you?*

He would hug her, wouldn't he. Run right out onto South Main to open the car door, hug her weeping wouldn't he.

Marianne whispered for Hewie to stop the car if he could, park at the curb. Or maybe she hadn't whispered aloud but he'd heard her nonetheless. Through a haze of blinding scintillating light she stared at the façade of MULVANEY ROOFING. Immediately she'd understood it wasn't open for business though not exactly empty. The front door locked, that unmistakable look of a locked door, and no one in sight. Where was Leah, her father's receptionist? Leah who'd been so sweet to Marianne, telling Michael Mulvaney how she wished she had a beautiful little girl like his. Marianne saw that there were no vehicles in the lot, either. Not a single truck?—MULVANEY ROOFING in curving white letters.

"Well. I guess no one's here right now. I guess—" Marianne straightened cautiously, adjusting her hat. Peering out at the building and blinking numbly. *He'd run out, he'd hug me, he loves me. If only he could see me!* But there was no one at Mulvaney Roofing, not a soul.

Farther down the block, at the box company warehouse, there was activity—a truck being loaded. And vehicles passing in the street in a jerky continuous stream. *If only he could see me.*

After a few minutes Marianne whispered to Hewie, "I guess—you can drive away, now."

Around the corner and along a street she didn't at first recognize, blinking tears from her eyes, except there was the old Blue Moon Café with a new smartly-bright blue moon swinging sign. Down to Third Street which was now one-way going the wrong way—a woman in sunglasses driving a handsome car—Suzi Quigley's mother?—Marianne quickly looked away. (She'd written to Suzi, and Suzi had written back, enrolled at Wells College, they'd kept up a correspondence for the first year then Suzi ceased replying to Marianne's letters and Marianne eventually ceased writing, too. But always in her heart she would be Suzi's friend. And Merissa's, and Bonnie's. And Trisha's most of all.) On Fifth Street easing downhill past the attractive Trinity Episcopal Church she'd visited once, for Sunday service, with a friend, which appeared unchanged; and Reynolds' Funeral Home; and a large pink-limestone house, she'd imagined in childhood a mansion, now occupied by an insurance agency. And so on down the hill to the high school, needing to drive past the high school, already cringing and wincing as Hewie slowed the Dodge, sensitive to Marianne's unuttered wish as her lost lovely Molly-O had been on their good days. Hewie had to brake in any case as clusters of teenagers crossed the street heedless, brashly smiling young people Marianne seemed not to know. Not a single one! They would have been younger brothers and sisters of her classmates but she didn't recognize anyone. The girls so young-looking, and so pretty—cutting their eyes at Hewie—snug jeans, oversized sweaters, bright lipstick, permed-frizzy hair. The boys were so *young*—that was even more unsettling. Suddenly she saw one she knew—no, he only looked like lumbering-loutish Ike Rodman—swinging along the sidewalk, a baseball cap reversed on his head. A Jeepload of boys veered past Hewie, rudely honking, laughter in their wake; at the wheel, a dark-haired hawkish-profiled boy resembling Zachary Lundt. Marianne's temples throbbed. It was silly, an optic-neurological misfiring. As, new at Kilburn State, she'd kept seeing faces achingly familiar until at last the new faces drove out the old which they hadn't much resembled, really. Probably there was a term for such tricks of the eye, Patrick would be the one to ask.

But she'd lost contact with Patrick, too. He'd spoken vaguely of going off on a "field trip"—with some scientists—or maybe they were fellow dropouts from biology? You could ask Patrick a question point-blank and hear an answer but afterward you wouldn't know much more than you'd known at the start.

Even as Marianne was thinking of her brother, she was watching a tall blond boy trotting across a patch of scruffy lawn, eyeglasses winking. His solitary hurrying-away gait—he might have been Patrick Mulvaney, almost.

Marianne said, stammering, "Isn't it—funny, Hewie, people remind you of other people? Faces remind you of other faces? As if there aren't enough faces in the world to go around, exactly—" She remembered then that Judd was actually a student at Mt. Ephraim High, a sophomore; he'd be leaving the building at this time, except of course he was in Ransomville with their mother. *Only Corinne and her youngest showed up, of the precious Mulvaneys. There's a sorry tale there.* Marianne was saying, "My brother Judd, he's my youngest brother, he goes to school here. Maybe you met him, Hewie? Around Christmastime, last year? He and my mom came to visit me in Kilburn, we all had lunch together? They met Abelove. . . ." Her voice trailed off weakly.

If Hewie responded, Marianne couldn't make out what he said.

There appeared then, close by on the sidewalk, on Marianne's side of the car, Mr. Farolino, who'd taught biology to each of the Mulvaney children, in turn: one of Mt. Ephraim High's most popular teachers, admired and feared for his sarcastic wit. Mr. Farolino was loping along the walk—he lived near enough to school not to have to drive. He was carrying a briefcase battered as an old football at his side. How bald Mr. Farolino had become, though only Michael Mulvaney's age! How caved-in his chest, in a white nylon shirt with short fluttery sleeves! His expression was fixed in a fierce grin, eyes lifted to the horizon, to somewhere not in sight; clearly, he didn't want to be waylaid by departing students. But Marianne had hunched down in her seat at once, in terror of being seen. *And what if Mr. Farolino sees you? Why should it matter so much? Haven't you put that all behind you, silly sad vanity, along with everything else? Poor Button Mulvaney!* Taking for granted that everyone adored her, yes they must have been envious of her, "Button" Mulvaney and her close tight circle of friends, "Button" Mulvaney of High Point Farm, the Mulvaneys whom everyone in Mt. Ephraim knew and admired, how sad to be left out of their circle of friends, how sad not to be them, pity the plain girls of Mt. Ephraim High where being pretty and being popular were so crucial, pity the girls with blemished skins, no boyfriends, no personality-plus Dad and Mom, no good-looking brothers, girls whose pictures never appeared in the school newspaper or the *Mt. Ephraim Patriot-Ledger.* Girls like poor Della Rae Duncan, their smudged skin, hunted eyes. *That kind of a girl. Sad!*

Marianne wondered what had become of Della Rae. The family had lived in a trailer village on the Haggartsville Road, her brother Dwight had been killed in Vietnam. Della Rae had dropped out of school and had—what? Disappeared? Married? Last time Marianne asked Corinne about her, Corinne had murmured vaguely that she didn't know, hadn't the slightest idea.

Marianne said, "Oh, Hewie, it's as if—I've been gone a hundred years. As if I've died and come back and—"

Hewie had parked the Dodge at the curb, and was leaning over now to scowl at the buff-brick façade of Mt. Ephraim High. In mild disbelief he asked, "*You* went to school here, Marianne?" It was the first direct question from Hewie in hours, perhaps all day, and the tenor was unmistakable—*That place isn't good enough for you.*

Then, to High Point Farm.

With that strange fated compulsion with which swirling water is drawn down a drain, each discrete molecule and atom seemingly pressing for extinction, Marianne felt a wildness come over her—to see High Point Farm one more time. As beforehand she'd warned herself *No: you must not* even as she knew she would succumb, if once she and Hewie drove to Mt. Ephraim, only seven miles from the farm. *Just to say hello to Molly-O! I promise that's all.*

Shrewdly reasoning that since Corinne and Judd would still be in Ransomville, and Michael Sr. would surely not be at home at such an hour, no one would ever know.

She took a deep breath. "Hewie, please will you drive out into the country now? I'll tell you where."

Eager to be gone from the potholed constricting grid of Mt. Ephraim's streets as if he'd been feeling his passenger's pain, Hewie gunned the Dodge's motor at once.

And so—and so it happened, as in a dream, yet a dream not of Marianne's own volition, they drove out of Mt. Ephraim; a turn, another turn, past the Chautauqua & Buffalo depot, past the water tower with its heraldic Day-Glo scrawls and so to Route 119, the Haggartsville Road, en route to High Point Farm. *Just for a few minutes. No one will know.* Past Country Club Lane where Marianne's eyelids blinked as in a nervous spasm and Hillside Estates where certain of her former friends lived hidden now by a handsome scrim of rapidly grown poplars and Spohr's Lumber which had expanded, twice the size Marianne recalled but she wasn't looking, Mr. Spohr was one of those men who'd betrayed her father but she wasn't thinking of that, not now. *Family secrets you aren't supposed to know, of course you know.* The railroad tracks running parallel with Route 119 she found herself staring at entranced, for railroad tracks are neutral territory, lacking identity and history.

At High Point Road, where it forked off from the highway,

Marianne murmured, "Here!—" her breath failing, unable to speak she touched Hewie's arm—his knotty-muscled arm—it was the first time she had ever touched him, or any man of her present acquaintance, in their months of formally knowing each other at the Co-op and in these peculiar intense hours in his car, and the gesture was arguably not conscious—to indicate the road.

The Dodge sped onto High Point Road without slacking speed. As if it were the most natural thing in the world—Marianne bringing a college friend home to visit.

But: a balmy wind-crazed spring day. The sun shone blindingly in the sky from a thousand points, as if in a shattered mirror. As they ascended into the foothills, Hewie's big old Dodge began to quaver, rock, in the wind. *Because you're not wanted here: God is warning you.* At once Hewie slowed the car, for he was a careful, conscientious driver; not a boy but a young man of twenty-eight or -nine; danger alerted him, suffused his face with blood. Yet he glanced repeatedly from side to side, blinking at the view—more severe than the Ransomville countryside, the foothills of the Chautauqua Mountains were higher, more broken and discontinuous than that terrain. Marianne saw the Valley through Hewie's eyes and felt a frightened rapture: May fields planted in wheat, corn, soybeans, sloping down from the road; outcroppings of granite on the other, hilly side of the road, like ancient wounds that had never healed. Sudden drops, open vistas beyond an absurdly low guardrail. They were traversing the ridge of a glacier hill. Hewie pointed—"What's that?" In the distance, thirty miles away, chalky Mt. Cataract shone in the sunlight like a hand upraised in greeting. Or in warning.

The car rocked in the wind, Hewie shifted to second gear. Now he had broken the silence between them he seemed yet reluctant to speak, as if no mere uttered words could be equal to the sanctity of that intimate silence. His voice was thick, shy—"Where *is* this?— we keep climbing."

"Well, it's called High Point Road." Marianne laughed nervously, plucking at her hair beneath the crooked brim of the black straw hat.

"How much higher does it get? We're not going *there,* are we?"—pointing to an eroded cliffside rearing up a few miles ahead. Where clearly no one lived, and no road ascended.

"There? Oh, no. We just follow the road, a little farther."

"This is where you—lived?"

Lived. How sensitive Hewie was, for all his awkwardness. How subtle. Yet Marianne, suddenly clumsy, like an overgrown girl with awkward knees, elbows, could only laugh again, a sound in her own ears like breaking glass. "Well, yes. You could say so." Jamming her knuckles against her mouth to keep from crying.

Going home. To High Point Farm. Was it possible?

You know: impossible.

Oh but just to say hello! To Molly-O, and hug her. Stroke her cool damp nose. Just for a few minutes, I promise, who will know?

Recalling then how many times in the dreamless sleepless night she'd made this trip. High Point Road to High Point Farm. By phantom vehicle, no Mulvaney vehicle she could identify. Nor any driver she could identify, nor even see as she stared enraptured at the rushing countryside, the landscape of her childhood as imprinted in her soul as that soul's very essence and indeed indistinguishable from it. And often in these waking dreams she held Muffin in her arms. A restive, anxiously alert creature. Muffin she adored, when he'd been a soft heavy cat, and Muffin in more recent worrisome months when he'd begun to lose weight, grown amazingly lanky, long-tailed with a prominent spine. It was crucial that Marianne return Muffin safely home to High Point Farm but the danger was of course as with any cat regardless of how tamed docile and loving he might panic at any moment, struggle out of her arms, out of the vehicle and onto the rushing highway, even over the side of the guardrail— But Marianne always woke fully, bathed in sweat, before that happened.

Weeping half-angry with herself for being unable to bring the dream to a happy conclusion. Oh, how many times!

Abruptly and it always seemed rudely High Point Road changed from cracked and eroding blacktop to gravel and dirt, and now Hewie drove with increased concentration, diligence. At the Green Isle Co-op he was one of the patient, reliable workers; one of the "older" members; if he'd been casting his darkly shy sidelong glances at Marianne from time to time since early that morning, he ceased doing so now for maneuvering the wind-rattling Dodge, bearing his passenger to her mysterious destination, was work entrusted to him, a sacred duty and a privilege. *You wouldn't blow us both off the road, God? Not Hewie, oh please!* Jamming her knuckles against her mouth though whether to keep from crying or laughing she could not have said. It *was* ridiculous, to imagine for a split second that God could be so petty and vindictive; the God of all the ages, creator of all life on earth and it may be through the great universe, caring in such a fussy old-maidish way, about Marianne Mulvaney disobeying her parents' gravest wishes on the very day of her grandmother's funeral.

Now past the Pfenning farm, now past the shabby converted schoolhouse where a sprawling family lived, still the Zimmermans?—and as they approached High Point Farm Marianne began to feel faint. Her skeleton straining against her tight close-to-bursting transparent skin. *No, you don't dare: how do you dare, you! Not wanted here, a trespasser, thief.* Before she could comprehend what she was seeing her eye picked out the yellow-and-black realtor's sign FARM FOR SALE prominent and jarring beside the gravel drive.

Yes but you knew, you'd been told, warned. Patrick had told you and Judd had told you not once but numerous times. And Mom in her glimmering blurred way had mentioned it, *You know the farm's for sale, Dad's holding out for a decent price,* as if it were an issue already acknowledged, discussed. Just another neutral fact of Mulvaney family history.

In a trance of panic tinged with wonderment Marianne shut her icy fingers into fists and stared, stared greedily. Hewie had braked to a stop (seeing MULVANEY on the mailbox?) and stared wordless as well. There was a palpable excitement in the air, windblown, sunstruck, the dazzling-budding fragrance of spring. Wild-looking lilacs just past their fullest bloom and in the shallow roadside ditch a profusion of tiger lily stalks not yet in bloom, vividly green—by July the roadsides would be filled with them, bright-orange like savage dabs of paint. There was Corinne's proudly lettered, now slightly faded sign HIGH POINT FARM 1849 and yet more faded HIGH POINT ANTIQUES BARGAINS & BEAUTY! The antique sleigh with its slumping scarecrow figure seemed to have skidded farther downhill a few yards. There was the brook, almost hidden behind overgrown vegetation, and there was the little plank bridge. There, at the top of the hill, the house that was part fieldstone and part lavender, floating like a pastel drawing in a child's book.

Hewie, the undemonstrative one, whistled through his teeth, ran a big-knuckled hand through his hair. "*There?* That's your family's house?"

Marianne couldn't speak at first. Her lips were icy-cold, numb; she was frightened of fainting. Saying, almost inaudibly, "I—guess not. I mean, it is, but I can't go in. I made a mistake."

Hewie turned to stare at her. "What? Why?"

"I—just can't."

"Can't?" Hewie screwed up his face, not in impatience, nor even in surprise, or doubt; it was more a sort of perplexed sympathy, as if he might have anticipated such a response, all along. "You mean—you can't go *in*? You don't want us to drive up, and—go inside?"

"No! No, please."

There was a silence. Marianne heard Hewie breathing, or was it a sigh? He frowned, scowled—not at Marianne, at whom he'd ceased looking, but possibly at himself. You would expect this young man to reason with his distraught passenger, at least to express some disapproval of her mysterious self-hurtful behavior; it may have been even that Hewie was sifting through his head such a possibility, trying out words, phrases, yearning for the eloquence of, say, Abelove in such a circumstance, Abelove's moral certainty, yet failing; a young man of reserve, shyness and sullenness inextricably interwoven, he was not accustomed to such speech. As Marianne stammered, blushing, "I just remembered—my horse I'd wanted to see, to say hello to? She isn't here any longer. She's been sold. She's gone. Gone for years. I made a mistake. Hewie? I'm so sorry."

A dazzle of acid-sharp spring sunshine behind Hewie's startled head. Reflecting even on the dull plum-colored hood of the car with a sharpness that hurt the eyes.

What wasn't she seeing, so resolutely? Ugly unspeakable yellow-on-black sign FARM FOR SALE FARM FOR SALE FARM FOR SALE.

Hewie drew breath to speak, his mouth opened—he said nothing. Scratched his head vigorously, looking at her in that way of perplexed sympathy, even anguish; thinking, thinking very hard, giving off heat like a finely vibrating motor. For the first time then it came over Marianne, the fact of his physical being, his presence. Maleness. *A man, I've gone off with a man, alone with a man. All these hours alone with Hewie in his car. His car!* The revelation rose to a shriek in her head. She heard it in Corinne's astonished accusing voice. *But haven't you learned! You, Marianne Mulvaney! How could you be so careless, so reckless! You of all people!* It was true, Marianne hardly knew this young man she'd boldly asked to drive her all over the Chautauqua Valley on one wild-goose chase after another: Hewie Miner, the carpenter, one of the older drifting-along students in the

Green Isle Co-op, still many credits from graduating and then—what would his degree be in? Hewie had taken courses in agricultural science, hotel management, phys ed as it was somewhat contemptuously called, business administration, sociology, vocational arts education. His grades were *scraping-along* and he'd amassed any number of incompletes. When Marianne had first moved into the Co-op she'd heard a disquieting rumor about Hewie Miner that he'd been suspended from Kilburn State for a semester, or a year, for cheating; only later had she discovered that Hewie himself hadn't cheated, except technically—he'd loaned his earth science lab book to a friend unthinking enough to copy it verbatim (including errors) and they'd both been caught and disciplined. *Isn't that just like Hewie!* people said, shaking their heads. Marianne was one of the half dozen Co-op girls who frequently left cards and little gifts, anonymously, for people on their birthdays, especially people whose birthdays might otherwise be overlooked, you could look up birthdays in the Co-op register in Abelove's office and Marianne was always remembering birthdays of fellow members she didn't in fact know very well, like Hewie Miner for whom she'd left, anonymously, in his mailbox, a handmade card HAPPY BIRTHDAY TO A VERY SPECIAL FRIEND and a crocheted necktie (emerald green since Hewie's birthday was near St. Patrick's Day, very attractive, yet she'd never seen Hewie wear it) and somehow he'd known who had left these items and he'd been deeply moved, embarrassed, tongue-tied in Marianne's presence and Marianne had been slow to grasp that just possibly Hewie Miner whom girls looked after in muted longing yet in confidence that their longing wouldn't be returned had perhaps misunderstood her gesture? had interpreted it to mean something more personal than it did? but this thought, like the alarming realization of his physical presence, his maleness, and her being alone with him in his car in this remote place ran swiftly through her brain, and did not take hold. There was too much else to think of. Too much else assailing her.

She was saying, trying to explain, with her broken girl's laugh, plucking at her hair, "—Molly-O was my horse's name. I loved her so, she was so beautiful, her eyes, she was chestnut-red, a coat I loved to groom, she had a funny white patch on her nose and four white socks and a way of talking to me, like asking questions?—you know how horses are?—but, well—she's gone. I don't know where. My mom didn't want to tell me, she was afraid I might have gone to find her—I'm not what you'd call trustworthy." Now the truth was out, now Hewie knew, Marianne spoke rapidly, in a tumble of words. "I'm not what you'd call stable, or reliable. Nothing like you. I make mistakes, errors of judgment. I'm immature, and careless, I disappoint people. My family especially. My Dad, and my Mom. I've hurt them and there's not much I can do to make it right, not now. But there's no point in telling you and involving you, I'm sorry! I guess we should just drive back? To Kilburn? Is that all right, Hewie? We can stop somewhere and eat the lunch I packed but not on High Point Road, we'll have to stop on some other road, please is that all right? Hewie?" Pleading and apologetic and half-sickened at her own vanity in speaking in such a way, to Hewie Miner who was a young man of integrity. *I, I, I* as if anyone could be interested, in the slightest, in Marianne Mulvaney!

Quietly Hewie said, with a sidelong glance at her, a downturned little smile, shifting gears, preparing to turn around in the weedy-gravel driveway and continue on to wherever he was directed, "Hey, sure, Marianne. Didn't I say I'd drive you anywhere you wanted to go?"

They stopped at a roadside store somewhere south of Mt. Ephraim for three cans of soda (one for Marianne, two for Hewie) and on an unpaved road ate the lunch Marianne had prepared early that morning. Full-to-bursting tuna-salad sandwiches on nine-grain bread chewy as cake, carrot sticks, pickles, two Florida navel oranges, Marianne's special oatmeal cookies. Marianne was able to eat, some. Of course, Hewie was famished: devoured two and a half of the sandwiches, and all of the cookies. In the bright dazzling air, at the edge of a field of feathery-green sprouting shoots of sweet corn, Mt. Cataract in the distance, everything tasted fine. Marianne had removed her straw hat of mourning and kicked off her cardboard-stiff ballerina flats to wriggle her toes in the grass. Not thinking *How could you! if you'd been caught! like a trespasser, a thief!* Not recalling the nail driven into her heart at the sight of that ugly sign FARM FOR SALE. She was smiling, listening attentively to Hewie Miner who'd become suddenly talkative in that way of a shy boy let loose. He was saying, "*My* folks, they lived in so many places all over the country, I never could get homesick. My dad was a U.S. Army cook—he'd got so he hated food—it was whiskey he preferred—he was always getting transferred up and down the coast, or across the continent, from Florida to New Jersey, North Carolina to Texas, state of Washington to Michigan, turn around and we'd be in Florida again, same base, but everybody different. My mom took off, too—I mean, on her own—when she got fed up. She'd take my little brother and me when we were young, we'd go by bus. Trouble was, there wasn't any place we could go *to*, or if there was, like with some cousin of Mom's she'd been close to, as a girl, or thought she was, by the time we got there—as far away as Boulder, Colorado, once—" This was so long and impassioned a speech, Hewie got lost in it. He was staring at Marianne with his vivid dark eyes in a way that made her uneasy, it was so familiar somehow—the way Corinne had sometimes stared at Michael Sr. when he wasn't looking, or the way poor Silky had stared up at Mike Jr. with his doggy yearning eyes as Mike Jr. ignored him completely. "What I mean to say, Marianne, is—there are different kinds of homesickness, you know? To fit different kinds of families."

Hearing this, realizing he meant to console her, though not knowing nor presuming to know why she might need consolation, and not about to inquire, Marianne got into a fit of laughing so Hewie laughed, too—"What's funny, Marianne? I guess it *is* funny, isn't it?" though he was puzzled, how she laughed; jammed her knuckles against her mouth until suddenly tears leaked out acid-hot on her cheeks.

He would have consoled her then, taking hold of her hands, or wrapping his arms around her—but she turned quickly away, made him know she wanted to be alone.

Back in Kilburn, at the conclusion of this long, long day—almost thirteen hours together, nonstop!—Hewie told Marianne he hoped he would see more of her, especially any time she wanted to be driven anywhere, anywhere at all. He told her stammering slightly this had been the happiest day of his life. He told her he didn't want to embarrass her, or scare her, or—anything like that. He scratched the back of his neck vigorously, where his hair grew dark and bristly as a dog's. Face suffused with blood he managed to say matter-of-factly, "Hell, you know I love you, Marianne—it doesn't matter what you do, or did. Or think you did. Or anything you'd ask me to do for you, ever."

Marianne heard these words, or believed she did. Staring at the ground at Hewie's feet. Oh what, why?—after she'd told him?

How she was of no worth—worthless? There was a sickish roaring in her ears as of the wind of High Point Road. Though standing on firm ground in the Co-op driveway, she felt the earth quaver. She was searching her rattled brain for a decent reply, like pawing through a kitchen drawer of mismatched odds and ends, but came up with nothing better than a breathy scared-sounding, "Oh, Hewie—*thanks.*"

THE PROPOSAL

That night sleeping in drowning gasps and lunges, clawing her way repeatedly up out of a gouged-out hole in the earth. She'd wanted to cry for help but the words choked in her throat. Sometime during the night Muffin discreetly removed himself from her neck and shoulder to the foot of the bed, to sleep less disturbed, and when she woke to find him missing, the familiar furry warmth gone, in just that instant her heart contracted with a dread of the future profound as her dread of the past.

Not wanting to think of Hewie Miner. The terrible misconception he had of her. Sick with guilt that anyone might think she'd deliberately deceived him—oh, and he was so nice!

Amethyst said, twisting her mouth in a droll smile, "You mean Hewie actually *talked to you*? Well!"

And next morning there was Abelove requesting Marianne please to come into his office, he'd cancelled an appointment with a business associate in town. Abelove gravely agitated as Marianne hadn't seen him since the day Birk vanished from Earth. Quickly he shut the door behind Marianne, that door never shut, and stroked his beard murmuring, "Oh, Marianne!" in a sighing distracting way that made her uneasy as if she were hearing someone's private thoughts.

Instinctively, without even knowing what she said, Marianne whispered, "I'm—*sorry*."

She knew from Felice-Marie, Amethyst, Val Allan that Abelove had been asking after her through the previous day. Remarking, hurt, how Marianne and Hewie had "gone off unauthorized together," secretly it seemed, without informing anyone exactly where; at any rate, without informing *him*. In fact, Marianne had left a note for Abelove taped to his door explaining there was a family emergency, she'd been too hurried and rattled to explain anything further, even where she was going, and when Abelove could expect her back. How many tasks she'd left undone, how many crucial expediting calls, how she must have disappointed this kindly, generous man who'd entrusted her with responsibility approaching his own—Marianne didn't want to think. Stammering, as Abelove gazed at her with swimming-hurt reproachful eyes, as he'd never gazed at her before even in her imagination, "Abelove, I—just had to go to my grandmother's funeral. I couldn't stay away and I didn't have time to explain to you. I guess—I behaved irresponsibly. I'm sorry."

She felt a sudden tightness around her neck. Like a tethered creature, horse, dog, goat—aware only now of how closely she was leashed.

Abelove said solemnly, "Well. It's *over*, it *happened*, no need to dwell upon it. I'm so sorry to hear that your grandmother died, Marianne—please accept my condolences." He seemed about to approach her, perhaps to take her hands, and Marianne started away, just perceptibly; so he didn't follow. There came a painful pause as Marianne, examining the toe of her sneaker as it circled, and recircled, a beet-colored stain on Abelove's hemp carpet, dredged her brain for something to say. *Oh, well—Grandmother and I weren't close! She was ashamed of me I guess! In fact I wasn't even allowed at the funeral!* Abelove said, "I'm only concerned, Marianne, what it might indicate of the future."

"The f–future?"

"Your future at the Co-op."

Frightened, Marianne stared at Abelove as one might stare at a being who held all happiness, and all misery, in his hands. He was pacing restlessly, stroking and tugging at his beard. Wavy pale-blond hair to his thickset shoulders, grave forehead furrowed. He wore an almost-white long-sleeved shirt that appeared almost-ironed, fairly clean jeans, a leather belt and leather sandals from which his big, chunky white toes protruded—Abelove's going-to-town attire. He was huffily breathing as if he'd been pacing for some time working up words to say to Marianne. She feared his stern eyes swinging onto her, discovering too much.

Her guilt shone in her eyes, obviously. Bruised from what Corinne called *nuisance-tears*—just self-pity, exhausting and doing not a bit of good to another person. Her hair that had been combed and shining the previous day was tufts and snarls this morning like thistles sprouting from her head. Her skin was so tight across her face it ached. What did Abelove *see*? Marianne had thrown on clothes that morning without glancing at them—her usual slacks, a paint-stained T-shirt, gray-frayed sneakers.

"I need to know I can trust you, Marianne. That's the main thing."

"Oh, but—"

"Are you in love with him?"

"—Him?"

"Hewie Miner. Are you in love with him?"

Marianne was so surprised, she couldn't think how to reply. *In love? In love? I'm in love with you!*

Seeing Marianne's look of astonishment, her shrinking away like a frightened child, Abelove quickly changed the subject. In a gentler voice saying, "I'd been thinking of inviting you to share more responsibility with me, Marianne. To be—well, not just my personal assistant, like Birk, but someone more trusted. 'Associate director'— a new post." Through a roaring in her ears Marianne heard this man she so admired speak of her as if she were important: laying out words in his lecturer's way of deliberation and purpose you could almost see and would never dream of questioning, let alone contradicting. "You would have access to the Co-op's accounts, Marianne—as I do. You would have authority to make out checks, and to cash them. To bargain with our distributors. To negotiate contracts. The contract with the college food services is up for renewal, for instance—we'll want to renegotiate some of the terms. Yes, and you could come with me to visit potential donors—we'd make an excellent team, Marianne! You're intelligent and articulate and— when you make the effort—attractive—if perhaps you'd wear a dress, or a skirt? Stockings and shoes and—that black straw hat?" *Oh, had Abelove seen her? Had he been watching for her yesterday? Seen her early in the morning, clamping her hat to her head, hurrying to Hewie's car?* "And I've been thinking the Co-op should expand now that profits are rising. You seem to have such a way with you for 'expediting.' I've heard you on the phone! Our distributors ask about you! And here in the house, of course, everyone—likes you. I'd guess that every-one who has ever known you has—" Abelove paused, his voice nearly failing, "—fallen in love with you. Most of all, they—we—trust you."

Marianne was too taken by surprise, too disoriented, to do any-thing but stare at Abelove with a faint fixed smile.

Abelove hovered near, face ruddy with emotion. He spoke with the passion and purpose with which he spoke at Co-op meetings. "Our local reputation is excellent, Marianne, as you know, and it will continue to be excellent. However, we need more visibility. We need to display ourselves—a Green Isle open house, for instance. We might sponsor an arts and crafts fair and sell our products. And, maybe, hire ourselves out in work teams locally—housepainting, housecleaning, carpentry, lawn maintenance. Only think Marianne, of the markets we haven't tapped! Most of all, there's catering—weddings, anniversaries, even funeral breakfasts. We're locally famous for the high quality of our food and our congeniality. Mrs. Johanson, one of our most gener-ous donors, mentioned to me the other night at dinner that it would be wonderful if the Co-op could provide food for her niece's wed-ding—three hundred guests. At an estimated price of ninety dollars apiece. With additional charges, we're talking of approximately thirty thousand dollars! I couldn't disappoint her, I told her *yes*. And now—"

Marianne said, stunned, "Three hundred? Oh, dear—"

At Abelove's urging she'd sat; on the edge of the sofa; trying to keep up with Abelove's rapid speech. She had rarely seen him so ani-mated, such luminosity in his eyes. And he kept glancing at her in that anxious sidelong way of—was it Hewie?—that was making her even more uneasy.

Abruptly, seeing Marianne's reaction, Abelove changed the sub-ject. He began to talk of "ethical directives"—"philosophical first principles." He was no less animated, but more abstract, as if speak-ing not only to Marianne but through Marianne to a vast audience. "As a Harvard Ph.D. I became a neo-Malthusian but I consider my-self a revisionist neo-Malthusian. I see no contradiction between the grim teachings of Malthus and the teachings of Christ. Malthus was himself a clergyman, Church of England, as well as a mathematician; you know his hypothesis—there is an inevitable, deathly relation-ship between the quantity of food available and the number of mouths to consume it. If left unchecked, Malthus believed, population will always increase more rapidly than the means of food production. Plagues, famines, droughts, infanticide, wars—these are the means by which population has historically stabilized. It would seem almost that God is working through 'survival of the fittest'!— Nature's cruelty but the outward face of God's mathematical necessity! Basically, Malthus' gloomy hypothesis is correct; like Darwin's; the population of Earth, for instance, is expected to be a crushing six billion by the year 2000, and things have never been more perilous, more fraught with war. But Malthus for all his genius failed to conceive of mankind's *cooperation* in the face of such threat; oddly, he did not conceive of Christianity's basic principles put into operation, through science. My vision of the Green Isle Co-op is that it is a microcosm of the world. What works for us, can work for the world! We are dedicated to the principle of transcending competition and struggle. *All* are 'fittest.' Only there must be leadership, and dedication; hard work; abrogation of self. 'From each what he or she can give; to each—' "

"—'as he or she requires.' " But Marianne spoke mechanically, as if not hearing her own words.

Abelove broke off his speech and came quickly to her, and took her hands in his. Her small chill nail-bitten hands in his big warm hands. How strange it was, how abrupt to be touched like this, held! Marianne was so taken by surprise she didn't resist. In a now tremulous voice Abelove said, "Marianne, from the first I saw of you, I think I knew you were special. I never, never approach young women in the Co-op—that is a principle I've abided by since our founding, for obvious reasons. But I've been aware of you, Marianne—oh, yes! Your face, your eyes—the quietness, peace, purity! *Blessed are the pure in spirit, for they shall see God.* You are one of these, Marianne? Are you? I feel you've suffered."

"I—have? I don't think—"

"The only really good, pure person is one who has suffered with no thought of revenge, or vindication—*I* lack that strength, though recognize it in others. But I would never ask you how, Marianne. I would never wish to pry into your soul."

"But—"

Abelove leaned over Marianne, forehead furrowed, lightly beaded in sweat. His eyes were anxious. His face was mottled, in rosy splotches like something bloody reflected in water. "I think—I love you, Marianne. I—we—might live together?—might marry?" He was gripping Marianne's hands so tightly, she couldn't pull away; his earnestness held her, his certitude. You could see that, for him, saying a thing was the great effort; he could not anticipate that another might have a response, let alone one that resisted.

Marianne was saying, almost inaudibly, "Oh, Abelove, I don't—think so."

Abelove didn't hear. He took hold of her thin shoulders, stooped to kiss her. Abelove's warm dry kindly lips pressed against hers! Marianne pushed away, not hard, more in surprise than resistance, her eyes widened in alarm. Love? What was he saying? "—I have to be honest with you, Marianne," Abelove said quickly, "—I'm not altogether free—morally, I am—but not legally—I've been separated from a woman for years and, yes, there are children—two, teenagers—but things are worked out fairly, I believe—and there have been other women of course—not many, but a few—never here at the Co-op, I swear—never, till now. Always I've tried to be open, honest I think, as with you, Marianne. Are you shocked? You do feel something for me anyway, don't you? The way you've looked at me sometimes—you do love me, a little?"

Marianne stammered, "Yes, I—I guess so. I mean—"

"You do? Oh, Marianne—"

Squatting clumsily before her, thick-hammed, Abelove wrapped his strong arms around Marianne and kissed her again, more passionately than before. *Love! love! he loves me!* In astonishment she felt the man's body warm and yearning as any creature ravenous for affection, as she herself, perhaps—Abelove so *alive*, so *solid, compact*—the authority of his manly body against hers. She might have been snapped like a twig, invaded utterly. Abelove might have parted her stiff, dry lips with his, pushed his tongue into her mouth, but Marianne managed to slip from him, quick as a cat. Breathless, apologetic, she said, "Abelove, I—I have to leave, now. Thank you for all you've said but Felice-Marie, Amethyst are waiting for me—in the greenhouse—we have work to do—"

Preposterous: Abelove gazing at Marianne Mulvaney with such open emotion, yearning, why was she reminded of poor Silky?

She backed away, toward the door. Abelove followed almost humbly.

"You do love me a little, Marianne? You said?"

"Oh, yes," Marianne said nervously. "But right now I have to—"

"You're not in love with Hewie? Are you sure?"

"Am I—*sure?*"

"He didn't take advantage of you yesterday, did he? You were alone together all those hours. . . ."

"Advantage? Hewie?" Marianne was upset, incensed. "Hewie is as good and decent a man, Abelove, as *you.*"

She'd opened the door, desperate to escape before Abelove persuaded her to stay. He was saying, in a lowered voice, so that no one could overhear, a voice that was an echo of Marianne's own most secret yearning, "Will you come back, Marianne, as soon as you can? We'll go somewhere away from here to talk—we have so much to talk about! Marianne? *I love you.*"

Headlong in flight, Marianne was already out of earshot. Or almost.

Out of obscurity I came. To obscurity I can return.

RAG-QUILT LIFE

Who could have foreseen? Not Marianne Mulvaney herself. How, on the day following her attempted return to the Chautauqua Valley, the very day of Abelove's declaration of love for her, what Corinne had already shrewdly identified as her *rag-quilt life* would seriously begin.

No one at the Green Isle Co-op would have guessed why, nor would Abelove volunteer or offer any explanation. Stricken, humiliated, bewildered as he'd been when Birk had vanished, he'd gone to look for Marianne in the late afternoon—finding only Felice-Marie in their room, baffled as well. Where is Marianne? Abelove asked, trying to keep his voice level, and Felice-Marie shook her head numbly. She didn't know! She hadn't seen Marianne all day!

It was obvious that Marianne had packed most of her belongings, leaving behind only larger, unwieldy items (overcoat, boots, a scattering of hardcover textbooks); she'd taken her quilt, most of her paperback books, and her few clothes, apparently stuffed in a duffel bag. And, of course, she'd taken Muffin.

Where had they gone, without anyone observing?

Where had they gone, leaving no explanation or note of farewell?

"Vanished off the face of Earth"—Abelove's words had a grimly prophetic tone.

IV
HARD RECKONING

HARD RECKONING

This is a hard reckoning for a son to make. I'm not sure how to begin.

How Judd, too, went away—left my mom when she needed me. Thinking *I want my own life. I'm not just Mulvaney, I'm Judd.*

How I struck my dad, and was struck by him. Struck down, on my ass on the ground is frankly how you'd put it.

This was in Marsena, in the new place we came to live. That long wet spring 1980. I was seventeen, just transferred to the Marsena High School for the remainder of my junior year. *New kid* with no friends, and wanting none. Slouch-shouldered, scowling, a habit of shaking my head like a horse harassed by flies. If I smiled, which wasn't often, it was a quick come-and-gone twitch of the lips. Mom joked, sighing, "Judd, hon, you're becoming—well, some kind of *upright tic.*"

Looking at me, the youngest of the Mulvaneys, all that remained of her children at home, as if looking into a mirror.

When I say this is a hard reckoning I mean it's been like squeezing thick drops of blood from my veins. Just to set down what requires saying in some semblance of chronological order. For every statement of historic fact like *High Point Farm was finally sold, February 1980* or *The remaining Mulvaneys, Michael, Corinne, Judd, two aging dogs and three nervous cats, moved to a "split-level ranch" in a cornfield outside Marsena, New York* or *However many loans my father took out to relocate Mulvaney Roofing in Marsena, he was forced to declare bankruptcy anyway by June* strikes my ear like a lie, reverberating like tin. What actually happened was so much more complicated.

"A man gets to be the sum of his bad luck"—Dad was in the habit of saying, smiling bemused as he'd open another can of ale or, carefully so his hand wouldn't shake, pour something stronger and darker into a glass.

Trying to sell High Point Farm when real estate in the Chautauqua Valley was what the realtors called a buyer's market, and mortgage interest rates were high—that was *bad luck*. And Dad with debts to pay. Taking out loans, loans to repay loans, not always telling Mom what he was doing exactly, and maybe not always knowing himself; trying to negotiate a partnership with a roofer-sider in Yewville that finally fell through, and another with a businessman in Marsena that dragged on for weeks and finally fell through, too—*bad luck*. "It's like somebody, or something, is fixing the dice against me," Dad said, with his shrugging smile meant to indicate he wasn't much surprised, only just a little curious. He'd always been, in the old days, a man of *good luck*.

It was like the tragical-farcical Delta rescue mission in Iran, President Jimmy Carter's desperate jinxed attempt to free our hostages from their imprisonment in the center of Tehran under the directive of the Ayatollah Khomeini—in theory, the American military strategy might have worked, but in reality things went wrong. Badly wrong.

Mom watched TV nonstop when the terrible news broke on April 25, 1980. Our TV in a corner of the new, unfamiliar living room, reception wavering and ghostly. She wept for the eight young American servicemen who'd died in the helicopter crashes—men "chosen from all four branches of the armed services" as the Joint Chiefs of Staff so meticulously stated, and she wept for ashen-faced, badly shaken Jimmy Carter who was more and more looking like an ordinary man, a decent good Christian-Caucasian-American man as out of his depth in the riptide of history as a person not knowing how to swim in a deep, rough sea. What was this but American *bad luck*—smashed and burning helicopters, rubble where triumph might have been, an officially "aborted" mission and a rapid clumsy retreat to Egypt. Naked, exposed in the eyes of the entire world: what *shame*.

Mom said, wiping her eyes, "Oh, at least Mike wasn't one of them! Oh, thank you, God, at least for that."

Just to make the statement *High Point Farm was sold—finally!* doesn't give any true sense of that disjointed time in our lives that dragged on, and on, and on. There must have been thirty or forty "prospectives" who drove out to gawk at the property, in the company of a real estate agent; even more made appointments and were "no-shows." Some of the people who tramped through our house were locals with no intention to buy. You couldn't screen them out very well, the real estate agent explained to Mom. It's an open market, you've listed your house, in theory anyone can buy.

Like selling your soul. Once you make the decision, sign the contract, you can't back out.

Selling High Point Farm fell to Mom mainly. She was always on the telephone, or in a frenzy of housecleaning; wildly brushing at her hair, slipping on a sweater or jacket to cover her stained shirt. She had to play "Mrs. Mulvaney"—"the lady of the house"—when at last the awaited car or cars drove haltingly up the driveway. She had to be polite, smiling, hopeful and *never, never betray the misery she felt*. Never scream into these strangers' faces, "Go home! Go away! This is madness! Leave us alone!"

No, Corinne Mulvaney was a good sport about her own bad luck.

Michael Mulvaney Sr. was busy elsewhere. Not of a temperament to permit strangers to prowl through his property staring and assessing, shaking their heads at "needed repairs." To Dad, the potential buyers of the farm were "bloodsuckers" or "just plain suckers" depending on his mood.

As for me, Judd—I tried to stay out of everyone's way. If I was doing barn chores when the real estate agent showed up with whoever, I'd hide until they were gone; hardly breathing, my forehead pressed against a bale of hay. Sometimes I'd overhear snatches of conversations not meant for my ears—*Oh this is a run-down place isn't it, but so attractive, but how much would it cost to, but what a lot of work, oh but why would anyone in his right mind, yes but it's so beautiful out here, yes but it's so far out here, is it true the farm might be sold at auction, for bankruptcy? should we wait, until then?*

A knife blade turned in my heart. *I will never, never forgive you,* I thought. Not knowing who *you* was.

Over the many months the farm was for sale, the list price was frequently "readjusted"—downward. I'd overhear Mom on the phone, her hurt, faltering voice, "Oh, but I can't take that offer to my husband, I'm sorry I just can't. That offer is an insult—don't you know that offer is an insult?"

And, once, suddenly furious: "All right, then! I warned you! We will list High Point Farm with another realtor starting this minute! *Please do not attempt to contact us again!*" Slamming the receiver down so I felt the thrill of it along my spine.

Yayyyy Mom!

Eventually, though, in February 1980, after we'd about given up hope, a potential buyer made an offer that Mom dared bring to Dad. Only two thousand dollars below the list price. Dad shrugged and said, "Sure. How soon?"

So, High Point Farm was sold.

So, in March 1980 strangers came to live in the house in which Mulvaneys had lived since 1955. Supplanting Mulvaneys as if we'd never been. Hillside Estates people, a family of four plus a nervous little dachshund. Showy silver-gray BMW and canary-yellow Toyota station wagon. The adults were youngish middle-aged, the children, boy and girl, were ten and twelve. The father was a cardiologist at the new Chautauqua Medical Center, he claimed never to have heard of Dr. Oakley, now retired. It had long been his dream, he told Mom, to breed Black Angus cattle on a "dream-farm" like High Point. Both the children were "crazy for horses"—the girl had already begun riding lessons. The mother proudly described herself as a full-time housewife-mother and something of a perfectionist "bordering on the neurotic." She wore designer jeans, cashmere pullovers in bright, soft colors. She was almost beautiful in a way Corinne Mulvaney had never been. Deftly this woman met Mom's nervous chatter with shrewd questions about soil drainage, house maintenance, which "interesting" pieces of furniture, clocks, carpets, quilts, decorative objects Mom wanted to sell. Where Mom tried to quick-connect by searching out mutual friends or acquaintances, in the hopeful female way, this woman shook her head as if she'd never heard these names, smiled hard and directed the subject back to the purely practical. *Can't we be friends? Surely we're meant to be friends if you're buying this farm I love?* Mom pleaded in the face of one who held firm, having no sentiment to spare for strangers. Especially luckless strangers about whom the terrible word *bankruptcy* was being whispered.

Mom was rebuffed, hurt, chagrined. But after a while, being Mom, philosophical and even approving—"I understand her, of course! She's afraid I might turn out to be the kind of person who'd want to come back and visit, try to be friends. Some kind of crazy thing like that. I don't blame her at all!"

After so many months of delay and frustration, the sale was disconcertingly swift, the closing within fifteen days: the cardiologist and his perfectionist wife didn't require a mortgage but bought the property outright. And this, before they'd even sold their own house and five-acre lot in Hillside Estates. The day we moved into our new home in Marsena, Mom said, smiling, "There! Thank God that's behind us." She made a dismissive gesture in the vague direction of whatever it was we'd left.

The new house was only temporary of course. A tacky "split-level ranch" with glary-white aluminum siding like corrugated metal, "simulated redwood" trim, "picture window," carport on a two-third acre lot. The cement block basement showed peculiarly like bared gums in a giant mouth, only a few scrawny bushes grew around the house and there could not have been more than five spindly trees on the entire property. We were just outside the Marsena town limits, on a country highway where trucks traveled at sixty miles an hour, sometimes more, rattling everything not cemented in place, though the speed limit was fifty, and, inside the town limits, thirty-five. There were small doomed farms in the vicinity, several with FOR SALE signs out front. There was a large, busy Kmart a half mile away, there was a prosperous-looking Ford dealership, there was a mini-shopping center with 7-Eleven store, Exxon station, car wash. Marsena was a town of 3,400 people and where we'd live permanently Dad said but the house itself was temporary. He'd been in a hurry, pressed for time, had to make a quick decision on his own. A small down payment and a deal in which he took over the previous owner's mortgage without the intervention of lawyers. Just to find his family an interim house until, with the money realized from selling High Point Farm, he could reestablish Mulvaney Roofing and they could look around for a more suitable house. Maybe build?

Mom in her open-eyed daze, smiling at every surface in the new house, every remark put to her, murmured, "Oh, yes, Michael. That's always been our dream anyway—to build our own house."

High Point Antiques hadn't been abandoned exactly. Like Mulvaney Roofing, it was to be relocated in Marsena.

Except Mom hadn't much space for her precious things in the "split-level ranch" which was primarily a single floor sprawled out in a formula rectangle, living room/dining room/kitchen/"rec room"/three bedrooms at the rear of which two were small, meant for children. There was a toolshed beyond the carport only large enough to hold Dad's Toro lawn mower, the tractor, gardening tools, etc., and there was basement space immediately crammed with furniture that couldn't be fitted in upstairs and movers' crates, boxes, barrels that weren't unpacked, and would not be unpacked for a long time. There was an attic no larger than our corncrib at High Point Farm and this too was crammed solid. All the rooms of the new house were full to bursting with familiar things made strange and disturbing by their crowdedness and juxtaposition in this new setting, like an unwieldy nightmare into which an entire life has been shuffled out of impersonal malicious glee. "It's like the inside of a skull," Mom marveled, with her fluttery laugh. "We just have to deal with it one day, one hour at a time. We just have to keep calm and retain our sense of humor. We should think of it as camping out, sort of—not real. Just temporary. Oh, but that basement—I'm afraid even to *peek*." She shuddered, and laughed.

Mom did peek, though. And more. While Dad was out on business, and I was at school, she'd run back and forth, upstairs and down, checking to see if some beloved item (lamp, watercolor, pendulum clock, quilt, wine-colored crystal goblets, etc.) had been packed and brought along, a dog or two whimpering or yapping at her heels. (We had only Foxy and Little Boots, and of the cats only Snowball, Marmalade, and a pure black barn kitten, Sin, Mom had taken pity on and carried away with her to Marsena. The new owners of High Point Farm had been ambiguous about how they would deal with the ever-shifting population of semiferal barn cats and Mom dreaded the worst—"What if they hire old Zimmerman to come out and shoot them? What if that nasty old man suggests it? I wouldn't put it past him, or them. But I don't want to know about any of it. *Thank God that's behind us.*") There was a way she had of running with her eyes slitted almost shut, hair frizzed out gray-laced-with-red like a Hallowe'en wig and there was a way she had of abruptly halting because she'd forgotten where she was going; or, arriving there breathless, basement, attic, toolshed, back bedroom she'd swear she'd never seen before, and the view from the window of an empty weedy backyard ending at a ditch—she'd have forgotten why. She drew up lists of purchases to make in town (one of these, a replacement for poor Feathers who'd died just before the move) but lost the lists and had to draw them up again and this list too she'd mislay, or find crumpled with others in her pocket, handwriting unintelligible. *Make new friends (women!)* it looked like she'd scribbled on a scrap of paper. *Seek out new church (local!).* Naturally it fell to Mom to make arrangements with the telephone company for new phones, the gas and electric company, the oil delivery company, the Marsena public school district, the Marsena post office. The First Bank of Marsena—checking account, savings account. "Home owner's protection" for the new Mulvaney property at 193 Post Road, Marsena, New York. She rushed out intending to drive into town but found herself headed into the open country where, taking a wrong turn, she'd get lost for a half hour; or, on her way to the discount stores south of town, she'd find herself cruising the two-block Marsena downtown looking for a familiar storefront—some store she'd been shopping in for the past twenty years, in Mt. Ephraim. In the midst of so much confusion, why not take the animals for their much-procrastinated rabies and distemper shots? And little Sin, rapidly maturing, why not have her "fixed"? It would only save grief later. So single-handed, not even waiting for Judd to get back from school to help, Judd who was always Mom's assistant on these tumultuous outings, Mom hauled Foxy, Little Boots, Snowball, Marmalade, and Sin to a new vet six miles away—an adventure that would afterward require the thorough cleaning of the interior of the befouled station wagon, disinfectant and three Airwicks! *Well, we all had quite a time today* Mom would chuckle hoping to entertain her husband and her son when, and if, the three of them sat down together for dinner at the same time that evening. *Look at my war wounds!*—holding out her arms to show the scratches.

The looks on their faces!

There were those times when the telephone rang, and she could not locate a phone amid the clutter. She rushed, she stumbled—for what if it was Michael Sr., her beloved husband of whom she thought, worried obsessively as the mother of an infant if physically parted from the infant thinks and worries obsessively of the infant even when her mind appears to be fully engaged, if not obsessed, with other matters. Or what if it was news of him? During these mad dashes to the wall phone in the kitchen she hadn't time to fall but with fantastical grace and dexterity wrenched herself upright in midfall and continued running (dogs whimpering, yapping hysterically in her wake, cats scattering wide-eyed and plume-tailed) before the telephone ceased its querulous ringing—though frequently she was greeted with nothing more than a derisive dial tone, in any case. "Yes? Hello? Who is it? This is—" wondering for a blank moment what her name was before hanging up sadly, like a schoolgirl passed over by friends.

This is Corinne Mulvaney, please don't forget me.

In the weeks following the move from High Point Farm, a dozen times a day Mom had to restrain herself from calling the new woman of the house there. Oh, that woman! That—exploiter! Shrewdly seeing how trapped Corinne Mulvaney was, with her inventory of High Point Antiques and so much more furniture and belongings than she could ever fit into a "split-level ranch"—knowing how vulnerable Corinne was and how little time she had to sell her things elsewhere, this woman offered to "help out" as if buying an 1840 cast-iron Gothic Revival settee for $150 or a Colt Willow Ware bed for $200 or the exquisite little German ceramic clock in Marianne's old room for $60 was "helping out"! Oh, how she hated—but no, of course Corinne didn't *hate*. She was a Christian women to her finger- and toe-tips, to the deepest depths of her soul, she'd managed not to *hate* even those vicious enemies of Michael Mulvaney's, his former friends at the Mt. Ephraim Country Club who'd almost succeeded in putting him in prison. She'd managed not to *hate* even the Lundts, Morton and Cynthia Lundt who'd once been her friend who'd not only denied the brutal act their rapist son Zachary had perpetrated upon her daughter but had defended the son and vilified her daughter— even these people Corinne Mulvaney had managed not to *hate*.

These past few months, Corinne seemed to have lost contact with Marianne. She had an address for Marianne in Erie, Pennsylvania— unless, in the confusion of the move, she'd misplaced it. She had no telephone number. She knew of course that Marianne was no longer a student at Kilburn State and no longer a resident of the Green Island Co-op, or whatever it was called. Probably Marianne had transferred to another college? Was there a college in Erie, Pennsylvania? She'd ask Judd to look it up in the local library. Kilburn State was not a highly regarded college even within the New York State system and the Co-op—that character "Abelove" with his moist staring eyes and shimmering Christ-locks simply wasn't trustworthy. So it was just as well that Marianne had left. Corinne wasn't worried, much—hadn't time to worry about her scattered grown-up children any more than a mother cat about her scattered grown-up kittens telling herself *It's nature's way for them to scatter, to leave the nest* as Patrick had once said lecturing his family at mealtimes *it's the strategy by which nature assures that mammals won't interbreed with their siblings and weaken their genes—expulsion from the Garden of Eden, with a purpose* so she wasn't truly worried about Marianne, or Patrick either, both would contact her soon enough, she had no doubt.

Rag-quilt lives, both of them!—not what you'd have expected.

These days, Corinne almost envied them.

Then there was Mikey-Junior. Of course, you didn't dare call him that now. Marine Private First Class Mike Mulvaney Jr.—no mystery, at least, where *he* was. When people inquired, in the days when people inquired, his parents would say with pride, if uneasiness, considering the situation in Iran, that their eldest son was a Marine with a special training in electronics; they had snapshots to show of him in his dress uniform, remarkable photographs of a handsome clean-shaven young man with a somber smile, an air of conspicuous certainty and pride. Or was it the uniform, dazzling in its beauty? When Mike had first visited home, after his eleven-week boot camp at Parris Island, South Carolina, he'd had a difficult time adjusting to what he called the civilian world; he'd seemed uncomfortable with his own parents, pained at his father's drinking and smoking and even his posture, and eager to return to the Marines. Corinne had been so hurt! So shocked! And she'd let Mike Jr. know.

"How can you look at your own parents like you don't know us?" Corinne had demanded, and Mike Jr. had shifted his muscular shoulders in embarrassment, and looked her in the eye in a way new to him, a way she guessed he'd been trained to do, at the boot camp, as if he was about ready to salute, and said, "Mom, I guess I don't, in some weird way. It's like things are in code and the key's been lost."

Now Corinne looked at her son as if *he* were the stranger.

This past year, thank God, Mike was coming around. Worried about the farm and what Corinne had passed on to him of his dad's business problems (she'd spared him any news of the drinking, the second arrest, the trouble with that vindictive Judge Kirkland), Mike had begun to call home more often, and even to send postcards. He'd never been one to write letters, but postcards were just right, and they were from such exotic places as Gibraltar, Cairo, Saudi Arabia. Signed with just a carefully scripted *Mike*, usually. Though once, on the reverse of a card depicting a brilliantly blue Mediterranean Sea, he'd signed *Thinking of you & love, Mike*.

Michael, who'd long behaved as if he hadn't been missing his eldest son, was much moved by these cards. Especially *Thinking of you &*

love, Mike. So Mike Jr. was growing up, maturing!—it was a miracle, how the Marines had made a man (yes that sounded goddamned corny, but it seemed to be so) out of a hotheaded, immature kid who hadn't been able to get along with anyone except his drinking buddies. If to be *a man* is to be in control of oneself, and taking pride in the fact.

He, Michael Mulvaney Sr., the boy's own father, hadn't had the luck, good or bad, of serving in the U.S. armed forces. He might've been drafted into the Korean War—"conflict" was what they called it, in those days—except he'd married young, started having kids young. No telling what Michael Mulvaney might have learned.

What doesn't break you can teach you—right?

In the midst of so much worry about losing the farm, losing the business, Michael asked Corinne to locate the oldest snapshot album, dating back to—well, the beginning. They'd sit in the family room, each sipping beer, Michael grinning and laughing and shaking his head, tears in his eyes, lingering over the earliest pictures of High Point Farm, their young-marrieds pictures, Mikey-Junior at the age of a week in his beaming mom's arms, Mikey-Junior as a husky toddler gaping into the camera, Mikey-Junior at the age of four atop his first pony—what was that pony's name? Michael said, sighing, clamping a warm heavy hand on Corinne's knee, that long-married gesture meaning *We're in this together*, "Corinne, d'you think he'll ever come back? Try to work with me in the business? I wouldn't be so hard on him, now. I pushed too much, I guess. God, we could really be a team, Mike and me. If he'd give his old man a second chance."

Corinne laid her hand over Michael's. She said, smiling, "Well. Maybe. We can *pray*."

Thinking of such things like they'd happened years ago already and not just a few weeks back. For once life begins to accelerate it goes faster and faster. Probably, Patrick could explain that in scientific terms. Some equation of x, y, z.

She'd discover herself sitting on the steps of a basement stairs she didn't recognize. *Not* High Point Farm—this was different. No light on, and no purpose in her being there. She might have a cold coffee mug in her hands, or a screwdriver or sponge mop or Windex meaning she'd been going somewhere. But now just sitting here in the shadows, a shell-shocked woman of fifty, vague and smiling into the darkness below where ominous shapes of crates, barrels, up-ended tables and chairs slyly beckoned. Had she wandered into a mausoleum? Was this the Land of the Dead? "Mother, *you* aren't here, too, are you?" This was meant to be jokey, bravado. If Corinne Mulvaney could make only one person, herself, laugh— why, that meant everything was under control.

Or, stranger yet, she'd find herself shivering outside in some backyard she didn't know. In a chill mist or even light-falling snow. Was it getting to be spring, or just starting winter? A raw suburban-looking place, nearly without trees, oh how could people stand to live without trees?—you're so exposed to the sky. There was a country highway out front, diesel trucks thundering by. There was a neighboring house, split-level ranch with carport and glary-white aluminum siding, just the other side of the scrawny hedge. Foxy and Little Boots, hackles raised, barking their fool heads off at two psycho German shepherds beyond the hedge. Corinne was trying without success to get the damned tractor started, wanting to plow up some soil for a vegetable garden, flower beds. It was April, unless it was still March, but she was eager to begin. That yearning to feel the crumbly earth, dirt between her fingers. The hell with the tractor, probably it was out of gas. Michael wasn't tending to such things these days. She could use a shovel, a spade, a hoe. Oh, anything! Just to get the hard soil broken and tilled. You can set out lettuce just after St. Patrick's Day, in theory at least.

I'd come home from school and find Mom in such places. Crazy places like the backyard where, in a lightly falling snow, or a cold drizzle, there she was trying to spade the hard-packed earth. Mom in a soiled parka, slacks. I'd park my bike in the carport (it was a mile-and-a-half ride from school, even in the rough March wind those rides were usually my happiest times of day) and trot out back not so much hearing Mom talking to herself as seeing her, moving lips, short steamy puffs of breath. There came Judd's cheerful voice calling out, "Hey, Mom! What's up?" Mom would turn startled to stare at me as if for a moment she didn't recognize me, either. "Oh, Judd. Are you home from school, so soon? What on earth time *is* it?"—searching for her watch that wasn't on her wrist.

Take care of Mom. Be sure Mom doesn't crack up.

There was this voice instructing me, Judd Mulvaney's cheerful loud voice in my ears. I was open-eyed, I could see the way Dad was sliding, the way our lives were skidding. Like a runaway semi on a steep hill where the warning sign is TRUCKERS USE LOWER GEAR but it's too late for any warning. And the brakes are worn-out and not going to hold.

So I'd put away Mom's gardening tools in the shed, and get her to come back inside the house. If she'd been sitting in a trance on the basement stairs I'd tease her saying let's put some light on the subject!—switching on the light. And get her back upstairs, into the kitchen.

Now we could play TV Mom and teenaged son just home from school. He'd even bicycled home from school, he's such a good, clean-living simple country kid.

"Well, now!" Mom would say, rubbing her chapped hands, a pale neon-blue light coming up in her eyes, "—you must be famished, I bet. How about a snack—" opening the refrigerator door for me to rummage inside, maybe some milk, maybe orange juice, wedge of gelatinous cherry pie, "—but don't ruin your appetite for supper, please!"

Under Mom's watchful smiling eyes I'd squeeze into the breakfast "nook" with its Formica-top worn colorless from the elbows of the previous tenants of the house. I'd devour my delicious after-school snack for it's true I was famished.

The split-level ranch with the glary-white aluminum siding was not *home* and would never be *home*. I seemed to know that, as the rattled dogs and cats knew it, restlessly prowling and sniffing as if seeking their lost niches, trying to settle down for a nap but never quite comfortable. Little Boots was so nervous he'd gotten into the habit of snapping at me if I wriggled the loose skin at the nape of his neck as I'd always done. Foxy barked, barked, barked at invisible and inaudible dangers as fiercely as he barked at the thunderous diesels on the highway. We didn't have a canary now, poor Feathers had lived to a ripe old age of seven and then expired. Mom wanted to buy another canary or possibly even a parrot (someone to talk to, she said jokingly) but not right now—"We'd better wait till we get settled."

One sad day Marmalade disappeared. Mom called desperately for him, I bicycled for miles calling for him, "Marmalade! Oh kitty-kitty-kitty-kitty-KIT-TY!" but the wily old orange fellow was gone.

Another sad day, Dad backed the Lincoln over something bunchy and soft, as he called it, in the driveway—poor little Sin. Only six months old, and she'd just had her operation at the vet's. Mom wept for Sin harder than she'd wept for Marmalade who'd been with us so many years but, since he'd run away, might be considered a deserter.

"Sin never had a chance," Mom said, grieving so I thought she'd make herself sick. "Oh, why did we come here! This terrible, terrible place."

We buried little black Sin who'd never had a chance, just a limp soft-furred creature weighing less than four pounds, in the backyard near the single decent-sized tree, and that a weeping willow—the species of tree Dad hated, for the messes they make, and their propensity for cracking and shattering in the wind.

Home wasn't *home* and wasn't very real and that was fine with me. School was even less real. Like a TV program I'd switch on, stare at for a few seconds then switch off. Bullshit.

Back from Marsena High School I'd immediately shut out all memory of the place. Because we'd moved in midterm, in March, I had less than four months before summer recess and already I'd begun looking for after-school and Saturday work, freed at last from farm chores, and needing and wanting more to do; wanting to make some money of my own. *Money of my own!*—it was like a prayer. Maybe not being a farm kid any longer wasn't a hundred percent bad?

In the old days when I guess we had money, or anyway Mulvaney Roofing was prosperous, Dad loved to joke and tease about how much a farm like High Point cost, how much the "largely useless" animals cost, and his kids, and his wife's "notorious expenditures"—now he was facing bankruptcy he never spoke of money at all let alone joked about it.

Don't worry, Dad. I'll go to work, too. I can help out.

If we don't get along, I can move out, too! Just watch.

At seventeen, a transfer from Mt. Ephraim to Marsena, Judd Mulvaney was much observed, much discussed at Marsena High School. (You have to know what a backwater Marsena was, to understand that Mt. Ephraim High was considered "more sophisticated" by far. For one thing, it was roughly twice as large.) I possessed, in this new place, the arrogance of a certain kind of brainy male adolescent: not so smart as he thinks he is, but smart enough for the competition. I did my homework with contemptuous ease, wrote my tests quickly and carelessly. Sometimes I got high grades, sometimes not. I rarely volunteered to speak in class but if called upon I could provide correct and even impressive answers. Anyone who'd known Patrick would have seen that I'd taken on certain of his public ways—the haughty composure that disguised shyness, the frowning silence that intimidated others. I almost wished I wore glasses so that I could shove them against the bridge of my nose like Patrick.

Mind your own business, Judd. Make your own way. No one knows the Mulvaneys here.

I hardly remembered my teachers' names that first spring, let alone my classmates' names. It was a great feeling, actually—like that last scene in *Alice in Wonderland* Mom used to read to me when I was little, before I went to sleep, when Alice suddenly tosses the kings, queens, would-be executioners who've been threatening her into the air and discovers that they're just playing cards. *Who cares for you? You're nothing but a pack of cards!*

I'd always liked that as a little kid and as a seventeen-year-old transfer from one life to another, I was liking it more and more all the time.

Take care of Mom. Be sure Mom doesn't crack up.
As for Dad—stay out of his way.

I don't want to misrepresent my father. There were days when he didn't drink much, or in any case didn't show the effects of drinking. Which were for him an anesthetized glare, on the edge of belligerence but lacking the energy to cross over. He'd come home exhausted, too tired to eat, crack a can or two of ale and drain them in a few minutes, fall into bed—and be up again the next morning by 6 A.M. He was a good man in his heart but stymied, frenzied, like a creature poked by spears, upright and flailing in a corner. If you got too close, to console, or hope to be consoled, you might be hurt.

At the time, I guess I hardened my heart against him. *He's a drunk. He's a fool. He's stupid. He doesn't give a shit about you or Mom.* Dad would order me to do something and I'd shrug sullenly and take my time doing it and Dad would give me a shove on the shoulder—oh, just a shove!—to show who's boss!—and my heart would flood with rage, adrenaline rushed through my skinny kid's body hot to bursting. I thought of the shotgun, the rifles now packed away somewhere in the basement amid the chaos of cartons, boxes, barrels *yes but I know where: I can find them* and it seemed to me the most natural thing, that a son might kill his father; to protect not just himself but his mother. *He's waiting to explode. Look what he did to Marianne. Erased her like she never existed. What makes you think he won't do the same fucking thing to you.*

I missed Patrick! My brother I loved, my brother I'd been led to think was my friend. Needing to talk to him for his intelligence, his wisdom. What had he said of our parents—they were casualties? Dad was like some poor creature whose life is being sucked out of him by a predator? By nature's plan? Yet Patrick had seemed to blame Dad anyway. He'd never forgiven him. When he called home, which was rare, it was never at a time Dad was likely to be home, only Mom and me. And Patrick had said he believed in evil.

I needed to talk to Patrick about what was happening to us which I didn't always understand and could not control. Even in a kid's fantasy I could not control. The deals Dad was always negotiating that always fell through. The lengthy telephone calls, the abrupt departures in the car; another missed dinner, and no explanation; long hours of absence explained by mysterious words—*laying the groundwork, connecting the dots.* One day Dad's old foreman Alex Flood had been rehired to work for him, and was going to move his family to Marsena; a few days later, Alex Flood had changed his mind, or Dad had changed his mind, and Alex was "out of the picture—permanently." One day there was a roofing supplier in Rochester with whom Dad was going to do business, a few days later the supplier was "out of the picture—permanently." In Marsena and vicinity, Dad seemed to have made a wide range of acquaintances already, businessmen, tradesmen, but predominantly men who worked with their hands, the kind of men he'd strike up friendly conversations with in local taverns, with whom he felt comfortable and could "respect" just as they "respected" him. But at the same time he spoke vaguely of people in this new place not liking him, not welcoming him—"They won't give me a chance. They don't really want me here. It's like somebody's been talking to them about me."

Carefully Mom said, "Michael, dear—who would be talking about you? Why?"

"You know who," Dad said. "And you know why."

These were the months, eventually years, my brother Patrick was out of contact with the family for long periods of time. I missed him so, tried to harden my heart against him, too, but could not.

Just when I'd thought I had a brother at last and I was a brother at last, I'd lost Patrick! God damn him.

Hurting Mom, too. Mom and Judd, two people who loved him.

I guess I was the only person on earth who might have understood why Patrick went away when he did. Sabotaging what looked to be a *summa cum laude* B.A. at Cornell. Disappointing his professors who'd had such hopes for him. But even I didn't really understand. He'd felt good about the *execution of justice*, that he hadn't killed Zachary Lundt after all, hadn't even hurt the bastard much. Said he felt free, would never need to punish any living creature again. And if Zachary had recognized Patrick, apparently he'd never told a soul.

Still, Patrick had disappeared. We'd receive postcards from him from time to time, forwarded from our old address. Postmarked California, Utah, Idaho. *Thinking of you & hoping all is well there. Sorry not to be in touch but will be calling soon I promise. Mom's birthday if possible. Sincerely & love patrick.* He was working with "learning-disabled children" in Oakland, California. Had a job in a fire watch station in Glacier Park, Montana. *Traveling & learning more than I'd ever thought possible. Feel such SHAME at my old self. Love to you all on my 22nd birthday (sorry to be missing it). Your son & brother patrick.* He was in Boulder, Colorado taking courses at the university in geology and archeology, he'd apprenticed himself to a Japanese woman potter. But soon then working as a hospital orderly in Denver, then again, a month later, in Fargo, North Dakota. *Promise will call soon. Am in good health & hope all is well with you. Making arrangements to return to Cornell & get the degree. Sorry for being out of contact & promise will call soon. Love pj.*

We waited to hear more about Patrick returning to Cornell, but—a long time passed.

We waited for him to call. And waited.

That Easter Sunday last year I'd done exactly as Patrick instructed. After Mom and I came home from church, after a harried lunch, I drove out saying I was going to visit a friend, went to the old abandoned cemetery on the Sandhill Road and found the rifle where Patrick had promised. I was scared as hell scurrying like a rabbit imagining police surveillance, somebody hiding amid the trees. But it was quiet, still, deserted like the country usually is, especially a lost old cemetery where the carved names of the dead have flattened out to almost nothing and weeds have grown taller than the tallest headstones. In nature, Patrick said, energy is never lost it's only reconverted, but a cemetery makes you wonder—so many people, so many lives, each one once thinking *Here I am, look at me! I'm something!* Yeah, right.

But there was Mike's .22 Winchester rifle neatly wrapped in the same canvas, shoved beneath some loose rock. Without letting the canvas fall back, I sniffed the gun barrel—it didn't seem to have been fired.

Not fired! Patrick hadn't fired the gun!

Not a *murder weapon* in my hands!

Of course, he might still have used the knife. There was that terrible possibility—Patrick might have used the knife. For what had my brother said, boasted—he was accustomed to "dissecting" animals in the lab? Was that actually what Patrick had said?

I carried the rifle back to High Point Farm, smuggled it into the house and back to Dad's cabinet, locked the cabinet door. I was desperate to hear from Patrick what had happened, but he didn't call until 10 P.M. that night, from Ithaca; and then he said only, tersely, "It's over—justice has been executed."

"But, Patrick—what happened?"

"Look, Judd: the less you know, the less you're involved. It's over."

"But what does that mean? Did you actually—"

"I don't think he'll ever tell anyone what happened even if he recognized me which I'm not convinced he did, or didn't—you understand?" Patrick was speaking rapidly. "It's over and I'm through and I might not be speaking to you or Mom for a while."

"But, Patrick—"

"Can't talk now, Judd. But *thanks*! And, hey—*I love you.*"

Quickly hanging up, before I could stammer any response.

So I'd think in the months and eventually years to come *Patrick loves me, what I'd risked was worth it.*

Which I still believe, to this day.

It was in early June just before the "incident" (as Mom would subsequently call it) between Dad and me, and maybe this had something to do with the incident, that, suddenly, Marianne was back in touch. Calling one Sunday evening as if nothing were wrong, and we hadn't heard from her in months.

"Oh, my goodness! Marianne," Mom exclaimed. "I picked up the phone and—my goodness, it's *you.*"

Pressing her hand against her heart, leaning against a doorframe.

Marianne was fine she said, living in Spartansburg in the very northwestern corner of Pennsylvania, south of Erie; her address was in care of a woman named Penelope Hagström, a poet, a philanthropist, in her sixties, a wonderful person for whom Marianne was "a sort of all-around assistant and friend." Miss Hagström was confined to a wheelchair, she'd been stricken with multiple sclerosis at the age of twenty-nine. She'd been engaged but the young man had broken it off and she'd never married, had no children and just a handful of distant, not very involved relatives. A wonderful person, Marianne reiterated, with high standards of integrity, behavior. Mom was guardedly pleased, hoped that Marianne was still managing to take some college courses?—and Marianne vaguely murmured yes, or she would be, soon, at a local community college. Mom hoped that Marianne was being paid "decently" by this Miss Hagström and that she wasn't being taken "criminal advantage of" as she'd been at the Green Island Co-op or whatever that place was called. In turn, Mom reported that our new house was just a little cramped, and the highway was closer than they would have liked (those damned trucks!—everything rattled including Corinne's teeth practically, she had to press a hand over one ear to talk on the phone), and Dad was having trouble finding the ideal location for the business, but otherwise things were fine, just fine! Everyone's health was fine! Marianne had numerous questions about the house, what did it look like, how large, what were the views from the windows, which pieces of furniture were in which rooms, which artworks on the walls? Did Mom remember that old painting "The Pilgrim" that Marianne had always liked so much? Mom said hurriedly that it had only been a print, not a painting, and she hadn't seen it for years—probably it had been tossed out with the mountain of trash when they'd moved. And there wasn't much point in describing the new house because it was just temporary, they planned to build a house of their own design— "Once your father gets Mulvaney Roofing back on its feet."

Every time I overheard Mom say this to whomever, a weird grin would crack over my face. *Back on its feet.* Like a drunk or a stroke victim who'd just crumpled.

On the phone with me, Marianne was cheerful, sunny-sounding. Questions about my new school, new friends I'd made, how did I like Marsena I managed to answer in the same tone, saying what sounded plausible. There was in the background beyond Marianne's voice a muted clatter like dishes being washed, cutlery—I had a quick flash of my twenty-one-year-old sister holding the phone receiver awkwardly between her shoulder and one ear as she stooped over a sink in someone's kitchen. Would she be wearing rubber gloves? Was her hair still so short, shorter than mine? I could see a gloomy high-ceilinged kitchen with glass-knob cupboards neatly lined with oilcloth, I could see a large chipped old gas stove, one of those old-fashioned refrigerators on legs, whirring motor on top like a pillbox hat. Elsewhere, in another part of the house, a chisel-faced gray-haired woman sat in a wheelchair, blanket tucked in tight over her knees, waiting for Marianne to *please hurry, to push her out into the garden before it gets too chill.* The walled garden was soft-rotted old brick, crumbling masonry. Wild ragged English ivy nibbled by aphids. Leggy black-spotted rosebushes. Was that scrawny speckled-white cat picking his way through the lichen, all backbone and tail, Muffin? Was Muffin still living? I was afraid to ask.

In a lowered voice, hurried as if she was running out of time, or in fact someone was calling her, Marianne said, "Muffin's in great shape, Judd. I forgot to tell Mom, so will you? Muffin says hello and he misses you all."

"Well—hello to Muffin, too. We miss him, too."

"He loves it here. It's so much more peaceful than the Co-op."

"It sounds sort of—busy."

"Have you heard from Patrick?"

"Oh, Patrick—he's in Denver studying geology, or—no, he's in Fargo, North Dakota working in a children's hospital—"

"Is he all right? Is he happy?"

"He sounds very happy. Not like Pinch at all."

"Can you give him my number? Next time he calls?"

"Do we have your number?"

There was a muffled sound in the background as of creaking, rolling. A door with hinges needing to be oiled—unless it was a voice. "Oh, dear—I guess I have to hang up now, Judd. Love you! Miss you!"

"Marianne, wait—"

"Love to Daddy, too—but don't tell him if he won't want to hear, please? Bye!"

And in an instant it all vanished—dishes being washed in a sink, humming-vibrating refrigerator, Miss Penelope Hagström in her wheelchair, Muffin picking his way through a stranger's walled garden, my sister Marianne with her head at a sharp angle holding a telephone receiver against her shoulder. Not even a dial tone, just a dead line.

Naturally Mom didn't tell Dad that Marianne had called, and I surely didn't. Nor did Mom say much about Marianne to me, even to fret aloud about why Marianne wasn't going to college, preparing for a career. Maybe she worried I might take up the conversation again in Dad's hearing. And Dad was in such a mood these days, swinging between lethargy and mania, it was hardly the right time to speak to him of Marianne.

But a few days after Marianne's call, there Mom was with a book she'd driven seventy miles to a Yewville bookstore to buy— *The Selected Poems of Penelope Hagström*. The publisher was a "real" New York publisher and the poems, Mom said, were difficult to understand but very good, she thought. In fact, profound.

"Oh, I'm so proud of Marianne," Mom said excitedly. "I'm thinking of calling some old friends, in Mt. Ephraim. Finally my daughter has been recognized by someone of *quality*."

∽✷∾

Next night was the "incident" between Dad and me.

In fact just for the record, I guess I feel guilty about this, there'd been plenty of "incidents" for a long time I'd tolerated in silence. I mean months, years of my father ordering me around, half the time in a sarcastic voice, as he'd never ordered Mike or Patrick. I felt that hurt as keenly as the hurt of being treated by my father like a dog. Well, worse—Dad had a soft spot for poor almost-blind Foxy. He'd never have been sarcastic to Foxy!

This was the night of June 11, a damp windy nothing-day, by coincidence exactly a month before my eighteenth birthday, when Mom's rattletrap old station wagon finally broke down and died. She'd been doing errands in Marsena and the motor just gave out, lucky for Mom practically in the front yard of Jimmy Ray Pluckett and his wife Nanci—"The Reverend *and* the Reverend of the New Church of Christ the Healer of Marsena, New York" (the Plucketts were both ordained ministers and had a dual appointment)—and even before the Buick's motor ceased sputtering, Jimmy Ray had trotted out to offer assistance. He was a tall rangy freckle-spotted man of any age between thirty and fifty, in khaki shorts and a sleeveless T-shirt. Not only did Jimmy Ray call a tow truck for Mom immediately, but when the mechanic told Mom the bad news that the motor was "beyond repair," Jimmy Ray and Nanci drove Mom out to the house, five miles away; and Nanci, a short plumpish woman with vivid eyes, offered to drive Mom wherever she needed to go next day, and the day after next—saying, with a child's frankness, that Mom looked like she'd about come to the end of her tether.

"And I know what a 'tether' is, around the neck," Nanci Pluckett said, stroking her neck reflectively, "—I have to confess, I been married before. *Not* to a Christian man."

To the Plucketts' embarrassment, Mom burst into tears. She wasn't used to being treated so *considerately*, she said, in a long while.

Then clamping her hand over her mouth, blinking appalled at her newfound friends. "Oh, my goodness, what did I say? I don't mean that at all. That's the most ridiculous *self-pity*."

The Plucketts gave Mom their joint card—identifying them as "The Reverend *and* the Reverend"—and told her to call them, any time. And to drop by the New Church of Christ the Healer which was just up the road from where her station wagon had died.

Dad missed supper that evening, didn't call to explain why, arrived home around 10 P.M. sullen and heavy-footed and in no mood for surprises. He'd seen, of course, that the Buick was missing from the driveway and naturally he wasn't happy about it. I heard him and Mom discussing the problem, calmly enough at first and then with more urgency as Dad's voice rose in volume with a beat like chopping wood. *Don't listen. Stay out of it. He can't seriously blame her—can he?* I was in "my" room at a back corner of the house, a room approximately the size of the old claw-footed bathtub we'd had at the farm, and I'd pushed my windows up as far as they could go so the exterior night seemed to be *in*. I was sprawled on my bed listening to a radio turned low and leafing through some paperbacks I'd brought home—"borrowed"—from the Miracle Mart where I worked four afternoons a week—a handbook *Backpacking in the Mountains: A Personal Odyssey*, a "pictorial biography" of John F. Kennedy, *Lovejoy's College Guide*. That was the way I read most things—three or four at once. Even Patrick's science magazines and books I'd appropriated, I was too restless and my mind too scattered to focus on just one. Even *The Selected Poems of Penelope Hagström* I'd looked into and agreed with Mom they were hard to understand but impressive and who knows?—maybe even profound.

After a while I couldn't pretend not to be hearing. My drunk bully-Dad cursing my Mom because *he's* a loser, *he's* a failure and a bankrupt and all the world's waiting to know.

So I run out there so scared I'm shaking and it's just then that Dad must've pushed or punched Mom, there's her cry of pain, "Oh!—

Michael—" and she's scrambling to escape, out the side door beneath the carport and Dad is grabbing at her, ripping a sleeve of her shirt, tugging at her hair—"God damn you *listen* to me, just for once *you listen to me!*" but Mom gets away, and Dad's right behind her, and huddled beneath the breakfast nook Foxy and Little Boots are barking in terror, I'm running into the kitchen and outside where my parents are struggling together, panting, Mom crying, I'm pulling at Dad's arm, you don't touch a man like Michael Mulvaney but I'm pulling at his fatty-muscled arm, "Don't hurt Mom! You're drunk! Leave her alone!" and Dad bares his teeth at me, a vein standing out on his forehead, a red-flushed sweaty face like a mask, one of those Polynesian devil-masks I'd seen in a book, and with one arm as if he's slinging a box of shingles onto a truck he swings me around, slams me against the side of the house, as Mom begs, "No. No. No. *No.* Michael, *no.*" There's a roaring in my ears but I'm flailing out at Dad—striking with my fists that haven't the force to counter the force coming at me—the sheer weight of my father, two hundred pounds so compact, bull-necked—I'm as tall as Dad now but fifty pounds lighter and he's practically laughing at me, contemptuous, loathing—"Who do you think you are! You punk! You're nothing! You and your brothers! Letting your father down! Insulting your father! Every one of you—ungrateful bastards!" His hard fist on the side of my head, my head's ringing, suddenly I'm sliding down the wall of the house, sitting on the cold cement floor of the carport, amazed touching my face that's slippery with blood. And Mom is bending over me, crying, "Oh Judd, oh honey, are you hurt?" and Dad backs off, disgusted, "You make me sick, both of you. Y'hear? You make me sick. Get a man in a trap, rat in a trap, his head in a vise, tangled in fucking barbed wire—"

His voice trails off muttering. He doesn't touch Mom again, luckily because I can't stop him if he does. He might kick, kick, kick me and I don't have strength enough even to crawl away. Instead he fumbles for his car keys in his pants pocket, drops them, gropes for them on the cement with a grunted obscenity, throws himself into the Lincoln and backs out skidding and seesawing to the highway with the twin manic German shepherds next door barking furiously in his wake and behind Mom and me in the kitchen our dogs are whimpering, that doggy-plaintive-helpless terror you know will smell exactly like dog pee when you get close enough.

ON MY OWN

Following that night, I moved out. I would live by myself in Marsena, I said. Yes I'd take Little Boots with me, I'd care for him in his old age. Yes I was strong enough, I could do it.

Never again under the same roof with Michael Mulvaney Sr. In fact it seemed to me that Michael Mulvaney Sr. had died, and another man had taken his place, not even resembling him that much, and maybe that's a good thing.

I had my job at Miracle Mart, and later on I'd get a better-paying job at the Milk Jug, and still later (though I could not have guessed such good luck, beforehand) a part-time job with the *Marsena Weekly Packet* whose editor was a brother of the English teacher at the high school I came to be friends with, my senior year—actual writing, reporting, my byline *Judd Mulvaney* there in print, and even being paid for it.

Beyond that, I'd graduate with honors from Marsena High School and go away to college, and be gone.

On my own at the age of not-even-eighteen.

Mom cried, cried. It wasn't as easy parting the way I'm making it sound. Because nothing between human beings isn't uncomplicated and there's no way to speak of human beings without simplifying and misrepresenting them. Mom cried but she helped me pack my things. Begged me to kneel with her and pray together to ask of God whether this was the right thing and quietly I said no.

"We're past prayer," I said. "We passed prayer a long time ago."

I thought she would protest but instead she sat heavily on the edge of the bed, and tried to smile at me. In a hoarse voice she said, "Yes, maybe it's better. Until he's himself again. You know one day he'll be himself again, you know that don't you?"

I stared at the toes of my sneakers. What did I know?—I was an arrogant scared kid.

"Your father loves you, honey. He loves you all, you know that don't you?"

"I don't know what I know."

They say the youngest kid of a family doesn't remember himself very clearly because he has learned to rely on the memories of others, who are older and thus possess authority. Where his memory conflicts with theirs, it's discarded as of little worth. What he believes to be his memory is more accurately described as a rag-bin of others' memories, their overlapping testimonies of things that happened before he was born, mixed in with things that happened after his birth, including him. So it wasn't a smart-ass remark, *I don't know what I know*. It was just the truth.

"It's just that he loses control sometimes. As soon as he gets the business established again, and gets back to work, you know how he loves to work, he'll be fine. The drinking is only temporary—it's like medicine for him, like he has a terrible headache and needs to anesthetize himself, you can sympathize with that, Judd, can't you? We might be the same way in his place. He's a good, decent man who only wants to provide for his family. He's told me how sorry he is, and he'd tell you except—well, you know how he is, how men are. He loves you no matter what he says or does, you know that don't you? He's been under so much pressure it's like his head, his skull, is being squeezed. Once, a long time ago, I read a story about an Italian worker who has a terrible, tragic accident on a construction site, a load of wet concrete overturns on him—'Christ in Concrete' was the title, I think—oh, I never forgot that story!—it was so real, so terrifying how the poor man was trapped—in hardening concrete that squeezed him to death, broke his bones and his skull and there was nothing anyone could do—" Mom spoke more and more rapidly, more breathlessly until I wanted to take hold of her hands and quiet her.

Thinking *Christ is anybody and nobody.*

Thinking *Love wears out, maybe. Maybe that's a good thing.*

I guess I started crying, too. But I wasn't going to change my mind.

I made Mom promise she'd call me, or come to where I was staying next time Dad got drunk or crazy, or if he threatened her. Don't wait for him to hit you, I said. She promised she would do this. She believed there would not be a next time because he'd been so sorry when he came back, and so scared of what he'd done, but yes she promised. And finally I did kneel with Mom, one last time, and we prayed together each of us in silence in the cramped little room at the rear of the "split-level ranch" on Post Road which was our last shared home even if it was never a home. Both Foxy and Little Boots crowded eagerly against us, nudged their damp anxious noses against us begging *Us, too! Us, too! Don't forget us, too!*

But Mom never called me. On June 21, first day of summer, Dad filed papers in the district civil court in Yewville applying for the privilege of bankruptcy. He'd had to hire a new lawyer—couldn't avoid it. Immediately the Mulvaneys' assets were "frozen"—the new house put on the market for resale—what humiliation my parents had to endure I would not learn until years later.

Their marriage, too, began to unravel—in ways I would not know, and did not wish to know.

For suddenly I was *on my own*! I'd thought I would be lonely, but in my new life I had no time for loneliness.

Living in a single furnished room (with lavatory, shower) on the top, third floor of a big old clapboard apartment house in the no-man's-land south side of Marsena. Near the railroad yard, about a mile from the high school. The building had once been a hotel, the Marsena Inn, a long time ago. Mostly it was welfare families who lived there, in the larger apartments on the ground floor. The siding was weatherworn brown the color of bleached winter grass, transparent strips of duct tape from the previous winter still flapped at some of the windows. A sagging veranda across the width of the building, the roof and posts overgrown with vivid orange bug-ridden trumpet vine. The building's custodian and his wife and children lived on the ground floor—the wife had set out geraniums in pots on the veranda, and a scattering of battered old wicker furniture, a carpet. There were clotheslines everywhere and except on rainy days laundry hanging up to dry. One of the elderly tenants tended a coop of scruffy chickens in the backyard. These chickens were all

Rhode Island Reds but diseased-looking, like old feather-dusters, bald on their heads and backs. There were two reigning, squawky roosters for about two dozen hens and both looked the worst for wear, with inflamed combs, scaly legs. On wet days, and it was a wet summer, a terrible stink wafted upward from the muddy floor of their coop at which they pecked, pecked, pecked chicken-fashion through the daylight hours—but I didn't mind, I was a farm boy used to such smells.

And quickly I would come to be friends with the old man who owned the chickens. He'd come to like me, too. And Little Boots he'd keep company with when I was away. He called me "Juddy-boy"—sometimes "Sonny" if he didn't exactly remember my name.

THE WHITE HORSE

He'd married young, that was his story. You don't know what your story is going to be until looking back.

Because he'd fallen in love with a girl strong enough to keep him faithful. And he'd wanted children with her as ballast, to keep his rocky little boat from careening off course, carried away by the first big swell. A son, another son, a daughter, and a third son. Their small limbs, warm and pulsing, unbelievable soft skin, faces eager with love for Daddy, for now *he was Daddy that was who he was*, holding him tight, holding him safe.

God, he'd loved them! Those kids. The first baby, named for him, had scared him a little, the love came so strong, and the love for the woman, so strong, he'd felt panic touch the base of his spine light as a stranger's fingertips *You did this, Mulvaney? that's your son? your responsibility for life?* But then it was all right. It was just life. It was American life. Look around, everybody's marrying young, it's an economic boom too, all world's watching in awe, post–World War II United States of America mushrooming up, up, up like the A-bomb cloud—*Sky's the limit!* Forty million American babies predicted for the Fifties. It was just life, normal life, and it was good.

Like God said gazing upon His creation in the Garden of Eden, it *was* good.

And then—they were gone.

The Mulvaneys who bore his name, not just the kids but the woman, too. (In fact, he'd been the one to move away. Just took off, threw a few things in the car, moved to Yewville. There gets a point, a man can't take it any longer.) Life started going fast, and faster, and he'd been taken by surprise. And not old, damn it, either—in his early fifties. Suddenly his little boat was in rough, unfriendly waters. Storm winds, heaving waves spinning him out of control. And there, above, on a bridge he'd have to pass under, there stood his father—his father he hadn't seen for a lifetime! The bridge was one of the old Pittsburgh bridges over the Allegheny River, he recognized the knotty black shape of it, the looming silhouette, and he recognized his father astonished that the man wasn't elderly but a man Michael's own age, his father was shouting at him, his voice forlorn yet angry, over these many years still angry, and the jaws thickset in the stubborn inviolable rectitude of the damned, and there was the upraised fist—*Go to hell, then! No son of mine.*

A father's curse! Michael Mulvaney Sr. had lived his entire adult life in the wake of his father's curse.

So too he'd sent his own daughter away, not with a curse but in the name of love. He believed, he would swear to his very death—it had been love.

And how strange time was. Once you veered away from shore, and flew along, borne by the river's current beneath the bridge and out to what looked like sea, as if it hadn't been the Allegheny after all but the mouth of a vast dark thundercloud-sea—somewhere you can't recognize. *What the hell is this? Who's making these decisions?*

After thirty years living a bachelor's life again. But the world wasn't a bachelor's world now. Not the world of Michael Mulvaney's young adulthood when he'd thumbed his nose at the old man, *Go to hell yourself!* and left Pittsburgh forever.

Now there was a confusion of times, places. It was like switching TV channels—you never knew where exactly you were, or how long you'd be there.

How Corinne had cried, cried. It wasn't like her, and it scared him. That first full day the three of them were in the new house in Marsena when Corinne hadn't the manic excitement of preparing to move, the great effort ahead. She'd cried like a helpless child *Where are our trees? Oh Michael, where are our trees?* As if she hadn't actually noticed until then, hadn't allowed herself to look, to know what the new property was: a plot of land less than an acre.

So he'd gotten good and drunk, left her there bawling. What good would it do, the two of them bawling together like sick calves?

Thinking *A man deserves some freedom for Christ's sake. A furlough.* If he wanted to drink, he'd drink. Fed up with being made to feel guilty every time he popped a can of ale, or stayed away missing a meal, or took the name of the Lord "in vain" making his Christian wife flinch. She wasn't his mother for Christ's sake.

The first place he lived was a good-sized furnished apartment overlooking Outwater Park, in Yewville. The second was a smaller apartment on Market Street, New Canaan. The third was a room and a half on East Street, Port Oriskany. He'd never again return to the Chautauqua Valley, that was a dead region to him now.

Working where he could. As often as he could. Nonunion, hourly wages. Sure he'd had serious problems of attitude, adjustment, at first. Michael Mulvaney's new status being not *employer* as he'd been for nearly thirty years but *employee.* A sensation like stepping into an elevator but there's no elevator there, just the shaft.

At first, he'd tried to get managerial jobs, salesman positions. But there were none of these jobs available, at least not for him. That look of belligerence in his face, the tight, taut mouth. He'd caught sight of himself once in a window, looked like a pike. Slamming along. Impatient, furious. Forcing a smile. A pike's smile. How quickly he was recognized: one glance at this job applicant entering an office not entirely clean-shaven, clothes just slightly rumpled, the hurt puckered furious pike-look in his eyes.

Sorry Mr. Mulvaney, that position has been taken.

Once, in Port Oriskany, a young bespectacled man smirked uttering these words *Sorry Mr. Mulvaney, that position has been taken* but Michael Mulvaney didn't slink away like a kicked dog, instead he leaned over the man's desk trembling with indignation shoving his fine-stubbled jaw and bared teeth into the bastard's face. *Yes? Taken by assholes like you?*

That story—how many times he'd tell it, for the remainder of his life. In how many bars and always it would get laughs. True belly laughs. Even the women, they'd laugh—he was a man who loved making a woman laugh.

It had done him good to see that prissy bastard cower, the quick fear in the bastard's eyes. One of the enemy. His comeback hadn't gotten him a job in that office nor any job ever again in which he would wear a fresh-laundered shirt, a tie and coat and gleaming leather shoes, and be called "Mr. Mulvaney." *He*, who'd once had capital and assets approaching two million dollars. But still it had done his soul good.

Two years, three years, five years—he would lose count. Ronald Reagan was President of the United States now and poor sad Jimmy Carter was not only gone but forgotten. Supplanted as if he'd never been.

Ashes to ashes, dust to dust.

Working where he could, where they'd hire him on. Scanning the HELP WANTED—MALE columns of the papers. Some employers knew him—which was good sometimes, bad others. He was a damned good worker but he did have a short fuse. He was good at giving orders but not so good at taking them. Where he couldn't be foreman, things didn't always work out. Crews of mostly younger men. Somedays, he wasn't in top physical condition. Hacking cough from those damned cigarettes he couldn't seem to kick, puffy boiled-looking face, the bleary no-color of eyes determined not to give away the *beat beat beat* of a hangover's pain. Also, his joints were giving him trouble—fingers, shoulders, knees. Also, he needed glasses but never got around to getting them.

Working where he could, and when. He let his employers know he'd had plenty of experience with roofing, siding, construction but he never went into details. *Last thing you want the bastards to know is who you are. Your true identity. No one wants to hire a man who, if there was justice in the world, deserves to be the one behind the desk hiring.*

For a while he was foreman for an Elmira roofing-siding company and that was a decent-paying job, nobody knowing the name Mulvaney. But there were "temperamental differences" with the owner so he moved on, to Cheektowaga, to Batavia, to Rochester. He couldn't hope to get into the trade union, too old and anyway you need to know the right people. Bastards have the unions shut up tight. Exactly why, as an employer, he'd hated the unions. Roused him to fury, those sons of bitches telling him, Michael Mulvaney, what to do. What hourly wages to pay, overtime and social security and pension and sick-time and the rest of it—bullshit. No man of integrity and pride can tolerate such intrusion.

Y'know what he hoped?—that Reagan would bust their asses, all of them. Starting with the air controllers and blitzing them all.

Sure he believed in the free market, "deregulation"—if that was what it sounded like, what it seemed to promise.

Life is dog-eat-dog, why not acknowledge it? He'd been cheated of the business he'd spent a lifetime building up, his farm-home had been taken from him, his family. Sucked dry and tossed down like a husk. His enemies ganging together against him, bringing him to ruin.

Blessed are the meek, blessed are the pure in heart—poor deluded Christians you want to laugh in their faces. Turn the other cheek?—you get walloped.

Michael! You don't mean that. That's hardening your heart to God, you know you're not such a man.

Which was exactly why he'd left her. Threw his things into the Lincoln and fled. A woman too good for him from the first and love shining in her eyes he didn't deserve and had never deserved and the strain of keeping up the deception was too much. Driven out into the world by a father's curse, aged eighteen.

I love you so, Michael. I wish I could give you peace, peace in your troubled heart.

Yes he knew she was praying for him—he could practically feel the vibrations in the air. Wanting to cup his hands and yell, in the direction of Marsena, *Stop! Cease and desist! Let me go!*

At least, he believed she was in Marsena. He hoped to hell she hadn't moved to Salamanca to live with that old maid-mutt cousin of hers Ethel.

Maybe she'd gone to live with Marianne. That thought, like a beacon shining too brightly into his eyes, he couldn't deal with.

High Point Farm. The memory of it, the lavender house atop a wooded hill. He couldn't deal with that, either.

It was in Rochester that his drinking gradually increased until such a time that he was never what you'd call sober nor was he (he believed) what you'd call drunk. If he drank just to this degree he could anesthetize himself so there was minimal danger of flashes of memory of High Point Farm; but if he drank too much, got sick to his stomach, vomiting and choking—there was that danger. And afterward a sensation of something spongy, swelling inside his head.

Oh, but he couldn't bear it!—the farm in its final days. The pickup had been sold. The barnyard was deserted. Weeds grew everywhere. Most of the animals and the fowl were gone—the new

tenants said they were "leery" of taking on the Mulvaneys' creatures, and preferred to populate the farm with their own. You can't
blame them, Corinne said, they're worried about—well, diseases.
But, God damn them to hell, Michael Mulvaney did blame them.

On Michael's last day at High Point Farm he'd tramped about
the property, alone. He saw a half dozen deer grazing in the back
pasture, drifting into the orchard. He saw that the pond had become
so shallow, choked with cattails and rushes, it was hardly more than
a declivity in the earth. And what a rank-rotting odor lifted from
it—you had to know something had died there, maybe a deer run to
death by dogs, only a part of the carcass remaining. But he didn't really know, and didn't want to know. Let the fastidious new tenants
deal with it.

In fact, Michael Mulvaney had moved out three days before
Corinne and Judd, before the moving van's arrival. He couldn't bear
to be a witness to the very end. His excuse was he had business in
Marsena and Corinne and Judd could oversee the actual moving,
the details; he'd be at the Marsena house, preparing for the arrival.
In the new house he slept on the floor in an old thermal sleeping
bag belonging to one of the children. He brought Foxy along with
him, for company. That, and a fresh quart bottle of whiskey.

Poor Foxy: whimpering and shivering in this new, unfamiliar
place. Why was his master behaving so strangely? Why was his master *alone*, sleeping on bare floorboards? The red setter Michael remembered as a puppy and then a sleek, slender young dog with
liquid-brown eyes was now thick-bodied, losing his eyesight, frequently off balance; he had a tendency to favor his right front paw,
though the vet couldn't find anything wrong with it. He was just
an old, aging dog. A dog's life is a speeded-up version of your own.
After a while, you can hardly bear to be a witness.

"It's a dog-eat-dog world, eh, Foxy? You're a dog, but you've
been shielded from it until now."

*I love you so, Michael darling. Why is it so hard now for you to
love me?*
These words were whispered, never spoken aloud. And then
only in the dark. When, under pretense of sleep, he could pretend
not to hear.

Yet he heard, and turned away; didn't care to hear again, so he
began to sleep elsewhere in the house. Another wife might have

screamed *Bankrupt! Failure! Impotent!* but never Corinne who had given her life to him, and would surely have died for him. Hadn't she sacrificed their only daughter to his blind, raging self-righteousness?

So Michael had stopped coming upstairs to their bedroom, to sleep in that bed, weeks and even months before the move to Marsena. Long before his actual declaration of bankruptcy. Maybe it had nothing to do with the collapse of Mulvaney Roofing and the public humiliation, maybe it was simply the wearing-down of their marriage. Like one of Corinne's "antique" clocks that one day ceased ticking.

Frequently Michael fell asleep on the sofa in the family room, or in Mike's room where the bed was neatly made, surfaces kept free of dust, in readiness for their Marine son should he come home to visit. (He'd come home only twice, in three years. For brief weekend visits.) He slept on top of the bed, inhaling a faint melancholy dog-odor—poor Silky, a ghostly presence. Drifting off to sleep amid shiny sports trophies and plaques, framed team photos signed by all the boys, laminated newspaper features and banner-headline clippings devoted to "MULE" MULVANEY. In that almost mystical state of consciousness that accompanies just the right degree of drunkenness Michael Mulvaney came to realize *It's a boy's world in America—but only if you're a winner.*

Once he woke with his feet tangled in the bedspread, alert and agitated. Somehow confused thinking *he* was Mule Mulvaney. Damned good-looking kid, but young. Smart-ass. What's required is a few punches to the jaw to wise a kid like that up.

❧

Married but no longer married. A husband and father but no longer. He'd taken away with him from the house in Marsena, carelessly dumped into a box with financial papers and documents, a handful of snapshots from Corinne's albums. Stone cold sober, he dared not look at these snapshots; drunk, he had no need.

There were women sympathetic to him, women he'd buy drinks for to whom he spoke not bitterly but bemusedly of his past life—you could sum it up, thirty years of it, in one word: *Betrayal.*

How exactly was he betrayed?—that's nobody's business.

Saying, *I don't discuss my personal life with anybody.*

In Rochester, he worked for Ace Roofing & Siding, not regular employment but when they called him. The business was run by a man given to dishonest tactics, cheating on estimates, inflating bills, substituting inferior materials where he knew he could get away with it. Michael Mulvaney saw, and saw that others of the work crew saw, but they said nothing. Ace hired nonunion workers, you had to be grateful. At this time Michael lived on a south-side street above the Golden Pavilion Chinese Restaurant & Takeout where sometimes he ate, pork-fried rice and "chow mein" which were the cheapest dishes on the menu and he'd drink from a bottle in a paper bag placed discreetly beside him in the booth. He was a sunburnt-looking man in his fifties with squinty eyes, deep creases in his cheeks, fleshy-muscled shoulders and arms, a hefty paunch growing out of his midriff like a giant fetus. He wore not workmen's clothes but rayon shirts, gabardine trousers. Not a visored work-cap but a fedora. He chain-smoked Camels, the first and second fingers of his right hand were stained the color of jaundice. Black raging moods swept over him like sudden storms in this part of New York State south of Lake Ontario but when he was in a good mood he was in a *good mood* and let the world know. Smiling at the shy Chinese waiter who looked like a kid of fourteen and even, when he had the cash, tipping generously—a one-dollar bill discreetly tucked beneath his plate. In the Golden Pavilion, sitting in his usual booth, he felt puls-ing-warm faded-pink neon light falling upon his face from the sign in the front window like the blessing of a God distant and rapidly receding as in that terrifying vast universe of which his son Patrick used to speak, with glib schoolboy pedantry, a lifetime ago.

Patrick. One who'd betrayed. As young as eleven, that frowning scrutiny had been unnerving. Gone away to fancy Cornell University and never returned. Four weeks before his graduation they'd received from him a terse, typed pronouncement on a sheet of paper with the letterhead CORNELL UNIVERSITY DEPT. OF BIOLOGY MEMO. The first words as if he'd spat into their faces. *When you read this I will be a thousand miles away.*

Corinne had almost fainted, reading these words thinking the boy had killed himself.

And there was Judd. Damn, it was heartbreaking, the mistakes he'd made with his youngest child—who'd turned stubborn, and hotheaded like his dad, moved out of the Marsena house and refused to speak to Michael. Well—let the kid go. He'd be sorry. Maybe he *was* sorry, right now. Serve him right.

And there was Marianne.

He could talk about his sons, his sons who'd betrayed him, but never about his daughter.

Once, he'd bloodied a woman's nose, she'd been pawing through his things and came across the hoard of mostly creased and torn snapshots and waved a snapshot of Marianne in his face asking was this his daughter. Might've killed her, he hadn't been so drunk.

Marianne he'd loved most. Who'd hurt him most. Betrayed. He could not always remember why, exactly. But there was a reason. *Michael Mulvaney always had reasons*. Oh, but never mind about Marianne—have another drink.

It was in the Golden Pavilion that he and Mike Jr. had a meal together. Their first in years, and it would be their last. Late August 1986. How Mike had tracked his elusive father down in Rochester, the elusive father didn't know and didn't inquire. It was a humid-sulfurous evening. About ninety degrees and a single antiquated air-conditioning unit vibrating at the rear of the narrow tunnel of a restaurant. The look in Mike Jr.'s eyes taking in this place his ravaged old dad was bringing him—just downstairs from where he lived! The look in Mike Jr.'s eyes taking in his ravaged old dad. Staring, and swallowing. For a moment speechless. They'd shaken hands, wasn't that what you did? Mike Mulvaney Jr. was a Marine sergeant now, a grown man, in neat pressed civilian clothes and his hair trimmed so it looked sculpted on his head. Yet those were a boy's eyes, a scared-son's eyes, seeing Michael Mulvaney after how many years.

"Not exactly the Blue Moon, eh?"—the old dad laughed wheezily, leading Mike to one of the sticky plastic booths. There was a smell of something brown-scorched in the stale-circulating air. They sat, and the effort began. Mike Jr. had to do most of the talking. He'd driven up from—the information drifted past, lost in the air conditioner's rattling. He was engaged to be married to—the girl's name was something bright and perky ending in *y*. The wedding was scheduled for—whenever. Michael Mulvaney who was playing the role of the ravaged old alcoholic dad in this TV sitcom nodded and grunted and grinned and cupped his hand obligingly to his ear. Blame it on the goddamned airconditioner, he was missing syllables now and then.

They must have ordered from the stained menus, for food was brought. Mike Jr. had splurged and ordered beef Szechwan-style and prawns in garlic sauce and General's Chicken. No liquor license so the old dad had brought his usual bottle of Gallo wine in a paper bag, poured into one of the teacups, would Mike like some?—thanks, Mike did not. After a moment's hesitation he'd declined buying a six-pack of cold beer up the street to drink with the meal. Explaining he had a long drive back that night to—wherever.

"Well. Good to see you, son."

"Good to see you, Dad."

Those eyes so like his own had been, once. A boy's eyes. Gazing at his dad in pity, misery, disbelief. *Dad? My dad? That's my dad? Michael Mulvaney?*

Polaroid snapshots were being passed across the table to the shaky-handed dad, or was it the air-conditioning unit that made everything seem to tremble? Dad picked them up, dropped them, squinting and grinning. Hard to see in this wavering light, his eyesight grown unreliable. Nor was it clear why exactly he was being shown these snapshots of happy strangers, why the transaction was important and what sort of response was expected. How seriously human beings took themselves!—it really became clear, when you're asked to examine pictures of strangers. Mike was identifying X, Y, Z. That girl with the name ending in *y*, and some others. Was Mike already married, and this was his new family? A pretty moonfaced girl with caramel-colored hair and bright lips smiling so happily you'd worry her face might crack. Cinched-in waist and heavy full breasts in a shimmering red dress that looked like liquid coalesced on her body. And there was Mike Jr. with this voluptuous girl, good-looking Marine-Mike, arms around each other's waists and both grinning like they'd won the lottery. Other scenes at what looked like a barbecue, unknown men, women, children some of them with caramel-colored hair and moon faces, grinning happy as lunatics on a Sunday outing. "Mighty pret-ty," the ravaged old dad said, sighing. Pushed the snapshots back at his son after a discreet interval of trying to figure them out.

Son and shaky-handed dad were eating, or going through the motions. Salty-gummy food, tasting of something brown-scorched. Always at the Golden Pavilion they brought you tea in a tin pot though you'd as soon drink warm piss.

Mike talked, and his dad gave every impression of listening, leaning forward, belly creased against the tabletop. In fact he was distracted wanting very badly to maintain his *good mood* in these trying circumstances. The *good mood* had been initiated early that day, as soon as he'd gotten out of bed in fact. An antidote to the other mood which was not good and which had a foul tarry taste. Hadn't worked in two weeks, his money about gone. Well, in fact gone. He'd had an accident, slipped and fell from a ladder onto a concrete drive practically smashing his kneecap, twisting his spine, his neck. Sure they claimed he'd been drinking and it was his fault, the sons of bitches. And the aching in all his joints, really bad in humid weather. And the spongy sensation in his head. But none of this was going to get him down, spoil his *good mood* he deserved. This evening with the only child of his marriage he guessed loved him any longer or at least tolerated him. So maintaining the *good mood* required concentration. Tricky as the performance of a high wire artist for whom the slightest misstep or even hesitation could be fatal. So he had to concentrate on the spacing of wine and food, food and wine, wine, food, and wine, mouthfuls in discreet alternation and succession. Though it was only the liquid that mattered: warm, tart, reverently swallowed, making its way down his gullet into what felt like the very cavity of his heart, empty, cavernous as the Grand Canyon, and yearning to be filled. Gallo, red. Sour-sickish aftertaste but cheap, couple of bucks a bottle. Did the job.

Then these words sprang out, with no warning.

The way he'd grabbed the youngest kid, Judd—slammed him against a wall.

"Eh, son—you're looking at your father like he's some kind of dog."

But he was grinning, chuckling at the kid's face. For Mike Jr., taken by surprise, looked guilty as hell.

Mike said quickly, "No, Dad! Hell—" his big-boned handsome face reddening, how like his mother, that instant blush, acknowledgment he'd been found out. Saying, shrugging, with a frowning glance at other customers in the restaurant, "—it's just that I have a hard time, sometimes, places like this, I mean the civilian world—not you, Dad, really. On the base you get used to a different atmosphere. Off base, things are—" staring at a couple close by, the woman obese, sallow-skinned, some sort of glittery rag tied around her head, laughing and swilling noodles out of a bowl, the man in a paint-stained undershirt, crinkly-haired, pigeon-chested, baring his gums and laughing loudly, drunk. In the booth behind Mike, an elderly Chinese man was coughing in prolonged spasms, rapid staccato barks that caused the Mulvaneys' booth to shake. "—kind of coming apart, you know? No purpose to them. Nobody seems to know what the hell they're doing, or why. Why they're even *alive*." His voice gave him away, quavering with contempt.

Ravaged old dad said, chuckling, "*You* do, eh?"

Long as he had his Gallo in its upright bottle snug against his thigh. Mellow, riding the crest of whatever happened.

"That's right, sir! I do."

"Which is—?"

"A Marine fulfills his responsibility, basically."

"Which is—?"

"On a day's basis, his assignment."

"Which is—?"

"What his superior officer tells him to do."

"I'll drink to that." Laughter radiated upward through the ravaged old dad's fleshy torso, making it quiver. He raised his scummy teacup in shaky fingers. Seeing the tight set of his son's jaws, the Marine disapproval, he said, genially, "Always knew I should've been a Marine. At the age you went in, I had what it takes—hard ass, harder head. But I got married instead, and by the time I was your age I was up to here in it." Drawing a swift crude forefinger beneath his chin.

Wondering suddenly how old his oldest child was, these days. Dear God, was Mike thirty?—thirty-*two*?

The son grimaced to signal perfunctory mirth, or shock and disgust at his dad's speech. He'd pushed his plate of indistinguishable lumps of food on gummy white rice, two-thirds uneaten, slightly away from him, now nudged it an inch further as if to distance himself from even its memory. Half-pleading, "Dad? Like I started to say before, I was just visiting Mom, and—"

Shrewd old dad had leapt ahead. "Look, son, say you'd been one of those servicemen sent to—where was it—Beirut?—Tehran? To rescue those hostages? Remember? Poor Jimmy Carter issues orders from the White House—some 'Joint Chiefs of Staff' palookas issue orders from the Pentagon—thousands of miles away in a godforsaken desert a dumb innocent American kid in uniform dies a horrible death in a flaming helicopter—fulfilling his assignment, eh? What his superior officer tells him to do? *You'd* have gone?" Words slurred as if clotted with phlegm but the point was valid, let the blustery kid deny it.

Saying, "Dad, those were *special units*. Of course I'd have gone if I was one of them, and qualified. A guy breaks his ass to get into one of those units, it's an honor. A secret mission like that, against the enemy, it's an *honor*." Mike spoke quickly, almost in embarrassment at having to explain something so obvious. "About Mom? Maybe you know she's back in Mt. Ephraim, in town? She's got a job with—"

"No, no. Don't avoid the issue, son." The shrewd old dad was creasing his forehead as if this were a public debate, two political candidates on TV. Speaking loudly so that others in the restaurant glanced around. "Those Iranians had a right to be sore as hell, in my opinion. They'd had a revolution and overthrew a dictator, a crook and a torturer, what's-his-name—the 'Shah.' And this character skips the country with millions of dollars and winds up in the United States and we protect him, of course—we're the saps! Exactly like in Vietnam we're the saps! All the Iranians want is this 'Shah' crook returned to them, for a trial and an execution, maybe some torture beforehand he's got coming to him, plus the money he and his glamor-gal wife stole, in exchange for the hostages, right? I'd say they had a valid point, wouldn't you?"

Mike said, trying to remain calm, "Dad, the Iranians are our *enemies*. We don't have diplomatic ties with them. They committed an *enemy action*, an act of *international terrorism*, kidnapping American citizens out of our embassy! You don't give in to terrorist blackmail, Dad."

"Yes, but look here, son: since the beginning of recorded history the military has been sending young men out to die for some cause or other and you can be sure it's always against 'enemies.' Sure it's a big deal at the time, sacrificing your life for your country, honors and medals and memorial services and all, but underneath it's just politicians sounding their mouths, right? Can you deny this? Your enemy is your ally a few years later—look at Japan and Germany. Your ally is your enemy—that's Iran! Maybe that's how it has to be, but when a man's got only one life, he's a fool to toss it like dice." How passionately Michael Mulvaney was speaking, his face heated, eyeballs bulging in their sockets. He who could go for days uttering no more than a few expedient words or epithets. But then spoiling the effect by fumbling for the Gallo bottle, splashing wine into the little cup and drinking.

Mike murmured, disgusted, "Christ, Dad—you're drunk."

"*That's* an answer? A rebuttal? You call that a rebuttal? Ronald Reagan could do better than that, improvising."

"Look, don't you want to hear about Mom, for Christ's sake? Your *wife*?"

"That's private, son. That's personal. I don't discuss my personal life with anyone."

"You know she thinks about you all the time? All these years? Keeps track of you? *Prays* for you?"

"No, no! No." Ravaged old dad in his rumpled rayon sports shirt, three-day beard and sweaty gleaming scalp, made a blind, confused gesture as if hoping to lift himself by brute strength from the table, except of course he was in a booth, and fell back down onto the seat, heaving and wheezing. "I'm on furlough from all that," he said. It came out a strange scared laugh.

"Dad, my God! What's happened to you?"

The spongy grapefruit inside his head. The ache in his breastbone. The wavering vision he hoped was in fact his eyes and not the actual world beyond his fingertips.

Was the meal ended? The Gallo bottle was just about empty. Which meant the *good mood* would be starting to wind down, soon. The ravaged old dad was anticipating the embarrassment of his Marine son taking pity on him, offering him money he'd be morally obliged to refuse, but he couldn't very well refuse the offer of a drink, could he? But had one been offered?

"Did you want to leave here? Where'd you like to go, son?"

"Leave? Go where?"

"Didn't you say—?"

"Say what?"

Oh, it was too much effort. Just pushing himself up out of the sticky-plastic booth was too much effort. Almost, he could lay his head down, face in his plate of gummy rice, and sleep.

Instead he surprised himself, as so often he did. As with a woman, striking up a conversation with a woman he didn't know, in a bar, or a park, even out on the street, he'd hear his voice unexpectedly fluent, even youthful. "Mikey, d'you remember that white horse you kids had? Long time ago, handsome fella, white horse, white mane, belonged to one of you boys, I think? I was trying to think the other night what was his name?"

Mike shook his head. "*White* horse? I don't think so."

"Sure! Sure we did. C'mon, name me some names."

As if this were a profound question and not another clumsy diversionary tactic, Mike frowned and cast his eyes to the flyspecked ceiling that looked as if it were made of cardboard and recited the names of horses long gone from High Point Farm and very likely from this earth. "Well, there was Crackerjack, my pony—then there was Junior Jones, then—" The names drifted past, confused with the rattling of the air-conditioning unit. Mike's dad gave every impression of listening hard, with that intent yet glazed look of a drunk holding onto his *good mood* as a drowning man might cling to the side of an overturned boat, but essentially Mike was going it alone. "—Prince, Red, Molly-O, Clover—you must've sold Judd's horse just before you sold the farm, didn't you? Who bought him?"

The ravaged old dad squinted at his son, bemused. "How in hell would I know who bought him? Ask your mom."

Time to say good night, good-bye. The meal was ended. A drink up the street was possibly forthcoming, the dad couldn't recall. He said, "Terrific meal, we'll be back," to the shy Chinese waiter hovering a few yards away, waiting to clear the table. This time, screwing up his face with the effort, the dad did successfully heave himself up out of the booth, lurching sideways—oh God, what a jolt of pain running from the base of his skull to the base of his spine. He was a sick, sick man. Mike was on his feet with military alacrity, holding the old man erect. "Dad? Hey? You all right?"—but the old man was already recovered, muttering to himself, in swaying motion headed for the door. There was a vague sense of an audience, outright stares and a wish (unless imagined?) that the ravaged old dad collapse on the floor but that refused to happen. The son had to stay behind to pay the check; out on the sidewalk in the soupy gray air, wiping his damp face on his shirtsleeves, rubbing his eyes savagely, the dad had time to recover, or almost. But oh God—the *good mood* was rapidly dribbling away like piss down a pant-leg.

Once the kid, what's-his-name, was gone, back to wherever he'd come from, that would be a relief. Too damned exhausting to love them, even to keep them straight.

Mike trotted to catch up with him. Practically towered over him. Gripping both his arms with steely fingers—"I'd better take you back to your place, Dad? Just to make sure you're all right."

Anxious Dad shaking his head, no thanks, no need. Ashamed of his pigsty room above the smelly restaurant and just possibly some female's things were there and anyway what business was it of the kid's? What business of any of them, if he wanted to crawl away like a gut-wounded deer and die alone in the woods?

At least Mike Jr. wasn't in his Marine officer's uniform, looking like he was arresting a citizen. Enough assholes gaping at them in the street as it was.

So they argued for a while. Past nine o'clock and the sky was still riddled with light like pale capillaries in dark-bruised flesh. The dad who was in fact Michael Mulvaney, his own independent person and not just the father of some pack of kids, was mumbling he had a friend to meet up the street, had to leave, but thanks for the meal, son—"We'll have to get together more often." This made Mike laugh as if it were meant to be witty, a TV gag line. He'd taken out his wallet, was offering the ravaged old dad some bills, and the dad was protesting, "No! No thanks, son," almost convincingly, "—you're an old married man now, soon there'll be babies and you'll need all the money you can get." Breaking off then to cough, as if coughing were a signal of sincerity, but there was a cigarette in his fingers and he'd inhaled wrong and the coughing veered out of control. *This is how you'll die* the bulletin came *puking up your lung-tissue*. But Mike was insisting that his dad accept the money, the kid's big-boned handsome face dark with blood and eyes glistening with misery. Maybe they'd decided all this beforehand? Life was trickier than TV, it seemed so often to be veering in the wrong direction, yet sometimes it veered in the right direction as if by accident. Certainly it was the case, the ravaged old dad couldn't deny it, he needed to purchase some new, decent clothes, also shoes, have his hair professionally cut and not hacked with a scissors by a shaky-handed woman friend, yes and check into a clinic—promise? "Well, maybe—" he assented, seeing the logic of it, from the son's perspective at least. Giving in then and the son in the tall muscled Marine-body slipped cash into his shyly opened hand.

"But only if it's a loan, Mike. That's understood?"

A black rushing-laughing sensation then like the wind in the chimneys at High Point Farm. As if you could be sucked up inside a chimney, blown up into the wild-windy sky and lost.

So in the end Mike did walk his ravaged old rubbery-legged dad up the filth-encrusted stairs to the furnished room above the Golden Pavilion Chinese Restaurant and Takeout. The pigsty room you wouldn't want to examine too closely. Poor Mike biting his lower lip, nostrils pinching. He pulled off his dad's laceless shoes, a few items of dirt-stiffened clothing, laid him onto the stained rumpled sheets where at once he began to snore, snort, wheeze, his head lolling like the head of a broken-necked goose. Waking a long time later to discover only six twenty-dollar bills stuffed in his pants pocket—a hundred twenty where he'd had a wild hope of five hundred at least. So the ravaged old man had humbled himself in the eyes of his eldest son and in his own eyes for so little, after all.

The white horse. So much more alive, vivid, than Michael Mulvaney who was but smoke.

Breathless daring to climb atop the white horse's bare muscled back, grip its mane in his fists, its sides with his knees. Suddenly they were moving, lurching—behind what appeared to be the pear orchard, now into the lane. Yes, clearly it was the lane. The white horse snorted, shook its head, bucking, prancing, kicking—trying to throw Michael Mulvaney off? Or merely testing him, as a horse will test any new, uncertain rider? The children were riding beside him on their horses, saddled horses, beneath the tall trees. So beautiful on their mounts, smiling and grave, there was Mikey-Junior no more than thirteen years old, there was Patrick about the same age, there was Marianne, and at the rear, his face blurred, the youngest, Judd—why, Michael hadn't seen his children riding their horses in years. His perfect children! He'd been born into the world to be the father of those children, suddenly it was clear! And at the fence Corinne grinning and waving, holding a camera, dear Corinne in that straw hat that looked as if a goat had been chomping on it, he'd swear he'd stolen it from her and replaced it with an identical hat, brand new. He was not a horseman like his children, yet there he was, on this amazing white horse—galloping after them in the lane. Pounding thudding hooves! The horse snorting, bucking! He saw that his children were outdistancing him, galloping toward the mountains. His heart was enormous in his chest, hurting him. He was gripping the horse's smoky white mane, gripping its heaving sides with his knees. He would not let go. He would never let go. He would not be thrown off. He was in full pursuit.

STUMP CREEK HILL

Her life was so haphazard, so flung together by impulse and stitched like a rag quilt, it was something of a shock to Marianne to realize that, four years and two months since the morning she'd walked up the lane to the Stump Creek Hill Animal Shelter & Hospital, a sick Muffin in her arms, *she was still there.*

Of course, Marianne had been given a job at the shelter, and living quarters were provided. And she'd fallen in love with the veterinarian who ran the place, Dr. Whittaker West. And Whit West—as everyone called him—seemed fond of Marianne, too.

So it was at Stump Creek Hill, a few miles south of the small town of Sykesville, Pennsylvania, itself about seventy-five miles south of the New York State border, that Marianne was living when, at last, as she'd almost given up hoping, Corinne telephoned to say, in a voice trembling with excitement and dread, "Oh Marianne! Honey! Your father wants to see you! How quickly can you get here?"

Marianne who'd just dashed to the phone, panting and sweaty, called inside from hosing down Delilah and Samson the elderly African elephants, hesitated only a moment, pressing the heel of her hand against her heart, and said, "I'll be right there, Mom! I'll leave right away."

She would drive! She would take the Chevy pickup, out there in the parking lot.

Corinne said, "Honey, wait—we're in Rochester. At the University Medical Clinic. *Hurry*."

So Marianne knew what it was, what it must be.
Hurry. Hurry. Hurry.
After twelve years of exile. *Hurry!*

This was October 1988. A Tuesday morning, and Whit West was away in Washington, unless it was Chicago, or—San Francisco? Marianne had helped prepare his speech to the conference of—Associated Humane Societies?—no, that had been the previous week. No matter. Whit was away and Marianne didn't have time to call him, to explain.

Since High Point Farm had been sold, Marianne had kept in contact with Corinne in a way you'd have to call sporadic. She'd meant to be more reliable, but somehow—well, things happened. She hadn't seen her mom in some time (didn't want to think how long!) and hadn't been back to the Chautauqua Valley since that terrible confused time of Grandmother Hausmann's funeral. How busy, how frantic their lives all were!—time just seemed to be rushing past, like Stump Creek after a rainstorm.

Marianne had to pinch herself to realize *I am twenty-nine years old*.

Not that she would have given this fact a second thought, except her friends and co-workers at the shelter had surprised her on the eve of her birthday a few weeks ago, with one of Whit's special-recipe birthday cakes (sugarless vanilla-sponge with orange peel) studded with so many tall burning candles they practically toppled off the cake's sides. Marianne had counted the candles, amazed. "Oh, dear. Am I really this old?" Whit laughed, and said, "*Old?* You've hardly begun, kid." Whit had become touchy since turning thirty-nine, in ways he tried to joke about.

It was true: for a while after she'd slipped away from Kilburn without telling anyone, including her family, Marianne had been out of touch with Corinne except now and then telephoning hastily from bus stations, pay phones—"Mom? Just Marianne, just to say hello!" Once she'd settled in Spartansburg and was working for Penelope Hagström, she and Corinne spoke together fairly regularly, once or twice a month; but then when Marianne had slipped away from Spartansburg, after things became too complicated there, again there was a confused jumbled time she was out of contact with every Mulvaney. She knew of the breakup of Corinne and Michael's marriage, which she couldn't quite believe, and which Corinne persisted in describing as "temporary, pending," and she knew what there was to be known of Mike, Patrick and Judd. What her brothers knew of her was less clear. She'd lost the narrative of herself, somehow. She'd become a girl who turned up places, stayed if she could get halfway decent employment and moved on if she couldn't; she made friends, sometimes very close friends, then with no warning, as if it wouldn't occur to her that anyone might miss her, moved on. Since the days of the Green Isle Co-op, she'd hardly given a thought to Hewie Miner, or Abelove. How long ago that all seemed! And Penelope Hagström had probably forgotten *her* by now. Anyway, Marianne hoped so.

True, Marianne sometimes felt a stab of guilt. Slipping away from Miss Hagström like that. Just a farewell note, and no explanation. Her things stuffed into a duffel bag, and poor startled Muffin in a cardboard box, and—she was gone. One year had melted into the next, and that into the next, and she'd felt the walls of the old house closing in. The problem was, Marianne Mulvaney was becoming too *important* there, somehow.

She'd been sad about leaving. The tall shuttered pale-limestone house on a tree-shaded residential street in Spartansburg—at first glance it looked daunting, even ugly, but there was a stern sort of beauty to it, as to Penelope Hagström herself. And Muffin had been so content there, dozing in one or another of his favorite spots, a faded-chintz window box, on a carpet beneath a never-touched Steinway grand piano in the living room, best of all in the rear walled garden where on warm days he lay stretched out to a lean, startling length, blinking benignly at butterflies hovering close by, even at quick-darting mice boldly scurrying across his line of vision. At Miss Hagström's, most days resembled most others, in an outward sense at least—cat paradise!

And Penelope Hagström, certainly, was a remarkable, even an extraordinary woman. A poet—a true lover of poetry—who could recite poems of Keats, Shelley, Dickinson, Yeats, Frost in a way that thrilled Marianne to hear. (Marianne was frequently invited to share meals with the lonely woman, and it was at such times that Penelope Hagström recited those poems she considered "luminous—illuminating to the soul.") Now in her early sixties, Miss Hagström had been wheelchair-bound for many years, though her multiple sclerosis seemed to be in remission at the present time. She had a ravaged, hawkish, rather noble face, her graying hair parted in the center and drawn back severely into a chignon—"My Emily Dickinson look, the best we plain girls can hope for." She was surprisingly robust in appearance, from the hips up, with an ample bosom, shoulders, arms; if you couldn't discern her sad sticklike legs beneath. Her voice was alternately melodic and shrill, sweetly reasonable and despotic. There had been other "girl assistants" preceding Marianne, and Marianne had no doubt there would be others to follow. Miss Hagström seemed to be fond of Marianne, and several times made inquiries into her family background ("But you must be from some*where* and some*one*, dear—we all are!"), which Marianne gently discouraged; she was always "promoting" her—and raising her modest salary by a few dollars; she encouraged Marianne to "cultivate friends your own age" in Spartansburg, but seemed pleased when Marianne stayed close to home. Yet she was a demanding, dictatorial presence, requiring help in small matters—getting into, and out of, "this damned chair"—and large—the organization of her study, including her vast correspondence that dated back to the mid-1940's, and hundreds, or thousands, of poetry manuscripts. (What a confusion this study had been, when Marianne first saw it! As if a hurricane had blown through.) She was always scolding Marianne to "Speak up! You'll make me think I'm going deaf and *I am not*" and even poor Muffin, for being "nervous as a cat"—which, in her presence, he was. She declared herself, however, a lover of animals, and gave lavish donations to the Humane Society. She declared herself "an opponent of organized religion" and resolutely did not give to local churches or church-related charities—"Let them pray to their Almighty God, if they think they're on such special terms with Him." She refused to see visitors who dropped by with no warning; yet complained of being lonely in Spartansburg, "ostracized for being a 'poetess.'" She was furious if her morning was interrupted (this was her time, from 9 A.M. until noon, for the intense work of composing poems) yet disappointed as a child when Marianne fetched the mail, and there was nothing interesting; no requests for interviews, visits, etc., which she would have probably refused. Or if an entire day passed, and often an entire day did, when no calls came in and Marianne had to report apologetically, "Nothing, Miss Hagström. Not a thing."

"Hmmm! Don't be redundant, Marianne," Miss Hagström said sharply.

Marianne looked up "redundant" in the dictionary, though she guessed she knew what it meant. *Superfluous, more than is needed.* In British usage, *out of work, laid off.* She supposed that was true enough of her. And Muffin, too.

Though in fact Marianne was kept busy by her wheelchair-bound employer. Confined to the first floor of the grand old house, Miss Hagström was debating whether to install a "chair-lift," or an elevator—she much preferred the view "from the upper storeys." There were weeks of telephone calls and visits from prospective builders, haggling over estimates, terms, guarantees, which Marianne had to monitor, but in the end, abruptly, Penelope Hagström decided not to install anything, after all. There was a period in late winter of 1983 when day followed day in gloom thick as molasses—"the dark night of the soul is *out there*"—and Miss Hagström charged Marianne with planning a two-week trip to Italy, which involved, as one might expect, though in fact it turned out to be even more complicated than one might expect, countless telephone calls to travel agents in various cities. Marianne, who usually enjoyed making calls for Miss Hagström, addressing a third party in the service of another, gradually became worn-out with the project, which entailed, of course, "provisions—ample provisions—for a 'handicapped' party" and which came to nothing in the end, as Marianne had suspected. If Penelope Hagström was uneasy about traveling to Pittsburgh, less than one hundred miles away, by limousine (she'd several times been invited by arts organizations to read her poetry there, and to attend a ceremony in her honor), it was not likely that she would make it to Rome, Florence, Venice and Palermo. When, one morning, Miss Hagström curtly informed Marianne, "I've decided—we're not going. Cancel any and all plans you've made," Marianne must have smiled with relief, for the older woman added, with a sly wink, "Hmmm! Sorry to disappoint you, dear."

Marianne laughed. *But you can't disappoint me! I don't love you.*

By slow degrees Marianne realized that she'd been hired by Miss Hagström partly to absorb the poet's "mistral moods" ("mistral" was a word Marianne did indeed have to look up in the dictionary— *strong cold dry northerly wind*), since none of the Hagström relatives, the few who remained in the Spartansburg area, had the patience for them. Except for a long-deceased mother, no one in the family "read"—certainly not poetry. Within the family, and locally, Penelope Hagström's identity was not that of a well-published and -acclaimed American poet, but that of a luckless young woman, never pretty, yet with an "interesting" face, who had succumbed at a young age to a mystery disease—"MS" the sinister, sibilant euphemism—and lost her handsome wellborn fiancé in one dismal season more than a quarter century ago. No one exactly blamed Penelope for "losing" the fiancé, any more than they blamed her for contracting a mystery disease, and yet—there was an air of subtle reproach beneath the Hagströms' concern for her, which Marianne, who spoke with the relatives mainly on the phone, could detect, and which angered her.

News of Penelope Hagström's poetry publications, critical essays on her work, even an award from the National Poetry Society— none of it seemed to matter much to the Hagströms. Their family money had come from coal mining and was now mainly invested in property, so far as Marianne knew; theirs was the domain of the *real*, and poetry had no place in it.

By degrees, Penelope Hagström began to expect more of Marianne. She'd been astonished at the way Marianne had organized her voluminous files of letters, manuscripts, drafts—"*You* did all this, Marianne?"—and impressed with Marianne's ease on the telephone, an instrument she "abhorred." She began to expect from Marianne a different, more qualitative involvement in her life and work, frequently calling for Marianne during the mornings and reading her drafts of new poems—"Now you must tell me what you think, Marianne, without equivocating. And look me in the eye." Her own eyes shone brightly, if sometimes a bit fanatically. In the sharp light of morning her skin had a curiously layered look, the soft flesh beneath the eyes deeply lined; her smile was quick and hard and sometimes not a smile at all. When she read her poetry aloud to Marianne, her voice deepened and took on a dramatic tenor that Marianne found distracting. Why was poetry always so intense? Why was everything heightened, made to seem so important? A line of poetry, a single word, even punctuation—why couldn't it just be—well, normal life? Marianne clasped her hands together in her lap, fidgeting, uneasy, worrying that the sharp-eyed older woman, so impatient with what she called "flimflam," could peer right into her eyes and read her unworthy thoughts.

She protested, "Oh, Miss Hagström—you can't expect me to 'critique' your poetry. I have only a high school diploma, I flunked out of college—"

Penelope Hagström, regal in her wheelchair, her hawkish face uplifted, said, "Of course I can, Marianne, and I do. You're an intelligent young woman. Much more intelligent, I've come to see, than you let on. To whom do you imagine I'm writing my poetry, if not to 'Marianne Mulvaney'? Not to the dear departed dead poets, I hope. Not to my 'archivist.' "

So, reluctantly, Marianne would offer an opinion: she liked a poem very much though she had to admit she didn't fully under-stand it; or, she didn't fully understand a poem but she liked it, very much. "But what are you truly thinking, Marianne?" Miss Hagström demanded, suspiciously. "I feel you're thinking some-thing sharp and shrewd."

Marianne, seated in the older woman's study with Muffin twined in her lap half-asleep, protested faintly, "But, Miss Hagström—why have any opinion at all? Can't poetry be just what it *is*?"

Coolly, Penelope Hagström said, "Nothing *is*, my dear. Only what our opinions make of it." She shuffled manuscript pages into a folder on her lap, indicating the poetry session had concluded.

Marianne fled in relief, carrying drowsy Muffin. Her cheeks burned, her heart beat swiftly. She thought *No! I could never believe that.*

Thinking *I must leave Spartansburg soon. It's time.*

Much as she admired Penelope Hagström, that remarkable woman. And had grown—almost—to love her. But Marianne was being mistaken for a person she was not, and could never be.

The end came abruptly only twelve days later. Miss Hagström made to Marianne an astonishing, wholly unexpected offer of a "pro-motion": Marianne would become associate director of the Hagström Foundation, as well as continue as Miss Hagström's personal assistant, at a considerably higher salary than the one she now received—"An executive salary, my dear." (The Lydia Charles Hagström Memorial Foundation for the Arts, which Penelope had established after her mother's death in 1967, awarded grants as high as twenty-five thou-sand dollars to arts organizations, literary journals, nonprofit theaters and the like, mainly in the Pittsburgh area. The director was a Pitts-burgh attorney with whom Marianne occasionally spoke on the phone but had never met.) This proposal was so alarming, Marianne felt faint. There was a buzzing in her ears as of muffled laughter. She began at once to shake her head. "Miss Hagström, thank you very much, but—"

"Go away and think it over, Marianne. Don't make a decision on the spot. Discuss it with Muffin, if you wish—I'm sure he's on my side!"

"But, Miss Hagström, I couldn't possibly take on such a—such responsibility. I don't have any executive experience. I have only—"

"I know: a high school diploma," Miss Hagström said briskly. "We've been through that, I think. Will you stop behaving in such a ridiculous schoolgirl manner, Marianne? That isn't you—*I happen to know that isn't you.*"

Marianne stared at the older woman, seated in her wheelchair as if it were a throne, her ravaged-handsome head uplifted, eyes shining.

"Who—who is it, then? I don't understand."

"*I* don't understand, I'm sure," Miss Hagström said. "But our subject is the Foundation. As you know, we receive many applications for grants each year, and are obliged to assess them carefully; your task would be to organize the files, which you do so superbly, in any case, and to help in the selection process. You might even travel to Pittsburgh occasionally, to interview applicants; or to see work we've subsidized—plays, art exhibits, children's puppet theater. Most of the work you would do from this house, of course, in an office of your own. Otherwise, I wouldn't hear of it! Wouldn't hear of losing you, I mean. I would miss you too much."

"I see," Marianne said, confused. "I'm sorry."

"Oh, don't be ridiculous, my dear! Go away and think about it and tell me 'yes' in the morning."

Marianne went away. But never spoke with Penelope Hagström again.

Instead, in stealth, very early the next morning, she hastily packed as many of her things as she could fit into her duffel bag, and sweet-talked dubious Muffin into allowing her to close him in a cardboard box liberally pierced with airholes. There was a housekeeper who lived on the premises, who would discover the note Marianne left for Penelope Hagström, on the dining room table. *Miss Hagström, I'm sorry but I find I must leave, right away! No need to bother about my last-month's salary, or whatever. I thank you for your kindness and Muffin thanks you, too.* Only later would Marianne recall, she'd forgotten to sign the note!

Well, anyway. That was done.

Unseen, Marianne slipped away from the tall shuttered pale-limestone house, and hiked a mile or so into the Spartansburg downtown, carrying her duffel bag and the cardboard box inside which Muffin mewed quizzically, thinking she would buy a ticket—two tickets?—at the Trailways bus station; then got to fretting what if pets weren't allowed on the bus? She was standing on a street corner where a farmer's pickup truck waited for a red light to change, and the farmer, middle-aged, kindly faced, called over to ask did she need a ride, and Marianne said gratefully yes she did, and climbed into the cab of the truck, tossing her duffel bag into the back and holding the cardboard box tight on her lap, and they drove off toward the country. The farmer said he was headed for Sykesville, and Marianne said that was fine. She was headachey from crying, and must have looked a sight—but she'd done the right thing, she'd prevented a terrible misunderstanding from taking place. She would miss Penelope Hagström, she hadn't had room to pack even one of the inscribed books the poet had given her, she was embarrassed of her rude behavior but she was excited, too—it was a mild showery-bright April day, and she'd never so much as heard of Sykesville before.

"That a cat you're carrying there, miss?" the farmer asked.

"His name is Muffin," Marianne said. She'd been poking her fingers through the airholes in the box, and Muffin licked them with his scratchy tongue, ticklish and cool.

In Sykesville, a country town half the size of Spartansburg, Marianne rented a whitewashed wood-frame cabin with a kitchen by the week at the Wayside Motor Court; got a job at a farm produce market less than a mile away by simply walking in and asking if help was needed. She would have been content to settle down in Sykesville, at least for a while, meeting new people, joining a new church, making a few friends including the wonderful woman Janie who, with her husband, owned the produce market, not much older than Marianne but already the mother of several children. And what beautiful children! There was even a young man "interested" in Marianne—in fact, two or three young men—but Marianne rarely went out except during daytime hours, and most days she worked at the market. And by midsummer she'd become increasingly distracted as Muffin began to behave strangely.

When Marianne returned to the cabin in the early evening, instead of trotting out eagerly to greet her, Muffin didn't appear at all. Marianne would call and call him, and sometimes he'd come, and sometimes he wouldn't. One evening the woman who owned the motor court told Marianne she'd seen Muffin descending the hill behind the cabin, where the ground was rocky, uneven, and littered with rusted cans and trash, and where, calling "Muffin? Muffin?" Marianne stumbled, trying not to give in to fear, or worse. Inside a scrubby woods, she sighted the cat, glimmering-white in the dusk, so strangely unmoving, of hardly more substance, at fifteen feet, than a scrap of paper. Why hadn't he come to her, hearing her pleading voice? Why didn't he acknowledge her now? Gazing at her instead with tawny imperturbable eyes. "Oh, what are you doing here? Oh, Muffin." Marianne waved away a swarm of mosquitoes, seeing that Muffin was sitting, or lying, in the grass, sphinx-style, forepaws neatly tucked beneath his chest, tail curving around his thin buttocks. She picked him up gently and held him. How thin he was! Yet how soft and fine his fur. He did not resist her; but neither was he kneading his paws against her as usual, nor did he begin to purr immediately.

Up in the cabin, with shaking fingers Marianne opened a can of cat-food tuna, Muffin's favorite, but Muffin merely sniffed sadly at it, and at his water bowl; and lay down on the floor as if he were very tired. "But, Muffin, you have to eat. If you don't eat—" Marianne's eyes stung with tears.

What had Corinne said?—*You'll just have to be realistic.*

Next day Marianne was fretful and distracted at work, and when she returned to the cabin it was as she'd feared—Muffin was again missing, and would not come when she called. Again she found him in the scrubby woods, except this time deeper into the woods. "Oh, Muffin. What's happening to you?" Marianne was close to tears. She picked Muffin up tenderly, hugging him to her chest. So thin! Hardly more than fur and bones. It took him longer today to begin purring and Marianne had the distinct notion he was doing it solely to humor her, to make her believe things were as they'd always been.

Up in the cabin, again Muffin refused to eat. Sniffed at his food as if he'd forgotten what food was. And again he lay on the floor, tawny eyes going inward.

Next day, Marianne was so distracted at the market, Janie asked her what on earth was wrong, and Marianne laughed lightly and said, "Just life, I guess." Janie had learned not to question Marianne too closely, and so asked nothing more.

Again when Marianne returned to the cabin, she had to hunt out Muffin in the woods, more remote than ever. And again he refused to eat, turning away with a look of disdain. It seemed to Marianne that his eyes that had always been so beautiful were going flat, dull.

"Muffin, can't you try? Oh, please *try.*"

Of course, Marianne had known for some time that Muffin wasn't "a hundred percent"—as Corinne used to say of an ailing person or animal—but she hadn't wanted to dwell upon it. She knew that Muffin was aging—in fact, old. Was he fifteen? Sixteen? Her mind went vague. She held him on her lap and petted him and wondered what would happen next even as her mind held to its vagueness, an upright wall of fog. She smiled recalling how, as foundling kittens never weaned, Muffin and his twin Big Tom had eaten so ravenously, and so often, everyone in the household was amazed. You would put food in the cats' plastic dishes, turn around for a moment, and next thing you knew—the dishes were licked clean, and the kittens were looking up expectantly, hungry for more. Dad marveled that the kittens ate more than he did, pound for pound. Patrick swore they were growing daily—hourly. When Mom had brought them home, from where they'd been abandoned on a country road, they'd been so tiny both could fit in the palm of her hand; at their heaviest, in the sleek, lustrous prime of mature cathood, they'd each weighed more than twenty pounds.

Now, Muffin probably weighted no more than seven pounds. Five?

Be realistic, Marianne.

Yes, she knew. But there'd be time to be realistic, wouldn't there, when there was no other choice?

So Marianne decided instead to take Muffin to the Stump Creek Hill Animal Shelter & Hospital, of which she'd been hearing such good things since coming to Sykesville. It was only a few miles away and next morning, early, she managed to get a ride with a local farmer, carrying Muffin not in the cardboard box but on her lap. The farmer was doubtful about just dropping her off at the end of the sandy driveway marked STUMP CREEK HILL ANIMAL SHELTER & HOSPITAL, wouldn't she want him to come by and pick her up, later?—but Marianne said no, thank you, she'd be fine. Walking then up the quarter-mile drive, Muffin in her arms, the two of them blinking and staring about them. A strange place—an old estate apparently, now given over to the care of animals; a broad stone house and a carriage house each weatherworn as aged grave markers, yet with bright yellow shutters and trim, and the front area overgrown and tangled as a jungle, lush with wild tiger lilies, goldenrod, and Queen Anne's lace. There were various outbuildings and sheds, and a graveled parking lot in which a half dozen vehicles were parked. To the rear was a yellow picket fence and twin gates marked ENTER and EXIT, leading to what appeared to be an outdoor zoo. Muffin's pale nose began to twitch with the raffish smell of animals. There was a sound of excited screeching, jabbering in the distance. Muffled barking. Marianne saw a gigantic bird—iridescent midnight blue, exquisitely beautiful, with a quivering feather crown and a long tail dragging in the dust—a peacock?—ambling across the parking lot, and in its wake a smaller pure-white bird—a peahen? Farther along the lane were several deer, a small loose tame herd. Marianne stared—at least two of the deer were young bucks, with only three legs.

Marianne let herself into the main house, through a door marked ANIMAL HOSPITAL PLEASE ENTER. She was in a veterinarian's waiting room with a shabby linoleum floor and an oilcloth-covered counter and several slightly scummy glass-fronted cages with hand-made signs ORPHANS! PLEASE ADOPT! inside which a number of small kittens slept, played with one another, stared through the glass. "Oh, look, Muffin! Aren't they sweet?" Marianne whispered. But Muffin scarcely looked, and Marianne herself could hardly bear to meet the kittens' eyes. A stringy-haired girl behind the counter, name tag RHODA, took Marianne's name and asked what the problem was, staring at Muffin, and Marianne explained, as clearly and brightly as she could, and it seemed to her, unless she imagined it, that the stringy-haired girl muttered, "Uh-oh," in a discouraged tone. There was no one ahead of Marianne, but the telephone rang, rang, rang for Rhoda to answer. After a few anxious minutes of studying a sun-faded poster PET OWNERS GUARD AGAINST RABIES! Marianne heard her name called, and quickly followed Rhoda into a frankly stale-smelling interior, a warren of rooms. At the end of a long corridor, as a door opened, there came a noisy clamor of barking and yipping, before the door swung shut again. Marianne hugged Muffin tight in case he should panic, but he didn't move, at all.

In one of the examining rooms was Dr. West, Whittaker West as he introduced himself, an impatient-looking man of moderate height, just slightly stoop-shouldered, in a soiled white jacket and khaki trousers. He hardly glanced at Marianne and surely hadn't heard her name as in the first instant his practiced eyes moved upon poor skinny Muffin—examined, assessed, made a judgment. "Your cat is seriously ill, I'm afraid. How old is he?"

"How old? I—don't know," Marianne stammered.

The vet muttered a skeptical reply. Brusquely he removed Muffin from Marianne's arms and set him upon the examination table, peered into his ears, his eyes, his mouth with a small lighted instrument;

examined his teeth; palpated his abdomen, at some length. As he examined Muffin he spoke to him, not in words but in murmurs, *Hmmm? hmmm? hmmm? hmmm?* Marianne spoke of Muffin's gradual loss of appetite and his loss of weight, his recent, strange behavior in the woods—"He's never done anything like that before, he isn't an outdoor cat." Dr. West grunted as if he'd heard it all before, or wasn't listening. Marianne saw with disapproval that he hadn't even troubled to put on rubber gloves, like any other vet; his fingers were covered in nicks and scratches, splashed with iodine. His nails were wide and blunt and edged with dirt. His hair, thinning at the crown, was thick, lank, rather greasy at the sides of his head, that dull dun color of a deer's winter coat. Marianne said, trying to be helpful, "I think he's somewhere beyond twelve years old. His fur is so clean and healthy, isn't it? So soft." She spoke pleadingly. Dr. West did not respond. "It's hard to believe he's sick, except for losing weight. His eyes are clear. He still purrs." "His eyes are possibly turning yellow," the vet said almost carelessly. "Jaundice." "Oh, no—they've always been golden-tawny. All his life." Again Dr. West muttered a skeptical, not quite audible reply. Marianne seemed to hear *Be realistic. Realistic!*

Through a haze of tears Marianne saw that the examination was over, unless it had been halted midway. The vet continued to stroke Muffin, with deft, practiced fingers, and Muffin, who for all his docility and shyness had sometimes panicked at the hands of other vets, lay unmoving, splay-legged, on the crinkly tissue paper covering the tabletop. Marianne too reached out to touch him—his bony head, the soft fur covering it. She wished that Muffin would glance up at her, in recognition of her, or simple acknowledgment; but he did not. Why, he seemed almost to be siding with this stranger, Whittaker West! There was some perverse stubborn maleness to it, a subtle repudiation of her. Marianne asked what seemed to be wrong with Muffin, and Dr. West said, shrugging, "He's old. Happens to us all." Marianne said, with childlike tenacity, "But what, exactly? It has to be something!" Dr. West said, "I can do a blood test, a urinalysis, but it's almost certain your cat is suffering from kidney failure. His bloodstream is slowly filling up with toxins. It's been happening for months." "Oh, but isn't there anything you can do?" Marianne asked. "Nothing *I* can do, at Stump Creek Hill," Dr. West said. Marianne said quickly, "Somewhere else, then? Could he be helped somewhere else?" For the first time, Dr. West looked at Marianne. She could not meet his frank, searching gaze; she was blinking tears from her eyes, frightened she might break down. How ashamed she was of herself, begging for Muffin's life as she would never have begged for her own. How Corinne would wring her hands if she knew, scolding *Be realistic, Marianne. Haven't I told you and told you!* Whittaker West, this stranger so familiarly kneading Muffin's fur, stroking his ears and the underside of his chin as if they were old, old friends, was looking at her sternly, saying, "An animal knows when its time has come. That's why—is it Muffin?—has been slipping away into the woods. He prefers a quiet, dark, private place in which to die. Wouldn't you? *I* would. Of course he loves you, but the part of him that loves you, or even knows you, is fading. His cat-self, his instinct is emerging. Why not let him follow his instinct? You can't be bringing him back forever, can you?" Marianne stammered, ashamed of her desperation, but persisting, "Oh, forever is such a long time. Isn't there some way Muffin can be helped, for just now?" "At the most, he probably wouldn't live for more than another six months," Dr. West said reluctantly. "And it's expensive." "I have money saved," Marianne said eagerly. She knew she didn't look exactly prosperous, in her rumpled T-shirt and denim cut-offs and sandals, summer wear for working at the farm market, but she'd brought along her wallet, thick with bills; her hands shook as she fumbled for it. "I could pay you ahead of time, Doctor. Oh, don't let him die!" "*I* can't do the procedure here, we don't have the facilities. There's a clinic in Pittsburgh that might do it—a kind of dialysis. Blood-cleansing," Dr. West said. And Marianne said, her eyes shining with hope, "How soon can it be done, Dr. West? Today?"

There was a moment's silence. Marianne distinctly heard the vet grinding his teeth.

Finally he said, with a sigh, curtly, "You're in luck, miss. I happen to be driving to Pittsburgh later this morning with a van of ailing animals and I can take Muffin along. The procedure will involve not less than forty-eight hours and it isn't guaranteed, understand? You should be prepared for never seeing your cat alive again."

Marianne tried a smile, wavering and uncertain. "Oh, I'm prepared," she said brightly.

That lilting insincere brightness on the edge of despair: how like Corinne Mulvaney she was sounding!

So she said good-bye to Muffin, who scarcely responded, and hurried out. Thinking then that she should have left a deposit, a down payment, how would Dr. West know he could trust her?

★ ★ ★

In a daze then, vaguely smiling, Marianne wandered back through the parking lot, hoping for another glimpse of the peacock and his hen, and the herd of deer. There were chattering guinea hens and a high-stepping bantam rooster running loose, there was a scrawny black tomcat with two half-ears sunning himself on the hood of a battered Chevy pickup. Marianne petted him, daringly—you never can tell, with a strange cat—but he merely blinked at her, lazy and content. It was a heating-up sort of August morning, the kind that begins damp and almost cool and turns baking by noon. A happy, hopeful day. No ticket seller at the ENTRANCE gate, just an orange plastic container STUMP CREEK HILL ANIMALS NEED ALL YOU CAN GIVE THEM! so Marianne took a five-dollar bill from her wallet (yes, she'd saved plenty of money working as Penelope Hagström's assistant) and pushed it into the slot. The pungent smell of animals drew her. Manure and hay, that just-slightly-rancid-pleasurable smell. A sharper smell—what was it? the antiseptic spray they'd used, at the farm, when the cows calved?—but this was sweeter somehow. And someone had been mowing deep grass, a wet green pungent smell, laced with wild onion.

How much larger the Stump Creek Hill shelter was than Marianne had anticipated!—it must have covered acres. Visitors were starting to arrive, mothers with young children, retired-looking older couples. Not a very prosperous zoo, sort of shabby and blurred at the edges. Weeds poked through the sand paths, there were tall oaks badly in need of trimming. Droppings underfoot from the stray wandering tame deer, buzzing with flies. Marianne read a sun-faded poster: *Stump Creek Hill is the only federally and state-licensed zoo in the United States dedicated to the care of sick, injured, abandoned and elderly wildlife and domestic animals. Founded 1974 by Whittaker West. YOUR DONATIONS GREATLY APPRECIATED!* Marianne wandered from one animal compound to another, enthralled. She had never been in such a place before, nor had even heard of such a place. Her parents had taken them to zoos in Port Oriskany and Rochester, but those were very different—somehow so sad, you ended up wanting to leave early. But the Stump Creek Hill zoo was like home.

Each of the animals had not only a name but a story. There was King Sheba the mountain lion, mistreated as a cub in a Florida safari zoo and "retired" now to Stump Creek Hill—a huge-headed sand-colored cat with sleepy eyes, an enormous nose, matted mane.

There were Masha, Irina and Olga, capuchin monkeys "abandoned by the roadside" in North Carolina, crowding against the wire fence, peering at Marianne as if they recognized her. There was Hickory the blind mule pony from New Jersey. There was Big Ben the Bengal tiger "rescued" from a traveling circus in New Mexico, there was Rocky the silver fox, three-legged since "misfortune in a hunter's trap" in Maine, there was Lena the llama, "donated" by a circus owner when he discovered she had cataracts in both eyes—a shy creature, handsome, the size of a mature deer, with white facial markings and the thick, nappy fur of a well-worn teddy bear. There was Joker the rhesus monkey, "sole survivor" of a shut-down research institute in New Mexico. There was Big Girl the Vietnamese potbellied pig who'd "outgrown her owner's affections" and was donated to the zoo, an enormous gray creature, no eyes that Marianne could see, creased like a satchel and stretched out luxuriantly in the shade. There was Princess the jaguar, a beautiful black-spotted big cat discovered "abandoned and starved" by a roadside in Minnesota. There was Sweetheart the Adirondacks bobcat missing a leg, there was Hickey the hyena, another mistreated former zoo resident, there were Cinderella and Svengali the "Thoroughbred ex-trotters from Saratoga Springs." There were donkeys, sheep, goats in barn-yard pens and free-ranging fowl of all sorts—chickens, ducks, geese. Shyly tame, there were loose deer. The zoo's main attraction, apart from the big cats and the playful chattering monkeys, were Delilah and Samson the African elephants who had been slated for "termination" by their Oregon zoo owner unless a new home could be found for them, fast—"As devoted a married pair as you'll ever meet, and just look at the size of those feet!" Marianne laughed— she wondered if Whittaker West had written that. She wondered if the entire zoo was his—his idea, his scheme.

All that day, and it was a hot, dry, baking August day, Marianne wandered about the zoo. She helped staff workers scatter seed for the fowl; she helped a harassed young woman, name tag TRUDI, hose down the elephants and pigs. She'd forgotten to eat that morning, so made a meal, salty and delicious, of peanuts and popcorn from the vending machines marked BUY HERE TO FEED ANIMALS! washed down with a lukewarm Royal Crown soda. More visitors came, more children. The zoo was a popular place, it seemed. Marianne sat for a while on a rickety bench in the shade of a big oak, watching Ezra, Smoke, ChaCha and Fleur the black bears being fed by their attendants—bare-chested teenaged boys who reminded her so much of her brothers, years ago, she had to shut her eyes finally. Moved to another rickety bench to watch Bo, Peep, Louie and LaLa, wild Barbary sheep in their compound, until she dozed off. Midafternoon, late afternoon. Sun-dappled shade. She had nowhere to go. She had found her way here, and had nowhere to go. But no—of course she did—she'd forgotten the little whitewashed wood-frame cabin in the Wayside Motor Court in—where was it? Not Spartansburg, she'd left Spartansburg weeks ago. The name would come to her in a minute, not that she needed a name to find her way back. Not that it mattered where she was exactly since she'd be moving on soon. When Muffin was returned to her she would know more clearly what her plans might be.

She thought of this strange zoo, this haven for animals. The abandoned, the mistreated, the sick, the injured. "Survivors." What would Patrick think? It's ridiculous to be sentimental about animals, he'd said. The individual doesn't exist, only the species. And maybe not even the species, for long—every day, every hour, species are becoming extinct. Many of these species, animal, bird, reptile, amphibian, never known to Homo sapiens, at all.

Religion is a comforting fantasy, Patrick said. Christianity above all. Just another story people tell themselves so they're spared telling themselves the story they don't want to hear.

Marianne felt something nudge her elbow—"Oh, who are you? Are you hungry?" It was one of the tame deer. A young velvety-horned buck the size of a children's pony. There didn't appear to be anything wrong with the deer—it wasn't missing a leg, and didn't seem to be blind. Marianne laughed in delight, feeding it the remainder of her popcorn, which it ate quickly out of the palm of her hand. That damp ticklish sensation, so familiar.

Dr. West who'd seemed so impatient with her, begging for an aged cat's life, had told her to telephone next morning to hear how things had gone in Pittsburgh. Marianne fully intended to leave Stump Creek Hill and return to her dreary little rented cabin, and in the morning make that call, but somehow there she was lingering in the zoo; feeding more popcorn to the velvety-horned buck and a half dozen of his friends. Then she was feeding a bevy of long-necked white geese in a farther corner of the enclosure as an announcement came over a loudspeaker that the zoo was closing in five minutes. Then she was in a women's rest room not exactly hiding but hardly in view, either. Only at dusk did she emerge, feeling an immense sense of peace, tranquility. No Homo sapiens here now, except for her! She made a nighttime meal of more peanuts, popcorn, soda from the vending machines, climbed from a bench to the crotch of an oak tree and from the crotch of the tree to the roof of a shed behind Cinderella's and Svengali's compound where, very early the next morning, she was discovered just waking from a dazed, stuporous sleep—by Whittaker West himself, who stared at her in utter amazement. "Miss Mulvaney, what on earth are you doing *here*?"

Marianne said, faltering, though it was the simplest sort of truth, "I just thought, you know—it would be easier. If I didn't go so far away."

Muffin was brought back from the Pittsburgh clinic, his left foreleg shaved, where the intravenous needle had gone in. He would regain his lost appetite and some of his lost weight, and would live for another thirteen months. By the time he died, for the second time it almost seemed, Marianne would have joined the full-time staff of Stump Creek Hill and would have been living on the premises for most of those months. It was the most wonderful job, she never ceased to marvel, she'd ever had in her life: she answered the telephone, did both clerical and manual tasks in the office, helped design the new fund-raising flyer ("12 Good Reasons You Should Be Generous to Stump Creek Hill"—with photo inserts of twelve of the most appealing and photogenic resident animals); she helped in the dog- and cat-kennels, in which there were both private animals, temporary visitors, and animals for adoption; she helped with grounds maintenance in the zoo, which was her favorite work. She told Whit West she wished she'd gone to college, to study veterinary science; and of course Whit replied, in that contrary way of his, "Why speak in the past tense? There's nothing to stop you going, right now." Which made Marianne blush in confusion, and back off—that wasn't what she meant, at all.

Rhoda told her, "Don't be hurt by Whit, he doesn't mean to be rude. It's just how he *sounds*."

Stump Creek Hill Animal Shelter & Hospital had been established by Whit partly through a family inheritance and numerous solicited donations. The property itself, fifteen acres and a once-elegant English-style manor house, had been willed to Whit by an elderly widow whose eleven Siamese cats he'd treated for years—quite well, evidently. (One of the provisions of the widow's will was that the eleven Siamese should continue to live in the manor house exactly in the style to which they were accustomed, which Whit had no problem in obliging.) The widow's outraged relatives had contested the will and there had been a protracted lawsuit, with a good deal of publicity through western Pennsylvania—"In certain quarters I was made out to be a gigolo," Whit complained, "in others, St. Francis of Assisi." In the end, Stump Creek Hill had emerged ninety percent victorious. The gilt-ceilinged ballroom of the house was used for the kennels; the glass-topped conservatory was an aviary for injured, convalescent and "retired" birds (among them an African gray parrot and a snowy white cockatoo—amazing, intelligent birds of a kind new to Marianne); a former drawing room, still furnished with faded, plush-upholstered chairs and sofas, now wonderfully shredded, was the site of "Kitty City" (a haven for as many as fifty cats sponsored by the well-intentioned who either could not or did not wish to bring them home). Most of the many smaller rooms of the house were empty; a few staff members lived on the premises, the rest commuted to their nearby homes. When Marianne was hired on, Whit took her upstairs, throwing open doors to rooms he hadn't, it seemed, glanced into in a long time—"Take any room you want, if you can find one that's livable. And furniture, anything—use your imagination." Whit himself lived in the carriage house adjoining the veterinary. He was obsessed with the place, he acknowledged—maybe a little crazy. "The thought of going away, on a vacation for instance, if only for a few days, fills me with panic," he said.

Marianne said, "Oh, why would anyone ever want to leave *here*?"

She could not imagine such a prospect. In the several years between her moving into the manor house, in August 1984, and Corinne's sudden call summoning her to Rochester, in October 1988, Marianne would not have been away from Stump Creek Hill for more than a day.

So, inspired, Marianne put together a room for herself on the second floor of the house, overlooking the tall oaks of the zoo and with a view of the elephants' rocky compound. What a bliss of housewifery, furnishing her room with odd wonderful shabbily elegant pieces of furniture scattered through the house! If only Corinne could see! But Marianne hesitated to call her mother for months. And even then, she was reluctant to confide in Corinne too fully. For what was so precious to Marianne it seemed at times a dream she and Muffin had concocted together would appear less so to Corinne. "Rag-quilt life!" Corinne would sigh heavily over the phone. By implication, her own life was so fixed, so settled, so *defined*.

The "blood cleansing" had certainly worked magic on Muffin. Even Whit West was surprised. As soon as Muffin was returned to Marianne, and settled into his new quarters, he began to regain his health; within a few days he appeared normal, or nearly—the shaved foreleg gave him a somber look, which his gleaming white fur and addled, clownish markings did not dispel. Whit said warningly, "Now you know this is only a temporary respite, don't you, Marianne?" Marianne murmured yes. She was prepared to accept Muffin's second death, whenever. Thinking *I'm temporary, too. I don't expect anything more*.

At Stump Creek Hill, days melted into days, weeks into weeks and months in a frenzy of activity punctuated by oases of relative calm—"Therapeutic boredom," Whit called it. Boredom! None of his staff shared Whit's attitude: they were grateful for quiet, when it came. But in a place devoted to so many infirm and elderly creatures, with an emergency veterinary service to which people brought animals in desperate states (run over on the highway, for instance), there was little quiet. The ballroom-kennels were filled with yipping, yammering, yowling creatures like an anteroom of Hell. Thanks to Whittaker West's promotion of Stump Creek Hill, the shelter-zoo was known for hundreds of miles—through the Associated Humane Societies, across the continent—and so the telephone was forever ringing, people were forever driving up the sandy front lane with injured animals, strays, litters of unwanted puppies and kittens, ex-baby chicks and Easter bunnies grown to unwanted adult sizes. (Big Girl, the three-hundred-pound Vietnamese potbellied pig, had actually been given as a piglet to a child.) There were animals who were the casualties of other animals—severely dog-bitten dogs and cats, bucks terribly injured in rutting season by rival bucks—but most of the animal casualties, of course, were human afflicted. Starvation, mistreatment, actual torture. (Whit's boxer Luther had been, as a puppy, doused in kerosene and set on fire by boys.) After a few days at Stump Creek Hill, Marianne learned not to ask detailed questions. When someone told her bluntly, "Hey. You really don't want to know," she took them at their word.

When Marianne was new at answering calls, she had a conversation with a distraught woman who told her she was "doomed to die" despite surgery, radiation and chemotherapy, and what worried her most was the fate of her two cats. "Mimi and Fifi have no one but me. They're not young. What will happen to them? As soon as I'm gone—what will happen to them?" The woman broke down sobbing and it was all Marianne could do not to break down herself. Marianne promised she would personally take care of the cats. Without telling Whit, she drove ten miles to fetch them in the Chevy pickup—a pair of sleek-furred black cats with white-marbled markings and long tails prehensile as monkey tails. Their skeletal-thin mistress, weeping as she saw them off with Marianne, could have been no older than forty. She reminded Marianne of Corinne, fluttery eyelids and fingers, a steely resolve beneath. "I won't mind dying nearly so much if I know that Mimi and Fifi are in good hands," she said anxiously, and quite literally she seized Marianne's hands in hers. "You will promise? You will?" "Oh, yes," Marianne said, blinking away tears. "I promise." She drove back to Stump Creek Hill, Mimi and Fifi yowling in the backseat, in a wire carrier. *O God help us, what a world of suffering.*

When Whit came by later that afternoon, he discovered Marianne ashen-faced, kneeling on a floor in a back room of the office, trying to coax Mimi and Fifi out from their hiding place behind boxes of Nu-Plus Canine Kibble. She'd been crying and looked so desolate, Whit resisted whatever sardonic remark might have sprung to his lips. He asked her what on earth was wrong and Marianne told him about the terminally ill woman and her cats and she told him, too, she'd been reading some of the reports he'd filed with the Humane Society of the United States and the American Horse Protection Association, the unspeakable cruelty endured by horses shipped to slaughter was something she hadn't known about and she'd had a horse she'd loved and her parents had sold it and she wasn't sure she was strong enough or courageous enough for this work after all—and Whit interrupted, "Marianne, we're here to serve these animals, not ourselves. We're dedicated to making what remains of their lives reasonably happy and if you can do only a little, that little is of great worth to the animals involved. Right?" Marianne shook her head yes, no—she wasn't sure. She'd used up her last tissue and her nose was running badly. Whit said, cheerfully, "One day at a time! You'll see."

Just as, in time, Mimi and Fifi emerged from hiding, and were taken by Marianne upstairs to her room, to live, more or less harmoniously, with Muffin, so too in time Marianne came to share Whit's attitude. Or to see its logic. It was the attitude, the philosophy, of all of Whit's staff, at least those who didn't quickly burn out and depart. How they all admired, and were intimidated by, Dr. Whittaker West! He was one of those persons who seemed to thrive upon emergencies, tension, "challenge" as he called it. He travelled frequently to Philadelphia and Washington, D.C., to argue for legislation to "reduce animal suffering at the hands of mankind." He had the look of an impatient, ungainly bird—an ostrich, a stork—lank-limbed, quick-darting. His eyebrows were untidy tufts, hairs grew in his ears and nostrils. His forearms, bared in his soiled white coat, were a tangle of wiry dark hairs. His features were so motile, you couldn't say if he was an attractive man or homely; his manner so direct, eyes so glaring, it was difficult to "see" him at all. He bore scars on his face and arms from animal assaults over the years; the most prominent, a two-inch crescent moon above his left eye, was from a rabid bobcat. Marianne often did not look at him at all, even when he was speaking to her; like Penelope Hagström, Whit West was just too—*real*. And the trouble with such people was, they seemed always, simply by singling you out for attention, to make you *real*, too.

Whittaker West was said to be the son of a well-to-do Philadelphia businessman who'd owned Thoroughbreds and who had been involved in a scandal in the 1950s in which stables had been set afire, by a paid arsonist, to collect insurance money on racehorses not performing so well as their owner would have liked. He was said to have been badly hurt and embittered by an early, long-since terminated marriage—his former wife, also of a well-to-do Philadelphia family, had divorced him on grounds of mental cruelty, charging in divorce court that he'd preferred "the love of animals" to "the love of a spouse." There had been much local media attention, and embarrassment for Whit. That had been years ago, and of the present staff only Irma, a woman in her fifties, recalled Mrs. West: a glamorous, high-strung, fashionably dressed young woman who'd never seemed to approve of her husband's work, still less of his devotion to it. At that time, however, Whit lived with his wife in a real house and not on the estate grounds. Mrs. West came to visit rarely. When she did, she seemed invariably to find fault with the staff, or to suffer comical mishaps. Once she'd amazed Irma by rushing terrified into the office, staggering in high-heeled shoes, claiming that a "gigantic" peacock had screamed and flown straight at her head. The woman was white-faced, fainting, and Whit was quickly summoned, rushing out from the rear of the office, a fresh-bleeding welt in his cheek where a parrot had just gashed him with its beak. Mrs. West, seeing him, gave a strangled scream and fell heavily to the floor.

Oh, it was funny! Sad, but funny. For of course Whit was the one to be hurt, finally. But, Irma insisted, it *was* so—always when Mrs. West arrived in her sporty little white Fiat coupe, the peacocks seemed to be screaming that peacock-shriek that could break your eardrum. One of the feral tomcats would dart out to spray the gleaming white-walled Fiat tires and, sometimes, Mrs. West's slender ankles. If Mrs. West visited the zoo, the monkeys cavorted shamelessly, even squirted water at her from their fluted little mouths. Though Stump Creek Hill animals were generally past the age for mating, or distracted by infirmities, it would happen that, if Mrs. West appeared, two of the younger animals were mating, shamelessly, too, in full view. The water bucks were the worst! Other animals squabbled, fought—the younger barnyard goats and the younger roosters seemed always to be taunting and feinting at one another. It was always too windy at Stump Creek Hill, or raining in gusts; or hot, and sand flies were biting, unless it was horseflies, or mosquitoes from the marshy land bordering Stump Creek close by. If there was a sudden outbreak of fleas—fleas you could see, like antic punctuation marks leaping from the ground onto your legs—poor Mrs. West was sure to arrive before the situation was under control. She was sarcastic with the young women staff workers, imagining they had "designs" on her husband; yet she was too vain to imagine that Whit, in turn, could be attracted to any of them. Such a scruffy, stringy-haired, poor-white-trash-looking crew! Marianne asked, guardedly, for she did not want to appear curious, "What did Mrs. West look like, exactly?" and Irma said vehemently, "Exactly like a cheerleader. Very blond, self-assured. Miss Personality Plus, except when things didn't go her way. You could see that Whit must have married her for love, there wasn't a thing else they had in common."

Marianne caught sight of herself in a shiny surface—a sunburnt face that more resembled a boy's than a young woman's, eyebrows that might have needed plucking if she'd dared to look closely, flyaway hair grown to shoulder length and tied back carelessly in a ponytail. Her hands and forearms, too, were now finely nicked and scratched from animal encounters and stippled with who knows what sort of insect bites. She bit her lip, and laughed. No one would ever say of her, "Exactly like a cheerleader."

Marianne would not have said *I am in love with Whit West* but rather *If I was in love, it would be with Whit West.*

Did Whit sense? Could he guess? Marianne flushed with embarrassment when he teased her, in his merciless way, asking for instance if she'd like to accompany him to Washington to meet with one or another congressman—"He'd sit up and listen to *you*"—or to New York City on one of his whirlwind fund-raising weekends— "Separate suites at the Waldorf, I promise." (Suites! Waldorf! It was a joke, the Eco-Inn motels Whit managed to find wherever he travelled.) Marianne would laugh nervously, her gaze skidding sidelong, saying, "Well. Not just right now, Whit." Whit would say, "Why not, Marianne? You've done all the paperwork." Marianne would say, backing off, "I just don't think, you know, it's a good idea." Whit would say, laughing to show it was a joke, "Evidently not. Except—why not?" But Marianne would have fled to answer a ringing telephone, or to meet an animal owner bursting through the screen door with a pet in some stage of crisis. Whit never pursued Marianne beyond such jokey exchanges, which were part of the atmosphere of Stump Creek Hill, in any case. Always his tone was light, playful, kindly-meant. He was shrewd enough, seeing whatever it was in Marianne's face, a glimmer of panic, a stab of terror, to back away. He'd been a horseman as a boy and knew a spooked creature when he saw one: advance too quickly, it bolts away.

Marianne, on her part, was always watching for Whit. She was only really relaxed (did the others notice? she hoped not) when Whit was away and not expected back for a while. No chance of him slamming through a door, crying, "All right! Break's over! Back to work!"—as if in his absence they all just lazed around. No chance of running into him in the ballroom-kennel where it was so noisy, someone could come up right behind you and speak your name and you wouldn't hear. And at mealtimes where Whit often ate with the half dozen staff members who lived on the grounds, casual picnic-style meals around a handsome scroll-footed mahogany dining room table that was an elegant leftover from the manor house's prime days—and there was Whit in a blood-spattered jacket, two days'

growth of beard and dirt-edged fingernails, spooning out his specialty black bean–shiitake mushroom–red pepper quiche onto plates
and cursing the damned thing, as if, every time it turned out "runny
as dishwater" was the first time, a complete surprise and humiliation.
The laughter at these tossed-together meals was such that Marianne,
shy of her employer, found it difficult not to look at him—how
could you avoid it, with Whit clowning shameless as a child, his
good moods as dramatic and somehow *coercive* as the bad?

Quickly, Marianne had learned to watch out for Dr. Whittaker
West who'd impulsively hired her, hired and fired at Stump Creek
Hill as he liked to boast (but whom had he ever fired, however in-
competent? Irma couldn't name a name) so she could stay out of his
careening way if at all possible. Rhoda, Trudi, Irma, Gus, Steve,
Wiggles—they were always assuring Marianne, "Whit doesn't mean
it, that's just how he *sounds*." She knew he didn't mean it, yet what
he might mean was couched so slyly in what he didn't, like wheat
kernels amid chaff, she was left unnerved. There was an erotic, sexual
swagger to the man, in her presence—wasn't there? Or did she
imagine it? How much more pleasant to observe Whit unobserved,
at a safe distance: the way he walked, the slight stoop of his shoulders and neck, the angle at which he wore one or another of his
grimy STUMP CREEK HILL—SUPPORT 'EM! hats; the jerky motion of
his hands, arms, legs. The back of his head. Marianne admired even
his shadow! Yet she found it disagreeable to look Whit in the face
when he spoke to her. She feared him gazing impudently into her
soul and finding her out, whoever she was—as Penelope Hagström
had done. For Whit too was a poet. Not of language but of gesture.
The way he comforted animals so terrified their bodies shook like
vibrating motors, his battered big-knuckled hands holding them
firm. Murmuring and cajoling and even joking with them. The way
he wielded a needle, injecting vaccine or drawing blood—the deli-
cacy, the unerring firmness. The way, gripping an animal's taut jaws
from below with his left hand, he could position a capsule on the
animal's tongue so that the animal would swallow it effortlessly—the
most skittish and panicky of animals. When Muffin began at last to
fail, the second time, Whit insisted upon teaching Marianne this
technique, for the cat was susceptible to infections and required antibiotics several times a day. At first, Marianne's touch was too hesitant—Muffin shook her off, squirmed out of her grasp panicked and
tried to run away. "I'm afraid of hurting him," Marianne protested.

"Oh, don't be silly. It isn't that easy to hurt an animal," Whit said. He petted Muffin briskly to calm him and expertly gripped his jaws from beneath and pried them open. "See? Your turn, Marianne." So Marianne, shaky-fingered, tried, and tried, and at last succeeded; and Muffin swallowed his capsule. "Animals are basically wildlife," Whit said, with an air of approval. " 'Domestic' cats, dogs—just the surface ten percent is domesticated. The rest is nature. Right, Muf?" He rubbed the cat's ears and Muffin blinked up at him.

Marianne thought *They understand each other. But what is it they understand?*

And when finally Muffin did die, a few months later, very thin, his eyes tawny-yellow with jaundice, it was in Marianne's arms, as Whit injected him with a medicine that stopped his heart instantaneously. He had weakened, at the end, swiftly, in a matter of days. He'd simply stopped eating. He had not crept away to die in the woods as Marianne feared, had never ventured outdoors much at this new place, shy of the numerous feral cats who lived on the grounds; but dozed for long hours atop Marianne's bed, on her ragged old quilt. At night, he'd slept pressed against Marianne's leg, breathing thinly, twitching from time to time in such a way that Marianne, lying awake, wondered if he would live until morning. Marianne told Whit now, "We're ready. We're prepared for—it." Whit said gently, "Muffin is, Marianne, but are you?" She did not answer. Yet as Whit sank the thin needle into Muffin's bony shoulder, and the cat cringed, and went rigid, and immediately then limp, lifeless as a rag doll—Marianne held him firmly, and did not break down. *O my God, can this be? Can this really be happening?* She stared in astonishment at the now dead cat in her arms, his eyes open, blank. Yet she did not break down, at least at this time.

Whit was sitting on the edge of Marianne's brass bed, stroking Muffin's fur that was so soft and fine. Marianne could not bear to look at him yet saw a glistening on his cheeks. Whit said, "Muffin wasn't your only friend, Marianne." Marianne said calmly, "Well, I know that." Whit said, "He wasn't the only one who loves you, Marianne." "Well," said Marianne, now just slightly hesitating, as if at the edge of an abyss, yet calmly enough, "I know that, too."

INTENSIVE CARE

Was that Judd?—that tall, lean-limbed, staring young man?—waiting in the hospital corridor for Marianne, to hug her, and lead her into the intensive care unit, and was that Corinne?—hair gone unevenly gray, a powdery-pebbly gray, a hectic flush in her thin cheeks—rushing at Marianne, embracing her so hard Marianne felt the breath squeezed from her. "Oh, Marianne! Thank God you're here, honey! Dad's just waking up." The air in this place was chilled as a refrigerator. There was a humming on all sides. Marianne couldn't stop shivering. She and her mother were staring at each other with widened amazed eyes. Corinne whispered, "Don't be surprised, Marianne. Dad has had surgery to remove a cancerous lung, he's been delirious off and on since yesterday. He isn't the way you remember him." Marianne was dazed with exhaustion. She'd driven from Stump Creek Hill to the Medical Clinic, University of Rochester, three hundred miles nearly nonstop, more than six hours in the rattling Chevy pickup and much of the route along narrow country highways and in Rochester she hadn't known where the Medical Center was so she'd had to stop to ask directions several times, intimidated by so much traffic, intimidated by the size and complexity of the city in which she had never driven before and by the nightmare network of elevated expressways, *on* and *off* ramps, *exit only* lanes, praying aloud in a child's scared voice "Dear God, dear Jesus don't let my father die" and now as in a dream others had somehow entered and even appropriated she was being led forward by her mother, Mom she loved so! Mom she'd missed so! Mom gripping both Marianne's hands in hers, such cold anxious fingers!—and Marianne found herself inside not a room but a cubicle staring at a person in a raised bed amid glittering beeping instruments. Why, he was no one Marianne knew—was he? An ashy-skinned sunken-eyed sunken-cheeked man of some age beyond age. His hair was thin tin-colored strips across the waxy, vein-splattered dome of his scalp, there were clawed-looking creases in his cheeks, his eyes peered out wildly from deep bruised sockets. A transparent tube ran into his left nostril and tubes were attached to his shrunken arms and disappeared beneath the bedclothes covering his flat, yet bulky body. Marianne stared in disbelief even as Corinne murmured eagerly, "Michael? Darling? See who's here! She's come such a long way! It's Marianne." The man who was Michael Mulvaney Sr., the man who was Dad, Dad so changed, squinted at Marianne, as if a light blinded him. He tried to move his head on the raised pillow but the tube that ran into his nostril seemed to hold him in place. His right eye was badly blood-shot and not in focus. The air hummed with cold, with ventilators, with machines; a computer screen registered nervous zigzaggy blue lines. There was a subtle smell as of rotted oranges which Marianne recognized from the office at Stump Creek Hill and did not wish to identify.

Corinne urged Marianne forward. Marianne dared to take her father's hand that groped along the bed rail—such a thin, cold hand!—the bones seemingly hollow!—yet the fingers closed about hers with unexpected strength, urgency. Michael tried to speak, tried very hard but the sound came out garbled, a sound like drowning, terrible to hear. Marianne said, leaning over the bed, anxiously, yet smiling, "Daddy? It's me." He tugged at her hand as if by sheer strength he hoped to lift himself from the bed and break free of his restraints that seemed to confound him. At last he managed to mutter coherent words, phrases—"Where?—didn't want to—so tired—I want—God help—where is?—so tired so tired—" and abruptly then his strength waned, he sank back and shut his eyes, his breath hoarse. His grip on Marianne's hand loosened; she continued to hold it tight. "Daddy? Oh, Daddy, I'm so sorry," she said, resolute she would not cry, and for what seemed a long time the three of them waited for Michael to open his eyes again as he lay there in his bed drifting in sleep yet not peaceably, mouth working, eyeballs moving jerkily behind shut lids. He twitched, moaned, seemed to be arguing with someone. He was like one who has sunk beneath the surface of consciousness as beneath the surface of water floating there gathering his desperate strength to reemerge, to save himself. How close the surface was, yet how tough the membrane that trapped him beneath it! A nurse entered the cubicle and told them to wait outside and so they did, and again Corinne gripped Marianne's hands, staring at her almost greedily. It had not been clear to Marianne initially that her mother was so exhausted, even as she spoke in a strangely exhilarated voice, "Marianne, my goodness you're so grown up!—isn't she, Judd?—and your hair, oh dear your hair, oh but how pretty you are, Marianne—I know you're exhausted—I know this is a terrible surprise—Marianne you aren't married are you?—are you married, honey?—no?—I just, I—wondered—I mean, it's been so confused—I'm sorry not to have been a better mother but—I don't know what happened exactly—it was just something that happened, wasn't it?—no one ever decided—*I* never decided—I love you honey, thank you for coming—your Dad does want to speak to you, he told us—didn't he, Judd?—oh what a sad, terrible time for us—we can pray, that's all we can do, but it's a sad time, we have to be prepared the nurses have warned us. They've been so nice, so understanding, haven't they, Judd?" her eyes a pale wan blue washed out with fatigue, strangely lashless, naked in the bright fluorescent overhead light, and even as Judd murmured a reply she continued in her bright tumbling way, "Dad's been awake off and on since the surgery—you know his lung was removed?—a cancerous lung removed—that was nine days ago, imagine!—and he has recognized Judd and me most of the time—he has said some things we can understand and I know he can hear us and understand us, isn't that right, Judd?—but he's been angry, he doesn't know why he's here—he's angry too about someone stealing from him, taking money and snapshots from his room—oh, that terrible room!—Dad was staying at this terrible filthy hotel downtown, he'd collapsed on the street and had been here in the hospital for more than a week before anyone took the trouble to look through his things and call me—his own wife! his nearest of kin! Imagine!" turning to Judd who shrugged, as if embarrassed, and who said to Marianne, "Dad's 'indigent,' he's an alcoholic, a charity case, frankly I think we're lucky he's had this much care at all," and Corinne said quickly, "Oh yes, thank God, you're right, Judd is right of course, thank God his things weren't just dumped out on the street and my name and address lost, I'm grateful someone from the hospital did call, I'm grateful the doctors took him in and operated though there doesn't seem—now—anybody for me to talk to, exactly—the surgeon is never available—I never spoke with the surgeon at all—but the nurses *are* nice, so understanding and kind—and Dad isn't really insured any longer, *I'm* under a medical coverage with the county—where I work—but not Dad—oh Marianne, they removed a lung but they said it's too late, the cancer has spread to his brain, his kidneys—'metasized'—" and Judd said, gently, " 'Metastasized,' Mom." " 'Metastasized'—of course." Corinne had begun to cry silently, in that way that Marianne recalled for the first time in years; a mother's crying, stifled, soundless, secret so as not to disturb. If you cried so others could hear you were crying to be heard but a mother's crying was just the opposite, crying not to be heard. Yet, now, Corinne could not hide from her adult children. Judd said matter-of-factly to Marianne, in that way that was Whit's too, much of the time, as if the worst, the bluntest truth might as well be acknowledged, "He's just worn down, worn out. His liver has been affected, his heart—all the years of heavy drinking. Smoking caused the cancer but—it's obvious he'd been killing himself for years. Poor Dad!" Corinne said vehemently, tugging at Marianne's arm, "Oh he was a good man and he loved you, he loved you all, it was just he was led astray. He's only sixty-one years old, Marianne. Imagine! That's not old at all."

Marianne heard herself say, scarcely knowing what the words meant, "No, Mom. That's not old at all."

Later that day they returned to Michael Mulvaney's bedside in the chilled humming cubicle amid the bustle of Intensive Care. And another time Michael fought his way to the surface of consciousness, fixing his good, focussed eye upon Marianne, struggling to speak. Marianne said, "Daddy? I love you. Don't tire yourself, Daddy, just rest. Daddy, I'm so sorry." But Michael was squeezing her hand, trying with such urgency to speak, out of a garble of noises syllables of words emerged like pebbles in a rushing stream, and Marianne believed she heard her name—"Marianne"—unless it was "Marian"—but a name very like hers, almost identical, and clearly her father was looking at her, staring at her, he had recognized *her*, Marianne—hadn't he?

There came a final, feeble spasm of strength, his fingers clasping hers. Then again the dying man lost the thread of consciousness and sank back on the pillow.

In one of the patches of waiting that were like pleats in time, while Corinne remained at their father's bedside in case he should wake, Marianne and Judd, faint with hunger, had a quick meal in the hospital cafeteria; and afterward, grateful for each other's company like old friends who'd somehow forgotten how much they liked each other, went outside to walk for a half hour in the bright windy autumn air. How strangely vivid, how vast the world was—the sky so steeply overhead, just *there*. In a fluorescent chill-humming room, you could easily forget how the world, the sky were—*there*. Marianne said wonderingly, "Daddy did recognize me, I think. He did, Judd, didn't he? I'm not just imagining it?" and Judd said, "Yes, of course he did." Marianne laughed, embarrassed, biting at a thumbnail. "He called me 'Marian'—I think. Did you hear it?" Judd said, frowning, "He called you 'Marianne.' That's what I heard." Marianne said, "I guess he's forgiven me? I mean—he loves me again, he's not ashamed of me?" and Judd said, "Dad always loved you, Marianne. He wasn't ashamed exactly, it was—well, like Mom said it was just something that happened." Marianne repeated slowly, " 'Just something that happened.' " Judd said, "It's the way families are, sometimes. A thing goes wrong and no one knows how to fix it and years pass and—no one knows how to fix it." He spoke quickly, almost combatively. Marianne said, "Dad saw *me*. I'm sure he did." Judd said, "Marianne, for God's sake he said your name. Mom heard him, and so did I." When Marianne didn't reply, walking now swiftly with her head lowered, plucking at her long, untidy ponytail blowing in the wind, he added, with brotherly indulgence and impatience, as if this was an old family issue once again resurfacing when it ought to have been settled long ago, "He'd been asking for you, that's why Mom called you. He asked for 'Marianne'—I heard him, I swear—and he didn't ask for any of the rest of us, his sons, by name. Mom and I kind of worked out what he was trying to say, he wants to see Mike and Patrick, too, but couldn't remember their names exactly, or couldn't pronounce them—we're pretty sure. But your name, Marianne, he knew. Don't you believe me?"

So Marianne decided yes, she would believe him.

GONE

Cremate my body and scatter my ashes and that's the kindest thing you can do for me. Amen.

That gusty October morning. The sky pebbly-pale with streaks of vivid blue like swaths of a housepainter's brush.

Wind, wind. A high keening sound. Rocking the car as we ascended. On the rear seat of Mike's car, between Marianne and me, the box containing the remains of Michael Mulvaney Sr. Of about the size and proportions of a hat box.

I'd peeked, I had to know: these were sizable bone fragments, grit like chunks of gravel, as well as powdery fine "ashes."

It was the morning following the funeral in Rochester. We were silent mourners.

There was little to say that had not been said.

I did not say, bitterly *Where the hell is Patrick! I hate that bastard.*

We passed High Point Farm on our left but I was looking resolutely away and did not see. Or my eyes may have been shut tight.

Abruptly then High Point Road narrowed and became more rutted, jolting. In winter, snowplows wouldn't bother much with this stretch.

Dust rose in angry swirls in our wake.

By instinct Mike was taking us to the perfect place. I knew exactly where he'd park. No houses for miles, no one to drive by gawking curiously at us. *Mulvaneys? Back? What on earth are you doing here?*

A high windy glacier ridge overlooking a near-vertical drop of hundreds of feet, scarred-looking boulders strewn below, vivid patches of scarlet sumac. It was fall, a cold-tasting fall, the leaves having quickly turned bright, brilliant shades of orange, yellow, russet-red, to be quickly torn from the trees.

Dad's voice came teasing in my ears. *Be sure to keep the wind at your back, kid! Don't err at such a crucial time, you're not going to get a second chance.*

Scattering the earthly remains of Michael John Mulvaney, Sr. to the wind. And how swiftly the wind tore at them, a savage appetite. Hyena-keening, roaring up out of the Valley.

Mom said suddenly, "I can hear Dad laughing, can't you? Oh, this *is* funny—somehow. He'd think so."

Mike and I lifted the clumsy box, shaking out the last of the grit and ashes. As the wind took them, so roughly.

And gone.

EPILOGUE

REUNION:
FOURTH OF JULY 1993

The phone rang. I picked it up and it was Mom, breathless and hopeful as a girl—"Come for a Fourth of July cookout, Judd! Come for a Mulvaney family reunion! Come help Sable and me celebrate Alder Antiques and *independence*!"

It was mid-June, weeks ahead of time. Remarkable for my mom who usually telephoned to invite me over at the last minute. I said yes, of course I'd come, sounds like a great idea I said, but what's this about a Mulvaney family reunion? Mom insisted it was so—"All of you are coming. Including Patrick."

This, I let pass in silence. I asked what would she and Sable like me to bring? and Mom said, "Just yourself, honey! And, you know, if you had a, a—"

"A girl? But I don't."

"Well—you know."

"Maybe I'll acquire a girl between now and then," I said, teasing, "—how's that?"

"Bring yourself and whoever you'd like. This will be our first annual Mulvaney family reunion."

I must have sighed. Did I believe for a fraction of a second that Patrick would show up? After fourteen years?

Marianne and Whit, sure; Mike and Vicky, yes probably; but Patrick?—never.

Mom said reproachfully, as if I'd spoken aloud, "Judd, this time he's *promised*. We were just now talking on the phone."

Mom and Patrick were in touch sporadically. The last news I had of Patrick firsthand, he was living in Berkeley, California and training to be a therapist of some kind. Or was he training others to be therapists? So far as I knew he'd never finished his degree at Cornell. He'd been out of contact with us at the time of Dad's death, which was why he hadn't come to the funeral and helped us scatter Dad's ashes—though possibly he wouldn't have come, anyway. All these years, he hadn't come east to see us and if Mom suggested flying out to see him he'd seem to vaporize, disappear. I had a picture of swirling molecules where a human figure had been, so dissolved into its elements there could be no identity.

Still, Mom had gotten it into her head that Patrick would be coming for the reunion on July Fourth. Yes he'd promised, and he was even planning to bring a friend; a woman friend, Mom believed, though she was vague about this as no doubt Patrick had been purposefully vague in telling her. He'd be traveling all that distance by motorcycle, backpacking en route. "Can you imagine, Judd? P.J. on a motorcycle!" Mom was incredulous and hopeful as a girl.

I said, "Frankly, Mom, no, I can't imagine."

In Chautauqua Falls where I now live, and work as editor of the *Chautauqua Falls Journal*, I went shopping on the morning of July Fourth, buying a bushel of sweet corn at a farm stand, selecting the ears individually, carefully. I went to our local beer and wine store and bought six-packs of beer, ale, soda pop. Then to a food store filling the cart with giant bags of potato chips and pretzels, costly little containers of dip ("Mexican Fiesta Hot Sauce," "Spicy Authentic Indian Curry") feeling generous, elated, giddy and anxious, and the girl at the checkout counter, who knew me, laughed and said, "Looks like *you're* going to a Fourth of July cookout!" and I said, proudly, "That's almost right, yes. It's a family reunion, too."

My fingers so mysteriously numb, one of the tins slipped and tumbled to the floor.

ALDER ANTIQUES
BARGAINS & BEAUTY!

Mom's new home, which she shared with her friend Sable Mills, was on a hillside on New Canaan Road, about six miles south of Mt. Ephraim and eighteen miles southwest of High Point Farm. I'd seen my mom's place a number of times of course, since Chautauqua Falls was only forty miles away, and in fact I'd helped her move in; I'd helped her and Sable fix up the property, and given my advice about whom to hire for renovations. (Not that they listened, much. And if they'd asked my advice at the outset, which of course they had not, I'd have advised them not to buy the property at all. I suppose I take after my dad, viewing ramshackle "quaint" farms in the Valley with an unsentimental male eye, not my mom's romantic farm-girl eye.) Still, I have to admit the place is attractive. The house and outbuildings and pastures, what you can see from the narrow country road. That pert little barn freshly painted an eye-catching royal blue with the sign ALDER ANTIQUES prominently displayed.

"My dream," Mom would say, giving her voice a lightly ironic lilt so you'd know she meant to make fun of herself, even as it was all so terribly serious, "—my heart's desire. If only we don't go bankrupt!"

Oh, it was just a coincidence, Mom insisted, that Alder Creek, beautiful Alder Creek, narrow and treacherously swift-flowing, was less than a mile away from the property, traversing New Canaan Road; the same Alder Creek that ran through our old High Point Farm property to the north.

The Alder Creek of my boyhood. That trickling splashing sound of water over rocks; a sound like voices in the distance, murmurous, questioning.

But Mom insisted it was just a coincidence. "Sable and I fell in love with the property, and just had to have it," Mom said, and Sable added, emphatically, "Love at first sight!"

The house was just a modest farmhouse, the kind of place my dad would have rolled his eyes at, saying it's hardly worthwhile for the owner to install a new roof. But Mom and her friend bought it with a bank loan and paid for enough renovations to make it habitable, dividing it "straight across the middle, the kitchen between." Living with a dog, numerous cats and a pair of canaries they'd managed to get through not one winter, but two. The house was two storeys, rotted-looking clapboard siding, a tilting stone chimney, badly sagging porches at front and rear. A dank cellar with an earthen floor. The barn had been in good enough condition to be converted into a shop—ALDER ANTIQUES—painted a bold eye-catching blue like no other barn on the New Canaan Road. On the roof was a row of old-fashioned school desks of the kind connected by runners, like a toboggan. "They were dismantling the one-room schoolhouse in Ransomville, where I'd gone for eight grades. Imagine!" Mom told me. "So Sable and I drove over for the auction, and came away with so many wonderful things, we had to rent a U-Haul." They'd bought the faded-nearly-colorless American flag from the school, the old potbellied wood-burning stove that had heated the single school-room, tattered old "readers" and anthologies of long-forgotten patri-otic authors. "The only drawback is," Mom admitted, "—once you get to love these old things, you can't bear to part with them."

In good weather, there was placed beside the antique shop's front door a dressmaker's dummy with an hourglass figure in an elegant satin-and-lace wedding gown with a five-foot train, circa 1910, faded to the color of weak tea. Sable Mills says dryly of this artifact, "It sure does help to be headless and lacking a crotch if you're about to be a bride."

And Mom would murmur, blushing, "Oh, Sable! Really."

Corinne Mulvaney's specialty at Alder Antiques was refinishing furniture, re-covering cushions, etc.; Sable's specialty was repairing rattan, wicker, etc. Corinne's inclination was for hominess, house-keeping; Sable's for keeping accounts, business. The one was all breathy sweetness on the phone, the other staccato as a machine gun, thrilling in her own decisiveness. Sable was a good-looking trim woman of five feet one, brassy-dyed hair, cruel-stylish ear clamps, magenta lipstick, flashy sporty clothes, expensive high-heeled boots. She'd had experience selling "antique" furniture and clothes off and on over a period of twenty years. She too had grown children, in fact several grandchildren, and she too was unmarried at the present time. She liked to discomfort my mother by remarking she hadn't any idea if her ex-husbands (yes, plural: three) were living or dead, nor any great desire to be illuminated on the score. "When I'm finished with a person, I'm finished," Sable boasted, drawing a forefinger across her throat, "—whether *he* is, or not."

Mom would glance at me, tremulously. Both of us thinking of Dad.

I don't know what Mom told Sable Mills about Dad. About our family. I'm inclined to think she's told Sable very little. For what are the words with which to summarize a lifetime, so much crowded confused happiness terminated by such stark slow-motion pain?

The vision of the wind off High Point Road, bearing bone, grit, ash away into infinity.

So Mom and her friend Sable Mills teamed up to buy the three-acre Alder Creek property, house and barn and a few ramshackle outbuildings, in the summer of 1991, and began ALDER ANTIQUES with Sable's savings and a bank loan; if they weren't exaggerating or embellishing, they would have repaid the loan completely by July 4, 1993—"Independence Day! So come help celebrate."

I was proud of Mom, and hopeful for her. After Dad's death she'd gone through a bad spell. Not actively unhappy and never complaining, certainly not what you'd call depressed, but for a long time just not herself.

It was during this time Mom's hair turned silver, glittering like mica, and seemed even to have lost its kinky wave. She wore it plaited into a thick braid that swung between her shoulder blades. She'd become a striking woman after whom people glanced admiringly on the street as if wondering: *Who's that?* I must have observed the change so gradually, the way I register changes in myself, my own face that isn't a boy's face any longer (I would be thirty years old, July 11!)—there was never a moment when I actually *saw*.

Marianne and I discussed Mom on the phone. I remarked, how long ago and far away it seemed, now—lanky carroty-haired Whistle making such a commotion in the kitchen. "The way she'd call us down for breakfast—remember? 'WAKE UP! RISE 'N' SHINE, KIDDOS!' "

But Marianne, nursing Willy even as we spoke, said gently, "You know, Judd, maybe Mom doesn't want to be 'Mom' right now. Maybe she's taking time out."

Then Sable Mills came into Mom's life like a hurricane. And no looking back.

After Dad left her, and the property out in Marsena was repossessed, Mom came to live in Mt. Ephraim where people knew her, and liked her. There came a succession of slow dull safe jobs—in the Mt. Ephraim Public Library, in a day-care center, at the Chautauqua County Bureau of Records where eventually she would be promoted to office manager. She lived in an apartment building downtown and of course she was miserable there—Corinne Mulvaney, in a pokey little apartment with no lawn! And no animals! She had many women friends, and of course she had church (in fact, she continued to drive over to Marsena, to Sunday services at the New Church of Christ the Healer, where the Reverends Pluckett had been so kind to her in her time of need), yes she was lonely sometimes when she allowed herself to think of her losses, but of course she was a Christian, and an adult; an optimist, and a farmer's-daughter pragmatist; she knew not to dwell upon what can't be changed.

And there was her "antiquarian" soul.

Always going, with women friends or alone, to auctions in the Valley, to rummage sales, flea markets. Once she drove all the way to Chautauqua Falls—eighty miles round trip—to attend an estate auction, where most of the items were far out of her price range; I met her there and took her to dinner afterward and she said, apologetically, yet defiantly, "Judd, I know you disapprove, you think it's a silly waste of time, but, well—I'm *looking*. I'll never stop *looking*."

On the tip of my tongue was a son's embarrassed question—*For God's sake, Mom, at your age looking for what?*

She bought things sparingly, and always small items, for of course she hadn't much room in her pokey little apartment; but always at the back of her mind she was planning, plotting how to start a shop of her own again. It happened that she and a brassy-haired woman of some age between forty-five and fifty-five who favored brightly colored cloche hats, snug-fitting jodhpurs, lizard-skin boots became aware of each other at auctions: Sable Mills was always outbidding Corinne Mulvaney for the same items, and Corinne looked with longing at the younger woman's acquisitions. The more forlorn, left-behind kinds of things—a badly frayed silk fan in the shape of a butterfly, a heavy ceramic teapot on whose curved surface someone (children?) had mischievously scratched their initials, a packet of love letters from a World War I soldier to someone named Samantha, a soiled needlepoint pillow in the shape of an elephant's head, complete with drooping tusks—the more likely Corinne and Sable were drawn to them. Sometimes out of apparent kindness, Sable would allow Corinne to outbid her; calling then across the room sotto voce, with malicious glee, "Whew! Thank God! Who in her right mind would want such junk!" Others were shocked but Corinne just laughed. She liked being teased, even mocked: no one ever behaved that way with her any longer. Since her husband had gone away she was always being treated, by her children especially, like some fragile about-to-shatter old *thing*.

So Corinne Mulvaney and Sable Mills came to be friends, going out for coffee, or drinks, or a meal, after one or another of these exhilarating exhausting frustrating auctions, and talking for hours. "My goodness, we have so much in common!" Corinne marveled. She and Sable had both lived in the Ransomville area as girls, Sable in town and Corinne in the country; they'd both married young, had children young, and lived alone now; their children were "grown and mainly scattered"; they had grandchildren (by this time Mike and Vicky had two children, Marianne and Whit had had their first baby) whom they adored but saw infrequently. What was most amazing to Corinne was the way in which her life and Sable's had intersected without their knowing. When they first met, Sable was forty-nine to Corinne's fifty-nine: she'd attended Ransomville High and had had certain of Corinne's old teachers, she'd swum on Saturdays at the Y where a certain female instructor had "tried to exert her will" on the girls, there was a librarian at the public library named Miss Grimsley—yes, truly that was the woman's name, both remembered how *grim* she was!—there were bus drivers, storekeepers, a miscellany of nameless people who had played marginal roles in both their lives, unremarked upon at the time of course but now, in recollection, how vividly *there*. And there were places, too—so many places! Sable had lived intermittently in Mt. Ephraim and knew the landscape, as she called it, like the back of her hand.

I was mystified why these "coincidences" meant so much to my mom and her lively new friend. As a reporter, though, I'd quickly learned to keep a neutral position: when in doubt, *don't express it*. Mom would explain excitedly, as if she and Sable had uncovered a long-sought mystery of nature, "Sable and I remember identical things as if, somehow, we'd been the identical person, at different times! The strange part of it is—isn't it, Sable?—we don't seem to have known anyone in common central or important to our lives, it's just these background people, like in a movie. Sable says she'd heard the name 'Mulvaney' many times—"

Sable interrupted, "Oh, for God's sake, 'Mulvaney' is such a well-known name around here, you'd have to be blind, deaf and dumb not to have heard of it."

But Corinne persisted, "—Yet Sable never set eyes on any of us, in person. All those years."

"Until you, sweetie," Sable said, winking.

She gave Corinne's fluttery hand a tap and the women laughed, laughed.

∽≫≪∼

When I arrived at Alder Creek it wasn't yet 3 P.M. and already cars, pickups, even bicycles were parked everywhere in the drive and on the grassy lawn. So many! What was Mom thinking of, calling this a family reunion? Scram, Mom's and Sable's antic beagle, came rushing at me, barking and sniffing excitedly, tail thumping. The first people I ran into were the Plucketts, hauling enormous watermelons up the drive—Jimmy Ray and Nanci and their three freckle-faced teenagers so alike in appearance I could never tell them apart—but the Plucketts, sunny, good-hearted people, wouldn't have expected me to remember their names, just called out, all smiles, "Judd, hello! Happy Fourth of July!" The next people I ran into were my gorgeous sister-in-law Vicky, Mrs. Mike Mulvaney Jr. with the caramel-colored hair—*very* pregnant—again—and her little girl Chrissy, my firstborn niece, for whom my heart always gave a lurch. Vicky cried, "Judd, aren't you looking handsome!" standing on tiptoe to give me a breathy little kiss, her basketball-belly poking against me, and I lifted Chrissy in my arms with a mock grunt—four years old already, what if she'd forgotten her Uncle Judd she hadn't seen in a year?—but she hadn't. And where was Mike?—playing softball, Vicky said, in the goat pasture. And there were damp smeary kiddy-kisses from two-year-old Davy, Mike and Vicky's other child, and there came rushing at me my sister Marianne in STUMP CREEK HILL yellow T-shirt and shorts, baby Molly Ellen in her arms, and three-year-old Willy toddling behind, and we hugged, and kissed, clutching at each other as always as if in the other's absence each of us had imagined catastrophes, and these phantoms to be laughed eagerly away, dispelled like bad dreams in daylight, and we exchanged a minute's quick news, and I saw that Marianne was in the prime of her young womanhood, the color restored to her skin, a fullness to her face, the stress lines eased, the liquidy yearning in the eyes eased, now she was thirty-four years old, and married, and a mother, and a devoted worker at Stump Creek Hill Animal Shelter & Hospital, and her life independent of all Mulvaneys if she should wish it. And what a husband she had!—I didn't always get along with bluff opinionated Whit West, but I admired him immensely. I asked, "Where's Whit? I don't hear him," and Marianne laughed, poked me reprovingly in the chest, and said, "He's on the phone. We haven't been here an hour—have we, Willy?—and already Whit is checking back. He was up late doing emergency surgery on Smoke—remember Smoke?—one of our black bears—an appendectomy. Oh but Judd," Marianne said, just remembering, "—he's here, he's actually *here*. And he has a *girl*." Marianne pointed toward the pasture where a rowdy game of softball was in progress.

I didn't need to ask who *he* was.

I said, "So Mom was right."

Marianne said, "Isn't Mom always right?—I mean, when she's serious."

Trembling with excitement I dumped my bushel basket of sweet corn and groceries onto the nearest picnic table, and snatched up a beer from an ice-packed tub, and hurried to the pasture behind the blue ALDER ANTIQUES barn where Effie and Eddie the coarse-haired black goats were watching the game, in a shady corner. I took my place beside them, climbing onto the fence. Of the fifteen or sixteen players, adults and teenagers, I recognized almost no one at first. I felt a pang of hurt, childish disappointment—why had Mom promised a Mulvaney family reunion, when so many strangers were being invited, too? I hoped that no one would sight me and invite me to join the game.

The pitcher was a stranger, or so I thought, one of Sable Mills' younger relatives?—in dark glasses, sinewy-lean and about my age, but fitter than I was, with hard tight compact arm- and shoulder-muscles, ropey-muscled legs gleaming fuzzily bronze, his hair sun-bleached and shaggy to his shoulders—*My God could this be Patrick?—my own brother?*—the thought flashed to me yet somehow in the excitement of the moment did not adhere. All eyes were on this man as with almost ritualistic earnestness, in the midst of much joking, laughing, clowning about of the players, he pitched underhand the dazzling-white softball to a figure crouched at bat—Sable Mills, herself—an energetic and feisty figure, yet not much of an athlete—Sable with her brassy hair newly cut in a virtual flattop, a wicked silver clamp on one ear, in black sleeveless sweater and matching jodhpurs that fitted her wiry body as if she'd been poured into them like melted wax. The pitches came courteously and it almost seemed unnaturally slow as if the ball were floating through a substance more solid than air yet managed to drop as it neared the plate in such a cunning way that Sable swung the bat with a grunt and missed, and a second time swung and missed, and the call was "Two strikes!"—the umpire was a neighboring farmer, an oldish man with a Father Time wispy beard and an air of quirky authority—and with the third pitch either Sable or the pitcher had so adjusted to each other that Sable was able to swing the bat and actually strike the ball, sending it scuttling at a sharp angle along the third-base line, an easy catch for a lanky teenaged boy (a second cousin of mine, a Hausmann from Ransomville) who scooped it up bare-handed and pitched it to the first baseman, a stout white-whiskered fellow whom I recognized as an antique shop proprietor in Mt. Ephraim, clearly not much of an athlete either as to groans and cheers he fumbled the catch, the ball bounced from his awkward hands and rolled away even as, with much attendant squealing, clapping, cheers Sable rushed to first base there to stand panting and triumphant. I saw Mom in center field—no mistaking that silvery-glittery hair—Mom in sunflower-print culottes and sandals—clapping, crying, "Hooray, Sable! Show these kids!" For her age, Corinne Mulvaney was in fact something of an athlete, capable and lithe and smart about conserving her energy. My eye snagged on the second baseman, or -woman—a petite dark girl, a stranger I was sure I'd never seen before, in fact like no one I'd ever encountered in the Chautauqua Valley, with olive-pale skin and perfect features and a Greek sailor cap tilted seductively over her forehead, though she was dressed like any teenager in T-shirt, jeans, sneakers without socks. Next at bat was a boy of about twelve, another of my distant cousins, the horsey-faced Hausmann look, and he seemed shy, so the pitcher sent several teasing-slow underhanded balls in such a way as to allow him, too, to connect on what would have been the third strike—a pop fly, unluckily, which the pitcher himself easily snatched from the air. By this time I'd been drawn into the mood of the game, cheering and clapping at virtually all the plays without discrimination. (I'd just noticed a familiar face among the specta-tors—was it "Aunt" Ethel Hausmann? Her hair now steely-gray, her figure grimly turnip-shaped in slacks and loose-fitting shirt but she appeared to be in a genial mood as if determined to have a good time.) There was a murmur of excited expectation as there came trotting to the plate my big brother Mike!—handing his beer can to a bystander as he took up the bat with a flourish and balanced it on the palm of his hand, "Mule" Mulvaney soaking up the quick round of applause, and gentlemanly-charitable enough, since he was probably the only real athlete on the field, to volunteer to bat southpaw. The lanky pitcher shoved his dark glasses against the bridge of his nose—his face was suntanned, lean—*Patrick? was it possible?—my brother who'd scorned all team sports?*—and coolly studied his formidable opponent. People were trailing over from the house to watch— Marianne with her children, Vicky and her children, Chrissy running crying, "Dad-dy! DAD-DY!" Even Effie and Eddie who'd been imperturbably munching grass paused to watch.

The pitcher wound up like an elastic knot, unleashed himself and the initial pitch, though underhand, flew across the plate conspicuously faster than the pitches directed at Mike's predecessors, and Mike swung, swung hard, and missed, coloring and laughing good-naturedly, leaning over to spit on the ground in mock-macho style, returned the bat to his shoulder with a determined look and again the pitch came flying fast, deviously dropping just as it crossed the plate, and again Mike swung and missed. "Mule" Mulvaney, soon to be forty: how was that possible? He'd been discharged several years before from the Marines with the rank of sergeant and was now a civil engineer with the state of Delaware, living with his family in Wilmington, husband and father and upstanding American citizen it would seem; something of a stranger to me now though I'd visited him and his family a few times in their upscale residential neighborhood, and saw him at least once a year in the company of Mom. Mike was still good-looking—what girls call, so vulgarly and poetically, a hunk—though his jowls had thickened and his fading-brown hair was receding severely from his forehead; not a heavy man but beefy-solid in the torso and abdomen in the way of a former athlete now easing into middle age. His skin burnt red as if with sun though he was genial, grinning. Another time the pitcher wound up, lanky and sinuous, and the ball came flying—"Too wide, outside! Ball one!" declared the umpire. And the next pitch too was declared a ball, and may even have been one. And the next pitch flew unerringly toward the plate—which was, in fact, a paper picnic plate— and Mike swung the bat with blind impulsive faith and there was a *crack!* as bat and ball connected and for a fraction of a second the ball seemed virtually to pause in midair before sailing up, up, up—as Mike began to run—and finally down into a grove of trees on the far side of the pasture, where squealing children ran to fetch it. There were manic cheers, applause as Mike trotted like royalty around the bases, blowing kisses to all, paused to take up Mom's hand and kiss it in the outfield, trotting then to third, and home, and my eyes seized with moisture thinking *How like Dad!* for it was as if Michael Mulvaney Sr. at the age of almost-forty had appeared before us, the glimmer of the man at least, the hazy sunstruck aura out of which Mike Jr.'s features smiled in triumph. So Mike trotted home, carrying Chrissy from third base, and I was whistling and applauding with the others, for so spectacular a home run in Mom's and Sable's goat pasture was something of an occasion, after all. I shaded my eyes then studying the stranger who was the pitcher standing abashed now but grinning, a good sport, too, as Mike trotted back to home, hands on his lean hips, the lenses of his dark glasses winking, and of course it was Patrick, who else but my lost brother Patrick? By this time Mom had seen me and cried, "Judd! There's Judd!" and Patrick turned blinking to see me, and ran over at once, and grabbed me in a bear hug like no imaginable gesture of P.J.'s, still less Pinch's, saying, his voice choked with emotion, "Jesus, kid! You're all grown up."

❧

Ringing the cowbell!—there on the back veranda of the clapboard farmhouse on the New Canaan Road, her hair turned completely silver and glittering like mica, braided into a single thick plait swinging between her shoulder blades, there was Corinne Mulvaney, sixty-two years old! Laughing like one of her own grandchildren, the color up in her cheeks, tugging the cord of the old gourd-shaped cowbell to summon us all to eat, at last.

It was nearing 6:30 P.M. but still bright as midday except in the shadows beneath the tall chestnut trees where picnic tables had been set, covered in bright American-flag paper runners. Fourth of July but no fireworks, no "explosive devices"—Mom and Sable had insisted. Just red-white-and-blue napkins, streamers. Tiny American flags fluttering from the veranda. Scram, in a delirium of joy at so many children, so much loving attention, wore an American-flag kerchief around his neck.

There were Whit and Marianne playful as newlyweds overseeing the grilling of hamburgers, hot dogs, and spicy Italian sausage at the pit barbecue, and there were Mom and Sable overseeing the preparation of chicken pieces brushed with Sable's Texas Hot Sauce, at the portable grill. On the buffet picnic table were enormous bowls of homemade salads, a platter heaped with raw vegetables beautiful as works of art—bell peppers, tomatoes, sliced cucumbers, zucchini and yellow squash from Mom's garden. There were platters of fresh-baked breads, muffins, biscuits. Ethel Hausmann's pineapple-glazed Virginia ham that must have weighed twenty pounds. A small gang of us husked the ears of sweet corn I'd brought, and my perky sister-in-law Vicky and I boiled them in the kitchen, in immense pots of water on Mom's and Sable's old-fashioned gas stove. Vicky set the timer—"Five minutes exactly! Overcooking makes corn mushy." Vicky had a bossy-flirty manner I'd have adored if I had been the type to fall in love with an older brother's wife. Saying, as we waited for the timer to ring, with an air of one imparting a secret, "Judd, I just can't get over your brother Patrick! He isn't at all what I'd expected." I asked, curious, what she'd expected, what Mike had led her to expect of Patrick, and she said, "Well, I guess I expected someone not so—*Mulvaney*." I asked, "But what is *Mulvaney*?" for the concept was genuinely baffling to me. Vicky said, stroking her belly that was so pert and round beneath her buttercup-yellow maternity smock, and fixing me with a look as if I must be joking, to ask such a question, "Why, you. All of you."

There were twenty-seven of us, adults, children, babies in high chairs and on laps, beneath the tall chestnut trees behind Mom's and Sable's house. The sky overhead glowed with a warm sepia cast as if flames licked beyond the scrim of cloud. Barn swifts soared and darted overhead—they nested under the eaves of the outbuildings, Mom explained, dozens of them, and neither she nor Sable had the heart to run them off.

Whit West rose to propose a toast to Corinne Mulvaney and Sable Mills and all the Mulvaneys present—naming us in turn, insisting we rise blushing in our places—and all the Hausmanns present—five, no six Hausmanns: how had Mom talked such unsociable folks into coming here today?—and the toast included, too, relatives of Sable Mills—of whom there were a half dozen—and people who'd come a long distance—who, in fact, had come the longest distance?—Whit West peered out among us like an affable just slightly bullying master of ceremonies until Patrick laughingly volunteered, "Katya and me, I suppose"—and we all applauded.

No wonder I was a little drunk, such a humming buzzing day! Cicadas shrieking out of the trees like an aberration of the inner ear.

Thinking *How did we get to this?—how do we deserve this?*

In late October it would be five years since Dad died. Five years. For Mike's and Marianne's children, who'd never known their grandfather, a lifetime.

Someone poked my shoulder, I turned and there came Mom, Marianne, Vicky and Sable bearing candlelit cakes, and everyone sang "Happy Birthday" loudly and it took me a beat or two to catch on—what was this? Feebly I protested my birthday wasn't until the eleventh but no one paid the slightest heed. What amazing cakes were presented to me—a three-tiered chocolate fudge, a carrot-pumpkin-ginger-yogurt pound cake (Whit West's special recipe), an angel food with stiff sculpted egg-white frosting, and a strawberry ice-cream cake in a heart-shaped tin. Each cake glimmered with candles—*thirty*? Which added up to a phantasmagoric *one hundred twenty*? "God, am I this old?" I groaned. Much laughter, as if I'd meant to be funny. I stood swaying at my place at the table, cheeks burning with self-consciousness, dazed, disoriented, I'd suspected nothing, not a thing, hadn't given any thought to my upcoming thirtieth birthday except a twinge of dread. *Once you turn thirty in America, you really are not a kid any longer. No more excuses!* Now came a flurry of kisses aimed at my face, Mulvaneys and others, my little nieces and nephews held up for special hugs—"Say 'Happy Birthday, Uncle Judd!' "—"Say 'I love you, Uncle Judd!' "—and a succession of blinding Polaroid flash-shots—"For posterity," Whit, whose camera it was, said, "—and to prove that you Mulvaneys all exist in the same time frame."

Witty Whit West! How well my brother-in-law knew us.

I was equal to the task, but just barely: blew out every candle of the one hundred twenty. I was applauded, cheered. I was prevailed upon to speak and I stood mute and blushing and stammered finally, "—Thanks! I'll never forget this, I guess," and they applauded anyway, as if I'd been brilliant. My head was buzzing like a hornets' hive, a roaring in my ears that was happiness on the brink of passing over into something else—terror, paralysis. Mom must have seen it in my face, that happiness that's almost too much to bear, she stood beside me lifting her glass, voice rapturous, "I'm just so, so happy every one of you is here! It just seems so amazing and wonderful and, well, a miracle, but I guess it's just ordinary life, how we all keep going, isn't it?"—suddenly stammering herself, and sniffing, and everyone laughed and quickly applauded and Sable leapt to her feet raising her glass, too, and cried, "You tell 'em, sweetheart! You're the girl who knows."

It was so, as Vicky had said. Patrick had become a Mulvaney at last, in his long exile from home.

Unless it was California that had loosened and lightened him? Even sun-bleached his hair that grew long and shaggy to his shoulders. Tanned him dark as a walnut from spending so much time outdoors he said, backpacking in the mountains of northern California, hiking along the Monterey Coast. He and Katya had made the journey east on Patrick's 1988 Honda in a looping route up through northern Nevada and Utah and southern Wyoming, taking fifteen days. He had a month's leave from the Berkeley Institute of Child Development, where he was assistant to the director; he'd developed a technique for treating autistic children, and seemed to be, so far as I could gather, a licensed physical therapist as well—"Our work is continuously experimental, and evolving, there's no point in trying to define it." Katya was a graduate student in mathematics at UC–Berkeley, the Russian-born daughter of Jews who'd been allowed to emigrate out of the Soviet Union in the mid-Sixties, both of them scientists at Cal Tech. When Patrick introduced me to Katya, she smiled shyly at me from beneath her oversized Greek sailor's cap, lovely thick-lashed black eyes, and said, "Oh, Judd!—I have heard so much about you, from Patrick."

I said, "You have? What?"

Katya bit her lower lip. Like a child who has blundered into inviting more attention than she'd wished.

Patrick just laughed. "Go on, Katya, tell him. What?"

Amazing how the Pinch-crease had vanished from between Patrick's eyebrows, as if it had never been. My brother was more boyish at the age of thirty-five than he'd been at fifteen.

"Well—" Katya smiled at me hesitantly, and frowned, and touched one of her delicate earlobes where a tiny gold stud gleamed, "—he has said, you are a good brother. He loves you very much."

I laughed, embarrassed. "Well."

Impossible to say *Patrick hey: I love you.*

Patrick I'm angry as hell at you, I'll never forgive you for abandoning us but now you're back, now I've seen you and touched you I guess I love you again, so that's it.

Patrick laughed, and let his hand fall on my shoulder. Brotherly, affectionate. As if I'd spoken aloud.

Now he'd come back to us, it was as if that old Patrick, and those old sorrows, had never been.

I saw how powerfully, it must have been erotically, passionate my brother and the young Russian-born woman were; even as they spoke with others, their eyes drifted back onto each other. Their favored stance was side by side, Patrick's arm around Katya's slender waist and her fingers hooked in companionable intimacy in the belt of his khaki shorts. Was I jealous, a little? Envious? At supper, Katya sat between Patrick and Marianne and across from me; I kept stealing glances at her, so quiet amid the noisy gathering she might almost have been overlooked. She and Patrick nudged against each other unconsciously, bare arms touching, caressing. Without the Greek sailor cap, Katya looked even younger. She must have been no more than twenty-five or -six. Her black hair was wound in several long thin braids around her head, wisps of hair springing from them like tiny question marks. Around her neck were several thin gold chains. I wondered how long she and Patrick had been together, how they'd met. How unexpected, my brother in love.

Katya saw me looking at her, and smiled shyly. "Judd? Your former house?—'High Point Farm'? I hope to see it tomorrow, Patrick says we must go. To look."

"Well, it's changed. It isn't the same now."

"Not the same?"

"The house has been painted white. The front yard has been 'landscaped.' Some of the big old oaks are down."

Patrick overheard, and said, "You've been back, Judd?"

"Not really." I was embarrassed, speaking with such bitterness. "I've driven by a few times, parked on the road. But not recently."

"What about Mom?"

We looked to the head of the table where Mom was lifting a sleep-dazed Molly Ellen in her arms. The baby's mouth gleamed smilingly with wet and her bare feet paddled like a frog's. Mom's face was suffused with emotion, tenderness. Lanky rawboned Whistle had gone, and who had taken her place?—a silvery-haired woman of sixty-two with a ravaged throat but a surprisingly smooth face for one who'd spent so much time outdoors with no care for outward appearances.

"No."

"She hasn't tried to make friends with the new owners?"

"Mom has better things to do."

For a while then Patrick brooded in silence. I guessed he might want to change the subject, as Mike shrank visibly from speaking of the farm, why rake over that old hurt, and had never taken Vicky and his children anywhere near it. Nor had Marianne, of course— oh, the Wests were always too busy! Whit was a dynamo of a man, living in *present time*.

I thought I would change the subject, and asked Katya how she and Patrick had met. Katya colored pleasurably, for this was a good memory, and said, in her lightly accented English, what sounded like, "At a hunger strike." I cupped my hand to my ear, not certain I'd heard correctly. "A—what?" Katya laughed at the expression on my face, and said, "Yes, a hunger strike, in Oakland." Patrick said, "It was more than just a hunger strike, it was an active demonstration, too. The Berkeley Peace Coalition was demonstrating to protest Oakland police brutality against ethnic minorities, and some of us were arrested for blocking the street in front of police headquarters and that's how Katya and I met. In the back of a van." Patrick spoke so matter-of-factly, I responded in kind, to show how I took such bizarre information in stride, "Well, was the strike effective?" and Patrick smiled at me, yet with his old Pinch hauteur, a just perceptible curl of the upper lip just so you'd know what the perimeters of his new tolerance were, "About as effective as you'd expect any feeble human action to be in this galaxy that's a river of blind matter rushing at four hundred miles per second toward the Hydra-Centaurus supercluster of galaxies."

Katya winced, and bit her lower lip, her gaze plummeting. As if in embarrassment of me, that I should ask Patrick such a question.

"Oh! Oh, Mommy!"—it was little Willy, that excitable child. One of Mom's and Sable's cats, a sleek sand-colored tom named Tiger, had darted brazenly along the table to seize in his jaws Willy's part-eaten hamburger where it lay on a paper plate, and leapt with it to the ground before anyone could prevent him. Willy, who of all children you'd expect to be used to animals, tugged at his mother and cried, "Oh, Mommy, the bad kitty!" Marianne laughed, and kissed his forehead, and said, "Now, honey, you know better—no kitties are *bad*. And you weren't going to finish that, anyway."

So whatever we'd been discussing, almost heatedly, Patrick, Katya, and Judd, was deflected, and dropped.

★ ★ ★

Whit was saying, "Darwin leaves too many crucial questions unresolved. Of course I respect his genius, and I understand the magnitude of his contribution to knowledge, but his isn't a concise, coherent theory like Einstein's that can be tested, confirmed or refuted. It's pure abstraction, ultimately," and Patrick said, with an air of incredulity, "Abstraction? The theory is based upon minute observations!" and Whit said, waving a forefinger, "But the minutiae of a thousand thousand observations fail to add up to a single demonstrable equation," and Patrick, beginning to become impatient, protested, "Science can't be held to a single paradigm, 'science' can be many points of perspective," and Whit said, more excitedly, the moon-shaped scar in his forehead squinching with intensity like a third eye, "Hell it can't! It *should*!" and Patrick said, leaning forward on his elbows, glasses winking in the candlelight, "It wasn't until Darwin that a changing, 'evolving' theory of history was seriously conceived, before Darwin all of history was frozen, the species were frozen, this 'Mind precedes Being' superstition, God precedes His creation, centuries of Platonic nonsense," and Whit said excitedly, "So they were deluded! So they were wrong about almost everything! So time isn't cyclical so far as we can measure it! That doesn't mean there isn't any guiding intelligence behind the forms of nature, that the extraordinary forms we discover in nature aren't purposeful," and Patrick said, excitedly too, "Look, there's plenty of disorder, too, in nature," and Whit said, laughing, glancing about to see how his listeners were appreciating his performance, "Tell me about it, kid!—I'm 'Dr. West,' I'm the poor besieged sucker who knows about disorder," and Patrick said, "Where there's design there *is* purpose, but how did the purpose arise?—out of accident, millions of advantageous accidents over millions of years," and Whit said, "Oh, hell. I know that's Darwinian sacred script but I happen to subscribe to Fred Hoyle's belief—you know who Hoyle is, the maverick Brit scientist?—'I'd as easily believe that a 747 jet was assembled out of a junkyard by a passing tornado as that "natural selection" can account for a single specimen in nature,' " and Patrick said, exasperated, running his hands through his shaggy hair that looked now wild, windswept, "Whit, come *on*. That's just wishful thinking," and Whit grinned, sliding an arm around Patrick's shoulders and giving his hair a shake, as if the two of them were old pals, brothers-in-law who'd been quarrelling in this vein for decades, to the amusement of their families, neither able to budge the other an inch, "That's the best kind of thinking, Patrick—wishful. You'll learn."

Fireflies!—children were darting to catch the tiny insects, cupped in their hands.

The sun had set behind the dense flaming tree line. In the tall unmowed grass at the edge of the clearing, dozens of fireflies appeared winking like distant galaxies.

It was then Mike called out from the next table, in a teasing singsong he'd never outgrown, "Hey Mom, remember?—fireflies," and Mom looked around, smiling, puzzled, "Fireflies? What about them?" and Patrick said, with juvenile slyness, "Come on, Mom: fireflies. You must remember," and Marianne gave a little cry, clapped her hand to her mouth and laughed and said, "Oh, Mom, of course you remember," and I joined in laughing, it came to me in a rush, "Fireflies, Mom—c'mon, sure you remember," and Mom was staring at us, each in turn, sensing a joke but perplexed, "Why, no, what?" and in a chorus we Mulvaney children cried, "Ransomville! The snowstorm! Grandma Hausmann! 'Providence'!" and at last Mom remembered, and must have blushed though by candlelight we couldn't see, "Oh, yes. But that happened in winter, you know—that wasn't summer, like now," and we laughed harder, we'd never heard anything so funny, and Mom began to laugh too, quaking with laughter like pain, pleading in an undertone, for Sable was out of earshot saying good-bye to relatives of hers who were leaving, "Oh, but please don't tell Sable, she'd tease me mercilessly forever! *Please.*"

Laughing so hard, tears leaking from my eyes. There's the danger of cracking like aged brittle crockery.

It was around that time I drifted from the party, needing to escape for a few minutes. I wasn't drunk but my head was ringing like the cowbell.

Walking blindly in this place I knew to be my mom's new home but which I didn't exactly recognize like one of those dreams in which a familiar landscape is subtly yet irrevocably altered. Thinking *If this is another time, then who am I?* I'd gotten to be proud of myself for the personality I'd built, piece by piece like shingling a roof. Precisely overlapping, imbricating to prevent water damage. Not that I'd allow Mom to boast about me in my presence, so young! already editor of a newspaper! nor did I give much thought to my professional accomplishments, such as they were. But I'd built a damned sturdy personality for myself, damned if I was going to dismantle it.

Beyond the antique barn that was lit from within for the evening's festivities, a floating glowing ark. Beyond the goat pasture where the animals dozed on their feet. Beyond the clearing where there was a narrow brook, a tributary of Alder Creek. I stood for a while inhaling deep calming breaths filling my lungs with the sobriety of night.

There was a movement, a rustling in the underbrush. Twenty feet away I saw a doe and two fawns at the brook, drinking. Fawns are born in June so these were scarcely a month old, on slender legs, sides streaked with white. What is the purpose, in nature, of a fawn's streaked sides? What is the purpose, in nature, of a deer's tail, flashing white when it's upturned, as the deer flees? What possible design, intelligence? Yet how could any of this be merely accident? I stood absolutely still, scarcely daring to breathe yet fairly quickly the doe became aware of me, saw or smelled or simply sensed me, and I lifted a hand in slow gentle mute acknowledgment of our fellowship and doe and fawns contemplated me gravely before turning, the doe first, the fawns immediately following, and disappearing into the underbrush.

I heard footsteps behind me, a voice—"Judd?"

It was Patrick. He caught up with me, we stood for a while together in silence, staring at the brook. I felt a childish stab of satisfaction he'd left Katya behind. Just for now.

Finally I said, my voice oddly weak, pleading, "I'm just not used to it anymore, I guess. So many people." Patrick made a sound meaning he understood. I said, "It's like happiness is a balloon and the balloon is somehow my head and it's being blown up bigger and bigger and I'm scared as hell it's going to burst and I'll be left with nothing but scraps of rubber."

Patrick said, thoughtfully, "Yes, right. I feel exactly the same way."

"Being angry, resentful—that's easier, somehow."

"To a degree."

I realized I was fearful of Patrick asking me questions that must be asked, yet not now. I would talk to him tomorrow, the next day—all the days to come! I would never let him go again and I would tell him everything in my heart. I would tell him how Marianne had never known, had never guessed. What had been done for her sake. For the family's sake. I would tell him that so far as I knew, Zachary Lundt had kept the secret, too; if in fact he'd recognized Patrick in his disguise. I would tell him that neither Mom nor I knew anything of the Lundts now, we'd put all that behind us. I would tell him that Dad had insisted upon cremation, that had been his last coherent request. Overriding Mom's pleas. His hoarse adamant words *Cremate my body and scatter my ashes and that's the kindest thing you can do for me. Amen.* How at the end before lapsing into his final delirium he'd been assured and even dignified in that old bulldog way of Michael Mulvaney Sr. wanting to get a job finished, over and done. That was why there was no cemetery plot anywhere. No gravestone. No memorial.

All this I would tell my brother. In time.

Patrick said, as if he'd been hearing my thoughts, "After I left that day, Easter Sunday, remember?—it all just drained out of me. Like poison draining out of my blood. Like I'd been sick, infected, and hadn't known it until the poison was gone. I don't regret any of it, though. I think revenge must be good. The Greeks knew—how blood calls out for blood. I think it must be inborn, in our genes, the instinct for 'justice.' The need to restore balance. I could have torn his throat out with my teeth, almost. But, well . . ." He shrugged. His voice trailed off. I saw a shimmering movement of white in the woods, a patch of movement, and wondered if the doe had returned, or would return. But we were alone.

Patrick laughed. "Bet you didn't think I'd make it for the family reunion, right?"

I protested, "Oh, no, Patrick—I had a premonition, actually, you would."

On the way back, Patrick took me to his and Katya's campsite in a grove of trees above a turn in the New Canaan Road, about fifty yards from Mom's and Sable's house. His motorcycle was parked on the hillside just below. He'd taken out of his pocket what appeared to be a Swiss army knife and switched on the pencil-thin flashlight attachment to illuminate the Honda, which was a two-seater, a 1988 model and fairly battered. "Ever ridden one of these?" he asked, and when I said no, he said, "Tomorrow, then. You are staying over tonight, aren't you?" I said I wasn't sure and he said, "Oh, come on. Mom's counting on it, all her kids under one roof." I pointed out that he wouldn't be under the same roof with the rest of us and he said, in his old, contrary way, "At breakfast I will. Count on it."

With big-brotherly zeal then, as if all adult complexities of emotion might as well be shrugged off, for the moment at least, Patrick lifted the mosquito-net flap of the tent, and led me inside. Both of us had to bend, and then to squat, the tent was no more than five feet at its pitch. Patrick spoke proudly of the tent which was made of "breathable" nylon with a collapsible fiberglass pole. He'd bought it at an Army-Navy store in Berkeley—"A real bargain." There was a damp-grassy fragrance here mixed with something delicate and sweet I wanted to think was Katya's cologne or even her hair. I saw Katya's hair unbraided, unwound and brushed shining around her face. Patrick was saying, again as if in response to my unuttered thoughts, that he'd introduced Katya to camping out, backpacking shortly after they met. He loved her very much, he said, she was the first woman he'd ever been able to love and that only at the age of thirty-two and he'd been frightened it would never happen but somehow it had, it does, in time.

There was a moment of silence between us. I understood that I wasn't expected to say anything, not a word. As if we'd been like this, at such ease with each other, for all of the fourteen years we'd lost.

Patrick showed me by flashlight a first aid kit small enough to fit in a jacket pocket. Waterproof candles, a waterproof lantern. Everything so wonderfully small, compact. He and Katya shared a single sleeping bag, nylon, with flannel lining you could unzip and remove, as of course they had, for summer. And look, Patrick said, pleasure in his voice, at this pocket-sized weather radio that provided up-to-the-minute bulletins twenty-four hours a day from the National Weather Service. As if a demonstration were necessary Patrick switched on the radio and at once a man's voice intoned through pulses of static, "—prevailing winds out of the north-northeast from Saskatchewan, twenty to twenty-five miles an hour, at the airport in Billings, Montana temperature sixty-four degrees Fahrenheit and barometer steady at—" and there was Patrick smiling happily, squatting in his nylon tent showing his kid brother a pocket-sized weather radio that was in fact a miracle of technology, what relief in having access to detailed weather facts twenty-four hours a day 365 days a year, you have only to switch on a tiny button to hear so solemn and incantatory a recitation of simple unassailable facts beyond all human subjectivity, will, yearning. I laughed, poking Patrick in the arm, had to laugh at that expression in his face he'd had when we were boys, when we were the Mulvaneys.

P.S.

Ideas,
interviews
& features . . .

About the author

About the book

Read on

The Continuity of Generations

Joyce Carol Oates talks to Sarah O'Reilly

How personal a work is *We Were the Mulvaneys*?

Like most of my novels, it is a mixture of fiction, memories (of my girlhood growing up on a farm in upstate New York, though one considerably smaller than the Mulvaneys' picture book farm), and imagined experiences of 'real' individuals whose lives seem to me exemplary. For instance, I had two friends who'd endured what is now called 'date rape' but which had no name at the time; I have a friend whose parents 'disowned' her (for marrying someone of another religion); I know of people whose families were rent in two by such incidents, then united again once the patriarch passed away. Like much of my writing, *We Were the Mulvaneys* is a celebration of the continuity of the generations, the ascendancy of the young and the inevitable passing-away of the old. But the characters in the novel are all fictitious, utterly.

Can you talk a little about how readers have reacted to the book?

Since this was an Oprah selection, I had hundreds, perhaps even thousands, of reactions. The most moving was meeting women who embraced me and told me that I'd told their 'story' as they could not have told it. The most distressing was being told by a tearful woman that if her daughter had been able to read my novel in time, she would not have committed suicide.

It is something of a surprise to writers like myself, who spend a great deal of time on formalist matters like structure and language, that few readers seem to care about technique, and react primarily in terms of emotional identifications with characters.

What was it like to be involved in the Oprah book club phenomenon?
The most immediate consequence of having appeared on the Oprah show is that, in public places, especially, for me, airports, you are recognized by total strangers, and find yourself smiled at much more readily. This 'recognition' experience lasts for a few weeks, then fades. In a more lasting way, you are likely to have gained some readers who would never have read your work before, though it might have been suitable for them. When I appeared on the show, the women guests whom Oprah had selected to discuss my novel were touchingly avid readers: they were not reading in order to criticize, but in order to experience. They were not reading as a matter of duty but in what might be called a quest for knowledge. The purely formal, 'literary' side of writing, which is what most writers concentrate upon, is ▶

6 Like much of my writing, *We Were the Mulvaneys* is a celebration of the continuity of the generations, the ascendancy of the young and the inevitable passing-away of the old. 9

The Continuity of Generations
(continued)

◀ scarcely registered by these readers, who look to 'realistic characters' with whom they can identify, and 'realistic stories' that throw light upon their own lives. Because of its narrative voice, as well as its realistic characters and story, *We Were the Mulvaneys* was the sort of novel which could resonate with such readers.

The novel contains incredibly beautiful, elegiac evocations of animals, the natural landscape, and the old farm. Can you talk a little about where you grew up and how the landscape of your youth infuses this novel?
Yes, it is certainly the landscape of my childhood and girlhood that is evoked here; in fact, this same landscape still exists. My feelings for animals have not changed at all with time. Muffin, for instance, was a 'real' cat – he is the hero of my first children's book *Come Meet Muffin!* (which I think, unfortunately, has not been published in the UK). Muffin's personality and his health crises were exactly as they are depicted in the novel, and Marianne's love for Muffin is very much my own.

Can you talk a little about why you chose an extract from Walt Whitman's 'Song of Myself' for your epigraph?
Whitman is suggesting the mystical continuity of the spirit, through the generations, in close, organic relationship to the earth. 'From ashes to ashes, dust to dust . . .' We are the very stuff of nature, of the landscape that surrounds us. I do think that

❝ Since this was an Oprah selection, I had hundreds, perhaps even thousands, of reactions. The most moving was meeting women who embraced me and told me that I'd told their 'story' as they could not have told it. ❞

landscapes acquire, for most of us, a symbolic and spiritual value that is more than mere sentiment.

At the heart of the Mulvaney family split is Marianne's ordeal. Can you explain why you chose *not* to fully describe that ordeal in the novel?
Marianne's experience is confused and incomplete. We are to identify with Marianne, and not really know what happened in this brutal, unexpected rape of a virginal young and naïve teenage girl in the mid-1970s. It is rare for me to write a fully detailed dramatic scene of any kind: far better for the reader to employ his or her imagination.

***We Were the Mulvaneys* unsparingly depicts the misogyny of many of the young men of Mt. Ephraim. In light of this was it difficult to write about Marianne's refusal to prosecute her attacker, and her feeling that the attack was partly her fault?**
It was very difficult to allow Marianne her forgiveness. Most of us, including the author, would prefer active prosecution, and some hope of justice and/or retribution. But there are many for whom such an action would be abhorrent, and Marianne's strong religious convictions are what give her the strength to forgive and to eventually recover from her trauma. In realistic terms, given the circumstances of the era, before even the designation 'date rape' existed, it would not have been at all likely that a prosecutor ▶

❛ When I appeared on the show, the women guests whom Oprah had selected to discuss my novel were touchingly avid readers: they were not reading in order to criticize, but in order to experience. ❜

LIFE
at a Glance

BORN

16 June,1938, in Lockport,
New York.

EDUCATION

Joyce Carol Oates
attended the same one-
room school as her
mother had attended in
rural upstate New York,
before being transferred
to a secondary school in
Lockport. In 1956 she
won a scholarship to
Syracuse University where
she studied English,
graduating in 1960. She
went on to earn a Master's
degree in a single year at
the University of
Wisconsin. In 1964
Oates's first novel, *With
Shuddering Fall*, was
published, when she
was 26.

CAREER

Oates's grandmother gave
her her first typewriter at
the age of 14 and she
began 'writing novel ▶

The Continuity of Generations
(continued)

◄ would have tried the case; if he had, the
jury would probably have acquitted the
defendant. Marianne was in fact sparing her
family a horrific public ordeal, but her
father's pride doesn't allow him to
comprehend this.

**You return to the issue of rape in your
more recent novel *Rape: A Love Story*. What
is it about the act that draws you to explore
it in your fiction?**

I find the legal circumstances fascinating,
and usually very disturbing for the victim.
Since there was no court case in *We Were the
Mulvaneys*, it seemed appropriate to pursue
a rape case in realistic terms in *Rape: A Love
Story*. (I wonder if anyone thinks that the
defence attorney in *Rape: A Love Story* is an
exaggerated portrait. I can assure you, he is
not. It isn't at all surprising that more than
fifty per cent of alleged rapes are never
reported.)

**At the close of *We Were the Mulvaneys* the
destructive father is fondly remembered.
Why end on this note?**

Michael Mulvaney was not a naturally
destructive man; he was a father who loved
his family, and whose pride was bound up
fatally in his family. I thought of him as a
kind of raging King Lear whose favourite
child, Cordelia, seems to have betrayed him.
It is only proper that Michael be
remembered as the father he'd been for most
of his children's lives, not as the defeated and
embittered alcoholic of his final months.

Marianne never stopped loving him, nor did Corinne. I would hope that the spiritual generosity of forgiveness is a more powerful and more valuable human attribute than the desire for revenge. ■

LIFE AT A
GLANCE (continued)

◄ after novel' throughout high school and college. After completing her MA in the early 1960s Oates and husband Raymond Smith (whom she met at the University of Wisconsin) settled in Detroit, Michigan, where Oates took up a teaching post at the University of Detroit. In 1968 she moved to the University of Windsor, and over the next decade published at a rate of two or three books a year. In 1978 she and her husband moved to Princeton, New Jersey, where Oates continues to teach in the university's creative writing programme to this day. To date she has published close to a hundred books, including novels, short stories and poetry. She has been three times nominated for the Pulitzer Prize and in 1996 she received the PEN/Malamud Award for 'a lifetime of literary achievement'.

LIVES
Joyce Carol Oates lives in New Jersey. ■

What is a Family except Memories?

by Joyce Carol Oates

THIS IS A question asked by Judd Mulvaney, the youngest of the Mulvaney children. I think it's a question we might all ask: Can there be a family without memories, or a family racked with heart-break and mystery in which memories are partly erased, denied? When I wrote *We Were the Mulvaneys*, I was just old enough to look back upon my own family life, and the lies of certain individuals close to how much pain they give, yet how much relief, even happiness, we may feel when at last the motive for secrecy has passed.

Readers have reacted in sharply contrasting ways to the dilemma at the heart of the novel: If a loving, family-oriented woman must choose between her husband and one of her children, whom does she choose? Corinne Mulvaney is a deeply, unself-consciously religious woman who acts out of love and duty, but also with an unquestioned sense of God's intentions. She doesn't think of herself or her own wishes but those of others; until the end of the novel, when she befriends an energetic, irrepressible woman named Sable, Corinne doesn't think of herself as an individual at all. She's Corinne Mulvaney, known to everyone as Michael Mulvaney's wife. Her behaviour will seem baffling, even unconscionable, to those who don't share her faith. I don't believe that, in her place, I would have acted as she did, but I don't judge her harshly. Perhaps I even envy her faith.

It happens in some families – perhaps many more than we know – that a 'split' occurs. A parent is hurt. It might be a father, as in this case; it might be a mother. Someone who is strong-willed, very loving, but also very dominating. Someone who, until the split occurs, you wouldn't expect to be so stubborn. So heartrendingly stubborn. This parent is hurt, or insulted, or thwarted, or 'disappointed'. This parent's pride is lacerated. And the individual, often a child, who has caused the rupture can't be easily forgiven. Maybe he or she doesn't wish to beg for forgiveness. Maybe he or she is as stubborn as the parent. And suddenly . . . the family is 'split'. People choose sides. People cease speaking to one another, sometimes for years. And only after a duration of time can things be made right again and healing begin again.

In lucky families, this is. Think of the many families who never heal, never forgive!

The Mulvaneys are a family in which the pride of one dominant individual is fatally injured, but they are also a family in which forgiveness finally, belatedly, occurs. I based this story on 'real-life' experiences, as the expression has it. Yet as I wrote the novel, it came to acquire a fairy-tale quality; it came, in time, to remind me, so very unexpectedly, of a Shakespearean tragedy in which no one is actually 'wrong' and yet all suffer. ▶

> ❛ As I wrote the novel, it came to acquire a fairy-tale quality; it came, in time, to remind me, so very unexpectedly, of a Shakespearean tragedy in which no one is actually 'wrong' and yet all suffer. ❜

What is a Family except Memories?
(continued)

◄ Two Mulvaney children, Marianne and her older brother Patrick, are among my favourite characters from my writing. They abide deep in my heart. I can 'see' them so vividly! Marianne is sweet, good-natured, docile, though in her own way stubborn; Patrick is the brainy boy, outspoken, rather a smart aleck within the family, but unswervingly honest and idealistic. He would die for his family. He would – almost – commit a terrible crime for his sister.

I wish I could claim to be as naturally 'good' as Marianne. I know that there are girls and women like Marianne. (Her character is based partly on one of my high-school friends.) I would like to hope that I could be magnanimous like Marianne, and forgive those who have wounded me, but I'm not sure that this is so. It's enough for me as the novelist to know and take solace in the fact that such individuals as Marianne do exist. I celebrate their generosity and goodness. I reach out to them: Thank you! Your being is an example to us all.

Finally, I have to say of *We Were the Mulvaneys* that it's the novel closest to my heart. Passages were transcribed in white heat, as in a fevered dream. I was scarcely inventing or imagining, only just 'remembering'. My writing is so much about homesickness. The rural landscapes and waterways of upstate New York, where I was born and grew up on a small, not very prosperous farm north of Lockport. The sights, smells and texture of life in a small town. The intense emotions of high-school life, ephemeral anxieties and joys.

6 When I wrote it, I was just old enough to look back upon my own family life, and the lies of certain individuals close to how much pain they give, yet how much relief, even happiness, we may feel when at last the motive for secrecy has passed. 9

10

The wounds that can cut deep, and scar for years, or a lifetime.

In *We Were the Mulvaneys* animals are almost as important as people. I wanted to show the tenderness in our relationships with cats, dogs, and horses. Especially cats. Marianne's cat Muffin was based on a real cat of that name and everything about him in the novel is, or was, true in life. Marianne's experience is exactly as mine was. Muffin's life was saved for thirteen miraculous months. Or, his death was forestalled. Exactly as in *We Were the Mulvaneys*, except that I was already married, and all the circumstances were different. This is a sentimental confession, but I may as well make it . . .

And so to continue in the vein of sentimental truth telling: Stump Creek Hill does exist, under another name, in southern New Jersey. It is an abandoned animal shelter 'dedicated to the care of sick, injured, abandoned, and elderly wildlife and domestic animals'. Just as this shelter saves the lives of numberless animals, so, too, in the novel it saves Marianne from isolation and despair. I wish there were more Mariannes in our midst, and I wish there were more Stump Creek Hills. In the meantime, we can do our best to support such selfless organizations, and, within a smaller, more domestic compass of activity, we can do our best to prevent the situations that cause such hurt to the innocent.

As Dr Whitaker West says, 'That's the best kind of thinking – wishful.' ∎

❛ It's the novel closest to my heart. Passages were transcribed in white heat, as in a fevered dream. I was scarcely inventing or imagining, only just 'remembering'. ❜

Have You Read?

Other books by Joyce Carol Oates

I'll Take You There

It is the 1960s, America's most turbulent decade, and Anelia is a student at Syracuse University, living away from home for the first time and searching for her place in the world. But in her quest for belonging in her new surroundings, Anelia discovers the risks, and curious rewards, of confronting the world. She is taken in, and then cruelly rejected, by a 'sisterhood' of her fellow students, falls recklessly in love with an older graduate student who happens to be black, and makes a journey westward when summoned by a figure from her past who she believed to be dead. *I'll Take You There* is a moving, wry, intense examination of how a girl becomes a young woman.

'Oates's precise and inspired writing is close to witchcraft'   JEANNE MOREAU

Middle Age: A Romance

A richly sympathetic yet unsparingly comic portrait of present-day affluent America, *Middle Age: A Romance* is the story of Salthill-on-Hudson. Half an hour outside New York, it is a place where the inhabitants are beautiful, rich – and middle-aged. When the enigmatic sculptor Adam Berendt dies suddenly, his death sends shock waves through the town. His loss and rumours of his possible lovers force the community to re-evaluate their lives. An intimately drawn group portrait and a wise chronicle of transformation and regeneration.

'Every single Oates novel I've read has added to my conviction that she is a genius'
JULIE MYERSON, *Independent on Sunday*

The Gravedigger's Daughter

The Gravedigger's Daughter tells the tale of Rebecca Schwart, born in the late 1930s to an immigrant family from Nazi Germany, just as they are arriving in America. The family settles in a small, bleak town in upstate New York, where the only job the father can get is as the town gravedigger and caretaker of the cemetery. Soon the town's prejudice and the family's own emotional frailty results in unspeakable tragedy. In the wake of this loss, and in an attempt to put her past behind her, young Rebecca Schwart moves on, across America and through a series of listless marriages, in search of somewhere, and someone, to whom she can belong.

'Exhilarating'   *Daily Mail*

High Lonesome: Selected Stories

A taste of Joyce Carol Oates's greatest short fiction, with eleven new works which offer an insight into what the *New York Times* called her 'intense and violent world of struggle'. ■

If You Liked This, Why Not Try More From *The Perennial Collection*

A Thousand Acres
Jane Smiley

WINNER OF THE PULITZER PRIZE

Larry Cook's farm is the largest in his county in Iowa, a tribute to his hard work and single-mindedness. Proud and possessive, his sudden decision to retire and hand over the farm to his three daughters is disarmingly uncharacteristic. When the youngest has misgivings he cuts her out – a decision that causes chaos.

'Powerful, poignant, intimate and involving'
New York Times

The Kitchen God's Wife
Amy Tan

Winnie Louis and Helen Kwong have kept each other's secrets since they met as young brides in the 1930s. Now Helen decides to unburden herself of everything and an angry Winnie realises she must be the first to tell her daughter Pearl about her past – about her childhood in China, the happy and desperate events that brought them to America, and the terrible truth even Helen does not know.

'Tan achieves what I want every novelist to achieve: she made me happy, she made me sad, made me think and made me learn'
MARGARET FORSTER

The Stone Diaries
Carol Shields

This is the poignant story of Daisy Goodwill, twentieth-century pilgrim, from her calamitous birth in Canada to her death in a Florida nursing home nearly ninety years later. Struggling to find her place in the world, she listens and observes, becoming a witness to her own life and death in this rich tale that reflects and illuminates our own unsettled era.

'I can think of few novels containing so much that is resonant and unforgettable, or that invite the reader to participate so fully and rewardingly' *Sunday Telegraph*

Empire of the Sun
JG Ballard

Made into a major motion picture by Steven Spielberg
SHORTLISTED FOR THE BOOKER PRIZE

Based on JG Ballard's own childhood, *Empire of the Sun* is the extraordinary account of a boy's life in Japanese-occupied wartime Shanghai – a mesmerising and hypnotically compelling novel of war, of starvation and survival, of internment camps and death marches, which blends searing honesty with an almost hallucinatory vision of a world thrown utterly out of joint. ▶

If You Liked This ... *(continued)*

◄ 'An incredible literary achievement and almost intolerably moving'

ANTHONY BURGESS

Eve Green
Susan Fletcher

WINNER OF THE WHITBREAD FIRST
NOVEL AWARD

Following the death of her mother, eight-year-old Evie is sent to a new life in rural Wales. With a sense of being lied to she sets out to discover her family's dark secret – unaware that when a local girl vanishes there is yet more darkness to come. Years later she remembers that first Welsh summer: her lies, her anger, her reckless search for Rosie's abductor and the lessons she learnt – about trust, identity, guilt and how to survive when love is gone.

'A passionate, intensely observed novel'

JULIE MYERSON

Purple Hibiscus
Chimamanda Ngozi Adichie

SHORTLISTED FOR THE ORANGE PRIZE
FOR FICTION

Fifteen-year-old Kambili lives in fear of her father, a charismatic yet violent Catholic patriarch, who is generous in the community but repressive at home. When Nigeria is shaken by a military coup, Kambili and her brother go to live at their aunt's home, a noisy place full of laughter. The visit will lift the silence from her world and unlock the terrible, bruising secret at the heart of her family life.

'An intoxicating story that is at once distinctly feminine, African and universal'
Observer

Beyond Black
Hilary Mantel

SHORTLISTED FOR THE ORANGE PRIZE FOR FICTION

Alison Hart, a medium by trade, tours the dormitory towns of London's orbital road with her flint-hearted sidekick, Colette, passing on messages from dead ancestors. But behind her plump, smiling persona is a desperate woman: the next life holds terrors she must conceal from her clients and her own waking hours are plagued by the spirits of men from her past. The more she tries to be rid of them the stronger they become . . .

'A masterpiece of wit'   *Independent* ■